Dec 25, 2000.

This one is to be read
only on a dark & stormy
night.

Love
Mom & Dad.

mjf

——What is a ghost? Stephen said with tingling energy. One who has faded into impalpability through death, through absence, through change of manners.

From James Joyce's *Ulysses*

The HAUNTED
OMNIBUS

edited and with a foreword by
ALEXANDER LAING
and illustrated by LYND WARD

MJF BOOKS
NEW YORK

Published by MJF Books
Fine Communications
Two Lincoln Square
60 West 66th Street
New York, NY 10023

Library of Congress Catalog Card Number 96-76466
ISBN 1-56731-119-9

This edition published by arrangement with Henry Holt & Company, Inc.

Manufactured in the United States of America on acid-free paper ∞

MJF Books and the MJF colophon are trademarks of Fine Creative Media, Inc.

10 9 8 7 6 5 4 3 2 1

ACKNOWLEDGMENTS

With the text of this book at last on the press, I feel bound to confess to a newly lenient opinion of all anthologists. The approval of an item for inclusion only begins the editorial task. If it is a work in copyright (most good stories are, that have appeared within the last fifty-six years) permission to reprint must be secured—and permission can be withheld, as I have ruefully discovered, for a number of unexpected reasons.

I had planned to include four of the tales of M. R. James, in recognition of the fact that he has written more good ghost stories than anyone else. His publishers have allowed me to use any two, but two only, as his ghost stories have recently been collected into an omnibus all his own.

Two stories by Thomas Burke were unavailable because their first appearance in book form had occurred within the present year.

I had received permission to use hitherto unpublished stories by Roger Burlingame and Norman Matson, but have been forced to omit them because their appearance in magazines has been delayed.

When I asked leave to use some of the incomparable ghost stories of Rudyard Kipling, he had recently died, and his agent was unable to secure the permission of Mrs Kipling. Fortunately, the stories in question—*"They," Wireless,* and *The Phantom Rickshaw*—are all easily obtainable in the same volume of the collected edition.

I am glad to say that every other story I very much wanted to include have been made available, and that in no case have financial considerations caused the exclusion of a desired title.

To Richmond A. Lattimore my thanks are most particularly due for permission to use a large portion of his as yet unpublished translation of *Beowulf*. It is my hope that the sample here offered will call Mr Lattimore's work to the attention of a publisher interested in presenting a great classic as readable literature rather than as an exercise in antique metrics.

So many friends have recommended their favorite ghost stories that I can but broadcast here a general message of thanks. I am chiefly indebted for usable suggestions to Basil Davenport, Professor W. K. Stewart, and Guy Endore.

Miss Adelaide A. Sherer has looked to the irksome details of securing permissions and typoscript copies with a patience very nearly—but happily not quite—saintly.

Some authors do more than to write about ghosts: they employ them. In this case the compiler's wife has acted as ghost-editor in much of the routine of preparing the typoscript, without even the solace of remuneration.

A. L.

Specific acknowledgments for the use of copyright material will be found on page 847.

FOREWORD

"ANNO 1670, not far from Cirencester, was an apparition: being demanded, whether a good spirit or a bad? returned no answer, but disappeared with a curious perfume and a most melodious twang. Mr W. Lilly believes it was a fairy."

So reports John Aubrey, in a volume of Miscellanies carefully prepared for the Lord Chief Justice in Eyre. Mr Lilly's reason for thinking it a fairy rather than a normal spook has not survived to us. Perhaps it was the perfume. At any rate, this mannerly visitant seems to have differed little in its conduct from the ghosts of recognizable persons described by Aubrey in the same work. Most of these also were reticent and in no way offensive. A number of them arrived on errands of good will, as witness that of the Laird Bocconi's versifying shade, in the account reprinted on page 187 herein.

But such kindly concepts of the nature ghosts, bolstered though they are by a high majority of reports from other veracious scholars of the period, still do not square with the notion of disembodied prowlers acquired by most of us in our casual studies. Spooks of the Raw Head and Bloody Bones persuasion, that went skirling across the Elizabethan stage, seem to have subsided in the latter 17th and early 18th Centuries, until they were Glendowered up again by Horace Walpole from the vasty deep. Should we infer from this that the malevolent ghost is a product of romantic fiction? Not altogether, surely; for savage religions always have depended largely upon a belief in the vengefulness of the dear departed. But the dawning age of reason, ushered in by Aubrey and his fellow members of the Royal Society, seems to have established it as a fact, on the basis of a painstaking census, that ghosts are by no means so bad a lot as they have been painted by the dramatists and other irresponsible romancers.

How then are we to account for the resurgence of horrid apparitions reported from all over the world—particularly from Germany—early in the last century? How but by calling them collectively another instance of nature following art? That is the best explanation I can give for the reappearance, in a society priding itself upon the advanced stage of its culture, of a completely primitive attitude toward ghosts. I do not mean to cast doubt upon the honesty of those who claimed to have met up with spooks of this vicious variety. After all, by strict definition, a ghost is the lingering personality of a dead individual, doomed for a certain term to walk the night; its visitations usually are confined to a brief period after the death of its body; so what would be more natural than that the ghosts of persons who had recently read Horace Walpole should have followed notions of behavior learnt from Horace Walpole's fictional ghosts?

This happily transient perversion of the unreal world by the fictional has almost run its course. Some contemporary devotees of the genre still would hold with Hoffmann and Tieck, and their less skillful, more gory imitators, that a ghost story as such is meant to play hob with the standard habits of nature—and that good ones should give proof of their power to reverse the ordinary state of affairs by quickly turning the reader's spine into a chord of quivering rubber, his blood into thin red sprigs of ice. But there is a general tendency nowadays to agree that the effort to be unremittingly horrendous defeats itself. The cannier recent writers of uncanny stories have shown themselves to be aware of this law, for very few of them have attempted to repeat their best performances in kind. It is notable that Henry James and W. W. Jacobs, who seem to have given us the two most widely remembered modern examples, were each satisfied with having done the thing once, superbly, and thereafter made sparing use of such themes. They realized that even fright, alas! can die of monotony.

Some of my masters and tutors in the art of collecting ghost stories have, I suspect, ignored this principle, and have erred in making too steady an effort to scare us all out of our wits.

This book proposes to correct such restrictive injustices to an ancient and various literary form. Therefore its intending purchaser, although that intention is regarded with the most sympathetic approval by the editor, should be warned in fairness that the methods of choice and arrangement followed herein are somewhat unorthodox. For example, it has usually been thought necessary, in prefacing similar collections, to let it subtly be known that the compiler has been guided by his own deep and abiding belief in ghosts. Such a belief would be an editorial virtue, no doubt, if all readers were equally believing. But I gather that mankind today splits about 50-50 on this question, and a gullible editor is hardly to be trusted to make selections for skeptics.

Yet a non-believer has as much right to enjoy a ghost story as anyone else. Dante's *Inferno* is not dependent for its effect upon a literal belief that the narrator's guide was in truth the shade of Virgil.

The following stories, then, have admittedly been gathered together by an unbeliever, on the theory that a fanciful narrative handled so skillfully as to overcome his unbelief during the period of reading should be even more impressive to those of the true faith. In this connection it should not be forgotten that all fiction is made up solely of apparitions. Some authors frankly people their tales with the identifiable ghosts of their living acquaintances. Others earnestly study to blend a single fictional composite from a variety of sources; or, if sufficiently lazy, they let their subconscious minds do the same job, unaided by intellect. But, since every character is only a figment of the author's imagination, and thus of the reader's, the fictional ghost must be a product of double distillation: great skill is required to make its first appearance convincing, and to maintain its relationship, as a remoter ghost, to characters who themselves are also ghostly.

Starting with that assumption, I have not been content to take any writer's word for it that a ghost has entered; I have required of him that he convince me by a judicious employment of the tricks of his trade. One story by Algernon Blackwood that is wanting in this respect has been included partly for the reason that it demonstrates the validity of my rule; for in it the author has declared his intention, through the mouth of his female narrator, to forgo the usual efforts that prepare us to accept the ghost as actual. As a result, the whole situation seems to be poppycock until the ghost's unusual request diverts our attention to the development and outcome of a fascinating literary conceit. Belatedly, it becomes a very good story indeed, but I suspect that many a reader has lost interest and has failed to finish it because of the author's calculated—but I think unwise—effort to gain verisimilitude by doing away with the early artifice essential to this kind of tale. An avowed believer, no doubt, can accept the situation from the beginning; but a skeptic cannot.

Such is the first factor of unorthodoxy against which the reader should be warned: The editor does not admit to a belief in ghosts. The second is an effort to justify my impression, acquired long before the task of editing this book was committed to me, that many of the best ghost stories are not terrifying at all. I am aware that this directly opposes the dictum of Montague Rhodes James, whose supernatural stories I find more consistently interesting than those of any other author who has confined himself to the field. Dr James holds that a ghost ought to be "malevolent or odious"; but I submit that he has been oddly mislead into a false critical position by the very excellence, in structure, of his own tales; for his ghosts are always incidental to an antiquarian theme of great interest in its own right, and are held in the background to pounce out upon us near the end. It is all over very quickly. Their malevolence or odiousness has no lasting effect. It is not to be inferred that I have frowned to exclusion upon the story of plain terror: rather I have tried to set such examples off to better effect by contrast with the quieter types. The stories and anecdotes all are arranged for consecutive reading.

(It may be well to explain in passing that the short quotations from John Aubrey, Sir Thomas Browne, Shakspere, and others, have no necessary pertinence to the stories they follow.)

The Ghost-Ship, by Richard Middleton, is offered in proof of my point that such a story can be excellent without being malevolent or odious at all. It is true that his bowsing nautical spooks had wily designs, and were to be bitterly judged in retrospect by the females of Fairfield; but I do not think that they could be so regarded by any fair-minded peruser of Middleton's yarn. The fact that A. E. Coppard's eerie and beautiful tales of the supernatural have been ignored by previous compilers of such books as this can be explained, I suppose, only on the assumption that they were found wanting in malevolent or odious apparitions. When Coppard wants to shock us, he sticks to real life, and does the job thoroughly. His ghost stories are properly nebulous; but to me the least of them is worth far more than all the chair-snatching tarradiddle of Bulwer-Lytton, and I have made room accordingly for several of Coppard's offerings by excluding that old stand-by of anthologists: *The Haunted and the Haunters.*

This brings up once more the question of orthodoxy in editing. It was my original intention to exclude all stories that have been consistently favored by other editors, not as a gesture of unseemly independence, but because most of the readers who would be predisposed to acquire the present volume would have read them before. However, a review of the collections made by Cynthia Asquith, Colin De La Mare, Joseph Lewis French, Arthur B. Reeve, Dorothy Scarborough, and Montague Summers—to name some of the best that have come to my attention—revealed that there has been much less duplication than I had assumed. As my publishers have generously put more space at my disposal than has ever been granted to such a book before, and as the total of frequently reprinted stories reaches a scant half dozen, the laboring of such an artificial distinction soon came to seem pointless. It so happens that all of the very well-known stories which I have included are less than sufficient to fill the surplus of pages which this volume contains over its bulkiest predecessor; so even the reader who has read all of them can still feel that he is getting his money's worth.

Oddly enough, the two stories which I have found to be the most widely remembered modern examples—at least among my own acquaintances—have been almost ignored by the anthologists mentioned above: *The Turn of the Screw* appears in none of their collections, and *The Monkey's Paw* in only one of them.

Consequently, I soon determined neither to include nor to exclude any story merely because it is well known. But if shorter pieces were to be fairly represented, there was room for only one really long story. *The Turn of the Screw* has been omitted in favor of *The Haunted Hotel* because the former is everywhere available in The Modern Library, whereas the latter is out of print and to my mind deserves revival as a tale combining the best features of the old-fashioned ghost story and the new. Considerations of space did not apply in the case of the other frequently-mentioned example, *The Monkey's Paw,* which is here solely because it impresses me as being the best thing of its kind that anyone has ever done. Equally famous, *The Haunted and the Haunters* has been rejected because it dates, because its ghosts do not behave in a fashion remotely resembling the behavior of those reported upon by eye-witnesses who are at least making an apparent effort to be honest, and finally, because it fails to measure up to a basic test which I shall now attempt to state in general terms:

A good ghost story should concern itself with matters worthy of our interest and attention if the ghost were never to appear at all. I say "should," not "must." There are exceptions, and it is a pleasure to admit that *The Monkey's Paw* is one of them: a pleasure and a warning, for the fact should not be overlooked that the plot of Jacobs' story is itself a far-wandering ghost, used with universal effectiveness in all ages and countries, from the nursery tale of Grimm to the smoking-room versions told by traveling salesmen who would be startled by the accusation that their shady yarn comes—as in fact it does—right out of *The Thousand Nights and a Night.*

A good ghost story, then, should present interesting persons in a situation worth reading about for its own sake. This is only fair to the ghost itself: The poor creature then has something worth haunting. Edith Wharton's *Afterward,* which also appears in Mr De La Mare's fine volume, excellently illustrates this contention. Looking back over it, we realize that the story could have been told in a fashion ignoring the supernatural element. The husband could have done what he presently did do, solely because he was "haunted" by his own private shame and regret, and his wife's gradual discovery of the reason for his conduct would be tragedy enough; but—and this is important—the addition of the ghost makes a good story better.

In the case of an author whose best level is repeated in several stories, I have favored examples that have been least often reprinted, but I have included no one's second-best merely because his best is too familiar.

The title, *The Haunted Omnibus,* has been interpreted broadly. The fact that in it someone is definitely haunted makes a tale eligible. The haunter does not need to be an orthodox spook.

It can be the reader's own task to decide whether the figures seen through the window in *The Yellow Wall Paper* were authentic ghosts—or, again, whether the definite bit of haunting that occurs in Poe's superb *The Tell-Tale Heart* is entirely the work of conscience.

The Foghorn might not properly belong in a book of "ghost stories," so labeled; but the haunting effects of fog and of the past, in the protagonist's mind, qualify it for *The Haunted Omnibus*.

Inclusion of A. E. Coppard's *The Cherry Tree* may seem to be based upon a far extension of my principle. But it does concern what I am pleased to think of as a ghost of a cherry tree; and there is the added reason that it is one of the few stories that have returned to haunt me, again and again, in memory. Also, in an age of unsuccessful attempts to write proletarian short stories, it ought to be brought forward as an entirely successful and heartbreaking example of the genre.

Anyone who looks over hundreds of such tales in succession (as I have recently been doing to refresh old memories, revise others, and make new discoveries) cannot ignore the fact that an intolerably large percentage of them turn upon the essentially childish device of giving to some character a physical peculiarity unknown to most of his fellows, and then allowing a person in the know to identify his ghost after death, through its possession of the same distinguishing mark. Bierce too frequently made use of this trick; and I have somewhat regretfully excluded what many consider his best tale, *The Middle Toe of the Right Foot*, because I am not convinced that he quite succeeds in covering up with artistry the penny-dreadful essentials of the plot. Reread for the first time in fifteen years, most of Bierce proved in some measure disappointing, perhaps because of his too laboriously apparent effort to present supernatural events in the noncommittal style of a newspaper man. But *An Occurrence at Owl Creek Bridge*, included herein, is free of that handicap.

It should be easily inferable from the foregoing remarks that the merits which I would claim for this collection do not include that of basic originality. Some of its worthy predecessors have been referred to above. It does contain, I believe, more ghostly material than any earlier compilation. It attempts a new editorial approach to an old genre, and if that approach is restrictive in one sense, it is generous in another. Not only does it include a good deal of matter which makes no pretence of being scary; it also extends the realm of choice farther afield than has hitherto been done, presenting stories from the ancients and the orient.

Most important of all, it opens the way, I hope, for a fairer appraisal of a literary type much sinned against in the recent past by its staunchest admirers and friends. A single manifestation of that type, and to my mind by no means the best one, has come to be praised as the real McCoy by devotees and dismissed by every-one else—just as the detective story has degenerated into a spe-cialized game for addicts. There is an aspect of injustice in men-tioning the two forms in the same sentence, for the ghost story has a far older and more honorable lineage. It has been employed in one form or another by almost all of the great writers of the world. The oldest story written down in our language is a ghost story; and for those who know its name better than its contents, I have included a self-sufficient episode from a new translation by Rich-mond Lattimore.

Thus it has been my chief aim to lift the ghost story out of the restriction that for a time made of it a mere shudder-producer and to prove by example that it is a varied and delightful, as well as a hackle-raising, form of literary art.

My learned friend, Professor George Loring Frost, whose opinion carries even greater weight than his chair, considers this one of the best—as it is surely one of the briefest—of ghost stories: Two gentlemen, strangers to each other, chanced at the end of a winter's afternoon to be wandering farther and farther down the darkening corridors of an ancient picture gallery. One of them, shivering slightly, said, "Rather spooky, isn't it?"

"Do you believe in ghosts?" countered the second.

"No," said the first speaker, "Do you?"

"Yes," said the other—and vanished.

Taking this excellent cue, the editor hereupon will vanish from the wheel, leaving the reader to proceed in his haunted omnibus alone.

A. L.

Hanover, N. H.
September 1936.

CONTENTS

CONTENTS

FROM THE URN BURIAL

THE particulars of future beings must needs be dark
unto ancient theories, which Christian philosophy yet deter-
mines but in a cloud of opinions. A dialogue between two
infants in the womb concerning the state of this world,
might handsomely illustrate our ignorance of the next,
whereof methinks we yet discourse in Plato's den, and are
but embryo philosophers.

—SIR THOMAS BROWNE

AUGUST HEAT

Technically, *August Heat* is one of the most ingenious stories I have ever read. Like another fine story by Professor Harvey, also used in this volume, it requires of the reader that he accept the possibility of certain improbable happenings. In this one, however, the probabilities are not stretched so far as in *The Beast With Five Fingers*. We are concerned here merely with a double coincidence, which, ghosts or no ghosts, *could* happen. Whether or not it did happen is a question we are inclined to forget in the fascination of a suspended climax of the first order. Here, as in *The Yellow Wall Paper*, the story purports to be written down by its chief character; but there is a slight technical flaw in the ending of Mrs Gilman's story that is avoided in this one. Can you find it?—EDITOR.

W. F. Harvey

AUGUST HEAT

PHENISTONE ROAD, CLAPHAM,
August 20th, 190–. I have had what I believe
to be the most remarkable day in my life, and while the events
are still fresh in my mind, I wish to put them down on paper as
clearly as possible.

Let me say at the outset that my name is James Clarence
Withencroft.

I am forty years old, in perfect health, never having known
a day's illness.

By profession I am an artist, not a very successful one, but I

3

earn enough money by my black-and-white work to satisfy my necessary wants.

My only near relative, a sister, died five years ago, so that I am independent.

I breakfasted this morning at nine, and after glancing through the morning paper I lighted my pipe and proceeded to let my mind wander in the hope that I might chance upon some subject for my pencil.

The room, though door and windows were open, was oppressively hot, and I had just made up my mind that the coolest and most comfortable place in the neighbourhood would be the deep end of the public swimming bath, when the idea came.

I began to draw. So intent was I on my work that I left my lunch untouched, only stopping work when the clock of St. Jude's struck four.

The final result, for a hurried sketch, was, I felt sure, the best thing I had done.

It showed a criminal in the dock immediately after the judge had pronounced sentence. The man was fat—enormously fat. The flesh hung in rolls about his chin; it creased his huge, stumpy neck. He was clean shaven (perhaps I should say a few days before he must have been clean shaven) and almost bald. He stood in the dock, his short, clumsy fingers clasping the rail, looking straight in front of him. The feeling that his expression conveyed was not so much one of horror as of utter, absolute collapse.

There seemed nothing in the man strong enough to sustain that mountain of flesh.

I rolled up the sketch, and without quite knowing why, placed it in my pocket. Then with the rare sense of happiness which the knowledge of a good thing well done gives, I left the house.

I believe that I set out with the idea of calling upon Trenton, for I remember walking along Lytton Street and turning to the right along Gilchrist Road at the bottom of the hill where the men were at work on the new tram lines.

From there onwards I have only the vaguest recollections of where I went. The one thing of which I was fully conscious was the awful heat, that came up from the dusty asphalt pavement as an almost palpable wave. I longed for the thunder promised by the great banks of copper-coloured cloud that hung low over the western sky.

I must have walked five or six miles, when a small boy roused me from my reverie by asking the time.

It was twenty minutes to seven.

When he left me I began to take stock of my bearings. I found myself standing before a gate that led into a yard bordered by a strip of thirsty earth, where there were flowers, purple stock and scarlet geranium. Above the entrance was a board with the inscription—

CHS. ATKINSON   MONUMENTAL MASON
WORKER IN ENGLISH AND ITALIAN MARBLES

From the yard itself came a cheery whistle, the noise of hammer blows, and the cold sound of steel meeting stone.

A sudden impulse made me enter.

A man was sitting with his back towards me, busy at work on a slab of curiously veined marble. He turned round as he heard my steps and stopped short.

It was the man I had been drawing, whose portrait lay in my pocket.

He sat there, huge and elephantine, the sweat pouring from his scalp, which he wiped with a red silk handkerchief. But though the face was the same, the expression was absolutely different.

He greeted me smiling, as if we were old friends, and shook my hand.

I apologised for my intrusion.

"Everything is hot and glary outside," I said. "This seems an oasis in the wilderness."

"I don't know about the oasis," he replied, "but it certainly is hot, as hot as hell. Take a seat, sir!"

He pointed to the end of the gravestone on which he was at work, and I sat down.

"That's a beautiful piece of stone you've got hold of," I said.

He shook his head. "In a way it is," he answered; "the surface here is as fine as anything you could wish, but there's a big flaw at the back, though I don't expect you'd ever notice it. I could never make really a good job of a bit of marble like that. It would be all right in the summer like this; it wouldn't mind the blasted heat. But wait till the winter comes. There's nothing quite like frost to find out the weak points in stone."

"Then what's it for?" I asked.

The man burst out laughing.

"You'd hardly believe me if I was to tell you it's for an exhibition, but it's the truth. Artists have exhibitions: so do grocers and butchers; we have them too. All the latest little things in headstones, you know."

He went on to talk of marbles, which sort best withstood wind and rain, and which were easiest to work; then of his garden and a new sort of carnation he had bought. At the end of every other minute he would drop his tools, wipe his shining head, and curse the heat.

I said little, for I felt uneasy. There was something unnatural, uncanny, in meeting this man.

I tried at first to persuade myself that I had seen him before, that his face, unknown to me, had found a place in some out-of-the-way corner of my memory, but I knew that I was practicing little more than a plausible piece of self-deception.

Mr. Atkinson finished his work, spat on the ground, and got up with a sigh of relief.

"There! what do you think of that?" he said, with an air of evident pride.

The inscription which I read for the first time was this—

SACRED TO THE MEMORY
OF
JAMES CLARENCE WITHENCROFT.
BORN JAN. 18TH, 1860.
HE PASSED AWAY VERY SUDDENLY
ON AUGUST 20TH, 190—
"In the midst of life we are in death."

For some time I sat in silence. Then a cold shudder ran down my spine. I asked him where he had seen the name.

"Oh, I didn't see it anywhere," replied Mr. Atkinson. "I

wanted some name, and I put down the first that came into my head. Why do you want to know?"

"It's a strange coincidence, but it happens to be mine."

He gave a long, low whistle.

"And the dates?"

"I can only answer for one of them, and that's correct."

"It's a rum go!" he said.

But he knew less than I did. I told him of my morning's work. I took the sketch from my pocket and showed it to him. As he looked, the expression of his face altered until it became more and more like that of the man I had drawn.

"And it was only the day before yesterday," he said, "that I told Maria there were no such things as ghosts!"

Neither of us had seen a ghost, but I knew what he meant.

"You probably heard my name," I said.

"And you must have seen me somewhere and have forgotten it! Were you at Clacton-on-Sea last July?"

I had never been to Clacton in my life. We were silent for some time. We were both looking at the same thing, the two dates on the gravestone, and one was right.

"Come inside and have some supper," said Mr. Atkinson.

His wife is a cheerful little woman, with the flaky red cheeks of the country-bred. Her husband introduced me as a friend of his who was an artist. The result was unfortunate, for after the sardines and watercress had been removed, she brought me out a Doré Bible, and I had to sit and express my admiration for nearly half an hour.

I went outside, and found Atkinson sitting on the gravestone smoking.

We resumed the conversation at the point we had left off.

"You must excuse my asking," I said, "but do you know of anything you've done for which you could be put on trial?"

He shook his head.

"I'm not a bankrupt, the business is prosperous enough. Three years ago I gave turkeys to some of the guardians at Christmas, but that's all I can think of. And they were small ones, too," he added as an afterthought.

He got up, fetched a can from the porch, and began to water the flowers. "Twice a day regular in the hot weather," he said, "and then the heat sometimes gets the better of the delicate ones. And ferns, good Lord! they could never stand it. Where do you live?"

I told him my address. It would take an hour's quick walk to get back home.

"It's like this," he said. "We'll look at the matter straight. If you go back home to-night, you take your chance of accidents. A cart may run over you, and there's always banana skins and orange peel, to say nothing of fallen ladders."

He spoke of the improbable with an intense seriousness that would have been laughable six hours before. But I did not laugh.

"The best thing we can do," he continued, "is for you to stay here till twelve o'clock. We'll go upstairs and smoke; it may be cooler inside."

To my surprise I agreed.

We are sitting in a long, low room beneath the eaves. Atkinson has sent his wife to bed. He himself is busy sharpening some tools at a little oilstone, smoking one of my cigars the while.

The air seems charged with thunder. I am writing this at a shaky table before the open window. The leg is cracked, and Atkinson, who seems a handy man with his tools, is going to mend it as soon as he has finished putting an edge on his chisel.

It is after eleven now. I shall be gone in less than an hour.

But the heat is stifling.

It is enough to send a man mad.

●

JUSTICE

(Second-Prize Winner in *The New Statesman*'s competition for a
Ghost Story in 200 words.)

THE MOVING clouds let through occasional gleams of
moonlight. Abel set out over the moor; its shapeless piles
of granite were wreathed in tatters of white mist. The
moorland path was the shortest way home. It was narrow
and rugged, but Abel knew it well and could even distinguish a few mist-clad landmarks. He would soon be among
the granite cairns.

The fitful moonlight made him stumble, and the path
seemed to wind more than he remembered. How thick the
mist was just here. If he lost the path he might go astray
on the open moor—but what would that matter? A robust
and sensible man such as he could come to no harm.

The moonlight made these rocks look rather horrible.
Perhaps they were not rocks. This could hardly be the right
path winding senselessly about like this. What was that
awful sound like laughter? Yet what had he to fear if this
place were evil—was he not an upright and godly man who
held no traffic with evil? If wicked spirits had power over
such men as he there would be no justice in it!

"That's true," said a voice behind him, "there isn't."

—"THE GIBSONS"

THE HALF PINT FLASK

The sort of scientist who will not admit the possibility of new facts and forces that may be brought within the realm of his understanding tomorrow, in spite of the history of new discoveries in the recent past, is as annoying to most of us as the hard-boiled business man who insists that everything on earth can be measured in terms of dollars and cents. The reader is apt to agree that Barksdale, desecrator of graves, got what was coming to him.—EDITOR.

DuBose Heyward

THE HALF
PINT FLASK

I picked up the book and regarded it with interest. Even its format suggested the author: the practical linen covered boards, the compact and exact paragraphing. I opened the volume at random. There he was again: "There can be no doubt;" "An undeniable fact," "I am prepared to assert." A statement in the preface leaped from the context and arrested my gaze:

"The primitive American Negro is of a deeply religious nature, demonstrating in his constant attendance at church, his fervent prayers, his hymns, and his frequent mention of the Deity that he has cast aside the last vestiges of his pagan background, and has unreservedly espoused the doctrine of Christianity."

I spun the pages through my fingers until a paragraph in the last chapter brought me up standing:

"I was hampered in my investigations by a sickness contracted on the island that was accompanied by a distressing insomnia, and, in its final stages, extreme delirium. But I already had sufficient evidence in hand to enable me to prove——"

Yes, there it was, fact upon fact. I was overwhelmed by the permanence, the unanswerable word of the printed page. In the face of it my own impressions became fantastic, discredited even in my own mind. In an effort at self-justification I commenced to rehearse my *impressions* of that preposterous month as opposed to Barksdale's *facts;* my feeling for effects and highly developed fiction writer's imagination on the one hand; and on the other, his cold record of a tight, three dimensional world as reported by his five good senses.

Sitting like a crystal gazer, with the book in my hand, I sent my memory back to a late afternoon in August, when, watching from the shore near the landing on Ediwander Island, I saw the "General Stonewall Jackson" slide past a frieze of palmetto trees, shut off her steam, and nose up to the tenuous little wharf against the ebb.

Two bare-footed Negroes removed a section of the rail and prepared to run out the gang plank. Behind them gathered the passengers for Ediwander landing: ten or a dozen Negroes back from town with the proceeds of a month's labor transformed into flaming calico, amazing bonnets, and new flimsy, yellow luggage; and trailing along behind them, the single white passenger.

I would have recognized my guest under more difficult circumstances and I experienced that inner satisfaction that comes from having a new acquaintance fit neatly into a preconceived pattern. The obstinacy of which I had been warned was evident in the thin immobile line of the mouth over the prognathous jaw. The eyes behind his thick glasses were a bright hard blue and moved methodically from object to object, allowing each its allotted time for classification then passing unhurriedly on to the next. He was so like the tabloid portrait in the letter of the club member who had sent him down that I drew the paper from my pocket and refreshed my memory with a surreptitious glance.

"He's the museum, or collector type," Spencer had written;

"spends his time collecting facts—some he sells—some he keeps to play with. Incidentally his hobby is American glass, and he has the finest private collection in the state."

We stood eyeing each other over the heads of the noisy landing party without enthusiasm. Then when the last Negro had come ashore he picked up his bag with a meticulousness that vaguely exasperated me, and advanced up the gang plank.

Perfunctory introductions followed: "Mr. Courtney?" from him, with an unnecessarily rising inflection; and a conventional "Mr. Barksdale, I presume," from me in reply.

The buckboard had been jogging along for several minutes before he spoke.

"Very good of Mr. Spencer to give me this opportunity," he said in a close clipped speech. "I am doing a series of articles on Negroid Primates, and I fancy the chances for observation are excellent here."

"Negroid Primates!" The phrase annoyed me. Uttered in that dissecting voice, it seemed to strip the human from the hundred or more Negroes who were my only company except during the duck season when the club members dropped down for the shooting.

"There are lots of Negroes here," I told him a little stiffly. "Their ancestors were slaves when the island was the largest rice plantation in South Carolina, and isolation from modern life has kept them primitive enough, I guess."

"Good!" he exclaimed. "I will commence my studies at once. Simple souls, I fancy. I should have my data within a month."

We had been traveling slowly through deep sand ruts that tugged at the wheels like an undertow. On either side towered serried ranks of virgin long-leaf pine. Now we topped a gentle rise. Before us was the last outpost of the forest crowning a diminishing ridge. The straight columned trees were bars against a released splendor of sunset sky and sea.

Impulsively I called his attention to it:

"Rather splendid, don't you think?"

He raised his face, and I was immediately cognizant of the keen methodical scrutiny that passed from trees to sea, and from sea back to that last wooded ridge that fell away into the tumble of dunes.

Suddenly I felt his wire-tight grasp about my arm.

"What's that?" he asked, pointing with his free hand. Then with an air of authority, he snapped: "Stop the cart. I've got to have a look at it."

"That won't interest you. It's only a Negro burying ground. I'll take you to the quarters tomorrow, where you can study your 'live primates.' "

But he was over the wheel with surprising alacrity and striding up the slight ascent to the scattered mounds beneath the pines.

The sunset was going quickly, dragging its color from the sky and sea, rolling up leagues of delicately tinted gauze into tight little bales of primary color, then draping these with dark covers for the night. In sharp contrast against the light the burying ground presented its pitiful emblems of the departed. Under the pine needles, in common with all Negro graveyards of the region, the mounds were covered with a strange litter of half-emptied medicine bottles, tin spoons, and other futile weapons that had failed in the final engagement with the last dark enemy.

Barksdale was puttering excitedly about among the graves, peering at the strange assortment of crockery and glass. The sight reminded me of what Spencer had said of the man's hobby and a chill foreboding assailed me. I jumped from the buckboard.

"Here," I called, "I wouldn't disturb those things if I were you!"

But my words went unheeded. When I reached Barksdale's side, he was holding a small flat bottle, half filled with a sticky black fluid, and was rubbing the earth from it with his coat sleeve. The man was electric with excitement. He held the flask close to his glasses, then spun around upon me.

"Do you know what this is?" he demanded, then rushed on triumphantly with his answer: "It's a first issue, half pint flask of the old South Carolina state dispensary. It gives me the only complete set in existence. Not another one in America. I had hoped that I might get on the trail of one down here. But to fall upon it like this!"

The hand that held the flask was shaking so violently that the little palmetto tree and single X that marked it described small agitated circles. He drew out his handkerchief and wrapped it up tenderly, black contents and all.

"Come," he announced, "we'll go now."

"Not so fast," I cautioned him. "You can't carry that away. It simply isn't done down here. We may have our moral lapses, but there are certain things that—well—can't be thought of. The graveyard is one. We let it alone."

He placed the little linen covered package tenderly in his inside pocket and buttoned his coat with an air of finality; then he faced me truculently.

"I have been searching for this flask for ten years," he asserted. "If you can find the proper person to whom payment should be made I will give a good price. In the meantime I intend to keep it. It certainly is of no use to anyone, and I shan't hesitate for a silly superstition."

I could not thrash him for it and I saw that nothing short of physical violence would remove it from his person. For a second I was tempted to argue with him; tell him why he should not take the thing. Then I was frustrated by my own lack of a reason. I groped with my instinctive knowledge that it was not to be done, trying to embody the abstract into something sufficiently concrete to impress him. And all the while I felt his gaze upon me, hard, very blue, a little mocking, absolutely determined.

Behind the low crest of the ridge sounded a single burst of laughter, and the ring of a trace chain. A strange panic seized me. Taking him by the arm I rushed him across the short distance to the buckboard and into his seat; then leaped across him and took up the lines.

Night was upon us, crowding forward from the recesses of the forest, pushing out beyond us through the last scattered trees, flowing over the sea and lifting like level smoke into the void of sky. The horse started forward, wrenching the wheels from the clutching sand.

Before us, coming suddenly up in the dusk, a party of field Negroes filled the road. A second burst of laughter sounded, warm now, volatile and disarming. It made me ashamed of my panic. The party passed the vehicle, dividing and flowing by on both sides of the road. The last vestiges of day brought out high lights on their long earth-polished hoes. Teeth were a white accent here and there. Only eyes, and fallen sockets under the brows of the very old, seemed to defy the fading glimmer, bringing the night in them from the woods. Laughter and soft Gullah words were warm in the air about us.

"Howdy, Boss."

"Ebenin', Boss."

The women curtsied in their high tucked up skirts; the men touched hat brims. Several mules followed, grotesque and incredible in the thickening dark, their trace chains dangling and chiming faintly.

The party topped the rise, then dropped behind it.

Silence, immediate and profound, as though a curtain had been run down upon the heels of the last.

"A simple folk," clipped out my companion. "I rather envy them starting out at zero, as it were, with everything to learn from our amazing civilization."

"Zero, hell!" I flung out. "They had created a Congo art before our ancestors drugged and robbed their first Indian."

Barksdale consigned me to limbo with his mocking, intolerable smile.

The first few days at the club were spent by my guest in going through the preliminary routine of the systematic writer. Books were unpacked and arranged in the order of study, loose-leaf folders were laid out, and notes made for the background of his thesis. He was working at a table in his bedroom which adjoined my own, and as I also used my sleeping apartment as a study for the fabrication of the fiction which, with my salary as manager of the club, discharged my financial obligations, I could not help seeing something of him.

On the morning of the second day I glanced in as I passed his door, and surprised him gloating over his find. It was placed on the table before him, and he was gazing fixedly at it. Unfortunately, he looked up; our glances met and, with a self-consciousness that smote us simultaneously, remained locked. Each felt that the subject had better remain closed—yet there the flask stood evident and unavoidable.

After a strained space of time I managed to step into the room, pick up a book and say casually:

"I am rather interested in Negroes myself. Do you mind if I see what you have here?"

While I examined the volume he passed behind me and put

the flask away, then came and looked at the book with me. " 'African Religions and Superstitions,' " he said, reading the title aloud; then supplemented:

"An interesting mythology for the American Negro, little more. The African Gullah Negro, from whom these are descended, believed in a God, you know, but he only created, then turned his people adrift to be preyed upon by malign spirits conjured up by their enemies. Really a religion, or rather a superstition, of senseless terror."

"I am not so sure of the complete obsoleteness of the old rites and superstitions," I told him, feeling as I proceeded that I was engaged in a useless mission. "I know these Negroes pretty well. For them, Plat-eye, for instance, is a very actual presence. If you will notice the cook you will see that she seems to get along without a prayer book, but when she goes home after dark she sticks a sulphur match in her hair. Sulphur is a charm against Plat-eye."

"Tell me," he asked with a bantering light in his hard eyes, "just what is Plat-eye?"

I felt that I was being laughed at and floundered ahead at the subject, anxious to be out of it as soon as possible.

"Plat-eye is a spirit which takes some form which will be particularly apt to lure its victims away. It is said to lead them into danger or lose them in the woods and, stealing their wits away, leave them to die alone."

He emitted a short acid laugh.

"What amusing rot. And I almost fancy you believe it."

"Of course I don't," I retorted but I experienced the feeling that my voice was over-emphatic and failed to convince.

"Well, well," he said, "I'm not doing folk lore but religion. So that is out of my province. But it is amusing and I'll make a note of it. Plat-eye, did you say?"

The next day was Thursday. I remember that distinctly because, although nearly a week's wages were due, the last servant failed to arrive for work in the morning. The club employed three of them; two women and a man. Even in the off season this was a justifiable expense, for a servant could be hired on Ediwander for four dollars a week. When I went to order breakfast the kitchen was closed, and the stove cold.

After a makeshift meal I went out to find the yard boy.

There were only a few Negroes in the village and these were women hoeing in the small garden patches before the cabins. There were the usual swarms of lean mongrel hounds, and a big sow lay nourishing her young in the warm dust of the road. The women looked up as I passed. Their soft voices, as they raised their heads one after another to say "Mornin', Boss," seemed like emanations from the very soil, so much a part of the earth did they appear.

But the curs were truculent that morning: strange, canny, candid little mongrels. If you want to know how you stand with a Negro, don't ask him—pat his dog.

I found Thomas, the hired boy, sitting before his cabin watching a buzzard carve half circles in the blue.

"When are you coming to work?" I demanded. "The day's half done."

"I gots de toot' ache, Boss. I can't git ober 'fore termorrer." The boy knew that I did not believe him. He also knew that I would not take issue with him on the point. No Negro on the island will say "no" to a white man. Call it "good form" if you will, but what Thomas had said to me was merely the code for "I'm through." I did not expect him and I was not disappointed.

Noon of the following day I took the buckboard, crossed the ferry to the mainland, and returned at dark with a cheerful wholesome Negress, loaned to me by a plantation owner, who answered for her faithfulness and promised that she would cook for us during the emergency. She got us a capital supper, retired to the room adjoining the kitchen that I had prepared for her, as I did not wish her to meet the Negroes in the village, and in the morning had vanished utterly. She must have left immediately after supper, for the bed was undisturbed.

I walked straight from her empty room to Barksdale's sanctum, entered, crossed to the closet where he had put the flask, and threw the door wide. The space was empty. I spun around and met his amused gaze.

"Thought I had better put it away carefully. It is too valuable to leave about."

Our glances crossed like the slide of steel on steel. Then suddenly my own impotence to master the situation arose and overwhelmed me. I did not admit it even to myself, but that moment saw what amounted to my complete surrender.

We entered upon the haphazard existence inevitable with two preoccupied men unused to caring for their own comfort: impossible makeshift meals, got when we were hungry; beds made when we were ready to get into them; with me, hours put into work that had to be torn up and started over the next day; with Barksdale, regular tours of investigation about the island and two thousand words a day, no more, no less, written out in longhand and methodically filed. We naturally saw less and less of each other—a fact which was evidently mutually agreeable.

It was therefore a surprise to me one night in the second week to leap from sleep into a condition of lucid consciousness and find myself staring at Barksdale who had opened the door between our rooms. There he stood like a bird of ill omen, tall and slightly stooping, with his ridiculous nightshirt and thin slightly bowed shanks.

"I'll leave this open if you don't mind," he said with a new note of apology in his voice. "Haven't been sleeping very well for a week or so, and thought the draft through the house might cool the air."

Immediately I knew that there was something behind the apparently casual action of the man. He was the type who could lie through conviction; adopt some expedient point of view, convince himself that it was the truth, then assert it as a fact; but he was not an instinctive liar, and that new apologetic note gave him away. For a while after he went back to bed, I lay wondering what was behind his request.

Then for the first time I felt it; but hemmed in by the appalling limitations of human speech, how am I to make the experience plain to others!

Once I was standing behind the organ of a great cathedral when a bass chord was pressed upon the keys; suddenly the air about me was all sound and movement. The demonstration that night was like this a little, except that the place of the sound was taken by an almost audible silence, and the vibrations were so violent as to seem almost a friction against the nerve terminals. The wave of movement lasted for several minutes, then it abated slowly. But this was the strange thing about it: the agitation was not dissipated into the air; rather it seemed to settle slowly, heavily, about my body, and to move upon my skin like the multitudinous crawling of invisible and indescribably loathsome vermin.

I got up and struck a light. The familiar disorder of the room sprang into high relief, reassuring me, telling me coolly not to be a fool. I took the lamp into Barksdale's room. There he lay, his eyes wide and fixed, braced in his bed with every muscle tense. He gave me the impression of wrenching himself out of invisible bonds as he turned and sat up on the edge of his bed.

"Just about to get up and work," he said in a voice that he could not manage to make casual. "Been suffering from insomnia for a week, and it's beginning to get on my nerves."

The strange sensation had passed from my body but the thought of sleep was intolerable. We went to our desks leaving the door ajar, and wrote away the four hours that remained until daylight.

And now a question arises of which due cognizance must be taken even though it may weaken my testimony. Is a man quite sane who has been without sleep for ten days and nights? Is he a competent witness? I do not know. And yet the phenomena that followed my first startled awakening entered into me and became part of my life experience. I live them over shudderingly, when my resistance is low and memory has its way with me. I know that they transpired with that instinctive certainty which lies back of human knowledge and is immune from the skepticism of the cynic.

After that first night the house was filled with the vibrations. I closed the door to Barksdale's room, hoping a superstitious hope that I would be immune. After an hour I opened it again, glad for even his companionship. Only while I was wide awake and driving my brain to its capacity did the agitation cease. At the first drowsiness it would commence faintly, then swell up and up, fighting sleep back from the tortured brain, working under leaden eyelids upon the tired eyes.

Ten days and nights of it! Terrible for me: devastating for Barksdale. It wasted him like a jungle fever.

Once when I went near him and his head had dropped forward on his desk in the vain hope of relief, I made a discovery. He was the *center*. The moment I bent over him my nerve terminals seemed to become living antennæ held out to a force that frayed and wasted them away. In my own room it was better. I went there and sat where I could still see him for what small solace there was in that.

I entreated him to go away, but with his insane obstinacy he would not hear of it. Then I thought of leaving him, confessing myself a coward—bolting for it. But again, something deeper than logic, some obscure tribal loyalty, held me bound. Two members of the same race; and out there the palmetto jungle, the village with its fires bronze against the midnight trees, the malign, the beleaguering presence. No, it could not be done.

But I did slip over to the mainland and arrange to send a wire to Spencer telling him to come and get Barksdale, that the man was ill.

During that interminable ten days and nights the fundamental difference between Barksdale and myself became increasingly evident. He would go to great pains to explain the natural causes of our malady.

"Simple enough," he would say, while his bloodshot eyes, fixed on me, shouted the lie to his words. "One of those damn swamp fevers. Livingstone complained of them, you will remember, and so did Stanley. Here in this sub-tropical belt we are evidently subject to the plague. Doubtless there is a serum. I should have inquired before coming down."

To this I said nothing, but I confess now, at risk of being branded a coward, that I had become the victim of a superstitious terror. Frequently when Barksdale was out I searched for the flask without finding the least trace of it. Finally I capitulated utterly and took to carrying a piece of sulphur next to my skin. Nothing availed.

The strange commotion in the atmosphere became more and more persistent. It crowded over from the nights into the days. It came at noon; any time that drowsiness fell upon our exhausted bodies it was there, waging a battle with it behind the closed lids. Only with the muscles tense and the eyes wide could one inhabit a static world. After the first ten days I lost count of time. There was a nightmare quality to its unbreakable continuity.

I remember only the night when I saw *her* in Barksdale's doorway, and I think that it must have been in the third week.

There was a full moon, I remember, and there had been unusual excitement in the village. I have always had a passion for moonlight and I stood long on the piazza watching the great disc change from its horizon copper to gold, then cool to silver as it swung up into the immeasurable tranquillity of the southern night. At first I thought that the Negroes must be having a dance, for I could hear the syncopation of sticks on a cabin floor, and the palmettos and moss-draped live oaks that grew about the buildings could be seen the full quarter of a mile away, a ruddy bronze against the sky from a brush fire. But the longer I waited listening the less sure I became about the nature of the celebration. The rhythm became strange, complicated; and the chanting that rose and fell with the drumming rang with a new, compelling quality, and lacked entirely the abandon of dancers.

Finally I went into my room, stretched myself fully dressed on the bed, and almost achieved oblivion. Then suddenly I was up again, my fists clenched, my body taut. The agitation exceeded anything that I had before experienced. Before me, across Barksdale's room, were wide open double doors letting on the piazza. They molded the moonlight into a square shaft that plunged through the darkness of the room, cold, white, and strangely substantial among the half-obliterated familiar objects. I had the feeling that it could be touched. That hands could be slid along its bright surface. It possessed itself of the place. It was the one reality in a swimming, nebulous cube. Then it commenced to tremble with the vibrations of the apartment.

And now the incredible thing happened. Incredible because belief arises in each of us out of the corroboration of our own life experience; and I have met no other white man who has beheld Plat-eye. I have no word, no symbol, which can awaken recognition. But who has not seen heat shaking upward from hot asphalt, shaking upward until the things beyond it wavered and quaked? That is the nearest approach in the material world. Only the thing that I witnessed was colored a cold blue, and it was heavy with the perfume of crushed jasmine flowers.

I stood, muscle locked to muscle by terror.

The center of the shaft darkened; the air bore upon me as though some external force exerted a tremendous pressure in an

effort to render an abstraction concrete: to mold moving unstable elements into something that could be seen—touched.

Suddenly it was done—accomplished. I looked—I saw *her*.

The shock released me, and I got a flare from several matches struck at once. Yellow light bloomed on familiar objects. I got the fire to a lamp wick, then looked again.

The shaft of moonlight was gone. The open doors showed only a deep blue vacant square. Beyond them something moved. The lamplight steadied, grew. It warmed the room like fire. It spread over the furniture, making it real again. It fell across Barksdale's bed, dragging my gaze with it. *The bed was empty.*

I got to the piazza just as he disappeared under a wide armed live oak. The Spanish moss fell behind him like a curtain. The place was a hundred yards away. When I reached it, all trace of him had vanished.

I went back to the house, built a rousing fire, lit all the lamps, and stretched myself in a deep chair to wait until morning.

Then! an automobile horn on Ediwander Island. Imagine that! I could not place it at first. It crashed through my sleep like the trump of judgment. It called me up from the abysses into which I had fallen. It infuriated me. It reduced me to tears. Finally it tore me from unutterable bliss, and held me blinking in the high noon, with my silly lamps still burning palely about me.

"You're a hell of a fellow," called Spencer. "Think I've got nothing to do but come to this jungle in summer to nurse you and Barksdale."

He got out of a big muddy machine and strode forward laughing. "Oh, well," he said, "I won't row you. It gave me a chance to try out the new bus. That's why I'm late. Thought I'd motor down. Had a hell of a time getting over the old ferry; but it was worth it to see the niggers when I started up on Ediwander. Some took to trees—one even jumped overboard."

He ended on a hearty burst of laughter. Then he looked at me and broke off short. I remember how his face looked then, close to mine, white and frightened.

"My God, man!" he exclaimed, "what's wrong? You aren't going to die on me, are you?"

"Not today," I told him. "We've got to find Barksdale first."

We could not get a Negro to help us. They greeted Spencer,

who had always been popular with them, warmly. They laughed their deep laughter—were just as they had always been with him. Mingo, his old paddler, promised to meet us in half an hour with a gang. They never showed up; and later, when we went to the village to find them, there was not a human being on the premises. Only a pack of curs there that followed us as closely as they dared and hung just out of boot reach, snapping at our heels.

We had to go it alone: a stretch of jungle five miles square, a large part of it accessible only with bush hooks and machetes. We dared not take time to go to the mainland and gather a party of whites. Barksdale had been gone over twelve hours when we started and he would not last long in his emaciated condition.

The chances were desperately against us. Spencer, though physically a giant, was soft from office life. I was hanging on to consciousness only by a tremendous and deliberate effort. We took food with us, which we ate on our feet during breathing spells, and we fell in our tracks for rest when we could go no farther.

At night, when we were eating under the high, white moon, he told me more of the man for whom we were searching.

"I ought to have written you more fully at the start. You'd have been sorry for him then, not angry with him. He does not suggest Lothario now, but he was desperately in love once.

"She was the most fantastically imaginative creature, quick as light, and she played in circles around him. He was never dull in those days. Rather handsome, in the lean Gibson manner; but he was always—well—matter of fact. She had all there was of him the first day, and it was hers to do as she pleased with. Then one morning she saw quite plainly that he would bore her. She had to have someone who could *play*. Barksdale could have died for her, but he could not play. Like that," and Spencer gave a snap of his fingers, "she jugged him. It was at a house party. I was there and saw it. She was the sort of surgeon who believes in amputation and she gave it to Barksdale there without an anæsthetic and with the crowd looking on.

"He changed after that. Wouldn't have anything he couldn't feel, see, smell. He had been wounded by something elusive, intangible. He was still scarred; and he hid behind the defenses of his five good senses. When I met him five years later he had gone in for facts and glass."

He stopped speaking for a moment. The August dark crowded closer, pressing its low, insistent nocturne against our ears. Then he resumed in a musing voice: "Strange the obsession that an imaginative woman can exercise over an unimaginative man. It is the sort of thing that can follow a chap to the grave. Celia's living in Europe now, married—children—but I believe that if she called him today he'd go. She was very beautiful, you know."

"Yes," I replied, "I know. Very tall, blonde, with hair fluffed and shining about her head like a madonna's halo. Odd way of standing too, with head turned to one side so that she might look at one over her shoulder. Jasmine perfume, heavy, almost druggy."

Spencer was startled: "You've seen her!"

"Yes, here. She came for Barksdale last night. I saw her as plainly as I see you."

"But she's abroad, I tell you."

I turned to Spencer with a sudden resolve: "You've heard the Negroes here talk of Plat-eye?"

He nodded.

"Well, I've got to tell you something whether you believe it or not. Barksdale got in wrong down here. Stole a flask from the graveyard. There's been hell turned loose ever since: fires and singing every night in the village and a lot more. I am sure now what it all meant—conjuring, and Plat-eye, of course, to lead Barksdale away and do him in, at the same time emptying the house so that it could be searched for the flask."

"But Celia; how could they know about her?"

"They didn't. But Barksdale knew. They had only to break him down and let his old obsession call her up. I probably saw her on the reflex from him, but I'll swear she was there."

Spencer was leaning toward me, the moon shining full upon his face. I could see that he believed.

"Thank God you see it," I breathed. "Now you know why we've got to find him soon."

In the hour just before dawn we emerged from the forest at the far side of the island. The moon was low and reached long fingers of pale light through the trees. The east was a swinging nebula of half light and vapor. A flight of immense blue heron broke suddenly into the air before us, hurling the mist back into our faces from their beating wings. Spencer, who was ahead of me, gave a cry and darted forward, disappearing behind a palmetto thicket.

I grasped my machete and followed.

Our quest had ended. Barksdale lay face downward in the marsh with his head toward the east. His hands flung out before him were already awash in the rising tide.

We dragged him to high ground. He was breathing faintly in spasmodic gasps, and his pulse was a tiny thread of movement under our finger tips. Two saplings and our coats gave us a makeshift litter, and three hours of stumbling, agonizing labor brought us with our burden to the forest's edge.

I waited with him there, while Spencer went for his car and some wraps. When he returned his face was a study.

"Had a devil of a time finding blankets," he told me, as we bundled Barksdale up for the race to town. "House looks as though a tornado had passed through it; everything out on the piazza, and in the front yard."

With what strength I had left I turned toward home. Behind me lay the forest, dark even in the summer noon; before me, the farthest hill, the sparse pines, and the tumble of mounds in the graveyard.

I entered the clearing and looked at the mound from which Barksdale had taken the flask. There it was again. While it had been gone the cavity had filled with water; now this had flooded out when the bottle had been replaced and still glistened grey on the sand, black on the pine needles.

I regained the road and headed for the club.

Up from the fields came the hands, dinner bound; fifteen or twenty of them; the women taking the direct sun indifferently upon their bare heads. Bright field hoes gleamed on shoulders. The hot noon stirred to deep laughter, soft Gullah accents:

"Mornin', Boss—howdy, Boss."

They divided and flowed past me, women curtsying, men touching hat brims. On they went; topped the ridge; dropped from view.

Silence, immediate and profound.

THE BRAHMAN, THE THIEF,
AND THE GHOST

In *The Ghost-Ship*, anchored elsewhere in this volume, we have one of the few English examples of a story in which ghosts and human beings live side by side, taking each other for granted. Such an atmosphere is more frequent in primitive tales. The spirits and fiends of the *Panchatantra* (originally composed in Kashmir 4,000 years ago) are on an equal footing with the living men—so far as the narrator's attitude toward them is concerned—as the following little episode from Arthur W. Ryder's translation will show.—EDITOR.

The Panchatantra
(Sanskrit)

THE BRAHMAN, THE THIEF, AND THE GHOST

There was once a poor Brahman in a certain place. He lived on presents, and always did without such luxuries as fine clothes and ointments and perfumes and garlands and gems and betel-gum. His beard and his nails were long, and so was the hair that covered his head and body. Heat, cold, rain, and the like had dried him up.

Then someone pitied him and gave him two calves. And the Brahman began when they were little and fed them on butter and oil and fodder and other things that he begged. So he made them very plump.

Then a thief saw them and the idea came to him at once: "I will steal these two cows from this Brahman." So he took a rope and set out at night. But on the way he met a fellow with a row of sharp teeth set far apart, with a high-bridged nose and uneven eyes, with limbs covered with knotty muscles, with hollow cheeks, with beard and body as yellow as a fire with much butter in it.

And when the thief saw him, he started with acute fear and said: "Who are you, sir?"

The other said: "I am a ghost named Truthful. It is now your turn to explain yourself."

The thief said: "I am a thief, and my acts are cruel. I am on my way to steal two cows from a poor Brahman."

Then the ghost felt relieved and said: "My dear sir, I take one meal every three days. So I will just eat this Brahman today. It is delightful that you and I are on the same errand."

So together they went there and hid, waiting for the proper moment. And when the Brahman went to sleep, the ghost started forward to eat him. But the thief saw him and said: "My dear sir, this is not right. You are not to eat the Brahman until I have stolen his two cows."

The ghost said: "The racket would most likely wake the Brahman. In that case all my trouble would be vain."

"But on the other hand," said the thief, "if any hindrance arises when you start to eat him, then I cannot steal the two cows either. First I will steal the two cows, then you may .eat the Brahman."

So they disputed, each crying "Me first! Me first!" And when they became heated, the hubbub waked the Brahman. Then the thief said: "Brahman, this is a ghost who wishes to eat you." And the ghost said: "Brahman, this is a thief who wishes to steal your two cows."

When the Brahman heard this, he stood up and took a good look. And by remembering a prayer to his favorite god, he saved his life from the ghost, then lifted a club and saved his two cows from the thief.

●

IT IS A riddle to me, how this story of oracles hath not wormed out of the world that doubtful conceit of spirits and witches; how so many learned heads should so far forget their metaphysics, and destroy the ladder and scale of creatures, as to question the existence of spirits: for my part, I have ever believed, and do now know, that there are witches. They that doubt of these, do not only deny them, but spirits; and are obliquely, and upon consequence a sort, not of infidels, but atheists. Those that, to confute their incredulity, desire to see apparitions, shall questionless never behold any, nor have the power to be so much as witches. The devil hath them already in a heresy as capital as witchcraft; and to appear to them, were but to convert them. Of all the delusions wherewith he deceives mortality, there is not any that puzzleth me more than the legerdemain of changelings. I do not credit those transformations of reasonable creatures into beasts, or that the devil hath a power to transpeciate a man into a horse, who tempted Christ, (as a trial of his divinity,) to convert but stones into bread. I could believe that spirits use with man the act of carnality, and that in both sexes: I conceive they may assume, steal, or contrive a body, wherein there may be action enough to content decrepit lust, or passion to satisfy more active veneries; yet in both without a possibility of generation: and therefore that opinion that Antichrist should be born of the tribe of Dan, by a conjunction with the devil, is ridiculous. . . .

—RELIGIO MEDICI

THE TREASURE OF ABBOT THOMAS

When *Ghost Stories of an Antiquary* was published, more than a quarter of a century ago, it was gleefully welcomed by a select circle of readers. Its fame has spread in the quiet, sure way that is marked by a call for another modest edition every three years or so. Antiquarian research is a field well-calculated to nourish ghosts; and Dr James has made ghost stories his specialty, in intervals between the preparation of learned catalogues describing the manuscript resources of a number of ancient libraries.—EDITOR.

M. R. James

THE TREASURE OF ABBOT THOMAS

I

Verum usque in præsentem diem multa gar-
riunt inter se Canonici de abscondito quodam istius Abbatis
Thomæ thesauro, quem sæpe, quanquam adhuc incassum, quæsi-
verunt Steinfeldenses. Ipsum enim Thomam adhuc florida in
ætate existentem ingentem auri massam circa monasterium defodisse
perhibent; de quo multoties interrogatus ubi esset, cum risu re-
spondere solitus erat: "Job, Johannes, et Zacharias vel vobis vel
posteris indicabunt"; idemque aliquando adiicere se inventuris
minime invisurum. Inter alia huius Abbatis opera, hoc memoria
præcipue dignum iudico quod fenestram magnam in orientali
parte alæ australis in ecclesia sua imaginibus optime in vitro depictis
impleverit: id quod et ipsius effigies et insignia ibidem posita demon-

strant. Domum quoque Abbatialem fere totam restauravit: puteo in atrio ipsius effosso et lapidibus marmoreis pulchre cælatis exornato. Decessit autem, morte aliquantulum subitanea perculsus, ætatis suæ anno lxxii^do, incarnationis vero Dominicæ mdxxix°.'

'I suppose I shall have to translate this,' said the antiquary to himself, as he finished copying the above lines from that rather rare and exceedingly diffuse book, the 'Sertum Steinfeldense Norbertinum'.[1] 'Well, it may as well be done first as last,' and accordingly the following rendering was very quickly produced:

'Up to the present day there is much gossip among the Canons about a certain hidden treasure of this Abbot Thomas, for which those of Steinfeld have often made search, though hitherto in vain. The story is that Thomas, while yet in the vigour of life, concealed a very large quantity of gold somewhere in the monastery. He was often asked where it was, and always answered, with a laugh: "Job, John, and Zechariah will tell either you or your successors." He sometimes added that he should feel no grudge against those who might find it. Among other works carried out by this Abbot I may specially mention his filling the great window at the east end of the south aisle of the church with figures admirably painted on glass, as his effigy and arms in the window attest. He also restored almost the whole of the Abbot's lodging, and dug a well in the court of it, which he adorned with beautiful carvings in marble. He died rather suddenly in the seventy-second year of his age, A.D. 1529.'

The object which the antiquary had before him at the moment was that of tracing the whereabouts of the painted windows of the Abbey Church of Steinfeld. Shortly after the Revolution, a very large quantity of painted glass made its way from the dissolved abbeys of Germany and Belgium to this country, and may now be seen adorning various of our parish churches, cathedrals, and private chapels. Steinfeld Abbey was among the most considerable of these involuntary contributors to our artistic possessions (I am quoting the somewhat ponderous preamble of the book which the antiquary wrote), and the greater part of the glass

---

[1] An account of the Premonstratensian abbey of Steinfeld, in the Eiffel, with lives of the Abbots, published at Cologne in 1712 by Christian Albert Erhard, a resident in the district. The epithet Norbertinum is due to the fact that St. Norbert was founder of the Premonstratensian Order.

from that institution can be identified without much difficulty by the help, either of the numerous inscriptions in which the place is mentioned, or of the subjects of the windows, in which several well-defined cycles or narratives were represented.

The passage with which I began my story had set the antiquary on the track of another identification. In a private chapel—no matter where—he had seen three large figures, each occupying a whole light in a window, and evidently the work of one artist. Their style made it plain that that artist had been a German of the sixteenth century; but hitherto the more exact localizing of them had been a puzzle. They represented—will you be surprised to hear it?—Job Patriarcha, Johannes Evangelista, Zacharias Propheta, and each of them held a book or scroll, inscribed with a sentence from his writings. These, as a matter of course, the antiquary had noted, and had been struck by the curious way in which they differed from any text of the Vulgate that he had been able to examine. Thus the scroll in Job's hand was inscribed: 'Auro est locus in quo absconditur' (for "conflatur"); [2] on the book of John was: 'Habent in vestimentis suis scripturam quam nemo novit' [3] (for "in vestimento scriptum," the following words being taken from another verse); and Zacharias had: 'Super lapidem unum septem oculi sunt' [4] (which alone of the three presents an unaltered text.).

A sad perplexity it had been to our investigator to think why these three personages should have been placed together in one window. There was no bond of connection between them, either historic, symbolic, or doctrinal, and he could only suppose that they must have formed part of a very large series of Prophets and Apostles, which might have filled, say, all the clerestory windows of some capacious church. But the passage from the 'Sertum' had altered the situation by showing that the names of the actual personages represented in the glass now in Lord D——'s chapel had been constantly on the lips of Abbot Thomas von Eschenhausen of Steinfeld, and that this Abbot had put up a painted window, probably about the year 1520, in the south aisle of his abbey church. It was no very wild conjecture that the three figures

[2] There is a place for gold where it is hidden.
[3] They have on their raiment a writing which no man knoweth.
[4] Upon one stone are seven eyes.

might have formed part of Abbot Thomas's offering; it was one which, moreover, could probably be confirmed or set aside by another careful examination of the glass. And, as Mr. Somerton was a man of leisure, he set out on pilgrimage to the private chapel with very little delay. His conjecture was confirmed to the full. Not only did the style and technique of the glass suit perfectly with the date and place required, but in another window of the chapel he found some glass, known to have been brought along with the figures, which contained the arms of Abbot Thomas von Eschenhausen.

At intervals during his researches Mr. Somerton had been haunted by the recollection of the gossip about the hidden treasure, and, as he thought the matter over, it became more and more obvious to him that if the Abbot meant anything by the enigmatical answer which he gave to his questioners, he must have meant that the secret was to be found somewhere in the window he had placed in the abbey church. It was undeniable, furthermore, that the first of the curiously-selected texts on the scrolls in the window might be taken to have a reference to hidden treasure.

Every feature, therefore, or mark which could possibly assist in elucidating the riddle which, he felt sure, the Abbot had set to posterity he noted with scrupulous care, and, returning to his Berkshire manor-house, consumed many a pint of the midnight-oil over his tracings and sketches. After two or three weeks, a day came when Mr. Somerton announced to his man that he must pack his own and his master's things for a short journey abroad, whither for the moment we will not follow him.

II

Mr. Gregory, the Rector of Parsbury, had strolled out before breakfast, it being a fine autumn morning, as far as the gate of his carriage-drive, with intent to meet the postman and sniff the cool air. Nor was he disappointed of either purpose. Before he had had time to answer more than ten or eleven of the miscellaneous questions propounded to him in the lightness of their hearts by his young offspring, who had accompanied him, the postman was seen approaching; and among the morning's budget was one letter bearing a foreign postmark and stamp (which became at once the object of an eager competition among the youthful Gregorys), and was addressed in an uneducated, but plainly an English hand.

When the Rector opened it, and turned to the signature, he realized that it came from the confidential valet of his friend and squire, Mr. Somerton. Thus it ran:

'HONOURD SIR,

Has I am in a great anxeity about Master I write at is Wish to Beg you Sir if you could be so good as Step over. Master Has add a Nastey Shock and keeps His Bedd. I never Have known Him like this but No wonder and Nothing will serve but you Sir. Master says would I mintion the Short Way Here is Drive to Cobblince and take a Trap. Hopeing I have maid all Plain, but am much Confused in Myself what with Anxiatey and Weakfulness at Night. If I might be so Bold Sir it will be a Pleasure to see a Honnest Brish Face among all These Forig ones.

I am Sir

Your obed^t Servt

William Brown.

'P.S.—The Villiage for Town I will not Turm It is name Steen-feld.'

The reader must be left to picture to himself in detail the surprise, confusion, and hurry of preparation into which the receipt of such a letter would be likely to plunge a quiet Berkshire parsonage in the year of grace 1859. It is enough for me to say that a train to town was caught in the course of the day, and that Mr. Gregory was able to secure a cabin in the Antwerp boat and a place in the Coblentz train. Nor was it difficult to manage the transit from that centre to Steinfeld.

I labour under a grave disadvantage as narrator of this story in that I have never visited Steinfeld myself, and that neither of the principal actors in the episode (from whom I derive my information) was able to give me anything but a vague and rather dismal idea of its appearance. I gather that it is a small place, with a large church despoiled of its ancient fittings; a number of rather ruinous great buildings, mostly of the seventeenth century, surround this church; for the abbey, in common with most of those on the Continent, was rebuilt in a luxurious fashion by its inhabitants at that period. It has not seemed to me worth while to lavish money on a visit to the place, for though it is probably far more attractive than either Mr. Somerton or Mr. Gregory thought it, there is evidently little, if anything, of first-rate interest to be seen —except, perhaps, one thing which I should not care to see.

The inn where the English gentleman and his servant were lodged is, or was, the only 'possible' one in the village. Mr. Gregory was taken to it at once by his driver, and found Mr. Brown waiting at the door. Mr. Brown, a model when in his Berkshire home of the impassive whiskered race who are known as confidential valets, was now egregiously out of his element, in a light tweed suit, anxious, almost irritable, and plainly anything but master of the situation. His relief at the sight of the 'honest British face' of his Rector was unmeasured, but words to describe it were denied him. He could only say:

'Well, I ham pleased, I'm sure, sir, to see you. And so I'm sure, sir, will master.'

'How *is* your master, Brown?' Mr. Gregory eagerly put in.

'I think he's better, sir, thank you; but he's had a dreadful time of it. I 'ope he's gettin' some sleep now, but——'

'What has been the matter—I couldn't make out from your letter? Was it an accident of any kind?'

'Well, sir, I 'ardly know whether I'd better speak about it. Master was very partickler he should be the one to tell you. But there's no bones broke—that's one thing I'm sure we ought to be thankful——'

'What does the doctor say?' asked Mr. Gregory.

They were by this time outside Mr. Somerton's bedroom door, and speaking in low tones. Mr. Gregory, who happened to be in front, was feeling for the handle, and chanced to run his fingers over the panels. Before Brown could answer, there was a terrible cry from within the room.

'In God's name, who is that?' were the first words they heard. 'Brown, is it?'

'Yes, sir—me, sir, and Mr. Gregory,' Brown hastened to answer, and there was an audible groan of relief in reply.

They entered the room, which was darkened against the afternoon sun, and Mr. Gregory saw, with a shock of pity, how drawn, how damp with drops of fear, was the usually calm face of his friend, who, sitting up in the curtained bed, stretched out a shaking hand to welcome him.

'Better for seeing you, my dear Gregory,' was the reply to the Rector's first question, and it was palpably true.

After five minutes of conversation Mr. Somerton was more his own man, Brown afterwards reported, than he had been for days. He was able to eat a more than respectable dinner, and talked confidently of being fit to stand a journey to Coblentz within twenty-four hours.

'But there's one thing,' he said, with a return of agitation which Mr. Gregory did not like to see, 'which I must beg you to do for me, my dear Gregory. Don't,' he went on, laying his hand on Gregory's to forestall any interruption—'don't ask me what it is, or why I want it done. I'm not up to explaining it yet; it would throw me back—undo all the good you have done me by coming. The only word I will say about it is that you run no risk whatever by doing it, and that Brown can and will show you to-morrow what it is. It's merely to put back—to keep—something—— No; I can't speak of it yet. Do you mind calling Brown?'

'Well, Somerton,' said Mr. Gregory, as he crossed the room to the door, "I won't ask for any explanations till you see fit to give them. And if this bit of business is as easy as you represent it to be, I will very gladly undertake it for you the first thing in the morning.'

'Ah, I was sure you would, my dear Gregory; I was certain I could rely on you. I shall owe you more thanks than I can tell. Now, here is Brown. Brown, one word with you.'

'Shall I go?' interjected Mr. Gregory.

'Not at all. Dear me, no. Brown, the first thing to-morrow morning—(you don't mind early hours, I know, Gregory)—you must take the Rector to—*there*, you know' (a nod from Brown, who looked grave and anxious), 'and he and you will put that back. You needn't be in the least alarmed; it's *perfectly* safe in the daytime. You know what I mean. It lies on the step, you know, where —where we put it.' (Brown swallowed dryly once or twice, and, failing to speak, bowed.) 'And—yes, that's all. Only this one other word, my dear Gregory. If you *can* manage to keep from questioning Brown about this matter, I shall be still more bound to you. To-morrow evening, at latest, if all goes well, I shall be able,

I believe, to tell you the whole story from start to finish. And now I'll wish you good night. Brown will be with me,—he sleeps here—and if I were you, I should lock my door. Yes, be particular to do that. They—they like it, the people here, and it's better. Good night, good night.'

They parted upon this, and if Mr. Gregory woke once or twice in the small hours and fancied he heard a fumbling about the lower part of his locked door, it was, perhaps, no more than what a quiet man, suddenly plunged into a strange bed and the heart of a mystery, might reasonably expect. Certainly he thought, to the end of his days, that he had heard such a sound twice or three times between midnight and dawn.

He was up with the sun, and out in company with Brown soon after. Perplexing as was the service he had been asked to perform for Mr. Somerton, it was not a difficult or an alarming one, and within half an hour from his leaving the inn it was over. What it was I shall not as yet divulge.

Later in the morning Mr. Somerton, now almost himself again, was able to start from Steinfeld; and that same evening, whether at Coblentz or at some intermediate stage on the journey I am not certain, he settled down to the promised explanation. Brown was present, but how much of the matter was ever really made plain to his comprehension he would never say, and I am unable to conjecture.

III

This was Mr. Somerton's story:

'You know roughly, both of you, that this expedition of mine was undertaken with the object of tracing something in connection with some old painted glass in Lord D——'s private chapel. Well, the starting-point of the whole matter lies in this passage from an old printed book, to which I will ask your attention.'

And at this point Mr. Somerton went carefully over some ground with which we are already familiar.

'On my second visit to the chapel,' he went on, 'my purpose was to take every note I could of figures, lettering, diamond-scratchings on the glass, and even apparently accidental markings. The first point which I tackled was that of the inscribed scrolls. I could not doubt that the first of these, that of Job—"There is a

place for the gold where it is hidden"—with its intentional alteration, must refer to the treasure; so I applied myself with some
confidence to the next, that of St. John—"They have on their vestures a writing which no man knoweth." The natural question will
have occurred to you: Was there an inscription on the robes of
the figures? I could see none; each of the three had a broad black
border to his mantle, which made a conspicuous and rather ugly
feature in the window. I was non-plussed, I will own, and but
for a curious bit of luck I think I should have left the search where
the Canons of Steinfeld had left it before me. But it so happened
that there was a good deal of dust on the surface of the glass, and
Lord D——, happening to come in, noticed my blackened hands,
and kindly insisted on sending for a Turk's head broom to clean
down the window. There must, I suppose, have been a rough piece
in the broom; anyhow, as it passed over the border of one of the
mantles, I noticed that it left a long scratch, and that some yellow
stain instantly showed up. I asked the man to stop his work for a
moment, and ran up the ladder to examine the place. The yellow
stain was there, sure enough, and what had come away was a thick
black pigment, which had evidently been laid on with the brush
after the glass had been burnt, and could therefore be easily
scraped off without doing any harm. I scraped, accordingly, and
you will hardly believe—no, I do you an injustice; you will have
guessed already—that I found under this black pigment two or
three clearly-formed capital letters in yellow stain on a clear
ground. Of course, I could hardly contain my delight.

'I told Lord D—— that I had detected an inscription which
I thought might be very interesting, and begged to be allowed
to uncover the whole of it. He made no difficulty about it whatever, told me to do exactly as I pleased, and then, having an engagement, was obliged—rather to my relief, I must say—to leave
me. I set to work at once, and found the task a fairly easy one. The
pigment, disintegrated, of course, by time, came off almost at a
touch, and I don't think that it took me a couple of hours, all
told, to clean the whole of the black borders in all three lights.
Each of the figures had, as the inscription said, "a writing on their
vestures which nobody knew."

'This discovery, of course, made it absolutely certain to my
mind that I was on the right track. And, now, what was the in-

scription? While I was cleaning the glass I almost took pains not to read the lettering, saving up the treat until I had got the whole thing clear. And when that *was* done, my dear Gregory, I assure you I could almost have cried from sheer disappointment. What I read was only the most hopeless jumble of letters that was ever shaken up in a hat. Here it is:

Job. DREVICIOPEDMOOMSMVIVLISLCAVIBASBATA-OVT

St. John. RDIIEAMRLESIPVSPODSEEIRSETTAAESGIAVN-NR

Zechariah. FTEEAILNQDPVAIVMTLEEATTOHIOONVMCA-AT.H.Q.E.

'Blank as I felt and must have looked for the first few minutes, my disappointment didn't last long. I realized almost at once that I was dealing with a cipher or cryptogram; and I reflected that it was likely to be of a pretty simple kind, considering its early date. So I copied the letters with the most anxious care. Another little point, I may tell you, turned up in the process which confirmed my belief in the cipher. After copying the letters on Job's robe I counted them, to make sure that I had them right. There were thirty-eight; and, just as I finished going through them, my eye fell on a scratching made with a sharp point on the edge of the border. It was simply the number xxxviii in Roman numerals. To cut the matter short, there was a similar note, as I may call it, in each of the other lights; and that made it plain to me that the glass-painter had had very strict orders from Abbot Thomas about the inscription, and had taken pains to get it correct.

'Well, after that discovery you may imagine how minutely I went over the whole surface of the glass in search of further light. Of course, I did not neglect the inscription on the scroll of Zecha-riah—"Upon one stone are seven eyes," but I very quickly con-cluded that this must refer to some mark on a stone which could only be found *in situ*, where the treasure was concealed. To be short, I made all possible notes and sketches and tracings, and then came back to Parsbury to work out the cipher at leisure. Oh, the agonies I went through! I thought myself very clever at first, for I made sure that the key would be found in some of the old books on secret writing. The "*Steganographia*" of Joachim Trithemius, who was an earlier contemporary of Abbot Thomas, seemed particularly promising; so I got that, and Selenius's "*Cryptographia*" and Bacon's "*de Augmentis Scientiarum*," and some more. But I could hit upon nothing. Then I tried the principle of the "most frequent letter," taking first Latin and then German as a basis. That didn't help, either; whether it ought to have done so, I am not clear. And then I came back to the window itself, and read over my notes, hoping almost against hope that the Abbot might himself have somewhere supplied the key I wanted. I could make nothing out of the colour or pattern of the robes. There were no landscape backgrounds with subsidiary objects; there was nothing in the canopies. The only resource possible seemed to be in the attitudes of the figures. "Job," I read: "scroll in left hand, forefinger of right hand extended upwards. John: holds inscribed book in left hand; with right hand blesses, with two fingers. Zechariah: scroll in left hand; right hand extended upwards, as Job, but with three fingers pointing up." In other words, I reflected, Job has *one* finger extended, John has *two*, Zechariah has *three*. May not there be a numeral key concealed in that? My dear Gregory,' said Mr. Somerton, laying his hand on his friend's knee, 'that *was* the key. I didn't get it to fit at first, but after two or three trials I saw what was meant. After the first letter of the inscription you skip *one* letter, after the next you skip *two*, and after that skip *three*. Now look at the result I got. I've underlined the letters which form words:

DREVICIOPEDMOOMSMVIVLISLCAVIBASBATAOVT
RDIIEAMRLESIPVSPODSEEIRSETTAAESGIAVNNR
FTEEAILNQDPVAIVMTLEEATTOHIOONVMCAAT.H.Q.E.

'Do you see it? "*Decem millia auri reposita sunt in puteo in at . . .*" (Ten thousand [pieces] of gold are laid up in a well in . . .), followed by an incomplete word beginning *at*. So far so good. I tried the same plan with the remaining letters; but it wouldn't work, and I fancied that perhaps the placing of dots after the three last letters might indicate some difference of procedure. Then I thought to myself, "Wasn't there some allusion to a well in the account of Abbot Thomas in that book the 'Ser-

tum' "? Yes, there was: he built a *puteus in atrio* (a well in the court). There, of course, was my word *atrio*. The next step was to copy out the remaining letters of the inscription, omitting those I had already used. That gave what you will see on this slip:

RVIIOPDOOSMVVISCAVBSBTAOTDIEAMLSIVSPDEERSE
TAEGIANRFEEALQDVAIMLEATTHOOVMCA.H.Q.E.

'Now, I knew what the first three letters I wanted were, namely, *rio*—to complete the word *atrio;* and, as you will see, these are all to be found in the first five letters. I was a little confused at first by the occurrence of two *i's*, but very soon I saw that every alternate letter must be taken in the remainder of the inscription. You can work it out for yourself; the result, continuing where the first "round" left off, is this:

"rio domus abbatialis de Steinfeld a me, Thoma, qui posui custo-dem super ea. Gare à qui la touche."

'So the whole secret was out:

"Ten thousand pieces of gold are laid up in the well in the court of the Abbot's house of Steinfeld by me, Thomas, who have set a guardian over them. *Gare à qui la touche.*"

'The last words, I ought to say, are a device which Abbot Thomas had adopted. I found it with his arms in another piece of glass at Lord D——'s, and he drafted it bodily into his cipher, though it doesn't quite fit in point of grammar.

'Well, what would any human being have been tempted to do, my dear Gregory, in my place? Could he have helped setting off, as I did, to Steinfeld, and tracing the secret literally to the fountain-head? I don't believe he could. Anyhow, I couldn't, and, as I needn't tell you, I found myself at Steinfeld as soon as the resources of civilization could put me there, and installed myself in the inn you saw. I must tell you that I was not altogether free from forebodings—on one hand of disappointment, on the other of danger. There was always the possibility that Abbot Thomas's well might have been wholly obliterated, or else that someone, ignorant of cryptograms, and guided only by luck, might have stumbled on the treasure before me. And then'—there was a very perceptible shaking of the voice here—'I was not entirely easy, I need not mind confessing, as to the meaning of the words about the guardian of the treasure. But, if you don't mind, I'll say no more about that until—until it becomes necessary.

'At the first possible opportunity Brown and I began exploring the place. I had naturally represented myself as being interested in the remains of the abbey, and we could not avoid paying a visit to the church, impatient as I was to be elsewhere. Still, it did interest me to see the windows where the glass had been, and especially that at the east end of the south aisle. In the tracery lights of that I was startled to see some fragments and coats-of-arms remaining—Abbot Thomas's shield was there, and a small figure with a scroll inscribed "Oculos habent, et non videbunt" (They have eyes, and shall not see), which, I take it, was a hit of the Abbot at his Canons.

'But, of course, the principal object was to find the Abbot's house. There is no prescribed place for this, so far as I know, in the plan of a monastery; you can't predict of it, as you can of the chapter-house, that it will be on the eastern side of the cloister, or, as of the dormitory, that it will communicate with a transept of the church. I felt that if I asked many questions I might awaken lingering memories of the treasure, and I thought it best to try first to discover it for myself. It was not a very long or difficult search. That three-sided court south-east of the church, with deserted piles of building round it, and grass-grown pavement, which you saw this morning, was the place. And glad enough I was to see that it was put to no use, and was neither very far from our inn nor overlooked by any inhabited building; there were only orchards and paddocks on the slopes east of the church. I can tell you that fine stone glowed wonderfully in the rather watery sunset that we had on the Tuesday afternoon.

'Next, what about the well? There was not much doubt about that, as you can testify. It is really a very remarkable thing. That curb is, I think, of Italian marble, and the carving I thought must be Italian also. There were reliefs, you will perhaps remember, of Eliezer and Rebekah, and of Jacob opening the well for Rachel, and similar subjects; but, by way of disarming suspicion, I suppose, the Abbot had carefully abstained from any of his cynical and allusive inscriptions.

'I examined the whole structure with the keenest interest, of course—a square well-head with an opening in one side; an arch over it, with a wheel for the rope to pass over, evidently in very good condition still, for it had been used within sixty years, or perhaps even later, though not quite recently. Then there was the question of depth and access to the interior. I suppose the depth was about sixty to seventy feet; and as to the other point, it really seemed as if the Abbot had wished to lead searchers up to the very door of his treasure-house, for, as you tested for yourself, there were big blocks of stone bonded into the masonry, and leading down in a regular staircase round and round the inside of the well.

'It seemed almost too good to be true. I wondered if there was a trap—if the stones were so contrived as to tip over when a weight was placed on them; but I tried a good many with my own weight and with my stick, and all seemed, and actually were, perfectly firm. Of course, I resolved that Brown and I would make an experiment that very night.

'I was well prepared. Knowing the sort of place I should have to explore, I had brought a sufficiency of good rope and bands of webbing to surround my body, and crossbars to hold to, as well as lanterns and candles and crowbars, all of which would go into a single carpet-bag and excite no suspicion. I satisfied myself that my rope would be long enough, and that the wheel for the bucket was in good working order, and then we went home to dinner.

'I had a little cautious conversation with the landlord, and made out that he would not be over-much surprised if I went out for a stroll with my man about nine o'clock, to make (Heaven forgive me!) a sketch of the abbey by moonlight. I asked no questions about the well, and am not likely to do so now. I fancy I know as much about it as anyone in Steinfeld: at least'—with a strong shudder—'I don't want to know any more.

'Now we come to the crisis, and, though I hate to think of it, I feel sure, Gregory, that it will be better for me in all ways to recall it just as it happened. We started, Brown and I, at about nine with our bag, and attracted no attention; for we managed to slip out at the hinder end of the inn-yard into an alley which brought us quite to the edge of the village. In five minutes we were at the well, and for some little time we sat on the edge of the well-head to make sure that no one was stirring or spying on us. All we heard was some horses cropping grass out of sight farther down the eastern slope. We were perfectly unobserved, and had plenty of light from the gorgeous full moon to allow us to get the rope properly fitted over the wheel. Then I secured the band round my body beneath the arms. We attached the end of the rope very securely to a ring in the stonework. Brown took the lighted lantern and followed me; I had a crowbar. And so we began to descend cautiously, feeling every step before we set foot on it, and scanning the walls in search of any marked stone.

'Half aloud I counted the steps as we went down, and we got as far as the thirty-eighth before I noted anything at all irregular in the surface of the masonry. Even here there was no mark, and I began to feel very blank, and to wonder if the Abbot's cryptogram could possibly be an elaborate hoax. At the forty-ninth step the staircase ceased. It was with a very sinking heart that I began retracing my steps, and when I was back on the thirty-eighth— Brown, with the lantern, being a step or two above me—I scrutinized the little bit of irregularity in the stone-work with all my might, but there was no vestige of a mark.

'Then it struck me that the texture of the surface looked just a little smoother than the rest, or, at least, in some way different. It might possibly be cement and not stone. I gave it a good blow with my iron bar. There was a decidedly hollow sound, though that might be the result of our being in a well. But there was more. A great flake of cement dropped on to my feet, and I saw marks on the stone underneath. I had tracked the Abbot down, my dear Gregory; even now I think of it with a certain pride. It took but a very few more taps to clear the whole of the cement away, and I saw a slab of stone about two feet square, upon which was engraven a cross. Disappointment again, but only for a moment. It was you, Brown, who reassured me by a casual remark. You said, if I remember right:

' "It's a funny cross; looks like a lot of eyes."

'I snatched the lantern out of your hand, and saw with inexpressible pleasure that the cross *was* composed of seven eyes, four in a vertical line, three horizontal. The last of the scrolls was explained in the way I had anticipated. Here was my "stone with the seven eyes." So far the Abbot's data had been exact, and, as I thought of this, the anxiety about the "guardian" returned upon me with increased force. Still, I wasn't going to retreat now.

'Without giving myself time to think, I knocked away the cement all round the marked stone, and then gave it a prise on the right side with my crowbar. It moved at once, and I saw that it was but a thin light slab, such as I could easily lift out myself, and that it stopped the entrance to a cavity. I did lift it out unbroken, and set it on the step, for it might be very important to us to be able to replace it. Then I waited for several minutes on the step just above. I don't know why, but I think to see if any dreadful thing would rush out. Nothing happened. Next I lit a candle, and very cautiously I placed it inside the cavity, with some idea of seeing whether there were foul air, and of getting a glimpse of what was inside. There *was* some foulness of air which nearly extinguished the flame, but in no long time it burned quite steadily. The hole went some little way back, and also on the right and left of the entrance, and I could see some rounded light-coloured objects within which might be bags. There was no use in waiting. I faced the cavity, and looked in. There was nothing immediately in the front of the hole. I put my arm in and felt to the right, very gingerly. . . .

'Just give me a glass of cognac, Brown. I'll go on in a moment, Gregory. . . .

'Well, I felt to the right, and my fingers touched something curved, that felt—yes—more or less like leather; dampish it was, and evidently part of a heavy, full thing. There was nothing, I must say, to alarm one. I grew bolder, and putting both hands in as well as I could, I pulled it to me, and it came. It was heavy, but moved more easily than I had expected. As I pulled it towards the entrance, my left elbow knocked over and extinguished the candle. I got the thing fairly in front of the mouth and began drawing it out. Just then Brown gave a sharp ejaculation and ran quickly up the steps with the lantern. He will tell you why in a moment. Startled as I was, I looked round after him, and saw him stand for a minute at the top and then walk away a few yards. Then I heard him call softly, "All right, sir," and went on pulling out the great bag, in complete darkness. It hung for an instant on the edge of the hole, then slipped forward on to my chest, and *put its arms round my neck.*

'My dear Gregory, I am telling you the exact truth. I believe I am now acquainted with the extremity of terror and repulsion which a man can endure without losing his mind. I can only just manage to tell you now the bare outline of the experience. I was conscious of a most horrible smell of mould, and of a cold kind of face pressed against my own, and moving slowly over it, and of several—I don't know how many—legs or arms or tentacles or something clinging to my body. I screamed out, Brown says, like a beast, and fell away backward from the step on which I stood, and the creature slipped downwards, I suppose, on to that same step. Providentially the band round me held firm. Brown did not lose his head, and was strong enough to pull me up to the top and get me over the edge quite promptly. How he managed it exactly I don't know, and I think he would find it hard to tell you. I believe he contrived to hide our implements in the deserted building near by, and with very great difficulty he got me back to the inn. I was in no state to make explanations, and Brown knows no German; but next morning I told the people some tale of having had a bad fall in the abbey ruins, which, I suppose, they believed. And now, before I go further, I should just like you to hear what Brown's experiences during those few minutes were. Tell the Rector, Brown, what you told me.'

'Well, sir,' said Brown, speaking low and nervously, 'it was just this way. Master was busy down in front of the 'ole, and I was 'olding the lantern and looking on, when I 'eard somethink drop in the water from the top, as I thought. So I looked up, and I see someone's 'ead lookin' over at us. I s'pose I must ha' said somethink, and I 'eld the light up and run up the steps, and my light shone right on the face. That was a bad un, sir, if ever I see one! A holdish man, and the face very much fell in, and larfin', as I thought. And I got up the steps as quick pretty nigh as I'm tellin' you, and when I was out on the ground there warn't a sign of any person. There 'adn't been the time for anyone to get away, let alone a hold chap, and I made sure he warn't crouching down by the well, nor nothink. Next thing I hear master cry out somethink 'orrible, and hall I see was him hanging out by the rope, and, as master says, 'owever I got him up I couldn't tell you.'

'You hear that, Gregory?' said Mr. Somerton. 'Now, does any explanation of that incident strike you?'

'The whole thing is so ghastly and abnormal that I must own it puts me quite off my balance; but the thought did occur to me that possibly the—well, the person who set the trap might have come to see the success of his plan.'

'Just so, Gregory, just so. I can think of nothing else so—*likely*, I should say, if such a word had a place anywhere in my story. I think it must have been the Abbot. . . . Well, I haven't much more to tell you. I spent a miserable night, Brown sitting up with me. Next day I was no better; unable to get up; no doctor to be had; and, if one had been available, I doubt if he could have done so much for me. I made Brown write off to you, and spent a second terrible night. And, Gregory, of this I am sure, and I think it affected me more than the first shock, for it lasted longer: there was someone or something on the watch outside my door the whole night. I almost fancy there were two. It wasn't only the faint noises I heard from time to time all through the dark hours, but there was the smell—the hideous smell of mould. Every rag I had had on me on that first evening I had stripped off and made Brown take it away. I believe he stuffed the things into the stove in his room; and yet the smell was there, as intense as it had been in the well; and, what is more, it came from outside the door. But with the first glimmer of dawn it faded out, and the sounds ceased, too; and so I was sure that if anyone could put back the stone, it or they would be powerless until someone else took it away again. I had to wait until you came to get that done. Of course, I couldn't send Brown to do it by himself, and still less could I tell anyone who belonged to the place.

'Well, there is my story; and if you don't believe it, I can't help it. But I think you do.'

'Indeed,' said Mr. Gregory, 'I can find no alternative. I *must* believe it! I saw the well and the stone myself, and had a glimpse, I thought, of the bags or something else in the hole. And, to be plain with you, Somerton, I believe my door was watched last night, too.'

'I dare say it was, Gregory; but, thank goodness, that is over. Have you, by the way, anything to tell about your visit to that dreadful place?'

'Very little,' was the answer. 'Brown and I managed easily enough to get the slab into its place, and he fixed it very firmly with the irons and wedges you had desired him to get, and we contrived to smear the surface with mud so that it looks just like the rest of the wall. One thing I did notice in the carving on the well-head, which I think must have escaped you. It was a horrid, grotesque shape—perhaps more like a toad than anything else, and there was a label by it inscribed with the two words, "Depositum custodi." ' [5]

●

In the life of JOHN DONNE, Dean of St. Paul's, London, writ by Isaak Walton.

AT THIS time of Mr. Donne's and his wife's living in Sir Robert Drury's house in Drury-Lane, the Lord Haye was, by King James, sent upon a glorious embassy to the then French King Henry the IV; and Sir Robert put on a sudden resolution to accompany him to the French Court, and to be present at his audience there. And Sir Robert put on as sudden a resolution, to subject Mr. Donne to be his companion in that journey; and his desire was suddenly made known to his wife, who was then with child, and otherwise under so dangerous a habit of body, as to her health, that she protested an unwillingness to allow him any absence from her; saying her divining soul boded her some ill in his absence, and therefore desired him not to leave her. This made Mr. Donne lay aside all thoughts of his journey, and really to resolve against it. But Sir Robert became restless in his persuasions for it, and Mr. Donne was so generous as to think he had sold his liberty, when he had received so many charitable kindnesses from him, and told his wife so; who, therefore, with an unwilling willingness, did give a faint consent to the journey, which

[5] 'Keep that which is committed to thee.'

was proposed to be but for two months: within a few days after this resolve, the Ambassador, Sir Robert, and Mr. Donne left London, and were the twelfth day got safe to Paris. Two days after their arrival there, Mr. Donne was left alone in the room where Sir Robert and he, with some others, had dined. To this place Sir Robert returned within half an hour; and as he left so he found Mr. Donne—alone, but in such an extacy, and so altered as to his looks, as amazed Sir Robert to behold him, insomuch as he earnestly desired Mr. Donne to declare what had befallen him in the short time of his absence? to which Mr. Donne was not able to make a present answer, but after a long and perplexed pause, said "I have seen a dreadful vision since I saw you: I have seen my dear wife pass twice by me through this room, with her hair hanging about her shoulders, and a dead child in her arms; this I have seen since I saw you." To which Sir Robert replied, "Sure sir, you have slept since I saw you, and this is the result of some melancholy dream, which I desire you to forget, for you are now awake." To which Mr. Donne's reply was, "I cannot be surer that I now live, than that I have not slept since I saw you, and am sure that at her second appearing, she stopt and lookt me in the face and vanished."——Rest and sleep had not altered Mr. Donne's opinion the next day, for he then affirmed this vision with a more deliberate, and so confirmed a confidence, that he inclined Sir Robert to a faint belief, that the vision was true. It is truly said, that desire and doubt have no rest, and it proved so with Sir Robert, for he immediately sent a servant to Drury-House, with a charge to hasten back and bring him word whether Mrs. Donne were alive? and if alive, in what condition she was as to her health. The twelfth day the messenger returned with this account—that he found and left Mrs. Donne very sad, sick in her bed, and that, after a long and dangerous labour, she had been delivered of a dead child: and upon examination, the abortion proved to be the same day, and about the very hour, that Mr. Donne affirmed he saw her pass by him in his chamber.

—QUOTED BY JOHN AUBREY

THE YELLOW WALL PAPER

Stories of self-revelation are commonly divided into two classes: those in which the narrator's secret is slowly revealed, and those in which the revelation comes as a startling climax. This one is of the former sort, but it has all the power of the latter, because the last few lines whip the brooding mental pictures into one of appalling physical action. *The Yellow Wall Paper* first appeared in *The New England Magazine* in 1895. Readers may be interested in comparing its structure with that of Poe's *The Tell-Tale Heart*, elsewhere in this volume.—EDITOR.

Charlotte Perkins Gilman

THE YELLOW WALL PAPER

It is very seldom that mere ordinary people like John and myself secure ancestral halls for the summer.

A colonial mansion, a hereditary estate, I would say a haunted house, and reach the height of romantic felicity,—but that would be asking too much of fate!

Still I will proudly declare that there is something queer about it.

Else, why should it be let so cheaply? And why have stood so long untenanted?

John laughs at me, of course, but one expects that in marriage.

John is practical in the extreme. He has no patience with faith, an intense horror of superstition, and he scoffs openly at any talk of things not to be felt and seen and put down in figures.

John is a physician, and *perhaps*—(I would not say it to a living soul, of course, but this is dead paper and a great relief to my mind)—*perhaps* that is one reason I do not get well faster.

You see, he does not believe I am sick!

And what can one do?

If a physician of high standing, and one's own husband, assures friends and relatives that there is really nothing the matter with one but temporary nervous depression,—a slight hysterical tendency,—what is one to do?

My brother is also a physician, and also of high standing, and he says the same thing.

So I take phosphates or phosphites,—whichever it is,—and tonics, and journeys, and air, and exercise, and am absolutely forbidden to "work" until I am well again.

Personally I disagree with their ideas.

Personally I believe that congenial work, with excitement and change, would do me good.

But what is one to do?

I did write for a while in spite of them; but it *does* exhaust me a good deal—having to be so sly about it, or else meet with heavy opposition.

I sometimes fancy that in my condition if I had less opposition and more society and stimulus—but John says the very worst thing I can do is to think about my condition, and I confess it always makes me feel bad.

So I will let it alone and talk about the house.

The most beautiful place! It is quite alone, standing well back from the road, quite three miles from the village. It makes me think of English places that you read about, for there are hedges, and walls and gates that lock, and lots of separate little houses for the gardeners and people.

There is a *delicious* garden! I never saw such a garden—large and shady, full of box-bordered paths, and lined with long grape-covered arbors with seats under them.

There were greenhouses, too, but they are all broken now.

There was some legal trouble, I believe, something about the heirs and co-heirs; anyhow, the place has been empty for years.

That spoils my ghostliness, I am afraid; but I don't care—there is something strange about the house—I can feel it.

I even said so to John one moonlight evening, but he said what I felt was a *draught*, and shut the window.

I get unreasonably angry with John sometimes. I'm sure I never used to be so sensitive. I think it is due to this nervous condition.

But John says if I feel so I shall neglect proper self-control; so I take pains to control myself—before him, at least, and that makes me very tired.

I don't like our room a bit. I wanted one downstairs that opened on the piazza and had roses all over the window, and such pretty, old-fashioned chintz hangings! but John would not hear of it.

He said there was only one window and not room for two beds, and no near room for him if he took another.

He is very careful and loving, and hardly lets me stir without special direction.

I have a schedule prescription for each hour in the day; he takes all care from me, and so I feel basely ungrateful not to value it more.

He said we came here solely on my account, that I was to have perfect rest and all the air I could get. "Your exercise depends on your strength, my dear," said he, "and your food somewhat on your appetite; but air you can absorb all the time." So we took the nursery, at the top of the house.

It is a big, airy room, the whole floor nearly, with windows that look all ways, and air and sunshine galore. It was nursery first and then playground and gymnasium, I should judge; for the windows are barred for little children, and there are rings and things in the walls.

The paint and paper look as if a boy's school had used it. It is stripped off—the paper—in great patches all around the head of my bed, about as far as I can reach, and in a great place on the other side of the room low down. I never saw a worse paper in my life.

One of those sprawling flamboyant patterns committing every artistic sin.

It is dull enough to confuse the eye in following, pronounced enough to constantly irritate, and provoke study, and when you follow the lame, uncertain curves for a little distance they suddenly commit suicide—plunge off at outrageous angles, destroy themselves in unheard-of contradictions.

The color is repellent, almost revolting; a smouldering, unclean yellow, strangely faded by the slow-turning sunlight.

It is a dull yet lurid orange in some places, a sickly sulphur tint in others.

No wonder the children hated it! I should hate it myself if I had to live in this room long.

There comes John, and I must put this away,—he hates to have me write a word.

We have been here two weeks, and I haven't felt like writing before, since that first day.

I am sitting by the window now, up in this atrocious nursery, and there is nothing to hinder my writing as much as I please, save lack of strength.

John is away all day, and even some nights when his cases are serious.

I am glad my case is not serious!

But these nervous troubles are dreadfully depressing.

John does not know how much I really suffer. He knows there is no *reason* to suffer, and that satisfies him.

Of course it is only nervousness. It does weigh on me so not to do my duty in any way!

I meant to be such a help to John, such a real rest and comfort, and here I am a comparative burden already!

Nobody would believe what an effort it is to do what little I am able—to dress and entertain, and order things.

It is fortunate Mary is so good with the baby. Such a dear baby!

And yet I *cannot* be with him, it makes me so nervous.

I suppose John never was nervous in his life. He laughs at me so about this wall paper!

At first he meant to repaper the room, but afterwards he said that I was letting it get the better of me, and that nothing was worse for a nervous patient than to give way to such fancies.

He said that after the wall paper was changed it would be the heavy bedstead, and then the barred windows, and then that gate at the head of the stairs, and so on.

"You know the place is doing you good," he said, "and really, dear, I don't care to renovate the house just for a three months' rental."

"Then do let us go downstairs," I said, "there are such pretty rooms there."

Then he took me in his arms and called me a blessed little goose, and said he would go down cellar if I wished, and would have it whitewashed into the bargain.

But he is right enough about the beds and windows and things.

It is as airy and comfortable a room as any one need wish, and of course, I would not be so silly as to make him uncomfortable just for a whim.

I'm really getting quite fond of the big room, all but that horrid paper.

Out of one window I can see the garden, those mysterious deep-shaded arbors, the riotous old-fashioned flowers, and bushes and gnarly trees.

Out of another I get a lovely view of the bay and a little private wharf belonging to the estate. There is a beautiful shaded lane that runs down there from the house. I always fancy I see people walking in these numerous paths and arbors, but John has cautioned me not to give way to fancy in the least. He says that with my imaginative power and habit of story-making a nervous weakness like mine is sure to lead to all manner of excited fancies, and that I ought to use my will and good sense to check the tendency. So I try.

I think sometimes that if I were only well enough to write a little it would relieve the press of ideas and rest me.

But I find I get pretty tired when I try.

It is so discouraging not to have any advice and companionship about my work. When I get really well John says we will ask Cousin Henry and Julia down for a long visit; but he says he would as soon put fire-works in my pillow-case as to let me have those stimulating people about now.

I wish I could get well faster.

But I must not think about that. This paper looks to me as if it *knew* what a vicious influence it had!

There is a recurrent spot where the pattern lolls like a broken neck and two bulbous eyes stare at you upside-down.

I got positively angry with the impertinence of it and the everlastingness. Up and down and sideways they crawl, and those absurd, unblinking eyes are everywhere. There is one place where two breadths didn't match, and the eyes go all up and down the line, one a little higher than the other.

I never saw so much expression in an inanimate thing before, and we all know how much expression they have!

I used to lie awake as a child and get more entertainment and terror out of blank walls and plain furniture than most children could find in a toy-store.

I remember what a kindly wink the knobs of our big old bureau used to have, and there was one chair that always seemed like a strong friend.

I used to feel that if any of the other things looked too fierce I could always hop into that chair and be safe.

The furniture in this room is no worse than inharmonious, however, for we had to bring it all from downstairs. I suppose when this was used as a playroom they had to take the nursery things out, and no wonder! I never saw such ravages as the children have made here.

The wall paper, as I said before, is torn off in spots, and it sticketh closer than a brother—they must have had perseverance as well as hatred.

Then the floor is scratched and gouged and splintered, the plaster itself is dug out here and there, and this great heavy bed, which is all we found in the room, looks as if it had been through the wars.

But I don't mind it a bit—only the paper.

There comes John's sister. Such a dear girl as she is, and so careful of me! I must not let her find me writing.

She is a perfect, an enthusiastic housekeeper, and hopes for no better profession. I verily believe she thinks it is the writing which made me sick!

But I can write when she is out, and see her a long way off from these windows.

There is one that commands the road, a lovely, shaded, winding road, and one that just looks off over the country. A lovely country, too, full of great elms and velvet meadows.

This wall paper has a kind of sub-pattern in a different shade, a particularly irritating one, for you can only see it in certain lights, and not clearly then.

But in the places where it isn't faded, and where the sun is just so, I can see a strange, provoking, formless sort of figure, that seems to sulk about that silly and conspicuous front design.

There's sister on the stairs!

Well, the Fourth of July is over! The people are all gone and I am tired out. John thought it might do me good to see a little company, so we just had mother and Nellie and the children down for a week.

Of course I didn't do a thing. Jennie sees to everything now.

But it tired me all the same.

John says if I don't pick up faster he shall send me to Weir Mitchell in the fall.

But I don't want to go there at all. I had a friend who was in his hands once, and she says he is just like John and my brother, only more so!

Besides, it is such an undertaking to go so far.

I don't feel as if it was worth while to turn my hand over for anything, and I'm getting dreadfully fretful and querulous.

I cry at nothing, and cry most of the time.

Of course I don't when John is here, or anybody else, but when I am alone.

And I am alone a good deal just now. John is kept in town very often by serious cases, and Jennie is good and lets me alone when I want her to.

So I walk a little in the garden or down that lovely lane, sit on the porch under the roses, and lie down up here a good deal.

I'm getting really fond of the room in spite of the wall paper. Perhaps *because* of the wall paper.

It dwells in my mind so!

I lie here on this great immovable bed—it is nailed down, I believe—and follow that pattern about by the hour. It is as good as gymnastics, I assure you. I start, we'll say, at the bottom, down in the corner over there where it has not been touched, and I determine for the thousandth time that I *will* follow that pointless pattern to some sort of a conclusion.

I know a little of the principles of design, and I know this thing was not arranged on any laws of radiation, or alternation, or repetition, or symmetry, or anything else that I ever heard of.

It is repeated, of course, by the breadths, but not otherwise.

Looked at in one way, each breadth stands alone, the bloated curves and flourishes—a kind of "debased Romanesque" with *delirium tremens*—go waddling up and down in isolated columns of fatuity.

But, on the other hand, they connect diagonally, and the sprawling outlines run off in great slanting waves of optic horror, like a lot of wallowing seaweeds in full chase.

The whole thing goes horizontally, too, at least it seems so, and I exhaust myself in trying to distinguish the order of its going in that direction.

They have used a horizontal breadth for a frieze, and that adds wonderfully to the confusion.

There is one end of the room where it is almost intact, and there, when the cross-lights fade and the low sun shines directly upon it, I can almost fancy radiation, after all—the interminable grotesques seem to form around a common centre and rush off in headlong plunges of equal distraction.

It makes me tired to follow it. I will take a nap, I guess.

I don't know why I should write this.

I don't want to.

I don't feel able.

And I know John would think it absurd. But I *must* say what I feel and think in some way—it is such a relief!

But the effort is getting to be greater than the relief.

Half the time now I am awfully lazy, and lie down ever so much.

John says I mustn't lose my strength, and has me take cod-liver oil and lots of tonics and things, to say nothing of ale and wine and rare meat.

Dear John! He loves me very dearly, and hates to have me sick. I tried to have a real earnest reasonable talk with him the other day, and tell him how I wished he would let me go and make a visit to Cousin Henry and Julia.

But he said I wasn't able to go, nor able to stand it after I got there; and I did not make out a very good case for myself, for I was crying before I had finished.

It is getting to be a great effort for me to think straight. Just this nervous weakness, I suppose.

And dear John gathered me up in his arms, and just carried me upstairs and laid me on the bed, and sat by me and read to me till he tired my head.

He said I was his darling and his comfort and all he had, and that I must take care of myself for his sake, and keep well.

He says no one but myself can help me out of it, that I must use my will and self-control and not let my silly fancies run away with me.

There's one comfort, the baby is well and happy, and does not have to occupy this nursery with the horrid wall paper.

If we had not used it that blessed child would have! What a fortunate escape! Why, I wouldn't have a child of mine, an impressionable little thing, live in such a room for worlds.

I never thought of it before, but it is lucky that John kept me here, after all. I can stand it so much easier than a baby, you see.

Of course I never mention it to them any more,—I am too wise,—but I keep watch of it all the same.

There are things in that paper that nobody knows but me, or ever will.

Behind that outside pattern the dim shapes get clearer every day.

It is always the same shape, only very numerous.

And it is like a woman stooping down and creeping about behind that pattern. I don't like it a bit. I wonder—I begin to think —I wish John would take me away from here!

It is so hard to talk with John about my case, because he is so wise, and because he loves me so.

But I tried it last night.

It was moonlight. The moon shines in all around, just as the sun does.

I hate to see it sometimes, it creeps so slowly, and always comes in by one window or another.

John was asleep and I hated to waken him, so I kept still

and watched the moonlight on that undulating wall paper till I felt creepy.

The faint figure behind seemed to shake the pattern, just as if she wanted to get out.

I got up softly and went to feel and see if the paper *did* move, and when I came back John was awake.

"What is it, little girl?" he said. "Don't go walking about like that—you'll get cold."

I thought it was a good time to talk, so I told him that I really was not gaining here, and that I wished he would take me away.

"Why, darling!" said he, "our lease will be up in three weeks, and I can't see how to leave before.

"The repairs are not done at home, and I cannot possibly leave town just now. Of course if you were in any danger I could and would, but you really are better, dear, whether you can see it or not. I am a doctor, dear, and I know. You are gaining flesh and color, your appetite is better. I feel really much easier about you."

"I don't weigh a bit more," said I, "nor as much; and my appetite may be better in the evening, when you are here, but it is worse in the morning, when you are away."

"Bless her little heart!" said he with a big hug; "she shall be as sick as she pleases. But now let's improve the shining hours by going to sleep, and talk about it in the morning."

"And you won't go away?" I asked gloomily.

"Why, how can I, dear? It is only three weeks more and then we will take a nice little trip of a few days while Jennie is getting the house ready. Really, dear, you are better!"

"Better in body, perhaps——" I began, and stopped short, for he sat up straight and looked at me with such a stern, reproachful look that I could not say another word.

"My darling," said he, "I beg of you, for my sake and for our child's sake, as well as for your own, that you will never for one instant let that idea enter your mind! There is nothing so dangerous, so fascinating, to a temperament like yours. It is a false and foolish fancy. Can you not trust me as a physician when I tell you so?"

So of course I said no more on that score, and we went to

sleep before long. He thought I was asleep first, but I wasn't—I lay there for hours trying to decide whether that front pattern and the back pattern really did move together or separately.

On a pattern like this, by daylight, there is a lack of sequence, a defiance of law, that is a constant irritant to a normal mind.

The color is hideous enough, and unreliable enough, and infuriating enough, but the pattern is torturing.

You think you have mastered it, but just as you get well under way in following, it turns a back somersault, and there you are. It slaps you in the face, knocks you down, and tramples upon you. It is like a bad dream.

The outside pattern is a florid arabesque, reminding one of a fungus. If you can imagine a toadstool in joints, an interminable string of toadstools, budding and sprouting in endless convolutions,—why, that is something like it.

That is, sometimes!

There is one marked peculiarity about this paper, a thing nobody seems to notice but myself, and that is that it changes as the light changes.

When the sun shoots in through the east window—I always watch for that first long, straight ray—it changes so quickly that I never can quite believe it.

That is why I watch it always.

By moonlight—the moon shines in all night when there is a moon—I wouldn't know it was the same paper.

At night in any kind of light, in twilight, candlelight, lamplight, and worst of all by moonlight, it becomes bars! The outside pattern, I mean, and the woman behind it is as plain as can be.

I didn't realize for a long time what the thing was that showed behind,—that dim sub-pattern,—but now I am quite sure it is a woman.

By daylight she is subdued, quiet. I fancy it is the pattern that keeps her so still. It is so puzzling. It keeps me quiet by the hour.

I lie down ever so much now. John says it is good for me, and to sleep all I can.

Indeed, he started the habit by making me lie down for an hour after each meal.

It is a very bad habit, I am convinced, for, you see, I don't sleep.

And that cultivates deceit, for I don't tell them I'm awake,—oh, no!

The fact is, I am getting a little afraid of John.

He seems very queer sometimes, and even Jennie has an inexplicable look.

It strikes me occasionally, just as a scientific hypothesis, that perhaps it is the paper!

I have watched John when he did not know I was looking, and come into the room suddenly on the most innocent excuses, and I've caught him several times *looking at the paper!* And Jennie too. I caught Jennie with her hand on it once.

She didn't know I was in the room, and when I asked her in a quiet, a very quiet voice, with the most restrained manner possible, what she was doing with the paper she turned around as if she had been caught stealing, and looked quite angry—asked me why I should frighten her so!

Then she said that the paper stained everything it touched, and that she had found yellow smooches on all my clothes and John's, and she wished we would be more careful!

Did not that sound innocent? But I know she was studying that pattern, and I am determined that nobody shall find it out but myself!

Life is very much more exciting now than it used to be. You see I have something more to expect, to look forward to, to watch. I really do eat better, and am more quiet than I was.

John is so pleased to see me improve! He laughed a little the other day, and said I seemed to be flourishing in spite of my wall paper.

I turned it off with a laugh. I had no intention of telling him that it was *because* of the wall paper—he would make fun of me. He might even want to take me away.

I don't want to leave now until I have found it out. There is a week more, and I think that will be enough.

I'm feeling ever so much better! I don't sleep much at night, for it is so interesting to watch developments; but I sleep a good deal in the daytime.

In the daytime it is tiresome and perplexing.

There are always new shoots on the fungus, and new shades of yellow all over it. I cannot keep count of them, though I have tried conscientiously.

It is the strangest yellow, that wall paper! It makes me think of all the yellow things I ever saw—not beautiful ones like buttercups, but old foul, bad yellow things.

But there is something else about that paper—the smell! I noticed it the moment we came into the room, but with so much air and sun it was not bad. Now we have had a week of fog and rain, and whether the windows are open or not the smell is here.

It creeps all over the house.

I find it hovering in the dining-room, skulking in the parlor, hiding in the hall, lying in wait for me on the stairs.

It gets into my hair.

Even when I go to ride, if I turn my head suddenly and surprise it—there is that smell!

Such a peculiar odor, too! I have spent hours in trying to analyze it, to find what it smelled like.

It is not bad—at first, and very gentle, but quite the subtlest, most enduring odor I ever met.

In this damp weather it is awful. I wake up in the night and find it hanging over me.

It used to disturb me at first. I thought seriously of burning the house—to reach the smell.

But now I am used to it. The only thing I can think of that it is like is the *color* of the paper—a yellow smell!

There is a very funny mark on this wall, low down, near the mopboard. A streak that runs around the room. It goes behind every piece of furniture, except the bed, a long, straight, even *smooch*, as if it had been rubbed over and over.

I wonder how it was done and who did it, and what they did it for. Round and round and round—round and round and round—it makes me dizzy!

I really have discovered something at last.

Through watching so much at night, when it changes so, I have finally found out.

The front pattern *does* move—and no wonder! The woman behind shakes it!

Sometimes I think there are a great many women behind, and sometimes only one, and she crawls around fast, and her crawling shakes it all over.

Then in the very bright spots she keeps still, and in the very shady spots she just takes hold of the bars and shakes them hard.

And she is all the time trying to climb through. But nobody could climb through that pattern—it strangles so; I think that is why it has so many heads.

They get through, and then the pattern strangles them off and turns them upside-down, and makes their eyes white!

If those heads were covered or taken off it would not be half so bad.

I think that woman gets out in the daytime!

And I'll tell you why—privately—I've seen her!

I can see her out of every one of my windows!

It is the same woman, I know, for she is always creeping, and most women do not creep by daylight.

I see her in that long shaded lane, creeping up and down. I see her in those dark grape arbors, creeping all around the garden.

I see her on that long road under the trees, creeping along, and when a carriage comes she hides under the blackberry vines.

I don't blame her a bit. It must be very humiliating to be caught creeping by daylight!

I always lock the door when I creep by daylight. I can't do it at night, for I know John would suspect something at once.

And John is so queer, now, that I don't want to irritate him. I wish he would take another room! Besides, I don't want anybody to get that woman out at night but myself.

I often wonder if I could see her out of all the windows at once.

But, turn as fast as I can, I can only see out of one at one time.

And though I always see her she *may* be able to creep faster than I can turn!

I have watched her sometimes away off in the open country, creeping as fast as a cloud shadow in a high wind.

If only that top pattern could be gotten off from the under one! I mean to try it, little by little.

I have found out another funny thing, but I sha'n't tell it this time! It does not do to trust people too much.

There are only two more days to get this paper off, and I believe John is beginning to notice. I don't like the look in his eyes.

And I heard him ask Jennie a lot of professional questions about me. She had a very good report to give.

She said I slept a good deal in the daytime.

John knows I don't sleep very well at night, for all I'm so quiet!

He asked me all sorts of questions, too, and pretended to be very loving and kind.

As if I couldn't see through him!

Still, I don't wonder he acts so, sleeping under this paper for three months.

It only interests me, but I feel sure John and Jennie are secretly affected by it.

Hurrah! This is the last day, but it is enough. John is to stay in town over night, and won't be out until this evening.

Jennie wanted to sleep with me—the sly thing! but I told her I should undoubtedly rest better for a night all alone.

That was clever, for really I wasn't alone a bit! As soon as it was moonlight, and that poor thing began to crawl and shake the pattern, I got up and ran to help her.

I pulled and she shook, I shook and she pulled, and before morning we had peeled off yards of that paper.

A strip about as high as my head and half around the room.

And then when the sun came and that awful pattern began to laugh at me I declared I would finish it to-day!

We go away to-morrow, and they are moving all my furniture down again to leave things as they were before.

Jennie looked at the wall in amazement, but I told her merrily that I did it out of pure spite at the vicious thing.

She laughed and said she wouldn't mind doing it herself, but I must not get tired.

How she betrayed herself that time!

But I am here, and no person touches this paper but me— not *alive!*

She tried to get me out of the room—it was too patent! But I said it was so quiet and empty and clean now that I believed I would lie down again and sleep all I could; and not to wake me even for dinner—I would call when I woke.

So now she is gone, and the servants are gone, and the things are gone, and there is nothing left but that great bedstead nailed down, with the canvas mattress we found on it.

We shall sleep downstairs to-night, and take the boat home to-morrow.

I quite enjoy the room, now it is bare again.

How those children did tear about here!

This bedstead is fairly gnawed!

But I must get to work.

I have locked the door and thrown the key down into the front path.

I don't want to go out, and I don't want to have anybody come in, till John comes.

I want to astonish him.

I've got a rope up here that even Jennie did not find. If that woman does get out, and tries to get away, I can tie her!

But I forgot I could not reach far without anything to stand on!

This bed will *not* move!

I tried to lift and push it until I was lame, and then I got so angry I bit off a little piece at one corner—but it hurt my teeth.

Then I peeled off all the paper I could reach standing on the floor. It sticks horribly and the pattern just enjoys it! All those strangled heads and bulbous eyes and waddling fungus growths just shriek with derision!

I am getting angry enough to do something desperate. To jump out of the window would be admirable exercise, but the bars are too strong even to try.

Besides, I wouldn't do it. Of course not. I know well enough that a step like that is improper and might be misconstrued.

I don't like to *look* out of the windows even—there are so many of those creeping women, and they creep so fast.

I wonder if they all come out of that wall paper, as I did?

But I am securely fastened now by my well-hidden rope— you don't get *me* out in the road there!

I suppose I shall have to get back behind the pattern when it comes night, and that is hard!

It is so pleasant to be out in this great room and creep around as I please!

I don't want to go outside. I won't, even if Jennie asks me to.

For outside you have to creep on the ground, and everything is green instead of yellow.

But here I can creep smoothly on the floor, and my shoulder just fits in that long smooch around the wall, so I cannot lose my way.

Why, there's John at the door!

It is no use, young man, you can't open it!

How he does call and pound!

Now he's crying for an axe.

It would be a shame to break down that beautiful door!

"John, dear!" said I in the gentlest voice, "the key is down by the front steps, under a plantain leaf!"

That silenced him for a few moments.

Then he said—very quietly indeed, "Open the door, my darling!"

"I can't," said I. "The key is down by the front door, under a plantain leaf!"

And then I said it again, several times, very gently and slowly, and said it so often that he had to go and see, and he got it, of course, and came in. He stopped short by the door.

"What is the matter?" he cried. "For God's sake, what are you doing?"

I kept on creeping just the same, but I looked at him over my shoulder.

"I've got out at last," said I, "in spite of you and Jennie! And I've pulled off most of the paper, so you can't put me back!"

Now why should that man have fainted? But he did, and right across my path by the wall, so that I had to creep over him every time!

●

I MUST NOT forget an apparition in my country, which appeared several times to Doctor Turbernile's sister, at Salisbury; which is much talked of. One married a second wife, and contrary to the agreement and settlement at the first wife's marriage, did wrong the children by the first venter. The settlement was hid behind a wainscot in the chamber where the Doctor's sister did lie: and the apparition of the first wife did discover it to her. By which means right was done to the first wife's children. The apparition told her that she wandered in the air, and was now going to God. Dr. Turbernile (oculist) did affirm this to be true. See Mr. Glanvill's *Sadducismus Triumphatus*.

—JOHN AUBREY

●

WHAT WE have inherited from our fathers and mothers is not all that 'walks in us.' There are all sorts of dead ideas and lifeless old beliefs. They have no tangibility, but they haunt us all the same and we can not get rid of them. Whenever I take up a newspaper I seem to see Ghosts gliding between the lines. Ghosts must be all over the country, as thick as the sands of the sea.

—HENRIK IBSEN

THE KING OF THE WORLD

Inquiry would reveal, I think, that this story by A. E. Coppard is one of his earliest. It is one of the three or four stories in his first book that seem to belong to a more fanciful period than the others: a very pure example of the far-away and long-ago atmosphere that characterized college short stories before the rise of the late, desperate realism. Such an atmosphere, dangerous for the imitative writer, has a strange distinction of its own when employed by so fine an artist as Coppard.—EDITOR.

A. E. Coppard

THE KING OF
THE WORLD

Once upon a time, yes, in the days of King Sennacherib, a young Assyrian captain, valiant and desirable, but more hapless than either, fleeing in that strange rout of the armies against Judah, was driven into the desert. Daily his company perished from him until he alone, astride a camel, was left searching desperately through a boundless desert for the loved plains of Shinar, sweet with flocks and rich with glittering cities. The desolation of ironic horizons that he could never live to pierce hung hopelessly in remote unattainable distances, endless as the blue sky. The fate of his comrades had left upon him a small pack of figs and wine, but in that uncharted wilderness it was but a pitiable parrying of death's last keen stroke. There was no balm or succour

75

in that empty sky; blue it was as sapphires, but savage with rays that scourged like flaming brass. Earth itself was not less empty, and the loneliness of his days was an increasing bitterness. He was so deeply forgotten of men, and so removed from the savour of life, from his lost country, the men he knew, the women he loved, their temples, their markets and their homes, that it seemed the gods had drawn that sweet and easy world away from his entangled feet.

But at last upon a day he was astonished and cheered by the sight of a black butterfly flickering in the air before him, and towards evening he espied a giant mound lying lonely in the east. He drove his camel to it, but found only a hill of sand whirled up by strange winds of the desert. He cast himself from the camel's back and lay miserably in the dust. His grief was extreme, but in time he tended his tired beast and camped in the shadow of the hill. When he gave himself up to sleep the night covering them was very calm and beautiful, the sky soft and streaming with stars; it seemed to his saddened mind that the desert and the deep earth were indeed dead, and life and love only in that calm enduring sky. But at midnight a storm arose with quickening furies that smote the desert to its unseen limits, and the ten thousand stars were flung into oblivion; winds flashed upon him with a passion more bitter than a million waves, a terror greater than hosts of immediate enemies. They grasped and plunged him into gulfs of darkness, heaped mountains upon him, lashed him with thongs of snakes and scattered him with scimitars of unspeakable fear. His soul was tossed in the void like a crushed star and his body beaten into the dust with no breath left him to bemoan his fate. Nevertheless by a miracle his soul and body lived on.

It was again day when he recovered, day in the likeness of yesterday, the horizons still infinitely far. Long past noon, the sun had turned in the sky; he was alone. The camel was doubtless buried in the fathoms he himself had escaped, but a surprising wonder greeted his half-blinded eyes; the hill of sand was gone, utterly, blown into the eternal waste of the desert, and in its track stood a strange thing—a shrine. There was a great unroofed pavement of onyx and blue jasper, large enough for the floor of a temple, with many life-size figures, both men and women, standing upon it all carved in rock and facing, at the sacred end, a giant pillared in black basalt, seven times the height of a man. The sad captain divined at once that this was the lost shrine of Namu-Sarkkon, the dead god of whom tradition spoke in the ancient litanies of his country. He heaved himself painfully from the grave of sand in which he had lain half-buried, and staggering to the pavement leaned in the shade of one of those figures fronting the dead god. In a little time he recovered and ate some figs which he carried in a leather bag at his hip, and plucked the sand from his eyes and ears and loosened his sandals and gear. Then he bowed himself for a moment before the black immobile idol, knowing that he would tarry here now until he died.

Namu-Sarkkon, the priestless god, had been praised of old time above all for his gifts of joy. Worshippers had gathered from the cities of Assyria at this his only shrine, offering their souls for a gift to him who, in his time and wisdom, granted their desires. But Namu-Sarkkon, like other gods, was a jealous god, and, because the hearts of mankind are vain and destined to betrayal, he turned the bodies of his devotees into rock and kept them pinioned in stone for a hundred years, or for a thousand years, according to the nature of their desires. Then if the consummation were worthy and just, the rock became a living fire, the blood of eternity quickened the limbs, and the god released the body full of youth and joy. But what god lives for ever? Not Namu-Sarkkon. He grew old and forgetful; his oracle was defamed. Stronger gods supplanted him and at last all power departed save only from one of his eyes. That eye possessed the favour of eternity, but only so faintly that the worshipper when released from his trap of stone lived at the longest but a day, some said even but an hour. None could then be found to exchange the endurances of the world for so brief a happiness. His worship ceased, Namu-Sarkkon was dead, and the remote shrine being lost to man's heart was lost to man's eyes. Even the tradition of its time and place had become a mere fantasy, but the whirlwinds of uncounted years sowing their sands about the shrine had left it blameless and unperishable, if impotent.

Recollecting this, the soldier gazed long at the dead idol. Its smooth huge bulk, carved wonderfully, was still without blemish and utterly cleansed of the sand. The strange squat body with the benign face stood on stout legs, one advanced as if about to stride

forward to the worshipper, and one arm outstretched offered the
sacred symbol. Then in a moment the Assyrian's heart leaped
within him; he had been staring at the mild eyes of the god—
surely there was a movement in one of the eyes! He stood erect,
trembling, then flung himself prostrate before Namu-Sarkkon, the
living god! He lay long, waiting for his doom to eclipse him, the
flaming swords of the sun scathing his weary limbs, the sweat
from his temples dripping in tiny pools beside his eyes. At last he
moved, he knelt up, and shielding his stricken eyes with one arm
he gazed at the god, and saw now quite clearly a black butterfly
resting on the lid of one of Sarkkon's eyes, inflecting its wings.
He gave a grunt of comprehension and relief. He got up and went
among the other figures. Close at hand they seemed fashioned
of soft material, like camphor or wax, that was slowly dissolving,
leaving them little more than stooks of clay, rough clod-like shapes
of people, all but one figure which seemed fixed in coloured marble, a woman of beauty so wondrous to behold that the Assyrian
bent his head in praise before her, though but an image of stone.
When he looked again at it the black butterfly from the eyelid of
the god fluttered between them and settled upon the girl's delicately carved lips for a moment, and then away. Amazedly watching it travel back to the idol he heard a movement and a sigh behind him. He leaped away, with his muscles distended, his fingers
outstretched, and fear bursting in his eyes. The beautiful figure
had moved a step towards him, holding out a caressing hand, calling him by his name, his name!

"Talakku! Talakku!"

She stood thus almost as if again turned to stone, until his fear
left him and he saw only her beauty, and knew only her living
loveliness in a tunic of the sacred purple fringed with tinkling
discs, that was clipped to her waist with a zone of gold and veiled,
even in the stone, her secret hips and knees. The slender feet were
guarded with pantoffles of crimson hide. Green agates in strings
of silver hung beside her brows, depending from a filet of gems
that crowned and confined the black locks tightly curled. Buds
of amber and coral were bound to her dusky wrists with threads of
copper, and between the delicacy of her brown breasts an amulet
of beryl, like a blue and gentle star, hung from a necklace made
of balls of opal linked with amethysts.

"Wonder of god! who are you?" whispered the warrior; but while he was speaking she ran past him sweetly as an antelope to the dark god. He heard the clicking of her beads and gems as she bent in reverence kissing the huge stone feet of Sarkkon. He did not dare to approach her although her presence filled him with rapture; he watched her obeisant at the shrine and saw that one of her crimson shoes had slipped from the clinging heel. What was she—girl or goddess, phantom or spirit of the stone, or just some lunatic of the desert? But whatever she was it was marvellous, and the marvel of it shocked him; time seemed to seethe in every channel of his blood. He heard her again call out his name as if from very far away.

"Talakku!"

He hastened to lift her from the pavement, and conquering his tremors he grasped and lifted her roughly, as a victor might hale a captive.

"Pretty antelope, who are you?"

She turned her eyes slowly upon his—this was no captive, no phantom—his intrepid arms fell back weakly to his sides.

"You will not know me, O brave Assyrian captain," said the girl gravely. "I was a weaver in the city of Eridu. . . ."

"Eridu!" It was an ancient city heard of only in the old poems of his country, as fabulous as snow in Canaan.

"Ai . . . it is long since riven into dust. I was a slave in Eridu, not . . . not a slave in spirit . . ."

"Beauty so rare is nobility enough," he said shyly.

"I worshipped god Namu-Sarkkon—behold his shrine. Who loves Namu-Sarkkon becomes what he wishes to become, gains what he wishes to gain."

"I have heard of these things," exclaimed the Assyrian. "What did you gain, what did you wish to become?"

"I worshipped here desiring in my heart to be loved by the King of the World."

"Who is he?"

She dropped her proud glances to the earth before him.

"Who was this King of the World?"

Still she made no reply, nor lifted her eyes.

"Who are these figures that stand with us here?" he asked.

"Dead, all dead," she sighed, "their destinies have closed. Only I renew the destiny."

She took his hand and led him among the wasting images.

"Merchants and poets, dead; princesses and slaves, dead; soldiers and kings, they look on us with eyes of dust, dead, all dead. I alone of Sarkkon's worshippers live on enduringly; I desired only love. I feed my spirit with new desire. I am the beam of his eye."

"Come," said the Assyrian suddenly, "I will carry you to Shinar; set but my foot to that lost track . . . will you?"

She shook her head gravely; "All roads lead to Sarkkon."

"Why do we tarry here? Come."

"Talakku, there is no way hence, no way for you, no way for me. We have wandered into the boundless. What star returns from the sky, what drop from the deep?"

Talakku looked at her with wonder, until the longing in his heart lightened the shadow of his doom.

"Tell me what I must do," he said.

She turned her eyes towards the dark god. "He knows," she cried, seizing his hands and drawing him towards the idol, "Come, Talakku."

"No, no!" he said in awe, "I cannot worship there. Who can deny the gods of his home and escape vengeance? In Shinar, beloved land, goes not one bee unhived nor a bird without a bower. Shall I slip my allegiance at every gust of the desert?"

For a moment a look of anguish appeared in her eyes.

"But if you will not leave this place," he continued gently, "Suffer me to stay."

"Talakku, in a while I must sink again into the stone."

"By all the gods I will keep you till I die," he said. "One day at least I will walk in Paradise."

"Talakku, not a day, not an hour; moments, moments, there are but moments now."

"Then, I am but dead," he cried, "for in that stone your sleeping heart will never dream of me."

"O, you whip me with rods of lilies. Quick, Talakku." He knew in her urgent voice the divining hope with which she wooed him. Alas for the Assyrian, he was but a man whose dying lips are slaked with wise honey. He embraced her as in a dream under the knees of towering Sarkkon. Her kisses, wrapt in the delicate veils of love, not the harsh brief glister of passion, were more lulling than a thousand songs of lost Shinar, but the time's sweet swiftness pursued them. Her momentary life had flown like a rushing star, swift and delighting but doomed. From the heel of the god a beetle of green lustre began to creep towards them.

"Farewell, Talakku," cried the girl. She stood again in her place before Namu-Sarkkon. "Have no fear, Talakku, prince of my heart. I will lock up in your breast all my soft unsundering years. Like the bird of fire they will surely spring again."

He waited, dumb, beside her, and suddenly her limbs compacted into stone once more. At the touch of his awed fingers her breast burned with the heat of the sun instead of the wooing blood. Then the vast silence of the world returned upon him; he looked in trembling loneliness at the stark sky, the unending desert, at the black god whose eye seemed to flicker balefully at him. Talakku turned to the lovely girl, but once more amazement gathered in all his veins. No longer stood her figure there—in its place he beheld only a stone image of himself.

"This is the hour, O beauteous one!" murmured the Assyrian, and, turning again towards the giant, he knelt in humility. His body wavered, faltered, suddenly stiffened, and then dissolved into a little heap of sand.

The same wind that unsealed Namu-Sarkkon and his shrine returning again at eve covered anew the idol and its figures, and the dust of the Assyrian captain became part of the desert for evermore.

●

PEREZ

The conception of an author haunted by a character of his own creation is not a new one. It is a variety of the Pygmalion legend that has intrigued a number of good writers. But W. L. George, in making his unhappy hero's Frankenstein-monster the avenger of a lax attitude toward artistic integrity, has contributed a new twist. I am not sure that the ending does not violate the very principle defended by the ghostly Perez; but if so, it points the more certain proof that Love will find a way.—EDITOR.

W. L. George

PEREZ

"And that," said Mr. Warlingham, holding up a few sheets of quarto paper, "is the end. The end," he repeated meditatively, his fingers playing with the manuscript as he could not bear to hand it to his secretary.

"May I congratulate you, Mr. Warlingham?" said Miss Medhurst. "I'm sure it will be a great success. A greater success than any of your novels." Mr. Warlingham raised a modest hand, and Miss Medhurst hastened to repair possible error. "I didn't mean that your novels haven't been successful; no one could say that; you remember how America went mad over '*The Four Frontiersmen*' . . . and there was '*Juliana*' too: eleven editions in nine weeks!"

"You forget the private limited edition on Japan paper," said Mr. Warlingham with some severity. "Yes, I haven't done badly." The novelist leant back in his armchair, finger-tips joined, staring at the ceiling with a certain complacency. He was a shortish, stoutish man aged about forty, with a rosy complexion, well-kept hands, a neatly clipped moustache and a noticeable baldness. Upon his rather thick, not unpleasant mouth lingered a little private smile, as if he were remembering obstacles easily overcome, were listing in his mind past triumphs; as if confident in merits that had not been overlooked by praise. Mr. Warlingham was successful. Mr. Warlingham looked successful. Then again he played with those manuscript sheets. He had dictated the whole of the book to Miss Medhurst except the last page, for he knew that the highest skill is obtained only when the hand labours with the brain. Still, at that moment, Mr. Warlingham was conscious of some uneasiness. It was an indefinable feeling which had come upon him during the last few days, a sense of . . . how could he put it? secret criticism? No, not exactly that. True, he had found that last page incredibly difficult to write; he had been held back by some doubt which his mind could not analyse. And now the strange sensation grew stronger. He felt as if he were not alone, as if something faintly hostile stood by his side. He wrinkled his brows crossly. "Ridiculous," he murmured. Indeed, his surroundings were strictly normal. Here he sat in his familiar study, his typical study: the deep red and blue carpet, the crowded bookshelves, the excellent appliances, the files, the scales, the typewriter in the corner, everything in his comfortable room cried out to him that he sat in the midst of ordinary life. But then? What? Tired, he supposed. Anyhow he mustn't brood.

"Well," said Mr. Warlingham, briskly, "here are the last sheets, Miss Medhurst. Please type them out, and I will revise them with the rest."

Miss Medhurst held out a wiry little hand and took the manuscript with an air of devotion. Her author's words thrilled her always, but, conveyed in his own handwriting, they took on an air of sanctity. Then Mr. Warlingham reached across the desk and took back the sheets. "I will read you the last page," he said, and Miss Medhurst wondered at a tone of defiance which had come into his voice. She could not know that Mr. Warlingham was re-

acting against a sudden growth of that secret feeling. As he gave
her the sheets he had again experienced it, and determined to read
the page aloud. After all there *might* be something wrong with
the stuff.

"Oh," she gasped, "please do. Like that," she added hurriedly.
"I shan't make any mistakes in typing." But a faint flush rose in
her pale cheeks as she grew conscious of her own excitement. Miss
Medhurst was of indeterminable age, between thirty and forty;
she was small, thin, with little features that had once been pretty;
dressed always in dark colours she looked even more insignificant
than she was; her hair was of a neutral brown shade; only her
eyes, that all mankind could, if it cared, describe as yellow-grey,
grew large and soft as she gazed upon the man whose secretary
she had been for ten years, yet was still to her marvellous and
inspired. Mr. Warlingham did not observe any change in those
neutral eyes. He cleared his throat, and read. The first few sentences Miss Medhurst did not hear, for her heart beat fast, but
after a moment the old spell worked, and as in a purple cloud the
phrases of Mr. Warlingham took shape for her:

". . . The six men stood undecided about the long shape that
lay upon the ground. It was as if they feared to touch that sumptu-
ously wild buccaneer, heavy-breeched, scarlet-sashed, so dark, and
fierce, and beautiful, lest the slightest movement should release the
mortal spark that lingered still in the faintly heaving breast. At
last Moreno spoke: 'We cannot leave him here,' he said. 'The sun
is too hot.'

"Indeed, from the purple vault above, the Mexican sun fell
like a heavy hand, and the air was filled with the buzzing of insects; the air was crowded with life; Moreno, pitiless and crime-
stained, felt his heart grow big and painful as he thought that
nature was filled with life, yet could not afford another hour to
Perez, Perez the man without fear, his comrade who lay there
dying. 'Come,' he said gently, 'let us carry him into the house.'

"A few minutes later they stood a little away from the bedside. Perez breathed more hurriedly. He grew yet paler, and
Moreno stepped forward, an anguish upon him. Then for one
moment his comrade opened his eyes, those soft, lustrous eyes;
his lips twisted into a crooked smile as for the last time he met
the gaze of Moreno; but, very slowly, his head sank down and

was still. Thus he lay, his dark face sharp outlined against the pillow, as an ancient bronze, his black beard erect, in death defiant as in life.

"Moreno fell upon his knees: 'Good-bye, eagleheart, good-bye,' he cried. One by one the others stole away; Perez lay still and aloof. And his soul, winging its way through space, carried as a last memory the sound of his comrade's weeping."

Miss Medhurst did not move; her yellow-grey eyes were dim, for she too loved the eaglehearted buccaneer. So she did not notice that as Mr. Warlingham pronounced the last word, he started so violently that his knees rapped against the desk. Nor did she see him furtively glance to the right and left, his eyes dilated, or fumble for his handkerchief with an unsteady hand. For Mr. Warlingham had distinctly heard a voice, a loud, indignant voice. And what it said was: "Nonsense!"

Nonsense? Somebody had said: "Nonsense." With sudden suspicion Mr. Warlingham stared at Miss Medhurst, then was ashamed, for his secretary sat in the same rapt attitude, and her eyes were swimming in tears. But then? what? Oh, if only his hand wouldn't shake so. Wherever had he put his handkerchief? He swore silently, still casting into the corners of the room a frightened gaze.

"It's wonderful," murmured Miss Medhurst, "wonderful. Oh, it'll be a great success. It's better than anything Henry James ever did. It's better than Hall Caine. But why must Perez die? Yes, I suppose it's artistic truth and that he had to die, that . . ."

"Miss Medhurst," said Mr. Warlingham in a voice suddenly metallic and laboured, "if you don't mind . . . I won't do any more to-day . . . I'm not very well."

She bent forward with quick sympathy: "Yes, of course, work like yours takes all your strength. I'll go. And, please, please, Mr. Warlingham, rest. Go into the Park. And I'm sure a tonic . . ."

Mr. Warlingham was not listening. He sat with clenched hands: when Miss Medhurst said, "Why must Perez die?" a voice had grumbled: "He didn't."

II

For a long time Mr. Warlingham sat with his face in his hands. The silence was complete, no ghostly voice assailed his ears, but at any moment he knew that it might speak. Haunted! he was haunted. An hour passed while his excited brain revolved horrid stories; he thought of phantoms that rattle chains, of the death dog, of riding witches. At length, only, as the study grew dark and he hurriedly switched on the electric light, he forced himself into a balanced state of mind.

"This won't do," he said aloud. "If I go on like this I'll get worse, and then . . ." he shuddered, "I'll find myself in a private nursing home, to call it by a polite name. How can you be so absurd?" he asked himself. "You let yourself become the prey of your nerves just because you're a little overworked; Old Medhurst is right; she's been at me for months to take a rest. Anyhow . . ." Mr. Warlingham suddenly grew defiant and addressed the wall: "Speak up! Now's your chance. I'm listening." There was no reply, and, nearly comforted, Mr. Warlingham got into his evening clothes and went to his club. He ate an excellent dinner; conscious of the rights of an invalid he drank a pint of champagne. This helped him to find the company attractive; his satisfaction was increased after dinner, for he made up a four at bridge with Draycott, Lord Langwith and the club bore, and as fortune gave him almost uniformly good hands he grew to like the club bore. At twelve o'clock Mr. Warlingham unlocked his front door, meeting the darkness with a slight tremor that passed away at once; faintly conscious of uneasiness as he undressed, he for a moment feared that he would have the horrors. But he slept almost at once, and awoke only to find that his valet had gone out, leaving by his side his letters, the newspapers, and the morning tea, while brilliant spring sunshine lit up every part of the room. Almost at once he remembered.

"Ah," he thought, as he stretched, "I feel better," and began to drink his tea. Then, quite suddenly, as the cup fell crashing and unnoticed to the ground, Mr. Warlingham found his brow wet. Somebody was standing at the foot of his bed. He clenched his fists, staring. Yes, this was no illusion. The door had not opened, and yet a man stood looking at him with a disagreeable expression. Mr. Warlingham made a violent effort to speak, but found his tongue palsied. Then a voice, the familiar voice that had haunted him, grew audible:

"Well," said the shape. "Surprised to see me, I suppose." Mr. Warlingham did not reply. "You've given me a lot of trouble," the Thing went on; "materialising isn't as easy as you novelists make out. When I think of the weeks of bother I've had over this business, I've a good mind . . ." It visibly snarled. "Still, that's not what I've really come for. Warlingham, that ending of yours is nonsense. Bunkum. Pure bunkum."

"What do you want?" asked Mr. Warlingham feebly, for this insult to his literary powers galvanised him.

"I want you to alter the ending. And you'll do it, sure as my name's Perez."

Mr. Warlingham still stared at the Thing. Perez! He had known at once that tall, black-bearded shape with the lustrous, dark eyes, had recognised the full trousers and the scarlet sash. His buccaneer! But this was awful. Was he going mad? Perez was talking again.

"Look here," he said. "I've got no time to waste. It's all I can do to hold my molecules together, so let's get down to business. That ending of yours is bunkum because I didn't die. Understand? *I didn't die.* It's quite true that Moreno, whom you have the audacity to call my friend, the scab who cheated me out of thirty-three dollars at euchre last night, so that I had to let the moonlight through him . . . Well, Moreno, as I was saying, carried me in. But that's where what you call your imagination failed. Mercedes was in the house; for a fortnight she fed me on milk and I got perfectly well. As soon as I felt strong enough I murdered her and took charge of her savings, which I am glad to say were considerable."

"You . . . murdered the woman who saved your life!" cried Mr. Warlingham, his fear expelled by surprise.

"Of course. You may think it ungrateful of me. But I'm not a respectable character; you made me like that, and if I killed Mercedes it's your fault."

"Well! I like your cheek," said Mr. Warlingham. "You say that Mercedes . . ."

"I'm tired of Mercedes," grumbled Perez. "And don't interrupt. With her savings I went to Mexico City and bought myself a small saloon at No. 11, Calle Berganza. I'm doing quite well; I've a man to help me, and by and by, I expect to develop a bit. Before

I'm done I'll be running a big cafe; I'll call it the Cafe Warlingham. I'll always be pleased to see you. My place is near the street
car depot. So you see your ending won't do."

For a moment, Mr. Warlingham was silent. He was still frightened, but interested. "All this," he said, loftily, "has nothing to do
with me."

"Nothing to do with you? Don't be silly. You've no right
to create a character and end him up wrong. Especially you've no
right to kill him off to save yourself the trouble of writing a few
hundred pages more."

"I'd like to see you do it," protested Mr. Warlingham. "You
talk as if one could write a few hundred pages in a week."

"Nothing to do with me. Anyhow I didn't die. I'm alive to-
day, so your ending isn't true; it isn't artistic truth."

"What!" shouted Mr. Warlingham, springing up in bed, "you
dare to stand there and lecture me on artistic truth. Please remember whom you're talking to."

"Don't brag; keep that for Miss Medhurst. Obviously the ending's inartistic; if you'll just look up Chapter VIII and observe the
psychology of . . ."

Here the discussion grew confused, and Mr. Warlingham
found himself at a disadvantage, for Perez knew a great many
things about the psychology of the other characters (and of
Perez) which had never occurred to the novelist. They ended by
shouting.

"Thoroughly inartistic. . . ."

"I know more about novels than you'll . . ."

"I want another seven chapters at least."

"Leave the room at once, sir."

There was a tap at the door. As Mr. Warlingham sank down
upon the pillow the valet came in and said: "Your bath is ready,
sir," then withdrew, Perez being obviously invisible to him.

"All right," said Perez. "Go and have your bath. I know you
think best in your bath. Besides, every molecule of me is aching,
so I'll dissolve for an hour or so. But," he added, threateningly,
"I'll come back and resume the discussion. I'll teach you . . ."
He began to grow dim. "You'll thank me for this some day." The
voice grew faint. "I'll teach you artistic truth."

III

"Mr. Warlingham," said Miss Medhurst as she buttoned her gloves prior to going out to lunch, "please don't think me impertinent, but I'm sure you're working too hard. You *must* have a holiday."

"You mean," said the novelist in an acid tone, "that my work isn't up to standard."

"I don't mean anything of the kind," protested the little spinster. "I think you're wonderful. Only I thought yesterday, and again this morning . . . well, you know you had to stop dictating, and . . ."

"Yes, I know, I know." Mr. Warlingham had indeed been paralysed for several minutes while Perez stood behind Miss Medhurst's chair and made ferocious faces. When at last Mr. Warlingham decided to affront him and tremblingly resumed an incoherent dictation, Perez had punctuated every other sentence with loud cries of "Rot!" while Miss Medhurst shrank from her author's livid face. "Inspiration," she thought, "is a beautiful, terrible thing."

"Just for a few days." Miss Medhurst's tone grew wheedling, and as she bent forward her yellow-grey eyes grew tender. "In the country. Think of it; here is the spring. Daffodils, primroses and . . . daffodils in the fields."

"Perhaps I will," said Mr. Warlingham harshly. "I'll see whether he . . . I mean, I'll see how I feel."

But the days that followed brought no improvement in Mr. Warlingham's condition. Perez had begun by appearing twice in one day; within a week he took to materialising every four hours or so. This seemed to please the phantom: "I say, Warlie, old boy," he remarked as he leaned against the tobacconist's counter while his victim tried to buy cigarettes, "this materialising isn't as difficult as it looks. It's a matter of practice; now that I know how to control my molecules I can bring it off every two hours. In time I may be able to keep it up day and night; then I'll never have to leave you at all."

Mr. Warlingham groaned and rushed out of the shop, leaving his change in front of the amazed salesman, Perez running by his side with long, easy strides.

"Steady," said the phantom, "there's no hurry. You won't get away from me."

Soon Mr. Warlingham realised that Perez was right. He appeared in the Park and followed his author all the way to the publisher, arguing incessantly. He was beginning to develop theories: "You've made a mess of the whole thing," said Perez. "On thinking it over carefully I don't think I should have killed Pepita before eloping with Inez. As for Isabel, I rather think I shot her father, so you should say in Chapter V . . ."

"I wish you'd go away," moaned Mr. Warlingham. "If you go on bothering me I'll burn the book and you'll be snuffed out."

"I shan't. You'll write it over again in the right way. Now, Warlie, pull yourself together. I'll make a celebrity of you when you've learned artistic truth."

Thereupon followed acrid argument, for Mr. Warlingham no longer feared Perez; he merely looked upon him as an intolerable nuisance whose literary criticisms outraged his pride. But on this occasion the victim soon was silenced, for a policeman turned round and stared as Mr. Warlingham told the empty air not to be a fool. As time passed the oppressor almost realised his threats; his molecular control became so great that in one day he managed to lunch with Mr. Warlingham, to make a fifth at bridge (which cost Mr. Warlingham a good deal of money and the friendship of his partner) and to enter a crowded omnibus where he sat upon an unmoved old lady and loudly lectured the apparently blind and deaf passengers on the defects of Mr. Warlingham's style. The author felt a dull brutalisation creep over him; Miss Medhurst openly wept. "He doesn't seem to care about anything," she whimpered to herself; "I don't think he hears."

She was wrong. Mr. Warlingham heard too much. His ruddy colour was leaving him, and his waistcoat began to sag. "I'm wasting away," he thought, and did not care. But his nervous system was working independently of his will, and only his pride forbade that he should surrender to the ever more insistent Perez; an incident brought about the breakdown. Mr. Warlingham went to a fashionable lunch party and found himself seated between a very pretty American Duchess and a well-known actress. Anxious to make himself agreeable he garnished his conversation with epigrams, and for a time all went well; he was alone. Who could say?

perhaps it was all over. Then he saw Perez, seated on the rose bowl, his heavy boots in the middle of a basket of crystallised violets. He seemed to enjoy the scene, but as Mr. Warlingham remarked: "Don't do unto others as you would be done by, for they may not have the same taste," the phantom informed the party that the epigram was not by Mr. Warlingham, but by Mr. Bernard Shaw. For a few minutes the novelist ground his teeth and plodded on his witty way, but the shameless Perez gravely followed every epigram by: "As Whistler put it," or "That's the best thing Anatole France ever said"; at last Mr. Warlingham grew blackly silent. Later the American Duchess confided to her husband that after the first ten minutes well-known novelists turned out to be dull dogs. Meanwhile Mr. Warlingham sat in his study, his face in his hands, while Miss Medhurst fluttered about him. "Tell me what's the matter," she implored. Mr. Warlingham looked at her wildly; perhaps something of her immense tenderness touched him, for suddenly he spoke.

"Don't think me mad . . . I don't know what to do. It keeps following me about, and arguing. Oh, what shall I do?" The horror of the past days was released as he told Miss Medhurst everything, little details of time and place, literary arguments the phantom had used, and gripping the wiry little hand that trembled and yielded he cried out as a child: "Oh, I'm right, I'm right, tell me I'm right."

"Yes," whispered Miss Medhurst. "Of course you're right. Who could teach you anything? Don't alter your novel; it doesn't belong to you, it belongs to humanity. But you are overwrought, worn out. I'm going to pack for you, and you must go to the seaside for a week. Promise?"

Mr. Warlingham nodded. He did not notice that for a moment his secretary laid upon his arm fingers light as a butterfly's wing.

A week later Miss Medhurst entered the study, her heart beating. Oh how ill he looked! "Well?" she asked tensely.

"It's no good," said Mr. Warlingham in a gloomy tone. "Perez and I went . . . bathing."

For a moment Miss Medhurst was tempted to laugh, then was ashamed. This was terrible. The man chosen of the muses was dying before her eyes; worse, his reason was dying, because of a wretched illusion. Oh, if she could only take it upon herself! She wrung her little hard hands, and as she peered into corners, seized by a sense of the uncanny, the hatred of a true partisan held her: if only Perez could appear to her . . . she would outrage him, blot him out. Yes, blot him out. The words raised in the little spinster an incredible excitement; medical memories taken from the newspapers invaded her mind, wonderful cures brought about by suggestion, by self-suggestion. *By self-suggestion!* Aghast at her own audacity, she put her hand on the stricken man's shoulder.

"Mr. Warlingham," she whispered, "do you hear me? It is an illusion. Do you understand it is an illusion?"

"Yes," said the novelist, without raising his eyes.

"Then if it is an illusion, let us face it. Prove to yourself that it is only an illusion."

"Prove?" uttered Mr. Warlingham. "How?"

"He said he lived in Mexico, that he kept a saloon. Well . . . go and see. Go to Mexico."

"Go to Mexico," shouted Mr. Warlingham, leaping to his feet.

"Yes. Go. Go and see. It's an illusion. When you get there, very likely you'll find a bank at the address he gave you. And then you'll know it was only an illusion. You'll be free."

Mr. Warlingham thought for a long time, then gently took her hand and said: "Perhaps you're right. But don't let me go alone. Come with me."

IV

A sickly man wrapped in a travelling rug staggered on to the platform, hanging with a curious air of helplessness to the arm of a slim, capable little woman. Behind them, in procession, came several swarthy porters laden with baggage; the commissionaire of the *Hotel de las Cuatro Naciones*, disguised as a full general, led the way. The little woman erupted into the Spanish she had acquired on board ship, directed the porters to wait with the *equipaje*, gave the commissionaire five pesos to help the heavy luggage through the customs, and gently led the grey-faced man to the waiting omnibus.

"Now, Mr. Warlingham," she said, briskly, half an hour later. "You must stay in bed and rest. Nothing can be done to-day; first you must sleep. I must go to my hotel, but I'll come back for dinner. You'll stay in bed? Promise?"

"All right," said Mr. Warlingham, wearily. He shut his eyes as if half-asleep or exhausted. With a sudden fond gesture Miss Medhurst smoothed the creases from the pillow and left the room.

But she stayed only a few minutes at her hotel, just long enough to wash her thin, intelligent face, and to smile as she powdered her nose, for this was a new habit. For a moment, on the steps, she shrank from the broad expanse of the *plaza*, crowded with black-garbed men crowned by sombreros, bareheaded women whose hair shone like oiled silk, lounging *peones*, wild, half-Indian, always about to be run over by the prancing buggy horses or the clanging electric cars. Then she clenched her little fists and called a cab. Her course was fixed in advance; the driver must carry her to a church selected from the plan of Mexico City and must inevitably pass through the Calle Berganza; yet she would not arouse suspicion by naming the street of doom. Her excitement was so powerful that the broad, white streets became to her mere symbols. She saw only name plates: *C. de Tampico* . . . *C. de Santa Fe* . . . then at last, in a mist, *C. Berganza* . . . 27 . . . 25 . . . a little street of old, mean houses . . . 19 . . . a dog rooting in a dustbin . . . 13 . . .

She passed number 11, was conscious horribly of the bush over the door. Indeed it was not a bank, but a little bar. Miss Medhurst ground her teeth, as she dropped her sunshade in the road, stopped the driver by a violent tug at the coat-tail (for not a word of Spanish could she remember) leaped out, ran back. As she bent she stared into the little bar. For a moment she could see nothing through the dirty panes, then a shape. Miss Medhurst tottered as she walked away with the sunshade: she had recognised the tall, dark man, with the soft eyes and the black beard.

All through the night Miss Medhurst tossed in the high Spanish bed. Perez! It was Perez. It was madness, death for Mr. Warlingham. Miss Medhurst wept into the pillow, bit it so as not to scream. And later she lit all the candles, seized by the dread of the supernatural. When morning came and she crept to the *Cuatro Naciones* she was paler than Mr. Warlingham. As she came in he was speaking to the shade, and for a moment she thought that she too could now glimpse Perez against the flowered curtain. Mad!

Both mad! But a savage purpose told her to gain time, to make Mr. Warlingham dress, to drive him wildly through the town, into the suburbs, only to gain time to think. The novelist did not resist, seemed to have lost even the desire to hasten to the place of trial, or to flee from it. Obediently, when lunch was done, he lay down for a siesta. All he said was:

"If you're going out, remember this is Mexico and take your revolver." He had given her the weapon and loaded it himself. For Mr. Warlingham's novels were slightly sensational, and he expected life to equal them. Miss Medhurst went out into the heat that struck up from the stones (she remembered Mr. Warlingham's metaphor) like a heavy hand. She hardly felt it, nor the molten shafts of light from the purple sky. She sped through the deserted streets, a grim, earnest little figure, careless of sights, on the route of yesterday. At the corner of Calle Berganza she paused, then ran. Number 11 stood open, and without an apparent tremor she went in. As her eyes, sun-blind, recovered sight, she took in the few details, the wooden tables, the few iron chairs, the counter, the armchair on which slumbered the man of destiny. Her limbs shook, but Miss Medhurst rapped a table with her knuckles until Perez half opened his eyes.

"*Te!*" she said harshly, "*con leche.*"

Perez stared at her. Tea? with milk? At half-past two? He expressed this view. Also the *mozo* had gone home for a siesta. He was alone in the cafe.

"*Te con leche,*" snapped Miss Medhurst.

Perez reflected that she was English, therefore a lunatic, therefore also rich, and after some time brought in an amazingly vile liquid. The little spinster watched his face, his hands. "Am I mad?" she thought. Then: "No, it is he." She drank the tea. She had nothing to say. This was the end. And yet she could not go. Time, gain time; she must. Desperately she asked if this were an old inn.

"*No se,*" replied Perez sleepily.

She found herself explaining that her employer was an antiquarian who studied old inns. Might she visit the inn? Perez was about to refuse, but observed in Miss Medhurst's hand a twenty pesos note. Lunatic, he thought, shrugged his shoulders, and led the way up steep wooden stairs.

They stood in a dark, shuttered bedroom. A carved oak chest

ran up to the black beams. On the mantelpiece stood a cheap statuette of a saint. In an alcove she saw the high, white bed.

"The carpet," said Perez, proudly pointing to the horror from Brussels, "is new." He turned to her, smiling. She did not know what had happened. She did not know what she did. She heard a shot, a cry, found herself, laughing and crying, on her knees by the side of the man she had slain, found her tiny strength tenfold multiplied as she hauled him to the bed, set upon the pillow the limp head. But before she fled through the lonely, brilliant streets, she thrust the revolver into the relaxed hand.

She found Mr. Warlingham up and excited.

"Where have you been all this time? I've been waiting," he cried crossly. "I feel so funny. I was talking to him a quarter of an hour ago, and he vanished in the middle of a word. Oh, I feel so ill."

"Come with me," said Miss Medhurst, firmly. "Come now. I have found the way. Now! quick; hurry!"

Her new cunning told her to make him walk, to arouse no notice. That cunning led her and her trembling charge into the bar where a dirty *mozo* now sat and smoked. It told her to make her scanty Spanish incomprehensible, until at last the *mozo* said he must fetch his master. He called up the wooden stairs, and Miss Medhurst's fingers entered like claws into Mr. Warlingham's arm. There was no reply. "*Senor!*" called the *mozo* again. Again no reply. The man's feet sounded loud as he went up the stairs. A moment later they heard him cry out, and as if drawn by a predominant will they ran up the stairs.

"Ah!" screamed the waiter.

But there was no horror in Mr. Warlingham's face. With enraptured eyes he gazed at the long, red-sashed body, at the black beard that stood erect, outlined against the pillow. Colour had rushed into his cheeks. He looked erect, confident in his fame.

"I was right!" he cried. "It was artistic truth!" His voice rose; he shouted into a realm now devoid of phantoms. "I was right! Right! Artistically right!"

●

Sɪʀ Wᴀʟᴛᴇʀ Lᴏɴɢ of Draycot, (grandfather of Sir James Long) had two wives; the first a daughter of Sir Thomas Packington in Worcestershire; by whom he had a son: his second wife was a daughter of Sir John Thynne of Long-Leat; by whom he had several sons and daughters. The second wife did use much artifice to render the son by the first wife, (who had not much Promethean fire) odious to his father; she would get her acquaintance to make him drunk; and then expose him in that condition to his father; in fine, she never left off her attempts, till she got Sir Walter to disinherit him. She laid the scene for doing this at Bath, at the assizes, where was her brother Sir Egrimond Thynne, an eminent serjeant at law, who drew the writing; and his clerk was to sit up all night to engross it; as he was writing, he perceived a shadow on the parchment, from the candle; he looked up, and there appeared a hand, which immediately vanished; he was startled at it, but thought it might be only his fancy, being sleepy; so he writ on. By and by a fine white hand interposed between the writing and the candle (he could discern it was a woman's hand) but vanished as before; I have forgot, it appeared a third time. But with that the clerk threw down his pen, and would engross no more, but goes and tells his master of it, and absolutely refuses to do it. But it was done by somebody, and Sir Walter was prevailed with to seal and sign it. He lived not long after; and his body did not go quiet to the grave, it being arrested at the church porch by the trustees of the first lady. The heir's relations took his part, and commenced a suit against Sir Walter (the second son), and compelled him to accept of a moiety of the estate; so the eldest son kept South-Wroxhall, and Sir Walter, the second son, Dray-Cernes, &c. This was about the middle of the reign of King James I.

—Jᴏʜɴ Aᴜʙʀᴇʏ

THE WENDIGO

Algernon Blackwood, as I have discovered while worrying my friends for news of their favorite ghost stories, has staunch partisans and earnest belittlers. Such an author can consider himself far luckier than one whose followers are supplemented only by those who are indifferent. I suspect that the two groups will argue more sharply over *The Wendigo* than over any of his other stories. It seems to make nature-lovers very uneasy in their minds; but is that not, after all, the primary function of a ghost story?— EDITOR.

Algernon
Blackwood

THE
WENDIGO

I

A considerable number of hunting parties were out that year without finding so much as a fresh trail; for the moose were uncommonly shy, and the various Nimrods returned to the bosoms of their respective families with the best excuses the facts or their imaginations could suggest. Dr. Cathcart, among others, came back without a trophy; but he brought instead the memory of an experience which he declares was worth all the bull-moose that had ever been shot. But then Cathcart, of

Aberdeen, was interested in other things besides moose—amongst them the vagaries of the human mind. This particular story, however, found no mention in his book on *Collective Hallucination* for the simple reason (so he confided once to a fellow colleague) that he himself played too intimate a part in it to form a competent judgment of the affair as a whole. . . .

Besides himself and his guide, Hank Davis, there was young Simpson, his nephew, a divinity student destined for the "Wee Kirk" (then on his first visit to Canadian backwoods), and the latter's guide, Défago. Joseph Défago was a French "Canuck," who had strayed from his native Province of Quebec years before, and had got caught in Rat Portage when the Canadian Pacific Railway was a-building; a man who, in addition to his unparalleled knowledge of woodcraft and bush-lore, could also sing the old *voyageur* songs and tell a capital hunting yarn into the bargain. He was deeply susceptible, moreover, to that singular spell which the wilderness lays upon certain lonely natures, and he loved the wild solitudes with a kind of romantic passion that amounted almost to an obsession. The life of the backwoods fascinated him—whence, doubtless, his surpassing efficiency in dealing with their mysteries.

On this particular expedition he was Hank's choice. Hank knew him and swore by him. He also swore at him, "jest as a pal might," and since he had a vocabulary of picturesque, if utterly meaningless, oaths, the conversation between the two stalwart and hardy woodsmen was often of a rather lively description. This river of expletives, however, Hank agreed to dam a little out of respect for his old "hunting boss," Dr. Cathcart, whom of course he addressed after the fashion of the country as "Doc," and also because he understood that young Simpson was already a "bit of a parson." He had, however, one objection to Défago, and one only—which was, that the French Canadian sometimes exhibited what Hank described as "the output of a cursed and dismal mind," meaning apparently that he sometimes was true to type, Latin type, and suffered fits of a kind of silent moroseness when nothing could induce him to utter speech. Défago, that is to say, was imaginative and melancholy. And, as a rule, it was too long a spell of "civilization" that induced the attacks, for a few days of the wilderness invariably cured them.

This, then, was the party of four that found themselves in

camp the last week in October of that "shy moose year" 'way up
in the wilderness north of Rat Portage—a forsaken and desolate
country. There was also Punk, an Indian, who had accompanied
Dr. Cathcart and Hank on their hunting trips in previous years,
and who acted as cook. His duty was merely to stay in camp,
catch fish, and prepare venison steaks and coffee at a few minutes'
notice. He dressed in the worn-out clothes bequeathed to him by
former patrons, and except for his coarse black hair and dark
skin, he looked in these city garments no more like a real redskin
than a stage negro looks like a real African. For all that, however,
Punk had in him still the instincts of his dying race; his taciturn
silence and his endurance survived; also his superstition.

The party round the blazing fire that night were despondent,
for a week had passed without a single sign of recent moose discovering itself. Défago had sung his song and plunged into a story,
but Hank, in bad humour, reminded him so often that "he kep'
mussing-up the fac's so, that it was 'most all nothin' but a petred-
out lie," that the Frenchman had finally subsided into a sulky
silence which nothing seemed likely to break. Dr. Cathcart and his
nephew were fairly done after an exhausting day. Punk was washing up the dishes, grunting to himself under the lean-to of branches,
where he later also slept. No one troubled to stir the slowly dying
fire. Overhead the stars were brilliant in a sky quite wintry, and
there was so little wind that ice was already forming stealthily
along the shores of the still lake behind them. The silence of the
vast listening forest stole forward and enveloped them.

Hank broke in suddenly with his nasal voice.

"I'm in favour of breaking new ground to-morrow, Doc," he
observed with energy, looking across at his employer. "We don't
stand a dead Dago's chance about here."

"Agreed," said Cathcart, always a man of few words. "Think
the idea's good."

"Sure pop, it's good," Hank resumed with confidence.
"S'pose, now, you and I strike west, up Garden Lake way for a
change! None of us ain't touched that quiet bit o' land yet——"

"I'm with you."

"And you, Défago, take Mr. Simpson along in the small canoe,
skip across the lake, portage over into Fifty Island Water, and
take a good squint down that thar southern shore. The moose

'yarded' there like hell last year, and for all we know they may be doin' it agin this year jest to spite us."

Défago, keeping his eyes on the fire, said nothing by way of reply. He was still offended, possibly, about his interrupted story.

"No one's been up that way this year, an' I'll lay my bottom dollar on *that!*" Hank added with emphasis, as though he had a reason for knowing. He looked over at his partner sharply. "Better take the little silk tent and stay away a couple o' nights," he concluded, as though the matter were definitely settled. For Hank was recognized as general organizer of the hunt, and in charge of the party.

It was obvious to any one that Défago did not jump at the plan, but his silence seemed to convey something more than ordinary disapproval, and across his sensitive dark face there passed a curious expression like a flash of firelight—not so quickly, however, that the three men had not time to catch it. "He funked for some reason, *I* thought," Simpson said afterwards in the tent he shared with his uncle. Dr. Cathcart made no immediate reply, although the look had interested him enough at the time for him to make a mental note of it. The expression had caused him a passing uneasiness he could not quite account for at the moment.

But Hank, of course, had been the first to notice it, and the odd thing was that instead of becoming explosive or angry over the other's reluctance, he at once began to humour him a bit.

"But there ain't no *speshul* reason why no one's been up there this year," he said, with a perceptible hush in his tone; "not the reason *you* mean, anyway! Las' year it was the fires that kep' folks out, and this year I guess—I guess it jest happened so, that's all!" His manner was clearly meant to be encouraging.

Joseph Défago raised his eyes a moment, then dropped them again. A breath of wind stole out of the forest and stirred the embers into a passing blaze. Dr. Cathcart again noticed the expression in the guide's face, and again he did not like it. But this time the nature of the look betrayed itself. In those eyes, for an instant, he caught the gleam of a man scared in his very soul. It disquieted him more than he cared to admit.

"Bad Indians up that way?" he asked, with a laugh to ease matters a little, while Simpson, too sleepy to notice this subtle by-play, moved off to bed with a prodigious yawn; "or,—or anything wrong with the country?" he added, when his nephew was out of hearing.

Hank met his eye with something less than his usual frankness.

"He's jest skeered," he replied good-humouredly, "skeered stiff about some ole feery tale! That's all, ain't it, ole pard?" And he gave Défago a friendly kick on the moccasined foot that lay nearest the fire.

Défago looked up quickly, as from an interrupted reverie, a reverie, however, that had not prevented his seeing all that went on about him.

"Skeered—*nuthin'!*" he answered, with a flush of defiance. "There's nuthin' in the Bush that can skeer Joseph Défago, and don't you forget it!" And the natural energy with which he spoke made it impossible to know whether he told the whole truth or only a part of it.

Hank turned towards the doctor. He was just going to add something when he stopped abruptly and looked round. A sound close behind them in the darkness made all three start. It was old Punk, who had moved up from his lean-to while they talked and now stood there just beyond the circle of firelight—listening.

" 'Nother time, Doc!" Hank whispered, with a wink, "when the gallery ain't stepped down into the stalls!" And, springing to his feet, he slapped the Indian on the back and cried noisily, "Come up t' the fire an' warm yer dirty red skin a bit." He dragged him towards the blaze and threw more wood on. "That was a mighty good feed you give us an hour or two back," he continued heartily, as though to set the man's thoughts on another scent, "and it ain't Christian to let you stand there freezin' yer ole soul to hell while we're gettin' all good an' toasted!" Punk moved in and warmed his feet, smiling darkly at the other's volubility which he only half understood, but saying nothing. And presently Dr. Cathcart, seeing that further conversation was impossible, followed his nephew's example and moved off to the tent, leaving the three men smoking over the now blazing fire.

It is not easy to undress in a small tent without waking one's companion, and Cathcart, hardened and warm-blooded as he was in spite of his fifty odd years, did what Hank would have described as "considerable of his twilight" in the open. He noticed, during the process, that Punk had meanwhile gone back to his lean-to, and that Hank and Défago were at it hammer and tongs, or, rather, hammer and anvil, the little French Canadian being the anvil. It was all very like the conventional stage picture of Western melodrama: the fire lighting up their faces with patches of alternate red and black; Défago, in slouch hat and moccasins in the part of the "badlands" villain; Hank, open-faced and hatless, with that reckless fling of his shoulders, the honest and deceived hero; and old Punk, eavesdropping in the background, supplying the atmosphere of mystery. The doctor smiled as he noticed the details; but at the same time something deep within him—he hardly knew what —shrank a little, as though an almost imperceptible breath of warning had touched the surface of his soul and was gone again before he could seize it. Probably it was traceable to that "scared expression" he had seen in the eyes of Défago; "probably"—for this hint of fugitive emotion otherwise escaped his usually so keen analysis. Défago, he was vaguely aware, might cause trouble somehow. . . . He was not as steady a guide as Hank, for instance. . . . Further than that he could not get . . .

He watched the men a moment longer before diving into the stuffy tent where Simpson already slept soundly. Hank, he saw, was swearing like a mad African in a New York nigger saloon; but it was the swearing of "affection." The ridiculous oaths flew freely now that the cause of their obstruction was asleep. Presently he put his arm almost tenderly upon his comrade's shoulder, and they moved off together into the shadows where their tent stood faintly glimmering. Punk, too, a moment later followed their example and disappeared between his odorous blankets in the opposite direction.

Dr. Cathcart then likewise turned in, weariness and sleep still fighting in his mind with an obscure curiosity to know what it was had scared Défago about the country up Fifty Island Water way,—wondering, too, why Punk's presence had prevented the completion of what Hank had to say. Then sleep overtook him. He would know to-morrow. Hank would tell him the story while they trudged after the elusive moose.

Deep silence fell about the little camp, planted there so audaciously in the jaws of the wilderness. The lake gleamed like a sheet of black glass beneath the stars. The cold air pricked. In the draughts of night that poured their silent tide from the depths of the forest, with messages from distant ridges and from lakes just beginning to freeze, there lay already the faint, bleak odours of coming winter. White men, with their dull scent, might never have divined them; the fragrance of the wood-fire would have concealed from them these almost electrical hints of moss and bark and hardening swamp a hundred miles away. Even Hank and Défago, subtly in league with the soul of the woods as they were, would probably have spread their delicate nostrils in vain. . . .

But an hour later, when all slept like the dead, old Punk crept from his blankets and went down to the shore of the lake like a shadow—silently, as only Indian blood can move. He raised his head and looked about him. The thick darkness rendered sight of small avail, but, like the animals, he possessed other senses that darkness could not mute. He listened—then sniffed the air. Motionless as a hemlock-stem he stood there. After five minutes again he lifted his head and sniffed, and yet once again. A tingling of the wonderful nerves that betrayed itself by no outer sign, ran through him as he tasted the keen air. Then, merging his figure into the surrounding blackness in a way that only wild men and animals understand, he turned, still moving like a shadow, and went stealthily back to his lean-to and his bed.

And soon after he slept, the change of wind he had divined stirred gently the reflection of the stars within the lake. Rising among the far ridges of the country beyond Fifty Island Water, it came from the direction in which he had stared, and it passed over the sleeping camp with a faint and sighing murmur through the tops of the big tree that was almost too delicate to be audible. With it, down the desert paths of night, though too faint, too high even for the Indian's hair-like nerves, there passed a curious, thin odour, strangely disquieting, an odour of something that seemed unfamiliar—utterly unknown.

The French Canadian and the man of Indian blood each stirred uneasily in his sleep just about this time, though neither of them woke. Then the ghost of that unforgettably strange odour passed away and was lost among the leagues of tenantless forest beyond.

II

In the morning the camp was astir before the sun. There had been a light fall of snow during the night and the air was sharp. Punk had done his duty betimes, for the odours of coffee and fried bacon reached every tent. All were in good spirits.

"Wind's shifted!" cried Hank vigorously, watching Simpson and his guide already loading the small canoe. "It's across the lake —dead right for you fellers. And the snow'll make bully trails! If there's any moose mussing around up thar, they'll not get so much as a tail-end scent of you with the wind as it is. Good luck, Monsieur Défago!" he added, facetiously giving the name its French pronunciation for once, "*bonne chance!*"

Défago returned the good wishes, apparently in the best of spirits, the silent mood gone. Before eight o'clock old Punk had the camp to himself, Cathcart and Hank were far along the trail that led westwards, while the canoe that carried Défago and Simpson, with silk tent and grub for two days, was already a dark speck bobbing on the bosom of the lake, going due east.

The wintry sharpness of the air was tempered now by a sun that topped the wooded ridges and blazed with a luxurious warmth upon the world of lake and forest below; loons flew skimming through the sparkling spray that the wind lifted; divers shook their dripping heads to the sun and popped smartly out of sight again; and as far as eye could reach rose the leagues of endless, crowding Bush, desolate in its lonely sweep and grandeur, untrodden by foot of man, and stretching its mighty and unbroken carpet right up to the frozen shores of Hudson Bay.

Simpson, who saw it all for the first time as he paddled hard in the bows of the dancing canoe, was enchanted by its austere beauty. His heart drank in the sense of freedom and great spaces just as his lungs drank in the cool and perfumed wind. Behind him in the stern seat, singing fragments of his native chanties, Défago steered the craft of birchbark like a thing of life, answering cheerfully all his companion's questions. Both were gay and lighthearted. On such occasions men lose the superficial, worldly distinctions; they become human beings working together for a common end. Simpson, the employer, and Défago, the employed, among these primitive forces, were simply—two men, the "guider," and the "guided." Superior knowledge, of course, assumed control, and the younger man fell without a second thought into the quasi-subordinate position. He never dreamed of objecting when Défago dropped the "Mr.," and addressed him as "Say, Simpson," or "Simpson, boss," which was invariably the case before they reached the farther shore after a stiff paddle of twelve miles against a head wind. He only laughed, and liked it; then ceased to notice it at all.

For this "divinity student" was a young man of parts and character, though as yet, of course, untravelled; and on this trip—the first time he had seen any country but his own and little Switzerland—the huge scale of things somewhat bewildered him. It was one thing, he realized, to hear about primeval forests, but quite another to see them. While to dwell in them and seek acquaintance with their wild life was, again, an initiation that no intelligent man could undergo without a certain shifting of personal values hitherto held for permanent and sacred.

Simpson knew the first faint indication of this emotion when he held the new .303 rifle in his hands and looked along its pair of faultless, gleaming barrels. The three days' journey to their headquarters, by lake and portage, had carried the process a stage farther. And now that he was about to plunge beyond even the fringe of wilderness where they were camped into the virgin heart of uninhabited regions as vast as Europe itself, the true nature of the situation stole upon him with an effect of delight and awe that his imagination was fully capable of appreciating. It was himself and Défago against a multitude—at least, against a Titan!

The bleak splendours of these remote and lonely forests rather overwhelmed him with the sense of his own littleness. That stern quality of the tangled backwoods which can only be described as merciless and terrible, rose out of these far blue woods swimming upon the horizon, and revealed itself. He understood the silent warning. He realized his own utter helplessness. Only Défago, as a symbol of a distant civilization where man was master, stood between him and a pitiless death by exhaustion and starvation.

It was thrilling to him, therefore, to watch Défago turn over the canoe upon the shore, pack the paddles carefully underneath, and then proceed to "blaze" the spruce stems for some distance on either side of an almost invisible trail, with the careless remark thrown in, "Say, Simpson, if anything happens to me, you'll find the canoe all correc' by these marks;—then strike doo west into the sun to hit the home camp agin, see?"

It was the most natural thing in the world to say, and he said it without any noticeable inflexion of the voice, only it happened to express the youth's emotions at the moment with an utterance that was symbolic of the situation and of his own helplessness as a factor in it. He was alone with Défago in a primitive world: that was all. The canoe, another symbol of man's ascendancy, was now to be left behind. Those small yellow patches, made on the trees by the axe, were the only indications of its hiding-place.

Meanwhile, shouldering the packs between them, each man carrying his own rifle, they followed the slender trail over rocks and fallen trunks and across half-frozen swamps; skirting numerous lakes that fairly gemmed the forest, their borders fringed with mist; and towards five o'clock found themselves suddenly on the edge of the woods, looking out across a large sheet of water in front of them, dotted with pine-clad islands of all describable shapes and sizes.

"Fifty Island Water," announced Défago wearily, "and the sun jest goin' to dip his bald old head into it!" he added, with unconscious poetry; and immediately they set about pitching camp for the night.

In a very few minutes, under those skilful hands that never made a movement too much or a movement too little, the silk tent stood taut and cosy, the beds of balsam boughs ready laid, and a brisk cooking-fire burned with the minimum of smoke. While the young Scotchman cleaned the fish they had caught trolling behind the canoe, Défago "guessed" he would "jest as soon" take a turn through the Bush for indications of moose. "*May* come across a trunk where they bin and rubbed horns," he said, as he moved off, "or feedin' on the last of the maple leaves,"—and he was gone.

His small figure melted away like a shadow in the dusk, while Simpson noted with a kind of admiration how easily the forest absorbed him into herself. A few steps, it seemed, and he was no longer visible.

Yet there was little underbrush hereabouts; the trees stood somewhat apart, well spaced; and in the clearings grew silver-birch and maple, spearlike and slender, against the immense stems of spruce and hemlock. But for occasional prostrate monsters, and the boulders of grey rock that thrust uncouth shoulders here and there out of the ground, it might well have been a bit of park in the Old Country. Almost, one might have seen in it the hand of man. A little to the right, however, began the great burnt section, miles in extent, proclaiming its real character—*brulé*, as it is called, where the fires of the previous year had raged for weeks, and the blackened stumps now rose gaunt and ugly, bereft of branches, like gigantic match-heads stuck into the ground, savage and desolate beyond words. The perfume of charcoal and rain-soaked ashes still hung faintly about it.

The dusk rapidly deepened; the glades grew dark; the crackling of the fire and the wash of little waves along the rocky lake shore were the only sounds audible. The wind had dropped with the sun, and in all that vast world of branches nothing stirred. Any moment, it seemed, the woodland gods, who are to be worshipped in silence and loneliness, might sketch their mighty and terrific outlines among the trees. In front, through doorways pillared by huge straight stems, lay the stretch of Fifty Island Water, a crescent-shaped lake some fifteen miles from tip to tip, and perhaps five miles across where they were camped. A sky of rose and saffron, more clear than any atmosphere Simpson had ever known, still dropped its pale streaming fires across the waves, where the islands—a hundred, surely, rather than fifty—floated like the fairy barques of some enchanted fleet. Fringed with pines, whose crests fingered most delicately the sky, they almost seemed to move upwards as the light faded—about to weigh anchor and navigate the pathways of the heavens instead of the currents of their native and desolate lake.

And strips of coloured cloud, like flaunting pennons, signalled their departure to the stars. . . .

The beauty of the scene was strangely uplifting. Simpson smoked the fish and burnt his fingers into the bargain in his efforts to enjoy it and at the same time tend the frying-pan and the fire. Yet, ever at the back of his thoughts, lay that other aspect of the wilderness: the indifference to human life, the merciless spirit of desolation which took no note of man. The sense of his utter loneliness, now that even Défago had gone, came close as he looked about him and listened for the sound of his companion's returning footsteps.

There was pleasure in the sensation, yet with it a perfectly comprehensible alarm. And instinctively the thought stirred in him: "What should I—*could* I, do—if anything happened and he did not come back——?"

They enjoyed their well-earned supper, eating untold quantities of fish, and drinking unmilked tea strong enough to kill men who had not covered thirty miles of hard "going," eating little on the way. And when it was over, they smoked and told stories round the blazing fire, laughing, stretching weary limbs, and discussing plans for the morrow. Défago was in excellent spirits, though disappointed at having no signs of moose to report. But it was dark and he had not gone far. The *brulé*, too, was bad. His clothes and hands were smeared with charcoal. Simpson, watching him, realized with renewed vividness their position—alone together in the wilderness.

"Défago," he said presently, "these woods, you know, are a bit too big to feel quite at home in—to feel comfortable in, I mean! . . . Eh?" He merely gave expression to the mood of the moment; he was hardly prepared for the earnestness, the solemnity even, with which the guide took him up.

"You've hit it right, Simpson, boss," he replied, fixing his searching brown eyes on his face, "and that's the truth, sure. There's no end to 'em—no end at all." Then he added in a lowered tone as if to himself, "There's lots found out *that*, and gone plumb to pieces!"

But the man's gravity of manner was not quite to the other's liking; it was a little too suggestive for this scenery and setting; he was sorry he had broached the subject. He remembered suddenly how his uncle had told him that men were sometimes stricken with a strange fever of the wilderness, when the seduction of the uninhabited wastes caught them so fiercely that they went forth, half fascinated, half deluded, to their death. And he had a shrewd idea that his companion held something in sympathy with that queer type. He led the conversation on to other topics, on to Hank and the doctor, for instance, and the natural rivalry as to who should get the first sight of moose.

"If they went doo west," observed Défago carelessly, "there's sixty miles between us now—with ole Punk at halfway house eatin' himself full to bustin' with fish and corfee." They laughed together over the picture. But the casual mention of those sixty miles again made Simpson realize the prodigious scale of this land where they hunted; sixty miles was a mere step; two hundred little more than a step. Stories of lost hunters rose persistently before his memory. The passion and mystery of homeless and wandering men, seduced by the beauty of great forests, swept his soul in a way too vivid to be quite pleasant. He wondered vaguely whether it was the mood of his companion that invited the unwelcome suggestion with such persistence.

"Sing us a song, Défago, if you're not too tired," he asked; "one of those old *voyageur* songs you sang the other night." He handed his tobacco pouch to the guide and then filled his own pipe, while the Canadian, nothing loth, sent his light voice across the lake in one of those plaintive, almost melancholy chanties with which lumbermen and trappers lessen the burden of their labour. There was an appealing and romantic flavour about it, something that recalled the atmosphere of the old pioneer days when Indians and wilderness were leagued together, battles frequent, and the Old Country farther off than it is to-day. The sound travelled pleasantly over the water, but the forest at their backs seemed to swallow it down with a single gulp that permitted neither echo nor resonance.

It was in the middle of the third verse that Simpson noticed something unusual—something that brought his thoughts back with a rush from far-away scenes. A curious change had come into the man's voice. Even before he knew what it was, uneasiness caught him, and looking up quickly, he saw that Défago, though still singing, was peering about him into the Bush, as though he heard or saw something. His voice grew fainter—dropped to a hush—then ceased altogether. The same instant, with a movement amazingly alert, he started to his feet and stood upright—*sniffing the air*. Like a dog scenting game, he drew the air into his nostrils in short, sharp breaths, turning quickly as he did so in all directions, and finally "pointing" down the lake shore, eastwards. It was a performance unpleasantly suggestive and at the same time singularly dramatic. Simpson's heart fluttered disagreeably as he watched it.

"Lord, man! How you made me jump!" he exclaimed, on his feet beside him the same instant, and peering over his shoulder into the sea of darkness. "What's up? Are you frightened——?"

Even before the question was out of his mouth he knew it was foolish, for any man with a pair of eyes in his head could see that the Canadian had turned white down to his very gills. Not even sunburn and the glare of the fire could hide that.

The student felt himself trembling a little, weakish in the knees. "What's up?" he repeated quickly. "D'you smell moose? Or anything queer, anything—wrong?" He lowered his voice instinctively.

The forest pressed round them with its encircling wall; the nearer tree-stems gleamed like bronze in the firelight; beyond that —blackness, and, so far as he could tell, a silence of death. Just behind them a passing puff of wind lifted a single leaf, looked at it, then laid it softly down again without disturbing the rest of the covey. It seemed as if a million invisible causes had combined just to produce that single visible effect. *Other* life pulsed about them —and was gone.

Défago turned abruptly; the livid hue of his face had turned to a dirty grey.

"I never said I heered—or smelt—nuthin'," he said slowly and emphatically, in an oddly altered voice that conveyed somehow a touch of defiance. "I was only—takin' a look round—so to speak. It's always a mistake to be too previous with yer questions." Then he added suddenly with obvious effort, in his more natural voice, "Have you got the matches, Boss Simpson?" and proceeded to light the pipe he had half filled just before he began to sing.

Without speaking another word they sat down again by the fire, Défago changing his side so that he could face the direction the wind came from. For even a tenderfoot could tell that. Défago changed his position in order to hear and smell—all there was to be heard and smelt. And, since he now faced the lake with his back to the trees it was evidently nothing in the forest that had sent so strange and sudden a warning to his marvellously trained nerves.

"Guess now I don't feel like singing any," he explained presently of his own accord. "That song kinder brings back memories that's troublesome to me; I never oughter've begun it. It sets me on t' imagining things, see?"

Clearly the man was still fighting with some profoundly moving emotion. He wished to excuse himself in the eyes of the other. But the explanation, in that it was only a part of the truth, was a lie, and he knew perfectly well that Simpson was not deceived by it. For nothing could explain away the livid terror that had dropped over his face while he stood there sniffing the air. And nothing—no amount of blazing fire, or chatting on ordinary subjects—could make that camp exactly as it had been before. The shadow of an unknown horror, naked if unguessed, that had flashed for an instant in the face and gestures of the guide, had also communicated itself, vaguely and therefore more potently, to his companion. The guide's visible efforts to dissemble the truth only made things worse. Moreover, to add to the younger man's uneasiness, was the difficulty, nay, the impossibility he felt of asking questions, and also his complete ignorance as to the cause. . . . Indians, wild animals, forest fires—all these, he knew, were wholly out of the question. His imagination searched vigorously, but in vain. . . .

Yet, somehow or other, after another long spell of smoking, talking and roasting themselves before the great fire, the shadow that had so suddenly invaded their peaceful camp began to lift. Perhaps Défago's efforts, or the return of his quiet and normal attitude accomplished this; perhaps Simpson himself had exaggerated the affair out of all proportion to the truth; or possibly the vigorous air of the wilderness brought its own powers of healing. Whatever the cause, the feeling of immediate horror seemed to have passed away as mysteriously as it had come, for nothing occurred to feed it. Simpson began to feel that he had permitted himself the unreasoning terror of a child. He put it down partly to a certain subconscious excitement that this wild and immense scenery generated in his blood, partly to the spell of solitude, and partly to overfatigue. That pallor in the guide's face was, of course, uncommonly hard to explain, yet it *might* have been due in some way to an effect of firelight, or his own imagination. . . . He gave it the benefit of the doubt; he was Scotch.

When a somewhat unordinary emotion has disappeared, the mind always finds a dozen ways of explaining away its causes. . . . Simpson lit a last pipe and tried to laugh to himself. On getting home to Scotland it would make quite a good story. He did not realize that this laughter was a sign that terror still lurked in the recesses of his soul—that, in fact, it was merely one of the conventional signs by which a man, seriously alarmed, tries to persuade himself that he is *not* so.

Défago, however, heard that low laughter and looked up with surprise on his face. The two men stood, side by side, kicking the embers about before going to bed. It was ten o'clock—a late hour for hunters to be still awake.

"What's ticklin' yer?" he asked in his ordinary tone, yet gravely.

"I—I was thinking of our little toy woods at home, just at that moment," stammered Simpson, coming back to what really dominated his mind, and startled by the question, "and comparing them to—to all this," and he swept his arm round to indicate the Bush.

A pause followed in which neither of them said anything.

"All the same I wouldn't laugh about it, if I was you," Défago added, looking over Simpson's shoulder into the shadows. "There's places in there nobody won't never see into—nobody knows what lives in there either."

"Too big—too far off?" The suggestion in the guide's manner was immense and horrible.

Défago nodded. The expression on his face was dark. He, too, felt uneasy. The younger man understood that in a *hinterland* of this size there might well be depths of wood that would never in the life of the world be known or trodden. The thought was not exactly the sort he welcomed. In a loud voice, cheerfully, he suggested that it was time for bed. But the guide lingered, tinkering with the fire, arranging the stones needlessly, doing a dozen things that did not really need doing. Evidently there was something he wanted to say, yet found it difficult to "get at."

"Say, you, Boss Simpson," he began suddenly, as the last shower of sparks went up into the air, "you don't—smell nothing, do you—nothing pertickler, I mean?" The commonplace question, Simpson realized, veiled a dreadfully serious thought in his mind. A shiver ran down his back.

"Nothing but this burning wood," he replied firmly, kicking again at the embers. The sound of his own foot made him start.

"And all the evenin' you ain't smelt—nothing?" persisted the guide, peering at him through the gloom; "nothing extrordiny, and different to anything else you ever smelt before?"

"No, no, man; nothing at all!" he replied aggressively, half angrily.

Défago's face cleared. "That's good!" he exclaimed with evident relief. "That's good to hear."

"Have *you?*" asked Simpson sharply, and the same instant regretted the question.

The Canadian came closer in the darkness. He shook his head. "I guess not," he said, though without overwhelming conviction. "It must've been jest that song of mine that did it. It's the song they sing in lumber-camps and god-forsaken places like that, when they're skeered the Wendigo's somewheres around, doin' a bit of swift travellin'——"

"And what's the Wendigo, pray?" Simpson asked quickly, irritated because again he could not prevent that sudden shiver of the nerves. He knew that he was close upon the man's terror and the cause of it. Yet a rushing passionate curiosity overcame his better judgment, *and* his fear.

Défago turned swiftly and looked at him as though he were suddenly about to shriek. His eyes shone, but his mouth was wide open. Yet all he said, or whispered rather, for his voice sank very low, was——

"It's nuthin'—nuthin' but what those lousy fellers believe when they've bin hittin' the bottle too long—a sort of great animal that lives up yonder," he jerked his head northwards, "quick as lightning in its tracks, an' bigger'n anything else in the Bush, an' ain't supposed to be very good to look at—*that's all!*"

"A backwoods' superstition—" began Simpson, moving hastily towards the tent in order to shake off the hand of the guide that clutched his arm. "Come, come, hurry up for God's sake, and get the lantern going! It's time we were in bed and asleep if we're to be up with the sun to-morrow. . . ."

The guide was close on his heels. "I'm coming," he answered out of the darkness, "I'm coming." And after a slight delay he appeared with the lantern and hung it from a nail in the front pole of the tent. The shadows of a hundred trees shifted their places quickly as he did so, and when he stumbled over the rope, diving swiftly inside, the whole tent trembled as though a gust of wind struck it.

The two men lay down, without undressing, upon their beds

of soft balsam boughs, cunningly arranged. Inside, all was warm and cosy, but outside the world of crowding trees pressed close about them, marshalling their million shadows, and smothering the little tent that stood there like a wee white shell facing the ocean of tremendous forest.

Between the two lonely figures within, however, there pressed another shadow that was *not* a shadow from the night. It was the Shadow cast by the strange Fear, never wholly exorcised, that had leaped suddenly upon Défago in the middle of his singing. And Simpson, as he lay there, watching the darkness through the open flap of the tent, ready to plunge into the fragrant abyss of sleep, knew first that unique and profound stillness of a primeval forest when no wind stirs . . . and when the night has weight and substance that enters into the soul to bind a veil about it. . . . Then sleep took him. . . .

III

Thus it seemed to him, at least. Yet it was true that the lap of the water, just beyond the tent door, still beat time with his lessening pulses when he realized that he was lying with his eyes open and that another sound had recently introduced itself with cunning softness between the splash and murmur of the little waves.

And, long before he understood what this sound was, it had stirred in him the centres of pity and alarm. He listened intently, though at first in vain, for the running blood beat all its drums too noisily in his ears. Did it come, he wondered, from the lake, or from the woods? . . .

Then, suddenly, with a rush and a flutter of the heart, he knew that it was close beside him in the tent; and, when he turned over for a better hearing, it focussed itself unmistakably not two feet away. It was a sound of weeping; Défago upon his bed of branches was sobbing in the darkness as though his heart would break, the blankets evidently stuffed against his mouth to stifle it.

And his first feeling, before he could think or reflect, was the rush of a poignant and searching tenderness. This intimate, human sound, heard amid the desolation about them, woke pity. It was so incongruous, so pitifully incongruous—and so vain! Tears—in this vast and cruel wilderness: of what avail? He thought of a little child crying in mid-Atlantic. . . . Then, of course, with fuller realization, and the memory of what had gone before, came the descent of the terror upon him, and his blood ran cold.

"Défago," he whispered quickly, "what's the matter?" He tried to make his voice very gentle. "Are you in pain—unhappy——?" There was no reply, but the sounds ceased abruptly. He stretched his hand out and touched him. The body did not stir.

"Are you awake?" for it occurred to him that the man was crying in his sleep. "Are you cold?" He noticed that his feet, which were uncovered, projected beyond the mouth of the tent. He spread an extra fold of his own blankets over them. The guide had slipped down in his bed, and the branches seemed to have been dragged with him. He was afraid to pull the body back again, for fear of waking him.

One or two tentative questions he ventured softly, but though he waited for several minutes there came no reply, nor any sign of movement. Presently he heard his regular and quiet breathing, and putting his hand again gently on the breast, felt the steady rise and fall beneath.

"Let me know if anything's wrong," he whispered, "or if I can do anything. Wake me at once if you feel—queer."

He hardly knew quite what to say. He lay down again, thinking and wondering what it all meant. Défago, of course, had been crying in his sleep. Some dream or other had afflicted him. Yet never in his life would he forget that pitiful sound of sobbing, and the feeling that the whole awful wilderness of woods listened. . . .

His own mind busied itself for a long time with the recent events, of which *this* took its mysterious place as one, and though his reason successfully argued away all unwelcome suggestions, a sensation of uneasiness remained, resisting ejection, very deep-seated—peculiar beyond ordinary.

IV

But sleep, in the long run, proves greater than all emotions. His thoughts soon wandered again; he lay there, warm as toast, exceedingly weary; the night soothed and comforted, blunting the edges of memory and alarm. Half-an-hour later he was oblivious of everything in the outer world about him.

Yet sleep, in this case, was his great enemy, concealing all approaches, smothering the warning of his nerves.

As, sometimes, in a nightmare events crowd upon each others' heels with a conviction of dreadfullest reality, yet some inconsistent detail accuses the whole display of incompleteness and disguise, so the events that now followed, though they actually happened, persuaded the mind somehow that the detail which could explain them had been overlooked in the confusion, and that therefore they were but partly true, the rest delusion. At the back of the sleeper's mind something remains awake, ready to let slip the judgment, "All this is not *quite* real; when you wake up you'll understand."

And thus, in a way, it was with Simpson. The events, not wholly inexplicable or incredible in themselves, yet remain for the man who saw and heard them a sequence of separate acts of cold horror, because the little piece that might have made the puzzle clear lay concealed or overlooked.

So far as he can recall, it was a violent movement, running downwards through the tent towards the door, that first woke him and made him aware that his companion was sitting bolt upright beside him—quivering. Hours must have passed, for it was the pale gleam of the dawn that revealed his outline against the canvas. This time the man was not crying; he was quaking like a leaf; the trembling he felt plainly through the blankets down the entire length of his own body. Défago had huddled down against him for protection, shrinking away from something that apparently concealed itself near the door-flaps of the little tent.

Simpson thereupon called out in a loud voice some question or other—in the first bewilderment of waking he does not remember exactly what—and the man made no reply. The atmosphere and feeling of true nightmare lay horribly about him, making movement and speech both difficult. At first, indeed, he was not sure where he was—whether in one of the earlier camps, or at home in his bed at Aberdeen. The sense of confusion was very troubling.

And next—almost simultaneous with his waking, it seemed—the profound stillness of the dawn outside was shattered by a most uncommon sound. It came without warning, or audible approach; and it was unspeakably dreadful. It was a voice, Simpson declares, possibly a human voice; hoarse yet plaintive—a soft, roaring voice

close outside the tent, overhead rather than upon the ground, of immense volume, while in some strange way most penetratingly and seductively sweet. It rang out, too, in three separate and distinct notes, or cries, that bore in some odd fashion a resemblance, far-fetched yet recognizable, to the name of the guide: "*Dé—fa—go!*"

The student admits he is unable to describe it quite intelligently, for it was unlike any sound he had ever heard in his life, and combined a blending of such contrary qualities. "A sort of windy, crying voice," he calls it, "as of something lonely and untamed, wild and of abominable power. . . ."

And, even before it ceased, dropping back into the great gulfs of silence, the guide beside him had sprung to his feet with an answering though unintelligible cry. He blundered against the tent-pole with violence, shaking the whole structure, spreading his arms out frantically for more room, and kicking his legs impetuously free of the clinging blankets. For a second, perhaps two, he stood upright by the door, his outline dark against the pallor of the dawn; then, with a furious, rushing speed, before his companion could move a hand to stop him, he shot with a plunge through the flaps of canvas—and was gone. And as he went—so astonishingly fast that the voice could actually be heard dying in the distance—he called aloud in tones of anguished terror that at the same time held something strangely like the frenzied exultation of delight——

"Oh! oh! My feet of fire! My burning feet of fire! Oh! oh! This height and fiery speed!"

And then the distance quickly buried it, and the deep silence of very early morning descended upon the forest as before.

It had all come about with such rapidity that, but for the evidence of the empty bed beside him Simpson could almost have believed it to have been the memory of a nightmare carried over from sleep. He still felt the warm pressure of that vanished body against his side; there lay the twisted blankets in a heap; the very tent yet trembled with the vehemence of the impetuous departure. The strange words rang in his ears, as though he still heard them in the distance—wild language of a suddenly stricken mind. Moreover, it was not only the senses of sight and hearing that reported uncommon things to his brain, for even while the man cried and ran, he had become aware that a strange perfume, faint yet pungent, pervaded the interior of the tent. And it was at this point, it seems, brought to himself by the consciousness that his nostrils were taking this distressing odour down into his throat, that he found his courage, sprang quickly to his feet—and went out.

The grey light of dawn that dropped, cold and glimmering, between the trees revealed the scene tolerably well. There stood the tent behind him, soaked with dew; the dark ashes of the fire, still warm; the lake, white beneath a coating of mist, the islands rising darkly out of it like objects packed in wool; and patches of snow beyond among the clearer spaces of the Bush—everything cold, still, waiting for the sun. But nowhere a sign of the vanished guide—still, doubtless, flying at frantic speed through the frozen woods. There was not even the sound of disappearing footsteps, nor the echoes of the dying voice. He had gone—utterly.

There was nothing; nothing but the sense of his recent presence, so strongly left behind about the camp; *and*—this penetrating, all-pervading odour.

And even this was now rapidly disappearing in its turn. In spite of his exceeding mental perturbation, Simpson struggled hard to detect its nature, and define it, but the ascertaining of an elusive scent, not recognized subconsciously and at once, is a very subtle operation of the mind. And he failed. It was gone before he could properly seize or name it. Approximate description, even, seems to have been difficult, for it was unlike any smell he knew. Acrid rather, not unlike the odour of a lion, he thinks, yet softer and not wholly unpleasing, with something almost sweet in it that reminded him of the scent of decaying garden leaves, earth, and the myriad, nameless perfumes that make up the odour of a big forest. Yet the "odour of lions" is the phrase with which he usually sums it all up.

Then—it was wholly gone, and he found himself standing by the ashes of the fire in a state of amazement and stupid terror that left him the helpless prey of anything that chose to happen. Had a musk-rat poked its pointed muzzle over a rock, or a squirrel scuttled in that instant down the bark of a tree, he would most likely have collapsed without more ado and fainted. For he felt about the whole affair the touch somewhere of a great Outer

Horror . . . and his scattered powers had not as yet had time to collect themselves into a definite attitude of fighting self-control.

Nothing did happen, however. A great kiss of wind ran softly through the awakening forest, and a few maple leaves here and there rustled tremblingly to earth. The sky seemed to grow suddenly much lighter. Simpson felt the cool air upon his cheek and uncovered head; realized that he was shivering with the cold; and, making a great effort, realized next that he was alone in the Bush —*and* that he was called upon to take immediate steps to find and succour his vanished companion.

Make an effort, accordingly, he did, though an ill-calculated and futile one. With that wilderness of trees about him, the sheet of water cutting him off behind, and the horror of that wild cry in his blood, he did what any other inexperienced man would have done in similar bewilderment: he ran about, without any sense of direction, like a frantic child, and called loudly without ceasing the name of the guide——

"Défago! Défago! Défago!" he yelled, and the trees gave him back the name as often as he shouted, only a little softened— "Défago! Défago! Défago!"

He followed the trail that lay for a short distance across the patches of snow, and then lost it again where the trees grew too thickly for snow to lie. He shouted till he was hoarse, and till the sound of his own voice in all that unanswering and listening world began to frighten him. His confusion increased in direct ratio to the violence of his efforts. His distress became formidably acute, till at length his exertions defeated their own object, and from sheer exhaustion he headed back to the camp again. It remains a wonder that he ever found his way. It was with great difficulty, and only after numberless false clues, that he at last saw the white tent between the trees, and so reached safety.

Exhaustion then applied its own remedy, and he grew calmer. He made the fire and breakfasted. Hot coffee and bacon put a little sense and judgment into him again, and he realized that he had been behaving like a boy. He now made another, and more successful attempt to face the situation collectedly, and, a nature naturally plucky coming to his assistance, he decided that he must first make as thorough a search as possible, failing success in which, he must find his way to the home camp as best he could and bring help.

And this was what he did. Taking food, matches and rifle with him, and a small axe to blaze the trees against his return journey, he set forth. It was eight o'clock when he started, the sun shining over the tops of the trees in a sky without clouds. Pinned to a stake by the fire he left a note in case Défago returned while he was away.

This time, according to a careful plan, he took a new direction, intending to make a wide sweep that must sooner or later cut into indications of the guide's trail and, before he had gone a quarter of a mile he came across the tracks of a large animal in the snow, and beside it the light and smaller tracks of what were beyond question human feet—the feet of Défago. The relief he at once experienced was natural, though brief; for at first sight he saw in these tracks a simple explanation of the whole matter: these big marks had surely been left by a bull moose that, wind against it, had blundered upon the camp, and uttered its singular cry of warning and alarm the moment its mistake was apparent. Défago, in whom the hunting instinct was developed to the point of uncanny perfection, had scented the brute coming down the wind hours before. His excitement and disappearance were due, of course, to—to his——

Then the impossible explanation at which he gasped faded, as common sense showed him mercilessly that none of this was true. No guide, much less a guide like Défago, could have acted in so irrational a way, going off even without his rifle . . . ! The whole affair demanded a far more complicated elucidation, when he remembered the details of it all—the cry of terror, the amazing language, the grey face of horror when his nostrils first caught the new odour; that muffled sobbing in the darkness, and—for this, too, now came back to him dimly—the man's original aversion for this particular bit of country. . . .

Besides, now that he examined them closer, these were not the tracks of a moose at all! Hank had explained to him the outline of a bull's hoofs, of a cow's or calf's, too, for that matter; he had drawn them clearly on a strip of birch bark. And these were wholly different. They were big, round, ample, and with no pointed outline as of sharp hoofs. He wondered for a moment whether bear-tracks were like that. There was no other animal he could think of, for caribou did not come so far south at this season, and, even if they did, would leave hoof-marks.

They were ominous signs—these mysterious writings left in the snow by the unknown creature that had lured a human being away from safety—and when he coupled them in his imagination with that haunting sound that broke the stillness of the dawn, a momentary dizziness shook his mind, distressing him again beyond belief. He felt the *threatening* aspect of it all. And, stooping down to examine the marks more closely, he caught a faint whiff of that sweet yet pungent odour that made him instantly straighten up again, fighting a sensation almost of nausea.

Then his memory played him another evil trick. He suddenly recalled those uncovered feet projecting beyond the edge of the tent, and the body's appearance of having been dragged towards the opening; the man's shrinking from something by the door when he woke later. The details now beat against his trembling mind with concerted attack. They seemed to gather in those deep spaces of the silent forest about him, where the host of trees stood waiting, listening, watching to see what he would do. The woods were closing round him.

With the persistence of true pluck, however, Simpson went forward, following the tracks as best he could, smothering these ugly emotions that sought to weaken his will. He blazed innumerable trees as he went, ever fearful of being unable to find the way back, and calling aloud at intervals of a few seconds the name of the guide. The dull tapping of the axe upon the massive trunks, and the unnatural accents of his own voice became at length sounds that he even dreaded to make, dreaded to hear. For they drew attention without ceasing to his presence and something was hunting himself down in the same way that he was hunting down another——

With a strong effort, he crushed the thought out the instant it rose. It was the beginning, he realized, of a bewilderment utterly diabolical in kind that would speedily destroy him.

Although the snow was not continuous, lying merely in shallow flurries over the more open spaces, he found no difficulty in following the tracks for the first few miles. They went straight as a ruled line wherever the trees permitted. The stride soon began to increase in length, till it finally assumed proportions that seemed absolutely impossible for any ordinary animal to have made. Like huge flying leaps they became. One of these he measured, and though he knew that "stretch" of eighteen feet must be somehow wrong, he was at a complete loss to understand why he found no signs on the snow between the extreme points. But what perplexed him even more, making him feel his vision had gone utterly awry, was that Défago's stride increased in the same manner, and finally covered the same incredible distances. It looked as if the great beast had lifted him with it and carried him across these astonishing intervals. Simpson, who was much longer in the limb, found that he could not compass even half the stretch by taking a running jump.

And the sight of these huge tracks, running side by side, silent evidence of a dreadful journey in which terror or madness had urged to impossible results, was profoundly moving. It shocked him in the secret depths of his soul. It was the most horrible thing his eyes had ever looked upon. He began to follow them mechanically, absent-mindedly almost, ever peering over his shoulder to see if he, too, were being followed by something with a gigantic tread. . . . And soon it came about that he no longer quite realized what it was they signified—these impressions left upon the snow by something nameless and untamed, always accompanied by the footmarks of the little French Canadian, his guide, his comrade, the man who had shared his tent a few hours before, chatting, laughing, even singing by his side. . . .

V

For a man of his years and inexperience, only a canny Scot, perhaps, grounded in common sense and established in logic, could have preserved even that measure of balance that this youth somehow or other did manage to preserve through the whole adventure. Otherwise, two things, he presently noticed, while forging pluckily ahead, must have sent him headlong back to the comparative safety of his tent, instead of only making his hands close more tightly upon the rifle-stock, while his heart, trained for the Wee Kirk, sent a wordless prayer winging its way to heaven. Both tracks, he saw, had undergone a change, and this change, so far as it concerned the footsteps of the man, was in some undecipherable manner—appalling.

It was in the bigger tracks he first noticed this, and for a long time he could not quite believe his eyes. Was it the blown leaves that produced odd effects of light and shade, or that the dry snow, drifting like finely-grounded rice about the edges, cast shadows and high lights? Or was it actually the fact that the great marks had become faintly coloured? For round about the deep, plunging holes of the animal there now appeared a mysterious, reddish tinge that was more like an effect of light than of anything that dyed the substance of the snow itself. Every mark had it, and had it increasingly—this indistinct fiery tinge that painted a new touch of ghastliness into the picture.

But when, wholly unable to explain or credit it, he turned his attention to the other tracks to discover if they, too, bore similar witness, he noticed that these had meanwhile undergone a change that was infinitely worse, and charged with far more horrible suggestion. For, in the last hundred yards or so, he saw that they had grown gradually into the semblance of the parent tread. Imperceptibly the change had come about, yet unmistakably. It was hard to see where the change first began. The result, however, was beyond question. Smaller, neater, more cleanly modelled, they formed now an exact and careful duplicate of the larger tracks beside them. The feet that produced them had, therefore, also changed. And something in his mind reared up with loathing and with terror as he saw it.

Simpson, for the first time, hesitated; then, ashamed of his alarm and indecision, took a few hurried steps ahead; the next instant stopped dead in his tracks. Immediately in front of him all signs of the trail ceased; both tracks came to an abrupt end. On all sides, for a hundred yards and more, he searched in vain for the least indication of their continuance. There was—nothing.

The trees were very thick just there, big trees all of them, spruce, cedar, hemlock; there was no underbrush. He stood, looking about him, all distraught; bereft of any power of judgment. Then he set to work to search again, and again, and yet again, but always with the same result: *nothing*. The feet that printed the surface of the snow thus far had now, apparently, left the ground!

And it was in that moment of distress and confusion that the whip of terror laid its most nicely calculated lash about his heart. It dropped with deadly effect upon the sorest spot of all, completely unnerving him. He had been secretly dreading all the time that it would come—and come it did.

Far overhead, muted by great height and distance, strangely thinned and wailing, he heard the crying voice of Défago, the guide.

The sound dropped upon him out of that still, wintry sky with an effect of dismay and terror unsurpassed. The rifle fell to his feet. He stood motionless an instant, listening as it were with his whole body, then staggered back against the nearest tree for support, disorganized hopelessly in mind and spirit. To him, in that moment, it seemed the most shattering and dislocating experience he had ever known, so that his heart emptied itself of all feeling whatsoever as by a sudden draught.

"Oh! oh! This fiery height! Oh, my feet of fire! My burning feet of fire . . . !" ran in far, beseeching accents of indescribable appeal this voice of anguish down the sky. Once it called—then silence through all the listening wilderness of trees.

And Simpson, scarcely knowing what he did, presently found himself running wildly to and fro, searching, calling, tripping over roots and boulders, and flinging himself in a frenzy of undirected pursuit after the Caller. Behind the screen of memory and emotion with which experience veils events, he plunged, distracted and half-deranged, picking up false lights like a ship at sea, terror in his eyes and heart and soul. For the Panic of the Wilderness had called to him in that far voice—the Power of untamed Distance—the Enticement of the Desolation that destroys. He knew in that moment all the pains of some one hopelessly and irretrievably lost, suffering the lust and travail of a soul in the final Loneliness. A vision of Défago, eternally hunted, driven and pursued across the skiey vastness of those ancient forests, fled like a flame across the dark ruin of his thoughts. . . .

It seemed ages before he could find anything in the chaos of his disorganized sensations to which he could anchor himself steady for a moment, and think. . . .

The cry was not repeated; his own hoarse calling brought no response; the inscrutable forces of the Wild had summoned their victim beyond recall—and held him fast.

Yet he searched and called, it seems, for hours afterwards, for it was late in the afternoon when at length he decided to abandon a useless pursuit and return to his camp on the shores of Fifty Island Water. Even then he went with reluctance, that crying voice still echoing in his ears. With difficulty he found his rifle and the homeward trail. The concentration necessary to follow the badly blazed trees, and a biting hunger that gnawed, helped to keep his mind steady. Otherwise, he admits, the temporary aberration he had suffered might have been prolonged to the point of positive disaster. Gradually the ballast shifted back again, and he regained something that approached his normal equilibrium.

But for all that the journey through the gathering dusk was miserably haunted. He heard innumerable following footsteps; voices that laughed and whispered; and saw figures crouching behind trees and boulders, making signs to one another for a concerted attack the moment he had passed. The creeping murmur of the wind made him start and listen. He went stealthily, trying to hide where possible, and making as little sound as he could. The shadows of the woods, hitherto protective or covering merely, had now become menacing, challenging; and the pageantry in his frightened mind masked a host of possibilities that were all the more ominous for being obscure. The presentiment of a nameless doom lurked ill-concealed behind every detail of what had happened.

It was really admirable how he emerged victor in the end; men of riper powers and experience might have come through the ordeal with less success. He had himself tolerably well in hand, all things considered, and his plan of action proves it. Sleep being absolutely out of the question, and travelling an unknown trail in the darkness equally impracticable, he sat up the whole of that night, rifle in hand, before a fire he never for a single moment allowed to die down. The severity of the haunted vigil marked his soul for life; but it was successfully accomplished; and with the very first signs of dawn he set forth upon the long return journey to the home-camp to get help. As before, he left a written note to explain his absence, and to indicate where he had left a plentiful *cache* of food and matches—though he had no expectation that any human hands would find them!

How Simpson found his way alone by lake and forest might

well make a story in itself, for to hear him tell it is to *know* the passionate loneliness of soul that a man can feel when the Wilderness holds him in the hollow of its illimitable hand—and laughs. It is also to admire his indomitable pluck.

He claims no skill, declaring that he followed the almost invisible trail mechanically, and without thinking. And this, doubtless, is the truth. He relied upon the guiding of the unconscious mind, which is instinct. Perhaps, too, some sense of orientation, known to animals and primitive men, may have helped as well, for through all that tangled region he succeeded in reaching the exact spot where Défago had hidden the canoe nearly three days before with the remark, "Strike doo west across the lake into the sun to find the camp."

There was not much sun left to guide him, but he used his compass to the best of his ability, embarking in the frail craft for the last twelve miles of his journey, with a sensation of immense relief that the forest was at last behind him. And, fortunately, the water was calm; he took his line across the centre of the lake instead of coasting round the shores for another twenty miles. Fortunately, too, the other hunters were back. The light of their fires furnished a steering-point without which he might have searched all night long for the actual position of the camp.

It was close upon midnight all the same when his canoe grated on the sandy cove, and Hank, Punk and his uncle, disturbed in their sleep by his cries, ran quickly down and helped a very exhausted and broken specimen of Scotch humanity over the rocks towards a dying fire.

VI

The sudden entrance of his prosaic uncle into this world of wizardry and horror that had haunted him without interruption now for two days and two nights, had the immediate effect of giving to the affair an entirely new aspect. The sound of that crisp "Hulloa, my boy! And what's up *now?*" and the grasp of that dry and vigorous hand introduced another standard of judgment. A revulsion of feeling washed through him. He realized that he had let himself "go" rather badly. He even felt vaguely ashamed of himself. The native hard-headedness of his race reclaimed him.

And this doubtless explains why he found it so hard to tell

that group round the fire—everything. He told enough, however, for the immediate decision to be arrived at that a relief party must start at the earliest possible moment, and that Simpson, in order to guide it capably, must first have food and, above all, sleep. Dr. Cathcart observing the lad's condition more shrewdly than his patient knew, gave him a very slight injection of morphine. For six hours he slept like the dead.

From the description carefully written out afterwards by this student of divinity, it appears that the account he gave to the astonished group omitted sundry vital and important details. He declares that, with his uncle's wholesome, matter-of-fact countenance staring him in the face, he simply had not the courage to mention them. Thus, all the search-party gathered, it would seem, was that Défago had suffered in the night an acute and inexplicable attack of mania, had imagined himself "called" by some one or something, and had plunged into the bush after it without food or rifle, where he must die a horrible and lingering death by cold and starvation unless he could be found and rescued in time. "In time," moreover, meant "at once."

In the course of the following day, however—they were off by seven, leaving Punk in charge with instructions to have food and fire always ready—Simpson found it possible to tell his uncle a good deal more of the story's true inwardness, without divining that it was drawn out of him as a matter of fact by a very subtle form of cross-examination. By the time they reached the beginning of the trail, where the canoe was laid up against the return journey, he had mentioned how Défago spoke vaguely of "something he called a 'Wendigo' "; how he cried in his sleep; how he imagined an unusual scent about the camp; and had betrayed other symptoms of mental excitement. He also admitted the bewildering effect of "that extraordinary" odour upon himself, "pungent and acrid like the odour of lions." And by the time they were within an easy hour of Fifty Island Water he had let slip the further fact —a foolish avowal of his own hysterical condition, as he felt afterwards—that he had heard the vanished guide call "for help." He omitted the singular phrases used, for he simply could not bring himself to repeat the preposterous language. Also, while describing how the man's footsteps in the snow had gradually assumed an exact miniature likeness of the animal's plunging tracks, he left out the fact that they measured a *wholly* incredible distance. It seemed a question, nicely balanced between individual pride and honesty, what he should reveal and what suppress. He mentioned the fiery tinge in the snow, for instance, yet shrank from telling that body and bed had been partly dragged out of the tent. . . .

With the net result that Dr. Cathcart, adroit psychologist that he fancied himself to be, had assured him clearly enough exactly where his mind, influenced by loneliness, bewilderment and terror, had yielded to the strain and invited delusion. While praising his conduct, he managed at the same time to point out where, when, and how his mind had gone astray. He made his nephew think himself finer than he was by judicious praise, yet more foolish than he was by minimizing the value of his evidence. Like many another materialist, that is, he lied cleverly on the basis of insufficient knowledge, *because* the knowledge supplied seemed to his own particular intelligence inadmissible.

"The spell of these terrible solitudes," he said, "cannot leave any mind untouched, any mind, that is, possessed of the higher imaginative qualities. It has worked upon yours exactly as it worked upon my own when I was your age. The animal that haunted your little camp was undoubtedly a moose, for the 'bell-ing' of a moose may have, sometimes, a very peculiar quality of sound. The coloured appearance of the big tracks was obviously a defect of vision in your own eyes produced by excitement. The size and stretch of the tracks we shall prove when we come to them. But the hallucination of an audible voice, of course, is one of the commonest forms of delusion due to mental excitement— an excitement, my dear boy, perfectly excusable, and, let me add, wonderfully controlled by you under the circumstances. For the rest, I am bound to say, you have acted with a splendid courage, for the terror of feeling oneself lost in this wilderness is nothing short of awful, and, had I been in your place, I don't for a moment believe I could have behaved with one quarter of your wisdom and decision. The only thing I find it uncommonly difficult to explain is—that—damned odour."

"It made me feel sick, I assure you," declared his nephew, "positively dizzy!" His uncle's attitude of calm omniscience, merely because he knew more psychological formulæ, made him slightly defiant. It was so easy to be wise in the explanation of an experience one has not personally witnessed. "A kind of desolate and terrible odour is the only way I can describe it," he concluded, glancing at the features of the quiet, unemotional man beside him.

"I can only marvel," was the reply, "that under the circumstances it did not seem to you even worse." The dry words, Simpson knew, hovered between the truth, and his uncle's interpretation of "the truth."

And so at last they came to the little camp and found the tent still standing, the remains of the fire, and the piece of paper pinned to a stake beside it—untouched. The *cache*, poorly contrived by inexperienced hands, however, had been discovered and opened— by musk rats, mink and squirrel. The matches lay scattered about the opening, but the food had been taken to the last crumb.

"Well, fellers, he ain't here," exclaimed Hank loudly after his fashion, "And that's as sartain as the coal supply down below! But whar he's got to by this time is 'bout as onsartain as the trade in crowns in t'other place." The presence of a divinity student was no barrier to his language at such a time, though for the reader's sake it may be severely edited. "I propose," he added, "that we start out at once an' hunt for'm like hell!"

The gloom of Défago's probable fate oppressed the whole party with a sense of dreadful gravity the moment they saw the familiar signs of recent occupancy. Especially the tent, with the bed of balsam branches still smoothed and flattened by the pressure of his body, seemed to bring his presence near to them. Simpson, feeling vaguely as if his word where somehow at stake, went about explaining particulars in a hushed tone. He was much calmer now, though overwearied with the strain of his many journeys. His uncle's method of explaining—"explaining away," rather—the details still fresh in his haunted memory helped, too, to put ice upon his emotions.

"And that's the direction he ran off in," he said to his two companions, pointing in the direction where the guide had vanished that morning in the grey dawn. "Straight down there he ran like a deer, in between the birch and the hemlock. . . ."

Hank and Dr. Cathcart exchanged glances.

"And it was about two miles down there, in a straight line," continued the other, speaking with something of the former terror in his voice, "that I followed his trail to the place where—it stopped —dead!"

"And where you heered him callin' an' caught the stench, an' all the rest of the wicked entertainment," cried Hank, with a volubility that betrayed his keen distress.

"And where your excitement overcame you to the point of producing illusions," added Dr. Cathcart under his breath, yet not so low that his nephew did not hear it.

It was early in the afternoon, for they had travelled quickly, and there were still a good two hours of daylight left. Dr. Cathcart and Hank lost no time in beginning the search, but Simpson was too exhausted to accompany them. They would follow the blazed marks on the trees, and where possible, his footsteps. Meanwhile the best thing he could do was to keep a good fire going, and rest.

But after something like three hours' search, the darkness already down, the two men returned to camp with nothing to report. Fresh snow had covered all signs, and though they had followed the blazed trees to the spot where Simpson had turned back, they had not discovered the smallest indications of a human being —or for that matter, of an animal. There were no fresh tracks of any kind; the snow lay undisturbed.

It was difficult to know what was best to do, though in reality there was nothing more they *could* do. They might stay and search for weeks without much chance of success. The fresh snow destroyed their only hope, and they gathered round the fire for supper, a gloomy and despondent party. The facts, indeed, were sad enough, for Défago had a wife at Rat Portage, and his earnings were the family's sole means of support.

Now that the whole truth in all its ugliness was out, it seemed useless to deal in further disguise or pretence. They talked openly of the facts and probabilities. It was not the first time, even in the experience of Dr. Cathcart, that a man had yielded to the singular seduction of the Solitudes and gone out of his mind; Défago, moreover, was predisposed to something of the sort, for he already had the touch of melancholia in his blood, and his fibre was weakened by bouts of drinking that often lasted for weeks at a time. Something on this trip—one might never know precisely what—had sufficed to push him over the line, that was all. And he had gone,

gone off into the great wilderness of trees and lakes to die by starvation and exhaustion. The chances against his finding camp again were overwhelming; the delirium that was upon him would also doubtless have increased, and it was quite likely he might do violence to himself and so hasten his cruel fate. Even while they talked, indeed, the end had probably come. On the suggestion of Hank, his old pal, however, they proposed to wait a little longer and devote the whole of the following day, from dawn to darkness, to the most systematic search they could devise. They would divide the territory between them. They discussed their plan in great detail. All that men could do they would do.

And, meanwhile, they talked about the particular form in which the singular Panic of the Wilderness had made its attack upon the mind of the unfortunate guide. Hank, though familiar with the legend in its general outline, obviously did not welcome the turn the conversation had taken. He contributed little, though that little was illuminating. For he admitted that a story ran over all this section of country to the effect that several Indians had "seen the Wendigo" along the shores of Fifty Island Water in the "fall" of last year, and that this was the true reason of Défago's disinclination to hunt there. Hank doubtless felt that he had in a sense helped his old pal to death by over-persuading him. "When an Indian goes crazy," he explained, talking to himself more than to the others, it seemed, "it's always put that he's 'seen the Wendigo.' An' pore old Défaygo was superstitious down to his very heels . . . !"

And then Simpson, feeling the atmosphere more sympathetic, told over again the full story of his astonishing tale; he left out no details this time; he mentioned his own sensations and gripping fears. He only omitted the strange language used.

"But Défago surely had already told you all these details of the Wendigo legend, my dear fellow," insisted the doctor. "I mean, he had talked about it, and thus put into your mind the ideas which your own excitement afterwards developed?"

Whereupon Simpson again repeated the facts. Défago, he declared, had barely mentioned the beast. He, Simpson, knew nothing of the story, and, so far as he remembered, had never even read about it. Even the word was unfamiliar.

Of course he was telling the truth, and Dr. Cathcart was reluctantly compelled to admit the singular character of the whole affair. He did not do this in words so much as in manner, however. He kept his back against a good, stout tree; he poked the fire into a blaze the moment it showed signs of dying down; he was quicker than any of them to notice the least sound in the night about them—a fish jumping in the lake, a twig snapping in the bush, the dropping of occasional fragments of frozen snow from the branches overhead where the heat loosened them. His voice, too, changed a little in quality, becoming a shade less confident, lower also in tone. Fear, to put it plainly, hovered close about that little camp, and though all three would have been glad to speak of other matters, the only thing they seemed able to discuss was this—the source of their fear. They tried other subjects in vain; there was nothing to say about them. Hank was the most honest of the group; he said next to nothing. He never once, however, turned his back to the darkness. His face was always to the forest, and when wood was needed he didn't go farther than was necessary to get it.

VII

A wall of silence wrapped them in, for the snow, though not thick, was sufficient to deaden any noise, and the frost held things pretty tight besides. No sound but their voices and the soft roar of the flames made itself heard. Only, from time to time, something soft as the flutter of a pine-moth's wings went past them through the air. No one seemed anxious to go to bed. The hours slipped towards midnight.

"The legend is picturesque enough," observed the doctor after one of the longer pauses, speaking to break it rather than because he had anything to say, "for the Wendigo is simply the Call of the Wild personified, which some natures hear to their own destruction."

"That's about it," Hank said presently. "An' there's no misunderstandin' when you hear it. It calls you by name right 'nough."

Another pause followed. Then Dr. Cathcart came back to the forbidden subject with a rush that made the others jump.

"The allegory *is* significant," he remarked, looking about him into the darkness, "for the Voice, they say, resembles all the minor sounds of the Bush—wind, falling water, cries of animals, and so forth. And, once the victim hears *that*—he's off for good, of course! His most vulnerable points, moreover, are said to be the feet and the eyes; the feet, you see, for the lust of wandering, and the eyes for the lust of beauty. The poor beggar goes at such a dreadful speed that he bleeds beneath the eyes, and his feet burn."

Dr. Cathcart, as he spoke, continued to peer uneasily into the surrounding gloom. His voice sank to a hushed tone.

"The Wendigo," he added, "is said to burn his feet—owing to the friction, apparently caused by its tremendous velocity—till they drop off, and new ones form exactly like its own."

Simpson listened in horrified amazement; but it was the pallor on Hank's face that fascinated him most. He would willingly have stopped his ears and closed his eyes, had he dared.

"It don't always keep to the ground neither," came in Hank's slow, heavy drawl, "for it goes so high that he thinks the stars have set him all a-fire. An' it'll take great thumpin' jumps some-times, an' run along the tops of the trees, carrying its partner with it, an' then droppin' him jest as a fish-hawk 'll drop a pickerel to kill it before eatin'. An' its food, of all the muck in the whole Bush is—moss!" And he laughed, a short, unnatural laugh. "It's a moss-eater, is the Wendigo," he added, looking up excitedly into the faces of his companions. "Moss-eater" he repeated, with a string of the most out-landish oaths he could invent.

But Simpson now understood the true purpose of all this talk. What these two men, each strong and "experienced" in his own way, dreaded more than anything else was—silence. They were talking against time. They were also talking against darkness, against the invasion of panic, against the admission reflection might bring that they were in an enemy's country—against anything, in fact, rather than allow their inmost thoughts to assume control. He himself, already initiated by the awful vigil with terror, was be-yond both of them in this respect. He had reached the stage where he was immune. But these two, the scoffing, analytical doctor, and the honest, dogged backwoodsman, each sat trembling in the depths of his being.

Thus the hours passed; and thus, with lowered voices and a kind of taut inner resistance of spirit, this little group of humanity sat in the jaws of the wilderness and talked foolishly of the terrible

and haunting legend. It was an unequal contest, all things considered, for the wilderness had already the advantage of first attack
—and of a hostage. The fate of their comrade hung over them with
a steadily increasing weight of oppression that finally became in-
supportable.

It was Hank, after a pause longer than the preceding ones
that no one seemed able to break, who first let loose all this
pent-up emotion in very unexpected fashion, by springing suddenly to his feet and letting out the most ear-shattering yell imagi-
nable into the night. He could not contain himself any longer, it
seemed. To make it carry even beyond an ordinary cry he interrupted its rhythm by shaking the palm of his hand before his
mouth.

"That's for Défago," he said, looking down at the other two
with a queer, defiant laugh, "for it's my belief"—the sandwiched
oaths may be omitted—"that my ole partner's not far from us at
this very minute."

There was a vehemence and recklessness about his performance that made Simpson, too, start to his feet in amazement, and
betrayed even the doctor into letting the pipe slip from between
his lips. Hank's face was ghastly, but Cathcart's showed a sudden
weakness—a loosening of all his faculties, as it were. Then a momentary anger blazed into his eyes, and he too, though with
deliberation born of habitual self-control, got upon his feet and
faced the excited guide. For this was unpermissible, foolish, dangerous, and he meant to stop it in the bud.

What might have happened in the next minute or two one
may speculate about, yet never definitely know, for in the instant
of profound silence that followed Hank's roaring voice, and as
though in answer to it, something went past through the darkness
of the sky overhead at terrific speed—something of necessity very
large, for it displaced much air, while down between the trees
there fell a faint and windy cry of a human voice, calling in tones
of indescribable anguish and appeal——

"Oh, oh! This fiery height! Oh, oh! My feet of fire! My burning feet of fire!"

White to the very edge of his shirt, Hank looked stupidly
about him like a child. Dr. Cathcart uttered some kind of unintelligible cry, turning as he did so with an instinctive movement

of blind terror towards the protection of the tent, then halting in the act as though frozen. Simpson, alone of the three, retained his presence of mind a little. His own horror was too deep to allow of any immediate reaction. He had heard that cry before.

Turning to his stricken companions, he said almost calmly——

"That's exactly the cry I heard—the very words he used!"

Then, lifting his face to the sky, he cried aloud, "Défago, Défago! Come down here to us! Come down——!"

And before there was time for anybody to take definite action one way or another, there came the sound of something dropping heavily between the trees, striking the branches on the way down, and landing with a dreadful thud upon the frozen earth below. The crash and thunder of it was really terrific.

"That's him, s'help me the good Gawd!" came from Hank in a whispering cry half choked, his hand going automatically towards the hunting-knife in his belt. "And he's coming! He's coming!" he added, with an irrational laugh of terror, as the sounds of heavy footsteps crunching over the snow became distinctly audible, approaching through the blackness towards the circle of light.

And while the steps, with their stumbling motion, moved nearer and nearer upon them, the three men stood round that fire, motionless and dumb. Dr. Cathcart had the appearance as of a man suddenly withered; even his eyes did not move. Hank, suffering shockingly, seemed on the verge again of violent action; yet did nothing. He, too, was hewn of stone. Like stricken children they seemed. The picture was hideous. And, meanwhile, their owner still invisible, the footsteps came closer, crunching the frozen snow. It was endless—too prolonged to be quite real—this measured and pitiless approach. It was accursed.

VIII

Then at length the darkness, having thus laboriously conceived, brought forth—a figure. It drew forward into the zone of uncertain light where fire and shadows mingled, not ten feet away; then halted, staring at them fixedly. The same instant it started forward again with the spasmodic motion as of a thing moved by wires, and coming up closer to them, full into the glare of the fire, they perceived then that—it was a man; and apparently that this man was—Défago.

Something like a skin of horror almost perceptibly drew down in that moment over every face, and three pairs of eyes shone through it as though they saw across the frontiers of normal vision into the Unknown.

Défago advanced, his tread faltering and uncertain; he made his way straight up to them as a group first, then turned sharply and peered close into the face of Simpson. The sound of a voice issued from his lips——

"Here I am, Boss Simpson. I heered some one calling me." It was a faint, dried-up voice, made wheezy and breathless as by immense exertion. "I'm havin' a reg'lar hell-fire kind of a trip, I am." And he laughed, thrusting his head forward into the other's face.

But that laugh started the machinery of the group of wax-work figures with the wax-white skins. Hank immediately sprang forward with a stream of oaths so far-fetched that Simpson did not recognize them as English at all, but thought he had lapsed into Indian or some other lingo. He only realized that Hank's presence, thrust thus between them, was welcome—uncommonly welcome. Dr. Cathcart, though more calmly and leisurely, advanced behind him, heavily stumbling.

Simpson seems hazy as to what was actually said and done in those next few seconds, for the eyes of that detestable and blasted visage peering at such close quarters into his own utterly bewildered his senses at first. He merely stood still. He said nothing. He had not the trained will of the older men that forced them into action in defiance of all emotional stress. He watched them moving as behind a glass, that half destroyed their reality: it was dreamlike; perverted. Yet, through the torrent of Hank's meaningless phrases, he remembers hearing his uncle's tone of authority —hard and forced—saying several things about food and warmth, blankets, whisky and the rest; . . . and, further, that whiffs of that penetrating, unaccustomed odour, vile, yet sweetly bewildering, assailed his nostrils during all that followed.

It was no less a person than himself, however—less experienced and adroit than the others though he was—who gave indistinctive utterance to the sentence that brought a measure of relief into the ghastly situation by expressing the doubt and thought in each one's heart.

It *is*—YOU, isn't it, Défago?" he asked under his breath, horror breaking his speech.

And at once Cathcart burst out with the loud answer before the other had time to move his lips. "Of course it is! Of course it is! Only—can't you see—he's nearly dead with exhaustion, cold and terror? Isn't *that* enough to change a man beyond all recognition?" It was said in order to convince himself as much as to convince the others. And continually, while he spoke and acted, he held a handkerchief to his nose. That odour pervaded the whole camp.

For the "Défago" who sat huddled by the big fire, wrapped in blankets, drinking hot whisky and holding food in wasted hands, was no more like the guide they had last seen alive than the picture of a man of sixty is like the daguerreotype of his early youth in the costume of another generation. Nothing really can describe that ghastly caricature, that parody, masquerading there in the firelight as Défago. From the ruins of the dark and awful memories he still retains, Simpson declares that the face was more animal than human, the features drawn about into wrong proportions, the skin loose and hanging, as though he had been subjected to extraordinary pressures and tensions. It made him think vaguely of those bladder-faces blown up by the hawkers on Ludgate Hill, that change their expression as they swell, and as they collapse emit a faint and wailing imitation of a voice. Both face and voice suggested some such abominable resemblance. But Cathcart long afterwards, seeking to describe the indescribable, asserts that thus might have looked a face and body that had been in air so rarefield that, the weight of atmosphere being removed, the entire structure threatened to fly asunder and become—*incoherent*. . . .

It was Hank, though all distraught and shaking with a tearing volume of emotion he could neither handle nor understand, who brought things to a head without more ado. He went off to a little distance from the fire, apparently so that the light should not dazzle him too much, and shading his eyes for a moment with both hands, shouted in a loud voice that held anger and affection dreadfully mingled——

"You ain't Défaygo! You ain't Défaygo at all! I don't give a—

damn, but that ain't you, my ole pal of twenty years!" He glared upon the huddled figure as though he would destroy him with his eyes. "An' if it is I'll swab the floor of hell with a wad of cotton-wool on a toothpick, s'help me the good Gawd!" he added, with a violent fling of horror and disgust.

It was impossible to silence him. He stood there shouting like one possessed, horrible to see, horrible to hear—*because it was the truth.* He repeated himself in fifty different ways, each more out-landish than the last. The woods rang with echoes. At one time it looked as if he meant to fling himself upon "the intruder," for his hand continually jerked towards the long hunting-knife in his belt.

But in the end he did nothing, and the whole tempest com-pleted itself very nearly with tears. Hank's voice suddenly broke, he collapsed on the ground, and Cathcart somehow or other per-suaded him at last to go into the tent and lie quiet. The remainder of the affair, indeed, was witnessed by him from behind the canvas, his white and terrified face peeping through the crack of the tent door-flap.

Then Dr. Cathcart, closely followed by his nephew who so far had kept his courage better than all of them, went up with a determined air and stood opposite to the figure of Défago hud-dled over the fire. He looked him squarely in the face and spoke. At first his voice was firm.

"Défago, tell us what's happened—just a little, so that we can know how best to help you?" he asked in a tone of authority, almost of command. And at that point, it *was* command. At once afterwards, however, it changed in quality, for the figure turned up to him a face so piteous, so terrible and so little like humanity, that the doctor shrank back from him as from something spirit-ually unclean. Simpson, watching close behind him, says he got the impression of a mask that was on the verge of dropping off, and that underneath they would discover something black and diabolical, revealed in utter nakedness. "Out with it, man, out with it!" Cathcart cried, terror running neck and neck with entreaty. "None of us can stand this much longer . . . !" It was the cry of instinct over reason.

And then "Défago," smiling *whitely*, answered in that thin

and fading voice that already seemed passing over into a sound of quite another character——

"I seen that great Wendigo thing," he whispered, sniffing the air about him exactly like an animal. "I been with it too——"

Whether the poor devil would have said more, or whether Dr. Cathcart would have continued the impossible cross-examination cannot be known, for at that moment the voice of Hank was heard yelling at the top of his voice from behind the canvas that concealed all but his terrified eyes. Such a howling was never heard.

"His feet! Oh, Gawd, his feet! Look at his great changed—feet!"

Défago, shuffling where he sat, had moved in such a way that for the first time his legs were in full light and his feet were visible. Yet Simpson had no time, himself, to see properly what Hank had seen. And Hank has never seen fit to tell. That same instant, with a leap like that of a frightened tiger, Cathcart was upon him, bundling the folds of blanket about his legs with such speed that the young student caught little more than a passing glimpse of something dark and oddly massed where moccasined feet ought to have been, and saw even that but with uncertain vision.

Then, before the doctor had time to do more, or Simpson time to even think a question, much less ask it, Défago was standing upright in front of them, balancing with pain and difficulty, and upon his shapeless and twisted visage an expression so dark and so malicious that it was, in the true sense, monstrous.

"Now *you* seen it too," he wheezed, "you seen my fiery, burning feet! And now—that is, unless you kin save me an' prevent —it's 'bout time for——"

His piteous and beseeching voice was interrupted by a sound that was like the roar of wind coming across the lake. The trees overhead shook their tangled branches. The blazing fire bent its flames as before a blast. And something swept with a terrific, rushing noise about the little camp and seemed to surround it entirely in a single moment of time. Défago shook the clinging blankets from his body, turned towards the woods behind, and with the same stumbling motion that had brought him—was gone: gone, before any one could move muscle to prevent him, gone with an amazing, blundering swiftness that left no time to act. The darkness positively swallowed him; and less than a dozen seconds later, above the roar of the swaying trees and the shout of the sudden wind, all three men, watching and listening with stricken hearts, heard a cry that seemed to drop down upon them from a great height of sky and distance——

"Oh, oh! This fiery height! Oh, oh! My feet of fire! My burning feet of fire . . . !" then died away, into untold space and silence.

Dr. Cathcart—suddenly master of himself, and therefore of the others—was just able to seize Hank violently by the arm as he tried to dash headlong into the Bush.

"But I want ter know,——you!" shrieked the guide. "I want ter see! That ain't him at all, but some——devil that's shunted into his place . . . !"

Somehow or other—he admits he never quite knew how he accomplished it—he managed to keep him in the tent and pacify him. The doctor, apparently, had reached the stage where reaction had set in and allowed his own innate force to conquer. Certainly he "managed" Hank admirably. It was his nephew, however, hitherto so wonderfully controlled, who gave him most cause for anxiety, for the cumulative strain had now produced a condition of lachrymose hysteria which made it necessary to isolate him upon a bed of boughs and blankets as far removed from Hank as was possible under the circumstance.

And there he lay, as the watches of that haunted night passed over the lonely camp, crying startled sentences, and fragments of sentences, into the folds of his blankets. A quantity of gibberish about speed and height and fire mingled oddly with biblical memories of the class-room. "People with broken faces all on fire are coming at a most awful, awful, pace towards the camp!" he would moan one minute; and the next would sit up and stare into the woods, intently listening, and whisper, "How terrible in the wilderness are—are the feet of them that——" until his uncle came across to change the direction of his thoughts and comfort him.

The hysteria, fortunately, proved but temporary. Sleep cured him, just as it cured Hank.

Till the first signs of daylight came, soon after five o'clock, Dr. Cathcart kept his vigil. His face was the colour of chalk, and there were strange flushes beneath the eyes. An appalling terror of the soul battled with his will all through those silent hours. These were some of the outer signs. . . .

At dawn he lit the fire himself, made breakfast, and woke the others, and by seven they were well on their way back to the home camp—three perplexed and afflicted men, but each in his own way having reduced his inner turmoil to a condition of more or less systematized order again.

IX

They talked little, and then only of the most wholesome and common things, for their minds were charged with painful thoughts that clamoured for explanation, though no one dared refer to them. Hank, being nearest to primitive conditions, was the first to find himself, for he was also less complex. In Dr. Cathcart "civilization" championed his forces against an attack singular enough. To this day, perhaps, he is not *quite* sure of certain things. Anyhow, he took longer to "find himself."

Simpson, the student of divinity, it was who arranged his conclusions probably with the best, though not most scientific, appearance of order. Out there, in the heart of unreclaimed wilderness, they had surely witnessed something crudely and essentially primitive. Something that had survived somehow the advance of humanity had emerged terrifically, betraying a scale of life still monstrous and immature. He envisaged it rather as a glimpse into prehistoric ages, when superstitions, gigantic and uncouth, still oppressed the hearts of men; when the forces of nature were still untamed, the Powers that may have haunted a primeval universe not yet withdrawn. To this day he thinks of what he termed years later in a sermon "savage and formidable Potencies lurking behind the souls of men, not evil perhaps in themselves, yet instinctively hostile to humanity as it exists."

With his uncle he never discussed the matter in detail, for the barrier between the two types of mind made it difficult. Only once, years later, something led them to the frontier of the subject—of a single detail of the subject, rather——

"Can't you even tell me what—*they* were like?" he asked; and the reply, though conceived in wisdom, was not encouraging, "It is far better you should not try to know, or to find out."

"Well—that odour . . . ?" persisted the nephew. "What do you make of that?"

Dr. Cathcart looked at him and raised his eyebrows.

"Odours," he replied, "are not so easy as sounds and sights of telepathic communication. I make as much, or as little, probably, as you do yourself."

He was not quite so glib as usual with his explanations. That was all.

At the fall of day, cold, exhausted, famished, the party came to the end of the long portage and dragged themselves into a camp that at first glimpse seemed empty. Fire there was none, and no Punk came forward to welcome them. The emotional capacity of all three was too over-spent to recognize either surprise or annoyance; but the cry of spontaneous affection that burst from the lips of Hank, as he rushed ahead of them towards the fireplace, came probably as a warning that the end of the amazing affair was not quite yet. And both Cathcart and his nephew confessed afterwards that when they saw him kneel down in his excitement and embrace something that reclined, gently moving, beside the extinguished ashes, they felt in their very bones that this "something" would prove to be Défago—the true Défago, returned.

And so, indeed, it was.

It is soon told. Exhausted to the point of emaciation, the French Canadian—what was left of him, that is,—fumbled among the ashes, trying to make a fire. His body crouched there, the weak fingers obeying feebly the instinctive habit of a lifetime with twigs and matches. But there was no longer any mind to direct the simple operation. The mind had fled beyond recall. And with it, too, had fled memory. Not only recent events, but all previous life was a blank.

This time it was the real man, though incredibly and horribly shrunken. On his face was no expression of any kind whatever—fear, welcome, or recognition. He did not seem to know who it was that embraced him, or who it was that fed, warmed and spoke to him the words of comfort and relief. Forlorn and broken beyond all reach of human aid, the little man did meekly as he was bidden. The "something" that had constituted him "individual" had vanished for ever.

In some ways it was more terribly moving than anything they had yet seen—that idiot smile as he drew wads of coarse moss from his swollen cheeks and told them that he was "a damned moss eater"; the continued vomiting of even the simplest food; and, worst of all, the piteous and childish voice of complaint in which he told them that his feet pained him—"burn like fire"—which was natural enough when Dr. Cathcart examined them and found that both were dreadfully frozen. Beneath the eyes there were faint indications of recent bleeding.

The details of how he survived the prolonged exposure, of where he had been, or of how he covered the great distance from one camp to the other, including an immense detour of the lake on foot since he had no canoe—all this remains unknown. His memory had vanished completely. And before the end of the winter whose beginning witnessed this strange occurrence, Défago, bereft of mind, memory and soul, had gone with it. He lingered only a few weeks.

And what Punk was able to contribute to the story throws no further light upon it. He was cleaning fish by the lake shore about five o'clock in the evening—an hour, that is, before the search party returned—when he saw this shadow of the guide picking its way weakly into camp. In advance of him, he declares, came the faint whiff of a certain singular odour.

That same instant old Punk started for home. He covered the entire journey of three days as only Indian blood could have covered it. The terror of a whole race drove him. He knew what it all meant. Défago had "seen the Wendigo."

●

●

Some say no evil thing that walks by night,
In fog or fire, by lake or moorish fen,
Blue meagre hag, or stubborn unlaid ghost
That breaks his magic chains at curfew time,
No goblin, or swart fairy of the mine,
Hath hurtful power o'er true virginity.

—JOHN MILTON

●

THE MATTER of this collection is beyond human reach: we being miserably in the dark, as to the œconomy of the invisible world, which knows what we do, or incline to, and works upon our passions, and sometimes is so kind as to afford us a glimpse of its præscience.

—JOHN AUBREY

THE FURNISHED ROOM

O. Henry was so contemptuous of Ward McAllister's phrase "the Four Hundred" that, when he mocked it in his book-title *The Four Million*, he referred to McAllister in a roundabout fashion, not by name. O. Henry, the great champion of drama in the commonplace, takes the lower depths of the commonplace for his setting in this story. But his matter-of-fact attitude does not extend to the ghost. The ghost is real, and no injury is done to an O. Henry surprise ending by admitting this in advance.—EDITOR.

O. Henry

THE
FURNISHED
ROOM

Restless, shifting, fugacious as time itself is a certain vast bulk of the population of the red brick district of the lower West Side. Homeless, they have a hundred homes. They flit from furnished room to furnished room, transients forever—transients in abode, transients in heart and mind. They sing "Home, Sweet Home" in ragtime; they carry their *lares et penates* in a bandbox; their vine is entwined about a picture hat; a rubber plant is their fig tree.

Hence the houses of this district, having had a thousand dwellers, should have a thousand tales to tell, mostly dull ones, no doubt; but it would be strange if there could not be found a ghost or two in the wake of all these vagrant guests.

One evening after dark a young man prowled among these crumbling red mansions, ringing their bells. At the twelfth he rested his lean hand-baggage upon the step and wiped the dust from his hat-band and forehead. The bell sounded faint and far away in some remote, hollow depths.

To the door of this, the twelfth house whose bell he had rung, came a housekeeper who made him think of an unwholesome, surfeited worm that had eaten its nut to a hollow shell and now sought to fill the vacancy with edible lodgers.

He asked if there was a room to let.

"Come in," said the housekeeper. Her voice came from her throat; her throat seemed lined with fur. "I have the third floor back, vacant since a week back. Should you wish to look at it?"

The young man followed her up the stairs. A faint light from no particular source mitigated the shadows of the halls. They trod noiselessly upon a stair carpet that its own loom would have forsworn. It seemed to have become vegetable; to have degenerated in that rank, sunless air to lush lichen or spreading moss that grew in patches to the staircase and was viscid under the foot like organic matter. At each turn of the stairs were vacant niches in the wall. Perhaps plants had once been set within them. If so they had died in that foul and tainted air. It may be that statues of the saints had stood there, but it was not difficult to conceive that imps and devils had dragged them forth in the darkness and down to the unholy depths of some furnished pit below.

"This is the room," said the housekeeper, from her furry throat. "It's a nice room. It ain't often vacant. I had some most elegant people in it last summer—no trouble at all, and paid in advance to the minute. The water's at the end of the hall. Sprowls and Mooney kept it three months. They done a vaudeville sketch. Miss B'retta Sprowls—you may have heard of her—Oh, that was just the stage names—right there over the dresser is where the marriage certificate hung, framed. The gas is here, and you see there is plenty of closet room. It's a room everybody likes. It never stays idle long."

"Do you have many theatrical people rooming here?" asked the young man.

"They comes and goes. A good proportion of my lodgers is connected with the theatres. Yes, sir, this is the theatrical district.

Actor people never stays long anywhere. I get my share. Yes, they comes and they goes."

He engaged the room, paying for a week in advance. He was tired, he said, and would take possession at once. He counted out the money. The room had been made ready, she said, even to towels and water. As the housekeeper moved away he put, for the thousandth time, the question that he carried at the end of his tongue.

"A young girl—Miss Vashner—Miss Eloise Vashner—do you remember such a one among your lodgers? She would be singing on the stage, most likely. A fair girl, of medium height, and slender, with reddish, gold hair and a dark mole near her left eyebrow."

"No, I don't remember the name. Them stage people has names they change as often as their rooms. They comes and they goes. No, I don't call that one to mind."

No. Always no. Five months of ceaseless interrogation and the inevitable negative. So much time spent by day in questioning managers, agents, schools and choruses; by night among the audiences of theatres from all-star casts down to music halls so low that he dreaded to find what he most hoped for. He who had loved her best had tried to find her. He was sure that since her disappearance from home this great, water-girt city held her somewhere, but it was like a monstrous quicksand, shifting its particles constantly, with no foundation, its upper granules of to-day buried to-morrow in ooze and slime.

The furnished room received its latest guest with a first glow of pseudo-hospitality, a hectic, haggard, perfunctory welcome like the specious smile of a demirep. The sophistical comfort came in reflected gleams from the decayed furniture, the ragged brocade upholstery of a couch and two chairs, a foot-wide cheap pier glass between the two windows, from one or two gilt picture frames and a brass bedstead in a corner.

The guest reclined, inert, upon a chair, while the room, confused in speech as though it were an apartment in Babel, tried to discourse to him of its divers tenantry.

A polychromatic rug like some brilliant-flowered rectangular, tropical islet lay surrounded by a billowy sea of soiled matting. Upon the gay-papered wall were those pictures that pursue the homeless one from house to house—The Huguenot Lovers, The First Quarrel, The Wedding Breakfast, Psyche at the Fountain. The mantel's chastely severe outline was ingloriously veiled behind some pert drapery drawn rakishly askew like the sashes of the Amazonian ballet. Upon it was some desolate flotsam cast aside by the room's marooned when a lucky sail had borne them to a fresh port—a trifling vase or two, pictures of actresses, a medicine bottle, some stray cards out of a deck.

One by one, as the characters of a cryptograph become explicit, the little signs left by the furnished room's procession of guests developed a significance. The threadbare space in the rug in front of the dresser told that lovely women had marched in the throng. Tiny finger prints on the wall spoke of little prisoners trying to feel their way to sun and air. A splattered stain, raying like a shadow of a bursting bomb, witnessed where a hurled glass or bottle had splintered with its contents against the wall. Across the pier glass had been scrawled with a diamond in staggering letters the name "Marie." It seemed that the succession of dwellers in the furnished room had turned in fury—perhaps tempted beyond forbearance by its garish coldness—and wreaked upon it their passions. The furniture was chipped and bruised; the couch, distorted by bursting springs, seemed a horrible monster that had been slain during the stress of some grotesque convulsion. Some more potent upheaval had cloven a great slice from the marble mantel. Each plank in the floor owned its particular cant and shriek as from a separate and individual agony. It seemed incredible that all this malice and injury had been wrought upon the room by those who had called it for a time their home; and yet it may have been the cheated home instinct surviving blindly, the resentful rage at false household gods that had kindled their wrath. A hut that is our own we can sweep and adorn and cherish.

The young tenant in the chair allowed these thoughts to file, soft-shod, through his mind, while there drifted into the room furnished sounds and furnished scents. He heard in one room a tittering and incontinent, slack laughter; in others the monologue of a scold, the rattling of dice, a lullaby, and one crying dully; above him a banjo tinkled with spirit. Doors banged somewhere, the elevated trains roared intermittently; a cat yowled miserably upon a back fence. And he breathed the breath of the house—a dank savour rather than a smell—a cold, musty effluvium as from underground vaults mingled with the reeking exhalations of linoleum and mildewed and rotten woodwork.

Then, suddenly, as he rested there, the room was filled with the strong, sweet odour of mignonette. It came as upon a single buffet of wind with such sureness and fragrance and emphasis that it almost seemed a living visitant. And the man cried aloud: "What, dear?" as if he had been called, and sprang up and faced about. The rich odour clung to him and wrapped him around. He reached out his arms for it, all his senses for the time confused and commingled. How could one be peremptorily called by an odour? Surely it must have been a sound. But, was it not the sound that had touched, that had caressed him?

"She has been in this room," he cried, and he sprang to wrest from it a token, for he knew he would recognize the smallest thing that had belonged to her or that she had touched. This enveloping scent of mignonette, the odour that she had loved and made her own—whence came it?

The room had been but carelessly set in order. Scattered upon the flimsy dresser scarf were half a dozen hairpins—those discreet, indistinguishable friends of womankind, feminine of gender, infinite of mood and uncommunicative of tense. These he ignored, conscious of their triumphant lack of identity. Ransacking the drawers of the dresser he came upon a discarded, tiny, ragged handkerchief. He pressed it to his face. It was racy and insolent with heliotrope; he hurled it to the floor. In another drawer he found odd buttons, a theatre programme, a pawn-broker's card, two lost marshmallows, a book on the divination of dreams. In the last was a woman's black satin hair-bow, which halted him, poised between ice and fire. But the black satin hair-bow also is femininity's demure, impersonal, common ornament, and tells no tales.

And then he traversed the room like a hound on the scent, skimming the walls, considering the corners of the bulging matting on his hands and knees, rummaging mantel and tables, the curtains and hangings, the drunken cabinet in the corner, for a visible sign, unable to perceive that she was there beside, around, against, within, above him, clinging to him, wooing him, calling him so poignantly through the finer senses that even his grosser ones became cognisant of the call. Once again he answered loudly: "Yes, dear!" and turned, wild-eyed, to gaze on vacancy, for he could not yet discern form and colour and love and outstretched arms in the odour of mignonette. Oh, God! whence that odour, and since when have odours had a voice to call? Thus he groped.

He burrowed in crevices and corners, and found corks and cigarettes. These he passed in passive contempt. But once he found in a fold of the matting a half-smoked cigar, and this he ground beneath his heel with a green and trenchant oath. He sifted the room from end to end. He found dreary and ignoble small records of many a peripatetic tenant; but of her whom he sought, and who may have lodged there, and whose spirit seemed to hover there, he found no trace.

And then he thought of the housekeeper.

He ran from the haunted room downstairs and to a door that showed a crack of light. She came out to his knock. He smothered his excitement as best he could.

"Will you tell me, madam," he besought her, "who occupied the room I have before I came?"

"Yes, sir. I can tell you again. 'Twas Sprowls and Mooney, as I said. Miss B'retta Sprowls it was in the theatres, but Missis Mooney she was. My house is well known for respectability. The marriage certificate hung, framed, on a nail over——"

"What kind of a lady was Miss Sprowls—in looks, I mean?"

"Why, black-haired, sir, short, and stout, with a comical face. They left a week ago Tuesday."

"And before they occupied it?"

"Why, there was a single gentleman connected with the draying business. He left owing me a week. Before him was Missis Crowder and her two children, they stayed four months; and back of them was old Mr. Doyle, whose sons paid for him. He kept the room six months. That goes back a year, sir, and further I do not remember."

He thanked her and crept back to his room. The room was dead. The essence that had vivified it was gone. The perfume of mignonette had departed. In its place was the old, stale odour of mouldy house furniture, of atmosphere in storage.

The ebbing of his hope drained his faith. He sat staring at the yellow, singing gaslight. Soon he walked to the bed and began to tear the sheets into ȿtrips. With the blade of his knife he drove them tightly into every crevice around windows and door. When all was snug and taut he turned out the light, turned the gas full on again and laid himself gratefully upon the bed.

It was Mrs. McCool's night to go with the can for beer. So she fetched it and sat with Mrs. Purdy in one of those subterranean retreats where house-keepers forgather and the worm dieth seldom.

"I rented out my third floor, back, this evening," said Mrs. Purdy, across a fine circle of foam. "A young man took it. He went up to bed two hours ago."

"Now, did ye, Missis Purdy, ma'am?" said Mrs. McCool, with intense admiration. "You do be a wonder for rentin' rooms of that kind. And did ye tell him, then?" she concluded in a husky whisper, laden with mystery.

"Rooms," said Mrs. Purdy, in her furriest tones, "are furnished for to rent. I did not tell him, Mrs. McCool."

"'Tis right ye are, ma'am; 'tis by renting rooms we kape alive. Ye have the rale sense for business, ma'am. There be many people will rayjict the rentin' of a room if they be tould a suicide has been after dyin' in the bed of it."

"As you say, we has our living to be making," remarked Mrs. Purdy.

"Yis, ma'am, 'tis true. 'Tis just one wake ago this day I helped ye lay out the third floor, back. A pretty slip of a colleen she was to be killin' herself wid the gas—a swate little face she had, Mrs. Purdy, ma'am."

"She'd a-been called handsome, as you say," said Mrs. Purdy, assenting but critical, "but for that mole she had a-growin' by her left eyebrow. Do fill up your glass again, Missis McCool."

THE SCREAMING SKULL

I point out in connection with Gertrude Atherton's *The Foghorn* that the stream-of-consciousness technic permits a kind of story, and a climactic effect, impossible in the epistolary manner. Midway between these two ways of writing there is a third: the monologue ostensibly spoken aloud to the reader while the action itself is occurring. It is interesting to see how skillfully Mr Crawford was able to get most of the effects of stream-of-consciousness writing in the following story of more than twenty-five years ago, when Joyce himself was still writing orthodox prose.— EDITOR.

F. Marion Crawford

THE SCREAMING SKULL

I have often heard it scream. No, I am not nervous, I am not imaginative, and I never believed in ghosts, unless that thing is one. Whatever it is, it hates me almost as much as it hated Luke Pratt, and it screams at me.

If I were you, I would never tell ugly stories about ingenious ways of killing people, for you never can tell but that some one at the table may be tired of his or her nearest and dearest. I have always blamed myself for Mrs. Pratt's death, and I suppose I was responsible for it in a way, though heaven knows I never wished her anything but long life and happiness. If I had not told that story she might be alive yet. That is why the thing screams at me, I fancy.

She was a good little woman, with a sweet temper, all things considered, and a nice gentle voice; but I remember hearing her shriek once when she thought her little boy was killed by a pistol that went off, though every one was sure that it was not loaded. It was the same scream; exactly the same, with a sort of rising quaver at the end; do you know what I mean? Unmistakable.

The truth is, I had not realised that the doctor and his wife were not on good terms. They used to bicker a bit now and then when I was here, and I often noticed that little Mrs. Pratt got very red and bit her lip hard to keep her temper, while Luke grew pale and said the most offensive things. He was that sort when he was in the nursery, I remember, and afterward at school. He was my cousin, you know; that is how I came by this house; after he died, and his boy Charley was killed in South Africa, there were no relations left. Yes, it's a pretty little property, just the sort of thing for an old sailor like me who has taken to gardening.

One always remembers one's mistakes much more vividly than one's cleverest things, doesn't one? I've often noticed it. I was dining with the Pratts one night, when I told them the story that afterwards made so much difference. It was a wet night in November, and the sea was moaning. Hush!—if you don't speak you will hear it now. . . .

Do you hear the tide? Gloomy sound, isn't it? Sometimes, about this time of year—hallo!—there it is! Don't be frightened, man—it won't eat you—it's only a noise, after all! But I'm glad you've heard it, because there are always people who think it's the wind, or my imagination, or something. You won't hear it again to-night, I fancy, for it doesn't often come more than once. Yes—that's right. Put another stick on the fire, and a little more stuff into that weak mixture you're so fond of. Do you remember old Blauklot the carpenter, on that German ship that picked us up when the *Clontarf* went to the bottom? We were hove to in a howling gale one night, as snug as you please, with no land within five hundred miles, and the ship coming up and falling off as regularly as clockwork—"Biddy te boor beebles ashore tis night, poys!" old Blauklot sang out, as he went off to his quarters with the sail-maker. I often think of that, now that I'm ashore for good and all.

Yes, it was on a night like this, when I was at home for a

spell, waiting to take the *Olympia* out on her first trip—it was on the next voyage that she broke the record, you remember—but that dates it. Ninety-two was the year, early in November.

The weather was dirty, Pratt was out of temper, and the dinner was bad, very bad indeed, which didn't improve matters, and cold, which made it worse. The poor little lady was very unhappy about it, and insisted on making a Welsh rarebit on the table to counteract the raw turnips and the half-boiled mutton. Pratt must have had a hard day. Perhaps he had lost a patient. At all events, he was in a nasty temper.

"My wife is trying to poison me, you see!" he said. "She'll succeed some day." I saw that she was hurt, and I made believe to laugh, and said that Mrs. Pratt was much too clever to get rid of her husband in such a simple way; and then I began to tell them about Japanese tricks with spun glass and chopped horsehair and the like.

Pratt was a doctor, and knew a lot more than I did about such things, but that only put me on my mettle, and I told a story about a woman in Ireland who did for three husbands before any one suspected foul play.

Did you never hear that tale? The fourth husband managed to keep awake and caught her, and she was hanged. How did she do it? She drugged them, and poured melted lead into their ears through a little horn funnel when they were asleep. . . . No— that's the wind whistling. It's backing up to the southward again. I can tell by the sound. Besides, the other thing doesn't often come more than once in an evening even at this time of year— when it happened. Yes, it was in November. Poor Mrs. Pratt died suddenly in her bed not long after I dined here. I can fix the date, because I got the news in New York by the steamer that followed the *Olympia* when I took her out on her first trip. You had the *Leofric* the same year? Yes, I remember. What a pair of old buffers we are coming to be, you and I. Nearly fifty years since we were apprentices together on the *Clontarf*. Shall you ever forget old Blauklot? "Biddy te boor beebles ashore, poys!" Ha, ha! Take a little more, with all that water. It's the old Hulstkamp I found in the cellar when this house came to me, the same I brought Luke from Amsterdam five-and-twenty years ago. He had never touched a drop of it. Perhaps he's sorry now, poor fellow.

Where did I leave off? I told you that Mrs. Pratt died suddenly—yes. Luke must have been lonely here after she was dead, I should think; I came to see him now and then, and he looked worn and nervous, and told me that his practice was growing too heavy for him, though he wouldn't take an assistant on any account. Years went on, and his son was killed in South Africa, and after that he began to be queer. There was something about him not like other people. I believe he kept his senses in his profession to the end; there was no complaint of his having made bad mistakes in cases, or anything of that sort, but he had a look about him——

Luke was a red-headed man with a pale face when he was young, and he was never stout; in middle age he turned a sandy grey, and after his son died he grew thinner and thinner, till his head looked like a skull with parchment stretched over it very tight, and his eyes had a sort of glare in them that was very disagreeable to look at.

He had an old dog that poor Mrs. Pratt had been fond of, and that used to follow her everywhere. He was a bull-dog, and the sweetest tempered beast you ever saw, though he had a way of hitching his upper lip behind one of his fangs that frightened strangers a good deal. Sometimes, of an evening, Pratt and Bumble —that was the dog's name—used to sit and look at each other a long time, thinking about old times, I suppose, when Luke's wife used to sit in that chair you've got. That was always her place, and this was the doctor's, where I'm sitting. Bumble used to climb up by the footstool—he was old and fat by that time, and could not jump much, and his teeth were getting shaky. He would look steadily at Luke, and Luke looked steadily at the dog, his face growing more and more like a skull with two little coals for eyes; and after about five minutes or so, though it may have been less, old Bumble would suddenly begin to shake all over, and all on a sudden he would set up an awful howl, as if he had been shot, and tumble out of the easy-chair and trot away, and hide himself under the side-board, and lie there making odd noises.

Considering Pratt's looks in those last months, the thing is not surprising, you know. I'm not nervous or imaginative, but I can quite believe he might have sent a sensitive woman into hysterics —his head looked so much like a skull in parchment.

At last I came down one day before Christmas, when my ship was in dock and I had three weeks off. Bumble was not about, and I said casually that I supposed the old dog was dead.

"Yes," Pratt answered, and I thought there was something odd in his tone even before he went on after a little pause. "I killed him," he said presently. "I could stand it no longer."

I asked what it was that Luke could not stand, though I guessed well enough.

"He had a way of sitting in her chair and glaring at me, and then howling." Luke shivered a little. "He didn't suffer at all, poor old Bumble," he went on in a hurry, as if he thought I might imagine he had been cruel. "I put dionine into his drink to make him sleep soundly, and then I chloroformed him gradually, so that he could not have felt suffocated even if he was dreaming. It's been quieter since then."

I wondered what he meant, for the words slipped out as if he could not help saying them. I've understood since. He meant that he did not hear that noise so often after the dog was out of the way. Perhaps he thought at first that it was old Bumble in the yard howling at the moon, though it's not that kind of noise, is it? Besides, I know what it is, if Luke didn't. It's only a noise after all, and a noise never hurt anybody yet. But he was much more imaginative than I am. No doubt there really is something about this place that I don't understand; but when I don't understand a thing, I call it a phenomenon, and I don't take it for granted that it's going to kill me, as he did. I don't understand everything, by long odds, nor do you, nor does any man who has been to sea. We used to talk of tidal waves, for instance, and we could not account for them; now we account for them by calling them submarine earthquakes, and we branch off into fifty theories, any one of which might make earthquakes quite comprehensible if we only knew what they were. I fell in with one of them once, and the ink-stand flew straight up from the table against the ceiling of my cabin. The same thing happened to Captain Lecky—I dare say you've read about it in his "Wrinkles." Very good. If that sort of thing took place ashore, in this room for instance, a nervous person would talk about spirits and levitation and fifty things that mean nothing, instead of just quietly setting it down as a "phenomenon" that has not been explained yet. My view of that voice, you see.

Besides, what is there to prove that Luke killed his wife? I would not even suggest such a thing to any one but you. After all, there was nothing but the coincidence that poor little Mrs. Pratt died suddenly in her bed a few days after I told that story at dinner. She was not the only woman who ever died like that. Luke got the doctor over from the next parish, and they agreed that she had died of something the matter with her heart. Why not? It's common enough.

Of course, there was the ladle. I never told anybody about that, and it made me start when I found it in the cupboard in the bedroom. It was new, too—a little tinned iron ladle that had not been in the fire more than once or twice, and there was some lead in it that had been melted, and stuck to the bottom of the bowl, all grey, with hardened dross on it. But that proves nothing. A country doctor is generally a handy man, who does everything for himself, and Luke may have had a dozen reasons for melting a little lead in a ladle. He was fond of sea-fishing, for instance, and he may have cast a sinker for a night-line; perhaps it was a weight for the hall clock, or something like that. All the same, when I found it I had a rather queer sensation, because it looked so much like the thing I had described when I told them the story. Do you understand? It affected me unpleasantly, and I threw it away; it's at the bottom of the sea a mile from the Spit, and it will be jolly well rusted beyond recognising if it's ever washed up by the tide.

You see, Luke must have bought it in the village, years ago, for the man sells just such ladles still. I suppose they are used in cooking. In any case, there was no reason why an inquisitive housemaid should find such a thing lying about, with lead in it, and wonder what it was, and perhaps talk to the maid who heard me tell the story at dinner—for that girl married the plumber's son in the village, and may remember the whole thing.

You understand me, don't you? Now that Luke Pratt is dead and gone, and lies buried beside his wife, with an honest man's tombstone at his head, I should not care to stir up anything that could hurt his memory. They are both dead, and their son, too. There was trouble enough about Luke's death, as it was.

How? He was found dead on the beach one morning, and there was a coroner's inquest. There were marks on his throat, but he had not been robbed. The verdict was that he had come to his end "By the hands or teeth of some person or animal unknown," for half the jury thought it might have been a big dog that had thrown him down and gripped his windpipe, though the skin of his throat was not broken. No one knew at what time he had gone out, nor where he had been. He was found lying on his back above high-water mark, and an old cardboard bandbox that had belonged to his wife lay under his hand, open. The lid had fallen off. He seemed to have been carrying home a skull in the box—doctors are fond of collecting such things. It had rolled out and lay near his head, and it was a remarkably fine skull, rather small, beautifully shaped and very white, with perfect teeth. That is to say, the upper jaw was perfect, but there was no lower one at all, when I first saw it.

Yes, I found it here when I came. You see, it was very white and polished, like a thing meant to be kept under a glass case, and the people did not know where it came from, nor what to do with it; so they put it back into the bandbox and set it on the shelf of the cupboard in the best bedroom, and of course they showed it to me when I took possession. I was taken down to the beach, too, to be shown the place where Luke was found, and the old fisherman explained just how he was lying, and the skull beside him. The only point he could not explain was why the skull had rolled up the sloping sand toward Luke's head instead of rolling downhill to his feet. It did not seem odd to me at the time, but I have often thought of it since, for the place is rather steep. I'll take you there to-morrow if you like—I made a sort of cairn of stones there afterward.

When he fell down, or was thrown down—whichever happened—the bandbox struck the sand, and the lid came off, and the thing came out and ought to have rolled down. But it didn't. It was close to his head, almost touching it, and turned with the face toward it. I say it didn't strike me as odd when the man told me; but I could not help thinking about it afterward, again and again, till I saw a picture of it all when I closed my eyes; and then I began to ask myself why the plaguy thing had rolled up instead of down, and why it had stopped near Luke's head instead of anywhere else, a yard away, for instance.

You naturally want to know what conclusion I reached, don't you? None that at all explained the rolling, at all events.

But I got something else into my head, after a time, that made me feel downright uncomfortable.

Oh, I don't mean as to anything surpernatural! There may be ghosts, or there may not be. If there are, I'm not inclined to believe that they can hurt living people except by frightening them, and, for my part, I would rather face any shape of ghost than a fog in the Channel when it's crowded. No. What bothered me was just a foolish idea, that's all, and I cannot tell how it began, nor what made it grow till it turned into a certainty.

I was thinking about Luke and his poor wife one evening over my pipe and a dull book, when it occurred to me that the skull might possibly be hers, and I have never got rid of the thought since. You'll tell me there's no sense in it, no doubt, that Mrs. Pratt was buried like a Christian and is lying in the churchyard where they put her, and that it's perfectly monstrous to suppose her husband kept her skull in her old bandbox in his bedroom. All the same, in the face of reason, and common sense, and probability, I'm convinced that he did. Doctors do all sorts of queer things that would make men like you and me feel creepy, and those are just the things that don't seem probable, nor logical, nor sensible to us.

Then, don't you see?—if it really was her skull, poor woman, the only way of accounting for his having it is that he really killed her, and did it in that way, as the woman killed her husbands in the story, and that he was afraid there might be an examination some day which would betray him. You see, I told that too, and I believe it had really happened some fifty or sixty years ago. They dug up the three skulls, you know, and there was a small lump of lead rattling about in each one. That was what hanged the woman. Luke remembered that, I'm sure. I don't want to know what he did when he thought of it; my taste never ran in the direction of horrors, and I don't fancy you care for them either, do you? No. If you did, you might supply what is wanting to the story.

It must have been rather grim, eh? I wish I did not see the whole thing so distinctly, just as everything must have happened. He took it the night before she was buried, I'm sure, after the coffin had been shut, and when the servant girl was asleep. I would bet anything, that when he'd got it, he put something under the sheet in its place, to fill up and look like it. What do you suppose he put there, under the sheet?

I don't wonder you take me up on what I'm saying! First I tell you that I don't want to know what happened, and that I hate to think about horrors, and then I describe the whole thing to you as if I had seen it. I'm quite sure that it was her work-bag that he put there. I remember the bag very well, for she always used it of an evening; it was made of brown plush, and when it was stuffed full it was about the size of—you understand. Yes, there I am, at it again! You may laugh at me, but you don't live here alone, where it was done, and you didn't tell Luke the story about the melted lead. I'm not nervous, I tell you, but sometimes I begin to feel that I understand why some people are. I dwell on all this when I'm alone, and I dream of it, and when that thing screams —well, frankly, I don't like the noise any more than you do, though I should be used to it by this time.

I ought not to be nervous. I've sailed in a haunted ship. There was a Man in the Top, and two-thirds of the crew died of the West Coast fever inside of ten days after we anchored; but I was all right, then and afterward. I have seen some ugly sights, too, just as you have, and all the rest of us. But nothing ever stuck in my head in the way this does.

You see, I've tried to get rid of the thing, but it doesn't like that. It wants to be there in its place, in Mrs. Pratt's bandbox in the cupboard in the best bedroom. It's not happy anywhere else. How do I know that? Because I've tried it. You don't suppose that I've not tried, do you? As long as it's there it only screams now and then, generally at this time of year, but if I put it out of the house it goes on all night, and no servant will stay here twenty-four hours. As it is, I've often been left alone and have been obliged to shift for myself for a fortnight at a time. No one from the village would ever pass a night under the roof now, and as for selling the place, or even letting it, that's out of the question. The old women say that if I stay here I shall come to a bad end myself before long.

I'm not afraid of that. You smile at the mere idea that any one could take such nonsense seriously. Quite right. It's utterly blatant nonsense, I agree with you. Didn't I tell you that it's only a noise after all when you started and looked round as if you expected to see a ghost standing behind your chair?

I may be all wrong about the skull, and I like to think that I am—when I can. It may be just a fine specimen which Luke got somewhere long ago, and what rattles about inside when you shake it may be nothing but a pebble, or a bit of hard clay, or anything. Skulls that have lain long in the ground generally have something inside them that rattles, don't they? No, I've never tried to get it out, whatever it is; I'm afraid it might be lead, don't you see? And if it is, I don't want to know the fact, for I'd much rather not be sure. If it really is lead, I killed her quite as much as if I had done the deed myself. Anybody must see that, I should think. As long as I don't know for certain, I have the consolation of saying that it's all utterly ridiculous nonsense, that Mrs. Pratt died a natural death and that the beautiful skull belonged to Luke when he was a student in London. But if I were quite sure, I believe I should have to leave the house; indeed I do, most certainly. As it is, I had to give up trying to sleep in the best bedroom where the cupboard is.

You ask me why I don't throw it into the pond—yes, but please don't call it a "confounded bugbear"—it doesn't like being called names.

There! Lord, what a shriek! I told you so! You're quite pale, man. Fill up your pipe and draw your chair nearer to the fire, and take some more drink. Old Hollands never hurt anybody yet. I've seen a Dutchman in Java drink half a jug of Hulstkamp in a morning without turning a hair. I don't take much rum myself, because it doesn't agree with my rheumatism, but you are not rheumatic and it won't damage you. Besides, it's a very damp night outside. The wind is howling again, and it will soon be in the south-west; do you hear how the windows rattle? The tide must have turned too, by the moaning.

We should not have heard the thing again if you had not said that. I'm pretty sure we should not. Oh yes, if you choose to describe it as a coincidence, you are quite welcome, but I would rather that you should not call the thing names again, if you don't mind. It may be that the poor little woman hears, and perhaps it hurts her, don't you know? Ghosts? No! You don't call anything a ghost that you can take in your hands and look at in broad daylight, and that rattles when you shake it. Do you, now? But it's something that hears and understands; there's no doubt about that.

I tried sleeping in the best bedroom when I first came to the house, just because it was the best and the most comfortable, but I had to give it up. It was their room, and there's the big bed she died in, and the cupboard is in the thickness of the wall, near the head, on the left. That's where it likes to be kept, in its bandbox. I only used the room for a fortnight after I came, and then I turned out and took the little room downstairs, next to the surgery, where Luke used to sleep when he expected to be called to a patient during the night.

I was always a good sleeper ashore; eight hours is my dose, eleven to seven when I'm alone, twelve to eight when I have a friend with me. But I could not sleep after three o'clock in the morning in that room—a quarter past, to be accurate—as a matter of fact, I timed it with my old pocket chronometer, which still keeps good time, and it was always at exactly seventeen minutes past three. I wonder whether that was the hour when she died?

It was not what you have heard. If it had been that I could not have stood it two nights. It was just a start and a moan and hard breathing for a few seconds in the cupboard, and it could never have waked me under ordinary circumstances, I'm sure. I suppose you are like me in that, and we are just like other people who have been to sea. No natural sounds disturb us at all, not all the racket of a square-rigger hove to in a heavy gale, or rolling on her beam ends before the wind. But if a lead pencil gets adrift and rattles in the drawer of your cabin table you are awake in a moment. Just so—you always understand. Very well, the noise in the cupboard was no louder than that, but it waked me instantly.

I said it was like a "start." I know what I mean, but it's hard to explain without seeming to talk nonsense. Of course you cannot exactly "hear" a person "start"; at the most, you might hear the quick drawing of the breath between the parted lips and closed teeth, and the almost imperceptible sound of clothing that moved suddenly though very slightly. It was like that.

You know how one feels what a sailing vessel is going to do, two or three seconds before she does it, when one has the wheel. Riders say the same of a horse, but that's less strange, because the horse is a live animal with feelings of its own, and only poets and landsmen talk about a ship being alive, and all that. But I have always felt somehow that besides being a steaming machine or a sailing machine for carrying weights, a vessel at sea is a sensitive instrument, and a means of communication between nature and man, and most particularly the man at the wheel, if she is steered by hand. She takes her impressions directly from wind and sea, tide and stream, and transmits them to the man's hand, just as the wireless telegraph picks up the interrupted currents aloft and turns them out below in the form of a message.

You see what I am driving at; I felt that something started in the cupboard, and I felt it so vividly that I heard it, though there may have been nothing to hear, and the sound inside my head waked me suddenly. But I really heard the other noise. It was as if it were muffled inside a box, as far away as if it came through a long-distance telephone; and yet I knew that it was inside the cupboard near the head of my bed. My hair did not bristle and my blood did not run cold that time. I simply resented being waked up by something that had no business to make a noise, any more than a pencil should rattle in the drawer of my cabin table on board ship. For I did not understand; I just supposed that the cupboard had some communication with the outside air, and that the wind had got in and was moaning through it with a sort of very faint screech. I struck a light and looked at my watch, and it was seventeen minutes past three. Then I turned over and went to sleep on my right ear. That's my good one; I'm pretty deaf with the other, for I struck the water with it when I was a lad in diving from the foretopsail yard. Silly thing to do, it was, but the result is very convenient when I want to go to sleep when there's a noise.

That was the first night, and the same thing happened again and several times afterward, but not regularly, though it was always at the same time, to a second; perhaps I was sometimes sleeping on my good ear, and sometimes not. I overhauled the cupboard and there was no way by which the wind could get in, or anything else, for the door makes a good fit, having been meant to keep out moths, I suppose; Mrs. Pratt must have kept her winter things in it, for it still smells of camphor and turpentine.

After about a fortnight I had had enough of the noises. So

far I had said to myself that it would be silly to yield to it and take the skull out of the room. Things always look differently by daylight, don't they? But the voice grew louder—I suppose one may call it a voice—and it got inside my deaf ear, too, one night. I realised that when I was wide awake, for my good ear was jammed down on the pillow, and I ought not to have heard a fog-horn in that position. But I heard that, and it made me lose my temper, unless it scared me, for sometimes the two are not far apart. I struck a light and got up, and I opened the cupboard, grabbed the bandbox and threw it out of the window, as far as I could.

Then my hair stood on end. The thing screamed in the air, like a shell from a twelve-inch gun. It fell on the other side of the road. The night was very dark, and I could not see it fall, but I know it fell beyond the road. The window is just over the front door, it's fifteen yards to the fence, more or less, and the road is ten yards wide. There's a thickset hedge beyond, along the glebe that belongs to the vicarage.

I did not sleep much more that night. It was not more than half an hour after I had thrown the bandbox out when I heard a shriek outside—like what we've had to-night, but worse, more despairing, I should call it; and it may have been my imagination, but I could have sworn that the screams came nearer and nearer each time. I lit a pipe, and walked up and down for a bit, and then took a book and sat up reading, but I'll be hanged if I can remember what I read nor even what the book was, for every now and then a shriek came up that would have made a dead man turn in his coffin.

A little before dawn some one knocked at the front door. There was no mistaking that for anything else, and I opened my window and looked down, for I guessed that some one wanted the doctor, supposing that the new man had taken Luke's house. It was rather a relief to hear a human knock after that awful noise.

You cannot see the door from above, owing to the little porch. The knocking came again, and I called out, asking who was there, but nobody answered, though the knock was repeated. I sang out again, and said that the doctor did not live here any longer. There was no answer, but it occurred to me that it might be some old country-man who was stone deaf. So I took my candle

and went down to open the door. Upon my word, I was not thinking of the thing yet, and I had almost forgotten the other noises.
I went down convinced that I should find somebody outside, on
the doorstep, with a message. I set the candle on the hall table, so
that the wind should not blow it out when I opened. While I was
drawing the old-fashioned bolt I heard the knocking again. It
was not loud, and it had a queer, hollow sound, now that I was
close to it, I remember, but I certainly thought it was made by
some person who wanted to get in.

It wasn't. There was nobody there, but as I opened the door
inward, standing a little on one side, so as to see out at once, something rolled across the threshold and stopped against my foot.

I drew back as I felt it, for I knew what it was before I looked
down. I cannot tell you how I knew, and it seemed unreasonable,
for I am still quite sure that I had thrown it across the road. It's
a French window, that opens wide, and I got a good swing when
I flung it out. Besides, when I went out early in the morning, I
found the bandbox beyond the thickset hedge.

You may think it opened when I threw it, and that the skull
dropped out; but that's impossible, for nobody could throw an
empty cardboard box so far. It's out of the question; you might
as well try to fling a ball of paper twenty-five yards, or a blown
bird's egg.

To go back, I shut and bolted the hall door, picked the thing
up carefully, and put it on the table beside the candle. I did that
mechanically, as one instinctively does the right thing in danger
without thinking at all—unless one does the opposite. It may seem
odd, but I believe my first thought had been that somebody might
come and find me there on the threshold while it was resting
against my foot, lying a little on its side, and turning one hollow
eye up at my face, as if it meant to accuse me. And the light and
shadow from the candle played in the hollows of the eyes as it
stood on the table, so that they seemed to open and shut at me.
Then the candle went out quite unexpectedly, though the door
was fastened and there was not the least draught; and I used up at
least half a dozen matches before it would burn again.

I sat down rather suddenly, without quite knowing why.
Probably I had been badly frightened, and perhaps you will admit
there was no great shame in being scared. The thing had come

home, and it wanted to go upstairs, back to its cupboard. I sat still and stared at it for a bit, till I began to feel very cold; then I took it and carried it up and set it in its place, and I remember that I spoke to it, and promised that it should have its bandbox again in the morning.

You want to know whether I stayed in the room till day-break? Yes, but I kept a light burning, and sat up smoking and reading, most likely out of fright; plain, undeniable fear, and you need not call it cowardice either, for that's not the same thing. I could not have stayed alone with that thing in the cupboard; I should have been scared to death, though I'm not more timid than other people. Confound it all, man, it had crossed the road alone, and had got up the doorstep and had knocked to be let in.

When the dawn came, I put on my boots and went out to find the bandbox. I had to go a good way round, by the gate near the highroad, and I found the box open and hanging on the other side of the hedge. It had caught on the twigs by the string, and the lid had fallen off and was lying on the ground below it. That shows that it did not open till it was well over; and if it had not opened as soon as it left my hand, what was inside it must have gone beyond the road too.

That's all. I took the box upstairs to the cupboard, and put the skull back and locked it up. When the girl brought me my breakfast she said she was sorry, but that she must go, and she did not care if she lost her month's wages. I looked at her, and her face was a sort of greenish, yellowish white. I pretended to be surprised, and asked what was the matter; but that was of no use, for she just turned on me and wanted to know whether I meant to stay in a haunted house, and how long I expected to live if I did, for though she noticed I was sometimes a little hard of hearing, she did not believe that even I could sleep through those screams again—and if I could, why had I been moving about the house and opening and shutting the front door, between three and four in the morning? There was no answering that, since she had heard me, so off she went, and I was left to myself. I went down to the village during the morning and found a woman who was willing to come and do the little work there is and cook my dinner, on condition that she might go home every night. As for me, I moved downstairs that day, and I have never tried to sleep in the best bedroom since. After a little while I got a brace of middle-aged Scotch servants from London, and things were quiet enough for a long time. I began by telling them that the house was in a very exposed position, and that the wind whistled round it a good deal in the autumn and winter, which had given it a bad name in the village, the Cornish people being inclined to superstition and telling ghost stories. The two hard-faced, sandy-haired sisters almost smiled, and they answered with great contempt that they had no great opinion of any Southern bogey whatever, having been in service in two English haunted houses, where they had never seen so much as the Boy in Gray, whom they reckoned no very particular rarity in Forfarshire.

They stayed with me several months, and while they were in the house we had peace and quiet. One of them is here again now, but she went away with her sister within the year. This one— she was the cook—married the sexton, who works in my garden. That's the way of it. It's a small village and he has not much to do, and he knows enough about flowers to help me nicely, besides doing most of the hard work; for though I'm fond of exercise, I'm getting a little stiff in the hinges. He's a sober, silent sort of fellow, who minds his own business, and he was a widower when I came here—Trehearn is his name, James Trehearn. The Scotch sisters would not admit that there was anything wrong about the house, but when November came they gave me warning that they were going, on the ground that the chapel was such a long walk from here, being in the next parish, and that they could not possibly go to our church. But the younger one came back in the spring, and as soon as the banns could be published she was married to James Trehearn by the vicar, and she seems to have had no scruples about hearing him preach since then. I'm quite satisfied, if she is! The couple live in a small cottage that looks over the churchyard.

I suppose you are wondering what all this has to do with what I was talking about. I'm alone so much that when an old friend comes to see me, I sometimes go on talking just for the sake of hearing my own voice. But in this case there is really a connection of ideas. It was James Trehearn who buried poor Mrs. Pratt, and her husband after her in the same grave, and it's not far from the back of his cottage. That's the connection in my mind, you see. It's plain enough. He knows something; I'm quite sure that he does, though he's such a reticent beggar.

Yes, I'm alone in the house at night now, for Mrs. Trehearn does everything herself, and when I have a friend the sexton's niece comes in to wait on the table. He takes his wife home every evening in winter, but in summer, when there's light, she goes by herself. She's not a nervous woman, but she's less sure than she used to be that there are no bogies in England worth a Scotchwoman's notice. Isn't it amusing, the idea that Scotland has a monopoly of the supernatural? Odd sort of national pride, I call that, don't you?

That's a good fire, isn't it? When driftwood gets started at last there's nothing like it, I think. Yes, we get lots of it, for I'm sorry to say there are still a great many wrecks about here. It's a lonely coast, and you may have all the wood you want for the trouble of bringing it in. Trehearn and I borrow a cart now and then, and load it between here and the Spit. I hate a coal fire when I can get wood of any sort. A log is company, even if it's only a piece of a deck-beam or timber sawn off, and the salt in it makes pretty sparks. See how they fly, like Japanese hand-fireworks! Upon my word, with an old friend and a good fire and a pipe, one forgets all about that thing upstairs, especially now that the wind has moderated. It's only a lull, though, and it will blow a gale before morning.

You think you would like to see the skull? I've no objection. There's no reason why you shouldn't have a look at it, and you never saw a more perfect one in your life, except that there are two front teeth missing in the lower jaw.

Oh yes—I had not told you about the jaw yet. Trehearn found it in the garden last spring when he was digging a pit for a new asparagus bed. You know we make asparagus beds six or eight feet deep here. Yes, yes—I had forgotten to tell you that. He was digging straight down, just as he digs a grave; if you want a good asparagus bed made, I advise you to get a sexton to make it for you. Those fellows have a wonderful knack at that sort of digging.

Trehearn had got down about three feet when he cut into a mass of white lime in the side of the trench. He had noticed that the earth was a little looser there, though he says it had not been disturbed for a number of years. I suppose he thought that even old lime might not be good for asparagus, so he broke it out and threw it up. It was pretty hard, he says, in biggish lumps, and out of sheer force of habit he cracked the lumps with his spade as they lay outside the pit beside him; the jawbone of a skull dropped out of one of the pieces. He thinks he must have knocked out the two front teeth in breaking up the lime, but he did not see them anywhere. He's a very experienced man in such things, as you may imagine, and he said at once that the jaw had probably belonged to a young woman, and that the teeth had been complete when she died. He brought it to me, and asked me if I wanted to keep it; if I did not, he said he would drop it into the next grave he made in the churchyard, as he supposed it was a Christian jaw, and ought to have decent burial, wherever the rest of the body might be. I told him that doctors often put bones into quicklime to whiten them nicely, and that I supposed Dr. Pratt had once had a little lime pit in the garden for that purpose, and had forgotten the jaw. Trehearn looked at me quietly.

"Maybe it fitted that skull that used to be in the cupboard upstairs, sir," he said. "Maybe Dr. Pratt had put the skull into the lime to clean it, or something, and when he took it out he left the lower jaw behind. There's some human hair sticking in the lime, sir."

I saw there was, and that was what Trehearn said. If he did not suspect something, why in the world should he have suggested that the jaw might fit the skull? Besides, it did. That's proof that he knows more than he cares to tell. Do you suppose he looked before she was buried? Or perhaps—when he buried Luke in the same grave——

Well, well, it's of no use to go over that, is it? I said I would keep the jaw with the skull, and I took it upstairs and fitted it into its place. There's not the slightest doubt about the two belonging together, and together they are.

Trehearn knows several things. We were talking about plastering the kitchen a while ago, and he happened to remember that it had not been done since the very week when Mrs. Pratt died. He did not say that the mason must have left some lime on the place, but he thought it, and that it was the very same lime he had found in the asparagus pit. He knows a lot. Trehearn is one of your silent beggars who can put two and two together. That grave is very near the back of his cottage, too, and he's one of the quickest men with a spade I ever saw. If he wanted to know the truth, he could, and no one else would ever be the wiser unless he chose to tell. In a quiet village like ours, people don't go and spend the night in the churchyard to see whether the sexton potters about by himself between ten o'clock and daylight.

What is awful to think of, is Luke's deliberation, if he did it; his cool certainty that no one would find him out; above all, his nerve, for that must have been extraordinary. I sometimes think it's bad enough to live in the place where it was done, if it really was done. I always put in the condition, you see, for the sake of his memory, and a little bit for my own sake, too.

I'll go upstairs and fetch the box in a minute. Let me light my pipe; there's no hurry! We had supper early, and it's only half-past nine o'clock. I never let a friend go to bed before twelve, or with less than three glasses—you may have as many more as you like, but you shan't have less, for the sake of old times.

It's breezing up again, do you hear? That was only a lull just now, and we are going to have a bad night.

A thing happened that made me start a little when I found that the jaw fitted exactly. I'm not very easily startled in that way myself, but I have seen people make a quick movement, drawing their breath sharply, when they had thought they were alone and suddenly turned and saw some one very near them. Nobody can call that fear. You wouldn't, would you? No. Well, just when I had set the jaw in its place under the skull, the teeth closed sharply on my finger. It felt exactly as if it were biting me hard, and I confess that I jumped before I realised that I had been pressing the jaw and the skull together with my other hand. I assure you I was not at all nervous. It was broad daylight, too, and a fine day, and the sun was streaming into the best bedroom. It would have been absurd to be nervous, and it was only a quick mistaken impression, but it really made me feel queer. Somehow it made me think of the funny verdict of the coroner's jury on Luke's death, "by the hand or teeth of some person or animal unknown." Ever since that I've wished I had seen those marks on his throat, though the lower jaw was missing then.

I have often seen a man do insane things with his hands that he does not realise at all. I once saw a man hanging on by an old awning stop with one hand, leaning backward, outboard, with all his weight on it, and he was just cutting the stop with the knife in his other hand when I got my arms round him. We were in mid-ocean, going twenty knots. He had not the smallest idea what he was doing; neither had I when I managed to pinch my finger between the teeth of that thing. I can feel it now. It was exactly as if it were alive and were trying to bite me. It would if it could, for I know it hates me, poor thing! Do you suppose that what rattles about inside is really a bit of lead? Well, I'll get the box down presently, and if whatever it is happens to drop out into your hands that's your affair. If it's only a clod of earth or a pebble, the whole matter would be off my mind, and I don't believe I should ever think of the skull again; but somehow I cannot bring myself to shake out the bit of hard stuff myself. The mere idea that it may be lead makes me confoundedly uncomfortable, yet I've got the conviction that I shall know before long. I shall certainly know. I'm sure Trehearn knows, but he's such a silent beggar.

I'll go upstairs now and get it. What? You had better go with me? Ha, ha! do you think I'm afraid of a bandbox and a noise? Nonsense!

Bother the candle, it won't light! As if the ridiculous thing understood what it's wanted for! Look at that—the third match. They light fast enough for my pipe. There, do you see? It's a fresh box, just out of the tin safe where I keep the supply on account of the dampness. Oh, you think the wick of the candle may be damp, do you? All right, I'll light the beastly thing in the fire. That won't go out, at all events. Yes, it sputters a bit, but it will keep lighted now. It burns just like any other candle, doesn't it? The fact is, candles are not very good about here. I don't know where they come from, but they have a way of burning low occasionally, with a greenish flame that spits tiny sparks, and I'm often annoyed by their going out of themselves. It cannot be helped, for it will be long before we have electricity in our village. It really is rather a poor light, isn't it?

You think I had better leave you the candle and take the lamp, do you? I don't like to carry lamps about, that's the truth. I never dropped one in my life, but I have always thought I might, and it's so confoundedly dangerous if you do. Besides, I am pretty well used to these rotten candles by this time.

You may as well finish that glass while I'm getting it, for I don't mean to let you off with less than three before you go to bed. You won't have to go upstairs, either, for I've put you in the old study next to the surgery—that's where I live myself. The fact is, I never ask a friend to sleep upstairs now. The last man who did was Crackenthorpe, and he said he was kept awake all night. You remember old Crack, don't you? He stuck to the Service, and they've just made him an admiral. Yes, I'm off now—unless the candle goes out. I couldn't help asking if you remembered Crackenthorpe. If any one had told us that the skinny little idiot he used to be was to turn out the most successful of the lot of us, we should have laughed at the idea, shouldn't we? You and I did not do badly, it's true—but I'm really going now. I don't mean to let you think that I've been putting it off by talking! As if there were anything to be afraid of! If I were scared, I should tell you so quite frankly, and get you to go upstairs with me.

Here's the box. I brought it down very carefully, so as not to disturb it, poor thing. You see, if it were shaken, the jaw might get separated from it again, and I'm sure it wouldn't like that. Yes, the candle went out as I was coming downstairs, but that was the draught from the leaky window on the landing. Did you hear anything? Yes, there was another scream. Am I pale, do you say? That's nothing. My heart is a little queer sometimes, and I went upstairs too fast. In fact, that's one reason why I really prefer to live altogether on the ground floor.

Wherever that shriek came from, it was not from the skull, for I had the box in my hand when I heard the noise, and here it is now; so we have proved definitely that the screams are produced by something else. I've no doubt I shall find out some day what makes them. Some crevice in the wall, of course, or a crack in a chimney, or a chink in the frame of a window. That's the way all ghost stories end in real life. Do you know, I'm jolly glad I thought of going up and bringing it down for you to see, for that last shriek settles the question. To think that I should have been so weak as to fancy that the poor skull could really cry out like a living thing!

Now I'll open the box, and we'll take it out and look at it under the bright light. It's rather awful to think that the poor lady used to sit there, in your chair, evening after evening, in just the same light, isn't it? But then—I've made up my mind that it's all rubbish from beginning to end, and that it's just an old skull that Luke had when he was a student; and perhaps he put it into the lime merely to whiten it, and could not find the jaw.

I made a seal on the string, you see, after I had put the jaw in its place, and I wrote on the cover. There's the old white label on it still, from the milliner's, addressed to Mrs. Pratt when the hat was sent to her, and as there was room I wrote on the edge: "A skull, once the property of the late Luke Pratt, M.D." I don't quite know why I wrote that, unless it was with the idea of explaining how the thing happened to be in my possession. I cannot help wondering sometimes what sort of hat it was that came in the bandbox. What colour was it, do you think? Was it a gay spring hat with a bobbing feather and pretty ribands? Strange that the very same box should hold the head that wore the finery —perhaps. No—we made up our minds that it just came from the hospital in London where Luke did his time. It's far better to look at it in that light, isn't it? There's no more connection between that skull and poor Mrs. Pratt than there was between my story about the lead and——

Good Lord! Take the lamp—don't let it go out, if you can help it—I'll have the window fastened again in a second—I say, what a gale! There, it's out! I told you so! Never mind, there's the firelight—I've got the window shut—the bolt was only half down. Was the box blown off the table? Where the deuce is it? There! That won't open again, for I've put up the bar. Good dodge, an old-fashioned bar—there's nothing like it. Now, you find the band-box while I light the lamp. Confound those wretched matches! Yes, a pipe spill is better—it must light in the fire—I hadn't thought of it—thank you—there we are again. Now, where's the box? Yes, put it back on the table, and we'll open it.

That's the first time I have ever known the wind to burst that window open; but it was partly carelessness on my part when I last shut it. Yes, of course I heard the scream. It seemed to go all round the house before it broke in at the window. That proves that it's always been the wind and nothing else, doesn't it? When it was not the wind, it was my imagination. I've always been a very imaginative man: I must have been, though I did not know it. As we grow older we understand ourselves better, don't you know?

I'll have a drop of the Hulstkamp neat, by way of an exception, since you are filling up your glass. That damp gust chilled me, and with my rheumatic tendency I'm very much afraid of a chill, for the cold sometimes seems to stick in my joints all winter when it once gets in.

By George, that's good stuff! I'll just light a fresh pipe, now that everything is snug again, and then we'll open the box. I'm so glad we heard that last scream together, with the skull here on the table between us, for a thing cannot possibly be in two places at the same time, and the noise most certainly came from outside, as any noise the wind makes must. You thought you heard it scream through the room after the window was burst open? Oh yes, so did I, but that was natural enough when everything was open. Of course we heard the wind. What could one expect?

Look here, please. I want you to see that the seal is intact before we open the box together. Will you take my glasses? No, you have your own. All right. The seal is sound, you see, and you can read the words of the motto easily. "Sweet and low"—that's it—because the poem goes on "Wind of the Western Sea," and says, "blow him again to me," and all that. Here is the seal on my watchchain, where it's hung for more than forty years. My poor little wife gave it to me when I was courting, and I never had any other. It was just like her to think of those words—she was always fond of Tennyson.

It's of no use to cut the string, for it's fastened to the box, so I'll just break the wax and untie the knot, and afterward we'll seal it up again. You see, I like to feel that the thing is safe in its place, and that nobody can take it out. Not that I should suspect Trehearn of meddling with it, but I always feel that he knows a lot more than he tells.

You see, I've managed it without breaking the string, though when I fastened it I never expected to open the bandbox again. The lid comes off easily enough. There! Now look!

What? Nothing in it? Empty? It's gone, man, the skull is gone!

No, there's nothing the matter with me. I'm only trying to collect my thoughts. It's so strange. I'm positively certain that it was inside when I put on the seal last spring. I can't have imagined that: it's utterly impossible. If I ever took a stiff glass with a friend now and then, I would admit that I might have made some idiotic mistake when I had taken too much. But I don't, and I never did. A pint of ale at supper and half a go of rum at bedtime was the most I ever took in my good days. I believe it's always we sober fellows who get rheumatism and gout! Yet there was my seal, and there is the empty bandbox. That's plain enough.

I say, I don't half like this. It's not right. There's something wrong about it, in my opinion. You needn't talk to me about super-natural manifestations, for I don't believe in them, not a little bit! Somebody must have tampered with the seal and stolen the skull. Sometimes, when I go out to work in the garden in summer, I leave my watch and chain on the table. Trehearn must have taken the seal then, and used it, for he would be quite sure that I should not come in for at least an hour.

If it was not Trehearn—oh, don't talk to me about the possi-bility that the thing has got out by itself! If it has, it must be some-where about the house, in some out-of-the-way corner, waiting. We may come upon it anywhere, waiting for us, don't you know? —just waiting in the dark. Then it will scream at me; it will shriek at me in the dark, for it hates me, I tell you!

The bandbox is quite empty. We are not dreaming, either of us. There, I turn it upside down.

What's that? Something fell out as I turned it over. It's on the floor, it's near your feet, I know it is, and we must find it. Help me to find it, man. Have you got it? For God's sake, give it to me, quickly!

Lead! I knew it when I heard it fall. I knew it couldn't be any-thing else by the little thud it made on the hearthrug. So it was lead after all, and Luke did it.

I feel a little bit shaken up—not exactly nervous, you know, but badly shaken up, that's the fact. Anybody would, I should think. After all, you cannot say that it's fear of the thing, for I went up and brought it down—at least, I believed I was bringing it down, and that's the same thing, and by George, rather than give in to such silly nonsense, I'll take the box upstairs again and put it back in its place. It's not that. It's the certainty that the poor little woman came to her end in that way, by my fault, because I told the story. That's what is so dreadful. Somehow, I had always hoped that I should never be quite sure of it, but there is no doubting it now. Look at that!

Look at it! That little lump of lead with no particular shape. Think of what it did, man! Doesn't it make you shiver? He gave her something to make her sleep, of course, but there must have been one moment of awful agony. Think of having boiling lead poured into your brain. Think of it. She was dead before she could scream, but only think of—oh! there it is again—it's just outside—I know it's just outside—I can't keep it out of my head!—oh!—oh!

You thought I had fainted? No, I wish I had, for it would have stopped sooner. It's all very well to say that it's only a noise, and that a noise never hurt anybody—you're as white as a shroud yourself. There's only one thing to be done, if we hope to close an eye to-night. We must find it and put it back into its bandbox and shut it up in the cupboard, where it likes to be. I don't know how it got out, but it wants to get in again. That's why it screams so awfully to-night—it was never so bad as this—never since I first——

Bury it? Yes, if we can find it, we'll bury it, if it takes us all night. We'll bury it six feet deep and ram down the earth over it, so that it shall never get out again, and if it screams, we shall hardly hear it so deep down. Quick, we'll get the lantern and look for it. It cannot be far away; I'm sure it's just outside—it was coming in when I shut the window, I know it.

Yes, you're quite right. I'm losing my senses, and I must get hold of myself. Don't speak to me for a minute or two; I'll sit quite still and keep my eyes shut and repeat something I know. That's the best way.

"Add together the altitude, the latitude, and the polar distance, divide by two and subtract the altitude from the half-sum; then add the logarithm of the secant of the latitude, the cosecant of the polar distance, the cosine of the half-sum and the sine of the half-sum minus the altitude"—there! Don't say that I'm out of my senses, for my memory is all right, isn't it?

Of course, you may say that it's mechanical, and that we

never forget the things we learned when we were boys and have used almost every day for a lifetime. But that's the very point. When a man is going crazy, it's the mechanical part of his mind that gets out of order and won't work right; he remembers things that never happened, or he sees things that aren't real, or he hears noises when there is perfect silence. That's not what is the matter with either of us, is it?

Come, we'll get the lantern and go round the house. It's not raining—only blowing like old boots, as we used to say. The lantern is in the cupboard under the stairs in the hall, and I always keep it trimmed in case of a wreck.

No use to look for the thing? I don't see how you can say that. It was nonsense to talk of burying it, of course, for it doesn't want to be buried; it wants to go back into its bandbox and be taken upstairs, poor thing! Trehearn took it out, I know, and made the seal over again. Perhaps he took it to the churchyard, and he may have meant well. I daresay he thought that it would not scream any more if it were quietly laid in consecrated ground, near where it belongs. But it has come home. Yes, that's it. He's not half a bad fellow, Trehearn, and rather religiously inclined, I think. Does not that sound natural, and reasonable, and well meant? He supposed it screamed because it was not decently buried—with the rest. But he was wrong. How should he know that it screams at me because it hates me, and because it's my fault that there was that little lump of lead in it?

No use to look for it, anyhow? Nonsense! I tell you it wants to be found—Hark! what's that knocking? Do you hear it? Knock —knock—knock—three times, then a pause, and then again. It has a hollow sound, hasn't it?

It has come home. I've heard that knock before. It wants to come in and be taken upstairs, in its box. It's at the front door.

Will you come with me? We'll take it in. Yes, I own that I don't like to go alone and open the door. The thing will roll in and stop against my foot, just as it did before, and the light will go out. I'm a good deal shaken by finding that bit of lead, and, besides, my heart isn't quite right—too much strong tobacco, per-haps. Besides, I'm quite willing to own that I'm a bit nervous to-night, if I never was before in my life.

That's right, come along! I'll take the box with me, so as not to come back. Do you hear the knocking? It's not like any other knocking I ever heard. If you will hold this door open, I can find the lantern under the stairs by the light from this room without bringing the lamp into the hall—it would only go out.

The thing knows we are coming—hark! It's impatient to get in. Don't shut the door till the lantern is ready, whatever you do. There will be the usual trouble with the matches, I suppose—no, the first one, by Jove! I tell you it wants to get in, so there's no trouble. All right with that door now; shut it, please. Now come and hold the lantern, for it's blowing so hard outside that I shall have to use both hands. That's it, hold the light low. Do you hear the knocking still? Here goes—I'll open just enough with my foot against the bottom of the door—now!

Catch it! it's only the wind that blows it across the floor, that's all—there's half a hurricane outside, I tell you! Have you got it? The bandbox is on the table. One minute, and I'll have the bar up. There!

Why did you throw it into the box so roughly? It doesn't like that, you know.

What do you say? Bitten your hand? Nonsense, man! You did just what I did. You pressed the jaws together with your other hand and pinched yourself. Let me see. You don't mean to say you have drawn blood? You must have squeezed hard, by Jove, for the skin is certainly torn. I'll give you some carbolic solution for it before we go to bed, for they say a scratch from a skull's tooth may go bad and give trouble.

Come inside again and let me see it by the lamp. I'll bring the bandbox—never mind the lantern, it may just as well burn in the hall, for I shall need it presently when I go up the stairs. Yes, shut the door if you will; it makes it more cheerful and bright. Is your finger still bleeding? I'll get you the carbolic in an instant; just let me see the thing.

Ugh! There's a drop of blood on the upper jaw. It's on the eye-tooth. Ghastly, isn't it? When I saw it running along the floor of the hall, the strength almost went out of my hands, and I felt my knees bending; then I understood that it was the gale, driving it over the smooth boards. You don't blame me? No, I should think not! We were boys together, and we've seen a thing or two, and we may just as well own to each other that we were both in a beastly funk when it slid across the floor at you. No wonder you pinched your finger picking it up, after that, if I did the same thing out of sheer nervousness, in broad daylight, with the sun streaming in on me.

Strange that the jaw should stick to it so closely, isn't it? I suppose it's the dampness, for it shuts like a vice—I have wiped off the drop of blood, for it was not nice to look at. I'm not going to try to open the jaws, don't be afraid! I shall not play any tricks with the poor thing, but I'll just seal the box again, and we'll take it upstairs and put it away where it wants to be. The wax is on the writing-table by the window. Thank you. It will be long before I leave my seal lying about again, for Trehearn to use, I can tell you. Explain? I don't explain natural phenomena, but if you choose to think that Trehearn had hidden it somewhere in the bushes, and that the gale blew it to the house against the door, and made it knock, as if it wanted to be let in, you're not thinking the impossible, and I'm quite ready to agree with you.

Do you see that? You can swear that you've actually seen me seal it this time, in case anything of the kind should occur again. The wax fastens the strings to the lid, which cannot possibly be lifted, even enough to get in one finger. You're quite satisfied, aren't you? Yes. Besides, I shall lock the cupboard and keep the key in my pocket hereafter.

Now we can take the lantern and go upstairs. Do you know? I'm very much inclined to agree with your theory that the wind blew it against the house. I'll go ahead, for I know the stairs; just hold the lantern near my feet as we go up. How the wind howls and whistles! Did you feel the sand on the floor under your shoes as we crossed the hall?

Yes—this is the door of the best bedroom. Hold up the lantern, please. This side, by the head of the bed. I left the cupboard open when I got the box. Isn't it queer how the faint odour of women's dresses will hang about an old closet for years? This is the shelf. You've seen me set the box there, and now you see me turn the key and put it into my pocket. So that's done!

Good-night. Are you sure you're quite comfortable? It's not much of a room, but I daresay you would as soon sleep here as upstairs to-night. If you want anything, sing out; there's only a lath and plaster partition between us. There's not so much wind on this side by half. There's the Hollands on the table, if you'll have one more nightcap. No? Well, do as you please. Good-night again, and don't dream about that thing, if you can.

The following paragraph appeared in the *Penraddon News*, 23rd November, 1906:

"MYSTERIOUS DEATH OF A RETIRED SEA CAPTAIN

"The village of Tredcombe is much disturbed by the strange death of Captain Charles Braddock, and all sorts of impossible stories are circulating with regard to the circumstances, which certainly seem difficult of explanation. The retired captain, who had successfully commanded in his time the largest and fastest liners belonging to one of the principal transatlantic steamship companies, was found dead in his bed on Tuesday morning in his own cottage, a quarter of a mile from the village. An examination was made at once by the local practitioner, which revealed the horrible fact that the deceased had been bitten in the throat by a human assailant, with such amazing force as to crush the windpipe and cause death. The marks of the teeth of both jaws were so plainly visible on the skin that they could be counted, but the perpetrator of the deed had evidently lost the two lower middle incisors. It is hoped that this peculiarity may help to iden-tify the murderer, who can only be a dangerous escaped maniac. The deceased, though over sixty-five years of age, is said to have been a hale man of considerable physical strength, and it is remarkable that no signs of any struggle were visible in the room, nor could it be ascertained how the murderer had entered the house. Warning has been sent to all the insane asylums in the United Kingdom, but as yet no information has been received regarding the escape of any dangerous patient.

"The coroner's jury returned the somewhat singular verdict that Captain Braddock came to his death 'by the hands or teeth of some person unknown.' The local surgeon is said to have expressed pri-vately the opinion that the maniac is a woman, a view he deduces from the small size of the jaws, as shown by the marks of the teeth. The whole affair is shrouded in mystery. Captain Braddock was a widower, and lived alone. He leaves no children."

(AUTHOR's NOTE.—Students of ghost lore and haunted houses will find the foundation of the foregoing story in the legends about a skull which is still pre-served in the farm-house called Bettiscombe Manor, situated, I believe, on the Dorsetshire coast.)

●

S<small>IR</small> W<small>ILLIAM</small> D<small>UGDALE</small> did farther inform me that Major General Middleton (since Lord) went into the Highlands of Scotland, to endeavour to make a party for King Charles I. An old gentleman (that was second-sighted) came and told him that his endeavour was good, but he would be unsuccessful: and moreover, "that they would put the King to death: And that several other attempts would be made, but all in vain: but that his son would come in, but not reign; but at last would be restored." This Lord Middleton had a great friendship with the Laird Bocconi, and they had made an agreement, that the first of them that died should appear to the other in extremity. The Lord Middleton was taken prisoner at Worcester fight, and was prisoner in the Tower of London, under three locks. Lying in bed pensive, Bocconi appeared to him; my Lord Middleton asked him if he were dead or alive? he said, dead, and that he was a ghost; and told him, that within three days he should escape, and he did so, in his wife's cloaths. When he had done his message, he gave a frisk, and said,

> *Givenni Givanni*, 'tis very strange,
> In the world to see so sudden a change.

And then gathered up and vanished. This account Sir William Dugdale had from the Bishop of Edinburgh. And this, and the former account he hath writ in a book of miscellanies, which I have seen, and is now reposited with other books of his in the Musæum at Oxford.

—J<small>OHN</small> A<small>UBREY</small>

THE MONKEY'S PAW

Once in a very long while we come upon a drama of the supernatural treated so skillfully that the stage direction "Enter the Ghost" never has to be written. "But," we say to ourselves at the finish, "it wasn't really a ghost—wasn't even meant to be." And then we wonder, "Or *was* it?" And we turn back again to reread more closely, seeking the author's own intention. And, having done so, we find that the mystery remains. It is that sort of echoing uncertainty, which distinguishes Mrs Wharton's *Afterward*, that also makes this shorter story linger long in the mind.—EDITOR.

W. W. Jacobs

THE MONKEY'S PAW

Without, the night was cold and wet, but in the small parlour of Laburnum Villa the blinds were drawn and the fire burned brightly. Father and son were at chess; the former, who possessed ideas about the game involving radical changes, putting his king into such sharp and unnecessary perils that it even provoked comment from the white-haired old lady knitting placidly by the fire.

"Hark at the wind," said Mr. White, who, having seen a fatal mistake after it was too late, was amiably desirous of preventing his son from seeing it.

"I'm listening," said the latter, grimly surveying the board as he stretched out his hand. "Check."

"I should hardly think that he'd come to-night," said his father, with his hand poised over the board.

"Mate," replied the son.

"That's the worst of living so far out," bawled Mr. White, with sudden and unlooked-for violence; "of all the beastly, slushy, out-of-the-way places to live in, this is the worst. Path's a bog, and the road's a torrent. I don't know what people are thinking about. I suppose because only two houses in the road are let, they think it doesn't matter."

"Never mind, dear," said his wife soothingly; "perhaps you'll win the next one."

Mr. White looked up sharply, just in time to intercept a knowing glance between mother and son. The words died away on his lips, and he hid a guilty grin in his thin grey beard.

"There he is," said Herbert White, as the gate banged to loudly and heavy footsteps came towards the door.

The old man rose with hospitable haste, and opening the door, was heard condoling with the new arrival. The new arrival also condoled with himself, so that Mrs. White said, "Tut, tut!" and coughed gently as her husband entered the room, followed by a tall, burly man, beady of eye and rubicund of visage.

"Sergeant-Major Morris," he said, introducing him.

The sergeant-major shook hands, and taking the proffered seat by the fire, watched contentedly while his host got out whisky and tumblers and stood a small copper kettle on the fire.

At the third glass his eyes got brighter, and he began to talk, the little family circle regarding with eager interest this visitor from distant parts, as he squared his broad shoulders in the chair, and spoke of wild scenes and doughty deeds; of wars and plagues, and strange peoples.

"Twenty-one years of it," said Mr. White, nodding at his wife and son. "When he went away he was a slip of a youth in the warehouse. Now look at him."

"He don't look to have taken much harm," said Mrs. White politely.

"I'd like to go to India myself," said the old man, "just to look round a bit, you know."

"Better where you are," said the sergeant-major, shaking his head. He put down the empty glass, and sighing softly, shook it again.

"I should like to see those old temples and fakirs and jugglers," said the old man. "What was that you started telling me the other day about a monkey's paw or something, Morris?"

"Nothing," said the soldier hastily. "Leastways nothing worth hearing."

"Monkey's paw?" said Mrs. White curiously.

"Well, it's just a bit of what you might call magic, perhaps," said the sergeant-major off-handedly.

His three listeners leaned forward eagerly. The vistor absent-mindedly put his empty glass to his lips and then set it down again. His host filled it for him.

"To look at," said the sergeant-major, fumbling in his pocket, "it's just an ordinary little paw, dried to a mummy."

He took something out of his pocket and proffered it. Mrs. White drew back with a grimace, but her son, taking it, examined it curiously.

"And what is there special about it?" enquired Mr. White as he took it from his son, and having examined it, placed it upon the table.

"It had a spell put on it by an old fakir," said the sergeant-major, "a very holy man. He wanted to show that fate ruled people's lives, and that those who interfered with it did so to their sorrow. He put a spell on it so that three separate men could each have three wishes from it."

His manner was so impressive that his hearers were conscious that their light laughter jarred somewhat.

"Well, why don't you have three, sir?" said Herbert White cleverly.

The soldier regarded him in the way that middle age is wont to regard presumptuous youth. "I have," he said quietly, and his blotchy face whitened.

"And did you really have the three wishes granted?" asked Mrs. White.

"I did," said the sergeant-major, and his glass tapped against his strong teeth.

"And has anybody else wished?" persisted the old lady.

"The first man had his three wishes. Yes," was the reply; "I don't know what the first two were, but the third was for death. That's how I got the paw."

His tones were so grave that a hush fell upon the group.

"If you've had your three wishes, it's no good to you now, then, Morris," said the old man at last. "What do you keep it for?"

The soldier shook his head. "Fancy, I suppose," he said slowly. "I did have some idea of selling it, but I don't think I will. It has caused enough mischief already. Besides, people won't buy. They think it's a fairy tale, some of them; and those who do think anything of it want to try it first and pay me afterward."

"If you could have another three wishes," said the old man, eyeing him keenly, "would you have them?"

"I don't know," said the other. "I don't know."

He took the paw, and dangling it between his forefinger and thumb, suddenly threw it upon the fire. White, with a slight cry, stooped down and snatched it off.

"Better let it burn," said the soldier solemnly.

"If you don't want it, Morris," said the other, "give it to me."

"I won't," said his friend doggedly. "I threw it on the fire. If you keep it, don't blame me for what happens. Pitch it on the fire again, like a sensible man."

The other shook his head and examined his new possession closely. "How do you do it?" he enquired.

"Hold it up in your right hand and wish aloud," said the sergeant-major, "but I warn you of the consequences."

"Sounds like the *Arabian Nights*," said Mrs. White, as she rose and began to set the supper. "Don't you think you might wish for four pairs of hands for me?"

Her husband drew the talisman from his pocket, and then all three burst into laughter as the sergeant-major, with a look of alarm on his face, caught him by the arm.

"If you must wish," he said gruffly, "wish for something sensible."

Mr. White dropped it back in his pocket, and placing chairs, motioned his friend to the table. In the business of supper the talisman was partly forgotten, and afterwards the three sat listening in an enthralled fashion to a second instalment of the soldier's adventures in India.

"If the tale about the monkey's paw is not more truthful than those he has been telling us," said Herbert, as the door closed behind their guest, just in time to catch the last train, "we shan't make much out of it."

"Did you give him anything for it, father?" enquired Mrs. White, regarding her husband closely.

"A trifle," said he, colouring slightly. "He didn't want it, but I made him take it. And he pressed me again to throw it away."

"Likely," said Herbert, with pretended horror. "Why, we're going to be rich, and famous, and happy. Wish to be an emperor, father, to begin with; then you can't be henpecked."

He darted round the table, pursued by the maligned Mrs. White armed with an antimacassar.

Mr. White took the paw from his pocket and eyed it dubiously. "I don't know what to wish for, and that's a fact," he said slowly. "It seems to me I've got all I want."

"If you only cleared the house, you'd be quite happy, wouldn't you!" said Herbert, with his hand on his shoulder. "Well, wish for two hundred pounds, then; that'll just do it."

His father, smiling shamefacedly at his own credulity, held up the talisman, as his son, with a solemn face, somewhat marred by a wink at his mother, sat down at the piano and struck a few impressive chords.

"I wish for two hundred pounds," said the old man distinctly.

A fine crash from the piano greeted the words, interrupted by a shuddering cry from the old man. His wife and son ran toward him.

"It moved," he cried, with a glance of disgust at the object as it lay on the floor. "As I wished, it twisted in my hand like a snake."

"Well, I don't see the money," said his son, as he picked it up and placed it on the table, "and I bet I never shall."

"It must have been your fancy, father," said his wife, regarding him anxiously.

He shook his head. "Never mind, though; there's no harm done, but it gave me a shock all the same."

They sat down by the fire again while the two men finished their pipes. Outside, the wind was higher than ever, and the old man started nervously at the sound of a door banging upstairs. A silence unusual and depressing settled upon all three, which lasted until the old couple arose to retire for the night.

"I expect you'll find the cash tied up in a big bag in the middle of your bed," said Herbert, as he bade them good night, "and something horrible squatting up on top of the wardrobe watching you as you pocket your ill-gotten gains."

He sat alone in the darkness, gazing at the dying fire, and seeing faces in it. The last face was so horrible and so simian that he gazed at it in amazement. It got so vivid that, with a little uneasy laugh, he felt on the table for a glass containing a little water to throw over it. His hand grasped the monkey's paw, and with a little shiver he wiped his hand on his coat and went up to bed.

II

In the brightness of the wintry sun next morning as it streamed over the breakfast table he laughed at his fears. There was an air of prosaic wholesomeness about the room which it had lacked on the previous night, and the dirty, shrivelled little paw was pitched on the side-board with a carelessness which betokened no great belief in its virtues.

"I suppose all old soldiers are the same," said Mrs. White. "The idea of our listening to such nonsense! How could wishes be granted in these days? And if they could, how could two hundred pounds hurt you, father?"

"Might drop on his head from the sky," said the frivolous Herbert.

"Morris said the things happened so naturally," said his father, "that you might if you so wished attribute it to coincidence."

"Well, don't break into the money before I come back," said Herbert as he rose from the table. "I'm afraid it'll turn you into a mean avaricious man, and we shall have to disown you."

His mother laughed, and following him to the door, watched him down the road; and returning to the breakfast table, was very merry at the expense of her husband's credulity. All of which did not prevent her from scurrying to the door at the postman's knock, nor prevent her from referring somewhat shortly to retired sergeant-majors of bibulous habits when she found that the post brought a tailor's bill.

"Herbert will have some more of his funny remarks, I expect, when he comes home," she said, as they sat at dinner.

"I dare say," said Mr. White, pouring himself out some beer; "but for all that, the thing moved in my hand; that I'll swear to."

"You thought it did," said the old lady soothingly.

"I say it did," replied the other. "There was no thought about it; I had just—What's the matter?"

His wife made no reply. She was watching the mysterious movements of a man outside, who, peering in an undecided fashion at the house, appeared to be trying to make up his mind to enter. In mental connection with the two hundred pounds, she noticed that the stranger was well dressed, and wore a silk hat of glossy newness. Three times he paused at the gate, and then walked on again. The fourth time he stood with his hand upon it, and then with sudden resolution flung it open and walked up the path. Mrs. White at the same moment placed her hands behind her, and hurriedly unfastening the strings of her apron, put that useful article of apparel beneath the cushion of her chair.

She brought the stranger, who seemed ill at ease, into the room. He gazed at her furtively, and listened in a preoccupied fashion as the old lady apologized for the appearance of the room, and her husband's coat, a garment which he usually reserved for the garden. She then waited as patiently as her sex would permit, for him to broach his business, but he was at first strangely silent.

"I—was asked to call," he said at last, and stooped and picked a piece of cotton from his trousers. "I come from 'Maw and Meggins'."

The old lady started. "Is anything the matter?" she asked breathlessly. "Has anything happened to Herbert? What is it? What is it?"

Her husband interposed. "There, there, mother," he said hastily. "Sit down, and don't jump to conclusions. You've not brought bad news, I'm sure, sir;" and he eyed the other wistfully.

"I'm sorry——" began the visitor.

"Is he hurt?" demanded the mother wildly.

The visitor bowed in assent. "Badly hurt," he said quietly, "but he is not in any pain."

"Oh, thank God!" said the old woman, clasping her hands. "Thank God for that! Thank——"

She broke off suddenly as the sinister meaning of the assurance dawned upon her, and she saw the awful confirmation of her fears in the other's averted face. She caught her breath, and turning to her slower-witted husband, laid a trembling old hand upon his. There was a long silence.

"He was caught in the machinery," said the visitor at length in a low voice.

"Caught in the machinery," repeated Mr. White, in a dazed fashion, "yes."

He sat staring blankly out at the window, and taking his wife's hand between his own, pressed it as he had been wont to do in their old courting days nearly forty years before.

"He was the only one left to us," he said, turning gently to the visitor. "It is hard."

The other coughed, and rising, walked slowly to the window. "The firm wished me to convey their sincere sympathy with you in your great loss," he said, without looking round. "I beg that you will understand I am only their servant and merely obeying orders."

There was no reply; the old woman's face was white, her eyes staring, and her breath inaudible; and on the husband's face was a look such as his friend the sergeant might have carried into his first action.

"I was to say that Maw and Meggins disclaim all responsibility," continued the other. "They admit no liability at all, but in consideration of your son's services, they wish to present you with a certain sum as compensation."

Mr. White dropped his wife's hand, and rising to his feet, gazed with a look of horror at his visitor. His dry lips shaped the words, "How much?"

"Two hundred pounds," was the answer.

Unconscious of his wife's shriek, the old man smiled faintly, put out his hands like a sightless man, and dropped, a senseless heap, to the floor.

III

In the huge new cemetery, some two miles distant, the old people buried their dead, and came back to the house steeped in shadow and silence. It was all over so quickly that at first they could hardly realise it, and remained in a state of expectation as though of something else to happen—something else which was to lighten this load, too heavy for old hearts to bear.

But the days passed, and expectation gave place to resignation —the hopeless resignation of the old, sometimes miscalled apathy. Sometimes they hardly exchanged a word, for now they had nothing to talk about, and their days were long to weariness.

It was about a week after, that the old man, waking suddenly in the night, stretched out his hand and found himself alone. The room was in darkness, and the sound of subdued weeping came from the window. He raised himself in bed and listened.

"Come back," he said tenderly. "You will be cold."

"It is colder for my son," said the old woman, and wept afresh.

The sound of her sobs died away on his ears. The bed was warm, and his eyes heavy with sleep. He dozed fitfully, and then slept until a sudden wild cry from his wife awoke him with a start.

"*The paw!*" she cried wildly. "The monkey's paw!"

He started up in alarm. "Where? Where is it? What's the matter?"

She came stumbling across the room toward him. "I want it," she said quietly. "You've not destroyed it?"

"It's in the parlour, on the bracket," he replied, marvelling. "Why?"

She cried and laughed together, and bending over, kissed his cheek.

"I only just thought of it," she said hysterically. "Why didn't I think of it before? Why didn't *you* think of it?"

"Think of what?" he questioned.

"The other two wishes," she replied rapidly. "We've only had one."

"Was not that enough?" he demanded fiercely.

"No," she cried triumphantly; "we'll have one more. Go down and get it quickly, and wish our boy alive again."

The man sat up in bed and flung the bedclothes from his quaking limbs. "Good God, you are mad!" he cried, aghast.

"Get it," she panted; "get it quickly, and wish—Oh, my boy, my boy!"

Her husband struck a match and lit the candle. "Get back to bed," he said unsteadily. "You don't know what you are saying."

"We had the first wish granted," said the old woman feverishly; "why not the second?"

"A coincidence," stammered the old man.

"Go and get it and wish," cried his wife, quivering with excitement.

The old man turned and regarded her, and his voice shook. "He has been dead ten days, and besides he—I would not tell you else, but—I could only recognize him by his clothing. If he was too terrible for you to see then, how now?"

"Bring him back," cried the old woman, and dragged him toward the door. "Do you think I fear the child I have nursed?"

He went down in the darkness, and felt his way to the parlour, and then to the mantelpiece. The talisman was in its place, and a horrible fear that the unspoken wish might bring his mutilated son before him ere he could escape from the room seized upon him, and he caught his breath as he found that he had lost the direction of the door. His brow cold with sweat, he felt his way round the table, and groping along the wall until he found himself in the small passage with the unwholesome thing in his hand.

Even his wife's face seemed changed as he entered the room. It was white and expectant, and to his fears seemed to have an unnatural look upon it. He was afraid of her.

"*Wish!*" she cried, in a strong voice.

"It is foolish and wicked," he faltered.

"*Wish!*" repeated his wife.

He raised his hand. "I wish my son alive again."

The talisman fell to the floor, and he regarded it fearfully. Then he sank trembling into a chair as the old woman, with burning eyes, walked to the window and raised the blind.

He sat until he was chilled with the cold, glancing occasionally at the figure of the old woman peering through the window. The candle-end, which had burned below the rim of the china candle-stick, was throwing pulsating shadows on the ceiling and walls, until, with a flicker larger than the rest, it expired. The old man, with an unspeakable sense of relief at the failure of the talisman, crept back to his bed, and a minute or two afterwards the old woman came silently and apathetically beside him.

Neither spoke, but lay silently listening to the ticking of the clock. A stair creaked, and a squeaky mouse scurried noisily through the wall. The darkness was oppressive, and after lying for some time screwing up his courage, he took the box of matches, and striking one, went downstairs for a candle.

At the foot of the stairs the match went out, and he paused to strike another; and at the same moment a knock, so quiet and stealthy as to be scarcely audible, sounded on the front door.

The matches fell from his hand and spilled in the passage. He stood motionless, his breath suspended until the knock was repeated. Then he turned and fled swiftly back to his room, and closed the door behind him. A third knock sounded through the house.

"*What's that?*" cried the old woman, starting up.

"A rat," said the old man in shaking tones—"a rat. It passed me on the stairs."

His wife sat up in bed listening. A loud knock resounded through the house.

"It's Herbert!" she screamed. "It's Herbert!"

She ran to the door, but her husband was before her, and catching her by the arm, held her tightly.

"What are you going to do?" he whispered hoarsely.

"It's my boy; it's Herbert!" she cried, struggling mechanically. "I forgot it was two miles away. What are you holding me for? Let go. I must open the door."

"For God's sake, don't let it in," cried the old man, trembling.

"You're afraid of your own son," she cried, struggling. "Let me go. I'm coming, Herbert; I'm coming."

There was another knock, and another. The old woman with a sudden wrench broke free and ran from the room. Her husband followed to the landing, and called after her appealingly as she hurried downstairs. He heard the chain rattle back and the bottom bolt drawn slowly and stiffly from the socket. Then the old woman's voice, strained and panting.

"The bolt," she cried loudly. "Come down. I can't reach it."

But her husband was on his hands and knees groping wildly on the floor in search of the paw. If he could only find it before the thing outside got in. A perfect fusillade of knocks reverberated through the house, and he heard the scraping of a chair as his wife put it down in the passage against the door. He heard the creaking of the bolt as it came slowly back, and at the same moment he found the monkey's paw, and frantically breathed his third and last wish.

The knocking ceased suddenly, although the echoes of it were still in the house. He heard the chair drawn back, and the door opened. A cold wind rushed up the staircase, and a long loud wail of disappointment and misery from his wife gave him courage to run down to her side, and then to the gate beyond. The street lamp flickering opposite shone on a quiet and deserted road.

●

SIR JOHN BURROUGHES being sent envoy to the Emperor by King Charles I. did take his eldest son Caisho Burroughes along with him, and taking his journey through Italy, left his son at Florence, to learn the language; where he having an intrigue with a beautiful courtesan (mistress of the Grand Duke), their familiarity became so public, that it came to the Duke's ear, who took a resolution to have him murdered; but Caisho having had timely notice of the Duke's design, by some of the English there, immediately left the city without acquainting his mistress with it, and came to England; whereupon the Duke being disappointed of his revenge, fell upon his mistress in most reproachful language; she on the other hand, resenting the sudden departure of her gallant, of whom she was most passionately enamoured, killed herself. At the same moment that she expired, she did appear to Caisho, at his lodgings in London; Colonel Remes * was then in bed with him, who saw her as well as he; giving him an account of her resentments of his ingratitude to her, in leaving her so suddenly, and

* This Colonel Remes was a Parliament man, and did belong to the wardrobe, *tempore Caroli* II.

exposing her to the fury of the Duke, not omitting her own tragical exit, adding withal, that he should be slain in a duel, which accordingly happened; and thus she appeared to him frequently, even when his younger brother (who afterwards was Sir John) was in bed with him. As often as she did appear, he would cry out with great shrieking, and trembling of his body, as anguish of mind, Saying, O God! here she comes, she comes, and at this rate she appeared till he was killed; she appeared to him the morning before he was killed. Some of my acquaintance have told me, that he was one of the most beautiful men in England, and very valiant, but proud and blood-thirsty.

This story was so common, that King Charles I. sent for Caisho Burroughes's father, whom he examined as to the truth of the matter; who did (together with Colonel Remes) aver the matter of fact to be true. So that the King thought it worth his while to send to Florence, to enquire at what time this unhappy lady killed herself; it was found to be the same minute that she first appeared to Caisho, being in bed with Colonel Remes. This relation I had from my worthy friend Mr. Monson, who had it from Sir John's own mouth, brother of Caisho; he had also the same account from his own father, who was intimately acquainted with old Sir John Burroughes and both his sons, and says, as often as Caisho related this, he wept bitterly.

—JOHN AUBREY

THE HORLA

Here is a story of equal worth for both skeptics and believers. Those who care to can consider it a study in the
approach of madness, marked by vividly imagined supernatural events; others can take the opposite view of cause
and effect, claiming that the madness results from genuine
visitations, or insisting that the man is not necessarily mad
at all. The author, no doubt, intended his average reader
to be torn equally between the two explanations, which is
one reason why the story is such a powerful and haunting
one.—EDITOR.

Guy de Maupassant

THE HORLA

May 8. What a lovely day! I have spent all the morning lying in the grass in front of my house, under the enormous plane tree that shades the whole of it. I like this part of the country and I like to live here because I am attached to it by old associations, by those deep and delicate roots which attach a man to the soil on which his ancestors were born and died, which attach him to the ideas and usages of the place as well as to the food, to local expressions, to the peculiar twang of the peasants, to the smell of the soil, of the villages and of the atmosphere itself.

I love my house in which I grew up. From my windows I can see the Seine which flows alongside my garden, on the other side of the high road, almost through my grounds, the great and wide Seine, which goes to Rouen and Havre, and is covered with boats passing to and fro.

On the left, down yonder, lies Rouen, that large town, with its blue roofs, under its pointed Gothic towers. These are innumerable, slender or broad, dominated by the spire of the cathedral, and full of bells which sound through the blue air on fine mornings, sending their sweet and distant iron clang even as far as my home; that song of the metal, which the breeze wafts in my direction, now stronger and now weaker, according as the wind is stronger or lighter.

What a delicious morning it was!

About eleven o'clock, a long line of boats drawn by a steam tug as big as a fly, and which scarcely puffed while emitting its thick smoke, passed my gate.

After two English schooners, whose red flag fluttered in space, there came a magnificent Brazilian three-master; it was perfectly white, and wonderfully clean and shining. I saluted it, I hardly knew why, except that the sight of the vessel gave me great pleasure.

May 12. I have had a slight feverish attack for the last few days, and I feel ill, or rather I feel low-spirited.

Whence come those mysterious influences which change our happiness into discouragement, and our self-confidence into diffidence? One might almost say that the air, the invisible air, is full of unknowable Powers whose mysterious presence we have to endure. I wake up in the best spirits, with an inclination to sing. Why? I go down to the edge of the water, and suddenly, after walking a short distance, I return home wretched, as if some misfortune were awaiting me there. Why? Is it a cold shiver which, passing over my skin, has upset my nerves and given me low spirits? Is it the form of the clouds, the color of the sky, or the color of the surrounding objects which is so changeable, that has troubled my thoughts as they passed before my eyes? Who can tell? Everything that surrounds us, everything that we see, without looking at it, everything that we touch, without knowing it, everything that we handle, without feeling it, all that we meet, without clearly distinguishing it, has a rapid, surprising and inexplicable effect upon us and upon our senses, and, through them, on our ideas and on our heart itself.

How profound that mystery of the Invisible is! We cannot fathom it with our miserable senses, with our eyes which are unable to perceive what is either too small or too great, too near to us, or too far from us—neither the inhabitants of a star nor of a drop of water; nor with our ears that deceive us, for they transmit to us the vibrations of the air in sonorous notes. They are fairies who work the miracle of changing these vibrations into sounds, and by that metamorphosis give birth to music, which makes the silent motion of nature musical . . . with our sense of smell which is less keen than that of a dog, . . . with our sense of taste which can scarcely distinguish the age of wine!

Oh! If we only had other organs which would work other miracles in our favor, what a number of fresh things we might discover around us!

May 16. I am ill, decidedly! I was so well last month! I am feverish, horribly feverish, or rather I am in a state of feverish enervation, which makes my mind suffer as much as my body. I have, continually, that horrible sensation of some impending danger, that apprehension of some coming misfortune, or of approaching death; that presentiment which is, no doubt, an attack of some illness which is still unknown, which germinates in the flesh and in the blood.

May 17. I have just come from consulting my physician, for I could no longer get any sleep. He said my pulse was rapid, my eyes dilated, my nerves highly strung, but there were no alarming symptoms. I must take a course of shower baths and of bromide of potassium.

May 25. No change! My condition is really very peculiar. As the evening comes on, an incomprehensible feeling of disquietude seizes me, just as if night concealed some threatening disaster. I dine hurriedly, and then try to read, but I do not understand the words, and can scarcely distinguish the letters. Then I walk up and down my drawing-room, oppressed by a feeling of confused and irresistible fear, the fear of sleep and fear of my bed.

About ten o'clock I go up to my room. As soon as I enter it I double-lock and bolt the door; I am afraid . . . of what? Up to the present time I have been afraid of nothing. . . . I open my cupboards, and look under my bed; I listen . . . to what? How strange it is that a simple feeling of discomfort, impeded or heightened circulation, perhaps the irritation of a nerve filament, a slight congestion, a small disturbance in the imperfect delicate functioning of our living machinery, may turn the most light-hearted of men into a melancholy one, and make a coward of the bravest? Then, I go to bed, and wait for sleep as a man might wait for the executioner. I wait for its coming with dread, and my heart beats and my legs tremble, while my whole body shivers beneath the warmth of the bed-clothes, until all at once I fall asleep, as though one should plunge into a pool of stagnant water in order to drown. I do not feel it coming on as I did formerly, this perfidious sleep which is close to me and watching me, which is going to seize me by the head, to close my eyes and annihilate me.

I sleep—a long time—two or three hours perhaps—then a dream —no—a nightmare lays hold on me. I feel that I am in bed and asleep . . . I feel it and I know it . . . and I feel also that somebody is coming close to me, is looking at me, touching me, is getting on to my bed, is kneeling on my chest, is taking my neck between his hands and squeezing it . . . squeezing it with all his might in order to strangle me.

I struggle, bound by that terrible sense of powerlessness which paralyzes us in our dreams; I try to cry out—but I cannot; I want to move—I cannot do so; I try, with the most violent efforts and breathing hard, to turn over and throw off this being who is crushing and suffocating me—I cannot!

And then, suddenly, I wake up, trembling and bathed in perspiration; I light a candle and find that I am alone, and after that crisis, which occurs every night, I at length fall asleep and slumber tranquilly till morning.

June 2. My condition has grown worse. What is the matter with me? The bromide does me no good, and the shower baths have no effect. Sometimes, in order to tire myself thoroughly, though I am fatigued enough already, I go for a walk in the forest of Roumare. I used to think at first that the fresh light and soft air, impregnated with the odor of herbs and leaves, would instill new blood into my veins and impart fresh energy to my heart. I turned into a broad hunting road, and then turned toward La Bouille, through a narrow path, between two rows of exceedingly tall trees, which placed a thick green, almost black, roof between the sky and me.

A sudden shiver ran through me, not a cold shiver, but a strange shiver of agony, and I hastened my steps, uneasy at being alone in the forest, afraid, stupidly and without reason, of the profound solitude. Suddenly it seemed to me as if I were being followed, that somebody was walking at my heels, close, quite close to me, near enough to touch me.

I turned round suddenly, but I was alone. I saw nothing behind me except the straight, broad path, empty and bordered by high trees, horribly empty; before me it also extended until it was lost in the distance, and looked just the same, terrible.

I closed my eyes. Why? And then I began to turn round on one heel very quickly, just like a top. I nearly fell down, and opened my eyes; the trees were dancing round me and the earth heaved; I was obliged to sit down. Then, ah! I no longer remembered how I had come! What a strange idea! What a strange, strange idea! I did not in the least know. I started off to the right, and got back into the avenue which had led me into the middle of the forest.

June 3. I have had a terrible night. I shall go away for a few weeks, for no doubt a journey will set me up again.

July 2. I have come back, quite cured, and have had a most delightful trip into the bargain. I have been to Mont Saint-Michel, which I had not seen before.

What a sight, when one arrives, as I did, at Avranches, toward the end of the day! The town stands on a hill, and I was taken into the public garden at the extremity of the town. I uttered a cry of astonishment. An extraordinarily large bay lay extended before me, as far as my eyes could reach, between two hills which were lost to sight in the mist; and in the middle of this immense yellow bay, under a clear, golden sky, a peculiar hill rose up, sombre and pointed in the midst of the sand. The sun had just disappeared, and under the still flaming sky appeared the outline of that fantastic rock which bears on its summit a fantastic monument.

At daybreak I went out to it. The tide was low, as it had been the night before, and I saw that wonderful abbey rise up before me as I approached it. After several hours' walking, I reached the enormous mass of rocks which supports the little town, dominated by the great church. Having climbed the steep and narrow street, I entered the most wonderful Gothic building that has ever been built to God on earth, as large as a town, full of low rooms which seem buried beneath vaulted roofs, and lofty galleries supported by delicate columns.

I entered this gigantic granite gem, which is as light as a bit of lace, covered with towers, with slender belfries with spiral staircases, which raise their strange heads that bristle with chimeras, with devils, with fantastic animals, with monstrous flowers, to the blue sky by day, and to the black sky by night, and are connected by finely carved arches.

When I had reached the summit I said to the monk who accompanied me: "Father, how happy you must be here!" And he replied: "It is very windy here, monsieur"; and so we began to talk while watching the rising tide, which ran over the sand and covered it as with a steel cuirass.

And then the monk told me stories, all the old stories belonging to the place, legends, nothing but legends.

One of them struck me forcibly. The country people, those belonging to the Mount, declare that at night one can hear voices talking on the sands, and then that one hears two goats bleating, one with a strong, the other with a weak voice. Incredulous people declare that it is nothing but the cry of the sea birds, which occasionally resembles bleatings, and occasionally, human lamentations; but belated fishermen swear that they have met an old shepherd wandering between tides on the sands around the little town. His head is completely concealed by his cloak and he is followed by a billy goat with a man's face, and a nanny goat with a woman's face, both having long, white hair and talking incessantly and quarreling in an unknown tongue. Then suddenly they cease and begin to bleat with all their might.

"Do you believe it?" I asked the monk. "I scarcely know," he replied, and I continued: "If there are other beings beside ourselves on this earth, how comes it that we have not known it long since, or why have *you* not seen them? How is that *I* have not seen them?" He replied: "Do we see the hundred-thousandth part of what exists? Look here; there is the wind, which is the strongest force in nature, which knocks down men, and blows down buildings, destroys cliffs and casts great ships on the rocks; the wind which kills, which whistles, which sighs, which roars—have you ever seen it, and can you see it? It exists for all that, however."

I was silent before this simple reasoning. That man was a philosopher, or perhaps a fool; I could not say which exactly, so I held my tongue. What he had said had often been in my own thoughts.

July 3. I have slept badly; certainly there is some feverish influence here, for my coachman is suffering in the same way as I am. When I went back home yesterday, I noticed his singular paleness, and I asked him: "What is the matter with you, Jean?" "The matter is that I never get any rest, and my nights devour my days. Since your departure, monsieur, there has been a spell over me."

However, the other servants are all well, but I am very much afraid of having another attack myself.

July 4. I am decidedly ill again; for my old nightmares have returned. Last night I felt somebody leaning on me and sucking my life from between my lips. Yes, he was sucking it out of my throat, like a leech. Then he got up, satiated, and I woke up, so exhausted, crushed and weak that I could not move. If this continues for a few days, I shall certainly go away again.

July 5. Have I lost my reason? What happened last night is so strange that my head wanders when I think of it!

I had locked my door, as I do now every evening, and then, being thirsty, I drank half a glass of water, and accidentally noticed that the water bottle was full up to the cut-glass stopper.

Then I went to bed and fell into one of my terrible sleeps, from which I was aroused in about two hours by a still more frightful shock.

Picture to yourself a sleeping man who is being murdered and who wakes up with a knife in his lung, and whose breath rattles, who is covered with blood, and who can no longer breathe and is about to die, and does not understand—there you have it.

Having recovered my senses, I was thirsty again, so I lit a candle and went to the table on which stood my water bottle. I lifted it up and tilted it over my glass, but nothing came out. It was empty! It was completely empty! At first I could not understand it at all, and then suddenly I was seized by such a terrible feeling that I had to sit down, or rather I fell into a chair! Then I sprang up suddenly to look about me; then I sat down again, overcome by astonishment and fear, in front of the transparent glass bottle!

I looked at it with fixed eyes, trying to conjecture, and my hands trembled! Somebody had drunk the water, but who? I? I without any doubt. It could surely only be I. In that case I was a somnambulist; I lived, without knowing it, that mysterious double life which makes us doubt whether there are not two beings in us, or whether a strange, unknowable and invisible being does not at such moments, when our soul is in a state of torpor, animate our captive body, which obeys this other being, as it obeys us, and more than it obeys ourselves.

Oh! Who will understand my horrible agony? Who will understand the emotion of a man who is sound in mind, wide awake, full of common sense, who looks in horror through the glass of a water bottle for a little water that disappeared while he was asleep? I remained thus until it was daylight, without venturing to go to bed again.

July 6. I am going mad. Again all the contents of my water bottle have been drunk during the night—or rather, I have drunk it!

But is it I? Is it I? Who could it be? Who? Oh! God! Am I going mad? Who will save me?

July 10. I have just been through some surprising ordeals. Decidedly I am mad! And yet! . . .

On July 6, before going to bed, I put some wine, milk, water, bread and strawberries on my table. Somebody drank—I drank—all the water and a little of the milk, but neither the wine, bread, nor the strawberries were touched.

On the seventh of July I renewed the same experiment, with the same results, and on July 8, I left out the water and the milk, and nothing was touched.

Lastly, on July 9, I put only water and milk on my table, taking care to wrap up the bottles in white muslin and to tie down the stoppers. Then I rubbed my lips, my beard and my hands with pencil lead, and went to bed.

Irresistible sleep seized me, which was soon followed by a terrible awakening. I had not moved, and there was no mark of lead on the sheets. I rushed to the table. The muslin round the bottles remained intact; I undid the string, trembling with fear. All the water had been drunk, and so had the milk! Ah! Great God! . . .

I must start for Paris immediately.

July 12. Paris. I must have lost my head during the last few days! I must be the plaything of my enervated imagination, unless I am really a somnambulist, or that I have been under the power of one of those hitherto unexplained influences which are called suggestions. In any case, my mental state bordered on madness, and twenty-four hours of Paris sufficed to restore my equilibrium.

Yesterday, after doing some business and paying some visits which instilled fresh and invigorating air into my soul, I wound up the evening at the *Théâtre-Français*. A play by Alexandre Dumas the younger was being acted, and his active and powerful imagination completed my cure. Certainly solitude is dangerous for active minds. We require around us men who can think and talk. When we are alone for a long time, we people space with phantoms.

I returned along the boulevards to my hotel in excellent spirits. Amid the jostling of the crowd I thought, not without irony, of my terrors and surmises of the previous week, because I had believed—yes, I had believed—that an invisible being lived beneath my roof. How weak our brains are, and how quickly they are terrified and led into error by a small incomprehensible fact.

Instead of saying simply: "I do not understand because I do not know the cause," we immediately imagine terrible mysteries and supernatural powers.

July 14. Fête of the Republic. I walked through the streets, amused as a child at the firecrackers and flags. Still it is very foolish to be merry on a fixed date, by Government decree. The populace is an imbecile flock of sheep, now stupidly patient, and now in ferocious revolt. Say to it: "Amuse yourself," and it amuses itself. Say to it: "Go and fight with your neighbor," and it goes and fights. Say to it: "Vote for the Emperor," and it votes for the Emperor, and then say to it: "Vote for the Republic," and it votes for the Republic.

Those who direct it are also stupid; only, instead of obeying men, they obey principles which can only be stupid, sterile, and false, for the very reason that they are principles, that is to say, ideas which are considered as certain and unchangeable, in this world where one is certain of nothing, since light is an illusion and noise is an illusion.

July 16. I saw some things yesterday that troubled me very much.

I was dining at the house of my cousin, Madame Sable, whose husband is colonel of the 76th Chasseurs at Limoges. There were two young women there, one of whom had married a medical man, Dr. Parent, who devotes much attention to nervous diseases and to the remarkable manifestations taking place at this moment under the influence of hypnotism and suggestion.

He related to us at some length the wonderful results obtained by English scientists and by the doctors of the Nancy school; and the facts which he adduced appeared to me so strange that I declared that I was altogether incredulous.

"We are," he declared, "on the point of discovering one of the most important secrets of nature; I mean to say, one of its most important secrets on this earth, for there are certainly others of a different kind of importance up in the stars, yonder. Ever since man has thought, ever since he has been able to express and write down his thoughts, he has felt himself close to a mystery which is impenetrable to his gross and imperfect senses, and he endeavors to supplement through his intellect the inefficiency of his senses. As long as that intellect remained in its elementary stage, these apparitions of invisible spirits assumed forms that were commonplace, though terrifying. Thence sprang the popular belief in the supernatural, the legends of wandering spirits, of fairies, of gnomes, ghosts, I might even say the legend of God; for our conceptions of the workman-creator, from whatever religion they may have come down to us, are certainly the most mediocre, the most stupid and the most incredible inventions that ever sprang from the terrified brain of any human beings. Nothing is truer than what Voltaire says: 'God made man in His own image, but man has certainly paid Him back in his own coin.'

"However, for rather more than a century men seem to have had a presentiment of something new. Mesmer and some others have put us on an unexpected track, and, especially within the last two or three years, we have arrived at really surprising results."

My cousin, who is also very incredulous, smiled, and Dr. Parent said to her: "Would you like me to try and send you to sleep, madame?" "Yes, certainly."

She sat down in an easy chair, and he began to look at her

fixedly, so as to fascinate her. I suddenly felt myself growing uncomfortable, my heart beating rapidly and a choking sensation in my throat. I saw Madame Sable's eyes becoming heavy, her mouth twitching and her bosom heaving, and at the end of ten minutes she was asleep.

"Go behind her," the doctor said to me, and I took a seat behind her. He put a visiting card into her hands, and said to her: "This is a looking-glass; what do you see in it?" And she replied: "I see my cousin." "What is he doing?" "He is twisting his mustache." "And now?" "He is taking a photograph out of his pocket." "Whose photograph is it?" "His own."

That was true, and the photograph had been given me that same evening at the hotel.

"What is his attitude in this portrait?" "He is standing up with his hat in his hand."

She saw, therefore, on that card, on that piece of white pasteboard, as if she had seen it in a mirror.

The young women were frightened, and exclaimed: "That is enough! Quite, quite enough!"

But the doctor said to Madame Sable authoritatively: "You will rise at eight o'clock to-morrow morning; then you will go and call on your cousin at his hotel and ask him to lend you five thousand francs which your husband demands of you, and which he will ask for when he sets out on his coming journey."

Then he woke her up.

On returning to my hotel, I thought over this curious séance, and I was assailed by doubts, not as to my cousin's absolute and undoubted good faith, for I had known her as well as if she were my own sister ever since she was a child, but as to a possible trick on the doctor's part. Had he not, perhaps, kept a glass hidden in his hand, which he showed to the young woman in her sleep, at the same time as he did the card? Professional conjurors do things that are just as singular.

So I went home and to bed, and this morning, at about half-past eight, I was awakened by my valet, who said to me: "Madame Sable has asked to see you immediately, monsieur." I dressed hastily and went to her.

She sat down in some agitation, with her eyes on the floor, and without raising her veil she said to me: "My dear cousin, I am going to ask a great favor of you." "What is it, cousin?" "I do not like to tell you, and yet I must. I am in absolute need of five thousand francs." "What, you?" "Yes, I, or rather my husband, who has asked me to procure them for him."

I was so thunderstruck that I stammered out my answers. I asked myself whether she had not really been making fun of me with Dr. Parent, if it was not merely a very well-acted farce which had been rehearsed beforehand. On looking at her attentively, however, all my doubts disappeared. She was trembling with grief, so painful was this step to her, and I was convinced that her throat was full of sobs.

I knew that she was very rich and I continued: "What! Has not your husband five thousand francs at his disposal? Come, think. Are you sure that he commissioned you to ask me for them?"

She hesitated for a few seconds, as if she were making a great effort to search her memory, and then she replied: "Yes . . . yes, I am quite sure of it." "He has written to you?"

She hesitated again and reflected, and I guessed the torture of her thoughts. She did not know. She only knew that she was to borrow five thousand francs of me for her husband. So she told a lie. "Yes, he had written to me." "When, pray? You did not mention it to me yesterday." "I received his letter this morning." "Can you show it me?" "No; no . . . no . . . it contained private matters . . . things too personal to ourselves . . . I burned it." "So your husband runs into debt?"

She hesitated again, and then murmured: "I do not know." Thereupon I said bluntly: "I have not five thousand francs at my disposal at this moment, my dear cousin."

She uttered a kind of cry as if she were in pain and said: "Oh! oh! I beseech you, I beseech you to get them for me. . . ."

She got excited and clasped her hands as if she were praying to me! I heard her voice change its tone; she wept and stammered, harassed and dominated by the irresistible order that she had received.

"Oh! oh! I beg you to . . . if you knew what I am suffering . . . I want them to-day."

I had pity on her: "You shall have them by and by, I swear to you." "Oh! thank you! thank you! How kind you are."

I continued: "Do you remember what took place at your

house last night?" "Yes." "Do you remember that Dr. Parent sent you to sleep?" "Yes." "Oh! Very well, then; he ordered you to come to me this morning to borrow five thousand francs, and at this moment you are obeying that suggestion."

She considered for a few moments, and then replied: "But as it is my husband who wants them——"

For a whole hour I tried to convince her, but could not succeed, and when she had gone I went to the doctor. He was just going out, and he listened to me with a smile, and said: "Do you believe now?" "Yes, I cannot help it." "Let us go to your cousin's."

She was already half asleep on a reclining chair, overcome with fatigue. The doctor felt her pulse, looked at her for some time with one hand raised toward her eyes, which she closed by degrees under the irresistible power of this magnetic influence, and when she was asleep, he said:

"Your husband does not require the five thousand francs any longer! You must, therefore, forget that you asked your cousin to lend them to you, and, if he speaks to you about it, you will not understand him."

Then he woke her up, and I took out a pocket book and said: "Here is what you asked me for this morning, my dear cousin." But she was so surprised that I did not venture to persist; nevertheless, I tried to recall the circumstance to her, but she denied it vigorously, thought I was making fun of her, and, in the end, very nearly lost her temper.

There! I have just come back, and I have not been able to eat any lunch, for this experiment has altogether upset me.

July 19. Many people to whom I told the adventure laughed at me. I no longer know what to think. The wise man says: "It may be!"

July 21. I dined at Bougival, and then I spent the evening at a boatmen's ball. Decidedly everything depends on place and surroundings. It would be the height of folly to believe in the supernatural on the Ile de la Grenouillière . . . but on top of Mont Saint-Michel? . . . and in India? We are terribly influenced by our surroundings. I shall return home next week.

July 30. I came back to my own house yesterday. Everything is going on well.

August 2. Nothing new; it is splendid weather, and I spend my days in watching the Seine flowing past.

August 4. Quarrels among my servants. They declare that the glasses are broken in the cupboards at night. The footman accuses the cook, who accuses the seamstress, who accuses the other two. Who is the culprit? It is a clever person who can tell.

August 6. This time I am not mad. I have seen . . . I have seen . . . I have seen! . . . I can doubt no longer . . . I have seen it! . . .

I was walking at two o'clock among my rose trees, in the full sunlight . . . in the walk bordered by autumn roses which are beginning to fall. As I stopped to look at a Géant de Bataille, which had three splendid blossoms, I distinctly saw the stalk of one of the roses near me bend, as if an invisible hand had bent it, and then break, as if that hand had picked it! Then the flower raised itself, following the curve which a hand would have described in carrying it toward a mouth, and it remained suspended in the transparent air, all alone and motionless, a terrible red spot, three yards from my eyes. In desperation I rushed at it to take it! I found nothing; it had disappeared. Then I was seized with furious rage against myself, for a reasonable and serious man should not have such hallucinations.

But was it an hallucination? I turned round to look for the stalk, and I found it at once, on the bush, freshly broken, between two other roses which remained on the branch. I returned home then, my mind greatly disturbed; for I am certain now, as certain as I am of the alternation of day and night, that there exists close to me an invisible being that lives on milk and water, that can touch objects, take them and change their places; that is, consequently, endowed with a material nature, although it is imperceptible to our senses, and that lives as I do, under my roof——

August 7. I slept tranquilly. He drank the water out of my decanter, but did not disturb my sleep.

I wonder if I am mad. As I was walking just now in the sun by the river side, doubts as to my sanity arose in me; not vague doubts such as I have had hitherto, but definite, absolute doubts. I have seen mad people, and I have known some who have been quite intelligent, lucid, even clear-sighted in every concern of life, except on one point. They spoke readily, clearly, profoundly on everything, when suddenly their mind struck upon the shoals of their madness and broke to pieces there, and scattered and floundered in that furious and terrible sea, full of rolling waves, fogs and squalls, which is called *madness*.

I certainly should think that I was mad, absolutely mad, if I were not conscious, did not perfectly know my condition, did not fathom it by analyzing it with the most complete lucidity. I should, in fact, be only a rational man who was laboring under an hallucination. Some unknown disturbance must have arisen in my brain, one of those disturbances which physiologists of the present day try to note and to verify; and that disturbance must have caused a deep gap in my mind and in the sequence and logic of my ideas. Similar phenomena occur in dreams which lead us among the most unlikely phantasmagoria, without causing us any surprise, because our verifying apparatus and our organ of control are asleep, while our imaginative faculty is awake and active. Is it not possible that one of the imperceptible notes of the cerebral keyboard had been paralyzed in me? Some men lose the recollection of proper names, of verbs, or of numbers, or merely of dates, in consequence of an accident. The localization of all the variations of thought has been established nowadays; why, then, should it be surprising if my faculty of controlling the unreality of certain hallucinations were dormant in me for the time being?

I thought of all this as I walked by the side of the water. The sun shone brightly on the river and made earth delightful, while it filled me with a love for life, for the swallows, whose agility always delights my eye, for the plants by the river side, the rustle of whose leaves is a pleasure to my ears.

By degrees, however, an inexplicable feeling of discomfort seized me. It seemed as if some unknown force were numbing and stopping me, were preventing me from going further, and were calling me back. I felt that painful wish to return which oppresses you when you have left a beloved invalid at home, and when you are seized with a presentiment that he is worse.

I, therefore, returned in spite of myself, feeling certain that I should find some bad news awaiting me, a letter or a telegram. There was nothing, however, and I was more surprised and uneasy than if I had had another fantastic vision.

August 8. I spent a terrible evening yesterday. He does not show himself any more, but I feel that he is near me, watching me, looking at me, penetrating me, dominating me, and more redoubtable when he hides himself thus than if he were to manifest his constant and invisible presence by supernatural phenomena. However, I slept.

August 9. Nothing, but I am afraid.

August 10. Nothing; what will happen to-morrow?

August 11. Still nothing; I cannot stop at home with this fear hanging over me and these thoughts in my mind; I shall go away.

August 12. Ten o'clock at night. All day long I have been trying to get away, and have not been able. I wished to accomplish this simple and easy act of freedom—to go out—to get into my carriage in order to go to Rouen—and I have not been able to do it. What is the reason?

August 13. When one is attacked by certain maladies, all the springs of our physical being appear to be broken, all our energies destroyed, all our muscles relaxed; our bones, too, have become as soft as flesh, and our blood as liquid as water. I am experiencing these sensations in my moral being in a strange and distressing manner. I have no longer any strength, any courage, any self-control, not even any power to set my own will in motion. I have no power left to will anything; but some one does it for me and I obey.

August 14. I am lost. Somebody possesses my soul and dominates it. Somebody orders all my acts, all my movements, all my thoughts. I am no longer anything in myself, nothing except an enslaved and terrified spectator of all the things I do. I wish to go out; I cannot. He does not wish to, and so I remain, trembling and distracted, in the armchair in which he keeps me sitting. I merely wish to get up and to rouse myself; I cannot! I am riveted to my chair, and my chair adheres to the ground in such a manner that no power could move us.

Then, suddenly, I must, I must go to the bottom of my garden to pick some strawberries and eat them, and I go there. I pick the strawberries and eat them! Oh, my God! My God! Is there a God? If there be one, deliver me! Save me! Succor me! Pardon! Pity! Mercy! Save me! Oh, what sufferings! What torture! What horror!

August 15. This is certainly the way in which my poor cousin was possessed and controlled when she came to borrow five thousand francs of me. She was under the power of a strange will which had entered into her, like another soul, like another parasitic and dominating soul. Is the world coming to an end?

But who is he, this invisible being that rules me? This unknowable being, this rover of a supernatural race?

Invisible beings exist, then! How is it, then, that since the beginning of the world they have never manifested themselves precisely as they do to me? I have never read of anything that resembles what goes on in my house. Oh, if I could only leave it, if I could only go away, escape, and never return! I should be saved, but I cannot.

August 16. I managed to escape to-day for two hours, like a prisoner who finds the door of his dungeon accidentally open. I suddenly felt that I was free and that he was far away, and so I gave orders to harness the horses as quickly as possible, and I drove to Rouen. Oh, how delightful to be able to say to a man who obeys you: "Go to Rouen!"

I made him pull up before the library, and I begged them to lend me Dr. Herrmann Herestauss' treatise on the unknown inhabitants of the ancient and modern world.

Then, as I was getting into my carriage, I intended to say: "To the railway station!" but instead of this I shouted—I did not say, but I shouted—in such a loud voice that all the passers-by turned round: "Home!" and I fell back on the cushion of my carriage, overcome by mental agony. He had found me again and regained possession of me.

August 17. Oh, what a night! What a night! And yet it seems to me that I ought to rejoice. I read until one o'clock in the morning! Herestauss, doctor of philosophy and theogony, wrote the history of the manifestation of all those invisible beings which hover round man, or of whom he dreams. He describes their origin, their domain, their power; but none of them resembles the one which haunts me. One might say that man, ever since he began to think, has had a foreboding fear of a new being, stronger than himself, his successor in this new world, and that, feeling his presence, and not being able to foresee the nature of that master, he has, in his terror, created the whole race of occult beings, of vague phantoms born of fear.

Having, therefore, read until one o'clock in the morning, I

went and sat down at the open window, in order to cool my forehead and my thoughts, in the calm night air. It was very pleasant and warm! How I should have enjoyed such a night formerly!

There was no moon, but the stars darted out their rays in the dark heavens. Who inhabits those worlds? What forms, what living beings, what animals are there yonder? What do the thinkers in those distant worlds know more than we do? What can they do more than we can? What do they see which we do not know? Will not one of them, some day or other, traversing space, appear on our earth to conquer it, just as the Norsemen formerly crossed the sea in order to subjugate nations more feeble than themselves?

We are so weak, so defenseless, so ignorant, so small, we who live on this particle of mud which revolves in a drop of water.

I fell asleep, dreaming thus in the cool night air, and when I had slept for about three-quarters of an hour, I opened my eyes without moving, awakened by I know not what confused and strange sensation. At first I saw nothing, and then suddenly it appeared to me as if a page of a book which had remained open on my table turned over of its own accord. Not a breath of air had come in at my window, and I was surprised, and waited. In about four minutes, I saw, I saw, yes, I saw with my own eyes, another page lift itself up and fall down on the others, as if a finger had turned it over. My armchair was empty, appeared empty, but I knew that he was there, he, and sitting in my place, and that he was reading. With a furious bound, the bound of an enraged wild beast that springs at its tamer, I crossed my room to seize him, to strangle him, to kill him! But before I could reach it, the chair fell over as if somebody had run away from me—my table rocked, my lamp fell and went out, and my window closed as if some thief had been surprised and had fled out into the night, shutting it behind him.

So he had run away; he had been afraid; he, afraid of me!

But—but—to-morrow—or later—some day or other—I should be able to hold him in my clutches and crush him against the ground! Do not dogs occasionally bite and strangle their masters?

August 18. I have been thinking the whole day long. Oh, yes, I will obey him, follow his impulses, fulfill all his wishes, show myself humble, submissive, a coward. He is the stronger; but the hour will come——

August 19. I know—I know—I know all! I have just read the following in the *Revue du Monde Scientifique:* "A curious piece of news comes to us from Rio de Janeiro. Madness, an epidemic of madness, which may be compared to that contagious madness which attacked the people of Europe in the Middle Ages, is at this moment raging in the Province of San-Paolo. The terrified inhabitants are leaving their houses, saying that they are pursued, possessed, dominated like human cattle by invisible, though tangible beings, a species of vampire, which feed on their life while they are asleep, and who, besides, drink water and milk without appearing to touch any other nourishment.

"Professor Don Pedro Henriquez, accompanied by several medical savants, has gone to the Province of San-Paolo, in order to study the origin and the manifestations of this surprising madness on the spot, and to propose such measures to the Emperor as may appear to him to be most fitted to restore the mad population to reason."

Ah! Ah! I remember now that fine Brazilian three-master which passed in front of my windows as it was going up the Seine, on the 8th day of last May! I thought it looked so pretty, so white and bright! That Being was on board of her, coming from there, where its race originated. And it saw me! It saw my house which was also white, and it sprang from the ship on to the land. Oh, merciful heaven!

Now I know, I can divine. The reign of man is over, and he has come. He who was feared by primitive man; whom disquieted priests exorcised; whom sorcerers evoked on dark nights, without having seen him appear, to whom the imagination of the transient masters of the world lent all the monstrous or graceful forms of gnomes, spirits, genii, fairies and familiar spirits. After the coarse conceptions of primitive fear, more clear-sighted men foresaw it more clearly. Mesmer divined it, and ten years ago physicians accurately discovered the nature of his power, even before he exercised it himself. They played with this new weapon of the Lord, the sway of a mysterious will over the human soul, which had become a slave. They called it magnetism, hypnotism, suggestion—what do I know? I have seen them amusing themselves like rash children with this horrible power! Woe to us! Woe to man! He has come, the—the—what does he call himself—the—I fancy that he is shouting out his name to me and I do not hear him—the—yes —he is shouting it out—I am listening—I cannot—he repeats it—the —Horla—I hear—the Horla—it is he—the Horla—he has come!

Ah! the vulture has eaten the pigeon; the wolf has eaten the lamb; the lion has devoured the sharp-horned buffalo; man has killed the lion with an arrow, with a sword, with gunpowder; but the Horla will make of man what we have made of the horse and of the ox; his chattel, his slave and his food, by the mere power of his will. Woe to us!

But, nevertheless, the animal sometimes revolts and kills the man who has subjugated it. I should also like—I shall be able to— but I must know him, touch him, see him! Scientists say that animals' eyes, being different from ours, do not distinguish objects as ours do. And my eye cannot distinguish this newcomer who is oppressing me.

Why? Oh, now I remember the words of the monk at Mont Saint-Michel: "Can we see the hundred-thousandth part of what exists? See here; there is the wind, which is the strongest force in nature, which knocks men, and bowls down buildings, uproots trees, raises the sea into mountains of water, destroys cliffs and casts great ships on the breakers; the wind which kills, which whistles, which sighs, which roars—have you ever seen it, and can you see it? It exists for all that, however!"

And I went on thinking; my eyes are so weak, so imperfect, that they do not even distinguish hard bodies, if they are as transparent as glass! If a glass without tinfoil behind it were to bar my way, I should run into it, just as a bird which has flown into a room breaks its head against the window-panes. A thousand things, moreover, deceive man and lead him astray. Why should it then be surprising that he cannot perceive an unknown body through which the light passes?

A new being! Why not? It was assuredly bound to come! Why should we be the last? We do not distinguish it any more than all the others created before us! The reason is, that its nature is more perfect, its body finer and more finished than ours, that ours is so weak, so awkwardly constructed, encumbered with organs that are always tired, always on the strain like machinery that is too complicated, which lives like a plant and like a beast, nourishing itself with difficulty on air, herbs and flesh, an animal machine which is a prey to maladies, to malformations, to decay; broken-winded, badly regulated, simple and eccentric, ingeniously badly made, at once a coarse and a delicate piece of workmanship, the rough sketch of a being that might become intelligent and grand.

We are only a few, so few in this world, from the oyster up to man. Why should there not be one more, once that period is passed which separates the successive apparitions from all the different species?

Why not one more? Why not, also, other trees with immense, splendid flowers, perfuming whole regions? Why not other elements besides fire, air, earth and water? There are four, only four, those nursing fathers of various beings! What a pity! Why are there not forty, four hundred, four thousand? How poor everything is, how mean and wretched! grudgingly produced, roughly constructed, clumsily made! Ah, the elephant and the hippopotamus, what grace! And the camel, what elegance!

But the butterfly, you will say, a flying flower? I dream of one that should be as large as a hundred worlds, with wings whose shape, beauty, colors and motion I cannot even express. But I see it—it flutters from star to star, refreshing them and perfuming them with the light and harmonious breath of its flight! And the people up there look at it as it passes in an ecstasy of delight!

What is the matter with me? It is he, the Horla, who haunts me, and who makes me think of these foolish things! He is within me, he is becoming my soul; I shall kill him!

August 19. I shall kill him. I have seen him! Yesterday I sat down at my table and pretended to write very assiduously. I knew quite well that he would come prowling round me, quite close to me, so close that I might perhaps be able to touch him, to seize him. And then—then I should have the strength of desperation; I should have my hands, my knees, my chest, my forehead, my teeth to strangle him, to crush him, to bite him, to tear him to pieces. And I watched for him with all my over-excited senses.

I had lighted my two lamps and the eight wax candles on my mantelpiece, as if with this light I could discover him.

My bedstead, my old oak post bedstead, stood opposite to me;

on my right was the fireplace; on my left, the door which was carefully closed, after I had left it open for some time in order to attract him; behind me was a very high wardrobe with a looking-glass in it, before which I stood to shave and dress every day, and in which I was in the habit of glancing at myself from head to foot every time I passed it.

I pretended to be writing in order to deceive him, for he also was watching me, and suddenly I felt—I was certain that he was reading over my shoulder, that he was there, touching my ear.

I got up, my hands extended, and turned round so quickly that I almost fell. Eh! well? It was as bright as at midday, but I did not see my reflection in the mirror! It was empty, clear, pro-found, full of light! But my figure was not reflected in it—and I, I was opposite to it! I saw the large, clear glass from top to bottom, and I looked at it with unsteady eyes; and I did not dare to ad-vance; I did not venture to make a movement, feeling that he was there, but that he would escape me again, he whose imperceptible body had absorbed my reflection.

How frightened I was! And then, suddenly, I began to see myself in a mist in the depths of the looking-glass, in a mist as it were a sheet of water; and it seemed to me as if this water were flowing clearer every moment. It was like the end of an eclipse. Whatever it was that hid me did not appear to possess any clearly defined outlines, but a sort of opaque transparency which gradu-ally grew clearer.

At last I was able to distinguish myself completely, as I do every day when I look at myself.

I had seen it! And the horror of it remained with me, and makes me shudder even now.

August 20. How could I kill it, as I could not get hold of it? Poison? But it would see me mix it with the water; and then, would our poisons have any effect on its impalpable body? No—no—no doubt about the matter——Then—then?——

August 21. I sent for a blacksmith from Rouen, and ordered iron shutters for my room, such as some private hotels in Paris have on the ground floor, for fear of burglars, and he is going to make me an iron door as well. I have made myself out a coward, but I do not care about that!

September 10. Rouen, Hôtel Continental. It is done—it is done
—but is he dead? My mind is thoroughly upset by what I have
seen.

Well then, yesterday, the locksmith having put on the iron
shutters and door, I left everything open until midnight, although
it was getting cold.

Suddenly I felt that he was there, and joy, mad joy, took
possession of me. I got up softly, and walked up and down for
some time, so that he might not suspect anything; then I took off
my boots and put on my slippers carelessly; then I fastened the
iron shutters, and, going back to the door, quickly double-locked it
with a padlock, putting the key into my pocket.

Suddenly I noticed that he was moving restlessly round me,
that in his turn he was frightened and was ordering me to let him
out. I nearly yielded; I did not, however, but, putting my back to
the door, I half opened it, just enough to allow me to go out backward, and as I am very tall my head touched the casing. I was sure
that he had not been able to escape, and I shut him up alone, quite
alone. What happiness! I had him fast. Then I ran downstairs; in
the drawing-room, which was under my bedroom, I took the two
lamps and I poured all the oil on the carpet, the furniture, everywhere; then I set fire to it and made my escape, after having carefully double-locked the door.

I went and hid myself at the bottom of the garden, in a clump
of laurel bushes. How long it seemed! How long it seemed! Everything was dark, silent, motionless, not a breath of air and not a star,
but heavy banks of clouds which one could not see, but which
weighed, oh, so heavily on my soul.

I looked at my house and waited. How long it was! I already
began to think that the fire had gone out of its own accord, or that
he had extinguished it, when one of the lower windows gave way
under the violence of the flames, and a long, soft, caressing sheet
of red flame mounted up the white wall, and enveloped it as far as
the roof. The light fell on the trees, the branches, and the leaves,
and a shiver of fear pervaded them also! The birds awoke, a dog
began to howl, and it seemed to me as if the day were breaking!
Almost immediately two other windows flew into fragments, and
I saw that the whole of the lower part of my house was nothing
but a terrible furnace. But a cry, a horrible, shrill, heartrending

cry, a woman's cry, sounded through the night, and two garret windows were opened! I had forgotten the servants! I saw their terror-stricken faces, and their arms waving frantically.

Then, overwhelmed with horror, I set off to run to the village, shouting: "Help! help! fire! fire!" I met some people who were already coming to the scene, and I returned with them.

By this time the house was nothing but a horrible and magnificent funeral pile, a monstrous funeral pile which lit up the whole country, a funeral pile where men were burning, and where he was burning also, He, He, my prisoner, that new Being, the new master, the Horla!

Suddenly the whole roof fell in between the walls, and a volcano of flames darted up to the sky. Through all the windows which opened on that furnace, I saw the flames darting, and I thought that he was there, in that kiln, dead.

Dead? Perhaps?—— His body? Was not his body, which was transparent, indestructible by such means as would kill ours?

If he were not dead?—— Perhaps time alone has power over that Invisible and Redoubtable Being. Why this transparent, unrecognizable body, this body belonging to a spirit, if it also has to fear ills, infirmities and premature destruction?

Premature destruction? All human terror springs from that! After man, the Horla. After him who can die every day, at any hour, at any moment, by any accident, came the one who would die only at his own proper hour, day, and minute, because he had touched the limits of his existence!

No—no—without any doubt—he is not dead—— Then—then—I suppose I must kill myself! . . .

LAURA

There are several ways in which an author can bring his characters to the point of conviction that there *are* such things as ghosts, and that ghosts are definitely at work about them. It is a well-worn formula to cite physical peculiarities of the living, recognized in the ghost. Saki's method in this story is more convincing: he gives a ghost the character and habits of the living, in a corporeal structure totally changed. There was no mistaking Laura, by her behavior, when she came back.—EDITOR.

Saki (H. H. Munro)

LAURA

You are not really dying, are you?" asked
Amanda.

"I have the doctor's permission to live till Tuesday," said
Laura.

"But today is Saturday; this is serious!" gasped Amanda.

"I don't know about it being serious; it is certainly Saturday,"
said Laura.

"Death is always serious," said Amanda.

"I never said I was going to die. I am presumably going to
leave off being Laura, but I shall go on being something. An animal
of some kind, I suppose. You see, when one hasn't been very good
in the life one has just lived, one reincarnates in some lower

organism. And I haven't been very good, when one comes to think of it. I've been petty and mean and vindictive and all that sort of thing when circumstances have seemed to warrant it."

"Circumstances never warrant that sort of thing," said Amanda hastily.

"If you don't mind my saying so," observed Laura, "Egbert is a circumstance that would warrant any amount of that sort of thing. You're married to him—that's different; you've sworn to love, honour, and endure him: I haven't."

'I don't see what's wrong with Egbert," protested Amanda.

"Oh, I dare say the wrongness has been on my part," admitted Laura dispassionately; "he has merely been the extenuating circumstance. He made a thin, peevish kind of fuss, for instance, when I took the collie puppies from the farm out for a run the other day."

"They chased his young broods of speckled Sussex and drove two sitting hens off their nests, besides running all over the flower beds. You know how devoted he is to his poultry and garden."

"Anyhow, he needn't have gone on about it for the entire evening and then have said, 'Let's say no more about it' just when I was beginning to enjoy the discussion. That's where one of my petty vindictive revenges came in," added Laura with an unrepentant chuckle; "I turned the entire family of speckled Sussex into his seedling shed the day after the puppy episode."

"How could you?" exclaimed Amanda.

"It came quite easy," said Laura; "two of the hens pretended to be laying at the time, but I was firm."

"And we thought it was an accident!"

"You see," resumed Laura, "I really *have* some grounds for supposing that my next incarnation will be in a lower organism. I shall be an animal of some kind. On the other hand, I haven't been a bad sort in my way, so I think I may count on being a nice animal, something elegant and lively, with a love of fun. An otter, perhaps."

"I can't imagine you as an otter," said Amanda.

"Well, I don't suppose you can imagine me as an angel, if it comes to that," said Laura.

Amanda was silent. She couldn't.

"Personally I think an otter life would be rather enjoyable," continued Laura; "salmon to eat all the year round, and the satisfaction of being able to fetch the trout in their own homes without having to wait for hours till they condescend to rise to the fly you've been dangling before them; and an elegant svelte figure——"

"Think of the otter hounds," interposed Amanda; "how dreadful to be hunted and harried and finally worried to death!"

"Rather fun with half the neighbourhood looking on, and anyhow not worse than this Saturday-to-Tuesday business of dying by inches; and then I should go on into something else. If I had been a moderately good otter I suppose I should get back into human shape of some sort; probably something rather primitive—a little brown, unclothed Nubian boy, I should think."

"I wish you would be serious," sighed Amanda; "you really ought to be if you're only going to live till Tuesday."

As a matter of fact Laura died on Monday.

"So dreadfully upsetting," Amanda complained to her uncle-in-law, Sir Lulworth Quayne. "I've asked quite a lot of people down for golf and fishing, and the rhododendrons are just looking their best."

"Laura always was inconsiderate," said Sir Lulworth; "she was born during Goodwood week, with an Ambassador staying in the house who hated babies."

"She had the maddest kind of ideas," said Amanda; "do you know if there was any insanity in her family?"

"Insanity? No, I never heard of any. Her father lives in West Kensington, but I believe he's sane on all other subjects."

"She had an idea that she was going to be reincarnated as an otter," said Amanda.

"One meets with those ideas of reincarnation so frequently, even in the West," said Sir Lulworth, "that one can hardly set them down as being mad. And Laura was such an unaccountable person in this life that I should not like to lay down definite rules as to what she might be doing in an after state."

"You think she really might have passed into some animal form?" asked Amanda. She was one of those who shape their opinions rather readily from the standpoint of those around them.

Just then Egbert entered the breakfast-room, wearing an air

of bereavement that Laura's demise would have been insufficient, in itself, to account for.

"Four of my speckled Sussex have been killed," he exclaimed, "the very four that were to go to the show on Friday. One of them was dragged away and eaten right in the middle of that carnation bed that I've been to such trouble and expense over. My best flower bed and my best fowls singled out for destruction; it almost seems as if the brute that did the deed had special knowledge how to be as devastating as possible in a short space of time."

"Was it a fox, do you think?" asked Amanda.

"Sounds more like a polecat," said Sir Lulworth.

"No," said Egbert, "there were marks of webbed feet all over the place, and we followed the tracks down to the stream at the bottom of the garden; evidently an otter."

Amanda looked quickly and furtively across at Sir Lulworth.

Egbert was too agitated to eat any breakfast, and went out to superintend the strengthening of the poultry yard defences.

"I think she might at least have waited till the funeral was over," said Amanda in a scandalized voice.

"It's her own funeral, you know," said Sir Lulworth; "it's a nice point in etiquette how far one ought to show respect to one's own mortal remains."

Disregard for mortuary convention was carried to further lengths next day; during the absence of the family at the funeral ceremony the remaining survivors of the speckled Sussex were massacred. The marauder's line of retreat seemed to have embraced most of the flower beds on the lawn, but the strawberry beds in the lower garden had also suffered.

"I shall get the otter hounds to come here at the earliest possible moment," said Egbert savagely.

"On no account! You can't dream of such a thing!" exclaimed Amanda. "I mean, it wouldn't do, so soon after a funeral in the house."

"It's a case of necessity," said Egbert; "once an otter takes to that sort of thing it won't stop."

"Perhaps it will go elsewhere now that there are no more fowls left," suggested Amanda.

"One would think you wanted to shield the beast," said Egbert.

"There's been so little water in the stream lately," objected Amanda, "it seems hardly sporting to hunt an animal when it has so little chance of taking refuge anywhere."

"Good gracious!" fumed Egbert, "I'm not thinking about sport. I want to have the animal killed as soon as possible."

Even Amanda's opposition weakened when, during church time on the following Sunday, the otter made its way into the house, raided half a salmon from the larder and worried it into scaly fragments on the Persian rug in Egbert's studio.

"We shall have it hiding under our beds and biting pieces out of our feet before long," said Egbert, and from what Amanda knew of this particular otter she felt that the possibility was not a remote one.

On the evening preceding the day fixed for the hunt Amanda spent a solitary hour walking by the banks of the stream, making what she imagined to be hound noises. It was charitably supposed by those who overheard her performance, that she was practising for farmyard imitations at the forthcoming village entertainment.

It was her friend and neighbour, Aurora Burret, who brought her news of the day's sport.

"Pity you weren't out; we had quite a good day. We found it at once, in the pool just below your garden."

"Did you—kill?" asked Amanda.

"Rather. A fine she-otter. Your husband got rather badly bitten in trying to 'tail it.' Poor beast, I felt quite sorry for it, it had such a human look in its eyes when it was killed. You'll call me silly, but do you know who the look reminded me of? My dear woman, what is the matter?"

When Amanda had recovered to a certain extent from her attack of nervous prostration Egbert took her to the Nile Valley to recuperate. Change of scene speedily brought about the desired recovery of health and mental balance. The escapades of an adventurous otter in search of a variation of diet were viewed in their proper light. Amanda's normally placid temperament reasserted itself. Even a hurricane of shouted curses, coming from her husband's dressing-room, in her husband's voice, but hardly in his usual vocabulary, failed to disturb her serenity as she made a leisurely toilet one evening in a Cairo hotel.

"What is the matter? What has happened?" she asked in amused curiosity.

"The little beast has thrown all my clean shirts into the bath! Wait till I catch you, you little——"

"What little beast?" asked Amanda, suppressing a desire to laugh; Egbert's language was so hopelessly inadequate to express his outraged feelings.

"A little beast of a naked brown Nubian boy," spluttered Egbert.

And now Amanda is seriously ill.

●

THE DEAD seem all alive in the human Hades of Homer, yet cannot well speak, prophesy, or know the living, except they drink blood, wherein is the life of man. And therefore the souls of Penelope's paramours, conducted by Mercury, chirped like bats, and those which followed Hercules made a noise but like a flock of birds.

—URN-BURIAL

●

To ONE Mr. Towes, who had been schoolfellow with Sir George Villers, the father of the first Duke of Buckingham, (and was his friend and neighbour) as he lay in his bed awake, (and it was daylight) came into his chamber, the phantom of his dear friend Sir George Villers. Said Mr. Towes to him, "Why, you are dead. What make you here?" Said the Knight, I am dead, but cannot rest in peace for the wickedness and abomination of my son George, at Court. I do appear to you, to tell him of it, and to advise and dehort him from his evil ways." Said Mr. Towes, "The Duke will not believe me, but will say that I am mad, or doat." Said Sir George, "Go to him from me, and tell him by such a token," (a mole) that he had in some secret place, which none but himself knew of. Accordingly Mr. Towes went to the Duke, who laughed at his message. At his return home the phantom appeared again, and told him that the Duke would be stabbed (he drew out a dagger) a quarter of a year after: "And you shall outlive him half a year; and the warning that you shall have of your death, will be, that your nose will fall a bleeding." All which accordingly fell out so. This account I have had (in the main) from two or three; but Sir William Dugdale affirms what I have here taken from him to be true, and that the apparition told him of several things to come, which proved true, e.g. of a prisoner in the Tower, that shall be honourably delivered. This Mr. Towes had so often the ghost of his old friend appear to him, that it was not at all terrible to him. He was surveyor of the works at Windsor, (by the favour of the Duke) being then sitting in the hall, he cried out, the Duke of Buckingham is stabbed: he was stabbed that very moment.

—JOHN AUBREY

THE WHITE PEOPLE

"If 'the forces symbolized by Pan' 'cannot be named, cannot be imagined,' the reader may remark that they also cannot thrill." So wrote a ghost-and-horror story reviewer not long ago in *The Literary Supplement* of the London *Times*. I agree, and I believe that many of Arthur Machen's otherwise fine stories suffer from a dependence upon horrors and bestialities hinted at too vaguely for our imaginations in a realistic age. The following story, however, avoids the difficulty skillfully by citing a child's diary throughout the central part of the narrative. All children have "secrets" from their elders, and the importantly secretive atmosphere in this case is all to the good.—EDITOR.

Arthur Machen

THE WHITE
PEOPLE

PROLOGUE

"Sorcery and sanctity," said Ambrose, "these are the only realities. Each is an ecstasy, a withdrawal from the common life."

Cotgrave listened, interested. He had been brought by a friend to this mouldering house in a northern suburb, through an old garden to the room where Ambrose the recluse dozed and dreamed over his books.

"Yes," he went on, "magic is justified of her children. There are many, I think, who eat dry crusts and drink water, with a joy infinitely sharper than anything within the experience of the 'practical' epicure."

"You are speaking of the saints?"

"Yes, and of the sinners, too. I think you are falling into the very general error of confining the spiritual world to the supremely good; but the supremely wicked, necessarily, have their portion in it. The merely carnal, sensual man can no more be a great sinner than he can be a great saint. Most of us are just indifferent, mixed-up creatures; we muddle through the world without realizing the meaning and the inner sense of things, and, consequently, our wickedness and our goodness are alike second-rate, unimportant."

"And you think the great sinner, then, will be an ascetic, as well as the great saint?"

"Great people of all kinds forsake the imperfect copies and go to the perfect originals. I have no doubt but that many of the very highest among the saints have never done a 'good action' (using the words in their ordinary sense). And, on the other hand, there have been those who have sounded the very depths of sin, who all their lives have never done an 'ill deed'."

He went out of the room for a moment, and Cotgrave, in high delight, turned to his friend and thanked him for the introduction.

"He's grand," he said. "I never saw that kind of lunatic before."

Ambrose returned with more whisky and helped the two men in a liberal manner. He abused the teetotal sect with ferocity, as he handed the seltzer, and pouring out a glass of water for himself, was about to resume his monologue, when Cotgrave broke in——

"I can't stand it, you know," he said, "your paradoxes are too monstrous. A man may be a great sinner and yet never do anything sinful! Come!"

"You're quite wrong," said Ambrose. "I never make paradoxes; I wish I could. I merely said that a man may have an exquisite taste in Romanée Conti, and yet never have even smelt four ale. That's all, and it's more like a truism than a paradox, isn't it? Your surprise at my remark is due to the fact that you haven't realized what sin is. Oh, yes, there is a sort of connexion between Sin with the capital letter, and actions which are commonly called sinful: with murder, theft, adultery, and so forth.

Much the same connexion that there is between the A, B, C and fine literature. But I believe that the misconception—it is all but universal—arises in great measure from our looking at the matter through social spectacles. We think that a man who does evil to *us* and to his neighbours must be very evil. So he is, from a social standpoint; but can't you realize that Evil in its essence is a lonely thing, a passion of the solitary, individual soul? Really, the average murderer, *qua* murderer, is not by any means a sinner in the true sense of the word. He is simply a wild beast that we have to get rid of to save our own necks from his knife. I should class him rather with tigers than with sinners."

"It seems a little strange."

"I think not. The murderer murders not from positive qualities, but from negative ones; he lacks something which non-murderers possess. Evil, of course, is wholly positive—only it is on the wrong side. You may believe me that sin in its proper sense is very rare; it is probable that there have been far fewer sinners than saints. Yes, your standpoint is all very well for practical, social purposes; we are naturally inclined to think that a person who is very disagreeable to us must be a very great sinner! It is very disagreeable to have one's pocket picked, and we pronounce the thief to be a very great sinner. In truth, he is merely an undeveloped man. He cannot be a saint, of course; but he may be, and often is, an infinitely better creature than thousands who have never broken a single commandment. He is a great nuisance to *us*, I admit, and we very properly lock him up if we catch him; but between his troublesome and unsocial action and evil—Oh, the connexion is of the weakest."

It was getting very late. The man who had brought Cotgrave had probably heard all this before, since he assisted with a bland and judicious smile, but Cotgrave began to think that his 'lunatic' was turning into a sage.

"Do you know," he said, "you interest me immensely? You think, then, that we do not understand the real nature of evil?"

"No, I don't think we do. We over-estimate it and we underestimate it. We take the very numerous infractions of our social 'bye-laws'—the very necessary and very proper regulations which keep the human company together—and we get frightened at the prevalence of 'sin' and 'evil'. But this is really nonsense. Take theft, for example. Have you any *horror* at the thought of Robin Hood, of the Highland caterans of the seventeenth century, of the moss-troopers, of the company promoters of our day?

"Then, on the other hand, we underrate evil. We attach such an enormous importance to the 'sin' of meddling with our pockets (and our wives) that we have quite forgotten the awfulness of real sin."

"And what is sin?" said Cotgrave.

"I think I must reply to your question by another. What would your feelings be, seriously, if your cat or your dog began to talk to you, and to dispute with you in human accents? You would be overwhelmed with horror. I am sure of it. And if the roses in your garden sang a weird song, you would go mad. And suppose the stones in the road began to swell and grow before your eyes, and if the pebble that you noticed at night had shot out stony blossoms in the morning?

"Well, these examples may give you some notion of what sin really is."

"Look here," said the third man, hitherto placid, "you two seem pretty well wound up. But I'm going home. I've missed my tram, and I shall have to walk."

Ambrose and Cotgrave seemed to settle down more profoundly when the other had gone out into the early misty morning and the pale light of the lamps.

"You astonish me," said Cotgrave. "I had never thought of that. If that is really so, one must turn everything upside down. Then the essence of sin really is——"

"In the taking of heaven by storm, it seems to me," said Ambrose. "It appears to me that it is simply an attempt to penetrate into another and higher sphere in a forbidden manner. You can understand why it is so rare. There are few, indeed, who wish to penetrate into other spheres, higher or lower, in ways allowed or forbidden. Men, in the mass, are amply content with life as they find it. Therefore there are few saints, and sinners (in the proper sense) are fewer still, and men of genius, who partake sometimes of each character, are rare also. Yes; on the whole, it is, perhaps, harder to be a great sinner than a great saint."

"There is something profoundly unnatural about sin? Is that what you mean?"

"Exactly. Holiness requires as great, or almost as great, an effort; but holiness works on lines that *were* natural once; it is an effort to recover the ecstasy that was before the Fall. But sin is an effort to gain the ecstasy and the knowledge that pertain alone to angels, and in making this effort man becomes a demon. I told you that the mere murderer is not *therefore* a sinner; that is true, but the sinner is sometimes a murderer. Gilles de Raiz is an instance. So you see that while the good and the evil are unnatural to man as he now is—to man the social, civilized being—evil is unnatural in a much deeper sense than good. The saint endeavours to recover a gift which he has lost; the sinner tries to obtain something which was never his. In brief, he repeats the Fall."

"But are you a Catholic?" said Cotgrave.

"Yes; I am a member of the persecuted Anglican Church."

"Then, how about those texts which seem to reckon as sin that which you would set down as a mere trivial dereliction?"

"Yes; but in one place the word 'sorcerers' comes in the same sentence, doesn't it? That seems to me to give the key-note. Consider: can you imagine for a moment that a false statement which saves an innocent man's life is a sin? No; very good, then, it is not the mere liar who is excluded by those words; it is, above all, the 'sorcerers' who use the material life, who use the failings incidental to material life as instruments to obtain their infinitely wicked ends. And let me tell you this: our higher senses are so blunted, we are so drenched with materialism, that we should probably fail to recognize real wickedness if we encountered it."

"But shouldn't we experience a certain horror—a terror such as you hinted we would experience if a rose tree sang—in the mere presence of an evil man?"

"We should if we were natural: children and women feel this horror you speak of, even animals experience it. But with most of us convention and civilization and education have blinded and deafened and obscured the natural reason. No, sometimes we may recognize evil by its hatred of the good—one doesn't need much penetration to guess at the influence which dictated, quite unconsciously, the 'Blackwood' review of Keats—but this is purely incidental; and, as a rule, I suspect that the Hierarchs of Tophet pass quite unnoticed, or, perhaps, in certain cases, as good but mistaken men."

"But you used the word 'unconscious' just now, of Keats's reviewers. Is wickedness ever unconscious?"

"Always. It must be so. It is like holiness and genius in this as in other points; it is a certain rapture or ecstasy of the soul; a transcendent effort to surpass the ordinary bounds. So, surpassing these, it surpasses also the understanding, the faculty that takes note of that which comes before it. No, a man may be infinitely and horribly wicked and never suspect it. But I tell you, evil in this, its certain and true sense, is rare, and I think it is growing rarer."

"I am trying to get hold of it all," said Cotgrave. "From what you say, I gather that the true evil differs generically from that which we call evil?"

"Quite so. There is, no doubt, an analogy between the two; a resemblance such as enables us to use, quite legitimately, such terms as the 'foot of the mountain' and the 'leg of the table.' And, sometimes, of course, the two speak, as it were, in the same language. The rough miner, or 'puddler,' the untrained, undeveloped 'tiger-man,' heated by a quart or two above his usual measure, comes home and kicks his irritating and injudicious wife to death. He is a murderer. And Gilles de Raiz was a murderer. But you see the gulf that separates the two? The 'word,' if I may so speak, is accidentally the same in each case, but the 'meaning' is utterly different. It is flagrant 'Hobson Jobson' to confuse the two, or rather, it is as if one supposed that Juggernaut and the Argonauts had something to do etymologically with one another. And no doubt the same weak likeness, or analogy, runs between all the 'social' sins and the real spiritual sins, and in some cases, perhaps, the lesser may be 'schoolmaster' to lead one on to the greater— from the shadow to the reality. If you are anything of a Theologian, you will see the importance of all this."

"I am sorry to say," remarked Cotgrave, "that I have devoted very little of my time to theology. Indeed, I have often wondered on what grounds theologians have claimed the title of Science of Sciences for their favourite study; since the 'theological' books I have looked into have always seemed to me to be concerned with feeble and obvious pieties, or with the kings of Israel and Judah. I do not care to hear about those kings."

Ambrose grinned.

"We must try to avoid theological discussion," he said. "I perceive that you would be a bitter disputant. But perhaps the 'dates of the kings' have as much to do with theology as the hobnails of the murderous puddler with evil."

"Then, to return to our main subject, you think that sin is an esoteric, occult thing?"

"Yes. It is the infernal miracle as holiness is the supernal. Now and then it is raised to such a pitch that we entirely fail to suspect its existence; it is like the note of the great pedal pipes of the organ, which is so deep that we cannot hear it. In other cases it may lead to the lunatic asylum, or to still stranger issues. But you must never confuse it with mere social misdoing. Remember how the Apostle, speaking of the 'other side,' distinguishes between 'charitable' actions and charity. And as one may give all one's goods to the poor, and yet lack charity; so, remember, one may avoid every crime and yet be a sinner."

"Your psychology is very strange to me," said Cotgrave, "but I confess I like it, and I suppose that one might fairly deduce from your premisses the conclusion that the real sinner might very possibly strike the observer as a harmless personage enough?"

"Certainly; because the true evil has nothing to do with social life or social laws, or if it has, only incidentally and accidentally. It is a lonely passion of the soul—or a passion of the lonely soul— whichever you like. If, by chance, we understand it, and grasp its full significance, then, indeed, it will fill us with horror and with awe. But this emotion is widely distinguished from the fear and the disgust with which we regard the ordinary criminal, since this latter is largely or entirely founded on the regard which we have for our own skins or purses. We hate a murderer, because we know that we should hate to be murdered, or to have any one that we like murdered. So, on the 'other side,' we venerate the saints, but we don't 'like' them as we like our friends. Can you persuade yourself that you would have 'enjoyed' St. Paul's company? Do you think that you and I would have 'got on' with Sir Galahad?

"So with the sinners, as with the saints. If you met a very evil man, and recognized his evil; he would, no doubt, fill you with horror and awe; but there is no reason why you should 'dislike' him. On the contrary, it is quite possible that if you could succeed in putting the sin out of your mind you might find the sinner capital company, and in a little while you might have to reason yourself back into horror. Still, how awful it is. If the roses and the lilies suddenly sang on this coming morning; if the furniture began to move in procession, as in De Maupassant's tale!"

"I am glad you have come back to that comparison," said Cotgrave, "because I wanted to ask you what it is that corresponds in humanity to these imaginary feats of inanimate things. In a word —what is sin? You have given me, I know, an abstract definition, but I should like a concrete example."

"I told you it was very rare," said Ambrose, who appeared willing to avoid the giving of a direct answer. "The materialism of the age, which has done a good deal to suppress sanctity, has done perhaps more to suppress evil. We find the earth so very comfortable that we have no inclination either for ascents or descents. It would seem as if the scholar who decided to 'specialize' in Tophet, would be reduced to purely antiquarian researches. No palaeontologist could show you a *live* pterodactyl."

"And yet you, I think, have 'specialized,' and I believe that your researches have descended to our modern times."

"You are really interested, I see. Well, I confess that I have dabbled a little, and if you like I can show you something that bears on the very curious subject we have been discussing."

Ambrose took a candle and went away to a far, dim corner of the room. Cotgrave saw him open a venerable bureau that stood there, and from some secret recess he drew out a parcel, and came back to the window where they had been sitting.

Ambrose undid a wrapping of paper, and produced a green book.

"You will take care of it?" he said. "Don't leave it lying about. It is one of the choicer pieces in my collection, and I should be very sorry if it were lost."

He fondled the faded binding.

"I knew the girl who wrote this," he said. "When you read it, you will see how it illustrates the talk we have had to-night. There is a sequel, too, but I won't talk of that."

"There was an odd article in one of the reviews some months ago," he began again, with the air of a man who changes the subject. "It was written by a doctor—Dr. Coryn, I think, was the name. He says that a lady, watching her little girl playing at the drawing-room window, suddenly saw the heavy sash give way and fall on the child's fingers. The lady fainted, I think, but at any rate the doctor was summoned, and when he had dressed the child's wounded and maimed fingers he was summoned to the mother. She was groaning with pain, and it was found that three fingers of her hand, corresponding with those that had been injured on the child's hand, were swollen and inflamed, and later, in the doctor's language, purulent sloughing set in."

Ambrose still handled delicately the green volume.

"Well, here it is," he said at last, parting with difficulty, it seemed, from his treasure.

"You will bring it back as soon as you have read it," he said, as they went out into the hall, into the old garden, faint with the odour of white lilies.

There was a broad red band in the east as Cotgrave turned to go, and from the high ground where he stood he saw that awful spectacle of London in a dream.

THE GREEN BOOK

The morocco binding of the book was faded, and the colour had grown faint, but there were no stains nor bruises nor marks of usage. The book looked as if it had been bought 'on a visit to London' some seventy or eighty years ago, and had somehow been forgotten and suffered to lie away out of sight. There was an old, delicate, lingering odour about it, such an odour as sometimes haunts an ancient piece of furniture for a century or more. The end-papers, inside the binding, were oddly decorated with coloured patterns and faded gold. It looked small, but the paper was fine, and there were many leaves, closely covered with minute, painfully formed characters.

I found this book (the manuscript began) in a drawer in the old bureau that stands on the landing. It was a very rainy day and I could not go out, so in the afternoon I got a candle and rummaged in the bureau. Nearly all the drawers were full of old dresses, but one of the small ones looked empty, and I found this book hidden right at the back. I wanted a book like this, so I took it to write in. It is full of secrets. I have a great many other books of secrets I have written, hidden in a safe place, and I am going to write here many of the old secrets and some new ones; but there are some I shall not put down at all. I must not write down the real names of the days and months which I found out a year ago, nor the way to make the Aklo letters, or the Chian language, or the great beautiful Circles, nor the Mao Games, nor the chief songs. I may write something about all these things but not the way to do them, for peculiar reasons. And I must not say who the Nymphs are, or the Dols, or Jeelo, or what voolas mean. All these are most secret secrets, and I am glad when I remember what they are, and how many wonderful languages I know, but there are some things that I call the secrets of the secrets of the secrets that I dare not think of unless I am quite alone, and then I shut my eyes, and put my hands over them and whisper the word, and the Alala comes. I only do this at night in my room or in certain woods that I know, but I must not describe them, as they are secret woods. Then there are the Ceremonies, which are all of them important, but some are more delightful than others—there are the White Ceremonies, and the Green Ceremonies, and the Scarlet Ceremonies. The Scarlet Ceremonies are the best, but there is only one place where they can be performed properly, though there is a very nice imitation which I have done in other places. Besides these, I have the dances, and the Comedy, and I have done the Comedy sometimes when the others were looking, and they didn't understand anything about it. I was very little when I first knew about these things.

When I was very small, and mother was alive, I can remember remembering things before that, only it has all got confused. But I remember when I was five or six I heard them talking about me when they thought I was not noticing. They were saying how queer I was a year or two before, and how nurse had called my mother to come and listen to me talking all to myself, and I was saying words that nobody could understand. I was speaking the Xu language, but I only remember a very few of the words, as it was about the little white faces that used to look at me when I was lying in my cradle. They used to talk to me, and I learnt their language and talked to them in it about some great white place where they lived, where the trees and the grass were all

white, and there were white hills as high up as the moon, and a
cold wind. I have often dreamed of it afterwards, but the faces
went away when I was very little. But a wonderful thing happened when I was about five. My nurse was carrying me on her
shoulder; there was a field of yellow corn, and we went through
it, it was very hot. Then we came to a path through a wood, and
a tall man came after us, and went with us till we came to a place
where there was a deep pool, and it was very dark and shady.
Nurse put me down on the soft moss under a tree, and she said:
"She can't get to the pond now." So they left me there, and I sat
quite still and watched, and out of the water and out of the wood
came two wonderful white people, and they began to play and
dance and sing. They were a kind of creamy white like the old
ivory figure in the drawing-room; one was a beautiful lady with
kind dark eyes, and a grave face, and long black hair, and she
smiled such a strange sad smile at the other, who laughed and
came to her. They played together, and danced round and round
the pool, and they sang a song till I fell asleep. Nurse woke me
up when she came back, and she was looking something like the
lady had looked, so I told her all about it, and asked her why she
looked like that. At first she cried, and then she looked very frightened, and turned quite pale. She put me down on the grass and
stared at me, and I could see she was shaking all over. Then she
said I had been dreaming, but I knew I hadn't. Then she made me
promise not to say a word about it to anybody, and if I did I
should be thrown into the black pit. I was not frightened at all,
though nurse was, and I never forgot about it, because when I
shut my eyes and it was quite quiet, and I was all alone, I could
see them again, very faint and far away, but very splendid; and
little bits of the song they sang came into my head, but I couldn't
sing it.

I was thirteen, nearly fourteen, when I had a very singular
adventure, so strange that the day on which it happened is always
called the White Day. My mother had been dead for more than
a year, and in the morning I had lessons, but they let me go out
for walks in the afternoon. And this afternoon I walked a new
way, and a little brook led me into a new country, but I tore my
frock getting through many bushes, and beneath the low branches
of trees, and up thorny thickets on the hills, and by dark woods

full of creeping thorns. And it was a long, long way. It seemed as if I was going on for ever and ever, and I had to creep by a place like a tunnel where a brook must have been, but all the water had dried up, and the floor was rocky, and the bushes had grown overhead till they met, so that it was quite dark. And I went on and on through that dark place; it was a long, long way. And I came to a hill that I never saw before. I was in a dismal thicket full of black twisted boughs that tore me as I went through them, and I cried out because I was smarting all over, and then I found that I was climbing, and I went up and up a long way, till at last the thicket stopped and I came out crying just under the top of a big bare place, where there were ugly grey stones lying all about' on the grass, and here and there a little twisted, stunted tree came out from under a stone, like a snake. And I went up, right to the top, a long way. I never saw such big ugly stones before; they came out of the earth some of them, and some looked as if they had been rolled to where they were, and they went on and on as far as I could see, a long, long way. I looked out from them and saw the country, but it was strange. It was winter time, and there were black terrible woods hanging from the hills all round; it was like seeing a large room hung with black curtains, and the shape of the trees seemed quite different from any I had ever seen before. I was afraid. Then beyond the woods there were other hills round in a great ring, but I had never seen any of them; it all looked black, and everything had a voor over it. It was all so still and silent, and the sky was heavy and grey and sad, like a wicked voorish dome in Deep Dendo. I went on into the dreadful rocks. There were hundreds and hundreds of them. Some were like horrid-grinning men; I could see their faces as if they would jump at me out of the stone, and catch hold of me, and drag me with them back into the rock, so that I should always be there. And there were other rocks that were like animals, creeping, horrible animals, putting out their tongues, and others were like words that I could not say, and others like dead people lying on the grass. I went on among them, though they frightened me, and my heart was full of wicked songs that they put into it; and I wanted to make faces and twist myself about in the way they did, and I went on and on a long way till at last I liked the rocks, and they didn't frighten me any more. I sang the songs I thought

of; songs full of words that must not be spoken or written down. Then I made faces like the faces on the rocks, and I twisted myself about like the twisted ones, and I lay down flat on the ground like the dead ones, and I went up to one that was grinning, and put my arms round him and hugged him. And so I went on and on through the rocks till I came to a round mound in the middle of them. It was higher than a mound, it was nearly as high as our house, and it was like a great basin turned upside down, all smooth and round and green, with one stone, like a post, sticking up at the top. I climbed up the sides, but they were so steep I had to stop or I should have rolled all the way down again, and I should have knocked against the stones at the bottom, and perhaps been killed. But I wanted to get up to the very top of the big round mound, so I lay down flat on my face, and took hold of the grass with my hands and drew myself up, bit by bit, till I was at the top. Then I sat down on the stone in the middle, and looked all round about. I felt I had come such a long, long way, just as if I were a hundred miles from home, or in some other country, or in one of the strange places I had read about in the "Tales of the Genie" and the "Arabian Nights," or as if I had gone across the sea, far away, for years and I had found another world that nobody had ever seen or heard of before, or as if I had somehow flown through the sky and fallen on one of the stars I had read about where everything is dead and cold and grey, and there is no air, and the wind doesn't blow. I sat on the stone and looked all round and down and round about me. It was just as if I was sitting on a tower in the middle of a great empty town, because I could see nothing all around but the grey rocks on the ground. I couldn't make out their shapes any more, but I could see them on and on for a long way, and I looked at them, and they seemed as if they had been arranged into patterns, and shapes, and figures. I knew they couldn't be, because I had seen a lot of them coming right out of the earth, joined to the deep rocks below, so I looked again, but still I saw nothing but circles, and small circles inside big ones, and pyramids, and domes, and spires, and they seemed all to go round and round the place where I was sitting, and the more I looked, the more I saw great big rings of rocks, getting bigger and bigger, and I stared so long that it felt as if they were all moving and turning, like a great wheel, and I was turning, too, in the middle. I got quite dizzy and queer in the head, and everything began to be hazy and not clear, and I saw little sparks of blue light, and the stones looked as if they were springing and dancing and twisting as they went round and round and round. I was frightened again, and I cried out loud, and jumped up from the stone I was sitting on, and fell down. When I got up I was so glad they all looked still, and I sat down on the top and slid down the mound, and went on again. I danced as I went in the peculiar way the rocks had danced when I got giddy, and I was so glad I could do it quite well, and I danced and danced along, and sang extraordinary songs that came into my head. At last I came to the edge of that great flat hill, and there were no more rocks, and the way went again through a dark thicket in a hollow. It was just as bad as the other one I went through climbing up, but I didn't mind this one, because I was so glad I had seen those singular dances and could imitate them. I went down, creeping through the bushes, and a tall nettle stung me on my leg, and made me burn, but I didn't mind it, and I tingled with the boughs and the thorns, but I only laughed and sang. Then I got out of the thicket into a close valley, a little secret place like a dark passage that nobody ever knows of, because it was so narrow and deep and the woods were so thick round it. There is a steep bank with trees hanging over it, and there the ferns keep green all through the winter, when they are dead and brown upon the hill, and the ferns there have a sweet, rich smell like what oozes out of fir trees. There was a little stream of water running down this valley, so small that I could easily step across it. I drank the water with my hand, and it tasted like bright, yellow wine, and it sparkled and bubbled as it ran down over beautiful red and yellow stones, so that it seemed alive and all colours at once. I drank it, and I drank more with my hand, but I couldn't drink enough, so I lay down and bent my head and sucked the water up with my lips. It tasted much better, drinking it that way, and a ripple would come up to my mouth and give me a kiss, and I laughed, and drank again, and pretended there was a nymph, like the one in the old picture at home, who lived in the water and was kissing me. So I bent low down to the water, and put my lips softly to it, and whispered to the nymph that I would come again. I felt sure it would not be common water, I was so glad when I got up and went on; and I danced again and went up and up the valley, under hanging hills. And when I came to the top, the ground rose up in front of me, tall and steep as a wall, and there was nothing but the green wall and the sky. I thought of "for ever and for ever, world without end, Amen"; and I thought I must have really found the end of the world, because it was like the end of everything, as if there could be nothing at all beyond, except the kingdom of Voor, where the light goes when it is put out, and the water goes when the sun takes it away. I began to think of all the long, long way I had journeyed, how I had found a brook and followed it, and followed it on, and gone through bushes and thorny thickets, and dark woods full of creeping thorns. Then I had crept up a tunnel under trees, and climbed a thicket, and seen all the grey rocks, and sat in the middle of them when they turned round, and then I had gone on through the grey rocks and come down the hill through the stinging thicket and up the dark valley, all a long, long way. I wondered how I should get home again, if I could ever find the way, and if my home was there any more, or if it were turned and everybody in it into grey rocks, as in the "Arabian Nights." So I sat down on the grass and thought what I should do next. I was tired, and my feet were hot with walking, and as I looked about I saw there was a wonderful well just under the high, steep wall of grass. All the ground round it was covered with bright, green, dripping moss; there was every kind of moss there, moss like beautiful little ferns, and like palms and fir trees, and it was all green as jewellery, and drops of water hung on it like diamonds. And in the middle was the great well, deep and shining and beautiful, so clear it looked as if I could touch the red sand at the bottom, but it was far below. I stood by it and looked in, as if I were looking in a glass. At the bottom of the well, in the middle of it, the red grains of sand were moving and stirring all the time, and I saw how the water bubbled up, but at the top it was quite smooth, and full and brimming. It was a great well, large like a bath, and with the shining, glittering green moss about it, it looked like a great white jewel, with green jewels all round. My feet were so hot and tired that I took off my boots and stockings, and let my feet down into the water, and the water was soft and cold, and when I got up I wasn't tired any more, and I felt I must go on, farther and farther, and see what was on the other side of the wall. I climbed up it very slowly, going sideways all the time, and when I got to the top and looked over, I was in the queerest country I had seen, stranger even than the hill of the grey rocks. It looked as if earth-children had been playing there with their spades, as it was all hills and hollows, and castles and walls made of earth and covered with grass. There were two mounds like big beehives, round and great and solemn, and then hollow basins, and then a steep mounting wall like the ones I saw once by the seaside where the big guns and the soldiers were. I nearly fell into one of the round hollows, it went away from under my feet so suddenly, and I ran fast down the side and stood at the bottom and looked up. It was strange and solemn to look up. There was nothing but the grey, heavy sky and the sides of the hollow; everything else had gone away, and the hollow was the whole world, and I thought that at night it must be full of ghosts and moving shadows and pale things when the moon shone down to the bottom at the dead of the night, and the wind wailed up above. It was so strange and solemn and lonely, like a hollow temple of dead heathen gods. It reminded me of a tale my nurse had told me when I was quite little; it was the same nurse that took me into the wood where I saw the beautiful white people. And I remembered how nurse had told me the story one winter night, when the wind was beating the trees against the wall, and crying and moaning in the nursery chimney. She said there was, somewhere or other, a hollow pit, just like the one I was standing in, everybody was afraid to go into it or near it, it was such a bad place. But once upon a time there was a poor girl who said she would go into the hollow pit, and everybody tried to stop her, but she would go. And she went down into the pit and came back laughing, and said there was nothing there at all, except green grass and red stones, and white stones and yellow flowers. And soon after people saw she had most beautiful emerald earrings, and they asked how she got them, as she and her mother were quite poor. But she laughed, and said her earrings were not made of emeralds at all, but only of green grass. Then, one day, she wore on her breast the reddest ruby that any one had ever seen, and it was as big as a hen's egg, and glowed and sparkled like a hot burning coal of fire. And they asked how she got it, as she and her mother were quite poor. But she laughed, and said it was not a ruby at all, but only a red stone. Then one

day she wore round her neck the loveliest necklace that any one
had ever seen, much finer than the queen's finest, and it was made
of great bright diamonds, hundreds of them, and they shone like
all the stars on a night in June. So they asked her how she got it,
as she and her mother were quite poor. But she laughed, and said
they were not diamonds at all, but only white stones. And one day
she went to the Court, and she wore on her head a crown of pure
angel-gold, so nurse said, and it shone like the sun, and it was much
more splendid than the crown the king was wearing himself, and
in her ears she wore the emeralds, and the big ruby was the brooch
on her breast, and the great diamond necklace was sparkling on her
neck. And the king and queen thought she was some great princess
from a long way off, and got down from their thrones and went
to meet her, but somebody told the king and queen who she was,
and that she was quite poor. So the king asked why she wore a
gold crown, and how she got it, as she and her mother were so
poor. And she laughed, and said it wasn't a gold crown at all,
but only some yellow flowers she had put in her hair. And the king
thought it was very strange, and said she should stay at the Court,
and they would see what would happen next. And she was so
lovely that everybody said that her eyes were greener than the
emeralds, that her lips were redder than the ruby, that her skin was
whiter than the diamonds, and that her hair was brighter than the
golden crown. So the king's son said he would marry her, and the
king said he might. And the bishop married them, and there was a
great supper, and afterwards the king's son went to his wife's
room. But just when he had his hand on the door, he saw a tall,
black man, with a dreadful face, standing in front of the door,
and a voice said——

> Venture not upon your life,
> This is mine own wedded wife.

Then the king's son fell down on the ground in a fit. And they
came and tried to get into the room, but they couldn't, and they
hacked at the door with hatchets, but the wood had turned hard
as iron, and at last everybody ran away, they were so frightened
at the screaming and laughing and shrieking and crying that came
out of the room. But next day they went in, and found there was
nothing in the room but thick black smoke, because the black

man had come and taken her away. And on the bed there were two knots of faded grass and a red stone, and some white stones, and some faded yellow flowers. I remembered this tale of nurse's while I was standing at the bottom of the deep hollow; it was so strange and solitary there, and I felt afraid. I could not see any stones or flowers, but I was afraid of bringing them away without knowing, and I thought I would do a charm that came into my head to keep the black man away. So I stood right in the very middle of the hollow, and I made sure that I had none of those things on me, and then I walked round the place, and touched my eyes, and my lips, and my hair in a peculiar manner, and whispered some queer words that nurse taught me to keep bad things away. Then I felt safe and climbed up out of the hollow, and went on through all those mounds and hollows and walls, till I came to the end, which was high above all the rest, and I could see that all the different shapes of the earth were arranged in patterns, something like the grey rocks, only the pattern was different. It was getting late, and the air was indistinct, but it looked from where I was standing something like two great figures of people lying on the grass. And I went on, and at last I found a certain wood, which is too secret to be described, and nobody knows of the passage into it, which I found out in a very curious manner, by seeing some little animal run into the wood through it. So I went in after the animal by a very narrow dark way, under thorns and bushes, and it was almost dark when I came to a kind of open place in the middle. And there I saw the most wonderful sight I have ever seen, but it was only for a minute, as I ran away directly, and crept out of the wood by the passage I had come by, and ran and ran as fast as ever I could, because I was afraid, what I had seen was so wonderful and so strange and beautiful. But I wanted to get home and think of it, and I did not know what might not happen if I stayed by the wood. I was hot all over and trembling, and my heart was beating, and strange cries that I could not help came from me as I ran from the wood. I was glad that a great white moon came up from over a round hill and showed me the way, so I went back through the mounds and hollows and down the close valley, and up through the thicket over the place of the grey rocks, and so at last I got home again. My father was busy in his study, and the servants had not told about my not coming home, though they were frightened, and wondered what they ought to do, so I told them I had lost my way, but I did not let them find out the real way I had been. I went to bed and lay awake all through the night, thinking of what I had seen. When I came out of the narrow way, and it looked all shining, though the air was dark, it seemed so certain, and all the way home I was quite sure that I had seen it, and I wanted to be alone in my room, and be glad over it all to myself, and shut my eyes and pretend it was there, and do all the things I would have done if I had not been so afraid. But when I shut my eyes the sight would not come, and I began to think about my adventures all over again, and I remembered how dusky and queer it was at the end, and I was afraid it must be all a mistake, because it seemed impossible it could happen. It seemed like one of nurse's tales, which I didn't really believe in, though I was frightened at the bottom of the hollow; and the stories she told me when I was little came back into my head, and I wondered whether it was really there what I thought I had seen, or whether any of her tales could have happened a long time ago. It was so queer; I lay awake there in my room at the back of the house, and the moon was shining on the other side towards the river, so the bright light did not fall upon the wall. And the house was quite still. I had heard my father come upstairs, and just after the clock struck twelve, and after the house was still and empty, as if there was nobody alive in it. And though it was all dark and indistinct in my room, a pale glimmering kind of light shone in through the white blind, and once I got up and looked out, and there was a great black shadow of the house covering the garden, looking like a prison where men are hanged; and then beyond it was all white; and the wood shone white with black gulfs between the trees. It was still and clear, and there were no clouds on the sky. I wanted to think of what I had seen but I couldn't, and I began to think of all the tales that nurse had told me so long ago that I thought I had forgotten, but they all came back, and mixed up with the thickets and the grey rocks and the hollows in the earth and the secret wood, till I hardly knew what was new and what was old, or whether it was not all dreaming. And then I remembered that hot summer afternoon, so long ago, when nurse left me by myself in the shade, and the white people came out of the water and out of the wood, and played, and danced, and sang, and I began to fancy that nurse told me about something like it before I saw them, only I couldn't recollect exactly what she told me. Then I wondered whether she had been the white lady, as I remembered she was just as white and beautiful, and had the same dark eyes and black hair; and sometimes she smiled and looked like the lady had looked, when she was telling me some of her stories, beginning with "Once on a time," or "In the time of the fairies." But I thought she couldn't be the lady, as she seemed to have gone a different way into the wood, and I didn't think the man who came after us could be the other, or I couldn't have seen that wonderful secret in the secret wood. I thought of the moon: but it was afterwards when I was in the middle of the wild land, where the earth was made into the shape of great figures, and it was all walls, and mysterious hollows, and smooth round mounds, that I saw the great white moon come up over a round hill. I was wondering about all these things, till at last I got quite frightened, because I was afraid something had happened to me, and I remembered nurse's tale of the poor girl who went into the hollow pit, and was carried away at last by the black man. I knew I had gone into a hollow pit too, and perhaps it was the same, and I had done something dreadful. So I did the charm over again, and touched my eyes and my lips and my hair in a peculiar manner, and said the old words from the fairy language, so that I might be sure I had not been carried away. I tried again to see the secret wood, and to creep up the passage and see what I had seen there, but somehow I couldn't, and I kept on thinking of nurse's stories. There was one I remembered about a young man who once upon a time went hunting, and all the day he and his hounds hunted everywhere, and they crossed the rivers and went into all the woods, and went round the marshes, but they couldn't find anything at all, and they hunted all day till the sun sank down and began to set behind the mountain. And the young man was angry because he couldn't find anything, and he was going to turn back, when just as the sun touched the mountain, he saw come out of a brake in front of him a beautiful white stag. And he cheered to his hounds, but they whined and would not follow, and he cheered to his horse, but it shivered and stood stock still, and the young man jumped off the horse and left the hounds and began to follow the white stag all alone. And soon it

was quite dark, and the sky was black, without a single star shining in it, and the stag went away into the darkness. And though
the man had brought his gun with him he never shot at the stag,
because he wanted to catch it, and he was afraid he would lose it
in the night. But he never lost it once, though the sky was so black
and the air was so dark, and the stag went on and on till the young
man didn't know a bit where he was. And they went through
enormous woods where the air was full of whispers and a pale,
dead light came out from the rotten trunks that were lying on the
ground, and just as the man thought he had lost the stag, he would
see it all white and shining in front of him, and he would run fast
to catch it, but the stag always ran faster, so he did not catch it.
And they went through the enormous woods, and they swam
across rivers, and they waded through black marshes where the
ground bubbled, and the air was full of will-o'-the-wisps, and the
stag fled away down into rocky narrow valleys, where the air was
like the smell of a vault, and the man went after it. And they went
over the great mountains, and the man heard the wind come down
from the sky, and the stag went on and the man went after. At
last the sun rose and the young man found he was in a country
that he had never seen before; it was a beautiful valley with a
bright stream running through it, and a great, big round hill in the
middle. And the stag went down the valley, towards the hill, and
it seemed to be getting tired and went slower and slower, and
though the man was tired, too, he began to run faster, and he was
sure he would catch the stag at last. But just as they got to the
bottom of the hill, and the man stretched out his hand to catch the
stag, it vanished into the earth, and the man began to cry; he was
so sorry that he had lost it after all his long hunting. But as he was
crying he saw there was a door in the hill, just in front of him,
and he went in, and it was quite dark, but he went on, as he
thought he would find the white stag. And all of a sudden it got
light, and there was the sky, and the sun shining, and birds singing
in the trees, and there was a beautiful fountain. And by the fountain a lovely lady was sitting, who was the queen of the fairies, and
she told the man that she had changed herself into a stag to bring
him there because she loved him so much. Then she brought out
a great gold cup, covered with jewels, from her fairy palace, and
she offered him wine in the cup to drink. And he drank, and the

more he drank the more he longed to drink, because the wine was enchanted. So he kissed the lovely lady, and she became his wife, and he stayed all that day and all that night in the hill where she lived, and when he woke he found he was lying on the ground, close to where he had seen the stag first, and his horse was there and his hounds were there waiting, and he looked up, and the sun sank behind the mountain. And he went home and lived a long time, but he would never kiss any other lady because he had kissed the queen of the fairies, and he would never drink common wine any more, because he had drunk enchanted wine. And sometimes nurse told me tales that she had heard from her great-grandmother, who was very old, and lived in a cottage on the mountain all alone, and most of these tales were about a hill where people used to meet at night long ago, and they used to play all sorts of strange games and do queer things that nurse told me of, but I couldn't understand, and now, she said, everybody but her great-grandmother had forgotten all about it, and nobody knew where the hill was, not even her great-grandmother. But she told me one very strange story about the hill, and I trembled when I remembered it. She said that people always went there in summer, when it was very hot, and they had to dance a good deal. It would be all dark at first, and there were trees there, which made it much darker, and people would come, one by one, from all directions, by a secret path which nobody else knew, and two persons would keep the gate, and every one as they came up had to give a very curious sign, which nurse showed me as well as she could, but she said she couldn't show me properly. And all kinds of people would come; there would be gentle folks and village folks, and some old people and boys and girls, and quite small children, who sat and watched. And it would all be dark as they came in, except in one corner where some one was burning something that smelt strong and sweet, and made them laugh, and there one would see a glaring of coals, and the smoke mounting up red. So they would all come in, and when the last had come there was no door any more, so that no one else could get in, even if they knew there was anything beyond. And once a gentleman who was a stranger and had ridden a long way, lost his path at night, and his horse took him into the very middle of the wild country, where everything was upside down, and there were dreadful marshes and great stones everywhere, and holes underfoot, and the trees looked like gibbet-posts, because they had great black arms that stretched out across the way. And this strange gentleman was very frightened, and his horse began to shiver all over, and at last it stopped and wouldn't go any farther, and the gentleman got down and tried to lead the horse, but it wouldn't move, and it was all covered with a sweat, like death. So the gentleman went on all alone, going farther and farther into the wild country, till at last he came to a dark place, where he heard shouting and singing and crying, like nothing he had ever heard before. It all sounded quite close to him, but he couldn't get in, and so he began to call, and while he was calling, something came behind him, and in a minute his mouth and arms and legs were all bound up, and he fell into a swoon. And when he came to himself, he was lying by the roadside, just where he had first lost his way, under a blasted oak with a black trunk, and his horse was tied beside him. So he rode on to the town and told the people there what had happened, and some of them were amazed; but others knew. So when once everybody had come, there was no door at all for anybody else to pass in by. And when they were all inside, round in a ring, touching each other, some one began to sing in the darkness, and some one else would make a noise like thunder with a thing they had on purpose, and on still nights people would hear the thundering noise far, far away beyond the wild land, and some of them, who thought they knew what it was, used to make a sign on their breasts when they woke up in their beds at dead of night and heard that terrible deep noise, like thunder on the mountains. And the noise and the singing would go on and on for a long time, and the people who were in a ring swayed a little to and fro; and the song was in an old, old language that nobody knows now, and the tune was queer. Nurse said her great-grand-mother had known some one who remembered a little of it, when she was quite a little girl, and nurse tried to sing some of it to me, and it was so strange a tune that I turned all cold and my flesh crept as if I had put my hand on something dead. Sometimes it was a man that sang and sometimes it was a woman, and sometimes the one who sang it did it so well that two or three of the people who were there fell to the ground shrieking and tearing with their hands. The singing went on, and the people in the ring kept sway-ing to and fro for a long time, and at last the moon would rise

over a place they called the Tole Deol, and came up and showed
them swinging and swaying from side to side, with the sweet thick
smoke curling up from the burning coals, and floating in circles
all around them. Then they had their supper. A boy and a girl
brought it to them; the boy carried a great cup of wine, and the
girl carried a cake of bread, and they passed the bread and the wine
round and round, but they tasted quite different from common
bread and common wine, and changed everybody that tasted
them. Then they all rose up and danced, and secret things were
brought out of some hiding place, and they played extraordinary
games, and danced round and round and round in the moonlight,
and sometimes people would suddenly disappear and never be
heard of afterwards, and nobody knew what had happened to
them. And they drank more of that curious wine, and they made
images and worshipped them, and nurse showed me how the images
were made one day when we were out for a walk, and we passed
by a place where there was a lot of wet clay. So nurse asked me
if I would like to know what those things were like that they made
on the hill, and I said yes. Then she asked me if I would promise
never to tell a living soul a word about it, and if I did I was to be
thrown into the black pit with the dead people, and I said I
wouldn't tell anybody, and she said the same thing again and again,
and I promised. So she took my wooden spade and dug a big lump
of clay and put it in my tin bucket, and told me to say if any
one met us that I was going to make pies when I went home. Then
we went on a little way till we came to a little brake growing
right down into the road, and nurse stopped, and looked up the
road and down it, and then peeped through the hedge into the
field on the other side, and then she said "Quick!" and we ran
into the brake, and crept in and out among the bushes till we had
gone a good way from the road. Then we sat down under a bush,
and I wanted so much to know what nurse was going to make with
the clay, but before she would begin she made me promise again
not to say a word about it, and she went again and peeped through
the bushes on every side, though the lane was so small and deep
that hardly anybody ever went there. So we sat down, and nurse
took the clay out of the bucket, and began to knead it with her
hands, and do queer things with it, and turn it about. And she hid
it under a big dock-leaf for a minute or two and then she brought

it out again, and then she stood up and sat down, and walked round
the clay in a peculiar manner, and all the time she was softly singing a sort of rhyme, and her face got very red. Then she sat down
again, and took the clay in her hands and began to shape it into a
doll, but not like the dolls I have at home, and she made the queerest doll I had ever seen, all out of the wet clay, and hid it under
a bush to get dry and hard, and all the time she was making it she
was singing these rhymes to herself, and her face got redder and
redder. So we left the doll there, hidden away in the bushes where
nobody would ever find it. And a few days later we went the same
walk, and when we came to that narrow, dark part of the lane
where the brake runs down to the bank, nurse made me promise
all over again, and she looked about, just as she had done before,
and we crept into the bushes till we got to the green place where
the little clay man was hidden. I remember it all so well, though
I was only eight, and it is eight years ago now as I am writing it
down, but the sky was a deep violet blue, and in the middle of the
brake where we were sitting there was a great elder tree covered
with blossoms, and on the other side there was a clump of mead-
owsweet, and when I think of that day the smell of the meadow-
sweet and elder blossom seems to fill the room, and if I shut my
eyes I can see the glaring sky, with little clouds very white floating
across it, and nurse who went away long ago sitting opposite me
and looking like the beautiful white lady in the wood. So we sat
down and nurse took out the clay doll from the secret place where
she had hidden it, and she said we must "pay our respects," and
she would show me what to do, and I must watch her all the time.
So she did all sorts of queer things with the little clay man, and
I noticed she was all streaming with perspiration, though we had
walked so slowly, and then she told me to "pay my respects," and
I did everything she did because I liked her, and it was such an
odd game. And she said that if one loved very much, the clay
man was very good, if one did certain things with it, and if one
hated very much, it was just as good, only one had to do different
things, and we played with it a long time, and pretended all sorts
of things. Nurse said her great-grandmother had told her all about
these images, but what we did was no harm at all, only a game.
But she told me a story about these images that frightened me very
much, and that was what I remembered that night when I was

lying awake in my room in the pale, empty darkness, thinking of
what I had seen and the secret wood. Nurse said there was once a
young lady of the high gentry, who lived in a great castle. And she
was so beautiful that all the gentlemen wanted to marry her, because she was the loveliest lady that anybody had ever seen, and
she was kind to everybody, and everybody thought she was very
good. But though she was polite to all the gentlemen who wished
to marry her, she put them off, and said she couldn't make up her
mind, and she wasn't sure she wanted to marry anybody at all.
And her father, who was a very great lord, was angry, though he
was so fond of her, and he asked her why she wouldn't choose a
bachelor out of all the handsome young men who came to the
castle. But she only said she didn't love any of them very much,
and she must wait, and if they pestered her, she said she would go
and be a nun in a nunnery. So all the gentlemen said they would
go away and wait for a year and a day, and when a year and a
day were gone, they would come back again and ask her to say
which one she would marry. So the day was appointed and they all
went away; and the lady had promised that in a year and a day
it would be her wedding day with one of them. But the truth was,
that she was the queen of the people who danced on the hill on
summer nights, and on the proper nights she would lock the door
of her room, and she and her maid would steal out of the castle
by a secret passage that only they knew of, and go away up to the
hill in the wild land. And she knew more of the secret things than
any one else, and more than any one knew before or after, because she would not tell anybody the most secret secrets. She
knew how to do all the awful things, how to destroy young men,
and how to put a curse on people, and other things that I could
not understand. And her real name was the Lady Avelin, but the
dancing people called her Cassap, which meant somebody very
wise, in the old language. And she was whiter than any of them
and taller, and her eyes shone in the dark like burning rubies; and
she could sing songs that none of the others could sing, and when
she sang they all fell down on their faces and worshipped her. And
she could do what they called the shib-show, which was a very
wonderful enchantment. She would tell the great lord, her father,
that she wanted to go into the woods to gather flowers, so he let
her go, and she and her maid went into the woods where nobody

came, and the maid would keep watch. Then the lady would lie
down under the trees and begin to sing a particular song, and she
stretched out her arms, and from every part of the wood great
serpents would come, hissing and gliding in and out among the
trees, and shooting out their forked tongues as they crawled up to
the lady. And they all came to her, and twisted round her, round
her body, and her arms, and her neck, till she was covered with
writhing serpents, and there was only her head to be seen. And she
whispered to them, and she sang to them, and they writhed round
and round, faster and faster, till she told them to go. And they all
went away directly, back to their holes, and on the lady's breast
there would be a most curious, beautiful stone, shaped something
like an egg, and coloured dark blue and yellow, and red, and green,
marked like a serpent's scales. It was called a glame stone, and
with it one could do all sorts of wonderful things, and nurse said
her great-grandmother had seen a glame stone with her own eyes,
and it was for all the world shiny and scaly like a snake. And the
lady could do a lot of other things as well, but she was quite fixed
that she would not be married. And there were a great many gentlemen who wanted to marry her, but there were five of them who
were chief, and their names were Sir Simon, Sir John, Sir Oliver,
Sir Richard, and Sir Rowland. All the others believed she spoke
the truth, and that she would choose one of them to be her man
when a year and a day was done; it was only Sir Simon, who was
very crafty, who thought she was deceiving them all, and he vowed
he would watch and try if he could find out anything. And though
he was very wise he was very young, and he had a smooth, soft
face like a girl's, and he pretended, as the rest did, that he would
not come to the castle for a year and a day, and he said he was
going away beyond the sea to foreign parts. But he really only
went a very little way, and came back dressed like a servant girl,
and so he got a place in the castle to wash the dishes. And he
waited and watched, and he listened and said nothing, and he hid
in dark places, and woke up at night and looked out, and he heard
things and he saw things that he thought were very strange. And
he was so sly that he told the girl that waited on the lady that he
was really a young man, and that he had dressed up as a girl because he loved her so very much and wanted to be in the same
house with her, and the girl was so pleased that she told him many

things, and he was more than ever certain that the Lady Avelin was deceiving him and the others. And he was so clever, and told the servant so many lies, that one night he managed to hide in the Lady's Avelin's room behind the curtains. And he stayed quite still and never moved, and at last the lady came. And she bent down under the bed, and raised up a stone, and there was a hollow place underneath, and out of it she took a waxen image, just like the clay one that I and nurse had made in the brake. And all the time her eyes were burning like rubies. And she took the little wax doll up in her arms and held it to her breast, and she whispered and she murmured, and she took it up and she laid it down again, and she held it high, and she held it low, and she laid it down again. And she said, "Happy is he that begat the bishop, that ordered the clerk, that married the man, that had the wife, that fashioned the hive, that harboured the bee, that gathered the wax that my own true love was made of." And she brought out of an aumbry a great golden bowl, and she brought out of a closet a great jar of wine, and she poured some of the wine into the bowl, and she laid her mannikin very gently in the wine, and washed it in the wine all over. Then she went to a cupboard and took a small round cake and laid it on the image's mouth, and then she bore it softly and covered it up. And Sir Simon, who was watching all the time, though he was terribly frightened, saw the lady bend down and stretch out her arms and whisper and sing, and then Sir Simon saw beside her a handsome young man, who kissed her on the lips. And they drank wine out of the golden bowl to-gether, and they ate the cake together. But when the sun rose there was only the little wax doll, and the lady hid it again under the bed in the hollow place. So Sir Simon knew quite well what the lady was, and he waited and he watched, till the time she had said was nearly over, and in a week the year and a day would be done. And one night, when he was watching behind the curtains in her room, he saw her making more wax dolls. And she made five, and hid them away. And the next night she took one out, and held it up, and filled the golden bowl with water, and took the doll by the neck and held it under the water. Then she said——

Sir Dickon, Sir Dickon, your day is done,
You shall be drowned in the water wan.

And the next day news came to the castle that Sir Richard had been drowned at the ford. And at night she took another doll and tied a violet cord round its neck and hung it up on a nail. Then she said——

> Sir Rowland, your life has ended its span,
> High on a tree I see you hang.

And the next day news came to the castle that Sir Rowland had been hanged by robbers in the wood. And at night she took another doll, and drove her bodkin right into its heart. Then she said——

> Sir Noll, Sir Noll, so cease your life,
> Your heart pierced with the knife.

And the next day news came to the castle that Sir Oliver had fought in a tavern, and a stranger had stabbed him to the heart. And at night she took another doll, and held it to a fire of charcoal till it was melted. Then she said——

> Sir John, return, and turn to clay,
> In fire of fever you waste away.

And the next day news came to the castle that Sir John had died in a burning fever. So then Sir Simon went out of the castle and mounted his horse and rode away to the bishop and told him everything. And the bishop sent his men, and they took the Lady Avelin, and everything she had done was found out. So on the day after the year and a day, when she was to have been married, they carried her through the town in her smock, and they tied her to a great stake in the market-place, and burned her alive before the bishop with her wax image hung round her neck. And people said the wax man screamed in the burning of the flames. And I thought of this story again and again as I was lying awake in my bed, and I seemed to see the Lady Avelin in the market-place, with the yellow flames eating up her beautiful white body. And I thought of it so much that I seemed to get into the story myself, and I fancied I was the lady, and that they were coming to take me to be burnt with fire, with all the people in the town looking at me. And I wondered whether she cared, after all the strange things she had done, and whether it hurt very much to be burned at the stake. I tried again and again to forget nurse's stories, and to remember the secret I had seen that afternoon, and what was in the secret wood, but I could only see the dark and a glimmering in the dark, and then it went away, and I only saw myself running, and then a great moon came up white over a dark round hill. Then all the old stories came back again, and the queer rhymes that nurse used to sing to me; and there was one beginning "Halsy cumsy Helen musty," that she used to sing very softly when she wanted me to go to sleep. And I began to sing it to myself inside of my head, and I went to sleep.

The next morning I was very tired and sleepy, and could hardly do my lessons, and I was very glad when they were over and I had had my dinner, as I wanted to go out and be alone. It was a warm day, and I went to a nice turfy hill by the river, and sat down on my mother's old shawl that I had brought with me on purpose. The sky was grey, like the day before, but there was a kind of white gleam behind it, and from where I was sitting I could look down on the town, and it was all still and quiet and white, like a picture. I remembered that it was on that hill that nurse taught me to play an old game called "Troy Town," in which one had to dance, and wind in and out on a pattern in the grass, and then when one had danced and turned long enough the other person asks you questions, and you can't help answering whether you want to or not, and whatever you are told to do you feel you have to do it. Nurse said there used to be a lot of games like that that some people knew of, and there was one by which people could be turned into anything you liked, and an old man her great-grandmother had seen had known a girl who had been turned into a large snake. And there was another very ancient game of dancing and winding and turning, by which you could take a person out of himself and hide him away as long as you liked, and his body went walking about quite empty, without any sense in it. But I came to that hill because I wanted to think of what had happened the day before, and of the secret of the wood. From the place where I was sitting I could see beyond the town, into the opening I had found, where a little brook had led me into an unknown country. And I pretended I was following the brook over again, and I went all the way in my mind, and at last I found the wood, and crept into it under the bushes, and then in the dusk I saw something that made me feel as if I were filled with fire, as if I wanted to dance and sing and fly up into the air, because I was changed and wonderful. But what I saw was not changed at all, and had not grown old, and I wondered again and again how such things could happen, and whether nurse's stories were really true, because in the daytime in the open air everything seemed quite different from what it was at night, when I was frightened, and thought I was to be burned alive. I once told my father one of her little tales, which was about a ghost, and asked him if it was true, and he told me it was not true at all, and that only common, ignorant people believed in such rubbish. He was very angry with nurse for telling me the story, and scolded her, and after that I promised her I would never whisper a word of what she told me, and if I did I should be bitten by the great black snake that lived in the pool in the wood. And all alone on the hill I wondered what was true. I had seen something very amazing and very lovely, and I knew a story, and if I had really seen it, and not made it up out of the dark, and the black bough, and the bright shining that was mounting up to the sky from over the great round hill, but had really seen it in truth, then there were all kinds of wonderful and lovely and terrible things to think of, so I longed and trembled, and I burned and got cold. And I looked down on the town, so quiet and still, like a little white picture, and I thought over and over if it could be true. I was a long time before I could make up my mind to anything; there was such a strange fluttering at my heart that seemed to whisper to me all the time that I had not made it up out of my head, and yet it seemed quite impossible, and I knew my father and everybody would say it was dreadful rubbish. I never dreamed of telling him or anybody else a word about it, because I knew it would be of no use, and I should only get laughed at or scolded, so for a long time I was very quiet, and went about thinking and wondering; and at night I used to dream of amazing things, and sometimes I woke up in the early morning and held out my arms with a cry. And I was frightened, too, because there were dangers, and some awful thing would happen to me, unless I took great care, if the story were true. These old tales were always in my head, night and morning, and I went over them and told them to myself over and over again, and went for walks in the places where nurse had told them to me; and when I sat in the nursery by the fire in the evenings I used to fancy nurse was sitting in the other chair, and telling me some wonderful story in a low voice, for fear anybody should be listening. But she used to like best to tell me about things when we were right out in the country, far from the house, because she said she was telling me such secrets, and walls have ears. And if it was something more than ever secret, we had to hide in brakes or woods; and I used to think it was such fun creeping along a hedge, and going very softly, and then we would get behind the bushes or run into the wood all of a sudden, when we were sure that noone was watching us; so we knew that we had our secrets quite all to ourselves, and nobody else at all knew anything about them. Now and then, when we had hidden ourselves as I have described, she used to show me all sorts of odd things. One day, I remember, we were in a hazel brake, over-looking the brook, and we were so snug and warm, as though it was April; the sun was quite hot, and the leaves were just coming out. Nurse said she would show me something funny that would make me laugh, and then she showed me, as she said, how one could turn a whole house upside down, without anybody being able to find out, and the pots and pans would jump about, and the china would be broken, and the chairs would tumble over of themselves. I tried it one day in the kitchen, and I found I could do it quite well, and a whole row of plates on the dresser fell off it, and cook's little work-table tilted up and turned right over "before her eyes," as she said, but she was so frightened and turned so white that I didn't do it again, as I liked her. And afterwards, in the hazel copse, when she had shown me how to make things tumble about, she showed me how to make rapping noises, and I learnt how to do that, too. Then she taught me rhymes to say on certain occasions, and peculiar marks to make on other occasions, and other things that her great-grandmother had taught her when she was a little girl herself. And these were all the things I was thinking about in those days after the strange walk when I thought I had seen a great secret, and I wished nurse were there for me to ask her about it, but she had gone away more than two years before, and nobody seemed to know what had become of her, or where she had gone. But I shall always remember those days if I live to be quite old, because all the time I felt so strange, wondering and doubting, and feeling quite sure

at one time, and making up my mind, and then I would feel quite
sure that such things couldn't happen really, and it began all over
again. But I took great care not to do certain things that might be
very dangerous. So I waited and wondered for a long time, and
though I was not sure at all, I never dared to try to find out. But
one day I became sure that all that nurse said was quite true, and
I was all alone when I found it out. I trembled all over with joy
and terror, and as fast as I could I ran into one of the old brakes
where we used to go—it was the one by the lane, where nurse
made the little clay man—and I ran into it, and I crept into it; and
when I came to the place where the elder was, I covered up my
face with my hands and lay down flat on the grass, and I stayed
there for two hours without moving, whispering to myself delicious, terrible things, and saying some words over and over again.
It was all true and wonderful and splendid, and when I remembered the story I knew and thought of what I had really seen, I
got hot and I got cold, and the air seemed full of scent, and flowers,
and singing. And first I wanted to make a little clay man, like the
one nurse had made so long ago, and I had to invent plans and
stratagems, and to look about, and to think of things beforehand,
because nobody must dream on anything that I was doing or going
to do, and I was too old to carry clay about in a tin bucket. At
last I thought of a plan, and I brought the wet clay to the brake,
and did everything that nurse had done, only I made a much finer
image than the one she had made; and when it was finished I did
everything that I could imagine and much more than she did,
because it was the likeness of something far better. And a few
days later, when I had done my lessons early, I went for the second
time by the way of the little brook that had led me into a strange
country. And I followed the brook, and went through the bushes,
and beneath the low branches of trees, and up thorny thickets
on the hill, and by dark woods full of creeping thorns, a long,
long way. Then I crept through the dark tunnel where the brook
had been and the ground was stony, till at last I came to the thicket
that climbed up the hill, and though the leaves were coming out
upon the trees, everything looked almost as black as it was on the
first day that I went there. And the thicket was just the same, and
I went up slowly till I came out on the big bare hill, and began
to walk among the wonderful rocks. I saw the terrible voor again

on everything, for though the sky was brighter, the ring of wild hills all around was still dark, and the hanging woods looked dark and dreadful, and the strange rocks were as grey as ever; and when I looked down on them from the great mound, sitting on the stone, I saw all their amazing circles and rounds within rounds, and I had to sit quite still and watch them as they began to turn about me, and each stone danced in its place, and they seemed to go round and round in a great whirl, as if one were in the middle of all the stars and heard them rushing through the air. So I went down among the rocks to dance with them and to sing extraordinary songs; and I went down through the other thicket, and drank from the bright stream in the close and secret valley, putting my lips down to the bubbling water; and then I went on till I came to the deep, brimming well among the glittering moss, and I sat down. I looked before me into the secret darkness of the valley, and behind me was the great high wall of grass, and all around me there were the hanging woods that made the valley such a secret place. I knew there was nobody here at all besides myself, and that no one could see me. So I took off my boots and stockings, and let my feet down into the water, saying the words that I knew. And it was not cold at all, as I expected, but warm and very pleasant, and when my feet were in it I felt as if they were in silk, or as if the nymph were kissing them. So when I had done, I said the other words and made the signs, and then I dried my feet with a towel I had brought on purpose, and put on my stockings and boots. Then I climbed up the steep wall, and went into the place where there are the hollows, and the two beautiful mounds, and the round ridges of land, and all the strange shapes. I did not go down into the hollow this time, but I turned at the end, and made out the figures quite plainly, as it was lighter, and I had remembered the story I had quite forgotten before, and in the story the two figures are called Adam and Eve, and only those who know the story understand what they mean. So I went on and on till I came to the secret wood which must not be described, and I crept into it by the way I had found. And when I had gone about halfway I stopped, and turned round, and got ready, and I bound the handkerchief tightly round my eyes, and made quite sure that I could not see at all, not a twig, nor the end of a leaf, nor the light of the sky, as it was an old red silk handkerchief with large yellow spots, that went round twice and covered my eyes, so that I could see nothing. Then I began to go on, step by step, very slowly. My heart beat faster and faster, and something rose in my throat that choked me and made me want to cry out, but I shut my lips, and went on. Boughs caught in my hair as I went, and great thorns tore me; but I went on to the end of the path. Then I stopped, and held out my arms and bowed, and I went round the first time, feeling with my hands, and there was nothing. I went round the second time, feeling with my hands and there was nothing. Then I went round the third time, feeling with my hands, and the story was all true, and I wished that the years were gone by, and that I had not so long a time to wait before I was happy for ever and ever.

Nurse must have been a prophet like those we read of in the Bible. Everything that she said began to come true, and since then other things that she told me of have happened. That was how I came to know that her stories were true and that I had not made up the secret myself out of my own head. But there was another thing that happened that day. I went a second time to the secret place. It was at the deep brimming well, and when I was standing on the moss I bent over and looked in, and then I knew who the white lady was that I had seen come out of the water in the wood long ago when I was quite little. And I trembled all over, because that told me other things. Then I remembered how sometime after I had seen the white people in the wood, nurse asked me more about them, and I told her all over again, and she listened, and said nothing for a long, long time, and at last she said, "You will see her again." So I understood what had happened and what was to happen. And I understood about the nymphs; how I might meet them in all kinds of places, and they would always help me, and I must always look for them, and find them in all sorts of strange shapes and appearances. And without the nymphs I could never have found the secret, and without them none of the other things could happen. Nurse had told me all about them long ago, but she called them by another name, and I did not know what she meant, or what her tales of them were about, only that they were very queer. And there were two kinds, the bright and the dark, and both were very lovely and very wonderful, and some people saw only one kind, and some only the other, but some saw them both. But usually the dark appeared first, and the bright ones came afterwards, and there were extraordinary tales about them. It was a day or two after I had come home from the secret place that I first really knew the nymphs. Nurse had shown me how to call them, and I had tried, but I did not know what she meant, and so I thought it was all nonsense. But I made up my mind I would try again, so I went to the wood where the pool was, where I saw the white people, and I tried again. The dark nymph, Alanna, came, and she turned the pool of water into a pool of fire. . . .

EPILOGUE

"That's a very queer story," said Cotgrave, handing back the green book to the recluse, Ambrose. "I see the drift of a good deal, but there are many things that I do not grasp at all. On the last page, for example, what does she mean by 'nymphs'?"

"Well, I think there are references throughout the manuscript to certain 'processes' which have been handed down by tradition from age to age. Some of these processes are just beginning to come within the purview of science, which has arrived at them —or rather at the steps which lead to them—by quite different paths. I have interpreted the reference to 'nymphs' as a reference to one of these processes."

"And you believe that there are such things?"

"Oh, I think so. Yes, I believe I could give you convincing evidence on that point. I am afraid you have neglected the study of alchemy. It is a pity, for the symbolism, at all events, is very beautiful, and moreover if you were acquainted with certain books on the subject, I could recall to your mind phrases which might explain a good deal in the manuscript that you have been reading."

"Yes; but I want to know whether you seriously think that there is any foundation of fact beneath these fancies. Is it not all a department of poetry; a curious dream which man has indulged himself?"

"I can only say that it is no doubt better for the great mass of people to dismiss it all as a dream. But if you ask my veritable belief—that goes quite the other way. No; I should not say belief, but rather knowledge. I may tell you that I have known cases in which men have stumbled quite by accident on certain of these 'processes,' and have been astonished by wholly unexpected results. In the cases I am thinking of there could have been no possibility of 'suggestion' or sub-conscious action of any kind. One might as well suppose a schoolboy 'suggesting' the existence of Æschylus to himself, while he plods mechanically through the declensions.

"But you have noticed the obscurity," Ambrose went on, "and in this particular case it must have been dictated by instinct, since the writer never thought that her manuscripts would fall into other hands. But the practice is universal, and for most excellent reasons. Powerful and sovereign medicines, which are, of necessity, virulent poisons also, are kept in a locked cabinet. The child may find the key by chance, and drink herself dead; but in most cases the search is educational, and the phials contain precious elixirs for him who has patiently fashioned the key for himself."

"You do not care to go into details?"

"No, frankly, I do not. No, you must remain unconvinced. But you saw how the manuscript illustrates the talk we had last week?"

"Is this girl still alive?"

"No. I was one of those who found her. I knew the father well; he was a lawyer, and had always left her very much to herself. He thought of nothing but deeds and leases, and the news came to him as an awful surprise. She was missing one morning; I suppose it was about a year after she had written what you have read. The servants were called, and they told things, and put the only natural interpretation on them—a perfectly erroneous one.

"They discovered that green book somewhere in her room, and I found her in the place that she described with so much dread, lying on the ground before the image."

"It was an image?"

"Yes; it was hidden by the thorns and the thick undergrowth that had surrounded it. It was a wild, lonely country; but you know what it was like by her description, though of course you will understand that the colours have been heightened. A child's imagination always makes the heights higher and the depths deeper than they really are; and she had, unfortunately for herself, something more than imagination. One might say, perhaps, that the picture in her mind which she succeeded in a measure in putting into words, was the scene as it would have appeared to an imaginative artist. But it is a strange, desolate land."

"And she was dead?"

"Yes. She had poisoned herself—in time. No; there was not a word to be said against her in the ordinary sense. You may recollect a story I told you the other night about a lady who saw her child's fingers crushed by a window?"

"And what was this statue?"

"Well, it was of Roman workmanship, of a stone that with the centuries had not blackened, but had become white and luminous. The thicket had grown up about it and concealed it, and in the Middle Ages the followers of a very old tradition had known how to use it for their own purposes. In fact it had been incorporated into the monstrous mythology of the Sabbath. You will have noted that those to whom a sight of that shining whiteness had been vouchsafed by chance, or rather, perhaps, by apparent chance, were required to blindfold themselves on their second approach. That is very significant."

"And is it there still?"

"I sent for tools, and we hammered it into dust and fragments."

"The persistence of tradition never surprises me," Ambrose went on after a pause. "I could name many an English parish where such traditions as that girl had listened to in her childhood are still existent in occult but unabated vigour. No, for me, it is the 'story' not the 'sequel,' which is strange and awful, for I have always believed that wonder is of the soul."

●

CONCERNING PHANTOMS

Most of the translators of Plinius Secundus have followed what may be the logical course, so far as exact sense is concerned, in making an almost exclusive use of the Latin words in English. I have taken the work of the Earl of Orrery, for this book, because Orrery makes a greater use of Anglo-Saxon roots than any of the other careful translators—and the Germanic languages in general seem best suited to the creation of a ghostly atmosphere. The reader will be interested to note that most of the circumstances and trappings of the typical ghost story of the Gothic renaissance appear in a story that was having mouth-to-mouth circulation nearly two millenniums earlier.
—EDITOR.

Pliny the Younger
(Latin)

CONCERNING PHANTOMS

Translated by John, Earl of Orrery

Our present leisure permits you to teach, and me to learn from you. I would therefore willingly know, if you are of opinion, that phantoms are real figures, and carry in them some kind of divinity; or are empty vain shadows, raised in our imaginations by the effect of fear?

An incident which happened, as I have been informed, to Curtius Rufus, was my first inducement to credit their reality. At a time, when his fortune was low, and his character in obscurity, he accompanied into Africa the person who was chosen governor. Towards the evening, while he was walking in a portico, the figure of a woman, fairer and larger than the human size, presented itself to him. He was much frightened. She said, she was Africa, who came to fortel him future events; adding, that he was destined to go to Rome, to enjoy high honours there; to return governor of the province, in which he then resided; and to die in that province. All these facts were fulfilled. It is farther reported, that the same figure met him upon the shore of Carthage, as he was coming out of a ship. It is certain, that as soon as he found himself ill, he gave up all hopes of recovery, although none of his friends despaired of his life. The remembrance of his past honours convinced him of his future end; which he judged was approaching from his former prosperity.

Consider now, if the following story is not as wonderful, and still more terrible than the former. I shall relate it in the manner, that I received it. There was at Athens a very large and spacious house; but of evil report, and fatal to the inhabitants. In the dead of night, the clinking of iron, and, upon closer attention, the rattling of chains was heard; first, at a great distance, and afterwards very near. A spectre immediately appeared, representing an old man, emaciated, and squalid. His beard long, his hair staring; bolts upon his legs; upon his hands chains; which he rattled, as he carried. From these circumstances the inhabitants, in all agonies of fear, continued watching during several melancholy and dreadful nights. Such constant watchings brought on distempers; illness was increased by fear, and death ensued; for even in the day, when the spectre was not visible, the representation of the image wandered before their eyes: so that the terror was of longer continuance, than the presence of the spectre. At length the house was deserted, and entirely left to the apparition. A bill however was posted up, to signify, that the house was either to be sold, or lett; in hopes that some person, ignorant of the calamity, might offer for it. Athenodorus, the philosopher, came at that time to Athens; he read the bill: the price surprised him: he suspected some bad cause to occasion the cheapness, and, upon inquiry, was informed of all the circumstances; by which he was so little deterred, that they were stronger inducements to hire it. When the evening came on, he ordered a bed to be prepared for him in the first apartment. He called for lights, for his table-books, and his pen. He sent all his servants into the farther parts of the house, and applied his eyes, his hands, and his whole attention to writing; lest, as he had heard of apparitions, his mind, if unemployed, might suggest to him idle fears, and represent false appearances. The beginning of the night was as silent there, as in other places. At length the irons clinked, and the chains rattled. Athenodorus neither lifted up his eyes, nor quitted his pen; but collecting his resolution, stopt his ears. The noise increased; it approached, as it was now heard at the threshold of the door, and immediately after within the room. The philosopher turned back his head, and saw the figure, which he observed to answer the description, that he had received of it. The apparition stood still, and beckoned with a finger, like a person, who calls another. Athenodorus signified, by the motion of his hand, that the ghost should stay a little; and again immediately applied himself to writing. The spectre rattled his chains over the head of the philosopher, who, looking back, saw him beckoning as before; and immediately taking up a light, followed him. The ghost went forward in a slow pace, as if encumbered by the chains; and afterwards turning into a court belonging to the house, immediately vanished, leaving the philosopher alone; who, finding himself thus deserted, pulled up some grass and leaves, and placed them as a signal to find the spot of ground. The next day he went to the magistrates; informed them of the event, and desired, that they would order the place to be dug up. Human bones were found buried there, and bound in chains. Time and the earth had mouldered away the flesh, and the skeleton only remained: which was publicly buried: and after the rites of sepulture, the house was no longer haunted. I give credit to these circumstances, as reported by others.

MARKHEIM

The visitant in *Markheim*, as in Poe's *William Wilson*, can be called—if you like—a symbol of conscience, of a doomed man's better self. But that interpretation is only one of several that are equally valid, and the author is wise enough not to give any obvious clue to his own intentions in the matter. At any rate, *Markheim* is haunted, and tempted; and if it seems at first that the tempter is the Devil, the reader's opinion about that is subject to alteration as the climax approaches.—EDITOR.

Robert Louis
Stevenson

MARKHEIM

"Yes," said the dealer, "our windfalls are of various kinds. Some customers are ignorant, and then I touch a dividend on my superior knowledge. Some are dishonest," and here he held up the candle, so that the light fell strongly on his visitor, "and in that case," he continued, "I profit by my virtue."

Markheim had but just entered from the daylight streets, and his eyes had not yet grown familiar with the mingled shine and darkness in the shop. At these pointed words, and before the near presence of the flame, he blinked painfully and looked aside.

The dealer chuckled. "You come to me on Christmas day," he resumed, "when you know that I am alone in my house, put up my shutters, and make a point of refusing business. Well, you will have to pay for that; you will have to pay for my loss of time, when I should be balancing my books; you will have to pay, besides, for a kind of manner that I remark in you to-day very strongly. I am the essence of discretion, and ask no awkward questions; but when a customer cannot look me in the eye, he has to pay for it." The dealer once more chuckled; and then, changing to his usual business voice, though still with a note of irony, "You can give, as usual, a clear account of how you came into the possession of the object?" he continued. "Still your uncle's cabinet? A remarkable collector, sir!"

And the little pale, round-shouldered dealer stood almost on tiptoe, looking over the top of his gold spectacles, and nodding his head with every mark of disbelief. Markheim returned his gaze with one of infinite pity, and a touch of horror.

"This time," said he, "you are in error. I have not come to sell, but to buy. I have no curios to dispose of; my uncle's cabinet is bare to the wainscot; even were it still intact, I have done well on the Stock Exchange, and should more likely add to it than otherwise, and my errand to-day is simplicity itself. I seek a Christmas present for a lady," he continued, waxing more fluent as he struck into the speech he had prepared; "and certainly I owe you every excuse for thus disturbing you upon so small a matter. But the thing was neglected yesterday; I must produce my little compliment at dinner; and, as you very well know, a rich marriage is not a thing to be neglected."

There followed a pause, during which the dealer seemed to weigh this statement incredulously. The ticking of many clocks among the curious lumber of the shop, and the faint rushing of the cabs in a near thoroughfare, filled up the interval of silence.

"Well, sir," said the dealer, "be it so. You are an old customer after all; and if, as you say, you have the chance of a good marriage, far be it from me to be an obstacle. Here is a nice thing for a lady now," he went on, "this hand-glass—fifteenth century, warranted; comes from a good collection, too; but I reserve the name, in the interests of my customer, who was, just like yourself, my dear sir, the nephew and sole heir of a remarkable collector."

The dealer, while he thus ran on in his dry and biting voice, had stooped to take the object from its place; and, as he had done so, a shock had passed through Markheim, a start both of hand and foot, a sudden leap of many tumultuous passions to the face. It passed as swiftly as it came, and left no trace beyond a certain trembling of the hand that now received the glass.

"A glass," he said hoarsely, and then paused, and repeated it more clearly. "A glass? For Christmas? Surely not?"

"And why not?" cried the dealer. "Why not a glass?"

Markheim was looking upon him with an indefinable expression. "You ask me why not?" he said. "Why, look here—look in it —look at yourself! Do you like to see it? No! nor I—nor any man."

The little man had jumped back when Markheim had so suddenly confronted him with the mirror; but now, perceiving there was nothing worse on hand, he chuckled. "Your future lady, sir, must be pretty hard favoured," said he.

"I ask you," said Markheim, "for a Christmas present, and you give me this—this damned reminder of years, and sins and follies —this hand-conscience! Did you mean it? Had you a thought in your mind? Tell me. It will be better for you if you do. Come, tell me about yourself. I hazard a guess now, that you are in secret a very charitable man?"

The dealer looked closely at his companion. It was very odd, Markheim did not appear to be laughing; there was something in his face like an eager sparkle of hope, but nothing of mirth.

"What are you driving at?" the dealer asked.

"Not charitable?" returned the other, gloomily. "Not charitable; not pious; not scrupulous; unloving, unbeloved; a hand to get money, a safe to keep it. Is that all? Dear God, man, is that all?"

"I will tell you what it is," began the dealer, with some sharpness, and then broke off again into a chuckle. "But I see this is a love-match of yours, and you have been drinking the lady's health."

"Ah!" cried Markheim, with a strange curiosity. "Ah, have you been in love? Tell me about that."

"I," cried the dealer. "I in love! I never had the time, nor have I the time to-day for all this nonsense. Will you take the glass?"

"Where is the hurry?" returned Markheim. "It is very pleasant to stand here talking; and life is so short and insecure that I would not hurry away from any pleasure—no, not even from so mild a one as this. We should rather cling, cling to what little we can get, like a man at a cliff's edge. Every second is a cliff, if you think upon it—a cliff a mile high—high enough, if we fall, to dash us out of every feature of humanity. Hence it is best to talk pleasantly. Let us talk of each other; why should we wear this mask? Let us be confidential. Who knows, we might become friends?"

"I have just one word to say to you," said the dealer. "Either make your purchase, or walk out of my shop."

"True, true," said Markheim. "Enough fooling. To business. Show me something else."

The dealer stooped once more, this time to replace the glass upon the shelf, his thin blond hair falling over his eyes as he did so. Markheim moved a little nearer, with one hand in the pocket of his greatcoat; he drew himself up and filled his lungs; at the same time many different emotions were depicted together on his face —terror, horror, and resolve, fascination and a physical repulsion; and through a haggard lift of his upper lip, his teeth looked out.

"This, perhaps, may suit," observed the dealer; and then, as he began to re-arise, Markheim bounded from behind upon his victim. The long, skewerlike dagger flashed and fell. The dealer struggled like a hen, striking his temple on the shelf, and then tumbled on the floor in a heap.

Time had some score of small voices in that shop, some stately and slow as was becoming to their great age; others garrulous and hurried. All these told out the seconds in an intricate chorus of tickings. Then the passage of a lad's feet, heavily running on the pavement, broke in upon these smaller voices and startled Markheim into the consciousness of his surroundings. He looked about him awfully. The candle stood on the counter, its flame solemnly wagging in a draught; and by that inconsiderable movement, the whole room was filled with noiseless bustle and kept heaving like a sea: the tall shadows nodding, the gross blots of darkness swelling and dwindling as with respiration, the faces of the portraits and the china gods changing and wavering like images in water. The inner door stood ajar, and peered into that leaguer of shadows with a long slit of daylight like a pointing finger.

From these fear-stricken rovings, Markheim's eyes returned to the body of his victim, where it lay both humped and sprawling,

incredibly small and strangely meaner than in life. In these poor, miserly clothes, in that ungainly attitude, the dealer lay like so much sawdust. Markheim had feared to see it, and, lo! it was nothing. And yet, as he gazed, this bundle of old clothes and pool of blood began to find eloquent voices. There it must lie; there was none to work the cunning hinges or direct the miracle of locomotion—there it must lie till it was found. Found! ay, and then? Then would this dead flesh lift up a cry that would ring over England, and fill the world with the echoes of pursuit. Ay, dead or not, this was still the enemy. "Time was that when the brains were out," he thought; and the first word struck into his mind. Time, now that the deed was accomplished—time, which had closed for the victim, had become instant and momentous for the slayer.

The thought was yet in his mind, when, first one and then another, with every variety of pace and voice—one deep as the bell from a cathedral turret, another ringing on its treble notes the prelude of a waltz—the clocks began to strike the hour of three in the afternoon.

The sudden outbreak of so many tongues in that dumb chamber staggered him. He began to bestir himself, going to and fro with the candle, beleaguered by moving shadows, and startled to the soul by chance reflections. In many rich mirrors, some of home designs, some from Venice or Amsterdam, he saw his face repeated and repeated, as it were an army of spies; his own eyes met and detected him; and the sound of his own steps, lightly as they fell, vexed the surrounding quiet. And still as he continued to fill his pockets, his mind accused him, with a sickening iteration, of the thousand faults of his design. He should have chosen a more quiet hour; he should have prepared an alibi; he should not have used a knife; he should have been more cautious, and only bound and gagged the dealer, and not killed him; he should have been more bold, and killed the servant also; he should have done all things otherwise; poignant regrets, weary, incessant toiling of the mind to change what was unchangeable, to plan what was now useless, to be the architect of the irrevocable past. Meanwhile, and behind all this activity, brute terrors, like the scurrying of rats in a deserted attic, filled the more remote chambers of his brain with riot; the hand of the constable would fall heavy on his shoulder, and his nerves would jerk like a hooked fish; or he beheld, in galloping defile, the dock, the prison, the gallows, and the black coffin.

Terror of the people in the street sat down before his mind like a besieging army. It was impossible, he thought, but that some rumour of the struggle must have reached their ears and set on edge their curiosity; and now, in all the neighbouring houses, he divined them sitting motionless and with uplifted ear—solitary people, condemned to spend Christmas dwelling alone on memories of the past, and now startlingly recalled from that tender exercise; happy family parties, struck into silence round the table, the mother still with raised finger: every degree and age and humour, but all, by their own hearths, prying and hearkening and weaving the rope that was to hang him. Sometimes it seemed to him he could not move too softly; the clink of the tall Bohemian goblets rang out loudly like a bell; and alarmed by the bigness of the ticking, he was tempted to stop the clocks. And then, again, with a swift transition of his terrors, the very silence of the place appeared a source of peril, and a thing to strike and freeze the passer-by; and he would step more boldly, and bustle aloud among the contents of the shop, and imitate, with elaborate bravado, the movements of a busy man at ease in his own house.

But he was now so pulled about by different alarms that, while one portion of his mind was still alert and cunning, another trembled on the brink of lunacy. One hallucination in particular took a strong hold on his credulity. The neighbour hearkening with white face beside his window, the passer-by arrested by a horrible surmise on the pavement—these could at worst suspect, they could not know; through the brick walls and shuttered windows only sounds could penetrate. But here, within the house, was he alone? He knew he was; he had watched the servant set forth sweethearting, in her poor best, "out for the day" written in every ribbon and smile. Yes, he was alone, of course; and yet, in the bulk of empty house about him, he could surely hear a stir of delicate footing—he was surely conscious, inexplicably conscious of some presence. Ay, surely; to every room and corner of the house his imagination followed it; and now it was a faceless thing, and yet had eyes to see with; and again it was a shadow of himself;

and yet again behold the image of the dead dealer, reinspired with cunning and hatred.

At times, with a strong effort, he would glance at the open door which still seemed to repel his eyes. The house was tall, the skylight small and dirty, the day blind with fog; and the light that filtered down to the ground storey was exceedingly faint, and showed dimly on the threshold of the shop. And yet, in that strip of doubtful brightness, did there not hang wavering a shadow?

Suddenly, from the street outside, a very jovial gentleman began to beat with a staff on the shop-door, accompanying his blows with shouts and railleries in which the dealer was continually called upon by name. Markheim, smitten into ice, glanced at the dead man. But no! he lay quite still; he was fled away far beyond ear-shot of these blows and shoutings; he was sunk beneath seas of silence; and his name, which would once have caught his notice above the howling of a storm, had become an empty sound. And presently the jovial gentleman desisted from his knocking and departed.

Here was a broad hint to hurry what remained to be done, to get forth from this accusing neighbourhood, to plunge into a path of London multitudes, and to reach, on the other side of day, that haven of safety and apparent innocence—his bed. One visitor had come: at any moment another might follow and be more obstinate. To have done the deed, and yet not to reap the profit, would be too abhorrent a failure. The money, that was now Markheim's concern; and as a means to that, the keys.

He glanced over his shoulder at the open door, where the shadow was still lingering and shivering; and with no conscious repugnance of the mind, yet with a tremor of the belly, he drew near the body of his victim. The human character had quite departed. Like a suit half-stuffed with bran, the limbs lay scattered, the trunk doubled, on the floor; and yet the thing repelled him. Although so dingy and inconsiderable to the eye, he feared it might have more significance to the touch. He took the body by the shoulders, and turned it on its back. It was strangely light and supple, and the limbs, as if they had been broken, fell into the oddest postures. The face was robbed of all expression; but it was as pale as wax, and shockingly smeared with blood about one temple. That was, for Markheim, the one displeasing circumstance.

It carried him back, upon the instant, to a certain fair day in a fishers' village; a gray day, a piping wind, a crowd upon the street, the blare of brasses, the booming of drums, the nasal voice of a ballad-singer; and a boy going to and fro, buried over head in the crowd and divided between interest and fear, until, coming out upon the chief place of concourse, he beheld a booth and a great screen with pictures, dismally designed, garishly coloured: Brownrigg with her apprentice; the Mannings with their murdered guest; Weare in the death-grip of Thurtell; and a score besides of famous crimes. The thing was as clear as an illusion; he was once again that little boy; he was looking once again, and with the same sense of physical revolt, at these vile pictures; he was still stunned by the thumping of the drums. A bar of that day's music returned upon his memory; and at that, for the first time, a qualm came over him, a breath of nausea, a sudden weakness of the joints, which he must instantly resist and conquer.

He judged it more prudent to confront than to flee from these considerations; looking the more hardily in the dead face, bending his mind to realise the nature and greatness of his crime. So little a while ago that face had moved with every change of sentiment, that pale mouth had spoken, that body had been all on fire with governable energies; and now, and by his act, that piece of life had been arrested, as the horologist, with interjected finger, arrests the beating of the clock. So he reasoned in vain; he could rise to no more remorseful consciousness; the same heart which had shuddered before the painted effigies of crime, looked on its reality unmoved. At best, he felt a gleam of pity for one who had been endowed in vain with all those faculties that can make the world a garden of enchantment, one who had never lived and who was now dead. But of penitence, no, not a tremor.

With that, shaking himself clear of these considerations, he found the keys and advanced towards the open door of the shop. Outside, it had begun to rain smartly; and the sound of the shower upon the roof had banished silence. Like some dripping cavern, the chambers of the house were haunted by an incessant echoing, which filled the ear and mingled with the ticking of the clocks. And, as Markheim approached the door, he seemed to hear, in answer to his own cautious tread, the steps of another foot withdrawing up the stair. The shadow still palpitated loosely on the threshold. He threw a ton's weight of resolve upon his muscles, and drew back the door.

The faint, foggy daylight glimmered dimly on the bare floor and stairs; on the bright suit of armour posted, halbert in hand, upon the landing; and on the dark wood-carvings, and framed pictures that hung against the yellow panels of the wainscot. So loud was the beating of the rain through all the house that, in Markheim's ears, it began to be distinguished into many different sounds. Footsteps and sighs, the tread of regiments marching in the distance, the chink of money in the counting, and the creaking of doors held stealthily ajar, appeared to mingle with the patter of the drops upon the cupola and the gushing of the water in the pipes. The sense that he was not alone grew upon him to the verge of madness. On every side he was haunted and begirt by presences. He heard them moving in the upper chambers; from the shop, he heard the dead man getting to his legs; and as he began with a great effort to mount the stairs, feet fled quietly before him and followed stealthily behind. If he were but deaf, he thought, how tranquilly he would possess his soul! And then again, and hearkening with ever fresh attention, he blessed himself for that unresting sense which held the outposts and stood a trusty sentinel upon his life. His head turned continually on his neck; his eyes, which seemed starting from their orbits, scouted on every side, and on every side were half-rewarded as with the tail of something nameless vanishing. The four-and-twenty steps to the first floor were four-and-twenty agonies.

On that first storey, the doors stood ajar, three of them like three ambushes, shaking his nerves like the throats of cannon. He could never again, he felt, be sufficiently immured and fortified from men's observing eyes; he longed to be home, girt in by walls, buried among bedclothes, and invisible to all but God. And at that thought he wondered a little, recollecting tales of other murderers and the fear they were said to entertain of heavenly avengers. It was not so, at least, with him. He feared the laws of nature, lest, in their callous and immutable procedure, they should preserve some damning evidence of his crime. He feared tenfold more, with a slavish, superstitious terror, some scission in the continuity of man's experience, some wilful illegality of nature. He played a game of skill, depending on the rules, calculating consequence from cause; and what if nature, as the defeated tyrant overthrew the chess-board, should break the mould of their succession? The like had befallen Napoleon (so writers said) when the winter changed the time of its appearance. The like might befall Markheim: the solid walls might become transparent and reveal his doings like those of bees in a glass hive; the stout planks might yield under his foot like quicksands and detain them in their clutch; ay, and there were soberer accidents that might destroy him: if, for instance, the house should fall and imprison him beside the body of his victim; or the house next door should fly on fire, and the firemen invade him from all sides. These things he feared; and, in a sense, these things might be called the hands of God reached forth against sin. But about God himself he was at ease; his act was doubtless exceptional, but so were his excuses, which God knew; it was there, and not among men, that he felt sure of justice.

When he had got safe into the drawing-room, and shut the door behind him, he was aware of a respite from alarms. The room was quite dismantled, uncarpeted besides, and strewn with packing-cases and incongruous furniture; several great pier-glasses, in which he beheld himself at various angles, like an actor on a stage; many pictures, framed and unframed, standing, with their faces to the wall; a fine Sheraton sideboard, a cabinet of marquetry, and a great old bed, with tapestry hangings. The windows opened to the floor; but by great good fortune the lower part of the shutters had been closed, and this concealed him from the neighbours. Here, then, Markheim drew in a packing-case before the cabinet, and began to search among the keys. It was a long business, for there were many; and it was irksome, besides; for, after all, there might be nothing in the cabinet, and time was on the wing. But the closeness of the occupation sobered him. With the tail of his eye he saw the door—even glanced at it from time to time directly, like a besieged commander pleased to verify the good estate of his defences. But in truth he was at peace. The rain falling in the street sounded natural and pleasant. Presently, on the other side, the notes of a piano were wakened to the music of a hymn, and the voices of many children took up the air and words. How stately, how comfortable was the melody! How fresh the youthful voices! Markheim gave ear to it smilingly, as he sorted out the keys; and his mind was thronged with answerable ideas and images; church-going children and the pealing of the high organ; children afield, bathers by the brookside, ramblers on the brambly common, kite-flyers in the windy and cloud-navigated sky; and then, at another cadence of the hymn, back again to church, and the somnolence of summer Sundays, and the high genteel voice of the parson (which he smiled a little to recall) and the painted Jacobean tombs, and the dim lettering of the Ten Commandments in the chancel.

And as he sat thus, at once busy and absent, he was startled to his feet. A flash of ice, a flash of fire, a bursting gush of blood, went over him, and then he stood transfixed and thrilling. A step mounted the stair slowly and steadily, and presently a hand was laid upon the knob, and the lock clicked, and the door opened.

Fear held Markheim in a vice. What to expect he knew not, whether the dead man walking, or the official ministers of human justice, or some chance witness blindly stumbling in to consign him to the gallows. But when a face was thrust into the aperture, glanced round the room, looked at him, nodded and smiled as if in friendly recognition, and then withdrew again, and the door closed behind it, his fear broke loose from his control in a hoarse cry. At the sound of this, the visitant returned.

"Did you call me?" he asked, pleasantly, and with that he entered the room and closed the door behind him.

Markheim stood and gazed at him with all his eyes. Perhaps there was a film upon his sight, but the outlines of the newcomer seemed to change and waver like those of the idols in the wavering candle-light of the shop, and at times he thought he knew him; and at times he thought he bore a likeness to himself; and always, like a lump of living terror, there lay in his bosom the conviction that this thing was not of the earth and not of God.

And yet the creature had a strange air of the commonplace, as he stood looking on Markheim with a smile; and when he added: "You are looking for the money, I believe?" it was in the tones of every-day politeness.

Markheim made no answer.

"I should warn you," resumed the other, "that the maid has left her sweetheart earlier than usual and will soon be here. If

Mr. Markheim be found in this house, I need not describe to him the consequences."

"You know me?" cried the murderer.

The visitor smiled. "You have long been a favourite of mine," he said; "and I have long observed and often sought to help you."

"What are you?" cried Markheim: "the devil?"

"What I may be," returned the other, "cannot affect the service I propose to render you."

"It can," cried Markheim; "it does! Be helped by you? No, never; not by you! You do not know me yet; thank God, you do not know me!"

"I know you," replied the visitant, with a sort of kind severity or rather firmness. "I know you to the soul."

"Know me!" cried Markheim. "Who can do so? My life is but a travesty and slander on myself. I have lived to belie my nature. All men do; all men are better than this disguise that grows about and stifles them. You see each dragged away by life, like one whom bravos have seized and muffled in a cloak. If they had their own control—if you could see their faces, they would be alto-gether different, they would shine out for heroes and saints! I am worse than most; myself is more overlaid; my excuse is known to me and God. But, had I the time, I could disclose myself."

"To me?" inquired the visitant.

"To you before all," returned the murderer. "I supposed you were intelligent. I thought—since you exist—you would prove a reader of the heart. And yet you would propose to judge me by my acts! Think of it; my acts! I was born and I have lived in a land of giants; giants have dragged me by the wrists since I was born out of my mother—the giants of circumstance. And you would judge me by my acts! But can you not look within? Can you not understand that evil is hateful to me? Can you not see within me the clear writing of conscience, never blurred by any wilful sophistry, although too often disregarded? Can you not read me for a thing that surely must be common as humanity— the unwilling sinner?"

"All this is very feelingly expressed," was the reply, "but it regards me not. These points of consistency are beyond my prov-ince, and I care not in the least by what compulsion you may have been dragged away, so as you are but carried in the right direction. But time flies; the servant delays, looking in the faces of the crowd and at the pictures on the hoardings, but still she keeps moving nearer; and remember, it is as if the gallows itself were striding towards you through the Christmas streets! Shall I help you; I, who know all? Shall I tell you where to find the money?"

"For what price?" asked Markheim.

"I offer you the service for a Christmas gift," returned the other.

Markheim could not refrain from smiling with a kind of bitter triumph. "No," said he, "I will take nothing at your hands; if I were dying of thirst, and it was your hand that put the pitcher to my lips, I should find the courage to refuse. It may be credulous, but I will do nothing to commit myself to evil."

"I have no objection to a death-bed repentance," observed the visitant.

"Because you disbelieve their efficacy!" Markheim cried.

"I do not say so," returned the other; "but I look on these things from a different side, and when the life is done my interest falls. The man has lived to serve me, to spread black looks under colour of religion, or to sow tares in the wheat-field, as you do, in a course of weak compliance with desire. Now that he draws so near to his deliverance, he can add but one act of service—to repent, to die smiling, and thus to build up in confidence and hope the more timorous of my surviving followers. I am not so hard a master. Try me. Accept my help. Please yourself in life as you have done hitherto; please yourself more amply, spread your elbows at the board; and when the night begins to fall and the curtains to be drawn, I tell you, for your greater comfort, that you will find it even easy to compound your quarrel with your conscience, and to make a truckling peace with God. I came but now from such a deathbed, and the room was full of sincere mourners, listening to the man's last words: and when I looked into that face, which had been set as a flint against mercy, I found it smiling with hope."

"And do you, then, suppose me such a creature?" asked Markheim. "Do you think I have no more generous aspirations than to sin, and sin, and sin, and, at last, sneak into heaven? My heart rises at the thought. Is this, then, your experience of man-

kind? or is it because you find me with red hands that you presume such baseness? and is this crime of murder indeed so impious
as to dry up the very springs of good?"

"Murder is to me no special category," replied the other. "All
sins are murder, even as all life is war. I behold your race, like
starving mariners on a raft, plucking crusts out of the hands of
famine and feeding on each other's lives. I follow sins beyond the
moment of their acting; I find in all that the last consequence is
death; and to my eyes, the pretty maid who thwarts her mother
with such taking graces on a question of a ball, drips no less visibly
with human gore than such a murderer as yourself. Do I say that
I follow sins? I follow virtues also; they differ not by the thickness
of a nail, they are both scythes for the reaping angel of Death.
Evil, for which I live, consists not in action, but in character. The
bad man is dear to me; not the bad act, whose fruits, if we could
follow them far enough down the hurtling cataract of the ages,
might yet be found more blessed than those of the rarest virtues.
And it is not because you have killed a dealer, but because you
are Markheim, that I offered to forward your escape."

"I will lay my heart open to you," answered Markheim.
"This crime on which you find me is my last. On my way to it I
have learned many lessons; itself is a lesson, a momentous lesson.
Hitherto I have been driven with revolt to what I would not; I
was a bond-slave to poverty, driven and scourged. There are
robust virtues that can stand in these temptations; mine was not
so: I had a thirst of pleasure. But to-day, and out of this deed, I
pluck both warning and riches—both the power and a fresh resolve to be myself. I become in all things a free actor in the world;
I begin to see myself all changed, these hands the agents of good,
this heart at peace. Something comes over me out of the past;
something of what I have dreamed on Sabbath evenings to the
sound of the church organ, of what I forecast when I shed tears
over noble books, or talked, an innocent child, with my mother.
There lies my life; I have wandered a few years, but now I see
once more my city of destination."

"You are to use this money on the Stock Exchange, I think?"
remarked the visitor; "and there, if I mistake not, you have already
lost some thousands?"

"Ah," said Markheim, "but this time I have a sure thing."

"This time, again, you will lose," replied the visitor quietly.

"Ah, but I keep back the half!" cried Markheim.

"That also you will lose," said the other.

The sweat started upon Markheim's brow. "Well, then, what matter?" he exclaimed. "Say it be lost, say I am plunged again in poverty, shall one part of me, and that the worse, continue until the end to override the better? Evil and good run strong in me, haling me both ways. I do not love the one thing, I love all. I can conceive great deeds, renunciations, martyrdoms; and though I be fallen to such a crime as murder, pity is no stranger to my thoughts. I pity the poor; who knows their trials better than myself? I pity and help them; I prize love, I love honest laughter; there is no good thing nor true thing on earth but I love it from my heart. And are my vices only to direct my life, and my virtues to lie without effect, like some passive lumber of the mind? Not so; good, also, is a spring of acts."

But the visitant raised his finger. "For six-and-thirty years that you have been in this world," said he, "through many changes of fortune and varieties of humour, I have watched you steadily fall. Fifteen years ago you would have started at a theft. Three years back you would have blenched at the name of murder. Is there any crime, is there any cruelty or meanness, from which you still recoil?—five years from now I shall detect you in the fact! Downward, downward, lies your way; nor can anything but death avail to stop you."

"It is true," Markheim said huskily, "I have in some degree complied with evil. But it is so with all: the very saints, in the mere exercise of living, grow less dainty, and take on the tone of their surroundings."

"I will propound to you one simple question," said the other; "and as you answer, I shall read to you your moral horoscope. You have grown in many things more lax; possibly you do right to be so; and at any account, it is the same with all men. But granting that, are you in any one particular, however trifling, more difficult to please with your own conduct, or do you go in all things with a looser rein?"

"In any one?" repeated Markheim, with an anguish of consideration. "No," he added, with despair, "in none! I have gone down in all."

"Then," said the visitor, "content yourself with what you are, for you will never change; and the words of your part on this stage are irrevocably written down."

Markheim stood for a long while silent, and indeed it was the visitor who first broke the silence. "That being so," he said, "shall I show you the money?"

"And grace?" cried Markheim.

"Have you not tried it?" returned the other. "Two or three years ago, did I not see you on the platform of revival meetings, and was not your voice the loudest in the hymn?"

"It is true," said Markheim; "and I see clearly what remains for me by way of duty. I thank you for these lessons from my soul; my eyes are opened, and I behold myself at last for what I am."

At this moment, the sharp note of the door-bell rang through the house; and the visitant, as though this were some concerted signal for which he had been waiting, changed at once in his demeanour.

"The maid!" he cried. "She has returned, as I forewarned you, and there is now before you one more difficult passage. Her master, you must say, is ill; you must let her in, with an assured but rather serious countenance—no smiles, no overacting, and I promise you success! Once the girl within and the door closed, the same dexterity that has already rid you of the dealer will relieve you of this last danger in your path. Thenceforward you have the whole evening—the whole night, if needful—to ransack the treasures of the house and to make good your safety. This is help that comes to you with the mask of danger. Up!" he cried: "up, friend; your life hangs trembling in the scales: up, and act!"

Markheim steadily regarded his counsellor. "If I be condemned to evil acts," he said, "there is still one door of freedom open—I can cease from action. If my life be an ill thing, I can lay it down. Though I be, as you say truly, at the beck of every small temptation, I can yet, by one decisive gesture, place myself beyond the reach of all. My love of good is damned to barrenness; it may, and let it be! But I have still my hatred of evil; and from that, to your galling disappointment, you shall see that I can draw both energy and courage."

The features of the visitor began to undergo a wonderful

and lovely change: they brightened and softened with a tender triumph; and, even as they brightened, faded and dislimned. But Markheim did not pause to watch or understand the transformation. He opened the door and went down-stairs very slowly, thinking to himself. His past went soberly before him; he beheld it as it was, ugly and strenuous like a dream, random as chance-medley —a scene of defeat. Life, as he thus reviewed it, tempted him no longer; but on the farther side he perceived a quiet haven for his bark. He paused in the passage, and looked into the shop, where the candle still burned by the dead body. It was strangely silent. Thoughts of the dealer swarmed into his mind, as he stood gazing. And then the bell once more broke out into impatient clamour.

He confronted the maid upon the threshold with something like a smile.

"You had better go for the police," said he: "I have killed your master."

●

JOHN EVELYN, ESQ., R.S.S., showed us at the Royal-Society, a note under Mr. Smith's hand, the curate of Deptford, that in November, 1679, as he was in bed sick of an ague, came to him the vision of a master of arts, with a white wand in his hand, and told him that if he did lie on his back three hours, viz. from ten to one, that he should be rid of his ague. He lay a good while on his back, but at last being weary he turned, and immediately the ague attacked him; afterwards he strictly followed the directions, and was perfectly cured. He was awoke, as it was in the day-time.

—JOHN AUBREY

●

A DUTCH prisoner at Woodbridge, in Suffolk, in the reign of K. Charles II. could discern Spirits; but others that stood by could not. The bell tolled for a man newly deceased. The prisoner saw his phantom, and did describe him to the Parson of the parish,* who was with him; exactly agreeing with the man for whom the bell tolled. Says the prisoner, now he is coming near to you, and now he is between you and the wall; the Parson was resolved to try it, and went to take the wall of him, and was thrown down; he could see nothing. This story is credibly told by several persons of belief.

—JOHN AUBREY

* Dr. Hooke, the Parson of the parish, has often told this story.

THE STORY OF MING-Y

The Story of Ming-Y was written more than fifty years ago; but it was as far from the realities of that day as from those of our own, and it is nearer to the modern than to the latter Victorian type of ghost story. There is no laboring to make the unbeliever say, "Well, it might just *possibly* happen." Hearn tells his story with straightforward simplicity, and with a sincerity that conveys much of the respectful Chinese attitude toward the shades of honorable ancestors, whether or not they are one's own.—EDITOR.

Lafcadio Hearn

THE STORY
OF MING-Y

Five hundred years ago, in the reign of the Emperor Houng-Wou, whose dynasty was *Ming*, there lived in the city of Genii, the city of Kwang-tchau-fu, a man celebrated for his learning and for his piety, named Tien-Pelou. This Tien-Pelou had one son, a beautiful boy, who for scholarship and for bodily grace and for polite accomplishments had no superior among the youths of his age. And his name was Ming-Y.

Now when the lad was in his eighteenth summer, it came to pass that Pelou, his father, was appointed Inspector of Public Instruction at the city of Tching-tou; and Ming-Y accompanied his parents thither. Near the city of Tching-tou lived a rich man of rank, a high commissioner of the government, whose name was

Tchang, and who wanted to find a worthy teacher for his children. On hearing of the arrival of the new Inspector of Public Instruction, the noble Tchang visited him to obtain advice in this matter; and happening to meet and converse with Pelou's accomplished son, immediately engaged Ming-Y as a private tutor for his family.

Now as the house of this Lord Tchang was situated several miles from town, it was deemed best that Ming-Y should abide in the house of his employer. Accordingly the youth made ready all things necessary for his new sojourn, and his parents, bidding him farewell, counselled him wisely, and cited to him the words of Lao-tseu and of the ancient sages:

"By a beautiful face the world is filled with love; but Heaven may never be deceived thereby. Shouldst thou behold a woman coming from the East, look thou to the West; shouldst thou perceive a maiden approaching from the West, turn thy eyes to the East."

If Ming-Y did not heed this counsel in after days, it was only because of his youth and the thoughtlessness of a naturally joyous heart.

And he departed to abide in the house of Lord Tchang, while the autumn passed, and the winter also.

When the time of the second moon of spring was drawing near, and that happy day which the Chinese call *Hoa-tchao*, or, "The Birthday of a Hundred Flowers," a longing came upon Ming-Y to see his parents; and he opened his heart to the good Tchang, who not only gave him the permission he desired, but also pressed into his hand a silver gift of two ounces, thinking that the lad might wish to bring some little memento to his father and mother. For it is the Chinese custom, on the feast of Hoa-tchao, to make presents to friends and relations.

That day all the air was drowsy with blossom perfume, and vibrant with the droning of bees. It seemed to Ming-Y that the path he followed had not been trodden by any other for many long years; the grass was tall upon it; vast trees on either side interlocked their mighty and mossgrown arms above him, beshadowing the way; but the leafy obscurities quivered with birdsong, and the deep vistas of the wood were glorified by vapours of gold, and odorous with flower-breathings as a temple with incense. The dreamy joy of the day entered into the heart of Ming-Y; and he

sat him down among the young blossoms, under the branches
swaying against the violet sky, to drink in the perfume and the
light, and to enjoy the great sweet silence. Even while thus re-
posing, a sound caused him to turn his eyes toward a shady place
where wild peach-trees were in bloom; and he beheld a young
woman, beautiful as the pinkening blossoms themselves, trying to
hide among them. Though he looked for a moment only, Ming-Y
could not avoid discerning the loveliness of her face, the golden
purity of her complexion, and the brightness of her long eyes that
sparkled under a pair of brows as daintily curved as the wings of
the silk-worm butterfly out-spread. Ming-Y at once turned his
gaze away, and, rising quickly, proceeded on his journey. But so
much embarrassed did he feel at the idea of those charming eyes
peeping at him through the leaves, that he suffered the money he
had been carrying in his sleeve to fall, without being aware of it.
A few moments later he heard the patter of light feet running behind him, and a woman's voice calling him by name. Turning his
face in great surprise, he saw a comely servant-maid, who said to
him, "Sir, my mistress bade me pick up and return to you this
silver which you dropped upon the road." Ming-Y thanked the
girl gracefully, and requested her to convey his compliments to
her mistress. Then he proceeded on his way through the perfumed
silence, athwart the shadows that dreamed along the forgotten
path, dreaming himself also, and feeling his heart beating with
strange quickness at the thought of the beautiful being that he
had seen.

It was just such another day when Ming-Y, returning by
the same path, paused once more at the spot where the gracious
figure had momentarily appeared before him. But this time he was
surprised to perceive, through a long vista of immense trees, a
dwelling that had previously escaped his notice—a country residence, not large, yet elegant to an unusual degree. The bright blue
tiles of its curved and serrated double roof, rising above the foliage,
seemed to blend their colour with the luminous azure of the day;
the green-and-gold designs of its carven porticos were exquisite
artistic mockeries of leaves and flowers bathed in sunshine. And
at the summit of terrace-steps before it, guarded by great porcelain
tortoises, Ming-Y saw standing the mistress of the mansion—the

idol of his passionate fancy—accompanied by the same waiting-maid who had borne to her his message of gratitude. While Ming-Y looked, he perceived that their eyes were upon him; they smiled and conversed together as if speaking about him; and, shy though he was, the youth found courage to salute the fair one from a distance. To his astonishment, the young servant beckoned him to approach; and opening a rustic gate half veiled by trailing plants bearing crimson flowers, Ming-Y advanced along the verdant alley leading to the terrace, with mingled feelings of surprise and timid joy. As he drew near, the beautiful lady withdrew from sight; but the maid waited at the broad steps to receive him, and said as he ascended:

"Sir, my mistress understands you wish to thank her for the trifling service she recently bade me do you, and requests that you will enter the house, as she knows you already by repute, and desires to have the pleasure of bidding you good day."

Ming-Y entered bashfully, his feet making no sound upon a matting elastically soft as forest moss, and found himself in a reception-chamber vast, cool, and fragrant with scent of blossoms freshly gathered. A delicious quiet pervaded the mansion; shadows of flying birds passed over the bands of light that fell through the half-blinds of bamboo; great butterflies, with pinions of fiery colour, found their way in, to hover a moment about the painted vases, and pass out again into the mysterious woods. And noiselessly as they, the young mistress of the mansion entered by another door, and kindly greeted the boy, who lifted his hands to his breast and bowed low in salutation. She was taller than he had deemed her, and supplely-slender as a beauteous lily; her black hair was interwoven with the creamy blossoms of the *chu-sha-kih;* her robes of pale silk took shifting tints when she moved, as vapours change hue with the changing of the light.

"If I be not mistaken," she said, when both had seated themselves after having exchanged the customary formalities of politeness, "my honoured visitor is none other than Tien-chou, surnamed Ming-Y, educator of the children of my respected relative, the High Commissioner Tchang. As the family of Lord Tchang is my family also, I cannot but consider the teacher of his children as one of my own kin."

"Lady," replied Ming-Y, not a little astonished, "may I dare to enquire the name of your honoured family, and to ask the relation which you hold to my noble patron?"

"The name of my poor family," responded the comely lady, "is *Ping*—an ancient family of the city of Tching-tou. I am the daughter of a certain Sië of Moun-hao; Sië is my name, likewise; and I was married to a young man of the Ping family, whose name was Khang. By this marriage I became related to your excellent patron; but my husband died soon after our wedding, and I have chosen this solitary place to reside in during the period of my widowhood."

There was a drowsy music in her voice, as of the melody of brooks, the murmurings of spring; and such a strange grace in the manner of her speech as Ming-Y had never heard before. Yet, on learning that she was a widow, the youth would not have presumed to remain long in her presence without a formal invitation; and after having sipped the cup of rich tea presented to him, he arose to depart. Sië would not suffer him to go so quickly.

"Nay, friend," she said, "stay yet a little while in my house, I pray you; for, should your honoured patron ever learn that you had been here, and that I had not treated you as a respected guest, and regaled you even as I would him, I know that he would be greatly angered. Remain at least to supper."

So Ming-Y remained, rejoicing secretly in his heart, for Sië seemed to him the fairest and sweetest being he had ever known, and he felt that he loved her more than his father and his mother. And while they talked the long shadows of the evening slowly blended into one violet darkness; the great citron-light of the sunset faded out; and those starry beings that are called the Three Councillors, who preside over life and death and the destinies of men, opened their cold bright eyes in the northern sky. Within the mansion of Sië the painted lanterns were lighted; the table was laid for the evening repast; and Ming-Y took his place at it, feeling little inclination to eat, and thinking only of the charming face before him. Observing that he scarcely tasted the dainties laid upon his plate, Sië pressed her young guest to partake of wine; and they drank several cups together. It was a purple wine, so cool that the cup into which it was poured became covered with vapoury dew; yet it seemed to warm the veins with strange fire. To Ming-Y, as he drank, all things became more luminous as by enchantment;

the walls of the chamber seemed to recede, and the roof to heighten; the lamps glowed like stars in their chains, and the voice of Sië floated to the boy's ears like some far melody heard through the spaces of a drowsy night. His heart swelled; his tongue loosened; and words flitted from his lips that he had fancied he could never dare to utter. Yet Sië sought not to restrain him; her lips gave no smile; but her long bright eyes seemed to laugh with pleasure at his words of praise, and to return his gaze of passionate admiration with affectionate interest.

"I have heard," she said, "of your rare talent, and of your many elegant accomplishments. I know how to sing a little, although I cannot claim to possess any musical learning; and now that I have the honour of finding myself in the society of a musical professor, I will venture to lay modesty aside, and beg you to sing a few songs with me. I should deem it no small gratification if you would condescend to examine my musical compositions."

"The honour and gratification, dear lady," replied Ming-Y, "will be mine; and I feel helpless to express the gratitude which the offer of so rare a favour deserves."

The serving-maid, obedient to the summons of a little silver gong, brought in the music and retired. Ming-Y took the manuscripts, and began to examine them with eager delight. The paper on which they were written had a pale yellow tint, and was light as a fabric of gossamer; but the characters were antiquely beautiful, as though they had been traced by the brush of Hei-song Che-Tchoo himself—that divine Genius of Ink, who is no bigger than a fly; and the signatures attached to the compositions were the signatures of Youen-tchin, Kao-pien, and Thou-mou—mighty poets and musicians of the Dynasty of Thang! Ming-Y could not repress a scream of delight at the sight of treasures so inestimable and so unique; scarcely could he summon resolution enough to permit them to leave his hands even for a moment.

"O Lady!" he cried, "these are veritably priceless things, surpassing in worth the treasures of all kings. This indeed is the handwriting of those great masters who sang five hundred years before our birth. How marvellously it has been preserved! Is not this the wondrous ink of which it was written: 'After centuries I remain firm as stone, and the letters that I make like lacquer'? And how divine the charm of this composition!—the song of Kao-pien, prince of poets, and Governor of Sze-tchouen five hundred years ago!"

"Kao-pien! darling Kao-pien!" murmured Sië, with a singular light in her eyes. "Kao-pien is also my favourite. Dear Ming-Y, let us chant his verses together, to the melody of old—the music of those grand years when men were nobler and wiser than to-day."

And their voices rose through the perfumed night like the voices of the wonder-birds—of the Fung-hoang—blending together in liquid sweetness. Yet a moment, and Ming-Y, overcome by the witchery of his companion's voice, could only listen in speechless ecstasy, while the lights of the chamber swam dim before his sight, and tears of pleasure trickled down his cheeks.

So the ninth hour passed; and they continued to converse, and to drink the cool purple wine, and to sing the songs of the years of Thang, until far into the night. More than once Ming-Y thought of departing; but each time Sië would begin, in that silver-sweet voice of hers, so wondrous a story of the great poets of the past, and of the women whom they loved, that he became as one entranced; or she would sing for him a song so strange that all his senses seemed to die except that of hearing. And at last, as she paused to pledge him in a cup of wine, Ming-Y could not restrain himself from putting his arm about her round neck and drawing her dainty head close to him, and kissing the lips that were so much ruddier than the wine. Then their lips separated no more; the night grew old, and they knew it not.

The birds awakened, the flowers opened their eyes to the rising sun, and Ming-Y found himself at last compelled to bid his lovely enchantress farewell. Sië, accompanying him to the terrace, kissed him fondly and said, "Dear boy, come hither as often as you are able—as often as your heart whispers you to come. I know you are not of those without faith and truth, who betray secrets; yet, being so young, you might also be sometimes thoughtless; and I pray you never to forget that only the stars have been the witness of our love. Speak of it to no living person, dearest; and take with you this little souvenir of our happy night."

And she presented him with an exquisite and curious little thing—a paper-weight in likeness of a couchant lion, wrought from a jade-stone yellow as that created by a rainbow in honour of

Kong-fu-tze. Tenderly the boy kissed the gift and the beautiful hand that gave it. "May the Spirits punish me," he vowed, "if ever I knowingly give you cause to reproach me, sweetheart!" And they separated with mutual vows.

That morning, on returning to the house of Lord Tchang Ming-Y told the first falsehood which had ever passed his lips. He averred that his mother had requested him thenceforward to pass his nights at home, now that the weather had become so pleasant; for, though the way was somewhat long, he was strong and active, and needed both air and healthy exercise. Tchang believed all Ming-Y said, and offered no objection. Accordingly the lad found himself enabled to pass all his evenings at the house of the beautiful Sië. Each night they devoted to the same pleasure which had made their first acquaintance so charming: they sang and conversed by turns; they played at chess—the learned game invented by Wu-Wang, which is an imitation of war; they composed pieces of eighty rhymes upon the flowers, the trees, the clouds, the streams, the birds, the bees. But in all accomplishments Sië far excelled her young sweetheart. Whenever they played at chess, it was always Ming-Y's general, Ming-Y's *tsiang*, who was surrounded and vanquished; when they composed verses, Sië's poems were ever superior to his in harmony of word-colouring, in elegance of form, in classic loftiness of thought. And the themes they selected were always the most difficult—those of the poets of the Thang Dynasty; the songs they sang were also the songs of five hundred years before—the songs of Youen-tchin, of Thoumou, of Kao-pien above all, high poet and ruler of the province of Sze-tchouen.

So the summer waxed and waned upon their love, and the luminous autumn came, with its vapours of phantom gold, its shadows of magical purple.

Then it unexpectedly happened that the father of Ming-Y, meeting his son's employer at Tching-tou, was asked by him: "Why must your boy continue to travel every evening to the city, now that the winter is approaching? The way is long, and when he returns in the morning he looks foredone with weariness. Why not permit him to slumber in my house during the season of snow?" And the father of Ming-Y, greatly astonished, responded: "Sir, my son has not visited the city, nor has he been to our house all this summer. I fear that he must have acquired wicked habits, and that he passes his nights in evil company—perhaps in gaming, or in drinking with the women of the flower-boats." But the High Commissioner returned:

"Nay! that is not to be thought of. I have never found any evil in the boy, and there are no taverns nor flower-boats nor any places of dissipation in our neighbourhood. No doubt Ming-Y has found some amiable youth of his own age with whom to spend his evenings, and only told me an untruth for fear that I would not otherwise permit him to leave my residence. I beg that you will say nothing to him until I shall have sought to discover this mystery; and this very evening I shall send my servant to follow after him, and to watch whither he goes."

Pelou readily assented to this proposal, and promising to visit Tchang the following morning, returned to his home. In the evening, when Ming-Y left the house of Tchang, a servant followed him unobserved at a distance. But on reaching the most obscure portion of the road the boy disappeared from sight as suddenly as though the earth had swallowed him. After having long sought after him in vain, the domestic returned in great bewilderment to the house, and related what had taken place. Tchang immediately sent a messenger to Pelou.

In the meantime Ming-Y, entering the chamber of his beloved, was surprised and deeply pained to find her in tears. "Sweetheart," she sobbed, wreathing her arms around his neck, "we are about to be separated for ever, because of reasons which I cannot tell you. From the very first I knew this must come to pass, and nevertheless it seemed to me for the moment so cruelly sudden a loss, so unexpected a misfortune that I could not prevent myself from weeping! After this night we shall never see each other again, beloved, and I know that you will not be able to forget me while you live; but I know also that you will become a great scholar, and that honours and riches will be showered upon you, and that some beautiful and loving woman will console you for my loss. And now let us speak no more of grief; but let us pass this last evening joyously, so that your recollection of me may not be a painful one, and that you may remember my laughter rather than my tears."

She brushed the bright drops away, and brought wine and music and the melodious *kin* of seven silken strings, and would not suffer Ming-Y to speak for one moment of the coming separation. And she sang him an ancient song about the calmness of summer lakes reflecting the blue of heaven only, and the calmness of the heart also, before the clouds of care and of grief and of weariness darken its little world. Soon they forgot their sorrow in the joy of song and wine; and those last hours seemed to Ming-Y more celestial than even the hours of their first bliss.

But when the yellow beauty of morning came their sadness returned, and they wept. Once more Sië accompanied her lover to the terrace steps; and as she kissed him farewell, she pressed into his hand a parting gift—a little brush-case of agate, wonderfully chiselled, and worthy the table of a great poet. And they separa-rated for ever, shedding many tears.

Still Ming-Y could not believe it was an eternal parting. "No!" he thought, "I shall visit her to-morrow; for I cannot live without her, and I feel assured that she cannot refuse to receive me." Such were the thoughts that filled his mind as he reached the house of Tchang, to find his father and his patron standing on the porch awaiting him. Ere he could speak a word, Pelou demanded:

"Son, in what place have you been passing your nights?"

Seeing that his falsehood had been discovered, Ming-Y dared not make any reply, and remained abashed and silent, with bowed head, in the presence of his father. Then Pelou, striking the boy violently with his staff, commanded him to divulge the secret; and at last, partly through fear of his parent, and partly through fear of the law which ordains that *"the son refusing to obey his father shall be punished with one hundred blows of the bamboo,"* Ming-Y faltered out the history of his love.

Tchang changed colour at the boy's tale. "Child," exclaimed the High Commissioner, "I have no relative of the name of Ping; I have never heard of the woman you describe; I have never heard even of the house which you speak of. But I know also that you cannot dare to lie to Pelou, your honoured father; there is some strange delusion in all this affair."

Then Ming-Y produced the gifts that Sië had given him—

the lion of yellow jade, the brush-case of carven agate, also some
original compositions made by the beautiful lady herself. The
astonishment of Tchang was now shared by Pelou. Both observed
that the brush-case of agate and the lion of jade bore the appearance of objects that had lain buried in the earth for centuries, and
were of a workmanship beyond the power of living man to imitate;
while the compositions proved to be veritable masterpieces of
poetry, written in the style of the poets of the Dynasty of Thang.

"Friend Pelou," cried the High Commissioner, "let us immediately accompany the boy to the place where he obtained these
miraculous things and apply the testimony of our senses to this
mystery; the boy is no doubt telling the truth; yet his story
passes my understanding." And all three proceeded toward the
place of the habitation of Sië.

But when they had arrived at the shadiest part of the road,
where the perfumes were most sweet and the mosses were green-
est, and the fruits of the wild peach flushed most pinkly, Ming-Y,
gazing through the groves, uttered a cry of dismay. Where the
azure-tiled roof had risen against the sky, there was now only
the blue emptiness of air; where the green-and-gold façade had
been, there was visible only the flickering of leaves under the
aureate autumn light; and where the broad terrace had extended,
could be discerned only a ruin—a tomb so ancient, so deeply
gnawed by moss, that the name graven upon it was no longer
decipherable. The home of Sië had disappeared.

All suddenly the High Commissioner smote his forehead with
his hand, and turning to Pelou, recited the well-known verse of
the ancient poet, Tching-Kou:

"*Surely the peach-flowers blossom over the tomb of Sië-
Thao.*"

"Friend Pelou," continued Tchang, "the beauty who bewitched your son was no other than she whose tomb stands there
in ruin before us! Did she not say she was wedded to Ping-Khang?
There is no family of that name, but Ping-Khang is indeed the
name of a broad alley in the city near. There was a dark riddle
in all that she said. She called herself Sië of Moun-Hiao; there is
no person of that name, there is no street of that name; but the
Chinese characters *Moun* and *Hiao*, placed together, form the

character, 'Kiao.' Listen! The alley Ping-Khang, situated in the street Kiao, was the place where dwelt the great courtesans of the Dynasty of Thang! Did she not sing the song of Kao-pien? And upon the brush-case and the paper-weight she gave your son, are there not characters which read, '*Pure object of art belonging to Kao of the city of Pho-hai*'? That city no longer exists; but the memory of Kao-pien remains, for he was governor of the province of Sze-tchouen, and a mighty poet. And when he dwelt in the land of Chou, was not his favourite the beautiful wanton Sië— Sië-Thao, unmatched for grace among all the women of her day? It was he who made her a gift of those manuscripts of song; it was he who gave her those objects of rare art. Sië-Thao died not as other women die. Her limbs may have crumbled to dust; yet something of her still lives in this deep wood, her Shadow still haunts this shadowy place."

Tchang ceased to speak. A vague fear fell upon the three. The thin mists of the morning made dim the distances of green, and deepened the ghostly beauty of the woods. A faint breeze passed by, leaving a trail of blossom-scent—a last odour of dying flowers—thin as that which clings to the silk of a forgotten robe; and, as it passed, the trees seemed to whisper across the silence, "*Sië-Thao.*"

Fearing greatly for his son, Pelou sent the lad away at once to the city of Kwang-tchau-fu. And there in after years, Ming-Y obtained high dignities and honours by reason of his talents and his learning; and he married the daughter of an illustrious house, by whom he became the father of sons and daughters famous for their virtues and their accomplishments. Never could he forget Sië-Thao; and yet it is said that he never spoke of her—not even to his children when they begged him to tell them the story of two beautiful objects that always lay upon his writing-table: a lion of yellow jade, and a brush-case of carven agate.

●

●

I MUST NOT forget an apparition in my country, which appeared several times to Doctor Turbernile's sister, at Salisbury; which is much talked of. One married a second wife, and contrary to the agreement and settlement at the first wife's marriage, did wrong the children by the first venter. The settlement was hid behind a wainscot in the chamber where the Doctor's sister did lie: and the apparition of the first wife did discover it to her. By which means right was done to the first wife's children. The apparition told her that she wandered in the air, and was now going to God. Dr. Turbernile (oculist) did affirm this to be true. See Mr. Glanvill's *Sadducismus Triumphatus*.

—JOHN AUBREY

THE BEAST WITH FIVE FINGERS

Not long ago, Basil Davenport wrote an article about ghost stories for *The Saturday Review of Literature*. In it, after a discussion of the inherent absurdities of *Frankenstein*, he said, "What a relief to be quite sympathetically terrified by a modern story like W. F. Harvey's 'The Beast With Five Fingers,' where the rules of the game . . . are clearly laid down. . . ." Here then is a ghost story in the modern manner, with no spooky properties or atmospherics except the beast with five fingers itself.—EDITOR.

W. F. Harvey

THE BEAST WITH FIVE FINGERS

When I was a little boy I once went with my father to call on Adrian Borlsover. I played on the floor with a black spaniel while my father appealed for a subscription. Just before we left my father said, "Mr. Borlsover, may my son here shake hands with you? It will be a thing to look back upon with pride when he grows to be a man."

I came up to the bed on which the old man was lying and put my hand in his, awed by the still beauty of his face. He spoke to me kindly, and hoped that I should always try to please my father. Then he placed his right hand on my head and asked for a blessing to rest upon me. "Amen!" said my father, and I followed him out of the room, feeling as if I wanted to cry. But my father was in excellent spirits.

"That old gentleman, Jim," said he, "is the most wonderful man in the whole town. For ten years he has been quite blind."

"But I saw his eyes," I said. "They were ever so black and shiny; they weren't shut up like Nora's puppies. Can't he see at all?"

And so I learnt for the first time that a man might have eyes that looked dark and beautiful and shining without being able to see.

"Just like Mrs. Tomlinson has big ears," I said, "and can't hear at all except when Mr. Tomlinson shouts."

"Jim," said my father, "it's not right to talk about a lady's ears. Remember what Mr. Borlsover said about pleasing me and being a good boy."

That was the only time I saw Adrian Borlsover. I soon forgot about him and the hand which he laid in blessing on my head. But for a week I prayed that those dark tender eyes might see.

"His spaniel may have puppies," I said in my prayers, "and he will never be able to know how funny they look with their eyes all closed up. Please let old Mr. Borlsover see."

Adrian Borlsover, as my father had said, was a wonderful man. He came of an eccentric family. Borlsovers' sons, for some reason, always seemed to marry very ordinary women, which perhaps accounted for the fact that no Borlsover had been a genius, and only one Borlsover had been mad. But they were great champions of little causes, generous patrons of odd sciences, founders of querulous sects, trustworthy guides to the by-path meadows of erudition.

Adrian was an authority on the fertilization of orchids. He had held at one time the family living at Borlsover Conyers, until a congenital weakness of the lungs obliged him to seek a less rigorous climate in the sunny south coast watering-place where I had seen him. Occasionally he would relieve one or other of the local clergy. My father described him as a fine preacher, who gave long and inspiring sermons from what many men would have considered unprofitable texts. "An excellent proof," he would add, "of the truth of the doctrine of direct verbal inspiration."

Adrian Borlsover was exceedingly clever with his hands. His penmanship was exquisite. He illustrated all his scientific papers, made his own woodcuts, and carved the reredos that is at present the chief feature of interest in the church at Borlsover Conyers. He had an exceedingly clever knack in cutting silhouettes for young ladies and paper pigs and cows for little children, and made more than one complicated wind instrument of his own devising.

When he was fifty years old Adrian Borlsover lost his sight. In a wonderfully short time he had adapted himself to the new conditions of life. He quickly learned to read Braille. So marvelous indeed was his sense of touch that he was still able to maintain his interest in botany. The mere passing of his long supple fingers over a flower was sufficient means for its identification, though occasionally he would use his lips. I have found several letters of his among my father's correspondence. In no case was there anything to show that he was afflicted with blindness, and this in spite of the fact that he exercised undue economy in the spacing of lines. Towards the close of his life the old man was credited with powers of touch that seemed almost uncanny: it has been said that he could tell at once the color of a ribbon placed between his fingers. My father would neither confirm nor deny the story.

I

Adrian Borlsover was a bachelor. His elder brother George had married late in life, leaving one son, Eustace, who lived in the gloomy Georgian mansion at Borlsover Conyers, where he could work undisturbed in collecting material for his great book on heredity.

Like his uncle, he was a remarkable man. The Borlsovers had always been born naturalists, but Eustace possessed in a special degree the power of systematizing his knowledge. He had received his university education in Germany, and then, after post-graduate work in Vienna and Naples, had traveled for four years in South America and the East, getting together a huge store of material for a new study into the processes of variation.

He lived alone at Borlsover Conyers with Saunders his secretary, a man who bore a somewhat dubious reputation in the district, but whose powers as a mathematician, combined with his business abilities, were invaluable to Eustace.

Uncle and nephew saw little of each other. The visits of

Eustace were confined to a week in the summer or autumn: long weeks, that dragged almost as slowly as the bath-chair in which the old man was drawn along the sunny sea front. In their way the two men were fond of each other, though their intimacy would doubtless have been greater had they shared the same religious views. Adrian held to the old-fashioned evangelical dogmas of his early manhood; his nephew for many years had been thinking of embracing Buddhism. Both men possessed, too, the reticence the Borlsovers had always shown, and which their enemies sometimes called hypocrisy. With Adrian it was a reticence as to the things he had left undone; but with Eustace it seemed that the curtain which he was so careful to leave undrawn hid something more than a half-empty chamber.

Two years before his death Adrian Borlsover developed, unknown to himself, the not uncommon power of automatic writing. Eustace made the discovery by accident. Adrian was sitting reading in bed, the forefinger of his left hand tracing the Braille characters, when his nephew noticed that a pencil the old man held in his right hand was moving slowly along the opposite page. He left his seat in the window and sat down beside the bed. The right hand continued to move, and now he could see plainly that they were letters and words which it was forming.

"Adrian Borlsover," wrote the hand, "Eustace Borlsover, George Borlsover, Francis Borlsover, Sigismund Borlsover, Adrian Borlsover, Eustace Borlsover, Saville Borlsover. B, for Borlsover. Honesty is the Best Policy. Beautiful Belinda Borlsover."

"What curious nonsense!" said Eustace to himself.

"King George the Third ascended the throne in 1760," wrote the hand. "Crowd, a noun of multitude; a collection of individuals —Adrian Borlsover, Eustace Borlsover."

"It seems to me," said his uncle, closing the book, "that you had much better make the most of the afternoon sunshine and take your walk now." "I think perhaps I will," Eustace answered as he picked up the volume. "I won't go far, and when I come back I can read to you those articles in *Nature* about which we were speaking."

He went along the promenade, but stopped at the first shelter, and seating himself in the corner best protected from the wind, he examined the book at leisure. Nearly every page was scored with a meaningless jungle of pencil marks: rows of capital letters, short words, long words, complete sentences, copy-book tags. The whole thing, in fact, had the appearance of a copy-book, and on a more careful scrutiny Eustace thought that there was ample evidence to show that the handwriting at the beginning of the book, good though it was, was not nearly so good as the handwriting at the end.

He left his uncle at the end of October, with a promise to return early in December. It seemed to him quite clear that the old man's power of automatic writing was developing rapidly, and for the first time he looked forward to a visit that combined duty with interest.

But on his return he was at first disappointed. His uncle, he thought, looked older. He was listless too, preferring others to read to him and dictating nearly all his letters. Not until the day before he left had Eustace an opportunity of observing Adrian Borlsover's new-found faculty.

The old man, propped up in bed with pillows, had sunk into a light sleep. His two hands lay on the coverlet, his left hand tightly clasping his right. Eustace took an empty manuscript book and placed a pencil within reach of the fingers of the right hand. They snatched at it eagerly; then dropped the pencil to unloose the left hand from its restraining grasp.

"Perhaps to prevent interference I had better hold that hand," said Eustace to himself, as he watched the pencil. Almost immediately it began to write.

"Blundering Borlsovers, unnecessarily unnatural, extraordinarily eccentric, culpably curious."

"Who are you?" asked Eustace, in a low voice.

"Never you mind," wrote the hand of Adrian.

"Is it my uncle who is writing?"

"Oh, my prophetic soul, mine uncle."

"Is it anyone I know?"

"Silly Eustace, you'll see me very soon."

"When shall I see you?"

"When poor old Adrian's dead."

"Where shall I see you?"

"Where shall you not?"

Instead of speaking his next question, Borlsover wrote it. "What is the time?"

The fingers dropped the pencil and moved three or four times across the paper. Then, picking up the pencil, they wrote: "Ten minutes before four. Put your book away, Eustace. Adrian mustn't find us working at this sort of thing. He doesn't know what to make of it, and I won't have poor old Adrian disturbed. *Au revoir.*"

Adrian Borlsover awoke with a start.

"I've been dreaming again," he said; "such queer dreams of leaguered cities and forgotten towns. You were mixed up in this one, Eustace, though I can't remember how. Eustace, I want to warn you. Don't walk in doubtful paths. Choose your friends well. Your poor grandfather——"

A fit of coughing put an end to what he was saying, but Eustace saw that the hand was still writing. He managed unnoticed to draw the book away. "I'll light the gas," he said, "and ring for tea." On the other side of the bed curtain he saw the last sentences that had been written.

"It's too late, Adrian," he read. "We're friends already; aren't we, Eustace Borlsover?"

On the following day Eustace Borlsover left. He thought his uncle looked ill when he said good-by, and the old man spoke despondently of the failure his life had been.

"Nonsense, uncle!" said his nephew. "You have got over your difficulties in a way not one in a hundred thousand would have done. Every one marvels at your splendid perseverance in teaching your hand to take the place of your lost sight. To me it's been a revelation of the possibilities of education."

"Education," said his uncle dreamily, as if the word had started a new train of thought, "education is good so long as you know to whom and for what purpose you give it. But with the lower orders of men, the base and more sordid spirits, I have grave doubts as to its results. Well, good-by, Eustace, I may not see you again. You are a true Borlsover, with all the Borlsover faults. Marry, Eustace. Marry some good, sensible girl. And if by any chance I don't see you again, my will is at my solicitor's. I've not left you any legacy, because I know you're well provided for, but I thought you might like to have my books. Oh, and there's just one other thing. You know, before the end people often lose control over themselves and make absurd requests. Don't pay any attention to them, Eustace. Good-by!" and he held out his hand. Eustace took it. It remained in his a fraction of a second longer than he had expected, and gripped him with a virility that was surprising. There was, too, in its touch a subtle sense of intimacy.

"Why, uncle!" he said, "I shall see you alive and well for many long years to come."

Two months later Adrian Borlsover died.

II

Eustace Borlsover was in Naples at the time. He read the obituary notice in the *Morning Post* on the day announced for the funeral.

"Poor old fellow!" he said. "I wonder where I shall find room for all his books."

The question occurred to him again with greater force when three days later he found himself standing in the library at Borlsover Conyers, a huge room built for use, and not for beauty, in the year of Waterloo by a Borlsover who was an ardent admirer of the great Napoleon. It was arranged on the plan of many college libraries, with tall, projecting bookcases forming deep recesses of dusty silence, fit graves for the old hates of forgotten controversy, the dead passions of forgotten lives. At the end of the room, behind the bust of some unknown eighteenth-century divine, an ugly iron corkscrew stair led to a shelf-lined gallery. Nearly every shelf was full.

"I must talk to Saunders about it," said Eustace. "I suppose that it will be necessary to have the billiard-room fitted up with book cases."

The two men met for the first time after many weeks in the dining-room that evening.

"Hullo!" said Eustace, standing before the fire with his hands in his pockets. "How goes the world, Saunders? Why these dress togs?" He himself was wearing an old shooting-jacket. He did not believe in mourning, as he had told his uncle on his last visit; and though he usually went in for quiet-colored ties, he wore this evening one of an ugly red, in order to shock Morton the butler, and to make them thrash out the whole question of mourning for themselves in the servants' hall. Eustace was a true Borlsover. "The world," said Saunders, "goes the same as usual, confoundedly slow. The dress togs are accounted for by an invitation from Captain Lockwood to bridge."

"How are you getting there?"

"I've told your coachman to drive me in your carriage. Any objection?"

"Oh, dear me, no! We've had all things in common for far too many years for me to raise objections at this hour of the day."

"You'll find your correspondence in the library," went on Saunders. "Most of it I've seen to. There are a few private letters I haven't opened. There's also a box with a rat, or something, inside it that came by the evening post. Very likely it's the six-toed albino. I didn't look, because I didn't want to mess up my things, but I should gather from the way it's jumping about that it's pretty hungry."

"Oh, I'll see to it," said Eustace, "while you and the Captain earn an honest penny."

Dinner over and Saunders gone, Eustace went into the library. Though the fire had been lit the room was by no means cheerful.

"We'll have all the lights on at any rate," he said, as he turned the switches. "And, Morton," he added, when the butler brought the coffee, "get me a screwdriver or something to undo this box. Whatever the animal is, he's kicking up the deuce of a row. What is it? Why are you dawdling?"

"If you please sir, when the postman brought it he told me that they'd bored the holes in the lid at the post-office. There were no breathin' holes in the lid, sir, and they didn't want the animal to die. That is all, sir."

"It's culpably careless of the man, whoever he was," said Eustace, as he removed the screws, "packing an animal like this in a wooden box with no means of getting air. Confound it all! I meant to ask Morton to bring me a cage to put it in. Now I suppose I shall have to get one myself."

He placed a heavy book on the lid from which the screws had been removed, and went into the billiard-room. As he came back into the library with an empty cage in his hand he heard the sound of something falling, and then of something scuttling along the floor.

"Bother it! The beast's got out. How in the world am I to find it again in this library!"

To search for it did indeed seem hopeless. He tried to follow the sound of the scuttling in one of the recesses where the animal seemed to be running behind the books in the shelves, but it was impossible to locate it. Eustace resolved to go on quietly reading. Very likely the animal might gain confidence and show itself. Saunders seemed to have dealt in his usual methodical manner with most of the correspondence. There were still the private letters.

What was that? Two sharp clicks and the lights in the hideous candelabra that hung from the ceiling suddenly went out.

"I wonder if something has gone wrong with the fuse," said Eustace, as he went to the switches by the door. Then he stopped. There was a noise at the other end of the room, as if something was crawling up the iron corkscrew stair. "If it's gone into the gallery," he said, "well and good." He hastily turned on the lights, crossed the room, and climbed up the stair. But he could see nothing. His grandfather had placed a little gate at the top of the stair, so that children could run and romp in the gallery without fear of accident. This Eustace closed, and having considerably narrowed the circle of his search, returned to his desk by the fire.

How gloomy the library was! There was no sense of intimacy about the room. The few busts that an eighteenth-century Borlsover had brought back from the grand tour, might have been in keeping in the old library. Here they seemed out of place. They made the room feel cold, in spite of the heavy red damask curtains and great gilt cornices.

With a crash two heavy books fell from the gallery to the floor; then, as Borlsover looked, another and yet another.

"Very well; you'll starve for this, my beauty!" he said. "We'll do some little experiments on the metabolism of rats deprived of water. Go on! Chuck them down! I think I've got the upper hand!" He turned once again to his correspondence. The letter was from the family solicitor. It spoke of his uncle's death and of the valuable collection of books that had been left to him in the will.

"There was one request," he read, "which certainly came as a surprise to me. As you know, Mr. Adrian Borlsover had left instructions that his body was to be buried in as simple a manner as possible at Eastbourne. He expressed a desire that there should be neither wreaths nor flowers of any kind, and hoped that his friends and relatives would not consider it necessary to wear mourning. The day before his death we received a letter canceling these instructions. He wished his body to be embalmed (he gave us the address of the men we were to employ—Pennifer, Ludgate Hill), with orders that his right hand was to be sent to you, stating that it was at your special request. The other arrangements as to the funeral remained unaltered."

"Good Lord!" said Eustace; "what in the world was the old boy driving at? And what in the name of all that's holy is that?"

Someone was in the gallery. Someone had pulled the cord attached to one of the blinds, and it had rolled up with a snap. Someone must be in the gallery, for a second blind did the same. Someone must be walking round the gallery, for one after the other the blinds sprang up, letting in the moonlight.

"I haven't got to the bottom of this yet," said Eustace, "but I will do so before the night is very much older," and he hurried up the corkscrew stair. He had just got to the top when the lights went out a second time, and he heard again the scuttling along the floor. Quickly he stole on tiptoe in the dim moonshine in the direction of the noise, feeling as he went for one of the switches. His fingers touched the metal knob at last. He turned on the electric light.

About ten yards in front of him, crawling along the floor, was a man's hand. Eustace stared at it in utter astonishment. It was moving quickly, in the manner of a geometer caterpillar, the fingers humped up one moment, flattened out the next; the thumb appeared to give a crab-like motion to the whole. While he was looking, too surprised to stir, the hand disappeared round the corner. Eustace ran forward. He no longer saw it, but he could hear it as it squeezed its way behind the books on one of the shelves. A heavy volume had been displaced. There was a gap in the row of books where it had got in. In his fear lest it should escape him again, he seized the first book that came to his hand and plugged it into the hole. Then, emptying two shelves of their contents, he took the wooden boards and propped them up in front to make his barrier doubly sure.

"I wish Saunders was back," he said; "one can't tackle this sort of thing alone." It was after eleven, and there seemed little likelihood of Saunders returning before twelve. He did not dare to leave the shelf unwatched, even to run downstairs to ring the bell. Morton the butler often used to come round about eleven to see that the windows were fastened, but he might not come. Eustace was thoroughly unstrung. At last he heard steps down below.

"Morton!" he shouted; "Morton!"

"Sir?"

"Has Mr. Saunders got back yet?"

"Not yet, sir."

"Well, bring me some brandy, and hurry up about it. I'm up here in the gallery, you duffer."

"Thanks," said Eustace, as he emptied the glass. "Don't go to bed yet, Morton. There are a lot of books that have fallen down by accident; bring them up and put them back in their shelves."

Morton had never seen Borlsover in so talkative a mood as on that night. "Here," said Eustace, when the books had been put back and dusted, "you might hold up these boards for me, Morton. That beast in the box got out, and I've been chasing it all over the place."

"I think I can hear it chawing at the books, sir. They're not valuable, I hope? I think that's the carriage, sir; I'll go and call Mr. Saunders."

It seemed to Eustace that he was away for five minutes, but it could hardly have been more than one when he returned with Saunders. "All right, Morton, you can go now. I'm up here, Saunders."

"What's all the row?" asked Saunders, as he lounged forward with his hands in his pockets. The luck had been with him all the evening. He was completely satisfied, both with himself and with Captain Lockwood's taste in wines. "What's the matter? You look to me to be in an absolute blue funk."

"That old devil of an uncle of mine," began Eustace—"oh, I can't explain it all. It's his hand that's been playing old Harry all the evening. But I've got it cornered behind these books. You've got to help me catch it."

"What's up with you, Eustace? What's the game?"

"It's no game, you silly idiot! If you don't believe me take out one of those books and put your hand in and feel."

"All right," said Saunders; "but wait till I've rolled up my sleeve. The accumulated dust of centuries, eh?" He took off his coat, knelt down, and thrust his arm along the shelf.

"There's something there right enough," he said. "It's got a funny stumpy end to it, whatever it is, and nips like a crab. Ah, no, you don't!" He pulled his hand out in a flash. "Shove in a book quickly. Now it can't get out."

"What was it?" asked Eustace.

"It was something that wanted very much to get hold of me. I felt what seemed like a thumb and forefinger. Give me some brandy."

"How are we to get it out of there?"

"What about a landing net?"

"No good. It would be too smart for us. I tell you, Saunders, it can cover the ground far faster than I can walk. But I think I see how we can manage it. The two books at the end of the shelf are big ones that go right back against the wall. The others are very thin. I'll take out one at a time, and you slide the rest along until we have it squashed between the end two."

It certainly seemed to be the best plan. One by one, as they took out the books, the space behind grew smaller and smaller. There was something in it that was certainly very much alive. Once they caught sight of fingers pressing outward for a way of escape. At last they had it pressed between the two big books.

"There's muscle there, if there isn't flesh and blood," said Saunders, as he held them together. "It seems to be a hand right enough, too. I suppose this is a sort of infectious hallucination. I've read about such cases before."

"Infectious fiddlesticks!" said Eustace, his face white with anger; "bring the thing downstairs. We'll get it back into the box."

It was not altogether easy, but they were successful at last. "Drive in the screws," said Eustace, "we won't run any risks. Put the box in this old desk of mine. There's nothing in it that I want. Here's the key. Thank goodness, there's nothing wrong with the lock."

"Quite a lively evening," said Saunders. "Now let's hear more about your uncle."

They sat up together until early morning. Saunders had no desire for sleep. Eustace was trying to explain and to forget: to conceal from himself a fear that he had never felt before—the fear of walking alone down the long corridor to his bedroom.

III

"Whatever it was," said Eustace to Saunders on the following morning, "I propose that we drop the subject. There's nothing to keep us here for the next ten days. We'll motor up to the Lakes and get some climbing."

"And see nobody all day, and sit bored to death with each other every night. Not for me, thanks. Why not run up to town? Run's the exact word in this case, isn't it? We're both in such a blessed funk. Pull yourself together, Eustace, and let's have another look at the hand."

"As you like," said Eustace; "there's the key." They went into the library and opened the desk. The box was as they had left it on the previous night.

"What are you waiting for?" asked Eustace.

"I am waiting for you to volunteer to open the lid. However, since you seem to funk it, allow me. There doesn't seem to be the likelihood of any rumpus this morning, at all events." He opened the lid and picked out the hand.

"Cold?" asked Eustace.

"Tepid. A bit below blood-heat by the feel. Soft and supple too. If it's the embalming, it's a sort of embalming I've never seen before. Is it your uncle's hand?"

"Oh, yes, it's his all right," said Eustace. "I should know those long thin fingers anywhere. Put it back in the box, Saunders. Never mind about the screws. I'll lock the desk, so that there'll be no chance of its getting out. We'll compromise by motoring up to town for a week. If we get off soon after lunch we ought to be at Grantham or Stamford by night."

"Right," said Saunders; "and to-morrow—Oh, well, by to-morrow we shall have forgotten all about this beastly thing."

If when the morrow came they had not forgotten, it was certainly true that at the end of the week they were able to tell a very vivid ghost story at the little supper Eustace gave on Hallow E'en.

"You don't want us to believe that it's true, Mr. Borlsover? How perfectly awful!"

"I'll take my oath on it, and so would Saunders here; wouldn't you, old chap?"

"Any number of oaths," said Saunders. "It was a long thin hand, you know, and it gripped me just like that."

"Don't, Mr. Saunders! Don't! How perfectly horrid! Now tell us another one, do. Only a really creepy one, please!"

"Here's a pretty mess!" said Eustace on the following day as he threw a letter across the table to Saunders. "It's your affair, though. Mrs. Merrit, if I understand it, gives a month's notice."

"Oh, that's quite absurd on Mrs. Merrit's part," Saunders replied. "She doesn't know what she's talking about. Let's see what she says."

"DEAR SIR," he read, "this is to let you know that I must give you a month's notice as from Tuesday the 13th. For a long time I've felt the place too big for me, but when Jane Parfit, and Emma Laidlaw go off with scarcely as much as an 'if you please,' after frightening the wits out of the other girls, so that they can't turn out a room by themselves or walk alone down the stairs for fear of treading on half-frozen toads or hearing it run along the passages at night, all I can say is that it's no place for me. So I must ask you, Mr. Borlsover, sir, to find a new housekeeper that has no objection to large and lonely houses, which some people do say, not that I believe them for a minute, my poor mother always having been a Wesleyan, are haunted.
"Yours faithfully,
"ELIZABETH MERRIT.
"P.S.—I should be obliged if you would give my respects to Mr. Saunders. I hope that he won't run no risks with his cold."

"Saunders," said Eustace, "you've always had a wonderful way with you in dealing with servants. You mustn't let poor old Merrit go."

"Of course she shan't go," said Saunders. "She's probably only angling for a rise in salary. I'll write to her this morning."

"No; there's nothing like a personal interview. We've had enough of town. We'll go back to-morrow, and you must work your cold for all it's worth. Don't forget that it's got on to the chest, and will require weeks of feeding up and nursing."

"All right. I think I can manage Mrs. Merrit."

But Mrs. Merrit was more obstinate than he had thought. She was very sorry to hear of Mr. Saunders's cold, and how he lay awake all night in London coughing; very sorry indeed. She'd change his room for him gladly, and get the south room aired. And wouldn't he have a basin of hot bread and milk last thing at night? But she was afraid that she would have to leave at the end of the month.

"Try her with an increase of salary," was the advice of Eustace.

It was no use. Mrs. Merrit was obdurate, though she knew of a Mrs. Handyside who had been housekeeper to Lord Gargrave, who might be glad to come at the salary mentioned.

"What's the matter with the servants, Morton?" asked Eustace that evening when he brought the coffee into the library. "What's all this about Mrs. Merrit wanting to leave?"

"If you please, sir, I was going to mention it myself. I have a confession to make, sir. When I found your note asking me to open that desk and take out the box with the rat, I broke the lock as you told me, and was glad to do it, because I could hear the animal in the box making a great noise, and I thought it wanted food. So I took out the box, sir, and got a cage, and was going to transfer it, when the animal got away."

"What in the world are you talking about? I never wrote any such note."

"Excuse me, sir, it was the note I picked up here on the floor on the day you and Mr. Saunders left. I have it in my pocket now."

It certainly seemed to be in Eustace's handwriting. It was written in pencil, and began somewhat abruptly.

"Get a hammer, Morton," he read, "or some other tool, and break open the lock in the old desk in the library. Take out the box that is inside. You need not do anything else. The lid is already open. Eustace Borlsover."

"And you opened the desk?"

"Yes, sir; and as I was getting the cage ready the animal hopped out."

"What animal?"

"The animal inside the box, sir."

"What did it look like?"

"Well, sir, I couldn't tell you," said Morton nervously; "my back was turned, and it was halfway down the room when I looked up."

"What was its color?" asked Saunders; "black?"

"Oh, no, sir, a grayish white. It crept along in a very funny way, sir. I don't think it had a tail."

"What did you do then?"

"I tried to catch it, but it was no use. So I set the rat-traps and kept the library shut. Then that girl Emma Laidlaw left the door open when she was cleaning, and I think it must have escaped."

"And you think it was the animal that's been frightening the maids?"

"Well, no, sir, not quite. They said it was—you'll excuse me, sir—a hand that they saw. Emma trod on it once at the bottom of the stairs. She thought then it was a half-frozen toad, only white. And then Parfit was washing up the dishes in the scullery. She wasn't thinking about anything in particular. It was close on dusk. She took her hands out of the water and was drying them absent-minded like on the roller towel, when she found that she was drying someone else's hand as well, only colder than hers."

"What nonsense!" exclaimed Saunders.

"Exactly, sir; that's what I told her; but we couldn't get her to stop."

"You don't believe all this?" said Eustace, turning suddenly towards the butler.

"Me, sir? Oh, no, sir! I've not seen anything."

"Nor heard anything?"

"Well, sir, if you must know, the bells do ring at odd times, and there's nobody there when we go; and when we go round to draw the blinds of a night, as often as not somebody's been there before us. But as I says to Mrs. Merrit, a young monkey might do wonderful things, and we all know that Mr. Borlsover has had some strange animals about the place."

"Very well, Morton, that will do."

"What do you make of it?" asked Saunders when they were alone. "I mean of the letter he said you wrote."

"Oh, that's simple enough," said Eustace. "See the paper it's written on? I stopped using that years ago, but there were a few odd sheets and envelopes left in the old desk. We never fastened up the lid of the box before locking it in. The hand got out, found a pencil, wrote this note, and shoved it through a crack on to the floor where Morton found it. That's plain as daylight."

"But the hand couldn't write?"

"Couldn't it? You've not seen it do the things I've seen," and he told Saunders more of what had happened at Eastbourne.

"Well," said Saunders, "in that case we have at least an explanation of the legacy. It was the hand which wrote unknown to your uncle that letter to your solicitor, bequeathing itself to you. Your uncle had no more to do with that request than I. In fact, it would seem that he had some idea of this automatic writing, and feared it."

"Then if it's not my uncle, what is it?"

"I suppose some people might say that a disembodied spirit had got your uncle to educate and prepare a little body for it. Now it's got into that little body and is off on its own."

"What are we to do?"

"We'll keep our eyes open," said Saunders, "and try to catch it. If we can't do that, we shall have to wait till the bally clock-work runs down. After all, if it's flesh and blood, it can't live for ever."

For two days nothing happened. Then Saunders saw it sliding down the banister in the hall. He was taken unawares, and lost a full second before he started in pursuit, only to find that the thing had escaped him. Three days later, Eustace, writing alone in the library at night, saw it sitting on an open book at the other end of the room. The fingers crept over the page, feeling the print as if it were reading; but before he had time to get up from his seat, it had taken the alarm and was pulling itself up the curtains. Eustace watched it grimly as it hung on to the cornice with three fingers, flicking thumb and forefinger at him in an expression of scornful derision.

"I know what I'll do," he said. "If I only get it into the open I'll set the dogs on to it."

He spoke to Saunders of the suggestion.

"It's a jolly good idea," he said; "only we won't wait till we find it out of doors. We'll get the dogs. There are the two terriers and the under-keeper's Irish mongrel that's on to rats like a flash. Your spaniel has not got spirit enough for this sort of game." They brought the dogs into the house, and the keeper's Irish mongrel chewed up the slippers, and the terriers tripped up Morton as he waited at table; but all three were welcome. Even false security is better than no security at all.

For a fortnight nothing happened. Then the hand was caught, not by the dogs, but by Mrs. Merrit's gray parrot. The bird was in the habit of periodically removing the pins that kept its seed and water tins in place, and of escaping through the holes in the side of the cage. When once at liberty Peter would show no inclination to return, and would often be about the house for days. Now, after six consecutive weeks of captivity, Peter had again discovered a new means of unloosing his bolts and was at large, exploring the tapestried forests of the curtains and singing songs in praise of liberty from cornice and picture rail.

"It's no use your trying to catch him," said Eustace to Mrs. Merrit, as she came into the study one afternoon towards dusk with a step-ladder. "You'd much better leave Peter alone. Starve him into surrender, Mrs. Merrit, and don't leave bananas and seed about for him to peck at when he fancies he's hungry. You're far too soft-hearted."

"Well, sir, I see he's right out of reach now on that picture rail, so if you wouldn't mind closing the door, sir, when you leave the room, I'll bring his cage in to-night and put some meat inside it. He's that fond of meat, though it does make him pull out his feathers to suck the quills. They *do* say that if you cook——"

"Never mind, Mrs. Merrit," said Eustace, who was busy writing. "That will do; I'll keep an eye on the bird."

There was silence in the room, unbroken but for the continuous whisper of his pen.

"Scratch poor Peter," said the bird. "Scratch poor old Peter!"

"Be quiet, you beastly bird!"

"Poor old Peter! Scratch poor Peter, do."

"I'm more likely to wring your neck if I get hold of you." He looked up at the picture rail, and there was the hand holding on to a hook with three fingers, and slowly scratching the head of the parrot with the fourth. Eustace ran to the bell and pressed it hard; then across to the window, which he closed with a bang. Frightened by the noise the parrot shook its wings preparatory to flight, and as it did so the fingers of the hand got hold of it by the throat. There was a shrill scream from Peter as he fluttered across the room, wheeling round in circles that ever descended, borne down under the weight that clung to him. The bird dropped at last quite suddenly, and Eustace saw fingers and feathers rolled into an inextricable mass on the floor. The struggle abruptly ceased as finger and thumb squeezed the neck; the bird's eyes rolled up to show the whites, and there was a faint, half-choked gurgle. But before the fingers had time to loose their hold, Eustace had them in his own.

"Send Mr. Saunders here at once," he said to the maid who came in answer to the bell. "Tell him I want him immediately."

Then he went with the hand to the fire. There was a ragged gash across the back where the bird's beak had torn it, but no blood oozed from the wound. He noticed with disgust that the nails had grown long and discolored.

"I'll burn the beastly thing," he said. But he could not burn it. He tried to throw it into the flames, but his own hands, as if restrained by some old primitive feeling, would not let him. And so Saunders found him pale and irresolute, with the hand still clasped tightly in his fingers.

"I've got it at last," he said in a tone of triumph.

"Good; let's have a look at it."

"Not when it's loose. Get me some nails and a hammer and a board of some sort."

"Can you hold it all right?"

"Yes; the thing's quite limp; tired out with throttling poor old Peter, I should say."

"And now," said Saunders when he returned with the things, "what are we going to do?"

"Drive a nail through it first, so that it can't get away; then we can take our time examining it."

"Do it yourself," said Saunders. "I don't mind helping you with guinea-pigs occasionally when there's something to be learned; partly because I don't fear a guinea-pig's revenge. This thing's different."

"All right, you miserable skunk. I won't forget the way you've stood by me."

He took up a nail, and before Saunders had realised what he was doing had driven in through the hand, deep into the board.

"Oh, my aunt," he giggled hysterically, "look at it now," for the hand was writhing in agonized contortions, squirming and wriggling upon the nail like a worm upon the hook.

"Well," said Saunders, "you've done it now. I'll leave you to examine it."

"Don't go, in heaven's name. Cover it up, man, cover it up! Shove a cloth over it! Here!" and he pulled off the antimacassar from the back of a chair and wrapped the board in it. "Now get the keys from my pocket and open the safe. Chuck the other things out. Oh, Lord, it's getting itself into frightful knots! and open it quick!" He threw the thing in and banged the door.

"We'll keep it there till it dies," he said. "May I burn in hell if I ever open the door of that safe again."

Mrs. Merrit departed at the end of the month. Her successor certainly was more successful in the management of the servants. Early in her rule she declared that she would stand no nonsense, and gossip soon withered and died. Eustace Borlsover went back to his old way of life. Old habits crept over and covered his new experience. He was, if anything, less morose, and showed a greater inclination to take his natural part in country society.

"I shouldn't be surprised if he marries one of these days," said Saunders. "Well, I'm in no hurry for such an event. I know Eustace far too well for the future Mrs. Borlsover to like me. It will be the same old story again: a long friendship slowly made —marriage—and a long friendship quickly forgotten."

IV

But Eustace Borlsover did not follow the advice of his uncle and marry. He was too fond of old slippers and tobacco. The cooking, too, under Mrs. Handyside's management was excellent, and she seemed, too, to have a heaven-sent faculty in knowing when to stop dusting.

Little by little the old life resumed its old power. Then came the burglary. The men, it was said, broke into the house by way of the conservatory. It was really little more than an attempt, for they only succeeded in carrying away a few pieces of plate from the pantry. The safe in the study was certainly found open and empty, but, as Mr. Borlsover informed the police inspector, he had kept nothing of value in it during the last six months.

"Then you're lucky in getting off so easily, sir," the man replied. "By the way they have gone about their business, I should say they were experienced cracksmen. They must have caught the alarm when they were just beginning their evening's work."

"Yes," said Eustace, "I suppose I am lucky."

"I've no doubt," said the inspector, "that we shall be able to trace the men. I've said that they must have been old hands at the game. The way they got in and opened the safe shows that. But there's one little thing that puzzles me. One of them was careless enough not to wear gloves, and I'm bothered if I know what he was trying to do. I've traced his finger-marks on the new varnish on the window sashes in every one of the downstairs rooms. They are very distinct ones too."

"Right hand or left, or both?" asked Eustace.

"Oh, right every time. That's the funny thing. He must have been a foolhardy fellow, and I rather think it was him that wrote that." He took out a slip of paper from his pocket. "That's what he wrote, sir. 'I've got out, Eustace Borlsover, but I'll be back before long.' Some gaol bird just escaped, I suppose. It will make it all the easier for us to trace him. Do you know the writing, sir?"

"No," said Eustace; "it's not the writing of anyone I know."

"I'm not going to stay here any longer," said Eustace to Saunders at luncheon. "I've got on far better during the last six months than ever I expected, but I'm not going to run the risk of seeing that thing again. I shall go up to town this afternoon. Get

Morton to put my things together, and join me with the car at Brighton on the day after to-morrow. And bring the proofs of those two papers with you. We'll run over them together."

"How long are you going to be away?"

"I can't say for certain, but be prepared to stay for some time. We've stuck to work pretty closely through the summer, and I for one need a holiday. I'll engage the rooms at Brighton. You'll find it best to break the journey at Hitchin. I'll wire to you there at the Crown to tell you the Brighton address."

The house he chose at Brighton was in a terrace. He had been there before. It was kept by his old college gyp, a man of discreet silence, who was admirably partnered by an excellent cook. The rooms were on the first floor. The two bedrooms were at the back, and opened out of each other. "Saunders can have the smaller one, though it is the only one with a fireplace," he said. "I'll stick to the larger of the two, since it's got a bathroom adjoining. I wonder what time he'll arrive with the car."

Saunders came about seven, cold and cross and dirty. "We'll light the fire in the dining-room," said Eustace, "and get Prince to unpack some of the things while we are at dinner. What were the roads like?"

"Rotten; swimming with mud, and a beastly cold wind against us all day. And this is July. Dear old England!"

"Yes," said Eustace, "I think we might do worse than leave dear old England for a few months."

They turned in soon after twelve.

"You oughtn't to feel cold, Saunders," said Eustace, "when you can afford to sport a great cat-skin lined coat like this. You do yourself very well, all things considered. Look at those gloves, for instance. Who could possibly feel cold when wearing them?"

"They are far too clumsy though for driving. Try them on and see," and he tossed them through the door on to Eustace's bed, and went on with his unpacking. A minute later he heard a shrill cry of terror. "Oh, Lord," he heard, "it's in the glove! Quick, Saunders, quick!" Then came a smacking thud. Eustace had thrown it from him. "I've chucked it into the bathroom," he gasped, "it's hit the wall and fallen into the bath. Come now if you want to help." Saunders, with a lighted candle in his hand, looked over the edge of the bath. There it was, old and maimed, dumb and blind, with a ragged hole in the middle, crawling, staggering, trying to creep up the slippery sides, only to fall back helpless.

"Stay there," said Saunders. "I'll empty a collar box or something, and we'll jam it in. It can't get out while I'm away."

"Yes, it can," shouted Eustace. "It's getting out now. It's climbing up the plug chain. No, you brute, you filthy brute, you don't! Come back, Saunders, it's getting away from me. I can't hold it; it's all slippery. Curse its claw! Shut the window, you idiot! The top too, as well as the bottom. You utter idiot! It's got out!" There was the sound of something dropping on to the hard flagstones below, and Eustace fell back fainting.

For a fortnight he was ill.

"I don't know what to make of it," the doctor said to Saunders. "I can only suppose that Mr. Borlsover has suffered some great emotional shock. You had better let me send someone to help you nurse him. And by all means indulge that whim of his never to be left alone in the dark. I would keep a light burning all night if I were you. But he *must* have more fresh air. It's perfectly absurd this hatred of open windows."

Eustace, however, would have no one with him but Saunders. "I don't want the other men," he said. "They'd smuggle it in somehow. I know they would."

"Don't worry about it, old chap. This sort of thing can't go on indefinitely. You know I saw it this time as well as you. It wasn't half so active. It won't go on living much longer, especially after that fall. I heard it hit the flags myself. As soon as you're a bit stronger we'll leave this place; not bag and baggage, but with only the clothes on our backs, so that it won't be able to hide anywhere. We'll escape it that way. We won't give any address, and we won't have any parcels sent after us. Cheer up, Eustace! You'll be well enough to leave in a day or two. The doctor says I can take you out in a chair to-morrow."

"What have I done?" asked Eustace. "Why does it come after me? I'm no worse than other men. I'm no worse than you, Saunders; you know I'm not. It was you who were at the bottom of that dirty business in San Diego, and that was fifteen years ago."

"It's not that, of course," said Saunders. "We are in the twentieth century, and even the parsons have dropped the idea of your old sins finding you out. Before you caught the hand in the library it was filled with pure malevolence—to you and all mankind. After you spiked it through with that nail it naturally forgot about other people, and concentrated its attention on you. It was shut up in the safe, you know, for nearly six months. That gives plenty of time for thinking of revenge."

Eustace Borlsover would not leave his room, but he thought that there might be something in Saunders's suggestion to leave Brighton without notice. He began rapidly to regain his strength.

"We'll go on the first of September," he said.

The evening of August 31st was oppressively warm. Though at midday the windows had been wide open, they had been shut an hour or so before dusk. Mrs. Prince had long since ceased to wonder at the strange habits of the gentlemen on the first floor. Soon after their arrival she had been told to take down the heavy curtains in the two bedrooms, and day by day the rooms had seemed to grow more bare. Nothing was left lying about.

"Mr. Borlsover doesn't like to have any place where dirt can collect," Saunders had said as an excuse. "He likes to see into all the corners of the room."

"Couldn't I open the window just a little?" he said to Eustace that evening. "We're simply roasting in here, you know."

"No, leave well alone. We're not a couple of boarding-school misses fresh from a course of hygiene lectures. Get the chessboard out."

They sat down and played. At ten o'clock Mrs. Prince came to the door with a note. "I am sorry I didn't bring it before," she said, "but it was left in the letter-box."

"Open it, Saunders, and see if it wants answering."

It was very brief. There was neither address nor signature.

"Will eleven o'clock to-night be suitable for our last appointment?"

"Who is it from?" asked Borlsover.

"It was meant for me," said Saunders. "There's no answer, Mrs. Prince," and he put the paper into his pocket. "A dunning letter from a tailor; I suppose he must have got wind of our leaving."

It was a clever lie, and Eustace asked no more questions. They went on with their game.

On the landing outside Saunders could hear the grandfather's clock whispering the seconds, blurting out the quarter-hours.

"Check!" said Eustace. The clock struck eleven. At the same time there was a gentle knocking on the door; it seemed to come from the bottom panel.

"Who's there?" asked Eustace.

There was no answer.

"Mrs. Prince, is that you?"

"She is up above," said Saunders; "I can hear her walking about the room."

"Then lock the door; bolt it too. Your move, Saunders."

While Saunders sat with his eyes on the chessboard, Eustace walked over to the window and examined the fastenings. He did the same in Saunders's room and the bathroom. There were no doors between the three rooms, or he would have shut and locked them too.

"Now, Saunders," he said, "don't stay all night over your move. I've had time to smoke one cigarette already. It's bad to keep an invalid waiting. There's only one possible thing for you to do. What was that?"

"The ivy blowing against the window. There, it's your move now, Eustace."

"It wasn't the ivy, you idiot. It was someone tapping at the window," and he pulled up the blind. On the outer side of the window, clinging to the sash, was the hand.

"What is it that it's holding?"

"It's a pocket-knife. It's going to try to open the window by pushing back the fastener with the blade."

"Well, let it try," said Eustace. "Those fasteners screw down; they can't be opened that way. Anyhow, we'll close the shutters. It's your move, Saunders. I've played."

But Saunders found it impossible to fix his attention on the game. He could not understand Eustace, who seemed all at once to have lost his fear. "What do you say to some wine?" he asked.

"You seem to be taking things coolly, but I don't mind confessing that I'm in a blessed funk."

"You've no need to be. There's nothing supernatural about that hand, Saunders. I mean it seems to be governed by the laws of time and space. It's not the sort of thing that vanishes into thin air or slides through oaken doors. And since that's so, I defy it to get in here. We'll leave the place in the morning. I for one have bottomed the depths of fear. Fill your glass, man! The windows are all shuttered, the door is locked and bolted. Pledge me my uncle Adrian! Drink, man! What are you waiting for?"

Saunders was standing with his glass half raised. "It can get in," he said hoarsely; "it can get in! We've forgotten. There's the fire-place in my bedroom. It will come down the chimney."

"Quick!" said Eustace, as he rushed into the other room; "we haven't a minute to lose. What can we do? Light the fire, Saunders. Give me a match, quick!"

"They must be all in the other room. I'll get them."

"Hurry, man, for goodness' sake! Look in the bookcase! Look in the bathroom! Here, come and stand here; I'll look."

"Be quick!" shouted Saunders. "I can hear something!"

"Then plug a sheet from your bed up the chimney. No, here's a match." He had found one at last that had slipped into a crack in the floor.

"Is the fire laid? Good, but it may not burn. I know—the oil from that old reading-lamp and this cotton-wool. Now the match, quick! Pull the sheet away, you fool! We don't want it now."

There was a great roar from the grate as the flames shot up. Saunders had been a fraction of a second too late with the sheet. The oil had fallen on to it. It, too, was burning.

"The whole place will be on fire!" cried Eustace, as he tried to beat out the flames with a blanket. "It's no good! I can't manage it. You must open the door, Saunders, and get help."

Saunders ran to the door and fumbled with the bolts. The key was stiff in the lock.

"Hurry!" shouted Eustace; "the whole place is ablaze!"

The key turned in the lock at last. For half a second Saunders stopped to look back. Afterwards he could never be quite sure as to what he had seen, but at the time he thought that something black and charred was creeping slowly, very slowly, from the masses of flames towards Eustace Borlsover. For a moment he thought of returning to his friend, but the noise and the smell of the burning sent him running down the passage crying, "Fire! Fire!" He rushed to the telephone to summon help, and then back to the bathroom—he should have thought of that before—for water. As he burst open the bedroom door there came a scream of terror which ended suddenly, and then the sound of a heavy fall.

●

THERE IS A tradition (which I have heard from persons of honour), that as the Protector Seymour and his Duchess were walking in the gallery at Sheen (in Surrey), both of them did see a hand with a bloody sword come out of the wall. He was afterwards beheaded.

—JOHN AUBREY

ADAM AND EVE AND PINCH ME

A. E. Coppard is to my taste one of the few great artists of the short story. If he should fail in his own time to take a place with us comparable to that of Tolstoi in Russia, or of de Maupassant in France, it will be because of a subtlety —where subtlety is called for—that never relents for considerations of popular taste. The following story should be read with the mind's full attention, as it tells of an adventure of the mind and spirit.—EDITOR.

A. E. Coppard

ADAM AND EVE AND PINCH ME

And in the whole of his days, vividly at the end of the afternoon—he repeated it again and again to himself —the kind country spaces had *never* absorbed *quite* so rich a glamour of light, so miraculous a bloom of clarity. He could feel streaming in his own mind, in his bones, the same crystalline brightness that lay upon the land. Thoughts and images went flowing through him as easily and amiably as fish swim in their pools; and as idly, too, for one of his speculations took up the theme of his family name. There was such an agreeable oddness about it, just as there was about all the luminous sky today, that it touched him as just a little remarkable. What *did* such a name connote, signify, or symbolize? It was a rann of a name, but it had euphony!

Then again, like the fish, his ambulating fancy flashed into other shallows, and he giggled as he paused, peering at the buds in the brake. Turning back towards his house again he could see, beyond its roofs, the spire of the Church tinctured richly as the vane: all round him was a new grandeur upon the grass of the fields, and the spare trees had shadows below that seemed to support them in the manner of a plinth, more real than themselves, and the dykes and any chance heave of the level fields were underlined, as if for special emphasis, with long shades of mysterious blackness.

With a little drift of emotion that had at other times assailed him in the wonder and ecstasy of pure light, Jaffa Codling pushed through the slit in the back hedge and stood within his own garden. The gardener was at work. He could hear the voices of the children about the lawn at the other side of the house. He was very happy, and the place was beautiful, a fine white many-windowed house rising from a lawn bowered with plots of mould, turretted with shrubs, and overset with a vast walnut tree. This house had deep clean eaves, a roof of faint coloured slates that, after rain, glowed dully, like onyx or jade, under the red chimneys, and half-way up at one end was a balcony set with black balusters. He went to a French window that stood open and stepped into the dining room. There was no-one within, and, on that lonely instant, a strange feeling of emptiness dropped upon him. The clock ticked almost as if it had been caught in some indecent act; the air was dim and troubled after that glory outside. Well, now, he would go up at once to the study and write down for his new book the ideas and images he had accumulated—beautiful rich thoughts they were —during that wonderful afternoon. He went to mount the stairs and he was passed by one of the maids; humming a silly song she brushed past him rudely, but he was an easy-going man—maids were unteachably tiresome—and reaching the landing he sauntered towards his room. The door stood slightly open and he could hear voices within. He put his hand upon the door . . . it would not open any further. What the devil . . . he pushed—like the bear in the tale—and he pushed, and he pushed—was there something against it on the other side? He put his shoulder to it . . . some wedge must be there, and *that* was extraordinary. Then his whole apprehension was swept up and whirled as by an avalanche— Mildred, his wife, was in there; he could hear her speaking to a man in fair soft tones and the rich phrases that could be used only by a woman yielding a deep affection for him. Codling kept still. Her words burned on his mind and thrilled him as if spoken to himself. There was a movement in the room, then utter silence. He again thrust savagely at the partly open door, but he could not stir it. The silence within continued. He beat upon the door with his fists, crying: "Mildred, Mildred!" There was no response, but he could hear the rocking arm chair commence to swing to and fro. Pushing his hand round the edge of the door he tried to thrust his head between the opening. There was not space for this, but he could just peer into the corner of a mirror hung near, and this is what he saw: the chair at one end of its swing, a man sitting in it, and upon one arm of it Mildred, the beloved woman, with her lips upon the man's face, caressing him with her hands. Codling made another effort to get into the room—as vain as it was violent. "Do you hear me, Mildred?" he shouted. Apparently neither of them heard him; they rocked to and fro while he gazed stupefied. What, in the name of God, . . . What this . . . was she bewitched . . . were there such things after all as magic, devilry!

He drew back and held himself quite steadily. The chair stopped swaying, and the room grew awfully still. The sharp ticking of the clock in the hall rose upon the house like the tongue of some perfunctory mocker. Couldn't they hear the clock? . . . Couldn't they hear his heart? He had to put his hand upon his heart, for, surely, in that great silence inside there, they would hear its beat, growing so loud now that it seemed almost to stun him! Then in a queer way he found himself reflecting, observing, analysing his own actions and intentions. He found some of them to be just a little spurious, counterfeit. He felt it would be easy, so perfectly easy to flash in one blast of anger and annihilate the two. He would do nothing of the kind. There was no occasion for it. People didn't really do that sort of thing, or, at least, not with a genuine passion. There was no need for anger. His curiosity was satisfied, quite satisfied, he was certain, he had not the remotest interest in the man. A welter of unexpected thoughts swept upon his mind as he stood there. As a writer of books he was often stimulated by the emotions and impulses of other people, and now his own surprise was beginning to intrigue him, leaving him, O, quite unstirred emotionally, but interesting him profoundly.

He heard the maid come stepping up the stairway again, humming her silly song. He did not want a scene, or to be caught eavesdropping, and so turned quickly to another door. It was locked. He sprang to one beyond it; the handle would not turn. "Bah! what's *up* with 'em?" But the girl was now upon him, carrying a tray of coffee things. "O, Mary!" he exclaimed casually, "I . . ." To his astonishment the girl stepped past him as if she did not hear or see him, tapped open the door of his study, entered, and closed the door behind her. Jaffa Codling then got really angry. "Hell! were the blasted servants in it!" He dashed to the door again and tore at the handle. It would not even turn, and, though he wrenched with fury at it, the room was utterly sealed against him. He went away for a chair with which to smash the effrontery of that door. No, he wasn't angry, either with his wife or this fellow—Gilbert, she had called him—who had a strangely familiar aspect as far as he had been able to take it in; but when one's servants . . . faugh!

The door opened and Mary came forth smiling demurely. He was a few yards further along the corridor at that moment. "Mary!" he shouted, "leave the door open!" Mary carefully closed it and turned her back on him. He sprang after her with bad words bursting from him as she went towards the stairs and flitted lightly down, humming all the way as if in derision. He leaped downwards after her three steps at a time, but she trotted with amazing swiftness into the kitchen and slammed the door in his face. Codling stood, but kept his hands carefully away from the door, kept them behind him. "No, no," he whispered cunningly, "there's something fiendish about door handles today, I'll go and get a bar, or a butt of timber," and, jumping out into the garden for some such thing, the miracle happened to him. For it was nothing else than a miracle, the unbelievable, the impossible, simple and laughable if you will, but having as much validity as any miracle can ever invoke. It was simple and laughable because by all the known physical laws he should have collided with his gardener, who happened to pass the window with his wheelbarrow as Codling jumped out on to the path. And it was unbelievable that they should not, and impossible that they *did* not collide; and it was miraculous, because Codling stood for a brief moment in the garden path and the wheelbarrow of Bond, its contents, and Bond himself passed apparently through the figure of Codling as if he were so much air, as if he were not a living breathing man but just a common ghost. There was no impact, just a momentary breathlessness. Codling stood and looked at the retreating figure going on utterly unaware of him. It is interesting to record that Codling's first feelings were mirthful. He giggled. He was jocular. He ran along in front of the gardener, and let him pass through him once more; then after him again; he scrambled into the man's barrow, and was wheeled about by this incomprehensible thick-headed gardener who was dead to all his master's efforts to engage his attention. Presently he dropped the wheelbarrow and went away, leaving Codling to cogitate upon the occurrence. There was no room for doubt, some essential part of him had become detached from the obviously not less vital part. He felt he was essential because he was responding to the experience, he was re-acting in the normal way to normal stimuli, although he happened for the time being to be invisible to his fellows and unable to communicate with them. How had it come about—this queer thing? How could he discover what part of him had cut loose, as it were? There was no question of this being death; death wasn't funny, it wasn't a joke; he had still all his human instincts. You didn't get angry with a faithless wife or joke with a fool of a gardener if you were dead, certainly not! He had realized enough of himself to know he was the usual man of instincts, desires, and prohibitions, complex and contradictory; his family history for a million or two years would have denoted that, not explicitly—obviously impossible—but suggestively. He had found himself doing things he had no desire to do, doing things he had a desire *not* to do, thinking thoughts that had no contiguous meaning, no meanings that could be related to his general experience. At odd times he had been chilled—aye, and even agreeably surprised—at the immense potential evil in himself. But still, this was no mere Jekyll and Hyde affair, that a man and his own ghost should separately inhabit the same world was a horse of quite another colour. The other part of him was alive and active somewhere . . . as alive . . . as alive . . . yes, as *he* was, but dashed if he knew where! What a lark when they got back to each other and compared notes! In his tales he had brooded over so many imagined personalities, followed in the track of so many psychological enigmas that he *had* felt at times a stranger to himself. What if, after all, that brooding had given him the faculty of projecting this figment of himself into the world of men. Or was he some unrealized latent element of being without its natural integument, doomed now to drift over the ridge of the world for ever. Was it his personality, his spirit? Then how was the dashed thing working? Here was he with the most wonderful happening in human experience, and he couldn't differentiate or disinter things. He was like a new Adam flung into some old Eden.

There was Bond tinkering about with some plants a dozen yards in front of him. Suddenly his three children came round from the other side of the house, the youngest boy leading them, carrying in his hand a small sword which was made, not of steel, but of some more brightly shining material; indeed it seemed at one moment to be of gold, and then again of flame, transmuting everything in its neighbourhood into the likeness of flame, the hair of the little girl Eve, a part of Adam's tunic; and the fingers of the boy Gabriel as he held the sword were like pale tongues of fire. Gabriel, the youngest boy, went up to the gardener and gave the sword into his hands, saying: "Bond, is this sword any good?" Codling saw the gardener take the weapon and examine it with a careful sort of smile; his great gnarled hands became immediately transparent, the blood could be seen moving diligently about the veins. Codling was so interested in the sight that he did not gather in the gardener's reply. The little boy was dissatisfied and repeated his question, "No, but Bond, *is* this sword any good?" Codling rose, and stood by invisible. The three beautiful children were grouped about the great angular figure of the gardener in his soiled clothes, looking up now into his face, and now at the sword, with anxiety in all their puckered eyes. "Well, Marse Gabriel," Codling could hear him reply, "as far as a sword goes, it may be a good un, or it may be a bad un, but, good as it is, it can never be anything but a bad thing." He then gave it back to them; the boy Adam held the haft of it, and the girl Eve rubbed the blade with curious fingers. The younger boy stood looking up at the gardener with unsatisfied gaze. "But, Bond, *can't* you say if this sword's any *good?*" Bond turned to his spade and trowels. "Mebbe the shape of it's wrong, Marse Gabriel, though it seems a pretty handy size." Saying this he moved off across the lawn. Gabriel turned to his brother and sister and took the sword from them; they all followed after the gardener and once more Gabriel made enquiry: "Bond, is this sword any *good?*" The gardener again took it and made a few passes in the air like a valiant soldier at exercise. Turning then, he lifted a bright curl from the head of Eve and cut it off with a sweep of the weapon. He held it up to look at it critically and then let it fall to the ground. Codling sneaked behind him and, picking it up, stood stupidly looking at it. "Mebbe, Marse Gabriel," the gardener was saying, "it ud be better made of steel, but it has a smartish edge on it." He went to pick up the barrow but Gabriel seized it with a spasm of anger, and cried out: "No, no, Bond, will you say, just yes or no, Bond, is this sword any *good?*" The gardener stood still, and looked down at the little boy, who repeated his question—"just yes or no, Bond!" "No, Marse Gabriel!" "Thank you, Bond!" replied the child with dignity, "That's all we wanted to know," and calling to his mates to follow him, he ran away to the other side of the house.

Codling stared again at the beautiful lock of hair in his hand, and felt himself grow so angry that he picked up a strange looking flower pot at his feet and hurled it at the retreating gardener. It struck Bond in the middle of the back and, passing clean through him, broke on the wheel of his barrow, but Bond seemed to be quite unaware of this catastrophe. Codling rushed after, and, taking the gardener by the throat, he yelled, "Damn you, will you tell me what all this means?" But Bond proceeded calmly about his work unnoticing, carrying his master about as if he were a clinging vapour, or a scarf hung upon his neck. In a few moments, Codling dropped exhausted to the ground. "What . . . O Hell . . . what, what am I to do?" he groaned. "What has happened to me? What shall I *do?* What *can* I do?" He looked at the broken flower pot. "Did I invent that?" He pulled out his watch. "That's a real watch, I hear it ticking, and it's six o'clock." Was he dead or disembodied or mad? What was this infernal lapse of identity? And who the devil, yes, who was it upstairs with Mildred? He jumped to his feet and hurried to the window; it was shut; to the door, it was fastened; he was powerless to open either. Well! well! this was experimental psychology with a vengeance, and he began to chuckle again. He'd have to write to McDougall about it. Then he turned and saw Bond wheeling across the lawn towards him again. "*Why* is that fellow always shoving that infernal green barrow around?" he asked, and, the fit of fury seizing him again, he rushed towards Bond, but, before he reached him, the three children danced into the garden again, crying, with great excitement, "Bond, O Bond!" The gardener stopped and set down the terrifying barrow; the children crowded about him, and Gabriel held out another shining thing, asking: "Bond, is this box any good?" The gardener took the box and at once his eyes lit up with interest and delight. "O, Marse Gabriel, where'd ye get it? Where'd ye get it?" "Bond," said the boy impatiently, "Is the box any *good?*" "Any good?" echoed the man, "Why, Marse Gabriel, Marse Adam, Miss Eve, look yere!" Holding it down in front of them, he lifted the lid from the box and a bright coloured bird flashed out and flew round and round above their heads. "O," screamed Gabriel with delight, "It's a kingfisher!" "That's what it is," said Bond, "a kingfisher!" "Where?" asked Adam. "Where?" asked Eve. "There it flies—round the fountain—see it? see it!" "No," said Adam. "No," said Eve.

"O, do, do, see it," cried Gabriel, "here it comes, it's coming!" and, holding his hands on high, and standing on his toes, the child cried out as happy as the bird which Codling saw flying above them.

"I can't see it," said Adam.

"Where is it, Gaby?" asked Eve.

"O, you stupids," cried the boy, "*There* it goes. There it goes . . . there . . . it's gone!"

He stood looking brightly at Bond, who replaced the lid.

"What shall we do now?" he exclaimed eagerly. For reply, the gardener gave the box into his hand, and walked off with the barrow. Gabriel took the box over to the fountain. Codling, unseen, went after him, almost as excited as the boy; Eve and her brother followed. They sat upon the stone tank that held the falling water. It was difficult for the child to unfasten the lid; Codling attempted to help him, but he was powerless. Gabriel looked up into his father's face and smiled. Then he stood up and said to the others:

"Now, *do* watch it this time."

They all knelt carefully beside the water. He lifted the lid and, behold, a fish like a gold carp, but made wholly of fire, leaped from the box into the fountain. The man saw it dart down into

the water, he saw the water bubble up behind it, he heard the hiss
that the junction of fire and water produced, and saw a little track
of steam follow the bubbles about the tank until the figure of the
fish was consumed and disappeared. Gabriel, in ecstasies, turned
to his sister with blazing happy eyes, exclaiming:

"There! Evey!"

"What was it?" asked Eve, nonchalantly, "I didn't see anything."

"More didn't I," said Adam.

"Didn't you see that lovely fish?"

"No," said Adam.

"No," said Eve.

"O, stupids," cried Gabriel, "it went right past the bottom of
the water."

"Let's get a fishin' hook," said Adam.

"No, no, no," said Gabriel, replacing the lid of the box.
"O no."

Jaffa Codling had remained on his knees staring at the water
so long that, when he looked around him again, the children had
gone away. He got up and went to the door, and that was closed;
the windows, fastened. He went moodily to a garden bench and sat
on it with folded arms. Dusk had begun to fall into the shrubs and
trees, the grass to grow dull, the air chill, the sky to muster its
gloom. Bond had overturned his barrow, stalled his tools in the
lodge, and gone to his home in the village. A curious cat came
round the house and surveyed the man who sat chained to his
seven-horned dilemma. It grew dark and fearfully silent. Was
the world emtpy now? Some small thing, a snail, perhaps, crept
among the dead leaves in the hedge, with a sharp, irritating noise.
A strange flood of mixed thoughts poured through his mind until
at last one idea disentangled itself, and he began thinking with
tremendous fixity of little Gabriel. He wondered if he could brood
or meditate, or "will" with sufficient power to bring him into the
garden again. The child had just vaguely recognized him for a
moment at the waterside. He'd try that dodge, telepathy was a
mild kind of a trick after so much of the miraculous. If he'd lost
his blessed body, at least the part that ate and smoked and talked
to Mildred . . . He stopped as his mind stumbled on a strange
recognition. . . . What a joke, of course . . . idiot . . . not to

have seen *that*. He stood up in the garden with joy . . . of course, *he* was upstairs with Mildred, it was himself, the other bit of him, that Mildred had been talking to. What a howling fool he'd been.

He found himself concentrating his mind on the purpose of getting the child Gabriel into the garden once more, but it was with a curious mood that he endeavoured to establish this relationship. He could not fix his will into any calm intensity of power, or fixity of purpose, or pleasurable mental ecstasy. The utmost force seemed to come with a malicious threatening splenetic "entreaty." That damned snail in the hedge broke the thread of his meditation; a dog began to bark sturdily from a distant farm; the faculties of his mind became joggled up like a child's picture puzzle, and he brooded unintelligibly upon such things as skating and steam engines, and Elizabethan drama so lapped about with themes like jealousy and chastity. Really now, Shakespeare's Isabella was the most consummate snob in . . . He looked up quickly to his wife's room and saw Gabriel step from the window to the balcony as if he were fearful of being seen. The boy lifted up his hands and placed the bright box on the rail of the balcony. He looked up at the faint stars for a moment or two, and then carefully released the lid of the box. What came out of it and rose into the air appeared to Codling to be just a piece of floating light, but as it soared above the roof he saw it grow to be a little ancient ship, with its hull and fully set sails and its three masts all of faint primrose flame colour. It cleaved through the air, rolling slightly as a ship through the wave, in widening circles above the house, making a curving ascent until it lost the shape of a vessel and became only a moving light hurrying to some sidereal shrine. Codling glanced at the boy on the balcony, but in that brief instant something had happened, the ship had burst like a rocket and released three coloured drops of fire which came falling slowly, leaving beautiful grey furrows of smoke in their track. Gabriel leaned over the rail with outstretched palms, and, catching the green star and the blue one as they drifted down to him, he ran with a rill of laughter back into the house. Codling sprang forward just in time to catch the red star; it lay vividly blasting his own palm for a monstrous second, and then, slipping through, was gone. He stared at the ground, at the balcony, the sky, and then heard an exclamation . . . his wife stood at his side.

"Gilbert! How you frightened me!" she cried, "I thought you were in your room; come along in to dinner." She took his arm and they walked up the steps into the dining room together. "Just a moment," said her husband, turning to the door of the room. His hand was upon the handle, which turned easily in his grasp, and he ran upstairs to his own room. He opened the door. The light was on, the fire was burning brightly, a smell of cigarette smoke about, pen and paper upon his desk, the Japanese bookknife, the gilt matchbox, everything all right, no one there. He picked up a book from his desk. . . . *Monna Vanna*. His bookplate was in it—*Ex Libris—Gilbert Cannister*. He put it down beside the green dish; two yellow oranges were in the green dish, and two most deliberately green Canadian apples rested by their side. He went to the door and swung it backwards and forwards quite easily. He sat on his desk trying to piece the thing together, glaring at the print and the book-knife and the smart matchbox, until his wife came up behind him exclaiming: "Come along, Gilbert!"

"Where are the kids, old man?" he asked her, and, before she replied, he had gone along to the nursery. He saw the two cots, his boy in one, his girl in the other. He turned whimsically to Mildred, saying, "There *are* only two, *are* there?" Such a question did not call for reply, but he confronted her as if expecting some assuring answer. She was staring at him with her bright beautiful eyes.

"Are there?" he repeated.

"How strange you should ask me that now!" she said. . . . "If you're a very good man . . . perhaps . . ."

"Mildred!"

She nodded brightly.

He sat down in the rocking chair, but got up again saying to her gently—"We'll call him Gabriel."

"But, suppose——"

"No, no," he said, stopping her lovely lips, "I know all about him." And he told her a pleasant little tale.

●

WHERE THEIR FIRE IS NOT QUENCHED

The theme of *Clorinda Walks in Heaven* is used in a very different fashion in this story, which was written at about the same time and published in *Uncanny Stories*, 1923. Coppard's version plays with a metaphysical concept, without passing judgment. Miss Sinclair is more seriously concerned with the moral problem of good and evil; and those who believe in orthodox conceptions of the afterlife would do well to ponder the rather grim outcome of this tale if they ever are tempted to make the unfortunate decision of Harriott Leigh.—EDITOR.

May Sinclair

WHERE THEIR FIRE IS NOT QUENCHED

There was nobody in the orchard. Harriott Leigh went out, carefully, through the iron gate into the field. She had made the latch slip into its notch without a sound.

The path slanted widely up to the field from the orchard gate to the stile under the elder tree. George Waring waited for her there.

Years afterwards, when she thought of George Waring she smelt the sweet, hot, wine-scent of the elder flowers. Years afterwards, when she smelt elder flowers she saw George Waring, with his beautiful, gentle face, like a poet's or a musician's, his black-blue eyes, and sleek, olive-brown hair. He was a naval lieutenant.

Yesterday he had asked her to marry him and she had consented. But her father hadn't, and she had come to tell him that and say good-bye before he left her. His ship was to sail the next day.

He was eager and excited. He couldn't believe that anything could stop their happiness, that anything he didn't want to happen could happen.

"Well?" he said.

"He's a perfect beast, George. He won't let us. He says we're too young."

"I was twenty last August," he said, aggrieved.

"And I shall be seventeen in September."

"And this is June. We're quite old, really. How long does he mean us to wait?"

"Three years."

"Three years before we can be engaged even—Why, we might be dead."

She put her arms round him to make him feel safe. They kissed; and the sweet, hot, wine-scent of the elder flowers mixed with their kisses. They stood, pressed close together, under the elder tree.

Across the yellow fields of charlock they heard the village clock strike seven. Up in the house a gong clanged.

"Darling, I must go," she said.

"Oh stay—stay *five* minutes."

He pressed her close. It lasted five minutes, and five more. Then he was running fast down the road to the station, while Harriott went along the field-path, slowly, struggling with her tears.

"He'll be back in three months," she said. "I can live through three months."

But he never came back. There was something wrong with the engines of his ship, the *Alexandra*. Three weeks later she went down in the Mediterranean, and George with her.

Harriott said she didn't care how soon she died now. She was quite sure it would be soon, because she couldn't live without him.

Five years passed.

The two lines of beech trees stretched on and on, the whole length of the Park, a broad green drive between. When you came to the middle they branched off right and left in the form of a cross, and at the end of the right arm there was a white stucco pavilion with pillars and a three-cornered pediment like a Greek temple. At the end of the left arm, the west entrance to the Park, double gates and a side door.

Harriott, on her stone seat at the back of the pavilion, could see Stephen Philpotts the very minute he came through the side door.

He had asked her to wait for him there. It was the place he always chose to read his poems aloud in. The poems were a pretext. She knew what he was going to say. And she knew what she would answer.

There were elder bushes in flower at the back of the pavilion, and Harriott thought of George Waring. She told herself that George was nearer to her now than he could ever have been, living. If she married Stephen she would not be unfaithful, because she loved him with another part of herself. It was not as though Stephen were taking George's place. She loved Stephen with her soul, in an unearthly way.

But her body quivered like a stretched wire when the door opened and the young man came towards her down the drive under the beech trees.

She loved him; she loved his slenderness, his darkness and sallow whiteness, his black eyes lighting up with the intellectual flame, the way his black hair swept back from his forehead, the way he walked, tiptoe, as if his feet were lifted with wings.

He sat down beside her. She could see his hands tremble. She felt that her moment was coming; it had come.

"I wanted to see you alone because there's something I must say to you. I don't quite know how to begin. . . ."

Her lips parted. She panted lightly.

"You've heard me speak of Sybill Foster?"

Her voice came stammering, "N-no, Stephen. Did you?"

"Well, I didn't mean to, till I knew it was all right. I only heard yesterday."

"Heard what?"

"Why, that she'll have me. Oh, Harriott—do you know what it's like to be terribly happy?"

She knew. She had known just now, the moment before he

told her. She sat there, stone-cold and stiff, listening to his rap-
tures, listening to her own voice saying she was glad.

Ten years passed.

Harriott Leigh sat waiting in the drawing-room of a small
house in Maida Vale. She had lived there ever since her father's
death two years before.

She was restless. She kept on looking at the clock to see if
it was four, the hour that Oscar Wade had appointed. She was
not sure that he would come, after she had sent him away yesterday.

She now asked herself, why, when she had sent him away
yesterday, she had let him come to-day. Her motives were not
altogether clear. If she really meant what she had said then, she
oughtn't to let him come to her again. Never again.

She had shown him plainly what she meant. She could see
herself, sitting very straight in her chair, uplifted by a passionate
integrity, while he stood before her, hanging his head, ashamed
and beaten; she could feel again the throb in her voice as she kept
on saying that she couldn't, she couldn't; he must see that she
couldn't; that no, nothing would make her change her mind; she
couldn't forget he had a wife; that he must think of Muriel.

To which he had answered savagely: "I needn't. That's all
over. We only live together for the look of the thing."

And she, serenely, with great dignity: "And for the look of
the thing, Oscar, we must leave off seeing each other. Please go."

"Do you mean it?"

"Yes. We must never see each other again."

And he had gone then, ashamed and beaten.

She could see him, squaring his broad shoulders to meet the
blow. And she was sorry for him. She told herself she had been
unnecessarily hard. Why shouldn't they see each other again, now
he understood where they must draw the line? Until yesterday the
line had never been very clearly drawn. To-day she meant to ask
him to forget what he had said to her. Once it was forgotten, they
could go on being friends as if nothing had happened.

It was four o'clock. Half-past. Five. She had finished tea,
and given him up when, between the half-hour and six o'clock, he
came.

He came as he had come a dozen times, with his measured,

deliberate, thoughtful tread, carrying himself well braced, with a sort of held-in arrogance, his great shoulders heaving. He was a man of about forty—broad and tall, lean-flanked and short-necked, his straight, handsome features showing small and even in the big square face and in the flush that swamped it. The close-clipped, reddish-brown moustache bristled forwards from the pushed-out upper lip. His small, flat eyes shone, reddish-brown, eager and animal.

She liked to think of him when he was not there, but always at the first sight of him she felt a slight shock. Physically, he was very far from her admired ideal. So different from George Waring and Stephen Philpotts.

He sat down, facing her.

There was an embarrassed silence, broken by Oscar Wade.

"Well, Harriott, you said I could come." He seemed to be throwing the responsibility on her.

"So I suppose you've forgiven me," he said.

"Oh, yes, Oscar, I've forgiven you."

He said she'd better show it by coming to dine with him somewhere that evening.

She could give no reason to herself for going. She simply went.

He took her to a restaurant in Soho. Oscar Wade dined well, even extravagantly, giving each dish its importance. She liked his extravagance. He had none of the mean virtues.

It was over. His flushed, embarrassed silence told her what he was thinking. But when he had seen her home, he left her at her garden gate. He had thought better of it.

She was not sure whether she were glad or sorry. She had had her moment of righteous exaltation and she had enjoyed it. But there was no joy in the weeks that followed. She had given up Oscar Wade because she didn't want him very much; and now she wanted him furiously, perversely, because she had given him up. Though he had no resemblance to her ideal, she couldn't live without him.

She dined with him again and again, till she knew Schnebler's Restaurant by heart, the white panelled walls picked out with gold; the white pillars, and the curling gold fronds of their capitals; the Turkey carpets, blue and crimson, soft under her feet;

the thick crimson velvet cushions, that clung to her skirts; the glitter of silver and glass on the innumerable white circles of the tables. And the faces of the diners, red, white, pink, brown, grey and sallow, distorted and excited; the curled mouths that twisted as they ate; the convoluted electric bulbs pointing, pointing down at them, under the red, crinkled shades. All shimmering in a thick air that the red light stained as wine stains water.

And Oscar's face, flushed with his dinner. Always, when he leaned back from the table and brooded in silence she knew what he was thinking. His heavy eyelids would lift; she would find his eyes fixed on hers, wondering, considering.

She knew now what the end would be. She thought of George Waring, and Stephen Philpotts, and of her life, cheated. She hadn't chosen Oscar, she hadn't really wanted him; but now he had forced himself on her she couldn't afford to let him go. Since George died no man had loved her, no other man ever would. And she was sorry for him when she thought of him going from her, beaten and ashamed.

She was certain, before he was, of the end. Only she didn't know when and where and how it would come. That was what Oscar knew.

It came at the close of one of their evenings when they had dined in a private sitting-room. He said he couldn't stand the heat and noise of the public restaurant.

She went before him, up a steep, red-carpeted stair to a white door on the second landing.

From time to time they repeated the furtive, hidden adventure. Sometimes she met him in the room above Schnebler's. Sometimes, when her maid was out, she received him at her house in Maida Vale. But that was dangerous, not to be risked too often.

Oscar declared himself unspeakably happy. Harriott was not quite sure. This was love, the thing she had never had, that she had dreamed of, hungered and thirsted for; but now she had it she was not satisfied. Always she looked for something just beyond it, some mystic, heavenly rapture, always beginning to come, that never came. There was something about Oscar that repelled her. But because she had taken him for her lover, she couldn't bring herself to admit that it was a certain coarseness. She looked another way and pretended it wasn't there. To justify herself, she fixed her mind on his good qualities, his generosities, his strength, the way he had built up his engineering business. She made him take her over his works, and show her his great dynamos. She made him lend her the books he read. But always, when she tried to talk to him he let her see that *that* wasn't what she was there for.

"My dear girl, we haven't time," he said. "It's waste of our priceless moments."

She persisted. "There's something wrong about it all if we can't talk to each other."

He was irritated. "Women never seem to consider that a man can get all the talk he wants from other men. What's wrong is our meeting in this unsatisfactory way. We ought to live together. It's the only sane thing. I would, only I don't want to break up Muriel's home and make her miserable."

"I thought you said she wouldn't care."

"My dear, she cares for her home and her position and the children. You forget the children."

Yes. She had forgotten the children. She had forgotten Muriel. She had left off thinking of Oscar as a man with a wife and children and a home.

He had a plan. His mother-in-law was coming to stay with Muriel in October and he would get away. He would go to Paris, and Harriott should come to him there. He could say he went on business. No need to lie about it; he *had* business in Paris.

He engaged rooms in an hotel in the rue de Rivoli. They spent two weeks there.

For three days Oscar was madly in love with Harriott and Harriott with him. As she lay awake she would turn on the light and look at him as he slept at her side. Sleep made him beautiful and innocent; it laid a fine, smooth tissue over his coarseness; it made his mouth gentle; it entirely hid his eyes.

In six days reaction had set in. At the end of the tenth day, Harriott, returning with Oscar from Montmartre, burst into a fit of crying. When questioned, she answered wildly that the Hotel Saint Pierre was too hideously ugly; it was getting on her nerves. Mercifully Oscar explained her state as fatigue following excitement. She tried hard to believe that she was miserable because her love was purer and more spiritual than Oscar's; but all the time she knew perfectly well she had cried from pure boredom. She was in love with Oscar, and Oscar bored her. Oscar was in love with her, and she bored him. At close quarters, day in and day out, each was revealed to the other as an incredible bore.

At the end of the second week she began to doubt whether she had ever been really in love with him.

Her passion returned for a little while after they got back to London. Freed from the unnatural strain which Paris had put on them, they persuaded themselves that their romantic temperaments were better fitted to the old life of casual adventure.

Then, gradually, the sense of danger began to wake in them. They lived in perpetual fear, face to face with all the chances of discovery. They tormented themselves and each other by imagining possibilities that they would never have considered in their first fine moments. It was as though they were beginning to ask themselves if it were, after all, worth while running such awful risks, for all they got out of it. Oscar still swore that if he had been free he would have married her. He pointed out that his intentions at any rate were regular. But she asked herself: Would I marry *him?* Marriage would be the Hotel Saint Pierre all over again, without any possibility of escape. But, if she wouldn't marry him, was she in love with him? That was the test. Perhaps it was a good thing he wasn't free. Then she told herself that these doubts were morbid, and that the question wouldn't arise.

One evening Oscar called to see her. He had come to tell her that Muriel was ill.

"Seriously ill?"

"I'm afraid so. It's pleurisy. May turn to pneumonia. We shall know one way or another in the next few days."

A terrible fear seized upon Harriott. Muriel might die of her pleurisy; and if Muriel died, she would have to marry Oscar. He was looking at her queerly, as if he knew what she was thinking, and she could see that the same thought had occurred to him and that he was frightened too.

Muriel got well again; but their danger had enlightened them. Muriel's life was now inconceivably precious to them both; she stood between them and that permanent union, which they dreaded and yet would not have the courage to refuse.

After enlightenment the rupture.

It came from Oscar, one evening when he sat with her in her drawing-room.

"Harriott," he said, "do you know I'm thinking seriously of settling down?"

"How do you mean, settling down?"

"Patching it up with Muriel, poor girl. . . . Has it never occurred to you that this little affair of ours can't go on for ever?"

"You don't want it to go on?"

"I don't want to have any humbug about it. For God's sake, let's be straight. If it's done, it's done. Let's end it decently."

"I see. You want to get rid of me."

"That's a beastly way of putting it."

"Is there any way that isn't beastly? The whole thing's beastly. I should have thought you'd have stuck to it now you've made it what you wanted. When I haven't an ideal, I haven't a single illusion, when you've destroyed everything you didn't want."

"What didn't I want?"

"The clean, beautiful part of it. The part *I* wanted."

"My part at least was real. It was cleaner and more beautiful than all that putrid stuff you wrapped it up in. You were a hypocrite, Harriott, and I wasn't. You're a hypocrite now if you say you weren't happy with me."

"I was never really happy. Never for one moment. There was always something I missed. Something you didn't give me. Perhaps you couldn't."

"No. I wasn't spiritual enough," he sneered.

"You were not. And you made me what you were."

"Oh, I noticed that you were always very spiritual *after* you'd got what you wanted."

"What I wanted?" she cried. "Oh, my God——"

"If you ever knew what you wanted."

"What—I—wanted," she repeated, drawing out her bitterness.

"Come," he said, "why not be honest? Face facts. I was awfully gone on you. You were awfully gone on me—once. We got tired of each other and it's over. But at least you might own we had a good time while it lasted."

"A good time?"

"Good enough for me."

"For you, because for you love only means one thing. Everything that's high and noble in it you dragged down to that, till there's nothing left for us but that. *That's* what you made of love."

Twenty years passed.

It was Oscar who died first, three years after the rupture. He did it suddenly one evening, falling down in a fit of apoplexy.

His death was an immense relief to Harriott. Perfect security had been impossible as long as he was alive. But now there wasn't a living soul who knew her secret.

Still, in the first moment of shock Harriott told herself that Oscar dead would be nearer to her than ever. She forgot how little she had wanted him to be near her, alive. And long before the twenty years had passed she had contrived to persuade herself that he had never been near to her at all. It was incredible that she had ever known such a person as Oscar Wade. As for their affair, she couldn't think of Harriott Leigh as the sort of woman to whom such a thing could happen. Schnebler's and the Hotel Saint Pierre ceased to figure among prominent images of her past. Her memories, if she had allowed herself to remember, would have clashed disagreeably with the reputation for sanctity which she had now acquired.

For Harriott at fifty-two was the friend and helper of the Reverend Clement Farmer, Vicar of St. Mary the Virgin, Maida Vale. She worked as a deaconess in his parish, wearing the uniform of a deaconess, the semi-religious gown, the cloak, the bonnet and veil, the cross and rosary, the holy smile. She was also secretary to the Maida Vale and Kilburn Home for Fallen Girls.

Her moments of excitement came when Clement Farmer, the lean, austere likeness of Stephen Philpotts, in his cassock and lace-bordered surplice, issued from the vestry, when he mounted the pulpit, when he stood before the altar rails and lifted up his arms in the Benediction; her moments of ecstasy when she received the Sacrament from his hands. And she had moments of calm happiness when his study door closed on their communion. All these moments were saturated with a solemn holiness.

And they were insignificant compared with the moment of her dying.

She lay dozing in her white bed under the black crucifix with the ivory Christ. The basins and medicine bottles had been cleared from the table by her pillow; it was spread for the last rites. The priest moved quietly about the room, arranging the candles, the Prayer Book and the Holy Sacrament. Then he drew a chair to her bedside and watched with her, waiting for her to come up out of her doze.

She woke suddenly. Her eyes were fixed upon him. She had a flash of lucidity. She was dying, and her dying made her supremely important to Clement Farmer.

"Are you ready?" he asked.

"Not yet. I think I'm afraid. Make me not afraid."

He rose and lit the two candles on the altar. He took down the crucifix from the wall and stood it against the foot-rail of the bed.

She sighed. That was not what she had wanted.

"You will not be afraid now," he said.

"I'm not afraid of the hereafter. I suppose you get used to it. Only it may be terrible just at first."

"Our first state will depend very much on what we are thinking of at our last hour."

"There'll be my confession," she said.

"And after it you will receive the Sacrament. Then you will have your mind fixed firmly upon God and your Redeemer. . . . Do you feel able to make your confession now, Sister? Everything is ready."

Her mind went back over her past and found Oscar Wade there. She wondered: Should she confess to him about Oscar Wade? One moment she thought it was possible; the next she knew that she couldn't. She could not. It wasn't necessary. For twenty years he had not been part of her life. No. She wouldn't confess about Oscar Wade. She had been guilty of other sins.

She made a careful selection.

"I have cared too much for the beauty of this world. . . . I have failed in charity to my poor girls. Because of my intense repugnance to their sin. . . . I have thought, often, about—people I love, when I should have been thinking about God."

After that she received the Sacrament.

"Now," he said, "there is nothing to be afraid of."

"I won't be afraid if—if you would hold my hand."

He held it. And she lay still a long time, with her eyes shut. Then he heard her murmuring something. He stooped close.

"This—is—dying. I thought it would be horrible. And it's bliss. . . . Bliss."

The priest's hand slackened, as if at the bidding of some wonder. She gave a weak cry.

"Oh—don't let me go."

His grasp tightened.

"Try," he said, "to think about God. Keep on looking at the crucifix."

"If I look," she whispered, "you won't let go my hand?"

"I will not let you go."

He held it till it was wrenched from him in the last agony.

She lingered for some hours in the room where these things had happened.

Its aspect was familiar and yet unfamiliar, and slightly repugnant to her. The altar, the crucifix, the lighted candles, suggested some tremendous and awful experience the details of which she was not able to recall. She seemed to remember that they had been connected in some way with the sheeted body on the bed; but the nature of the connection was not clear; and she did not associate the dead body with herself. When the nurse came in and laid it out, she saw that it was the body of a middle-aged woman. Her own living body was that of a young woman of about thirty-two.

Her mind had no past and no future, no sharp-edged, coherent memories, and no idea of anything to be done next.

Then, suddenly. the room began to come apart before her eyes, to split into shafts of floor and furniture and ceiling that shifted and were thrown by their commotion into different planes. They leaned slanting at every possible angle; they crossed and over-laid each other with a transparent mingling of dislocated perspectives, like reflections fallen on an interior seen behind glass.

The bed and the sheeted body slid away somewhere out of sight. She was standing by the door that still remained in position.

She opened it and found herself in the street, outside a building of yellowish-grey brick and freestone, with a tall slated spire.

Her mind came together with a palpable click of recognition. This object was the Church of St. Mary the Virgin, Maida Vale. She could hear the droning of the organ. She opened the door and slipped in.

She had gone back into a definite space and time, and recovered a certain limited section of coherent memory. She remembered the rows of pitch-pine benches, with their Gothic peaks and mouldings; the hanging rings of lights along the aisles of the nave; the high altar with its lighted candles, and the polished brass cross, twinkling. These things were somehow permanent and real, adjusted to the image that now took possession of her.

She knew what she had come there for. The service was over. The choir had gone from the chancel; the sacristan moved before the altar, putting out the candles. She walked up the middle aisle to a seat that she knew under the pulpit. She knelt down and covered her face with her hands. Peeping sideways through her fingers, she could see the door of the vestry on her left at the end of the north aisle. She watched it steadily.

Up in the organ loft the organist drew out the Recessional, slowly and softly, to its end in the two solemn, vibrating chords.

The vestry door opened and Clement Farmer came out, dressed in his black cassock. He passed before her, close, close outside the bench where she knelt. He paused at the opening. He was waiting for her. There was something he had to say.

She stood up and went towards him. He still waited. He didn't move to make way for her. She came close, closer than she had ever come to him, so close that his features grew indistinct. She bent her head back, peering short-sightedly, and found herself looking into Oscar Wade's face.

He stood still, horribly still, and close, barring her passage.

She drew back; his heaving shoulders followed her. He leaned forward, covering her with his eyes. She opened her mouth to scream and no sound came.

She was afraid to move lest he should move with her. The heaving of his shoulders terrified her.

One by one the lights in the side aisles were going out. The lights in the middle aisle would go next. They had gone. If she didn't get away she would be shut up with him there, in the appalling darkness.

She turned and moved towards the north aisle, groping, steadying herself by the book ledge.

When she looked back, Oscar Wade was not there.

Then she remembered that Oscar Wade was dead. Therefore, what she had seen was not Oscar; it was his ghost. He was dead; dead seventeen years ago. She was safe from him for ever.

When she came out on to the steps of the church she saw that the road it stood in had changed. It was not the road she remembered. The pavement on this side was raised slightly and covered in. It ran under a succession of arches. It was a long gallery walled with glittering shop windows on one side; on the other a line of tall grey columns divided it from the street.

She was going along the arcades of the rue de Rivoli. Ahead of her she could see the edge of an immense grey pillar jutting out. That was the porch of the Hotel Saint Pierre. The revolving glass doors swung forward to receive her; she crossed the grey, sultry vestibule under the pillared arches. She knew it. She knew the porter's shining, wine-coloured, mahogany pen on her left, and the shining, wine-coloured, mahogany barrier of the clerk's bureau on her right; she made straight for the great grey carpeted staircase; she climbed the endless flights that turned round and round the caged-in shaft of the well, past the latticed doors of the lift, and came up on to a landing that she knew, and into the long, ash-grey, foreign corridor lit by a dull window at one end.

It was there that the horror of the place came on her. She had no longer any memory of St. Mary's Church, so that she was unaware of her backward course through time. All space and time were here.

She remembered she had to go to the left, the left.

But there was something there; where the corridor turned by the window; at the end of all the corridors. If she went the other way she would escape it.

The corridor stopped there. A blank wall. She was driven back past the stairhead to the left.

At the corner, by the window, she turned down another long ash-grey corridor on her right, and to the right again where the night-light sputtered on the table-flap at the turn.

This third corridor was dark and secret and depraved. She

knew the soiled walls, and the warped door at the end. There was a sharp-pointed streak of light at the top. She could see the number on it now, 107.

Something had happened there. If she went in it would happen again.

Oscar Wade was in the room waiting for her behind the closed door. She felt him moving about in there. She leaned forward, her ear to the key-hole, and listened. She could hear the measured, deliberate, thoughtful footsteps. They were coming from the bed to the door.

She turned and ran; her knees gave way under her; she sank and ran on, down the long grey corridors and the stairs, quick and blind, a hunted beast seeking for cover, hearing his feet coming after her.

The revolving doors caught her and pushed her out into the street.

The strange quality of her state was this, that it had no time. She remembered dimly that there had once been a thing called time; but she had forgotten altogether what it was like. She was aware of things happening and about to happen; she fixed them by the place they occupied, and measured their duration by the space she went through.

So now she thought: If I could only go back and get to the place where it hadn't happened.

To get back farther——

She was walking now on a white road that went between broad grass borders. To the right and left were the long raking lines of the hills, curve after curve, shimmering in a thin mist.

The road dropped to the green valley. It mounted the humped bridge over the river. Beyond it she saw the twin gables of the grey house pricked up over the high, grey garden wall. The tall iron gate stood in front of it between the ball-topped stone pillars.

And now she was in a large, low-ceilinged room with drawn blinds. She was standing before the wide double bed. It was her father's bed. The dead body, stretched out in the middle under the drawn white sheet, was her father's body.

The outline of the sheet sank from the peak of the upturned

toes to the shin bone, and from the high bridge of the nose to the chin.

She lifted the sheet and folded it back across the breast of the dead man. The face she saw then was Oscar Wade's face, stilled and smoothed in the innocence of sleep, the supreme innocence of death. She stared at it, fascinated, in a cold, pitiless joy.

Oscar was dead.

She remembered how he used to lie like that beside her in the room in the Hotel Saint Pierre, on his back with his hands folded on his waist, his mouth half open, his big chest rising and falling. If he was dead, it would never happen again. She would be safe.

The dead face frightened her, and she was about to cover it up again when she was aware of a light heaving, a rhythmical rise and fall. As she drew the sheet up tighter, the hands under it began to struggle convulsively, the broad ends of the fingers appeared above the edge, clutching it to keep it down. The mouth opened; the eyes opened; the whole face stared back at her in a look of agony and horror.

Then the body drew itself forwards from the hips and sat up, its eyes peering into her eyes; he and she remained for an instant motionless, each held there by the other's fear.

Suddenly she broke away, turned and ran, out of the room, out of the house.

She stood at the gate, looking up and down the road, not knowing by which way she must go to escape Oscar. To the right, over the bridge and up the hill and across the downs she would come to the arcades of the rue de Rivoli and the dreadful grey corridors of the hotel. To the left the road went through the village.

If she could get further back she would be safe, out of Oscar's reach. Standing by her father's death-bed she had been young, but not young enough. She must get back to the place where she was younger still, to the Park and the green drive under the beech trees and the white pavilion at the cross. She knew how to find it. At the end of the village the high road ran right and left, east and west, under the Park walls; the south gate stood there at the top looking down the narrow street.

She ran towards it through the village, past the long grey

barns of Goodyer's farm, past the grocer's shop, past the yellow front and blue sign of the "Queen's Head," past the post office, with its one black window blinking under its vine, past the church and the yew-trees in the churchyard, to where the south gate made a delicate black pattern on the green grass.

These things appeared insubstantial, drawn back behind a sheet of air that shimmered over them like thin glass. They opened out, floated past and away from her; and instead of the high road and Park walls she saw a London street of dingy white façades, and instead of the south gate the swinging glass doors of Schnebler's Restaurant.

The glass doors swung open and she passed into the restaurant. The scene beat on her with the hard impact of reality: the white and gold panels, the white pillars and their curling gold capitals, the white circles of the tables, glittering, the flushed faces of the diners, moving mechanically.

She was driven forward by some irresistible compulsion to a table in the corner, where a man sat alone. The table napkin he was using hid his mouth, and jaw, and chest; and she was not sure of the upper part of the face above the straight, drawn edge. It dropped; and she saw Oscar Wade's face. She came to him, dragged, without power to resist; she sat down beside him, and he leaned to her over the table; she could feel the warmth of his red, congested face; the smell of wine floated towards her on his thick whisper.

"I knew you would come."

She ate and drank with him in silence, nibbling and sipping slowly, staving off the abominable moment it would end in.

At last they got up and faced each other. His long bulk stood before her, above her; she could almost feel the vibration of its power.

"Come," he said. "Come."

And she went before him, slowly, slipping out through the maze of the tables, hearing behind her Oscar's measured, deliberate, thoughtful tread. The steep, red-carpeted staircase rose up before her.

She swerved from it, but he turned her back.

"You know the way," he said.

At the top of the flight she found the white door of the room she knew. She knew the long windows guarded by drawn muslin blinds; the gilt looking-glass over the chimney-piece that reflected Oscar's head and shoulders grotesquely between two white porcelain babies with bulbous limbs and garlanded loins, she knew the sprawling stain on the drab carpet by the table, the shabby, infamous couch behind the screen.

They moved about the room, turning and turning in it like beasts in a cage, uneasy, inimical, avoiding each other.

At last they stood still, he at the window, she at the door, the length of the room between.

"It's no good your getting away like that," he said. "There couldn't be any other end to it—to what we did."

"But that *was* ended."

"Ended there, but not here."

"Ended for ever. We've done with it for ever."

"We haven't. We've got to begin again. And go on. And go on."

"Oh, no. No. Anything but that."

"There isn't anything else."

"We can't. We can't. Don't you remember how it bored us?"

"Remember? Do you suppose I'd touch you if I could help it? . . . That's what we're here for. We must. We must."

"No. No. I shall get away—now."

She turned to the door to open it.

"You can't," he said. "The door's locked."

"Oscar—what did you do that for?"

"We always did it. Don't you remember?"

She turned to the door again and shook it; she beat on it with her hands.

"It's no use, Harriott. If you got out now you'd only have to come back again. You might stave it off for an hour or so, but what's that in an immortality?"

"Immortality?"

"That's what we're in for."

"Time enough to talk about immortality when we're dead. . . . Ah——"

They were being drawn towards each other across the room, moving slowly, like figures in some monstrous and appalling dance, their heads thrown back over their shoulders, their faces turned from the horrible approach. Their arms rose slowly, heavy with intolerable reluctance; they stretched them out towards each other, aching, as if they held up an overpowering weight. Their feet dragged and were drawn.

Suddenly her knees sank under her; she shut her eyes; all her being went down before him in darkness and terror.

It was over. She had got away, she was going back, back, to the green drive of the Park, between the beech trees, where Oscar had never been, where he would never find her. When she passed through the south gate her memory became suddenly young and clean. She forgot the rue de Rivoli and the Hotel Saint Pierre; she forgot Schnebler's Restaurant and the room at the top of the stairs. She was back in her youth. She was Harriott Leigh going to wait for Stephen Philpotts in the pavilion opposite the west gate. She could feel herself, a slender figure moving fast over the grass between the lines of the great beech trees. The freshness of her youth was upon her.

She came to the heart of the drive where it branched right and left in the form of a cross. At the end of the right arm the white Greek temple, with its pediment and pillars, gleamed against the wood.

She was sitting on their seat at the back of the pavilion, watching the side door that Stephen would come in by.

The door was pushed open; he came towards her, light and young, skimming between the beech trees with his eager, tiptoeing stride. She rose up to meet him. She gave a cry.

"Stephen!"

It had been Stephen. She had seen him coming. But the man who stood before her between the pillars of the pavilion was Oscar Wade.

And now she was walking along the field-path that slanted from the orchard door to the stile; further and further back, to where young George Waring waited for her under the elder tree. The smell of the elder flowers came to her over the field. She could feel on her lips and in all her body the sweet, innocent excitement of her youth.

"George, oh, George?"

As she went along the field-path she had seen him. But the

man who stood waiting for her under the elder tree was Oscar Wade.

"I told you it's no use getting away, Harriott. Every path brings you back to me. You'll find me at every turn."

"But how did you get *here?*"

"As I got into the pavilion. As I got into your father's room, on to his death-bed. Because I *was* there. I am in all your memories."

"My memories are innocent. How could you take my father's place, and Stephen's, and George Waring's? You?"

"Because I did take them."

"Never. My love for *them* was innocent."

"Your love for me was part of it. You think the past affects the future. Has it never struck you that the future may affect the past? In your innocence there was the beginning of your sin. You *were* what you *were to be.*"

"I shall get away," she said.

"And, this time, I shall go with you."

The stile, the elder tree, and the field floated away from her. She was going under the beech trees down the Park drive towards the south gate and the village, slinking close to the right-hand row of trees. She was aware that Oscar Wade was going with her under the left-hand row, keeping even with her, step by step, and tree by tree. And presently there was grey pavement under her feet and a row of grey pillars on her right hand. They were walking side by side down the rue de Rivoli towards the hotel.

They were sitting together now on the edge of the dingy white bed. Their arms hung by their sides, heavy and limp, their heads drooped, averted. Their passion weighed on them with the unbearable, unescapable boredom of immortality.

"Oscar—how long will it last?"

"I can't tell you. I don't know whether *this* is one moment of eternity, or the eternity of one moment."

"It must end some time," she said. "Life doesn't go on for ever. We shall die."

"Die? We *have* died. Don't you know what this is? Don't you know where you are? This is death. We're dead, Harriott. We're in hell."

"Yes. There can't be anything worse than this."

"This isn't the worst. We're not quite dead yet, as long as we've life in us to turn and run and get away from each other; as long as we can escape into our memories. But when you've got back to the farthest memory of all and there's nothing beyond it —When there's no memory but this——

"In the last hell we shall not run away any longer; we shall find no more roads, no more passages, no more open doors. We shall have no need to look for each other.

"In the last death we shall be shut up in this room, behind that locked door, together. We shall lie here together, for ever and ever, joined so fast that even God can't put us asunder. We shall be one flesh and one spirit, one sin repeated for ever, and ever; spirit loathing flesh, flesh loathing spirit; you and I loathing each other."

"Why? Why?" she cried.

"Because that's all that's left us. That's what you made of love."

The darkness came down swamping, it blotted out the room. She was walking along a garden path between high borders of phlox and larkspur and lupin. They were taller than she was, their flowers swayed and nodded above her head. She tugged at the tall stems and had no strength to break them. She was a little thing.

She said to herself then that she was safe. She had gone back so far that she was a child again; she had the blank innocence of childhood. To be a child, to go small under the heads of the lupins, to be blank and innocent, without memory, was to be safe.

The walk led her out through a yew hedge on to a bright green lawn. In the middle of the lawn there was a shallow round pond in a ring of rockery cushioned with small flowers, yellow and white and purple. Gold-fish swam in the olive brown water. She would be safe when she saw the gold-fish swimming towards her. The old one with the white scales would come up first, pushing up his nose, making bubbles in the water.

At the bottom of the lawn there was a privet hedge cut by a broad path that went through the orchard. She knew what she would find there; her mother was in the orchard. She would lift her up in her arms to play with the hard red balls of the apples that hung from the trees. She had got back to the farthest memory of all; there was nothing beyond it.

There would be an iron gate in the wall of the orchard. It would lead into a field.

Something was different here, something that frightened her. An ash-grey door instead of an iron gate.

She pushed it open and came into the last corridor of the Hotel Saint Pierre.

●

CLIMAX FOR A GHOST STORY

"How EERIE!" said the girl, advancing cautiously. "—And what a heavy door!" She touched it as she spoke and it suddenly swung to with a click.

"Good Lord!" said the man, "I don't believe there's a handle inside. Why, you've locked us both in!"

"Not both of us. Only one of us," said the girl, and before his eyes she passed straight through the door, and vanished.

—I. A. IRELAND

THE SECOND KALANDAR'S TALE

A Kalandar is the Mahometan equivalent of a begging friar; and no-one will deny that the second Kalandar had good reason, after his adventures, to throw himself upon the bounty of his fellow men. I have rearranged the paragraphing for easier reading, and have omitted the notes, but Burton's text has not been altered. The episodes may give a helter-skelter effect, but so does the great book from which this section is taken. The entry of Shahrazad should not confuse the reader who comes here to the true *Nights* for the first time. She is the teller of all the stories, referred to only as each dawn breaks.—EDITOR.

Arabian Nights

THE SECOND KALANDAR'S TALE

Know, O my lady, that I was not born one-eyed and mine is a strange story; an it were graven with needle-graver on the eye-corners, it were a warner to whoso would be warned. I am a King, son of a King, and was brought up like a Prince. I learned intoning the Koran according the seven schools; and I read all manner books, and held disputations on their contents with the doctors and men of science; moreover I studied star-lore and the fair sayings of poets and I exercised myself in all branches of learning until I surpassed the people of my time; and my skill in calligraphy exceeded that of all the scribes; and my fame was bruited abroad over all climes and cities, and all the kings learned to know my name. Amongst others the King of Hind

heard of me and sent to my father to invite me to his court, with
offerings and presents and rarities such as befit royalties. So my
father fitted out six ships for me and my people; and we put to
sea and sailed for the space of a full month till we made the land.
Then we brought out the horses that were with us in the ships;
and, after loading the camels with our presents for the Prince, we
set forth inland. But we had marched only a little way, when behold, a dust-cloud up-flew, and grew until it walled the horizon
from view. After an hour or so the veil lifted and discovered beneath it fifty horsemen, ravening lions to the sight, in steel armour
dight. We observed them straightly and lo! they were cutters-off
of the highway, wild as wild Arabs. When they saw that we were
only four and had with us but the ten camels carrying the presents,
they dashed down upon us with lances at rest. We signed to them,
with our fingers, as it were saying, "We be messengers of the great
King of Hind, so harm us not!" but they answered on like wise,
"We are not in his dominions to obey nor are we subject to his
sway." Then they set upon us and slew some of my slaves and put
the lave to flight; and I also fled after I had gotten a wound, a
grievous hurt, whilst the Arabs were taken up with the money and
the presents which were with us. I went forth unknowing whither
I went, having become mean as I was mighty; and I fared on until
I came to the crest of a mountain where I took shelter for the night
in a cave. When day arose I set out again, nor ceased after this
fashion till I arrived at a fair city and a well-filled. Now it was the
season when Winter was turning away with his rime and to greet
the world with his flowers came Prime, and the young blooms were
springing and the streams flowed ringing, and the birds were
sweetly singing, as saith the poet concerning a certain city when
describing it:——

> A place secure from every thought of fear
> Safety and peace for ever lord it here:
> Its beauties seem to beautify its sons
> And as in Heaven its happy folk appear.

I was glad of my arrival for I was wearied with the way, and
yellow of face for weakness and want; but my plight was pitiable
and I knew not whither to betake me. So I accosted a Tailor sitting in his little shop and saluted him; he returned my salam, and

bade me kindly welcome and wished me well and entreated me gently and asked me of the cause of my strangerhood. I told him all my past from first to last; and he was concerned on my account and said, "O youth, disclose not thy secret to any: the King of this city is the greatest enemy thy father hath, and there is blood-wit between them and thou hast cause to fear for thy life." Then he set meat and drink before me; and I ate and drank and he with me; and we conversed freely till nightfall, when he cleared me a place in a corner of his shop and brought me a carpet and a coverlet. I tarried with him three days; at the end of which time he said to me, "Knowest thou no calling whereby to win thy living, O my son?" "I am learned in the law," I replied, "and a doctor of doctrine; an adept in art and science, a mathematician and a notable penman." He rejoined, "Thy calling is of no account in our city, where not a soul understandeth science or even writing or aught save money-making." Then said I, "By Allah, I know nothing but what I have mentioned;" and he answered, "Gird thy middle and take thee a hatchet and a cord, and go and hew wood in the wold for thy daily bread, till Allah send thee relief; and tell none who thou art lest they slay thee." Then he bought me an axe and a rope and gave me in charge to certain wood-cutters; and with these guardians I went forth into the forest, where I cut fuel-wood the whole of my day and came back in the evening bearing my bundle on my head. I sold it for half a dinar, with part of which I bought provisions and laid by the rest. In such work I spent a whole year and when this was ended I went out one day, as was my wont, into the wilderness; and, wandering away from my companions, I chanced on a thickly grown lowland in which there was an abundance of wood. So I entered and I found the gnarled stump of a great tree and loosened the ground about it and shovelled away the earth. Presently my hatchet rang upon a copper ring; so I cleared away the soil and behold, the ring was attached to a wooden trap-door. This I raised and there appeared beneath it a staircase. I descended the steps to the bottom and came to a door, which I opened and found myself in a noble hall strong of structure and beautifully built, where was a damsel like a pearl of great price, whose favour banished from my heart all grief and cark and care; and whose soft speech healed the soul in despair and captivated the wise and ware. Her figure measured five feet in height; her breasts were firm and upright; her cheek a very garden of delight; her colour lively bright; her face gleamed like dawn through curly tresses which gloomed like night, and above the snows of her bosom glittered teeth of a pearly white. As the poet said of one like her:——

> Slim-waisted loveling, jetty hair-encrowned
> A wand of willow on a sandy mound:

And as saith another:——

> Four things that meet not, save they here unite
> To shed my heart-blood and to rape my sprite:
> Brilliantest forehead; tresses jetty bright;
> Cheeks rosy red and stature beauty-dight.

When I looked upon her I prostrated myself before Him who had created her, for the beauty and loveliness He had shaped in her, and she looked at me and said, "Art thou man or Jinni?"

"I am a man," answered I, and she, "Now who brought thee to this place where I have abided five-and-twenty years without even yet seeing man in it?"

Quoth I (and indeed I found her words wonder-sweet, and my heart was melted to the core by them), "O my lady, my good fortune led me hither for the dispelling of my cark and care."

Then I related to her all my mishap from first to last, and my case appeared to her exceeding grievous; so she wept and said, "I will tell thee my story in my turn. I am the daughter of the King Ifitamus, lord of the Islands of Abnús, who married me to my cousin, the son of my paternal uncle; but on my wedding night an Ifrit named Jirjís bin Rajmús, first cousin that is, mother's sister's son, of Iblís, the Foul Fiend, snatched me up and, flying away with me like a bird, set me down in this place, whither he conveyed all I needed of fine stuffs, raiment and jewels and furniture, and meat and drink and other else. Once in every ten days he comes here and lies a single night with me, and then wends his way, for he took me without the consent of his family; and he hath agreed with me that if ever I need him by night or day, I have only to pass my hand over yonder two lines engraved upon the alcove, and he will appear to me before my fingers cease touching.

Four days have now passed since he was here; and, as there remain six days before he come again, say me, wilt thou abide with me five days, and go hence the day before his coming?"

I replied, "Yes, and yes again! O rare, if all this be not a dream!"

Hereat she was glad and, springing to her feet, seized my hand and carried me through an arched doorway to a Hammam-bath, a fair hall and richly decorate. I doffed my clothes, and she doffed hers; then we bathed and she washed me; and when this was done we left the bath, and she seated me by her side upon a high divan, and brought me sherbet scented with musk. When we felt cool after the bath, she set food before me and we ate and fell to talking; but presently she said to me, "Lay thee down and take thy rest, for surely thou must be weary."

So I thanked her, my lady, and lay down and slept soundly, forgetting all that had happened to me. When I awoke I found her rubbing and shampooing my feet; so I again thanked her and blessed her and we sat for awhile talking. Said she, "By Allah, I was sad at heart, for that I have dwelt alone underground for these five-and-twenty years; and praise be to Allah, who hath sent me some one with whom I can converse!" Then she asked, "O youth, what sayest thou to wine?" and I answered, "Do as thou wilt."

Whereupon she went to a cupboard and took out a sealed flask of right old wine and set off the table with flowers and scented herbs and began to sing these lines:—

> Had we known of thy coming we fain had dispread
> The cores of our hearts or the balls of our eyes;
> Our cheeks as a carpet to greet thee had thrown
> And our eyelids had strown for thy feet to betread.

Now when she finished her verse I thanked her, for indeed love of her had gotten hold of my heart and my grief and anguish were gone. We sat at converse and carousal till nightfall, and with her I spent the night—such night never spent I in all my life! On the morrow delight followed delight till midday, by which time I had drunken wine so freely that I had lost my wits, and stood up, staggering to the right and to the left, and said "Come, O my charmer, and I will carry thee up from this underground vault and deliver thee from the spell of thy Jinni."

She laughed and replied "Content thee and hold thy peace: of every ten days one is for the Ifrit and the other nine are thine."

Quoth I (and in good sooth drink had got the better of me), "This very instant will I break down the alcove whereon is graven the talisman and summon the Ifrit that I may slay him, for it is a practice of mine to slay Ifrits!"

When she heard my words her colour waxed wan and she said, "By Allah, do not!" and she began repeating:——

> This is a thing wherein destruction lies
> I rede thee shun it an thy wits be wise.

And these also:——

> O thou who seekest severance, draw the rein
> Of thy swift steed nor seek o'ermuch t' advance;
> Ah stay! for treachery is the rule of life,
> And sweets of meeting end in severance.

I heard her verse but paid no heed to her words, nay, I raised my foot and administered to the alcove a mighty kick.

And Shahrazad perceived the dawn of day and ceased to say her permitted say. When it was the 13th night, she said,

It hath reached me, O auspicious King, that the second Kalandar thus continued his tale to the lady:——But when, O my mistress, I kicked that alcove with a mighty kick, behold, the air starkened and darkened and thundered and lightened; the earth trembled and quaked and the world became invisible. At once the fumes of wine left my head: I cried to her, "What is the matter?" and she replied, "The Ifrit is upon us! did I not warn thee of this? By Allah, thou hast brought ruin upon me; but fly for thy life and go up by the way thou camest down!"

So I fled up the staircase; but, in the excess of my fear, I forgot sandals and hatchet. And when I had mounted two steps I turned to look for them, and lo! I saw the earth cleave asunder, and there arose from it an Ifrit, a monster of hideousness, who said to the damsel "What trouble and pother be this wherewith thou disturbest me? What mishap hath betided thee?"

"No mishap hath befallen me," she answered, "save that my breast was straitened and my heart heavy with sadness! so I drank a little wine to broaden it and to hearten myself; then I rose to obey a call of Nature, but the wine had gotten into my head and I fell against the alcove."

"Thou liest, like the whore thou art!" shrieked the Ifrit; and he looked around the hall right and left till he caught sight of my axe and sandals and said to her, "What be these but the belongings of some mortal who hath been in thy society?"

She answered, "I never set eyes upon them till this moment: they must have been brought by thee hither cleaving to thy garments."

Quoth the Ifrit, "These words are absurd; thou harlot! thou strumpet!"

Then he stripped her stark naked and, stretching her upon the floor, bound her hands and feet to four stakes, like one crucified; and set about torturing and trying to make her confess. I could not bear to stand listening to her cries and groans; so I climbed the stair on the quake with fear; and when I reached the top I replaced the trap-door and covered it with earth. Then repented I of what I had done with penitence exceeding; and thought of the lady and her beauty and loveliness, and the tortures she was suffering at the hands of the accursed Ifrit, after her quiet life of five-and-twenty years; and how all that had happened to her was for the cause of me. I bethought me of my father and his kingly estate and how I had become a woodcutter; and how, after my time had been awhile serene, the world had again waxed turbid and troubled to me. So I wept bitterly and repeated this couplet:——

> What time Fate's tyranny shall most oppress thee
> Perpend! one day shall joy thee, one distress thee!

Then I walked till I reached the home of my friend, the Tailor, whom I found most anxiously expecting me; indeed he was, as the saying goes, on coals of fire for my account. And when he saw me he said, "All night long my heart hath been heavy, fearing for thee from wild beasts or other mischances. Now praise be to Allah for thy safety!"

I thanked him for his friendly solicitude and, retiring to my

corner, sat pondering and musing on what had befallen me; and
I blamed and chided myself for my meddlesome folly and my
frowardness in kicking the alcove. I was calling myself to account
when behold, my friend, the Tailor, came to me and said, "O
youth, in the shop there is an old man, a Persian, who seeketh
thee: he hath thy hatchet and thy sandals which he had taken to
the woodcutters, saying, 'I was going out at what time the
Mu'azzin began the call to dawn-prayer, when I chanced upon
these things and know not whose they are; so direct me to their
owner.' The woodcutters recognized thy hatchet and directed
him to thee: he is sitting in my shop, so fare forth to him and
thank him and take thine axe and sandals."

When I heard these words I turned yellow with fear and felt
stunned as by a blow; and, before I could recover myself, lo! the
floor of my private room clove asunder, and out of it rose the
Persian who was the Ifrit. He had tortured the lady with exceeding
tortures, natheless she would not confess to him aught; so he took
the hatchet and sandals and said to her, "As surely as I am Jirjis
of the seed of Iblis, I will bring thee back the owner of this and
these!" Then he went to the woodcutters with the pretence
aforesaid and, being directed to me, after waiting a while in the
shop till the fact was confirmed, he suddenly snatched me up as a
hawk snatcheth a mouse and flew high in air; but presently descended and plunged with me under the earth (I being aswoon the
while), and lastly set me down in the subterranean palace wherein
I had passed that blissful night. And there I saw the lady stripped
to the skin, her limbs bound to four stakes and blood welling from
her sides. At the sight my eyes ran over with tears; but the Ifrit
covered her person and said, "O wanton, is not this man thy lover?"

She looked upon me and replied, "I wot him not nor have I
ever seen him before this hour!"

Quoth the Ifrit, "What! this torture and yet no confessing";
and quoth she, "I never saw this man in my born days, and it is
not lawful in Allah's sight to tell lies on him."

"If thou know him not," said the Ifrit to her, "take this sword
and strike off his head."

She hent the sword in hand and came close up to me; and I
signalled to her with my eyebrows, my tears the while flowing
adown my cheeks. She understood me and made answer, also by

signs, "How couldst thou bring all this evil upon me?" and I rejoined after the same fashion, "This is the time for mercy and forgiveness." And the mute tongue of my case spake aloud saying:——

> Mine eyes were dragomans for my tongue betied
> And told full clear the love I fain would hide:
> When last we met and tears in torrents railed
> For tongue struck dumb my glances testified:
> She signed with eye-glance while her lips were mute;
> I signed with fingers and she kenned th' implied:
> Our eyebrows did all duty 'twixt us twain;
> And we being speechless Love spake loud and plain.

Then, O my mistress, the lady threw away the sword and said, "How shall I strike the neck of one I wot not, and who hath done me no evil? Such deed were not lawful in my law!" and she held her hand.

Said the Ifrit, " 'Tis grievous to thee to slay thy lover; and, because he hath lain with thee, thou endurest these torments and obstinately refusest to confess. After this it is clear to me that only like loveth and pitieth like." Then he turned to me and asked me, "O man, haply thou also dost not know this woman"; whereto I answered, "And pray who may she be? assuredly I never saw her till this instant."

"Then take the sword," said he, "and strike off her head and I will believe that thou wottest her not and will leave thee free to go, and will not deal hardly with thee."

I replied, "That will I do"; and, taking the sword went forward sharply and raised my hand to smite. But she signed to me with her eyebrows, "Have I failed thee in aught of love; and is it thus that thou requitest me?"

I understood what her looks implied and answered her with an eye-glance, "I will sacrifice my soul for thee." And the tongue of the case wrote in our hearts these lines:—

> How many a lover with his eyebrows speaketh
> To his beloved, as his passion pleadeth;
> With flashing eyne his passion he inspireth
> And well she seeth what his pleading needeth.

How sweet the look when each on other gazeth;
And with what swiftness and how sure it speedeth:
And this with eyebrows all his passion writeth;
And that with eyeballs all his passion readeth.

Then my eyes filled with tears to overflowing and I cast the sword from my hand saying, "O mighty Ifrit and hero, if a woman lacking wits and faith deem it unlawful to strike off my head, how can it be lawful for me, a man, to smite her neck whom I never saw in my whole life? I cannot do such misdeed though thou cause me drink the cup of death and perdition."

Then said the Ifrit, "Ye twain show the good understanding between you; but I will let you see how such doings end."

He took the sword, and struck off the lady's hands first, with four strokes, and then her feet; whilst I looked on and made sure of death and she farewelled me with her dying eyes. So the Ifrit cried at her, "Thou whorest and makest me a wittol with thine eyes"; and struck her so that her head went flying. Then he turned to me and said, "O mortal, we have it in our law that, when the wife committeth advowtry it is lawful for us to slay her. As for this damsel I snatched her away on her bride-night when she was a girl of twelve and she knew no one but myself. I used to come to her once every ten days and lie with her the night, under the semblance of a man, a Persian; and when I was well assured that she had cuckolded me, I slew her. But as for thee I am not well satisfied that thou hast wronged me in her; nevertheless I must not let thee go unharmed; so ask a boon of me and I will grant it."

Then I rejoiced, O my lady, with exceeding joy and said, "What boon shall I crave of thee?" He replied, "Ask me this boon; into what shape I shall bewitch thee; wilt thou be a dog, or an ass or an ape?"

I rejoined (and indeed I had hoped that mercy might be shown me), "By Allah, spare me, that Allah spare thee for sparing a Moslem and a man who never wronged thee." And I humbled myself before him with exceeding humility, and remained standing in his presence, saying, "I am sore oppressed by circumstance." He replied, "Talk me no long talk, it is in my power to slay thee; but I give thee instead thy choice."

Quoth I, "O thou Ifrit, it would besit thee to pardon me even as the Envied pardoned the Envier." Quoth he, "And how was that?" and I began to tell him

The Tale Of The Envier And The Envied

They relate, O Ifrit, that in a certain city were two men who dwelt in adjoining houses, having a common party-wall; and one of them envied the other and looked on him with an evil eye, and did his utmost endeavour to injure him; and, albeit at all times he was jealous of his neighbour, his malice at last grew on him till he could hardly eat or enjoy the sweet pleasures of sleep. But the Envied did nothing save prosper; and the more the other strove to injure him, the more he got and gained and throve.

At last the malice of his neighbour and the man's constant endeavour to work him a harm came to his knowledge; so he said, "By Allah! God's earth is wide enough for its people"; and, leaving the neighbourhood, he repaired to another city where he bought himself a piece of land in which was a dried up draw-well, old and in ruinous condition. Here he built him an oratory and, furnishing it with a few necessaries, took up his abode therein, and devoted himself to prayer and worshipping Allah Almighty; and Fakirs and holy mendicants flocked to him from all quarters; and his fame went abroad through the city and that country side.

Presently the news reached his envious neighbour, of what good fortune had befallen him, and how the city notables had become his disciples; so he travelled to the place and presented himself at the holy man's hermitage, and was met by the Envied with welcome and greeting and all honour. Then quoth the Envier, "I have a word to say to thee; and this is the cause of my faring hither, and I wish to give thee a piece of good news; so come with me to thy cell."

Thereupon the Envied arose and took the Envier by the hand, and they went in to the inmost part of the hermitage; but the Envier said, "Bid thy Fakirs retire to their cells, for I will not tell thee what I have to say, save in secret where none may hear us."

Accordingly the Envied said to his Fakirs, "Retire to your private cells:" and, when all had done as he bade them, he set

out with his visitor and walked a little way until the twain reached
the ruinous old well. And as they stood upon the brink the Envier
gave the Envied a push which tumbled him headlong into it, unseen of any; whereupon he fared forth, and went his ways, thinking to have slain him.

Now this well happened to be haunted by the Jann who,
seeing the case, bore him up and let him down little by little, till
he reached the bottom, when they seated him upon a large stone.
Then one of them asked his fellows, "Wot ye who be this man?"
and they answered, "Nay."

"This man," continued the speaker, "is the Envied hight who,
flying from the Envier, came to dwell in our city, and here
founded this holy house, and he hath edified us by his litanies
and his lections of the Koran; but the Envier set out and journeyed
till he rejoined him, and cunningly contrived to deceive him and
cast him into the well where we now are. But the fame of this
good man hath this very night come to the Sultan of our city who
designeth to visit him on the morrow on account of his daughter."

"What aileth his daughter?" asked one, and another answered,
"She is possessed of a spirit; for Maymun, son of Damdam, is
madly in love with her; but, if this pious man knew the remedy,
her cure could be as easy as could be."

Hereupon one of them inquired, "And what is the medicine?"
and he replied, "The black tom-cat which is with him in the oratory hath, on the end of his tail, a white spot, the size of a dirham;
let him pluck seven white hairs from the spot, then let him fumi-
gate her therewith and the Marid will flee from her and not return; so she shall be sane for the rest of her life."

All this took place, O Ifrit, within earshot of the Envied
who listened readily. When dawn broke and morn arose in sheen
and shone, the Fakirs went to seek the Shaykh and found him
climbing up the wall of the well; whereby he was magnified in
their eyes. Then, knowing that naught save the black tom-cat
could supply him with the remedy required, he plucked the seven
tail-hairs from the white spot and laid them by him; and hardly
had the sun risen ere the Sultan entered the hermitage, with the
great lords of his estate, bidding the rest of his retinue to remain
standing outside.

The Envied gave him a hearty welcome, and seating him by his side asked him, "Shall I tell thee the cause of thy coming?"

The King answered, "Yes."

He continued, "Thou hast come upon pretext of a visitation, but it is in thy heart to question me of thy daughter."

Replied the King, " 'Tis even so, O thou holy Shaykh"; and the Envied continued, "Send and fetch her, and I trust to heal her forthright (an such it be the will of Allah!)."

The King in great joy sent for his daughter, and they brought her pinioned and fettered. The Envied made her sit down behind a curtain and taking out the hairs fumigated her therewith; whereupon that which was in her head cried out and departed from her.

The girl was at once restored to her right mind and veiling her face, said, "What hath happened and who brought me hither?"

The Sultan rejoiced with a joy that nothing could exceed, and kissed his daughter's eyes, and the holy man's hand; then, turning to his great lords, he asked, "How say ye! What fee deserveth he who hath made my daughter whole?" and all answered, "He deserveth her to wife"; and the King said, "Ye speak sooth!"

So he married him to her and the Envied thus became son-in-law to the King. And after a little the Wazir died and the King said, "Whom can I make Minister in his stead?"

"Thy son-in-law," replied the courtiers.

So the Envied became a Wazir; and after a while the Sultan also died and the lieges said, "Whom shall we make King?" and all cried, "The Wazir."

So the Wazir was forthright made Sultan, and he became King regnant, a true ruler of men.

One day as he had mounted his horse; and, in the eminence of his kinglihood, was riding amidst his Emirs and Wazirs and the Grandees of his realm his eye fell upon his old neighbour, the Envier, who stood afoot on his path; so he turned to one of his Ministers, and said, "Bring hither that man and cause him no affright."

The Wazir brought him and the King said, "Give him a thousand miskáls of gold from the treasury, and load him ten camels with goods for trade, and send him under escort to his own town."

Then he bade his enemy farewell and sent him away and forbore to punish him for the many and great evils he had done. See, O Ifrit, the mercy of the Envied to the Envier, who had hated him from the beginning and had borne him such bitter malice and never met him without causing him trouble; and had driven him from house and home, and then had journeyed for the sole purpose of taking his life by throwing him into the well. Yet he did not requite his injurious dealing, but forgave him and was bountiful to him. Then I wept before him, O my lady, with sore weeping, never was there sorer, and I recited:——

> Pardon my fault, for 'tis the wise man's wont
> All faults to pardon and revenge forgo:
> In sooth all manner faults in me contain,
> Then deign of goodness mercy-grace to show:
> Whoso imploreth pardon from on High
> Should hold his hand from sinners here below.

Said the Ifrit, "Lengthen not thy words! As to my slaying thee fear it not, and as to my pardoning thee hope it not; but from my bewitching thee there is no escape."

Then he tore me from the ground which closed under my feet and flew with me into the firmament till I saw the earth as a large white cloud or a saucer in the midst of the waters. Presently he set me down on a mountain, and taking a little dust, over which he muttered some magical words, sprinkled me therewith, saying, "Quit that shape and take thou the shape of an ape!"

And on the instant I became an ape, a tailless baboon, the son of a century.

Now when he had left me and I saw myself in this ugly and hateful shape, I wept for myself, but resigned my soul to the tyranny of Time and Circumstance, well weeting that Fortune is fair and constant to no man. I descended the mountain and found at the foot a desert plain, long and broad, over which I travelled for the space of a month till my course brought me to the brink of the briny sea. After standing there awhile, I was ware of a ship in the offing which ran before a fair wind making for the shore.

I hid myself behind a rock on the beach and waited till the ship drew near, when I leaped on board. I found her full of merchants and passengers and one of them cried, "O Captain, this ill-omened brute will bring us ill-luck!" and another said, "Turn this ill-omened beast out from among us"; the Captain said, "Let us kill it!" another said, "Slay it with the sword"; a third, "Drown it"; and a fourth, "Shoot it with an arrow." But I sprang up and laid hold of the Rais's skirt, and shed tears which poured down my chops.

The Captain took pity on me, and said, "O merchants! this ape hath appealed to me for protection and I will protect him; henceforth he is under my charge: so let none do him aught hurt or harm, otherwise there will be bad blood between us."

Then he entreated me kindly and whatsoever he said I understood and ministered to his every want and served him as a servant, albeit my tongue would not obey my wishes; so that he came to love me. The vessel sailed on, the wind being fair, for the space of fifty days; at the end of which we cast anchor under the walls of a great city wherein was a world of people, especially learned men, none could tell their number save Allah.

No sooner had we arrived than we were visited by certain Mameluke-officials from the King of that city; who, after boarding us, greeted the merchants and giving them joy of safe arrival said, "Our King welcometh you, and sendeth you this roll of paper, whereupon each and every of you must write a line. For ye shall know that the King's Minister, a calligrapher of renown, is dead, and the King hath sworn a solemn oath that he will make none Wazir in his stead who cannot write as well as he could."

He then gave us the scroll which measured ten cubits long by a breadth of one, and each of the merchants who knew how to write wrote a line thereon, even to the last of them; after which I stood up (still in the shape of an ape) and snatched the roll out of their hands. They feared lest I should tear it or throw it overboard; so they tried to stay me and scare me, but I signed to them that I could write, whereat all marvelled, saying, "We never yet saw an ape write."

And the Captain cried, "Let him write; and if he scribble and scrabble we will kick him out and kill him; but if he write fair and scholarly I will adopt him as my son; for surely I never yet saw a more intelligent and well-mannered monkey than he. Would Heaven my real son were his match in morals and manners."

I took the reed, and stretching out my paw, dipped it in ink
and wrote, in the hand used for letters, these two couplets:——

> Time hath recorded gifts she gave the great;
> But none recorded thine which be far higher;
> Allah ne'er orphan men by loss of thee
> Who be of Goodness mother, Bounty's sire.

And I wrote in Rayháni or larger letters elegantly curved:——

> Thou hast a reed of rede to every land,
> Whose driving causeth all the world to thrive;
> Nil is the Nile of Misraim by thy boons
> Who makest misery smile with fingers five.

Then I wrote in the Suls character:——

> There be no writer who from Death shall fleet;
> But what his hand hath writ men shall repeat:
> Write, therefore, naught, save what shall serve thee when
> Thou see't on Judgment-Day an so thou see't!

Then I wrote in the character Naskh:——

> When to sore parting Fate our love shall doom,
> To distant life by Destiny decreed,
> We cause the inkhorn's lips to 'plain our pains,
> And tongue our utterance with the talking reed.

And I wrote in the Túmár character:——

> Kingdom with none endures; if thou deny
> This truth, where be the Kings of earlier earth?
> Set trees of goodliness while rule endures,
> And when thou art fallen they shall tell thy worth.

And I wrote in the character of Muhakkak:——

> When oped the inkhorn of thy wealth and fame
> Take ink of generous heart and gracious hand;
> Write brave and noble deeds while write thou can
> And win thee praise from point of pen and brand.

Then I gave the scroll to the officials and, after we all had written our line, they carried it before the King. When he saw the paper no writing pleased him save my writing; and he said to the assembled courtiers, "Go seek the writer of these lines and dress him in a splendid robe of honour; then mount him on a she-mule, let a band of music precede him and bring him to the presence."

At these words they smiled and the King was wroth with them and cried, "O accursed! I give you an order and you laugh at me?"

"O King," they replied, "if we laugh 'tis not at thee and not without a cause."

"And what is it?" asked he; and they answered, "O king, thou orderest us to bring to thy presence the man who wrote these lines; now the truth is that he who wrote them is not of the sons of Adam, but an ape, a tailless baboon, belonging to the ship-captain."

Quoth he, "Is this true that you say?"

Quoth they, "Yea, by the rights of thy munificence!"

The King marvelled at their words and shook with mirth and said, "I am minded to buy this ape of the Captain."

Then he sent messengers to the ship with the mule, the dress, the guard and the state-drums, saying, "Not the less do you clothe him in the robe of honour and mount him on the mule and let him be surrounded by the guards and preceded by the band of music."

They came to the ship and took me from the Captain and robed me in the robe of honour and, mounting me on the she-mule, carried me in state-procession through the streets; whilst the people were amazed and amused. And folk said to one another, "Halloo! is our Sultan about to make an ape his Minister?" and came all agog crowding to gaze at me, and the town was astir and turned topsy-turvy on my account.

When they brought me up to the King and set me in his presence, I kissed the ground before him three times, and once before the High Chamberlain and great officers, and he bade me be seated, and I sat respectfully on shins and knees, and all who were present marvelled at my fine manners, and the King most of all. Thereupon he ordered the lieges to retire; and, when none

remained save the King's majesty, the Eunuch on duty and a
little white slave, he bade them set before me the table of food,
containing all manner of birds, whatever hoppeth and flieth and
treadeth in nest, such as quail and sand-grouse. Then he signed
me to eat with him; so I rose and kissed ground before him, then
sat me down and ate with him. And when the table was removed
I washed my hands in seven waters and took the reed-case and
reed; and wrote instead of speaking these couplets:——

Wail for the little partridges on porringer and plate;
Cry for the ruin of the fries and stews well marinate:
Keen as I keen for loved, lost daughters of the Katágrouse,
And omelette round the fair enbrownèd fowls agglomerate:
O fire in heart of me for fish, those deux poissons I saw,
Bedded on new made scones and cakes in piles to laniate.
For thee, O vermicelli! aches my very maw! I hold
Without thee every taste and joy are clean annihilate.
Those eggs have rolled their yellow eyes in torturing pains of fire
Ere served with hash and fritters hot, that delicatest cate.
Praisèd be to Allah for His baked and roast and ah! how good
This pulse, these pot-herbs steeped in oil with eysill combinate!
When hunger sated was, I elbow-propt fell back upon
Meat-pudding wherein gleamed the bangles that my wits amate.
Then woke I sleeping appetite to eat as though in sport
Sweets from brocaded trays and kickshaws most elaborate.
Be patient, soul of me! Time is a haughty, jealous wight;
To-day he seems dark-lowering and to-morrow far to sight.

Then I rose and seated myself at a respectful distance while
the King read what I had written, and marvelled, exclaiming, "O
the miracle, that an ape should be gifted with this graceful style
and this power of penmanship! By Allah, 'tis a wonder of
wonders!"

Presently they set before the King choice wines in flagons
of glass and he drank: then he passed on the cup to me; and I
kissed the ground and drank and wrote on it:——

With fire they boilèd me to loose my tongue,
And pain and patience gave for fellowship:
Hence comes it hands of men upbear me high
And honey-dew from lips of maid I sip!

And these also:——

> Morn saith to Night, "Withdraw and let me shine";
> So drain we draughts that dull all pain and pine:
> I doubt, so fine the glass, the wine so clear,
> If 'tis the wine in glass or glass in wine.

The King read my verse and said with a sigh, "Were these gifts
in a man, he would excel all the folk of his time and age!" Then
he called for the chess-board, and said, "Say, wilt thou play with
me?" and I signed with my head, "Yes."

Then I came forward and ordered the pieces and played with
him two games, both of which I won. He was speechless with
surprise; so I took the pen-case and, drawing forth a reed, wrote
on the board these two couplets:——

> Two hosts fare fighting thro' the livelong day,
> Nor is their battling ever finishèd,
> Until, when darkness girdeth them about,
> The twain go sleeping in a single bed.

The King read these lines with wonder and delight and said
to his Eunuch, "O Mukbil, go to thy mistress, Sitt al-Husn, and
say her, 'Come, speak the King who biddeth thee hither to take
thy solace in seeing this right wondrous ape!'"

So the Eunuch went out and presently returned with the lady
who, when she saw me veiled her face and said, "Oh my father!
hast thou lost all sense of honour? How cometh it thou art pleased
to send for me and show me to strange men?"

"O Sitt al-Husn," said he, "no man is here save this little foot-
page and the Eunuch who reared thee and I, thy father. From
whom, then, dost thou veil thy face?"

She answered, "This whom thou deemest an ape is a young
man, a clever and polite, a wise and learned and the son of a King;
but he is ensorcelled and the Ifrit Jirjaris, who is of the seed of
Iblis, cast a spell upon him, after putting to death his own wife the
daughter of King Ifitamus, lord of the islands of Abnus."

The King marvelled at his daughter's words and, turning to
me, said, "Is this true that she saith of thee?" and I signed by a
nod of my head the answer, "Yea, verily"; and wept sore.

Then he asked his daughter, "Whence knewest thou that he is ensorcelled?" and she answered, "O my dear papa, there was with me in my childhood an old woman, a wily one and a wise and a witch to boot, and she taught me the theory of magic and its practice; and I took notes in writing and therein waxed perfect, and have committed to memory an hundred and seventy chapters of egromantic formulas, by the least of which I could transport the stones of thy city behind the Mountain Kaf and the Circumambient Main, or make its site an abyss of the sea and its people fishes swimming in the midst of it."

"O my daughter," said her father, "I conjure thee, by my life, disenchant this young man, that I may make him my Wazir and marry thee to him, for indeed he is an ingenious youth and a deeply learned."

"With joy and goodly gree," she replied and, hending in hand an iron knife whereon was inscribed the name of Allah in Hebrew characters, she described a wide circle——

And Shahrazad perceived the dawn of day and ceased saying her permitted say. When it was the 14th night, she said,

It hath reached me, O auspicious King, that the Kalandar continued his tale thus:—— O my lady, the King's daughter hent in hand a knife whereon were inscribed Hebrew characters and described a wide circle in the midst of the palace-hall, and therein wrote in Cufic letters mysterious names and talismans; and she uttered words and muttered charms, some of which we understood and others we understood not. Presently the world waxed dark before our sight till we thought the sky was falling upon our heads, and lo! the Ifrit presented himself in his own shape and aspect. His hands were like many-pronged pitchforks, his legs like the masts of great ships, and his eyes like cressets of gleaming fire.

We were in terrible fear of him but the King's daughter cried at him, "No welcome to thee and no greeting, O dog!" whereupon he changed to the form of a lion and said, "O traitress, how is it thou has broken the oath we sware that neither should contraire other!"

"O accursed one," answered she, "how could there be a compact between me and the like of thee?"

Then said he, "Take what thou hast brought on thyself"; and the lion opened his jaws and rushed upon her; but she was too quick for him; and, plucking a hair from her head, waved it in the air muttering over it the while; and the hair straightway became a trenchant sword-blade, wherewith she smote the lion and cut him in twain. Then the two halves flew away in air and the head changed to a scorpion and the Princess became a huge serpent and set upon the accursed scorpion, and the two fought, coiling and uncoiling, a stiff fight for an hour at least. Then the scorpion changed to a vulture and the serpent became an eagle which set upon the vulture, and hunted him for an hour's time, till he became a black tom-cat, which miauled and grinned and spat. Thereupon the eagle changed into a piebald wolf and these two battled in the palace for a long time, when the cat, seeing himself overcome, changed into a worm and crept into a huge red pomegranate, which lay beside the jetting fountain in the midst of the palace hall.

Whereupon the pomegranate swelled to the size of a watermelon in air; and, falling upon the marble pavement of the palace, broke to pieces, and all the grains fell out and were scattered about till they covered the whole floor. Then the wolf shook himself and became a snow-white cock, which fell to picking up the grains purposing not to leave one; but by doom of destiny one seed rolled to the fountain edge and there lay hid. The cock fell to crowing and clapping his wings and signing to us with his beak as if to ask, "Are any grains left?"

But we understood not what he meant, and he cried to us with so loud a cry that we thought the place would fall upon us. Then he ran over all the floor till he saw the grain which had rolled to the fountain edge, and rushed eagerly to pick it up when behold, it sprang into the midst of the water and became a fish and dived to the bottom of the basin. Thereupon the cock changed to a big fish, and plunged in after the other, and the two disappeared for a while and lo! we heard loud shrieks and cries of pain which made us tremble. After this the Ifrit rose out of the water, and he was as a burning flame; casting fire and smoke from his mouth and eyes and nostrils. And immediately the Princess likewise came forth from the basin and she was one live coal of flaming lowe; and these two, she and he, battled for the space of an hour, until their fires entirely compassed them about and their thick smoke filled the palace.

As for us we panted for breath, being well-nigh suffocated, and we longed to plunge into the water fearing lest we be burnt up and utterly destroyed; and the King said, "There is no Majesty and there is no Might save in Allah the Glorious, the Great! Verily we are Allah's and unto Him are we returning! Would Heaven I had not urged my daughter to attempt the disenchantment of this ape-fellow, whereby I have imposed upon her the terrible task of fighting yon accursed Ifrit against whom all the Ifrits in the world could not prevail. And would Heaven we had never seen this ape, Allah never assain nor bless the day of his coming! We thought to do a good deed by him before the face of Allah, and to release him from enchantment, and now we have brought this trouble and travail upon our heart."

But I, O my lady, was tongue-tied and powerless to say a word to him. Suddenly, ere we were ware of aught, the Ifrit yelled out from under the flames and, coming up to us as we stood on the estrade, blew fire in our faces. The damsel overtook him and breathed blasts of fire at his face and the sparks from her and from him rained down upon us, and her sparks did us no harm, but one of his sparks alighted upon my eye and destroyed it making me a monocular ape; and another fell on the King's face scorching the lower half, burning off his beard and mustachios and causing his under teeth to fall out; while a third alighted on the Castrato's breast, killing him on the spot.

So we despaired of life and made sure of death when lo! a voice repeated the saying, "Allah is most Highest! Allah is most Highest! Aidance and victory to all who the Truth believe; and disappointment and disgrace to all who the religion of Mohammed, the Moon of Faith, unbelieve."

The speaker was the Princess who had burnt up the Ifrit, and he was become a heap of ashes. Then she came up to us and said, "Reach me a cup of water."

They brought it to her and she spoke over it words we understood not, and sprinkling me with it cried, "By virtue of the Truth, and by the Most Great name of Allah, I charge thee return to thy former shape."

And behold, I shook, and became a man as before, save that I had utterly lost an eye.

Then she cried out, "The fire! The fire! O my dear papa an

arrow from the accursed hath wounded me to the death, for I am not used to fight with the Jann; had he been a man I had slain him in the beginning. I had no trouble till the time when the pomegranate burst and the grains scattered, but I overlooked the seed wherein was the very life of the Jinni. Had I picked it up he had died on the spot, but as Fate and Fortune decreed, I saw it not; so he came upon me all unawares and there befell between him and me a sore struggle under the earth and high in air and in the water; and, as often as I opened on him a gate, he opened on me another gate and a stronger, till at last he opened on me the gate of fire, and few are saved upon whom the door of fire openeth. But Destiny willed that my cunning prevail over his cunning; and I burned him to death after I vainly exhorted him to embrace the religion of Al-Islam. As for me I am a dead woman; Allah supply my place to you!"

Then she called upon Heaven for help and ceased not to implore relief from the fire; when lo! a black spark shot up from her robed feet to her thighs; then it flew to her bosom and thence to her face. When it reached her face she wept and said, "I testify that there is no god but *the* God and that Mohammed is the Apostle of God!"

And we looked at her and saw naught but a heap of ashes by the side of the heap that had been the Ifrit.

We mourned for her and I wished I had been in her place, so had I not seen her lovely face who had worked me such weal become ashes; but there is no gainsaying the will of Allah.

When the King saw his daughter's terrible death, he plucked out what was left of his beard and beat his face and rent his raiment; and I did as he did and we both wept. Then came in the Chamberlains and Grandees who were amazed to find two heaps of ashes and the Sultan in a fainting fit; so they stood round him till he revived and told them what had befallen his daughter from the Ifrit; whereat their grief was right grievous and the women and the slave-girls shrieked and keened, and they continued their lamentations for the space of seven days. Moreover the King bade build over his daughter's ashes a vast vaulted tomb, and burn therein wax tapers and sepulchral lamps; but as for the Ifrit's ashes they scattered them on the winds, speeding them to the curse of Allah. Then the Sultan fell sick of a sickness that well-nigh brought him to his death for a month's space; and, when health returned to him and his beard grew again and he had been converted by the mercy of Allah to Al-Islam, he sent for me and said, "O youth, Fate had decreed for us the happiest of lives, safe from all the chances and changes of Time, till thou camest to us, when troubles fell upon us. Would to Heaven we had never seen thee and the foul face of thee! For we took pity on thee and thereby we have lost our all. I have on thy account first lost my daughter who to me was well worth an hundred men, secondly I have suffered that which befel me by reason of the fire and the loss of my teeth, and my Eunuch also was slain. I blame thee not, for it was out of thy power to prevent this: the doom of Allah was on thee as well as on us and thanks be to the Almighty for that my daughter delivered thee, albeit thereby she lost her own life! Go forth now, O my son, from this city, and suffice thee what hath befallen us through thee, even although 'twas decreed for us. Go forth in peace; and if I ever see thee again I will surely slay thee."

And he cried out at me. So I went forth from his presence, O my lady, weeping bitterly and hardly believing in my escape and knowing not whither I should wend. And I recalled all that had befallen me, my meeting the tailor, my love for the damsel in the palace beneath the earth, and my narrow escape from the Ifrit, even after he had determined to do me die; and how I had entered the city as an ape and was now leaving it a man once more. Then I gave thanks to Allah and said, "My eye and not my life!" and before leaving the place I entered the bath and shaved my poll and beard and mustachios and eyebrows; and cast ashes on my head and donned the coarse black woollen robe of a Kalandar. Then I fared forth, O my lady, and every day I pondered all the calamities which had betided me, and I wept and repeated these couplets:——

I am distraught, yet verily His ruth abides with me,
Tho' round me gather hosts of ills, whence come I cannot see:
Patient I'll be till Patience self with me impatient wax;
Patient for ever till the Lord fulfil my destiny:
Patient I'll bide without complaint, a wronged and vanquisht man;
Patient as sunparcht wight that spans the desert's sandy sea:
Patient I'll be till Aloe's self unwittingly allow
I'm patient under bitterer things than bitterest aloë:

No bitterer things than aloes or than patience for mankind;
Yet bitterer than the twain to me were Patience' treachery:
My sere and seamed and seared brow would dragoman my sore
If soul could search my sprite and there unsecret secrecy:
Were hills to bear the load I bear they'd crumble 'neath the weight;
'Twould still the roaring wind, 'twould quench the flame-tongue's
    flagrancy,
And whoso saith the world is sweet certès a day he'll see
With more than aloes' bitterness and aloes' pungency.

Then I journeyed through many regions and saw many a city intending for Baghdad, that I might seek audience, in the House of Peace, with the Commander of the Faithful and tell him all that had befallen me. I arrived here this very night and I found my brother in Allah, this first Kalandar, standing about as one perplexed; so I saluted him with "Peace be upon thee," and entered into discourse with him.

Presently up came our brother, this third Kalandar, and said to us, "Peace be with you! I am a stranger"; whereto we replied, "And we too be strangers, who have come hither this blessed night."

So we all three walked on together, none of us knowing the other's history, till Destiny drave us to this door and we came in to you. Such then is my story and my reason for shaving my beard and mustachios, and this is what caused the loss of my eye.

Said the house-mistress, "Thy tale is indeed a rare; so rub thy head and wend thy ways"; but he replied, "I will not budge till I hear my companions' stories."

●

DUKE. Against all sense do you importune her:
Should she kneel down in mercy of this fact,
Her brother's ghost his paved bed would break,
And take her hence in horror.

          —MEASURE FOR MEASURE

●

CALPHURNIA. Caesar, I never stood on ceremonies,
Yet now they fright me. There is one within,
Besides the things that we have heard and seen,
Recounts most horrid sights seen by the watch.
A lioness hath whelped in the streets;
And graves have yawn'd and yielded up their dead;
Fierce fiery warriors fought upon the clouds,
In ranks and squadrons and right form of war,
Which drizzled blood upon the Capitol;
The noise of battle hurtled in the air,
Horses did neigh, and dying men did groan,
And ghosts did shriek and squeal about the streets.
O Caesar! these are things beyond all use,
And I do fear them.

—JULIUS CAESAR

FULL FATHOM FIVE

Alexander Woollcott, whose *Shouts and Murmurs* has disappeared from the pages of *The New Yorker* and whose radio program *The Town Crier* has been heard in recent years in broadcast form throughout the land, has for long made it a specialty to trace word-of-mouth stories to their sources. What happened when he tried to do so with this one can be discovered in the course of the next few pages. It is a ghost story that has itself become a ghost.—EDITOR.

A l e x a n d e r
W o o l l c o t t

FULL
FATHOM
FIVE

This is the story just as I heard it the other evening—a ghost story told me as true. It seems that one chilly October night in the first decade of the present century, two sisters were motoring along a Cape Cod road, when their car broke down just before midnight and would go no further. This was in an era when such mishaps were both commoner and more hopeless than they are today. For these two, there was no chance of help until another car might chance to come by in the morning and give them a tow. Of a lodging for the night there was no hope, except a gaunt, unlighted, frame house which, with a clump of pine trees beside it, stood black in the moonlight, across a neglected stretch of frost-hardened lawn.

They yanked at its ancient bell-pull, but only a faint tinkle within made answer. They banged despairingly on the door panel, only to awaken what at first they thought was an echo, and then identified as a shutter responding antiphonally with the help of a nipping wind. This shutter was around the corner, and the ground-floor window behind it was broken and unfastened. There was enough moonlight to show that the room within was a deserted library, with a few books left on the sagging shelves and a few pieces of dilapidated furniture still standing where some departing family had left them, long before. At least the sweep of the electric flash which one of the women had brought with her showed them that on the uncarpeted floor the dust lay thick and trackless, as if no one had trod there in many a day.

They decided to bring their blankets in from the car and stretch out there on the floor until daylight, none too comfortable, perhaps, but at least sheltered from that salt and cutting wind. It was while they were lying there, trying to get to sleep, while, indeed, they had drifted halfway across the borderland, that they saw—each confirming the other's fear by a convulsive grip of the hand—saw standing at the empty fireplace, as if trying to dry himself by a fire that was not there, the wraithlike figure of a sailor, come dripping from the sea.

After an endless moment, in which neither woman breathed, one of them somehow found the strength to call out, "Who's there?" The challenge shattered the intolerable silence, and at the sound, muttering a little—they said afterwards that it was something between a groan and a whimper—the misty figure seemed to dissolve. They strained their eyes, but could see nothing between themselves and the battered mantelpiece.

Then, telling themselves (and, as one does, half believing it) that they had been dreaming, they tried again to sleep, and, indeed, did sleep until a patch of shuttered sunlight striped the morning floor. As they sat up and blinked at the gritty realism of the forsaken room, they would, I think, have laughed at their shared illusion of the night before, had it not been for something at which one of the sisters pointed with a kind of gasp. There, in the still undisturbed dust, on the spot in front of the fireplace where the apparition had seemed to stand, was a patch of water, a little, circular pool that had issued from no crack in the floor nor, as far as they could see, fallen from any point in the innocent ceiling. Near it in the surrounding dust was no footprint—their own or any other's—and in it was a piece of green that looked like seaweed. One of the women bent down and put her finger to the water, then lifted it to her tongue. The water was salty.

After that the sisters scuttled out and sat in their car, until a passerby gave them a tow to the nearest village. In its tavern at breakfast they gossiped with the proprietress about the empty house among the pine trees down the road. Oh, yes, it had been just that way for a score of years or more. Folks did say the place was spooky, haunted by a son of the family who, driven out by his father, had shipped before the mast and been drowned at sea. Some said the family had moved away because they could not stand the things they heard and saw at night.

A year later, one of the sisters told the story at a dinner party in New York. In the pause that followed a man across the table leaned forward.

"My dear lady," he said, with a smile, "I happen to be the curator of a museum where they are doing a good deal of work on submarine vegetation. In your place, I never would have left that house without taking the bit of seaweed with me."

"Of course you wouldn't," she answered tartly, "and neither did I."

It seems she had lifted it out of the water and dried it a little by pressing it against a window pane. Then she had carried it off in her pocketbook, as a souvenir. As far as she knew, it was still in an envelope in a little drawer of her desk at home. If she could find it, would he like to see it? He would. Next morning she sent it around by messenger, and a few days later it came back with a note.

"You were right," the note said, "this is seaweed. Furthermore, it may interest you to learn that it is of a rare variety which, as far as we know, grows only on dead bodies."

And that, my dears, is the story as I heard it the other evening, heard it from Alice Duer Miller who, in turn, had heard it five-and-twenty years before from Mrs. George Haven Putnam, sometime dean of Barnard College, and author of that admirable work, *The Lady*. To her I must go if—as I certainly did—I wanted more precise details. So to Mrs. Putnam I went, hat in hand and, as an inveterate reporter, showered her with questions. I wanted the names of the seaweed, of the curator, of the museum, of the two sisters, of the dead sailor, and of the nearby village on Cape Cod. I wanted a road-map marked with a cross to show the house in the grove of pines. I wanted—but the examination came to a dead stop at the sight of her obvious embarrassment. She was most graciously apologetic, but, really, what with this and what with that, she had forgotten the whole story. She could not even re-member—and thus it is ever with my life in science—who it was that had told it to her.

FOOTNOTE: More recently, the Curator of the Botanical Museum in St. Louis has assured me that this tale, whispered from neighbor to neighbor across the country, has become distorted in a manner offensive to students of submarine vegetation. According to him, the visitor from the sea was seen in a house in Woods Hole, Mass. He was a son of the house who had been drowned during his honeymoon off the coast of Australia. The seaweed picked up off the dusty floor of that New England mansion was of a variety which grows only off the Australian coast. The Curator even presented me with the actual seaweed. I regard it with mingled affection and skepticism, and keep it pressed between the pages of Bullfinch's *Mythology*.

●

VEX NOT his ghost: O, let him pass! he hates him much
That would upon the rack of this tough world
Stretch him out longer.
                              —KING LEAR

●

THE GHOST THAT MISSED ITS BONNET

IN THE village of Lodden, in England, about ten miles distant from Norwich, the upper storey of a thatched house was being repaired. During the upheaval a member of the family discovered in the attic an ancient bonnet. Not knowing what else to do with it, he gave it to the vicar's wife, who thought it would be a good idea to present it some day to the museum in Norwich. Several days later, however, before she had been able to carry her plan into action, the owner of the cottage came back to her and in great agitation asked for the bonnet back. "I haven't had a moment's peace since I gave it to you," he said, "the house is full of screams and wailings and strange noises!" So the lady relinquished the bonnet, and the ghost, satisfied with the return of its property, caused no more trouble.

—COMMUNICATED TO THE EDITOR BY MRS JOHN ALLSOP

AN OCCURRENCE AT OWL CREEK BRIDGE

There is no doubt whatever in my mind that this story is the best Bierce ever wrote; it proves him to have been alert to the psychological investigations of the latter 19th Century. No living man will ever be able to report upon the validity of the theory about which the story is built, but there are good reasons for supposing it to be possible, and Bierce unquestionably succeeds in the artistic task of making it convincing. It is a story of "haunting" as a mental quality, and not of ghosts.—EDITOR.

Ambrose Bierce

AN OCCUR-RENCE AT OWL CREEK BRIDGE

A man stood upon a railroad bridge in northern Alabama, looking down into the swift water twenty feet below. The man's hands were behind his back, the wrists bound with a cord. A rope closely encircled his neck. It was attached to a stout cross-timber above his head and the slack fell to the level of his knees. Some loose boards laid upon the sleepers supporting the metals of the railway supplied a footing for him and his executioners—two private soldiers of the Federal army, directed by a sergeant who in civil life may have been a deputy sheriff. At a short remove upon the same temporary platform was an officer in the uniform of his rank, armed. He was a captain. A sentinel at each end of the bridge stood with his rifle in the position known as "support," that is to say, vertical in front of the left shoulder, the hammer resting on the forearm thrown straight across the chest—a formal and unnatural position, enforcing an erect carriage of the body. It did not appear to be the duty of these two men to know what was occurring at the centre of the bridge; they merely blockaded the two ends of the foot planking that traversed it.

Beyond one of the sentinels nobody was in sight; the railroad ran straight away into a forest for a hundred yards, then, curving, was lost to view. Doubtless there was an outpost farther along. The other bank of the stream was open ground—a gentle acclivity topped with a stockade of vertical tree trunks, loop-holed for rifles, with a single embrasure through which protruded the muzzle of a brass cannon commanding the bridge. Midway of the slope between bridge and fort were the spectators—a single company of infantry in line, at "parade rest," the butts of the rifles on the ground, the barrels inclining slightly backward against the right shoulder, the hands crossed upon the stock. A lieutenant stood at the right of the line, the point of his sword upon the ground, his left hand resting upon his right. Excepting the group of four at the centre of the bridge, not a man moved. The company faced the bridge, staring stonily, motionless. The sentinels, facing the banks of the stream, might have been statues to adorn the bridge. The captain stood with folded arms, silent, observing the work of his subordinates, but making no sign. Death is a dignitary who when he comes announced is to be received with formal manifestations of respect, even by those most familiar with him. In the code of military etiquette silence and fixity are forms of deference.

The man who was engaged in being hanged was apparently about thirty-five years of age. He was a civilian, if one might judge from his habit, which was that of a planter. His features were good—a straight nose, firm mouth, broad forehead, from which his long, dark hair was combed straight back, falling behind his ears, to the collar of his well-fitting frock-coat. He wore a mustache and pointed beard, but no whiskers; his eyes were large and dark gray, and had a kindly expression which one would hardly have expected in one whose neck was in the hemp. Evidently this was no vulgar assassin. The liberal military code makes provision for hanging many kinds of persons, and gentlemen are not excluded.

The preparations being complete, the two private soldiers stepped aside and each drew away the plank upon which he had been standing. The sergeant turned to the captain, saluted and placed himself immediately behind that officer, who in turn moved apart one pace. These movements left the condemned man and the sergeant standing on the two ends of the same plank, which spanned three of the cross-ties of the bridge. The end upon which the civilian stood almost, but not quite, reached a fourth. This plank had been held in place by the weight of the captain; it was now held by that of the sergeant. At a signal from the former the latter would step aside, the plank would tilt and the condemned man go down between two ties. The arrangement commended itself to his judgment as simple and effective. His face had not been covered nor his eyes bandaged. He looked a moment at his "unsteadfast footing," then let his gaze wander to the swirling water of the stream racing madly beneath his feet. A piece of dancing driftwood caught his attention and his eyes followed it down the current. How slowly it appeared to move! What a sluggish stream!

He closed his eyes in order to fix his last thoughts upon his wife and children. The water, touched to gold by the early sun, the brooding mists under the banks at some distance down the stream, the fort, the soldiers, the piece of drift—all had distracted him. And now he became conscious of a new disturbance. Striking through the thought of his dear ones was a sound which he could neither ignore nor understand, a sharp, distinct, metallic percussion like the stroke of a blacksmith's hammer upon the anvil; it had the same ringing quality. He wondered what it was, and whether immeasurably distant or near by—it seemed both. Its recurrence was regular, but as slow as the tolling of a death knell. He awaited each stroke with impatience and—he knew not why— apprehension. The intervals of silence grew progressively longer; the delays became maddening. With their greater infrequency the sounds increased in strength and sharpness. They hurt his ear like the thrust of a knife; he feared he would shriek. What he heard was the ticking of his watch.

He unclosed his eyes and saw again the water below him. "If I could free my hands," he thought, "I might throw off the noose and spring into the stream. By diving I could evade the bullets and, swimming vigorously, reach the bank, take to the woods and get away home. My home, thank God, is as yet outside their lines; my wife and little ones are still beyond the invader's farthest advance."

As these thoughts, which have here to be set down in words, were flashed into the doomed man's brain rather than evolved from it the captain nodded to the sergeant. The sergeant stepped aside.

II

Peyton Farquhar was a well-to-do planter, of an old and highly respected Alabama family. Being a slave owner and like other slave owners a politician he was naturally an original secessionist and ardently devoted to the Southern cause. Circumstances of an imperious nature, which it is unnecessary to relate here, had prevented him from taking service with the gallant army that had fought the disastrous campaigns ending with the fall of Corinth, and he chafed under the inglorious restraint, longing for the release of his energies, the larger life of the soldier, the opportunity for distinction. That opportunity, he felt, would come, as it comes to all in war time. Meanwhile he did what he could. No service was too humble for him to perform in aid of the South, no adventure too perilous for him to undertake if consistent with the character of a civilian who was at heart a soldier, and who in good faith and without too much qualification assented to at least a part of the frankly villainous dictum that all is fair in love and war.

One evening while Farquhar and his wife were sitting on a rustic bench near the entrance to his grounds, a gray-clad soldier rode up to the gate and asked for a drink of water. Mrs. Farquhar was only too happy to serve him with her own white hands. While she was fetching the water her husband approached the dusty horseman and inquired eagerly for news from the front.

"The Yanks are repairing the railroads," said the man, "and are getting ready for another advance. They have reached the Owl Creek bridge, put it in order and built a stockade on the north bank. The commandant has issued an order, which is posted everywhere, declaring that any civilian caught interfering with the railroad, its bridges, tunnels or trains will be summarily hanged. I saw the order."

"How far is it to the Owl Creek bridge?" Farquhar asked.

"About thirty miles."

"Is there no force on this side of the creek?"

"Only a picket post half a mile out, on the railroad, and a single sentinel at this end of the bridge."

"Suppose a man—a civilian and student of hanging—should elude the picket post and perhaps get the better of the sentinel," said Farquhar, smiling, "what could he accomplish?"

The soldier reflected. "I was there a month ago," he replied. "I observed that the flood of last winter had lodged a great quantity of driftwood against the wooden pier at this end of the bridge. It is now dry and would burn like tow."

The lady had now brought the water, which the soldier drank. He thanked her ceremoniously, bowed to her husband and rode away. An hour later, after nightfall, he repassed the plantation, going northward in the direction from which he had come. He was a Federal scout.

III

As Peyton Farquhar fell straight downward through the bridge he lost consciousness and was as one already dead. From this state he was awakened—ages later, it seemed to him—by the pain of a sharp pressure upon his throat, followed by a sense of suffocation. Keen, poignant agonies seemed to shoot from his neck downward through every fibre of his body and limbs. These pains appeared to flash along well-defined lines of ramification and to beat with an inconceivably rapid periodicity. They seemed like streams of pulsating fire heating him to an intolerable temperature. As to his head, he was conscious of nothing but a feeling of fulness—of congestion. These sensations were unaccompanied by thought. The intellectual part of his nature was already effaced; he had power only to feel, and feeling was torment. He was conscious of motion. Encompassed in a luminous cloud, of which he was now merely the fiery heart, without material substance, he swung through unthinkable arcs of oscillation, like a vast pendulum. Then all at once, with terrible suddenness, the light about him shot upward with the noise of a loud plash; a frightful roar-

ing was in his ears, and all was cold and dark. The power of
thought was restored; he knew that the rope had broken and he
had fallen into the stream. There was no additional strangulation;
the noose about his neck was already suffocating him and kept the
water from his lungs. To die of hanging at the bottom of a river!
—the idea seemed to him ludicrous. He opened his eyes in the
darkness and saw above him a gleam of light, but how distant, how
inaccessible! He was still sinking, for the light became fainter and
fainter until it was a mere glimmer. Then it began to grow and
brighten, and he knew that he was rising toward the surface—
knew it with reluctance, for he was now very comfortable. "To be
hanged and drowned," he thought, "that is not so bad; but I do
not wish to be shot. No; I will not be shot; that is not fair."

He was not conscious of an effort, but a sharp pain in his wrist
apprised him that he was trying to free his hands. He gave the
struggle his attention, as an idler might observe the feat of a jug-
gler, without interest in the outcome. What splendid effort!—what
magnificent, what superhuman strength! Ah, that was a fine en-
deavor! Bravo! The cord fell away; his arms parted and floated
upward, the hands dimly seen on each side in the growing light.
He watched them with a new interest as first one and then the
other pounced upon the noose at his neck. They tore it away and
thrust it fiercely aside, its undulations resembling those of a water-
snake. "Put it back, put it back!" He thought he shouted these
words to his hands, for the undoing of the noose had been succeeded by the direst pang that he had yet experienced. His neck
ached horribly; his brain was on fire; his heart, which had been
fluttering faintly, gave a great leap, trying to force itself out at
his mouth. His whole body was racked and wrenched with an in-
supportable anguish! But his disobedient hands gave no heed to
the command. They beat the water vigorously with quick, downward strokes, forcing him to the surface. He felt his head emerge;
his eyes were blinded by the sunlight; his chest expanded convulsively, and with a supreme and crowning agony his lungs engulfed a great draught of air, which instantly he expelled in a
shriek!

He was now in full possession of his physical senses. They
were, indeed, preternaturally keen and alert. Something in the
awful disturbance of his organic system had so exalted and refined

them that they made record of things never before perceived. He felt the ripples upon his face and heard their separate sounds as they struck. He looked at the forest on the bank of the stream, saw the individual trees, the leaves and the veining of each leaf— saw the very insects upon them: the locusts, the brilliant-bodied flies, the gray spiders stretching their webs from twig to twig. He noted the prismatic colors in all the dewdrops upon a million blades of grass. The humming of the gnats that danced above the eddies of the stream, the beating of the dragon-flies' wings, the strokes of the water-spiders' legs, like oars which had lifted their boat—all these made audible music. A fish slid along beneath his eyes and he heard the rush of its body parting the water.

He had come to the surface facing down the stream; in a moment the visible world seemed to wheel slowly round, himself the pivotal point, and he saw the bridge, the fort, the soldiers upon the bridge, the captain, the sergeant, the two privates, his executioners. They were in silhouette against the blue sky. They shouted and gesticulated, pointing at him. The captain had drawn his pistol, but did not fire; the others were unarmed. Their movements were grotesque and horrible, their forms gigantic.

Suddenly he heard a sharp report and something struck the water smartly within a few inches of his head, spattering his face with spray. He heard a second report, and saw one of the sentinels with his rifle at his shoulder, a light cloud of blue smoke rising from the muzzle. The man in the water saw the eye of the man on the bridge gazing into his own through the sights of the rifle. He observed that it was a gray eye and remembered having read that gray eyes were keenest, and that all famous marksmen had them. Nevertheless, this one had missed.

A counter-swirl had caught Farquhar and turned him half round; he was again looking into the forest on the bank opposite the fort. The sound of a clear, high voice in a monotonous sing-song now rang out behind him and came across the water with a distinctness that pierced and subdued all other sounds, even the beating of the ripples in his ears. Although no soldier, he had frequented camps enough to know the dread significance of that deliberate, drawling, aspirated chant; the lieutenant on shore was taking a part in the morning's work. How coldly and pitilessly— with what an even, calm intonation, presaging, and enforcing tranquillity in the men—with what accurately measured intervals fell those cruel words:

"Attention, company! . . . Shoulder arms! . . . Ready! . . . Aim! . . . Fire!"

Farquhar dived—dived as deeply as he could. The water roared in his ears like the voice of Niagara, yet he heard the dulled thunder of the volley and, rising again toward the surface, met shining bits of metal, singularly flattened, oscillating slowly downward. Some of them touched him on the face and hands, then fell away, continuing their descent. One lodged between his collar and neck; it was uncomfortably warm and he snatched it out.

As he rose to the surface, gasping for breath, he saw that he had been a long time under water; he was perceptibly farther down stream—nearer to safety. The soldiers had almost finished reloading; the metal ramrods flashed all at once in the sunshine as they were drawn from the barrels, turned in the air, and thrust into their sockets. The two sentinels fired again, independently and ineffectually.

The hunted man saw all this over his shoulder; he was now swimming vigorously with the current. His brain was as energetic as his arms and legs; he thought with the rapidity of lightning.

"The officer," he reasoned, "will not make that martinet's error a second time. It is as easy to dodge a volley as a single shot. He has probably already given the command to fire at will. God help me, I cannot dodge them all!"

An appalling plash within two yards of him was followed by a loud, rushing sound, *diminuendo,* which seemed to travel back through the air to the fort and died in an explosion which stirred the very river to its deeps! A rising sheet of water curved over him, fell down upon him, blinded him, strangled him! The cannon had taken a hand in the game. As he shook his head free from the commotion of the smitten water he heard the deflected shot humming through the air ahead, and in an instant it was cracking and smashing the branches in the forest beyond.

"They will not do that again," he thought; "the next time they will use a charge of grape. I must keep my eye upon the gun; the smoke will apprise me—the report arrives too late; it lags behind the missile. That is a good gun."

Suddenly he felt himself whirled round and round—spinning

like a top. The water, the banks, the forests, the now distant bridge, fort and men—all were commingled and blurred. Objects were represented by their colors only; circular horizontal streaks of color—that was all he saw. He had been caught in a vortex and was being whirled on with a velocity of advance and gyration that made him giddy and sick. In a few moments he was flung upon the gravel at the foot of the left bank of the stream—the southern bank—and behind a projecting point which concealed him from his enemies. The sudden arrest of his motion, the abrasion of one of his hands on the gravel, restored him, and he wept with delight. He dug his fingers into the sand, threw it over himself in handfuls and audibly blessed it. It looked like diamonds, rubies, emeralds; he could think of nothing beautiful which it did not resemble. The trees upon the bank were giant garden plants; he noted a definite order in their arrangement, inhaled the fragrance of their blooms. A strange, roseate light shone through the spaces among their trunks and the wind made in their branches the music of æolian harps. He had no wish to perfect his escape—was content to remain in that enchanting spot until retaken.

A whiz and rattle of grapeshot among the branches high above his head roused him from his dream. The baffled cannoneer had fired him a random farewell. He sprang to his feet, rushed up the sloping bank, and plunged into the forest.

All that day he traveled, laying his course by the rounding sun. The forest seemed interminable; nowhere did he discover a break in it, not even a woodman's road. He had not known that he lived in so wild a region. There was something uncanny in the revelation.

By nightfall he was fatigued, footsore, famishing. The thought of his wife and children urged him on. At last he found a road which led him in what he knew to be the right direction. It was as wide and straight as a city street, yet it seemed untraveled. No fields bordered it, no dwelling anywhere. Not so much as the barking of a dog suggested human habitation. The black bodies of the trees formed a straight wall on both sides, terminating on the horizon in a point, like a diagram in a lesson in perspective. Overhead, as he looked up through this rift in the wood, shone great golden stars looking unfamiliar and grouped in strange constellations. He was sure they were arranged in some order which had a secret and malign significance. The wood on either side was full of singular noises, among which—once, twice, and again—he distinctly heard whispers in an unknown tongue.

His neck was in pain and lifting his hand to it he found it horribly swollen. He knew that it had a circle of black where the rope had bruised it. His eyes felt congested; he could no longer close them. His tongue was swollen with thirst; he relieved its fever by thrusting it forward from between his teeth into the cold air. How softly the turf had carpeted the untraveled avenue—he could no longer feel the roadway beneath his feet!

Doubtless, despite his suffering, he had fallen asleep while walking, for now he sees another scene—perhaps he has merely recovered from a delirium. He stands at the gate of his own home. All is as he left it, and all bright and beautiful in the morning sunshine. He must have traveled the entire night. As he pushes open the gate and passes up the wide white walk, he sees a flutter of female garments; his wife, looking fresh and cool and sweet, steps down from the veranda to meet him. At the bottom of the steps she stands waiting, with a smile of ineffable joy, an attitude of matchless grace and dignity. Ah, how beautiful she is! He springs forward with extended arms. As he is about to clasp her he feels a stunning blow upon the back of the neck; a blinding white light blazes all about him with a sound like the shock of a cannon —then all is darkness and silence!

Peyton Farquhar was dead; his body, with a broken neck, swung gently from side to side beneath the timbers of the Owl Creek bridge.

●

●

A MEMORABLE FANCY

I WAS IN A printing house in hell, and saw the method in which knowledge is transmitted from generation to generation.

In the first chamber was a dragon-man, clearing away the rubbish from a cave's mouth; within, a number of dragons were hollowing the cave.

In the second chamber was a viper folding round the rock and the cave, and others adorning it with silver, gold, and precious stones.

In the third chamber was an eagle with wings and feathers of air; he caused the inside of the cave to be infinite; around were numbers of eagle-like men, who built palaces in the immense cliffs. In the fourth chamber were lions of flaming fire raging around and melting the metals into living fluids.

In the fifth chamber were unnamed forms, which cast the metal into the expanse.

There they were received by men who occupied the sixth chamber, and took the forms of books, and were arranged in libraries.

—WILLIAM BLAKE

THE GHOST-SHIP

The equitable and friendly relationship between living and dead personalities in Fairfield gives the following story a quality I have found nowhere except in the work of Middleton. Even he was a one-story author, in this as well as in other respects. Most of his work is gloom-struck and embittered; but *The Ghost-Ship* alone should carry his memory happily onward long after some of his "significant" contemporaries have been embalmed in footnotes, from which no ghosts arise.—EDITOR.

Richard
Middleton

THE
GHOST-SHIP

Fairfield is a little village lying near the Portsmouth Road about half-way between London and the sea. Strangers who find it by accident now and then, call it a pretty, old-fashioned place; we who live in it and call it home don't find anything very pretty about it, but we should be sorry to live anywhere else. Our minds have taken the shape of the inn and the church and the green, I suppose. At all events we never feel comfortable out of Fairfield.

Of course the Cockneys, with their vasty houses and noise-ridden streets, can call us rustics if they choose, but for all that Fairfield is a better place to live in than London. Doctor says that when he goes to London his mind is bruised with the weight of the houses, and he was a Cockney born. He had to live there himself when he was a little chap, but he knows better now. You gentlemen may laugh—perhaps some of you come from London way—but it seems to me that a witness like that is worth a gallon of arguments.

Dull? Well, you might find it dull, but I assure you that I've listened to all the London yarns you have spun to-night, and they're absolutely nothing to the things that happen at Fairfield. It's because of our way of thinking and minding our own business. If one of your Londoners were set down on the green of a Saturday night when the ghosts of the lads who died in the war keep tryst with the lasses who lie in the churchyard, he couldn't help being curious and interfering, and then the ghosts would go somewhere where it was quieter. But we just let them come and go and don't make any fuss, and in consequence Fairfield is the ghostiest place in all England. Why, I've seen a headless man sitting on the edge of the well in broad daylight, and the children playing about his feet as if he were their father. Take my word for it, spirits know when they are well off as much as human beings.

Still, I must admit that the thing I'm going to tell you about was queer even for our part of the world, where three packs of ghost-hounds hunt regularly during the season, and blacksmith's great-grandfather is busy all night shoeing the dead gentlemen's horses. Now that's a thing that wouldn't happen in London, because of their interfering way, but blacksmith he lies up aloft and sleeps as quiet as a lamb. Once when he had a bad head he shouted down to them not to make so much noise, and in the morning he found an old guinea left on the anvil as an apology. He wears it on his watch-chain now. But I must get on with my story; if I start telling you about the queer happenings at Fairfield I'll never stop.

It all came of the great storm in the spring of '97, the year that we had two great storms. This was the first one, and I remember it very well, because I found in the morning that it had lifted the thatch of my pigsty into the widow's garden as clean as a boy's kite. When I looked over the hedge, widow—Tom Lamport's widow that was—was prodding for her nasturtiums with a daisy-grubber. After I had watched her for a little I went down to the "Fox and Grapes" to tell landlord what she had said to me.

Landlord he laughed, being a married man and at ease with the sex. "Come to that," he said, "the tempest has blowed something into my field. A kind of a ship I think it would be."

I was surprised at that until he explained that it was only a ghost-ship and would do no hurt to the turnips. We argued that it had been blown up from the sea at Portsmouth, and then we talked of something else. There were two slates down at the parsonage and a big tree in Lumley's meadow. It was a rare storm.

I reckon the wind had blown our ghosts all over England. They were coming back for days afterwards with foundered horses and as footsore as possible, and they were so glad to get back to Fairfield that some of them walked up the street crying like little children. Squire said that his great-grandfather's great-grandfather hadn't looked so dead-beat since the battle of Naseby, and he's an educated man.

What with one thing and another, I should think it was a week before we got straight again, and then one afternoon I met the landlord on the green and he had a worried face. "I wish you'd come and have a look at that ship in my field," he said to me; "it seems to me it's leaning real hard on the turnips. I can't bear thinking what the missus will say when she sees it."

I walked down the lane with him, and sure enough there was a ship in the middle of his field, but such a ship as no man had seen on the water for three hundred years, let alone in the middle of a turnip-field. It was all painted black and covered with carvings, and there was a great bay window in the stern for all the world like the Squire's drawing-room. There was a crowd of little black cannon on deck and looking out of her port-holes, and she was anchored at each end to the hard ground. I have seen the wonders of the world on picture-postcards, but I have never seen anything to equal that.

"She seems very solid for a ghost-ship," I said, seeing the landlord was bothered.

"I should say it's a betwixt and between," he answered, puzzling it over, "but it's going to spoil a matter of fifty turnips, and missus she'll want it moved." We went up to her and touched the side, and it was as hard as a real ship. "Now there's folks in England would call that very curious," he said.

Now I don't know much about ships, but I should think that

that ghost-ship weighed a solid two hundred tons, and it seemed to me that she had come to stay, so that I felt sorry for landlord, who was a married man. "All the horses in Fairfield won't move her out of my turnips," he said, frowning at her.

Just then we heard a noise on her deck, and we looked up and saw that a man had come out of her front cabin and was looking down at us very peaceably. He was dressed in a black uniform set out with rusty gold lace, and he had a great cutlass by his side in a brass sheath. "I'm Captain Bartholomew Roberts," he said, in a gentleman's voice, "put in for recruits. I seem to have brought her rather far up the harbor."

"Harbor!" cried landlord; "why, you're fifty miles from the sea."

Captain Roberts didn't turn a hair. "So much as that, is it?" he said coolly. "Well, it's of no consequence."

Landlord was a bit upset at this. "I don't want to be un-neighborly," he said, "but I wish you hadn't brought your ship into my field. You see, my wife sets great store on these turnips."

The captain took a pinch of snuff out of a fine gold box that he pulled out of his pocket, and dusted his fingers with a silk handkerchief in a very genteel fashion. "I'm only here for a few months," he said; "but if a testimony of my esteem would pacify your good lady I should be content," and with the words he loosed a great gold brooch from the neck of his coat and tossed it down to landlord.

Landlord blushed as red as a strawberry. "I'm not denying she's fond of jewelry," he said, "but it's too much for half a sack-ful of turnips." And indeed it was a handsome brooch.

The captain laughed. "Tut, man," he said, "it's a forced sale, and you deserve a good price. Say no more about it," and nodding good-day to us, he turned on his heel and went into the cabin. Landlord walked back up the lane like a man with a weight off his mind. "That tempest has blowed me a bit of luck," he said; "the missus will be main pleased with that brooch. It's better than blacksmith's guinea, any day."

Ninety-seven was Jubilee year, the year of the second Jubilee, you remember, and we had great doings at Fairfield, so that we hadn't much time to bother about the ghost-ship, though anyhow it isn't our way to meddle in things that don't concern us. Landlord, he saw his tenant once or twice when he was hoeing his turnips and passed the time of day, and landlord's wife wore her new brooch to church every Sunday. But we didn't mix much with the ghosts at any time, all except an idiot lad there was in the village, and he didn't know the difference between a man and a ghost, poor innocent! On Jubilee Day, however, somebody told Captain Roberts why the church bells were ringing, and he hoisted a flag and fired off his guns like a loyal Englishman. 'Tis true the guns were shotted, and one of the round shot knocked a hole in Farmer Johnstone's barn, but nobody thought much of that in such a season of rejoicing.

It wasn't till our celebrations were over that we noticed that anything was wrong in Fairfield. 'Twas shoemaker who told me first about it one morning at the "Fox and Grapes." "You know my great great-uncle?" he said to me.

"You mean Joshua, the quiet lad," I answered, knowing him well.

"Quiet!" said shoemaker indignantly. "Quiet you call him, coming home at three o'clock every morning as drunk as a magistrate and waking up the whole house with his noise."

"Why, it can't be Joshua!" I said, for I knew him for one of the most respectable young ghosts in the village.

"Joshua it is," said shoemaker; "and one of these nights he'll find himself out in the street if he isn't careful."

This kind of talk shocked me, I can tell you, for I don't like to hear a man abusing his own family, and I could hardly believe that a steady youngster like Joshua had taken to drink. But just then in came butcher Aylwin in such a temper that he could hardly drink his beer. "The young puppy! the young puppy!" he kept on saying; and it was some time before shoemaker and I found out that he was talking about his ancestor that fell at Senlac.

"Drink?" said shoemaker hopefully, for we all like company in our misfortunes, and butcher nodded grimly.

"The young noodle," he said, emptying his tankard.

Well, after that I kept my ears open, and it was the same story all over the village. There was hardly a young man among all the ghosts of Fairfield who didn't roll home in the small hours of the morning the worse for liquor. I used to wake up in the night and hear them stumble past my house, singing outrageous songs.

The worst of it was that we couldn't keep the scandal to ourselves, and the folk at Greenhill began to talk of "sodden Fairfield" and taught their children to sing a song about us:

> "Sodden Fairfield, sodden Fairfield, has no use for bread-
>   and-butter,
> Rum for breakfast, rum for dinner, rum for tea, and rum for
>   supper!"

We are easy-going in our village, but we didn't like that.

Of course we soon found out where the young fellows went
to get the drink, and landlord was terribly cut up that his tenant
should have turned out so badly, but his wife wouldn't hear of
parting with the brooch, so that he couldn't give the Captain notice
to quit. But as time went on, things grew from bad to worse, and
at all hours of the day you would see those young reprobates sleeping it off on the village green. Nearly every afternoon a ghost-
wagon used to jolt down to the ship with a lading of rum, and
though the older ghosts seemed inclined to give the Captain's
hospitality the go-by, the youngsters were neither to hold nor to
bind.

So one afternoon when I was taking my nap I heard a knock
at the door, and there was parson looking very serious, like a man
with a job before him that he didn't altogether relish. "I'm going
down to talk to the Captain about all this drunkenness in the village, and I want you to come with me," he said straight out.

I can't say that I fancied the visit much myself, and I tried
to hint to parson that as, after all, they were only a lot of ghosts,
it didn't very much matter.

"Dead or alive, I'm responsible for their good conduct," he
said, "and I'm going to do my duty and put a stop to this continued disorder. And you are coming with me, John Simmons." So
I went, parson being a persuasive kind of man.

We went down to the ship, and as we approached her I could
see the Captain tasting the air on deck. When he saw parson he
took off his hat very politely, and I can tell you that I was relieved
to find that he had a proper respect for the cloth. Parson acknowledged his salute and spoke out stoutly enough. "Sir, I should be
glad to have a word with you."

"Come on board, sir; come on board," said the Captain, and I could tell by his voice that he knew why we were there. Parson and I climbed up an uneasy kind of ladder, and the Captain took us into the great cabin at the back of the ship, where the bay-window was. It was the most wonderful place you ever saw in your life, all full of gold and silver plate, swords with jewelled scabbards, carved oak chairs, and great chests that look as though they were bursting with guineas. Even parson was surprised, and he did not shake his head very hard when the Captain took down some silver cups and poured us out a drink of rum. I tasted mine, and I don't mind saying that it changed my view of things entirely. There was nothing betwixt and between about that rum, and I felt that it was ridiculous to blame the lads for drinking too much of stuff like that. It seemed to fill my veins with honey and fire.

Parson put the case squarely ·to the Captain, but I didn't listen much to what he said; I was busy sipping my drink and looking through the window at the fishes swimming to and fro over landlord's turnips. Just then it seemed the most natural thing in the world that they should be there, though afterwards, of course, I could see that that proved it was a ghost-ship.

But even then I thought it was queer when I saw a drowned sailor float by in the thin air with his hair and beard all full of bubbles. It was the first time I had seen anything quite like that at Fairfield.

All the time I was regarding the wonders of the deep parson was telling Captain Roberts how there was no peace or rest in the village owing to the curse of drunkenness, and what a bad example the youngsters were setting to the older ghosts. The Captain listened very attentively, and only put in a word now and then about boys being boys and young men sowing their wild oats. But when parson had finished his speech he filled up our silver cups and said to parson, with a flourish, "I should be sorry to cause trouble anywhere where I have been made welcome, and you will be glad to hear that I put to sea to-morrow night. And now you must drink me a prosperous voyage." So we all stood up and drank the toast with honor, and that noble rum was like hot oil in my veins.

After that Captain showed us some of the curiosities he had brought back from foreign parts, and we were greatly amazed, though afterwards I couldn't clearly remember what they were. And then I found myself walking across the turnips with parson, and I was telling him of the glories of the deep that I had seen through the window of the ship. He turned on me severely. "If I were you, John Simmons," he said, "I should go straight home to bed." He has a way of putting things that wouldn't occur to an ordinary man, has parson, and I did as he told me.

Well, next day it came on to blow, and it blew harder and harder, till about eight o'clock at night I heard a noise and looked out into the garden. I dare say you won't believe me, it seems a bit tall even to me, but the wind had lifted the thatch of my pigsty into the widow's garden a second time. I thought I wouldn't wait to hear what widow had to say about it, so I went across the green to the "Fox and Grapes," and the wind was so strong that I danced along on tip-toe like a girl at the fair. When I got to the inn landlord had to help me shut the door; it seemed as though a dozen goats were pushing against it to come in out of the storm.

"It's a powerful tempest," he said, drawing the beer. "I hear there's a chimney down at Dickory End."

"It's a funny thing how these sailors know about the weather," I answered. "When Captain said he was going to-night, I was thinking it would take a capful of wind to carry the ship back to sea, but now here's more than a capful."

"Ah, yes," said landlord, "it's to-night he goes true enough and, mind you, though he treated me handsome over the rent, I'm not sure it's a loss to the village. I don't hold with gentrice who fetch their drink from London instead of helping local traders to get their living."

"But you haven't got any rum like his," I said, to draw him out.

His neck grew red above his collar, and I was afraid I'd gone too far, but after a while he got his breath with a grunt.

"John Simmons," he said, "if you've come down here this windy night to talk a lot of fool's talk, you've wasted a journey."

Well, of course, then I had to smooth him down with praising his rum, and Heaven forgive me for swearing it was better than Captain's. For the like of that rum no living lips have tasted save mine and parson's. But somehow or other I brought landlord round, and presently we must have a glass of his best to prove its quality.

"Beat that if you can!" he cried, and we both raised our glasses to our mouths, only to stop half-way and look at each other in amaze. For the wind that had been howling outside like an outrageous dog had all of a sudden turned as melodious as the carol-boys of a Christmas Eve.

"Surely that's not my Martha," whispered landlord; Martha being his great-aunt that lived in the loft over-head.

We went to the door, and the wind burst it open so that the handle was driven clean into the plaster of the wall. But we didn't think about that at the time; for over our heads, sailing very comfortably through the windy stars, was the ship that had passed the summer in landlord's field. Her portholes and her bay-window were blazing with lights, and there was a noise of singing and fiddling on her decks. "He's gone," shouted landlord above the storm, "and he's taken half the village with him!" I could only nod in answer, not having lungs like bellows of leather.

In the morning we were able to measure the strength of the storm, and over and above my pigsty there was damage enough wrought in the village to keep us busy. True it is that the children had to break down no branches for the firing that autumn, since the wind had strewn the woods with more than they could carry away. Many of our ghosts were scattered abroad, but this time very few came back, all the young men having sailed with Captain; and not only ghosts, for a poor half-witted lad was missing, and we reckoned that he had stowed himself away or perhaps shipped as cabin-boy, not knowing any better.

What with the lamentations of the ghost-girls and the grumbling of families who had lost an ancestor, the village was upset for a while, and the funny thing was that it was the folk who had complained most of the carryings-on of the youngsters, who made most noise now that they were gone. I hadn't any sympathy with shoemaker or butcher, who ran about saying how much they missed their lads, but it made me grieve to hear the poor bereaved girls calling their lovers by name on the village green at nightfall. It didn't seem fair to me that they should have lost their men a second time, after giving up life in order to join them, as like as not. Still, not even a spirit can be sorry for ever, and after a few months we made up our minds that the folk who had sailed in the ship were never coming back, and we didn't talk about it any more.

And then one day, I dare say it would be a couple of years after, when the whole business was quite forgotten, who should come trapesing along the road from Porstmouth but the daft lad who had gone away with the ship, without waiting till he was dead to become a ghost. You never saw such a boy as that in all your life. He had a great rusty cutlass hanging to a string at his waist, and he was tattooed all over in fine colors, so that even his face looked like a girl's sampler. He had a handkerchief in his hand full of foreign shells and old-fashioned pieces of small money, very curious, and he walked up to the well outside his mother's house and drew himself a drink as if he had been nowhere in particular.

The worst of it was that he had come back as soft-headed as he went, and try as we might we couldn't get anything reasonable out of him. He talked a lot of gibberish about keel-hauling and walking the plank and crimson murders—things which a decent sailor should know nothing about, so that it seemed to me that for all his manners Captain had been more of a pirate than a gentleman mariner. But to draw sense out of that boy was as hard as picking cherries off a crab-tree. One silly tale he had that he kept on drifting back to, and to hear him you would have thought that it was the only thing that happened to him in his life. "We was at anchor," he would say, "off an island called the Basket of Flowers, and the sailors had caught a lot of parrots and we were teaching them to swear. Up and down the decks, up and down the decks, and the language they used was dreadful. Then we looked up and saw the masts of the Spanish ship outside the harbor. Outside the harbor they were, so we threw the parrots into the sea and sailed out to fight. And all the parrots were drowned in the sea and the language they used was dreadful." That's the sort of boy he was, nothing but silly talk of parrots when we asked him about the fighting. And we never had a chance of teaching him better, for two days after he ran away again, and hasn't been seen since.

That's my story, and I assure you that things like that are happening at Fairfield all the time. The ship has never come back, but somehow as people grow older they seem to think that one of these windy nights she'll come sailing in over the hedges with all the lost ghosts on board. Well, when she comes, she'll be welcome. There's one ghost-lass that has never grown tired of waiting for her lad to return. Every night you'll see her out on the green, straining her poor eyes with looking for the mast-lights among the stars. A faithful lass you'd call her, and I'm thinking you'd be right.

Landlord's field wasn't a penny the worse for the visit, but they do say that since then the turnips that have been grown in it have tasted of rum.

●

I DO THINK that many mysteries ascribed to our own inventions, have been the courteous revelations of spirits; for those noble essences in heaven, bear a friendly regard unto their fellow-nature on earth; and therefore believe that those many prodigies and ominous prognostics, which forerun the ruins of states, princes, and private persons, are the charitable premonitions of good angels, which more careless enquiries term but the effects of chance and nature.

—RELIGIO MEDICI

WILLIAM WILSON

The psychic double, a "twin" who has no blood-relationship to the person he duplicates, has long fascinated the Germanic mind; and the German language contains a special word to describe him: *doppelganger*. The theme is rare in English. Poe has used it superbly, in one of his less well known tales. As is so often the case with the best ghost stories, the specter can be regarded by different readers in different ways. Is it a mere allegorical representation of William Wilson's conscience? or is it a valid spook? I prefer not to pass judgment.—EDITOR.

Edgar Allan Poe

WILLIAM WILSON

What say of it? what says CONSCIENCE *grim,*
That spectre in my path?
—CHAMBERLAYNE'S PHARRONID

Let me call myself, for the present, William
Wilson. The fair page now lying before me need not be sullied
with my real appellation. This has been already too much an object for the scorn—for the horror—for the detestation of my race.
To the uttermost regions of the globe have not the indignant
winds bruited its unparalleled infamy? Oh, outcast of all outcasts
most abandoned!—to the earth art thou not for ever dead? to its
honors, to its flowers, to its golden aspirations?—and a cloud, dense,
dismal, and limitless, does it not hang eternally between thy hopes
and heaven?

437

I would not, if I could, here or to-day, embody a record of my later years of unspeakable misery and unpardonable crime. This epoch—these later years—took unto themselves a sudden elevation in turpitude, whose origin alone it is my present purpose to assign. Men usually grow base by degrees. From me, in an instant, all virtue dropped bodily as a mantle. From comparatively trivial wickedness I passed, with the stride of a giant, into more than the enormities of an Elah-Gabalus. What chance—what one event brought this evil thing to pass, bear with me while I relate. Death approaches; and the shadow which foreruns him has thrown a softening influence over my spirit. I long, in passing through the dim valley, for the sympathy—I had nearly said for the pity—of my fellow men. I would fain have them believe that I have been, in some measure, the slave of circumstances beyond human control. I would wish them to seek out for me, in the details I am about to give, some little oasis of *fatality* amid a wilderness of error. I would have them allow—what they cannot refrain from allowing —that, although temptation may have ere-while existed as great, man was never *thus*, at least, tempted before—certainly, never *thus* fell. And is it therefore that he has never thus suffered? Have I not indeed been living in a dream? And am I not now dying a victim to the horror and the mystery of the wildest of all sublunary visions?

I am the descendant of a race whose imaginative and easily excitable temperament has at all times rendered them remarkable; and, in my earliest infancy, I gave evidence of having fully inherited the family character. As I advanced in years it was more strongly developed; becoming, for many reasons, a cause of serious disquietude to my friends, and of positive injury to myself. I grew self-willed, addicted to the wildest caprices, and a prey to the most ungovernable passions. Weak-minded, and beset with constitutional infirmities akin to my own, my parents could do but little to check the evil propensities which distinguished me. Some feeble and ill-directed efforts resulted in complete failure on their part, and, of course, in total triumph on mine. Thenceforward my voice was a household law; and at an age when few children have abandoned their leading strings, I was left to the guidance of my own will, and became, in all but name, the master of my own actions.

My earliest recollections of a school-life, are connected with a large, rambling, Elizabethan house, in a misty-looking village of England, where were a vast number of gigantic and gnarled trees, and where all the houses were excessively ancient. In truth, it was a dream-like and spirit-soothing place, that venerable old town. At this moment, in fancy, I feel the refreshing chilliness of its deeply-shadowed avenues, inhale the fragrance of its thousand shrubberies, and thrill anew with undefinable delight, at the deep hollow note of the church-bell, breaking, each hour, with sullen and sudden roar, upon the stillness of the dusky atmosphere in which the fretted Gothic steeple lay embedded and asleep.

It gives me, perhaps, as much of pleasure as I can now in any manner experience, to dwell upon minute recollections of the school and its concerns. Steeped in misery as I am—misery, alas! only too real—I shall be pardoned for seeking relief, however slight and temporary, in the weakness of a few rambling details. These, moreover, utterly trivial, and even ridiculous in themselves, assume, to my fancy, adventitious importance, as connected with a period and a locality when and where I recognize the first ambiguous monitions of the destiny which afterward so fully overshadowed me. Let me then remember.

The house, I have said, was old and irregular. The grounds were extensive, and a high and solid brick wall, topped with a bed of mortar and broken glass, encompassed the whole. This prison-like rampart formed the limit of our domain; beyond it we saw but thrice a week—once every Saturday afternoon, when, attended by two ushers, we were permitted to take brief walks in a body through some of the neighboring fields—and twice during Sunday, when we were paraded in the same formal manner to the morning and evening service in the one church of the village. Of this church the principal of our school was pastor. With how deep a spirit of wonder and perplexity was I wont to regard him from our remote pew in the gallery, as, with step solemn and slow, he ascended the pulpit! This reverend man, with countenance so demurely benign, with robes so glossy and so clerically flowing, with wig so minutely powdered, so rigid and so vast,—could this be he who, of late, with sour visage, and in snuffy habiliments, administered, ferule in hand, the Draconian laws of the academy? O gigantic paradox, too utterly monstrous for solution!

At an angle of the ponderous wall frowned a more ponderous

gate. It was riveted and studded with jagged iron spikes. What impressions of deep awe did it inspire! It was never opened save for the three periodical egressions and ingressions already mentioned; then, in every creak of its mighty hinges, we found a plenitude of mystery—a world of matter for solemn remark, or for more solemn meditation.

The extensive enclosure was irregular in form, having many capacious recesses. Of these, three or four of the largest constituted the play-ground. It was level, and covered with fine hard gravel. I well remember it had no trees, nor benches, nor any thing similar within it. Of course it was in the rear of the house. In front lay a small parterre, planted with box and other shrubs, but through this sacred division we passed only upon rare occasions indeed—such as a first advent to school or final departure thence, or perhaps, when a parent or friend having called for us, we joyfully took our way home for the Christmas or Midsummer holidays.

But the house!—how quaint an old building was this!—to me how veritable a palace of enchantment! There was really no end to its windings—to its incomprehensible subdivisions. It was difficult, at any given time, to say with certainty upon which of its two stories one happened to be. From each room to every other there were sure to be found three or four steps either in ascent or descent. Then the lateral branches were innumerable—inconceivable—and so returning in upon themselves, that our most exact ideas in regard to the whole mansion were not very far different from those with which we pondered upon infinity. During the five years of my residence here, I was never able to ascertain with precision, in what remote locality lay the little sleeping apartment assigned to myself and some eighteen or twenty other scholars.

The school-room was the largest in the house—I could not help thinking, in the world. It was very long, narrow, and dismally low, with pointed Gothic windows and a ceiling of oak. In a remote and terror-inspiring angle was a square enclosure of eight or ten feet, comprising the *sanctum*, "during hours," of our principal, the Reverend Dr. Bransby. It was a solid structure, with massy door, sooner than open which in the absence of the "Dominie," we would all have willingly perished by the *peine forte et dure*. In other angles were two other similar boxes, far less reverenced, indeed, but still greatly matters of awe. One of these was the pulpit of the "classical" usher, one of the "English and mathematical." Interspersed about the room, crossing and recrossing in endless irregularity, were innumerable benches and desks, black, ancient, and time-worn, piled desperately with much bethumbed books, and so beseamed with initial letters, names at full length, grotesque figures, and other multiplied efforts of the knife, as to have entirely lost what little of original form might have been their portion in days long departed. A huge bucket of water stood at one extremity of the room and a clock of stupendous dimensions at the other.

Encompassed by the massy walls of this venerable academy, I passed, yet not in tedium or disgust, the years of the third lustrum of my life. The teeming brain of childhood requires no external world of incident to occupy or amuse it; and the apparently dismal monotony of a school was replete with more intense excitement than my riper youth has derived from luxury, or my full manhood from crime. Yet I must believe that my first mental development had in it much of the uncommon—even much of the *outré*. Upon mankind at large the events of very early existence rarely leave in mature age any definite impression. All is gray shadow—a weak and irregular remembrance—an indistinct regathering of feeble pleasures and phantasmagoric pains. With me this is not so. In childhood I must have felt with the energy of a man what I now find stamped upon memory in lines as vivid, as deep, and as durable as the *exergues* of the Carthaginian medals.

Yet in fact—in the fact of the world's view—how little was there to remember! The morning's awakening, the nightly summons to bed; the connings, the recitations; the periodical half-holidays, and perambulations; the play-ground, with its broils, its pastimes, its intrigues;—these, by a mental sorcery long forgotten, were made to involve a wilderness of sensation, a world of rich incident, an universe of varied emotion, of excitement, the most passionate and spirit-stirring. *"Oh, le bon temps, que ce siècle de fer?"*

In truth, the ardor, the enthusiasm, and the imperiousness of my disposition, soon rendered me a marked character among my schoolmates, and by slow, but natural gradations, gave me an ascendancy over all not greatly older than myself;—over all with a single exception. This exception was found in the person of a scholar, who, although no relation, bore the same Christian and surname as myself;—a circumstance, in fact, little remarkable; for notwithstanding a noble descent, mine was one of those every-day appellations which seem, by prescriptive right, to have been, time out of mind, the common property of the mob. In this narrative I have therefore designated myself as William Wilson,—a fictitious title not very dissimilar to the real. My namesake alone, of those who in school phraseology constituted "our set," presumed to compete with me in the studies of the class—in the sports and broils of the play-ground—to refuse implicit belief in my assertions, and submission to my will—indeed, to interfere with my arbitrary dictation in any respect whatsoever. If there is on earth a supreme and unqualified despotism, it is the despotism of a master-mind in boyhood over the less energetic spirits of its companions.

Wilson's rebellion was to me a source of the greatest embarrassment; the more so as, in spite of the bravado with which in public I made a point of treating him and his pretensions, I secretly felt that I feared him, and could not help thinking the equality which he maintained so easily with myself, a proof of his true superiority; since not to be overcome cost me a perpetual struggle. Yet this superiority—even this equality—was in truth acknowledged by no one but myself; our associates, by some unaccountable blindness, seemed not even to suspect it. Indeed, his competition, his resistance, and especially his impertinent and dogged interference with my purposes, were not more pointed than private. He appeared to be destitute alike of the ambition which urged, and of the passionate energy of mind which enabled me to excel. In his rivalry he might have been supposed actuated solely by a whimsical desire to thwart, astonish, or mortify myself; although there were times when I could not help observing, with a feeling made up of wonder, abasement, and pique, that he mingled with his injuries, his insults, or his contradictions, a certain most inappropriate, and assuredly most unwelcome *affectionateness* of manner. I could only conceive this singular behavior to arise from a consummate self-conceit assuming the vulgar airs of patronage and protection.

Perhaps it was this latter trait in Wilson's conduct, conjoined with our identity of name, and the mere accident of our having entered the school upon the same day, which set afloat the notion that we were brothers, among the senior classes in the academy. These do not usually inquire with much strictness into the affairs of their juniors. I have before said, or should have said, that Wilson was not, in a most remote degree, connected with my family. But assuredly if we *had* been brothers we must have been twins; for, after leaving Dr. Bransby's, I casually learned that my namesake was born on the nineteenth of January, 1813—and this is a somewhat remarkable coincidence; for the day is precisely that of my own nativity.

It may seem strange that in spite of the continual anxiety occasioned me by the rivalry of Wilson, and his intolerable spirit of contradiction, I could not bring myself to hate him altogether. We had, to be sure, nearly every day a quarrel in which, yielding me publicly the palm of victory, he, in some manner, contrived to make me feel that it was he who had deserved it; yet a sense of pride on my part, and a veritable dignity on his own, kept us always upon what are called "speaking terms," while there were many points of strong congeniality in our tempers, operating to awake in me a sentiment which our position alone, perhaps, prevented from ripening into friendship. It is difficult, indeed, to define, or even to describe, my real feelings toward him. They formed a motley and heterogeneous admixture;—some petulant animosity, which was not yet hatred, some esteem, more respect, much fear, with a world of uneasy curiosity. To the moralist it will be necessary to say, in addition, that Wilson and myself were the most inseparable of companions.

It was no doubt the anomalous state of affairs existing between us, which turned all my attacks upon him, (and there were many, either open or covert) into the channel of banter or practical joke (giving pain while assuming the aspect of mere fun) rather than into a more serious and determined hostility. But my endeavors on this head were by no means uniformly successful, even when my plans were the most wittily concocted; for my namesake had much about him, in character, of that unassuming and quiet austerity which, while enjoying the poignancy of its own jokes, has no heel of Achilles in itself, and absolutely refuses to be laughed at. I could find, indeed, but one vulnerable point, and that, lying in a personal peculiarity, arising, perhaps, from constitutional disease, would have been spared by any antagonist less at his wit's end than myself;—my rival had a weakness in the faucial or guttural organs, which precluded him from raising his voice at any time *above a very low whisper*. Of this defect I did not fail to take what poor advantage lay in my power.

Wilson's retaliations in kind were many; and there was one form of his practical wit that disturbed me beyond measure. How his sagacity first discovered at all that so petty a thing would vex me, is a question I never could solve; but having discovered, he habitually practised the annoyance. I had always felt aversion to my uncourtly patronymic, and its very common, if not plebeian prænomen. The words were venom in my ears; and when, upon the day of my arrival, a second William Wilson came also to the academy, I felt angry with him for bearing the name, and doubly disgusted with the name because a stranger bore it, who would be the cause of its twofold repetition, who would be constantly in my presence, and whose concerns, in the ordinary routine of the school business, must inevitably, on account of the detestable coincidence, be often confounded with my own.

The feeling of vexation thus engendered grew stronger with every circumstance tending to show resemblance, moral or physical, between my rival and myself. I had not then discovered the remarkable fact that we were of the same age; but I saw that we were even singularly alike in general contour of person and outline of feature. I was galled, too, by the rumor touching a relationship, which had grown current in the upperforms. In a word, nothing could more seriously disturb me, (although I scrupulously concealed such disturbance), than any allusion to a similarity of mind, person, or condition existing between us. But, in truth, I had no reason to believe that (with the exception of the matter of relationship, and in the case of Wilson himself), this similarity had ever been made a subject of comment, or even observed at all by our schoolfellows. That *he* observed it in all its bearings, and as fixedly as I, was apparent; but that he could discover in such circumstances so fruitful a field of annoyance, can only be attributed, as I said before, to his more than ordinary penetration.

His cue, which was to perfect an imitation of myself, lay both in words and in actions; and most admirably did he play his part. My dress it was an easy matter to copy; my gait and general manner were, without difficulty, appropriated; in spite of his constitutional defect, even my voice did not escape him. My louder tones were, of course, unattempted, but then the key,—it was identical; *and his singular whisper, it grew the very echo of my own.*

How greatly this most exquisite portraiture harassed me (for it could not justly be termed a caricature), I will not now venture to describe. I had but one consolation—in the fact that the imitation, apparently, was noticed by myself alone, and that I had to endure only the knowing and strangely sarcastic smiles of my namesake himself. Satisfied with having produced in my bosom the intended effect, he seemed to chuckle in secret over the sting he had inflicted, and was characteristically disregardful of the public applause which the success of his witty endeavors might have so easily elicited. That the school, indeed, did not feel his design, perceive its accomplishment, and participate in his sneer, was, for many anxious months, a riddle I could not resolve. Perhaps the *gradation* of his copy rendered it not readily perceptible; or more possibly, I owed my security to the masterly air of the copyist, who, disdaining the letter (which in a painting is all the obtuse can see), gave but the full spirit of his original for my individual contemplation and chagrin.

I have already more than once spoken of the disgusting air of patronage which he assumed toward me, and of his frequent officious interference with my will. This interference often took the ungracious character of advice; advice not openly given, but hinted or insinuated. I received it with a repugnance which gained strength as I grew in years. Yet, at this distant day, let me do him the simple justice to acknowledge that I can recall no occasion when the suggestions of my rival were on the side of those errors or follies so usual to his immature age and seeming inexperience; that his moral sense, at least, if not his general talents and worldly wisdom, was far keener than my own; and that I might, to-day, have been a better and thus a happier man, had I less frequently rejected the counsels embodied in those meaning whispers which I then but too cordially hated and too bitterly despised.

As it was, I at length grew restive in the extreme under his distasteful supervision, and daily resented more and more openly, what I considered his intolerable arrogance. I have said that, in the first years of our connection as schoolmates, my feelings in regard to him might have been easily ripened into friendship; but, in the latter months of my residence at the academy, although the intrusion of his ordinary manner had, beyond doubt, in some measure, abated, my sentiments, in nearly similar proportion, partook very much of positive hatred. Upon one occasion he saw this, I think, and afterward avoided, or made a show of avoiding me.

It was about the same period, if I remember aright, that, in an altercation of violence with him, in which he was more than usually thrown off his guard, and spoke and acted with an openness of demeanor rather foreign to his nature, I discovered, or fancied I discovered, in his accent, in his air, and general appearance, a something which first startled, and then deeply interested me, by bringing to mind dim visions of my earliest infancy—wild, confused, and thronging memories of a time when memory herself was yet unborn. I cannot better describe the sensation which oppressed me, than by saying that I could with difficulty shake off the belief of my having been acquainted with the being who stood before me, at some epoch very long ago—some point of the past even infinitely remote. The delusion, however, faded rapidly as it came; and I mention it at all but to define the day of the last conversation I there held with my singular namesake.

The huge old house, with its countless subdivisions, had several large chambers communicating with each other, where slept the greater number of the students. There were, however (as must necessarily happen in a building so awkwardly planned), many little nooks or recesses, the odds and ends of the structure; and these the economic ingenuity of Dr. Bransby had also fitted up as dormitories; although, being the merest closets, they were capable of accommodating but a single individual. One of these small apartments was occupied by Wilson.

One night, about the close of my fifth year at the school, and immediately after the altercation just mentioned, finding every one wrapped in sleep, I arose from bed, and, lamp in hand, stole through a wilderness of narrow passages, from my own bedroom to that of my rival. I had long been plotting one of those ill-natured pieces of practical wit at his expense in which I had hitherto been so uniformly unsuccessful. It was my intention, now, to put my scheme in operation and I resolved to make him feel the whole extent of the malice with which I was imbued. Having reached his closet, I noiselessly entered, leaving the lamp, with a shade over it, on the outside. I advanced a step and listened to the sound of his tranquil breathing. Assured of his being asleep, I returned, took the light, and with it again approached the bed. Close curtains were around it, which, in the prosecution of my plan, I slowly and quietly withdrew, when the bright rays fell vividly upon the sleeper, and my eyes at the same moment, upon his countenance. I looked;—and a numbness, an iciness of feeling instantly pervaded my frame. My breast heaved, my knees tottered, my whole spirit became possessed with an objectless yet intolerable horror. Gasping for breath, I lowered the lamp in still nearer proximity to the face. Were these,—*these* the lineaments of William Wilson? I saw, indeed, that they were his, but I shook as if with a fit of the ague, in fancying they were not. What *was* there about them to confound me in this manner? I gazed;—while my brain reeled with a multitude of incoherent thoughts. Not thus he appeared—assuredly not *thus*—in the vivacity of his waking hours. The same name! the same contour of person! the same day of arrival at the academy! And then his dogged and meaningless imitations of my gait, my voice, my habits, and my manner! Was it, in truth, within the bounds of human possibility, that *what I now saw* was the result, merely, of the habitual practice of this sarcastic imitation? Awe-stricken, and with a creeping shudder, I extinguished the lamp, passed silently from the chamber, and left, at once, the halls of that old academy, never to enter them again.

After a lapse of some months, spent at home in mere idleness, I found myself a student at Eton. The brief interval had been sufficient to enfeeble my remembrance of the events at Dr. Bransby's, or at least to effect a material change in the nature of the feelings with which I remembered them. The truth—the tragedy—of the drama was no more. I could now find room to doubt the evidence of my senses; and seldom called up the subject at all but with wonder at the extent of human credulity, and a smile at the vivid force of the imagination which I hereditarily possessed. Neither was this species of skepticism likely to be diminished by the character of the life I led at Eton. The vortex of thoughtless folly into which I there so immediately and so recklessly plunged, washed away all but the froth of my past hours, ingulfed at once every solid or serious impression, and left to memory only the veriest levities of a former existence.

I do not wish, however, to trace the course of my miserable profligacy here—a profligacy which set at defiance the laws, while it eluded the vigilance of the institution. Three years of folly, passed without profit, had but given me rooted habits of vice, and added, in a somewhat unusual degree, to my bodily stature, when, after a week of soulless dissipation, I invited a small party of the most dissolute students to a secret carousal in my chambers. We met at a late hour of the night; for our debaucheries were to be faithfully protracted until morning. The wine flowed freely, and there were not wanting other and perhaps more dangerous seductions; so that the gray dawn had already faintly appeared in the east while our delirious extravagance was at its height. Madly flushed with cards and intoxication, I was in the act of insisting upon a toast of more than wonted profanity, when my attention was suddenly diverted by the violent, although partial, unclosing of the door of the apartment, and by the eager voice of a servant without. He said that some person, apparently in great haste, demanded to speak with me in the hall.

Wildly excited with wine, the unexpected interruption rather delighted than surprised me. I staggered forward at once, and a few steps brought me to the vestibule of the building. In this low and small room there hung no lamp; and now no light at all was admitted, save that of the exceedingly feeble dawn which made its way through the semi-circular window. As I put my foot over the threshold, I became aware of the figure of a youth about my own height, and habited in a white kerseymere morning frock, cut in the novel fashion of the one I myself wore at the moment. This the faint light enabled me to perceive; but the features of his face I could not distinguish. Upon my entering, he strode hurriedly up to me, and, seizing me by the arm with a gesture of petulant impatience, whispered the words "William Wilson" in my ear.

I grew perfectly sober in an instant.

There was that in the manner of the stranger, and in the tremulous shake of his uplifted finger, as he held it between my eyes and the light, which filled me with unqualified amazement; but it was not this which had so violently moved me. It was the pregnancy of solemn admonition in the singular, low, hissing utterance; and, above all, it was the character, the tone, *the key*, of those few, simple, and familiar, yet *whispered* syllables, which came with a thousand thronging memories of by-gone days, and struck upon my soul with the shock of a galvanic battery. Ere I could recover the use of my senses he was gone.

Although this event failed not of a vivid effect upon my disordered imagination, yet was it evanescent as vivid. For some weeks, indeed, I busied myself in earnest inquiry, or was wrapped in a cloud of morbid speculation. I did not pretend to disguise from my perception the identity of the singular individual who thus perseveringly interfered with my affairs, and harassed me with his insinuated counsel. But who and what was this Wilson?—and whence came he?—and what were his purposes? Upon neither of these points could I be satisfied—merely ascertaining, in regard to him, that a sudden accident in his family had caused his removal from Dr. Bransby's academy on the afternoon of the day in which I myself had eloped. But in a brief period I ceased to think upon the subject, my attention being all absorbed in a contemplated departure for Oxford. Thither I soon went, the uncalculating vanity of my parents furnishing me with an outfit and annual establishment which would enable me to indulge at will in the luxury already so dear to my heart—to vie in profuseness of expenditure with the haughtiest heirs of the wealthiest earldoms in Great Britain.

Excited by such appliances to vice, my constitutional temperament broke forth with redoubled ardor, and I spurned even the common restraints of decency in the mad infatuation of my revels. But it were absurd to pause in the detail of my extravagance. Let it suffice, that among spendthrifts I out-Heroded Herod, and that, giving name to a multitude of novel follies, I added no brief appendix to the long catalogue of vices then usual in the most dissolute university of Europe.

It could hardly be credited, however, that I had, even here, so utterly fallen from the gentlemanly estate, as to seek acquaintance with the vilest arts of the gambler by profession, and, having become an adept in his despicable science; to practice it habitually as a means of increasing my already enormous income at the expense of the weak-minded among my fellow-collegians. Such, nevertheless, was the fact. And the very enormity of this offence against all manly and honorable sentiment proved, beyond doubt, the main if not the sole reason of the impunity with which it was committed. Who, indeed, among my most abandoned associates, would not rather have disputed the clearest evidence of his senses, than have suspected of such courses, the gay, the frank, the generous William Wilson—the noblest and most liberal commoner at Oxford—him whose follies (said his parasites) were but the follies of youth and unbridled fancy—whose errors but inimitable whim—whose darkest vice but a careless and dashing extravagance?

I had been now two years successfully busied in this way, when there came to the university a young *parvenu* nobleman, Glendenning—rich, said report, as Herodes Atticus—his riches, too, as easily acquired. I soon found him of weak intellect, and, of course, marked him as a fitting subject for my skill. I frequently engaged him in play, and contrived, with the gambler's usual art, to let him win considerable sums, the more effectually to entangle him in my snares. At length, my schemes being ripe, I met him (with the full intention that this meeting should be final and decisive) at the chambers of a fellow-commoner (Mr. Preston), equally intimate with both, but who, to do him justice, entertained not even a remote suspicion of my design. To give to this a better coloring, I had contrived to have assembled a party of some eight or ten, and was solicitously careful that the introduction of cards should appear accidental, and originate in the proposal of my contemplated dupe himself. To be brief upon a vile topic, none of the low finesse was omitted, so customary upon similar occasions, that it is a just matter for wonder how any are still found so besotted as to fall its victim.

We had protracted our sitting far into the night, and I had at length effected the manoeuvre of getting Glendenning as my sole antagonist. The game, too, was my favorite *écarté*. The rest of the company, interested in the extent of our play, had abandoned their own cards, and were standing around us as spectators. The *parvenu*, who had been induced by my artifices in the early part of the evening, to drink deeply, now shuffled, dealt, or played, with a wild nervousness of manner for which his intoxication, I thought, might partially, but could not altogether account. In a very short period he had become my debtor to a large amount, when, having taken a long draught of port, he did precisely what

I had been coolly anticipating—he proposed to double our already extravagant stakes. With a well-feigned show of reluctance, and not until after my repeated refusal had seduced him into some angry words which gave a color of *pique* to my compliance, did I finally comply. The result, of course, did but prove how entirely the prey was in my toils: in less than an hour he had quadrupled his debt. For some time his countenance had been losing the florid tinge lent it by the wine; but now, to my astonishment, I perceived that it had grown to a pallor truly fearful. I say, to my astonishment. Glendenning had been represented to my eager inquiries as immeasurably wealthy; and the sums which he had as yet lost, although in themselves vast, could not, I supposed, very seriously annoy, much less so violently affect him. That he was overcome by the wine just swallowed, was the idea which most readily presented itself; and, rather with a view to the preservation of my own character in the eyes of my associates, than from any less interested motive, I was about to insist, peremptorily, upon a discontinuance of the play, when some expressions at my elbow from among the company, and an ejaculation evincing utter despair on the part of Glendenning, gave me to understand that I had effected his total ruin under circumstances which, rendering him an object for the pity of all, should have protected him from the ill offices even of a fiend.

What now might have been my conduct it is difficult to say. The pitiable condition of my dupe had thrown an air of embarrassed gloom over all; and, for some moments, a profound silence was maintained, during which I could not help feeling my cheeks tingle with the many burning glances of scorn or reproach cast upon me by the less abandoned of the party. I will even own that an intolerable weight of anxiety was for a brief instant lifted from my bosom by the sudden and extraordinary interruption which ensued. The wide, heavy folding doors of the apartment were all at once thrown open, to their full extent, with a vigorous and rushing impetuosity that extinguished, as if by magic, every candle in the room. Their light, in dying, enabled us just to perceive that a stranger had entered, about my own height, and closely muffled in a cloak. The darkness, however, was not total; and we could only *feel* that he was standing in our midst. Before any one of us could recover from the extreme astonishment into which this rudeness had thrown all, we heard the voice of the intruder.

"Gentlemen," he said, in a low, distinct, and never-to-be-forgotten *whisper* which thrilled to the very marrow of my bones, "Gentlemen, I make an apology for this behavior, because in thus behaving, I am fulfilling a duty. You are, beyond doubt, uninformed of the true character of the person who has to-night won at *écarté* a large sum of money from Lord Glendenning. I will therefore put you upon an expeditious and decisive plan of obtaining this very necessary information. Please to examine, at your leisure, the inner linings of the cuff of his left sleeve, and the several little packages which may be found in the somewhat capacious pockets of his embroidered morning wrapper."

While he spoke, so profound was the stillness that one might have heard a pin drop upon the floor. In ceasing, he departed at once, and as abruptly as he had entered. Can I—shall I describe my sensations? Must I say that I felt all the horrors of the damned? Most assuredly I had little time for reflection. Many hands roughly seized me upon the spot, and lights were immediately reprocured. A search ensued. In the lining of my sleeve were found all the court cards essential in *écarté*, and, in the pockets of my wrapper, a number of packs, fac-similes of those used at our sittings, with the single exception that mine were of the species called, technically, *arrondées;* the honors being slightly convex at the sides. In this disposition, the dupe who cuts, as customary, at the length of the pack, will invariably find that he cuts his antagonist an honor; while the gambler, cutting at the breadth, will, as certainly, cut nothing for his victim which may count in the records of the game.

Any burst of indignation upon this discovery would have affected me less than the silent contempt, or the sarcastic composure, with which it was received.

"Mr. Wilson," said our host, stooping to remove from beneath his feet an exceedingly luxurious cloak of rare furs, "Mr. Wilson, this is your property." (The weather was cold; and, upon quitting my own room, I had thrown a cloak over my dressing wrapper, putting it off upon reaching the scene of play.) "I presume it is supererogatory to seek here (eyeing the folds of the garment with a bitter smile) for any farther evidence of your skill. Indeed, we have had enough. You will see the necessity, I hope, of quitting Oxford—at all events, of quitting instantly my chambers."

Abased, humbled to the dust as I then was, it is probable that I should have resented this galling language by immediate personal violence, had not my whole attention been at the moment arrested by a fact of the most startling character. The cloak which I had worn was of a rare description of fur; how rare, how extravagantly costly, I shall not venture to say. Its fashion, too, was of my own fantastic invention; for I was fastidious to an absurd degree of coxcombry, in matters of this frivolous nature. When, therefore, Mr. Preston reached me that which he had picked up upon the floor, and near the folding-doors of the apartment, it was with an astonishment nearly bordering upon terror, that I perceived my own already hanging on my arm, (where I had no doubt unwittingly placed it,) and that the one presented me was but its exact counterpart in every, in even the minutest possible particular. The singular being who had so disastrously exposed me, had been muffled, I remembered, in a cloak; and none had been worn at all by any of the members of our party, with the exception of myself. Retaining some presence of mind, I took the one offered me by Preston; placed it, unnoticed, over my own; left the apartment with a resolute scowl of defiance; and, next morning ere dawn of day, commenced a hurried journey from Oxford to the continent, in a perfect agony of horror and shame.

I fled in vain. My evil destiny pursued me as if in exultation, and proved, indeed, that the exercise of its mysterious dominion had as yet only begun. Scarcely had I set foot in Paris, ere I had fresh evidence of the detestable interest taken by this Wilson in my concerns. Years flew, while I experienced no relief. Villain!— at Rome, with how untimely, yet with how spectral an officiousness, stepped he in between me and my ambition! at Vienna, too —at Berlin—and at Moscow! Where, in truth, had I *not* bitter cause to curse him within my heart? From his inscrutable tyranny did I at length flee, panic-stricken, as from a pestilence; and to the very ends of the earth *I fled in vain.*

And again, and again, in secret communion with my own spirit, would I demand the questions "Who is he?—whence came he?—and what are his objects?" But no answer was there found.

And now I scrutinized, with a minute scrutiny, the forms, and the methods, and the leading traits of his impertinent supervision. But even here there was very little upon which to base a conjecture. It was noticeable, indeed, that, in no one of the multiplied instances in which he had of late crossed my path, had he so crossed it except to frustrate those schemes, or to disturb those actions, which, if fully carried out, might have resulted in bitter mischief. Poor justification this, in truth, for an authority so imperiously assumed! Poor indemnity for natural rights of self-agency so pertinaciously, so insultingly denied.

I had also been forced to notice that my tormentor, for a very long period of time, (while scrupulously and with miraculous dexterity maintaining his whim of an identity of apparel with myself,) had so contrived it, in the execution of his varied interference with my will, that I saw not, at any moment, the features of his face. Be Wilson what he might, *this*, at least, was but the veriest of affectation, or of folly. Could he, for an instant, have supposed that, in my admonisher at Eton—in the destroyer of my honor at Oxford,—in him who thwarted my ambition at Rome, my revenge at Paris, my passionate love at Naples, or what he falsely termed my avarice in Egypt,—that in this, my arch-enemy and evil genius, I could fail to recognize the William Wilson of my school-days, —the name-sake, the companion, the rival,—the hated and dreaded rival at Dr. Bransby's? Impossible!—But let me hasten to the last eventful scene of the drama.

Thus far I had succumbed supinely to this imperious domination. The sentiment of deep awe with which I habitually regarded the elevated character, the majestic wisdom, the apparent omnipresence and omnipotence of Wilson, added to a feeling of even terror, with which certain other traits in his nature and assumptions inspired me, had operated, hitherto, to impress me with an idea of my own utter weakness and helplessness, and to suggest an implicit, although bitterly reluctant submission to his arbitrary will. But, of late days, I had given myself up entirely to wine; and its maddening influence upon my hereditary temper rendered me more and more impatient of control. I began to murmur,—to hesitate,—to resist. And was it only fancy which induced me to believe that, with the increase of my own firmness, that of my tormentor underwent a proportional diminution? Be this as it may,

I now began to feel the inspiration of a burning hope, and at length nurtured in my secret thoughts a stern and desperate resolution that I would submit no longer to be enslaved.

It was at Rome, during the Carnival of 18—, that I attended a masquerade in the palazzo of the Neapolitan Duke Di Broglio. I had indulged more freely than usual in the excesses of the wine-table; and now the suffocating atmosphere of the crowded rooms irritated me beyond endurance. The difficulty, too, of forcing my way through the mazes of the company contributed not a little to the ruffling of my temper; for I was anxiously seeking (let me not say with what unworthy motive) the young, the gay, the beautiful wife of the aged and doting Di Broglio. With a too un-scrupulous confidence she had previously communicated to me the secret of the costume in which she would be habited, and now, having caught a glimpse of her person, I was hurrying to make my way into her presence. At this moment I felt a light hand placed upon my shoulder, and that ever-remembered, low, damnable, *whisper* within my ear.

In an absolute frenzy of wrath, I turned at once upon him who had thus interrupted me, and seized him violently by the collar. He was attired, as I had expected, in a costume altogether similar to my own; wearing a Spanish cloak of blue velvet, begirt about the waist with a crimson belt sustaining a rapier. A mask of black silk entirely covered his face.

"Scoundrel!" I said, in a voice husky with rage, while every syllable I uttered seemed as new fuel to my fury; "scoundrel! impostor! accursed villain! you shall not—you *shall not* dog me unto death! Follow me, or I stab you where you stand!"—and I broke my way from the ball-room into a small ante-chamber adjoining, dragging him unresistingly with me as I went.

Upon entering, I thrust him furiously from me. He staggered against the wall, while I closed the door with an oath, and commanded him to draw. He hesitated but for an instant; then, with a slight sigh, drew in silence, and put himself upon his defence.

The contest was brief indeed. I was frantic with every species of wild excitement, and felt within my single arm the energy and power of a multitude. In a few seconds I forced him by sheer strength against the wainscoting, and thus, getting him at mercy, plunged my sword, with brute ferocity, repeatedly through and through his bosom.

At that instant some person tried the latch of the door. I hastened to prevent an intrusion, and then immediately returned to my dying antagonist. But what human language can adequately portray *that* astonishment, *that* horror which possessed me at the spectacle then presented to view? The brief moment in which I averted my eyes had been sufficient to produce, apparently, a material change in the arrangements at the upper or farther end of the room. A large mirror,—so at first it seemed to me in my confusion—now stood where none had been perceptible before; and as I stepped up to it in extremity of terror, mine own image, but with features all pale and dabbled in blood, advanced to meet me with a feeble and tottering gait.

Thus it appeared, I say, but was not. It was my antagonist—it was Wilson, who then stood before me in the agonies of his dissolution. His mask and cloak lay, where he had thrown them, upon the floor. Not a thread in all his raiment—not a line in all the marked and singular lineaments of his face which was not, even in the most absolute identity, *mine own!*

It was Wilson; but he spoke no longer in a whisper, and I could have fancied that I myself was speaking while he said:

"*You have conquered, and I yield. Yet henceforward art thou also dead—dead to the World, to Heaven, and to Hope! In me didst thou exist—and, in my death, see by this image, which is thine own, how utterly thou hast murdered thyself.*"

●

THE BEAUTIFUL Lady Diana Rich, daughter to the Earl of Holland, as she was walking in her father's garden at Kensington, to take the fresh air before dinner, about eleven o'clock, being then very well, met with her own apparition, habit, and every thing, as in a looking-glass. About a month after, she died of the small-pox. And it is said that her sister, the Lady Isabella Thynne, saw the like of herself also, before she died. This account I had from a person of honour.

—JOHN AUBREY

●

ST. AUGUSTINE heard a voice, saying, TOLLE, LEGE, take, read. He took up his bible, and dipt on Rom. 13. 13. "Not in rioting and drunkenness, not in chambering and wantonness." &c. And reformed his matters upon it.

—JOHN AUBREY

THE FEATHER CLOAK OF HAWAII

This tale—a free retelling of one of the best-beloved Hawaiian chants—should not be read with the expectation that it will end like a European romance. The ending is quite happy and proper, according to the ideas of Polynesian feudalism. Those who would like to pronounce the names somewhat as they would be spoken in the islands should remember that every vowel calls for a separate syllable, and that vowels unaccompanied by consonants are pronounced explosively, with a trace of an "h" sound following. The heroine's name is Kah-nee-kah-nee-ah-oo-la, the hero's, El-eh-ee-oh. Think of your throat as a little gate, expelling an equal puff of air for each syllable. There are no strong accents in Polynesian speech.—EDITOR.

Johannes C. Andersen

THE
FEATHER
CLOAK OF
HAWAII

The Hawaiians have a story of the feather
cloak that served as the first known pattern. Eleio was a *kukini*,
or trained runner, in the service of Kakaalaneo, chief of Maui. He
was not only a swift and tireless runner, but was also a *kahuna*,
initiated into the observances that enabled him to see spirits, that
made him skilled in medicine, and able to return a wandering
spirit to its dead body if the work of dissolution had not begun.

Eleio had been sent to Hana to fetch *awa* root for the chief,
and was expected to be back so that the chief might have his prepared drink for supper. Soon after leaving Olowalu Eleio saw
a beautiful young woman ahead of him. He hastened his steps, but
exert himself as he would, she kept the same distance between

them. Being the fleetest *kukini* of his time, it piqued him that a woman should be able to prevent his overtaking her, so he determined to capture her, and devoted all his energies to that object. She led him a long chase over rocks, hills, mountains, deep ravines, precipices, and gloomy streams, till they came to the cape of Hana-manuloa at Kahiki-nui, beyond Kaupo, where he caught her just at the entrance to a *puoa*—a kind of tower, made of bamboo, with a platform half-way up, where the dead bodies of persons of distinction were exposed to the elements.

When he caught her she turned to him and said, "Let me live! I am not human, but a spirit, and in this enclosure is my dwelling." He answered, "I have thought for some time that you were a spirit; no human being could have so outrun me."

She then said, "Let us be friends. In yonder house live my parents and relatives. Go to them and ask for a hog, rolls of *kapa*, some fine mats, and a feather cloak. Describe me to them, and tell them that I give all those things to you. The feather cloak is not finished; it is now only a fathom and a half square, and was intended to be two fathoms. There are in the house enough feathers and netting to finish it. Tell them to finish it for you." The spirit then disappeared.

Eleio entered the *puoa*, climbed on to the platform, and saw the dead body of the girl. She was in every way as beautiful as the spirit, and had apparently been dead but a short time. He left the *puoa* and hurried to the house pointed out as the home of her parents, and he saw a woman wailing, whom he recognized, from her resemblance, as the mother of the girl. He saluted her with an *aloha*. "I am a stranger here," said he, "but I had a travelling companion who guided me to yonder *puoa* and then disappeared." At these words the woman ceased her wailing and called to her husband, to whom she repeated what the stranger had said. "Does this house belong to you?" asked Eleio. "It does," they answered.

"Then," said Eleio, "my message is to you." He repeated to them the message of the young girl, and they willingly agreed to give up all the things which their loved daughter had herself thus given away. But when they spoke of killing the hog, and making a feast of him, he said, "Wait a little, and let me ask if all these people round about me are your friends?"

They answered, "They are our relatives, the uncles, aunts,

and cousins of the spirit who seems to have chosen you either as husband or as brother."

"Will they do your bidding in everything?" he asked.

The parents answered that they could be relied on. He directed them to build a large arbour, to be entirely covered with ferns, ginger, *maile, ieie*—sweet and odorous foliage of the islands. An altar was to be erected at one end of the arbour and appropriately decorated. The order was willingly carried out, men, women, and children working with a will, so that in a couple of hours the whole structure was finished. He then directed the hog to be cooked, also red and white fish, red, white, and black cocks, and varieties of banana called *lele* and *maoli* to be placed on the altar. He directed all women and children to enter their houses and assist with their prayers, all pigs, chickens, and dogs to be hidden in dark houses to keep them quiet, and that strict silence be kept. The men at work were asked to remember the gods, and to invoke their assistance for Eleio.

He then started for Hana, pulled up a couple of bushes of *awa* of Kaeleku, famous for its medicinal virtue, and was back again before the hog was cooked. The *awa* was prepared, and when everything was ready for the feast he offered all to the gods and prayed for their assistance in what he was about to perform.

The spirit of the girl had been lingering near him all the time, seeming to be attracted to him, but of course invisible to every one else. When he had finished his invocation he turned and caught the spirit, and holding his breath and invoking the gods he hurried to the *puoa*, followed by the parents, who now began to understand that he was about to attempt the *kapuku*, or restoration of the dead to life. Arrived at the *puoa*, he placed the spirit against the insteps of the girl and pressed it firmly in, meanwhile continuing his invocation. The spirit entered its former body kindly enough until it came to the knees, when it refused to go farther, fearing pollution, but Eleio by the strength of his prayers induced it to go farther, and farther, the father, mother, and male relatives assisting with their prayers, and at length the spirit was persuaded to take entire possession of the body, and the girl came to life again.

She was submitted to the usual ceremonies of purification by the priest, after which she was led to the prepared arbour, where there was a happy reunion. They feasted on the food prepared for the gods, whose guests they were, enjoying the material essence of the food after its spiritual essence had been accepted by the gods.

After the feast the feather cloak, the rolls of fine *kapa*, the beautiful mats, were brought and displayed to Eleio; and the father said to him, "Take as wife the woman you have restored, and remain here with us; and you shall be our son, sharing equally in the love we have for her."

But Eleio, thinking of his chief, said, "No, I accept her as a charge; but, for wife, she is worthy to be one for a higher in rank. If you will trust her to my care, I will take her to my master; for her beauty and her charms make her worthy to be his wife and our queen."

"She is yours to do with as you will," said the father. "It is as if you had created her; for without you where would she be now? We ask only this, that you will always remember that you have parents and relatives here, and a home whenever you may wish it."

Eleio then requested that the feather cloak be finished for him before he returned to the chief. All who could work feathers set about it at once, including the girl herself, whose name, Eleio now learned, was Kanikani-aula. When it was finished he set out on his return, accompanied by the girl, and taking the feather cloak and the *awa* that remained after a portion had been used during his incantations. They travelled slowly, according to the strength of Kanikani-aula, who now, in the body, could not equal the speed she had possessed as a spirit.

Arriving at Launi-upoko, Eleio turned to her and said, "You wait here, hidden in the bushes, while I go on alone. If by sundown I do not return, I shall be dead. You know the road by which we came; return then to your people. But if all goes well I shall be back in a little while."

He then went on, and when he reached Makila, on the confines of Lahaina, he saw a number of people heating an *imu*, or ground oven. On perceiving him they seized and started to bind him, saying it was the order of the chief that he should be roasted alive; but he ordered them away with the request, "Let me die at the feet of my master," and went on.

When at last he stood before Kakaalaneo the chief said to him,

"How is this? Why are you not cooked alive as I ordered? How came you to pass my guards?"

The runner answered, "It was the wish of the slave to die, if die he must, at the feet of his master; but if so, it would be an irreparable loss to you, my master; for I have that with me which will add to your fame, now and to posterity."

"And what is that?" asked the King.

Eleio unrolled his bundle, and displayed to the astonished chief the glories of the feather cloak, a garment unknown till then. Needless to say, he was pardoned and restored to favour, the *awa* he had brought from Hana being reserved for the chief's special use in his offerings to the gods that evening.

When the chief heard the whole story of the reason for the absence of Eleio he ordered the girl to be brought, that he might see her, and express gratitude for the wonderful garment. When she arrived he was so charmed with her appearance, with her manner and conversation, that he asked her to become his queen.

NOTE

Mr. Andersen adds, "This feather cloak, known as the Ahu o Kakaalaneo, is said to be preserved in the Bernice P. Bishop Museum at Honolulu. The Hawaiian name of the feather cloak is *ahuula*. The doubled vowel signifies the dropping of a consonant, usually *K*; the equivalent word, and the equivalent garment in Maori, is *kahukura*. The Hawaiian garment was made of red or yellow feathers on a netted foundation, and was a gorgeous object; the Maori cloak was made of red feathers from the underwing of the *kaka*, on a plaited foundation of silky flax-fibre. There were other feather cloaks, an especially valuable one being the *kahukiwi*, made from feathers of the *kiwi*, fixed on upside down, or quill pointing downward, so that the droop of the hairlike feather gave the appearance of a full fur."

THE GENTLEMAN FROM AMERICA

Here we have a story within a story, from the author's first book, *Mayfair* (1925); and it may seem to some readers that the facetious insert is more nearly in the true Arlen manner than are its surroundings. Certainly the insert has a good enough plot of its own, and could have been made into a first-rate horror story with a little different handling. American readers should forgive Mr Arlen for making his gentleman from America use such phrases as *"tall hat,"* and *"put the wind up,"*—trifles which should not be permitted to detract from the enjoyment of a very skillfully told tale.—EDITOR.

Michael Arlen

THE GENTLE-MAN FROM AMERICA

It is told by a decayed gentleman at the sign of "The Leather Butler," which is in Shepherd's Market, which is in Mayfair, how one night three men behaved in a most peculiar way; and one of them was left for dead.

Towards twelve o'clock on a night in the month of November some years ago, three men were ascending the noble stairway of a mansion in Grosvenor Square. The mansion, although appointed in every detail—to suit, however, a severe taste—had yet a sour atmosphere, as of a house long untenanted but by caretakers.

The first of the men, for they ascended in single file, held aloft a kitchen candlestick, whilst his companions made the best progress they could among the deep shadows that the faulty light cast on the oaken stairway. He who went last, the youngest of the three, said gaily:

"Mean old bird, my aunt! Cutting off the electric light just because she is away."

"Fur goodness' sake!" said the other.

The leader, whose face the candlelight revealed as thin almost to asceticism, a face white and tired, finely moulded but soiled in texture by the dissipations of a man of the world, contented himself with a curt request to his young friend not to speak so loud.

It was, however, the gentleman in between the two whom it will advantage the reader to consider. This was an unusually tall and strongly-built man. Yet it was not his giant stature, but rather the assurance of his bearing, which was remarkable. His very clothes sat on his huge frame with an air of firmness, of finality, that, as even a glance at his two companions would show, is deprecated by English tailors, whose inflexible formula it is that the elegance of the casual is the only possible elegance for the gentleman of the mode. While his face had that weathered, yet untired and eager look which is the enviable possession of many Americans, and is commonly considered to denote, for reasons not very clearly defined, the quality known as poise. Not, however, that this untired and eager look is, as some have supposed, the outward sign of a lack of interest in dissipation, but rather of an enthusiastic and naïve curiosity as to the varieties of the same. The gentleman from America looked, in fine, to be a proper man; and one who, in his early thirties, had established a philosophy of which his comfort and his assurance of retaining it were the two poles, his easy perception of humbug the pivot, and his fearlessness the latitude and longitude.

It was on the second landing that the leader, whose name was Quillier, and on whom the dignity of an ancient baronetcy seemed to have an almost intolerably tiring effect, flung open a door. He did not pass into the room, but held the candlestick towards the gentleman from America. And his manner was so impersonal as to be almost rude, which is a fault of breeding when it is bored.

"The terms of the bet," said Quillier, "are that this candle must suffice you for the night. That is understood?"

"Sure, why not?" smiled the gentleman from America. "It's

a bum bet, and it looks to me like a bum candle. But do I care? No, sir!"

"Further," continued the impersonal, pleasant voice, "that you are allowed no matches, and therefore cannot relight the candle when it has gone out. That if you can pass the night in that room, Kerr-Anderson and I pay you five hundred pounds. And *vice versa.*"

"That's all right, Quillier. We've got all that." The gentleman from America took the candle from Quillier's hand and looked into the room, but with no more than faint interest. In that faulty light little could be seen but the oak panelling, the heavy hangings about the great bed, and a steel engraving of a Meissonier duellist lunging at them from a wall nearby.

"Seldom," said he, "have I seen a room look less haunted——"

"Ah," vaguely said Sir Cyril Quillier.

"But," said the gentleman from America, "since you and Kerr-Anderson insist on presenting me with five hundred pounds for passing the night in it, do I complain? No, sir!"

"Got your revolver?" queried young Kerr-Anderson, a chubby youth whose profession was dining out.

"That is so," said the gentleman from America.

Quillier said: "Well, Puce, I don't mind telling you that I had just as soon this silly business was over. I have been betting all my life, but I have always had a preference for those bets which did not turn on a man's life or death——"

"Say, listen, Quillier, you can't frighten me with that junk!" snapped Mr. Puce.

"My aunt," said young Kerr-Anderson, "will be very annoyed if anything happens and she gets to hear of it. She hates a corpse in her house more than any one I know. You're sure you are going on with it, Puce?"

"Boy, if Abraham Lincoln was to come up this moment and tell me Queen Anne was dead, I'd be as sure he was speaking the truth as that I'm going to spend this night in this old haunted room of your aunt's. Yes, sir! And now I'll give you good-night, boys. Warn your mothers to be ready to give you five hundred pounds to hand on to Howard Cornelius Puce."

"I like Americans," said Quillier vaguely. "They are so enthusiastic. Good-night, Puce, and God bless you. I hope you have better luck than the last man who spent a night in that room. He was strangled. Good-night, my friend."

"Aw, have a heart!" growled Mr. Puce. "You get a guy so low with your talk that I feel I could put on a tall hat and crawl under a snake."

II

The gentleman from America, alone in the haunted room, lost none of his composure. Indeed, if anything disturbed him at all, it was that, irritated by Quillier's manner at a dinner-party a few nights before, and knowing Quillier to be a bankrupt wastrel, he had allowed himself to be dared into this silly adventure and had thus deprived himself for one night of the amenities of his suite at Claridge's Hotel. Five hundred pounds more or less did not matter very much to Mr. Puce: although, to be sure, it was some consolation to know that five hundred pounds more or less must matter quite a deal to *Sir* Cyril Quillier, for all his swank. Mr. Puce, like a good American, following the Gospel according to Mr. Sinclair Lewis, always stressed the titles of any of his acquaintance.

Now, he contented himself with a very cursory examination of the dim, large room; he rapped, in an amateurish way, on the oak panels, here and there for any sign of any "secret passage junk," but succeeded only in soiling his knuckles, and it was only when, fully clothed, he had thrown himself on the great bed that it occurred to him that five hundred pounds sterling was quite a pretty sum to have staked about a damfool haunted room.

The conclusion that naturally leapt to one's mind, thought Mr. Puce, was that the room must have something the matter with it, else would a hawk like Quillier have bet money on its qualities of terror? Mr. Puce had, indeed, suggested, when first the bet was put forward, that five hundred pounds was perhaps an unnecessary sum to stake on so idiotic a fancy; but Quillier had said in a very tired way that he never bet less than five hundred on anything, but that if Mr. Puce preferred to bet with poppycock and chicken-food, he, Quillier, would be pleased to introduce him to some very jolly children of his acquaintance.

Such thoughts persuaded Mr. Puce to rise and examine more carefully the walls and appointments of the room. But as the furniture was limited to the barest necessities, and as the oak-panelled walls appeared in the faint light to be much the same as any other walls, the gentleman from America swore vaguely and again reclined on the bed. It was a very comfortable bed.

He had made up his mind, however, that he would not sleep. He would watch out, thought Mr. Puce, for any sign of this ghost, and he would listen with the ears of a coyote, thought Mr. Puce, for any hint of those rapping noises, rude winds, musty odours, clanking of chains, and the like, with which, so Mr. Puce had always understood, the family ghosts of Britishers invariably heralded their foul appearance.

Mr. Puce, you can see, did not believe in ghosts. He could not but think, however, that some low trick might be played on him, since on the honour of *Sir* Cyril Quillier, peer though he was—for Mr. Puce, like a good American, could never get the cold dope on all this fancy title stuff—he had not the smallest reliance. But as to the supernatural, Mr. Puce's attitude was always a wholesome scepticism—and a rather aggressive scepticism at that, as Quillier had remarked with amusement when he had spoken of the ghost in, as he had put it, the house of Kerr-Anderson's aunt. Quillier had said:

"There are two sorts of men on whom ghosts have an effect: those who are silly enough to believe in them, and those who are silly enough not to believe in them."

Mr. Puce had been annoyed at that. He detested clever back-chat. "I'll tell the world," Mr. Puce had said, "that a plain American has to go to a drug-store after a conversation with you."

Mr. Puce, lying on the great bed, whose hangings depressed him, examined his automatic and found it good. He had every intention of standing no nonsense, and an automatic nine-shooter is, as Mr. Puce remembered having read somewhere, an Argument. Indeed, Mr. Puce was full of those dour witticisms about the effect of a "gun" on everyday life which go to make the less pretentious "movies" so entertaining; although, to be sure, he did not know more than a very little about guns. Travellers have remarked, however, that the exciting traditions behind a hundred-percent American nationality have given birth in even the most gentle citizens of that great republic to a feeling of familiarity with "guns," as such homely phrases as "slick with the steel mit," "doggone son of a gun," and the like, go to prove.

Mr. Puce placed the sleek little automatic on a small table by the bed, on which stood the candle and, as he realised for the first time, a book. One glance at the paper-jacket of the book was enough to convince the gentleman from America that its presence there must be one of Quillier's tired ideas. It showed a woman of striking, if conventional, beauty, fighting for her life with a shape which might or might not be the wraith of a blood-hound but which was certainly something quite outside a lovely woman's daily experience. Mr. Puce laughed. The book was called, *Tales of Terror for Tiny Tots*, by Ivor Pelham Marlay.

The gentleman from America was a healthy man, and needed his sleep; and it was therefore with relief that he turned to Mr. Marley's absurd-looking book as a means of keeping himself awake. The tale at which the book came open was called *The Phantom Footsteps*; and Mr. Puce prepared himself to be entertained, for he was not of those who read for instruction. He read:

THE PHANTOM FOOTSTEPS

The tale of The Phantom Footsteps is still whispered with awe and loathing among the people of that decayed but genteel district of London known to those who live in it as Belgravia and to others as Pimlico.

Julia and Geraldine Biggot-Baggot were twin sisters who lived with their father, a widower, in a town in Lancashire called Wigan, or it may have been called Bolton. The tale finds Julia and Geraldine in their nineteenth year, and it also finds them in a very bad temper, for they were yearning for a more spacious life than can be found in Wigan, or it might be, Bolton. This yearning their neighbours found all the more inexplicable since the parents of the girls were of Lancashire stock, their mother having been a Biggot from Wigan and their father a Baggot from Bolton.

The reader can imagine with what excess of gaiety Julia and Geraldine heard one day from their father that he had inherited a considerable property from a distant relation; and the reader can go on imagining the exaltation of the girls when they heard that the property included a mansion in Belgravia, since that for which they had always yearned most was to enjoy, from a central situation, the glittering life of the metropolis.

The father preceded them from Wigan, or was it Bolton? He was a man of a tidy disposition, and wished to see that everything in the Belgravia house was ready against his daughters' arrival. When Julia and Geraldine did arrive, however, they were admitted by a genial old person of repellent aspect and disagreeable odour, who informed them that she was doing a bit of charring about the house but would be gone by the evening. Their father, she added, had gone into the country to engage servants, but would be back the next day; and he had instructed her to tell Julia and Geraldine not to be nervous of sleeping alone in a strange house, and that there was nothing to be afraid of, and that he would, anyhow, be back with them first thing in the morning.

Now Julia and Geraldine, though twins, were of vastly different temperaments; for whereas Julia was a girl of gay and indomitable spirit who knew not fear, Geraldine suffered from agonies of timidity and knew nothing else. When, for instance, night fell and found them alone in the house, Julia could scarcely contain her delight at the adventure; while it was with difficulty that Geraldine could support the tremors that shook her girlish frame.

Imagine, then, how differently they were affected when, as they lay in bed in their room towards the top of the house, they distinctly heard from far below a noise, as of some one moving. Julia sat up in bed, intent, unafraid, curious. Geraldine swooned.

"It's only a cat," Julia whispered. "I'm going down to see."

"Don't!" sighed Geraldine. "For pity's *sake* don't leave me, Julia!"

"Oh, don't be so childish!" snapped Julia. "Whenever there's the chance of the least bit of fun you get shivers down your spine. But as you are so frightened I will lock the door from the outside and take the key with me, so that no one can get in when I am not looking. Oh, I hope it's a burglar! I'll give him the fright of his life, see if I don't."

And the indomitable girl went, feeling her way to the door in darkness, for to have switched on the light would have been to warn the intruder, if there was one, that the house was inhabited; whereas it was the plucky girl's conceit to turn the tables on the burglar, if there was one, by suddenly appearing to him as an avenging phantom; for having done not a little district-visiting in Wigan, or, possibly, Bolton, no one knew better than Julia of the depths of base superstition among the vulgar.

A little calmed by her sister's nonchalance, Geraldine lay still as a mouse in the darkness, with her pretty head beneath the bed-clothes. From without came not a sound, and the very stillness of the house had impelled Geraldine to a new access of terror had she not concentrated on the works of Mr. Rudyard Kipling, which tell of the grit of the English people.

Then, as though to test the grit of the English people in the most abominable way, came a dull noise from below. Geraldine restrained a scream, lay breathless in the darkness. The dull noise, however, was not repeated, and presently Geraldine grew a little calmer, thinking that maybe her sister had dropped a slipper or something of the sort. But the reader can imagine into what terror the poor girl had been plunged had she been a student of the detective novels of the day, for then she must instantly have recognised the dull noise as a dull thud, and what can a dull thud mean but one thing?

It was as she was praying a prayer to Our Lady that her ears grew aware of footsteps ascending the stairs. Her first feeling was one of infinite relief. Of course Julia had been right, and there had been nothing downstairs but a cat or, perhaps, a dog. And now Julia was returning, and in a second they would have a good laugh together. Indeed, it was all Geraldine could do to restrain herself from jumping out of bed to meet her sister, when she was assailed by a terrible doubt; and on the instant her mind grew so charged with fear that she could no longer hold back her sobs. Suppose it was not Julia ascending! Suppose—"Oh, God!" sobbed Gerald-ine.

Transfixed with terror, yet hopeful of the best, the poor girl could not even command herself to reinsert her head beneath the sheets. And always the ascending steps came nearer. As they approached the door, she thought she would die of uncertainty. But as the key was fitted into the lock she drew a deep breath of relief —to be at once shaken by the most acute agony of doubt, so that she had given anything in the world to be back again in Wigan, or, even better, Bolton.

"Julia!" she sobbed. "Julia!"

For the door had opened, the footsteps were in the room, and Geraldine thought she recognised her sister's maidenly tread. But why did Julia not speak, why this intolerable silence? Geraldine, peer as hard as she might, could make out nothing in the darkness. The footsteps seemed to fumble in their direction, but came always nearer to the bed, in which poor Geraldine lay more dead than alive. Oh, why did Julia not speak, just to reassure her?

"Julia!" sobbed Geraldine. "Julia!"

The footsteps seemed to fumble about the floor with an indecision maddening to Geraldine's distraught nerves. But at last they came beside the bed—and there they stood! In the awful silence Geraldine could hear her heart beating like a hammer on a bell.

"Oh!" the poor girl screamed. "What is it, Julia? Why don't you speak?"

But never a sound nor a word gave back the livid silence, never a sigh nor a breath, though Julia must be standing within a yard of the bed.

"Oh, she is only trying to frighten me, the beast!" poor Geraldine thought; and, unable for another second to bear the cruel silence, she timidly stretched out a hand to touch her sister —when, to her infinite relief, her fingers touched the white rabbit-fur with which Julia's dressing-gown was delicately trimmed.

"You beast, Julia!" she sobbed and laughed. Never a word, however, came from the still shape. Geraldine, impatient of the continuation of a joke which seemed to her in the worst of taste, raised her hand from the fur, that she might touch her sister's face; but her fingers had risen no farther than Julia's throat when they touched something wet and warm, and with a scream of indescribable terror Geraldine fainted away.

When Mr. Biggot-Baggot admitted himself into the house early the next morning, his eyes were assailed by a dreadful sight. At the foot of the stairs was a pool of blood, from which, in a loathsome trail, drops of blood wound up the stairway.

Mr. Biggot-Baggot, fearful lest something out of the way had happened to his beloved daughters, rushed frantically up the stairs.

The trail of blood led to his daughters' room; and there, in the doorway, the poor gentleman stood appalled, so foul was the sight that met his eyes. His beloved Geraldine lay on the bed, her hair snow-white, her lips raving with the shrill fancies of a maniac. While on the floor beside the bed lay stretched, in a pool of blood, his beloved Julia, her head half-severed from her trunk.

The tragic story unfolded only when the police arrived. It then became clear that Julia, her head half-severed from her body, and therefore a corpse, had yet, with indomitable purpose, come upstairs to warn her timid sister against the homicidal lunatic who, just escaped from an asylum near by, had penetrated into the house. However, the police consoled the distracted father not a little by pointing out that the escape of the homicidal lunatic from the asylum had done some good, insomuch as there would now be room in an asylum near her home for Geraldine.

III

When the gentleman from America had read the last line of *The Phantom Footsteps* he closed the book with a slam and, in his bitter impatience with the impossible work, was making to hurl it across the room, when, unfortunately, his circling arm overturned the candle. The candle, of course, went out.

"Aw hell!" said Mr. Puce bitterly, and he thought: "Another good mark to *Sir* Cyril Quillier! Won't I Sir him one some day! For only a lousy guy with a face like a drummer's overdraft would have bought a damfool book like that."

The tale of *The Phantom Footsteps* had annoyed him very much; but what annoyed him even more was the candle's extinction, for the gentleman from America knew himself too well to bet a nickel on his chances of remaining awake in a dark room.

He did, however, manage to keep awake for some time merely by concentrating on wicked words: on Quillier's face, and how its tired, mocking expression would change for the better were his, Puce's, foot to be firmly pressed down on its surface, and on Julia and Geraldine. For the luckless twins, by the almost criminal idiocy with which they were presented, kept walking about Mr. Puce's mind; and as he began to nod to the demands of a healthy and tired body he could not resist wondering if their home-town had been Wigan or Bolton and if Julia's head had been severed from ear to ear or only half-way. . . .

When he awoke, it was the stillness of the room that impressed his sharply-awakened senses. The room was very still.

"Who's there!" snapped Mr. Puce. Then, really awake, laughed at himself. "Say, what would plucky little Julia have done?" he thought, chuckling. "Why, got up and looked!"

But the gentleman from America discovered in himself a reluctance to move from the bed. He was very comfortable on the bed. Besides, he had no light and could see nothing if he did move. Besides, he had heard nothing at all, not the faintest noise. He had merely awoken rather more sharply than usual. . . .

Suddenly, he sat up on the bed, his back against the oak head. Something had moved in the room. He was certain something had moved. Somewhere by the foot of the bed.

"Aw, drop that!" laughed Mr. Puce.

His eyes peering into the darkness, Mr. Puce stretched his right hand to the table on which stood the automatic. The gesture reminded him of Geraldine's when she had touched the white rabbit-fur. Aw, Geraldine nothing! These idiotic twins kept chasing about a man's mind. The gentleman from America grasped the automatic firmly in his hand. His hand felt as though it had been born grasping an automatic.

"I want to tell you," said Mr. Puce into the darkness, "that some one is now going to have something coming to him, her, or it."

It was quite delicious, the feeling that he was not frightened. He had always known he was a helluva fellow. But he had never been quite certain. Now he was certain. He was regular.

But, if anything had moved, it moved no more. Maybe, though, nothing had moved at all, ever. Maybe it was only his half-awakened senses that had played him a trick. He was rather sorry if that was so. He was just beginning to enjoy the evening.

The room was very still. The gentleman from America could only hear himself breathing.

Something moved again, distinctly.

"What the hell!" snapped Mr. Puce.

He levelled the automatic towards the foot of the bed.

"I will now," said Mr. Puce grimly, "shoot."

The room was very still. The gentleman from America wished, forcibly, that he had a light. It was no good leaving the bed without a light. He'd only fall over the infernal thing, whatever it was. What would plucky little Julia have done? Aw, Julia nothing! He strained his ears to catch another movement, but he could only hear himself breathing—in sharp, short, gasps! The gentleman from America pulled himself together.

"Say, listen!" he snapped into the darkness. "I am going to count ten. I am then going to shoot. In the meanwhile you can make up your mind whether or not you are going to stay right here to watch the explosion. One. Two. Three. Four. . . ."

Then Mr. Puce interrupted himself. He had to. It was so funny. He laughed. He heard himself laugh, and again it was quite delicious, the feeling that he was not frightened. And wouldn't they laugh, the boys at the Booster Club back home, when he sprung this yarn on them! He could hear them. Oh, Boy! Say, listen, trying to scare him, Howard Cornelius Puce, with a ghost like that! Aw, it was like shooting craps with a guy that couldn't count. Poor old Quillier! Never bet less than five hundred on anything, didn't he, the poor boob! Well, there wasn't a ghost made, with or without a head on him, that could put the wind up Howard Puce. No, sir!

For, as his eyes had grown accustomed to the darkness, and helped by the mockery of light that the clouded, moonless night just managed to thrust through the distant window, the gentleman from America had been able to make out a form at the foot of the bed. He could only see its upper half, and that appeared to end above the throat. The phantom had no head. Whereas, Julia's head had been only half-severed from ——Aw, what the hell!

"A family like the Kerr-Andersons," began Mr. Puce, chuckling—but suddenly found, to his astonishment, that he was shouting at the top of his voice; anyhow, it sounded so. However, he began again, much lower, but still chuckling:

"Say, listen, Mr. Ghost, a family like the Kerr-Andersons might have afforded a head and a suit of clothes for their family ghost. Sir, you are one big bum phantom!" Again unaccountably, Mr. Puce found himself shouting at the top of his voice. "I am going on counting," he added grimly.

And, his automatic levelled at the thing's heart, the gentleman from America went on counting. His voice was steady.

"Five . . . six. . . ."

He sat crouched at the head of the bed, his eyes never off the thing's breast. Phantom nothing! He didn't believe in that no-head bunk. What the hell! He thought of getting a little nearer the foot of the bed and catching the thing a whack on that invisible head of his, but decided to stay where he was.

"Seven . . . eight. . . ."

He hadn't seen the hands before. Gee, some hands! And arms! Holy Moses, he'd got long arms to him, he had. . . .

"Nine!" said the gentleman from America.

Christopher and Columbus, but this would make some tale back home! Yes, sir! Not a bad idea of Quillier's that, though! Those arms. Long as old glory . . . long as the bed! Not bad for *Sir* Cyril Quillier, that idea. . . .

"Ten, you swine!" yelled the gentleman from America, and fired.

Some one laughed. Mr. Puce quite distinctly heard himself laughing, and that made him laugh again. Fur goodness' sake, what a shot! Missed from that distance!

His eyes, as he made to take aim again, were bothered by the drops of sweat from his forehead. "Aw, what the hell!" said Mr. Puce, and fired again.

The silence after the second shot was like a black cloud on the darkness. Mr. Puce thought out the wickedest word he knew, and said it. Well, he wasn't going to miss again. No sir! His hand was steady as iron, too. Iron was his second name. And again the gentleman from America found it quite delicious, the feeling that he was not frightened. Attaboy! The drops of sweat from his forehead bothered him, though. Aw, what the hell, that was only excitement.

He raised his arm for the third shot. Jupiter and Jane, but he'd learn that ghost to stop ghosting! He was certainly sorry for that ghost. He wished, though, that he could concentrate more on the actual body of the headless thing. There it was, darn it, at the foot of the bed, staring at him—well, it would have been staring at him if it had a head. Aw, of course it had a head! It was only Quillier with his lousy face in a black wrap. *Sir* Cyril Quillier'd get one piece of lead in him this time, though. His own fault, the bastard.

"Say, listen, Quillier," said the gentleman from America. "I want to tell you that unless you quit, you are a corpse. Now I mean it, sure as my name is Howard Cornelius Puce. I have been shooting to miss so far. Yes, sir. But I am now *an*noyed. You get me, kid?"

If only though he could concentrate more on the body of the thing. His eyes kept wandering to the hands and arms. Gee, but they sure were long, those arms! As long as the bed, no less. Just long enough for the hands to get at him from the foot of the bed. And that's what they were at, what's more! Coming nearer! What the hell! They were moving, those doggone arms, nearer and nearer. . . .

Mr. Puce fired again.

That was no miss. He knew that was no miss. Right through the heart, that little boy must have gone. In that darkness he couldn't see more than just the shape of the thing. But it was still now. The arms were still. They weren't moving any more. The gentleman from America chuckled. That one had shown him it's a wise little ghost that stops ghosting. Yes, sir! It would fall in a moment, dead as Argentine mutton.

Mr. Puce then swore. Those arms were moving again. The hands weren't a yard from him now. What the hell! They were for his throat, God-dammit.

"The swine!" sobbed the gentleman from America, and fired again. But he wouldn't wait this time. No, sir! He'd let that ghost have a ton of lead. Mr. Puce fired again. Those hands weren't half a yard from his throat now. No good shooting at the hands though. Thing was to get the thing through the heart. Mr. Puce fired the sixth bullet. Right into the thing's chest. The sweat bothered his eyes. "Aw, hell!" said Mr. Puce. He wished the bed was a bit longer. He couldn't get back any more. Those arms. . . . Holy Moses, long as hell, weren't they! Mr. Puce fired the seventh, eighth . . . ninth. Right into the thing. The revolver fell from Mr. Puce's shaking fingers. Mr. Puce heard himself screaming.

IV

Towards noon on a summer's day several years later two men were sitting before an inn some miles from the ancient town of Lincoln. Drawn up in the shade of a towering ash was a large grey touring-car, covered with dust. On the worn table stood two tankards of ale. The travellers rested in silence and content, smoking.

The road by which the inn stood was really no more than a lane, and the peace of the motorists was not disturbed by the traffic of a main road. Indeed, the only human being visible was a distant speck on the dust, coming towards them. He seemed, however, to be making a good pace, for he soon drew near.

"If," said the elder of the two men, in a low, tired voice, "if we take the short cut through Carmion Wood, we will be at Malmanor for lunch."

"Then you'll go short-cutting alone," said the other firmly. "I've heard enough tales about Carmion Wood to last me a lifetime without my adding one more to them. And as for spooks, one is enough for this child in one lifetime, thanks very much."

The two men, for lack of any other distraction, watched the pedestrian draw near. He turned out to be a giant of a man; and had, apparently, no intention of resting at the inn. The very air of the tall pedestrian was a challenge to the lazy content of the sunlit noon. He was walking at a great pace, his felt hat swinging from his hand. A giant he was; his hair greying, his massive face set with assurance.

"By all that's holy!" gasped the elder of the two observers. A little lean gentleman that was, with a lined face which had been handsome in a striking way but for the haggard marks of the dissipations of a man of the world. He had only one arm, and that added a curiously flippant air of devilry to his little, lean, sardonic person.

"Puce!" yelled the other, a young man with a chubby, good-humoured face. "Puce, you silly old ass! Come here at once!"

The giant swung round at the good-natured cry, stared at the two smiling men. Then the massive face broke into the old, genial smile by which his friends had always known and loved the gentleman from America, and he came towards them with hand outstretched.

"Well, boys!" laughed Mr. Puce. "This is one big surprise. But it's good to see you again, I'll say that."

"The years have rolled on, Puce, the years have rolled on," sighed Quillier in his tired way, but warmly enough he shook the gentleman from America with his one hand.

"They certainly have!" said Mr. Puce, mopping his brow and smiling down on the two. "And by the look of that arm, Quillier, I'll say you're no stranger to war."

"Sit down, old Puce, and have a drink," laughed Kerr-Anderson. Always gay, was Kerr-Anderson.

But the gentleman from America seemed, as he stood there, uncertain. He glanced down the way he had come. Quillier, watching him, saw that he was fagged out. Eleven years had made a great difference to Mr. Puce. He looked old, worn, a wreck of the hearty giant who was once Howard Cornelius Puce.

"Come, sit down, Puce," he said kindly, and quite briskly, for him. "Do you realise, man, that it's eleven years since that idiotic night? What are you doing? Taking a walking-tour?"

Mr. Puce sat down on the stained bench beside them. His massive presence, his massive smile, seemed to fill the whole air about the two men.

"Walking-tour? That is so, more or less," smiled Mr. Puce; and, with a flash of his old humour: "I want to tell you boys that I am the daughter of the King of Egypt, but I am dressed as a man because I am travelling *incognito*. Eleven years is it, since we met? A whale of a time, eleven years!"

"Why, there's been quite a war since then," chuckled Kerr-Anderson. "But still that night seems like last night. I *am* glad to see you again, old Puce! But, by Heaven, we owe you one for giving us the scare of our lives! Don't we, Quillier?"

"That's right, Puce," smiled Quillier. "We owe you one all right. But I am heartily glad that it was only a shock you had, and that you were quite yourself after all. And so here we are gathered together again by blind chance, eleven years older, eleven years wiser. Have a drink, Puce?"

The gentleman from America was looking from one to the other of the two. The smile on the massive face seemed one of utter bewilderment. Quillier was shocked at the ravages of a mere eleven years on the man's face.

"I gave you two a scare!" echoed Mr. Puce. "Aw, put it to music, boys! What the hell! How the blazes did I give you two a scare?"

Kerr-Anderson was quite delighted to explain. The scare of eleven years ago was part of the fun of to-day. Many a time he had told the tale to while away the boredom of Flanders and Mesopotamia, and had often wanted to let old Puce in on it to enjoy the joke on Quillier and himself, but had never had the chance to get hold of him.

They had thought, that night, that Puce was dead. Quillier, naked from the waist up, had rushed down to Kerr-Anderson, waiting in the dark porch, and had told him that Puce had kicked the bucket. Quillier had sworn like nothing on earth as he dashed on his clothes. Awkward, Puce's corpse, for Quillier and Kerr-Anderson. Quillier, thank Heaven, had had the sense not to leave the empty revolver on the bed. They shoved back all the ghost properties into a bag. And as, of course, the house wasn't Kerr-Anderson's aunt's house at all, but Johnny Paramour's, who was away, they couldn't be so easily traced. Still, awkward for them, very. They cleared the country that night, Quillier swearing all the way about the weak hearts of giants. And it wasn't until the Orient Express had pitched them out at Vienna that they saw in the Continental *Daily Mail* that an American of the name of Puce had been found by the caretaker in the bedroom of a house in Grosvenor Square, suffering from shock and nervous breakdown. Poor old Puce! Gool old Puce! But he'd had the laugh on them all right. . . .

And heartily enough the gentleman from America appeared to enjoy the joke on Quillier and Kerr-Anderson.

"That's good!" he laughed. "That's very good!"

"Of course," said Quillier in his tired, deprecating way, "we took the stake, this boy and I. For if you hadn't collapsed you would certainly have run out of that room like a Mussulman from a ham-sandwich."

"That's all right," laughed Mr. Puce. "But what I want to know, Quillier, is how you got me so scared?"

Kerr-Anderson says now that Puce was looking at Quillier

quite amiably. Full in the face, and very close to him, but quite amiably. Quillier smiled, in his deprecating way.

"Oh, an old trick, Puce! A black rag over the head, a couple of yards of stuffed cloth for arms——"

"Aw, steady!" said Mr. Puce. But quite amiably. "Say, listen, I shot at you! Nine times. How about that?"

"Dear, oh, dear!" laughed Kerr-Anderson. But that was the last time he laughed that day.

"My dear Puce," said Quillier gently, slightly waving his one arm. "That is the oldest trick of all. I was in a panic all the time that you would think of it and chuck the gun at my head. Those bullets in your automatic were blanks."

Kerr-Anderson isn't at all sure what exactly happened then. All he remembers is that Puce's huge face had suddenly gone crimson, which made his hair stand out shockingly white; and that Puce had Quillier's fragile throat between his hands; and that Puce was roaring and spitting into Quillier's blackening face.

"Say, listen, you Quillier! You'd scare me like that, would you! You'd scare me with a chicken's trick like that, would you! And you'd strangle me, eh? You swine, you *Sir* Cyril Quillier, you, right here's where the strangling comes in, and it's me that's going to do it——"

Kerr-Anderson hit out and yelled. Quillier was helpless with his one arm, the giant's grip on his throat. The woman who kept the inn had hysterics. Puce roared blasphemies. Quillier was doubled back over the small table, Puce on top of him, tightening his death-hold. Kerr-Anderson hit, kicked, bit, yelled.

Suddenly there were shouts from all around.

"For God's sake, quick!" sobbed Kerr-Anderson. "He's almost killed him."

"Aw, what the hell!" roared Puce.

The men in dark uniforms had all they could do to drag him away from that little, lean, blackened, unconscious thing. Then they manacled Puce. Puce looked sheepish, and grinned at Kerr-Anderson.

Two of the six men in dark uniforms helped to revive Quillier.

"Drinks," gasped Kerr-Anderson to the woman who kept the inn.

"Say, give me one," begged the gentleman from America. Huge, helpless, manacled, he stood sheepishly among his uniformed captors. Kerr-Anderson stared at them. Quillier was reviving.

"Get's like that," said the head-warder indifferently. "Gave us the slip this morning. Certain death for some one. Homicidal maniac, that's 'im! And he's the devil to hold. Been like that eleven years. Got a shock, I fancy. Keeps on talking about a sister of his called Julia who was murdered, and how he'll be revenged for it. . . ."

Kerr-Anderson had turned away. Quillier suddenly sobbed: "God have mercy on us!" The gentleman from America suddenly roared with laughter.

"Can't be helped," said the head-warder. "Sorry you were put to trouble, sir. Good-day, gentlemen. Glad it was no worse."

●

MR. BROGRAVE, of Hamel, near Puckridge in Hertford-shire, when he was a young man, riding in a lane in that county, had a blow given him on his cheek: (or head) he looked back and saw that nobody was near behind him; anon, he had such another blow, I have forgot if a third. He turned back, and fell to the study of the law; and was afterwards a Judge. This account I had from Sir John Pen-ruddocke of Compton-Chamberlain, (our neighbour) whose Lady was Judge Brograve's niece.

—JOHN AUBREY

●

T. M. Esq., an old acquaintance of mine, hath assured me that about a quarter of a year after his first wife's death, as he lay in bed awake with his grand-child, his wife opened the closet-door, and came into the chamber by the bedside, and looked upon him and stooped down and kissed him; her lips were warm, he fancied they would have been cold. He was about to have embraced her, but was afraid it might have done him hurt. When she went from him, he asked her when he should see her again? she turned about and smiled, but said nothing. The closet door striked as it used to do, both at her coming in and going out. He had every night a great coal fire in his chamber, which gave a light as clear almost as a candle. He was hypochondriacal; he married two wives since, the latter end of his life was uneasy.

—JOHN AUBREY

THE STORY OF GLAM

The saga from which this episode has been taken was formally composed at some time close to the year 1250 A.D., but it is thought to describe for the most part a sequence of genuine events that had occurred just after Iceland accepted Christianity, precisely at the end of the first Christian millennium. Glam has propensities very like those of Grendel, and Grettir, in dealing with this later spook, seems to have had knowledge of the methods used against Grendel by Beowulf. Ghosts of the gloomy north, by and large, seem to have been exceedingly tough and substantial. The thin spirits that have no physical powers come from softer lands.—EDITOR.

The Grettissaga
(Scandinavian)

THE STORY OF GLAM

There was a man named Thorhall living in Thorhallsstad in Forsæludal, up from Vatnsdal. He was the son of Grim, the son of Thorhall, the son of Fridmund, who was the first settler in Forsæludal. Thorhall's wife was named Gudrun; they had a son named Grim and a daughter named Thurid who were just grown up. Thorhall was fairly wealthy, especially in live-stock. His property in cattle exceeded that of any other man. He was not a chief, but an honest bondi nevertheless. He had great difficulty in getting a shepherd to suit him because the place was haunted. He consulted many men of experience as to what he should do, but nobody gave him any advice which was of any use. Thorhall had good horses, and went every summer to the

Thing. On one occasion at the All-Thing he went to the booth of the Lawman Skapti the son of Thorodd, who was a man of great knowledge and gave good counsel to those who consulted him. There was a great difference between Thorodd the father and Skapti the son in one respect. Thorodd possessed second sight, but was thought by some not to be straight, whereas Skapti gave to every man the advice which he thought would avail him, if he followed it exactly, and so earned the name of Father-betterer.

So Thorhall went to Skapti's booth, where Skapti, knowing that he was a man of wealth, received him graciously, and asked what the news was.

"I want some good counsel from you," said Thorhall.

"I am little fit to give you counsel," he replied; "but what is it that you need?"

"It is this: I have great difficulty in keeping my shepherds. Some get injured and others cannot finish their work. No one will come to me if he knows what he has to expect."

Skapti answered: "There must be some evil spirit abroad if men are less willing to tend your flocks than those of other men. Now since you have come to me for counsel, I will get you a shepherd. His name is Glam, and he came from Sylgsdale in Sweden last summer. He is a big strong man, but not to everybody's mind."

Thorhall said that did not matter so long as he looked after the sheep properly. Skapti said there was not much chance of getting another if this man with all his strength and boldness should fail. Then Thorhall departed. This happened towards the end of the Thing.

Two of Thorhall's horses were missing, and he went himself to look for them, which made people think he was not much of a man. He went up under Sledaass and south along the hill called Armannsfell. Then he saw a man coming down from Godaskog bringing some brushwood with a horse. They met and Thorhall asked him his name. He said it was Glam. He was a big man with an extraordinary expression of countenance, large grey eyes and wolf-grey hair. Thorhall was a little startled when he saw him, but soon found out that this was the man who had been sent to him.

"What work can you do best?" he asked.

Glam said it would suit him very well to mind sheep in the winter.

"Will you mind my sheep?" Thorhall asked. "Skapti has given you over to me."

"My service will only be of use to you if I am free to do as I please," he said. "I am rather cross-grained when I am not well pleased."

"That will not hurt me," said Thorhall. "I shall be glad if you will come to me."

"I can do so," he said. "Are there any special difficulties?"

"The place seems to be haunted."

"I am not afraid of ghosts. It will be the less dull."

"You will have to risk it," said Thorhall. "It will be best to meet it with a bold face."

Terms were arranged and Glam was to come in the autumn. Then they parted. Thorhall found his horses in the very place where he had just been looking for them. He rode home and thanked Skapti for his service.

The summer passed. Thorhall heard nothing of his shepherd and no one knew anything about him, but at the appointed time he appeared at Thorhallsstad. Thorhall treated him kindly, but all the rest of the household disliked him, especially the mistress. He commenced his work as shepherd, which gave him little trouble. He had a loud hoarse voice. The beasts all flocked together whenever he shouted at them. There was a church in the place, but Glam never went to it. He abstained from mass, had no religion, and was stubborn and surly. Every one hated him.

So the time passed till the eve of Yule-tide. Glam rose early and called for his meal. The mistress said: "It is not proper for Christian men to eat on this day, because to-morrow is the first day of Yule and it is our duty to fast to-day."

"You have many superstitions," he said; "but I do not see that much comes from them. I do not know that men are any better off than when there was nothing of that kind. The ways of men seemed to me better when they were called heathen. I want my food and no foolery."

"I am certain," she said, "that it will fare ill with you to-day if you commit this sin."

Glam told her that she should bring his food, or that it would be the worse for her. She did not dare to do otherwise than as he bade her. When he had eaten he went out, his breath smelling abominably. It was very dark; there was driving snow, the wind was howling and it became worse as the day advanced. The shepherd's voice was heard in the early part of the day, but less later on. Blizzards set in and a terrific storm in the evening. People went to mass and so the time passed. In the evening Glam did not return. They talked about going out to look for him, but the storm was so violent and the night so dark that no one went. The night passed and still he had not returned; they waited till the time for mass came. When it was full day some of the men set forth to search. They found the animals scattered everywhere in the snow and injured by the weather; some had strayed into the mountains. Then they came upon some well-marked tracks up above in the valley. The stones and earth were torn up all about as if there had been a violent tussle. On searching further they came upon Glam lying on the ground a short distance off. He was dead; his body was as black as Hel and swollen to the size of an ox. They were overcome with horror and their hearts shuddered within them. Nevertheless they tried to carry him to the church, but could not get him any further than the edge of a gully a short way off. So they left him there and went home to report to the bondi what had happened. He asked what could have caused Glam's death. They said they had tracked him to a big place like a hole made by the bottom of a cask thrown down and dragged along up below the mountains which were at the top of the valley, and all along the track were great drops of blood. They concluded that the evil spirit which had been about before must have killed Glam, but that he had inflicted wounds upon it which were enough, for that spook was never heard of again. On the second day of the festival they went out again to bring in Glam's body to the church. They yoked oxen to him, but directly the downward incline ceased and they came to level ground, they could not move him; so they went home again and left him. On the third day they took a priest with them, but after searching the whole day they failed to find him. The priest refused to go again, and when he was not with them they found Glam. So they gave up the attempt to bring him to the church and buried him where he was under a cairn of stones.

It was not long before men became aware that Glam was not easy in his grave. Many men suffered severe injuries; some who saw him were struck senseless and some lost their wits. Soon after the festival was over, men began to think they saw him about their houses. The panic was great and many left the neighborhood. Next he began to ride on the house-tops by night, and nearly broke them to pieces. Almost night and day he walked, and people would scarcely venture up the valley, however pressing their business. The district was in a grievous condition.

In the spring Thorhall procured servants and built a house on his lands. As the days lengthened out the apparitions became less, until at midsummer a ship sailed up the Hunavatn in which was a man named Thorgaut. He was a foreigner, very tall and powerful: he had the strength of two men. He was travelling on his own account, unattached, and being without money was looking out for employment. Thorhall rode to the ship, saw him and asked if he would take service with him. Thorgaut said he would indeed, and that there would be no difficulties.

"You must be prepared," said Thorhall, "for work which would not be fitting for a weak-minded person, because of the apparitions which have been there lately. I will not deceive you about it."

"I shall not give myself up as lost for the ghostlings," he said. "Before I am scared some others will not be easy. I shall not change my quarters on that account."

The terms were easily arranged and Thorgaut was engaged for the sheep during the winter. When the summer had passed away he took over charge of them, and was on good terms with everybody. Glam continued his rides on the roofs. Thorgaut thought it very amusing and said the thrall must come nearer if he wished to frighten him. Thorhall advised him not to say too much, and said it would be better if they did not come into conflict.

Thorgaut said: "Surely all the spirit has gone out of you. I shall not fall dead in the twilight for stories of that sort."

Yule was approaching. On the eve the shepherd went out with his sheep. The mistress said: "Now I hope that our former experiences will not be repeated."

"Have no fear for that, mistress," he said. "There will be something worth telling of if I come not back."

Then he went out to his sheep. The weather was rather cold and there was a heavy snowstorm. Thorgaut usually returned when it was getting dark, but this time he did not come. The people went to church as usual, but they thought matters looked very much as they did on the last occasion. The bondi wanted them to go out and search for the shepherd, but the church-goers cried off, and said they were not going to trust themselves into the power of trolls in the night; the bondi would not venture out and there was no search. On Yule day after their meal they went out to look for the shepherd, and first went to Glam's cairn, feeling sure that the shepherd's disappearance must be due to him. On approaching the cairn they saw an awful sight; there was the shepherd, his neck broken, and every bone in his body torn from its place. They carried him to the church and no one was molested by Thorgaut.

Glam became more rampageous than ever. He was so riotous that at last everybody fled from Thorhallsstad, excepting the bondi and his wife.

Thorhall's cowherd had been a long time in his service and he had become attached to him: for this reason and because he was a careful herdsman he did not want to part with him. The man was very old and thought it would be very troublesome to have to leave; he saw, too, that everything the bondi possessed would be ruined if he did not stay to look after them. One morning after midwinter the mistress went to the cow-house to milk the cows as usual. It was then full day, for no one would venture out of doors till then, except the cowherd, who went directly it was light. She heard a great crash in the cow-house and tremendous bellowing. She rushed in, shouting that something awful, she knew not what, was going on in the cow-house. The bondi went out and found the cattle all goring each other. It seemed not canny there, so he went into the shed and there saw the cowherd lying on his back with his head in one stall and his feet in the other. He went up and felt him, but saw at once that he was dead with his back broken. It had been broken over the flat stone which separated the two stalls. Evidently it was not safe to remain any longer on his estate, so he fled with everything that he could carry away. All the live-stock which he left behind him was killed by Glam. After that Glam went right up the valley and raided every farm as far as Tunga, while Thorhall stayed with his friends during the rest of the winter. No one could venture up the valley with a horse or a dog, for it was killed at once. As the spring went on and the sun rose higher in the sky the spook diminished somewhat, and Thorhall wanted to return to his land, but found it not easy to get servants. Nevertheless, he went and took up his abode at Thorhallsstad. Directly the autumn set in, everything began again, and the disturbances increased. The person most attacked was the bondi's daughter, who at last died of it. Many things were tried out but without success. It seemed likely that the whole of Vatnsdal would be devastated unless help could be found.

We have now to return to Grettir, who was at home in Bjarg during the autumn which followed his meeting with Warrior-Bardi at Thoreyjargnup. When the winter was approaching, he rode north across the neck to Vididal and stayed at Audunarstad. He and Audun made friends again; Grettir gave him a valuable battle-axe and they agreed to hold together in friendship. Audun had long lived there, and had many connections. He had a son named Egill, who married Ulfheid the daughter of Eyjolf, the son of Gudmund; their son Eyjolf, who was killed at the All-Thing, was the father of Orm, the chaplain of Bishop Thorlak.

Grettir rode to the North to Vatnsdal and went on a visit to Tunga, where dwelt his mother's brother, Jokull the son of Bard, a big strong man and exceedingly haughty. He was a mariner, very cantankerous, but a person of much consideration. He welcomed Grettir, who stayed three nights with him. Nothing was talked about but Glam's walking, and Grettir inquired minutely about all particulars. Jokull told him that no more was said than had really happened.

"Why, do you want to go there?" he asked.

Grettir said that it was so. Jokull told him not to do it.

"It would be a most hazardous undertaking," he said. "Your kinsmen incur a great risk with you as you are. There does not seem to be one of the younger men who is your equal. It is ill dealing with such a one as Glam. Much better fight with human men than with goblins of that sort."

Grettir said he had a mind to go to Thorhallsstad and see how things were. Jokull said: "I see there is no use in dissuading you. The saying is true that *Luck is one thing, brave deeds another.*"

"*Woe stands before the door of one but enters that of another*," answered Grettir. "I am thinking how it may fare with you yourself before all is done."

"It may be," said Jokull, "that we both see what is before us, and yet we may not alter it."

Then they parted, neither of them well pleased with the other's prophetic saying.

Grettir rode to Thorhallsstad where he was welcomed by the bondi. He asked Grettir whither he was bound, and Grettir said he wished to spend the night there if the bondi permitted. Thorhall said he would indeed be thankful to him for staying there.

"Few," he said, "think it a gain to stay here for any time. You must have heard tell of the trouble that is here, and I do not want you to be inconvenienced on my account. Even if you escape unhurt yourself, I know for certain that you will lose your horse, for no one can keep his beast in safety who comes here."

Grettir said there were plenty more horses to be had if anything happened to this one.

Thorhall was delighted at Grettir's wishing to remain, and received him with both hands. Grettir's horse was placed securely under lock and key and they both went to bed. The night passed without Glam showing himself.

"Your being here has already done some good," said Thorhall. "Glam has always been in the habit of riding on the roof or breaking open the doors every night, as you can see from the marks."

"Then," Grettir said, "either he will not keep quiet much longer, or he will remain so more than one night. I will stay another night and see what happens."

Then they went to Grettir's horse and found it had not been touched. The bondi thought that all pointed to the same thing. Grettir stayed a second night and again the thrall did not appear. The bondi became hopeful and went to see the horse. There he found the stable broken open, the horse dragged outside and every bone in his body broken. Thorhall told Grettir what had occurred and advised him to look to himself, for he was a dead man if he waited for Glam.

Grettir answered: "I must not have less for my horse than a sight of the thrall."

The bondi said there was no pleasure to be had from seeing him: "He is not like any man. I count every hour a gain that you are here."

The day passed, and when the hour came for going to bed Grettir said he would not take off his clothes, and lay down on a seat opposite to Thorhall's sleeping apartment. He had a rough fur cloak over him with one end of it fastened under his feet and the other drawn over his head so that he could see through the neck-hole. He set his feet against a strong bench which was in front of him. The frame-work of the outer door had been all broken away and some bits of wood had been rigged up roughly in its place. The partition which had once divided the hall from the entrance passage was all broken, both above the cross-beam and below, and all the bedding had been upset. The place was scarcely habitable. There was a light burning in the hall by night.

When about a third part of the night had passed Grettir heard a loud noise. Something was tearing through the house, riding above the hall and kicking with its heels until the timbers cracked again. This went on for some time, and then it came down towards the door. The door opened and Grettir saw the thrall stretching in an enormously big and ugly head. Glam moved slowly in, and on passing the door stood upright, reaching to the roof. He came down the hall holding the cross-beam with his hand and peering along the hall. The bondi uttered no sound, having heard quite enough of what had gone on outside. Grettir lay quite still and did not move. Glam saw a heap of something in the seat, came further into the hall and seized the cloak tightly with his hand. Grettir pressed his foot against the plank and the cloak held firm. Glam tugged at it again still more violently, but it did not give way. A third time he pulled, this time with both hands and with such force that he pulled Grettir up out of the seat, and between them the cloak was torn in two. Glam looked at the bit which he held in his hand and wondered much who could pull like that against him. Suddenly Grettir sprang under his arms, seized him round the waist and squeezed his back with all his might, intend-

ing in that way to bring him down, but the thrall wrenched his
arms till he staggered from the violence. Then Grettir fell back
to another bench. The benches flew about and everything was
shattered around them. Glam wanted to get out, but Grettir tried
to prevent him by stemming his foot against anything he could
find. Nevertheless Glam succeeded in getting him outside the hall.
Then a terrific struggle began, the thrall trying to drag him out
of the house, and Grettir saw that however hard he was to deal
with in the house, he would be worse outside, so he strove with all
his might to keep him from getting out. Then Glam made a desperate effort and gripped Grettir tightly towards him, forcing him
to the porch. Grettir saw that he could not put his foot against
it, and with a sudden movement he dashed into the thrall's arms
and set both his feet against a stone which was fastened in the
ground at the door. For that Glam was not prepared, since he
had been tugging to drag Grettir towards him; he reeled backwards and tumbled hindforemost out of the door, tearing away
the lintel with his shoulder and shattering the roof, the rafters and
the frozen thatch. Head over heels he fell out of the house and
Grettir fell on the top of him. The moon was shining very bright
outside, with light clouds passing over it and hiding it now and
again. At the moment when Glam fell the moon shone forth, and
Glam turned his eyes up towards it. Grettir himself has told us
that that sight was the only one which ever made him tremble.
What with fatigue and all else that he had endured, when he saw
the horrible rolling of Glam's eyes his heart sank so utterly that
he had not strength to draw his sword, but lay there well-nigh betwixt life and death. Glam possessed more malignant power than
most fiends, and he now spoke in this wise:

"You have expended much energy, Grettir, in your contest
with me. Nor is that to be wondered at, though you will have
little joy thereof. And now I tell you that you shall possess only
half the strength and firmness of heart that were decreed to you
if you had not striven with me. The might which was yours till
now I am not able to take away, but it is in my power to ordain
that never shall you grow stronger than you are now. Nevertheless your might is sufficient, as many shall find to their cost.
Hitherto you have earned fame through your deeds, but henceforth there shall fall upon you exile and battle; your deeds shall

turn to evil and your guardian-spirit shall forsake you. You will be outlawed and your lot shall be to dwell ever alone. And this I lay upon you, that these eyes of mine shall be ever before your vision. You will find it hard to live alone, and at last it shall drag you to death."

When the thrall had spoken the faintness which had come over Grettir left him. He drew his short sword, cut off Glam's head and laid it between his thighs. Then the bondi came out, having put on his clothes while Glam was speaking, but he did not venture to come near until he was dead. Thorhall praised God and thanked Grettir warmly for having laid this unclean spirit. Then they set to work and burned Glam to cold cinders, bound the ashes in a skin and buried them in a place far away from the haunts of man or beast. Then they went home, the day having nearly broken. Grettir was very stiff and lay down to rest. Thorhall sent for some men from the next farm and let them know how things had fared. They all realised the importance of Grettir's deed when they heard of it; all agreed that in the whole country side for strength and courage and enterprise there was not the equal of Grettir the son of Asmund.

Thorhall bade a kindly farewell to Grettir and dismissed him with a present of a fine horse and proper clothes, for all that he had been wearing were torn to pieces. They parted in friendship. Grettir rode to Ass in Vatnsdal and was welcomed by Thorvald, who asked him all about his encounter with Glam. Grettir told him everything and said that never had his strength been put to trial as it had been in their long struggle. Thorvald told him to conduct himself discreetly; if he did so he might prosper, but otherwise he would surely come to disaster. Grettir said that his temper had not improved, that he had even less discretion than before, and was more impatient of being crossed. In one thing a great change had come over him; he had become so frightened of the dark that he dared not go anywhere alone at night. Apparitions of every kind came before him. It has since passed into an expression, and men speak of "Glam's eyes" or "Glam visions" when things appear otherwise than as they are.

Having accomplished his undertaking Grettir rode back to Bjarg and spent the winter at home.

THE GHOSTS OF WULAKAI

This is an example of the true ghost story—narrated as fact and retold faithfully by the explorer and anthropologist who heard it from the lips of an old Manchu. I have dropped into the text two lines of asterisks to set off the ghost story proper from the factual matter preceding and following. Readers with no anthropological curiosity can skip the third section, but the first is a useful explanatory prologue to the tale itself. This story first appeared in *Asia* magazine, March, 1934. Owen Lattimore's excellent travel books, *The Desert Road to Turkestan* and *High Tartary*, give a modern view of the regions traversed by the ghosts of Wulakai.— EDITOR.

Owen Lattimore
(Manchurian)

THE GHOSTS
OF WULAKAI

One night, with the frost cracking outside and the fire (for once) going well inside, the Old Man and I were sitting with thimble-sized cups of heated grain-spirit in front of us. The Old Man asked about my former travels—not because he was really interested, but just to be polite. I spoke of Mongolia and then of Chinese Turkistan and mentioned the Six Cities of Ili, the Ili River and the spruce forests and high pastures of the Heavenly Mountains.

"Hi!" he said, looking really interested, "you have been there?" I said I had indeed.

"Ili, in Turkistan," said the Old Man to himself, and then recited the names of places and tribes and garrisons on the Road

North of the Heavenly Mountains, as if he had been there himself.

"How is it you know so much of Ili," I asked him, "distant from us by a road of many months?"

"What house in Wulakai does not know of Ili!" he said. "It was from Ili that the ghosts came back. Ha-hai! That was a terrible year!"

"Now, when would that be?" I said casually. "Would it be in those years when the Mohammedans rebelled? Probably you were yet small." The Old Man had stopped talking and was dreaming by himself, far away from the present. I was afraid that in calling back his attention I might call him away from his memories.

He was a Manchu; a man who looked even older than his years, because of much hardship; and very dirty. His eyes were bleared with smoke from the niggardly fires that the poor use, and many of his teeth were gone, so that he mumbled. He looked a beggar, but he was no such thing. His dignity and manners were of a kind that is found only with high breeding and an old tradition. He never forgot that his ancestors had been captains in the Manchu armies that conquered China, nearly three hundred years ago, and that in the following generations his clan had furnished generals and high officials to the Empire, rulers of provinces and wardens of turbulent frontiers. The clan graveyard lay a little distant from the town, out in the fields, watched over by a few cedars. On great stone tablets, which stood out bleakly in the bright air that glitters over the snow of Kirin Province in the depth of winter, were inscribed in Manchu and Chinese the names, honors and dignities of the chief men of the clan.

He had lived all his sixty-four years in Wulakai, on the bank of the Sungari, whose Manchu name is the name of that great river of stars we call the Milky Way and the Chinese call the River of Heaven. The people of the little town are almost all Manchu. They are conservative and stubborn, but at the same time bold and independent. Although they have long forgotten the Manchu language, they have not forgotten that they belong to the oldest and noblest Manchu stock. They regard Peiping as a kind of suburb which Wulakai officials used to frequent. When we first came to Wulakai, they received us with a perfectly obvious rude intolerance which made it plain that they had no use for inquisitive foreigners and that, if we meant to stay, we had better shift for ourselves. We had to prove that we were fit to associate with them before they would associate with us.

However, through the courtesy of the Governor of Kirin, we found quarters in the little school deserted for the long winter holiday. It had once been the Manchu school, where sons of Bannermen intended for the public service had learned a smattering of their own forgotten language. I found a Manchu teacher and settled down to study. It was a quaint experience; for to the teacher himself Manchu was as dead as Greek, but he knew it well, in a school-book way, and we made good progress.

My wife and I were quartered in a room that measured ten feet by twelve. Most of it was built up into a *k'ang*, or brick stove-bed, heated by a flue. This left only a narrow "well" at the front of the room in which to move around. In this room we lived and cooked and ate and slept and received visitors; and here I studied Manchu. The Old Man was the caretaker of the school. He lived next to us, in a tiny, dark hole of a room. He cherished an old sword that hung over his bed. He had been rich and had sons; now he was childless and dependent on charity. He had nothing to eat but scraps from the table of relatives, poor enough themselves; but he cooked the scraps afresh and served them to himself in separate courses, in broken cast-away crockery, and dined always with formality, as a gentleman should. We saw to it, without seeming to patronize him, that at least while we were there he had more to eat and more fuel to warm his lair. He decided, after a while, that we were above the ordinary run of barbarian; and at last that we were socially presentable. He would come and sit in our room for a while at night and drink a little *shao chiu* and ask what progress I was making in Manchu and perhaps talk a while.

Thus it happened that we heard the tale of the Ghosts of Wulakai. It goes back to the savage wars of the great Mohammedan Rebellion, which broke out in 1862 and lasted until 1877. It is said that in this rebellion the province of Kansu lost fifteen million people, leaving only one million alive, and that in Chinese Turkistan ten million people died. The story links together Manchuria and Chinese Turkistan, the deep forests of the Northeast and the wilds of Central Asia, more than two thousand miles or more of desert, mountain and nomad pasture; and it throws a light on the distant campaigns of the Bannermen on whom rested the military power of the Manchu Empire.

*　　*　　*　　*　　*　　*　　*

"Yes," said the Old Man, rousing out of his memories; "I was small, but I knew the men of those times and spoke with them. I was born in the fourth year of T'ung Chih, and it was in the seventh year of T'ung Chih (1869) that the ghosts came back from the Ili campaign, to which had gone two companies of men, levied among the Banner troops of Wulakai and the hamlets that lie near it. Of these, fifty men were under the command of I Ho; and that man was a man of one clan with me.

"They went, and no word came back. It was not like now, with post and telegraph. Not so easy. When they went, they went. Then the word did come back. Those thieves—the rebels—had taken them in ambush and slaughtered them. The names of the killed were proclaimed, and the villages mourned. Their bodies could never be returned; how could they, from so far? It was a journey of many months.

"Then, one night at the ferry over the Sungari below Wulakai, the men were awakened by shouting; the ferryboat was wanted. They grumbled, but one said, 'Some one calls for the ferry,' and one put on his gown and went and unbarred the gate and looked across the river. He looked and could see nothing; but he could hear bridles jingling. He called but got no answer. Then they spoke among themselves and said: 'Perhaps it would be as well to go across. Who knows? There are horses; it may be troops or despatch-riders.' With that, they took the boat and poled across the river; but, when they got to the landing on the far bank, they could see nothing. They called again, but there was no answer. They were frightened and looked at one another; and then they heard bridles jingling again. Thereupon the men said, 'Let us go back, quickly; this is no good business.' But the headman of the ferry (and he was my father's brother) said: 'No! This is some special business. There is something else in this. Did they not call? Put the boat alongside and hold it steady with poles on the stream side.'

"Thus then they did; and the boat, as they waited, sank a little and rocked, as if a horse had got aboard. This happened again and again and many times. Then my uncle said, 'If there are no more, we will ferry across.' There was no more rocking; so they went from the landing stage and ferried across. Yet all this time no horses were in the boat; nothing at all, yet they heard bridles jingling. When they got to their own side, they put the boat against the landing, fixed the gangplanks for disembarking, cleared the way as if for passengers to go on shore and steadied the boat as before. Then the boat swayed and rose, as it would when a horse got out—would it not? For those brutes, they weigh plenty. And again the boat stirred and rose; and again and again. One of the men in the ferry, whose heart was more clever, counted, and it was exactly fifty.

"When all were ashore they heard bridles jingling again, and stirrups, as if men were mounting into the saddle. Then their passengers rode away in a body. Thus those who had died in battle came home from the Ili war.

"But listen again. It was later on the same night that I Ho came home. He had to ride from Wulakai across three streams that flow into the Sungari. The first two of these he could ford, but at the last he had to use the ferry, right across from his own hamlet and his own home. It was a small ferry; a little boat with one man.

"There again the ferryman woke when he heard calling; but when he got up he could see nothing; and he listened, but he could hear nothing—only something that seemed to him like the jingling of a bridle when a horse shakes his head. He called, but there was no one that answered. He thought he would not go across; but then he thought: 'It may be troops or despatch-riders. I had better go over to see.'

"With that, he poled the boat over to the far bank and looked and called; but there was no one. No man was there, but, when he listened again, it was true he could hear bridles jingling. At first he was frightened—ha! he jumped, all right!—but he was a bold man. 'All right,' he said, and he called out, 'If there is anybody there, I'll put my boat alongside, and you may come aboard.' Then he put the boat alongside and steadied it with his punting pole, and in a moment it sank and swayed, as if a man had led a horse on board.

" 'Slowly, slowly!' said the ferryman. 'If there are any more of you, I'll come back again; but don't any more come on just now or you'll drown the lot of us.' He was a bold fellow, that, who could talk to devils like a devil.

"He ferried his unseen passenger across, and, as the horse was disembarked, the boat swayed once more as it lost the weight. The ferryman went back again across the river. He brought over four men in all, and the last of them was I Ho.

"Now, when the first three riders had landed, they went up a lane that led around two sides of the home of I Ho, their bridles jingling as they rode. Then one of them took his riding whip and with the handle of it knocked on the gate. The people in the house heard and called out, 'What business have you, coming like this in the middle of the night?' But there was no answer, only the knocking at the gate. Then they called again, being afraid, and they heard an answer, 'When the master of the house has come, who does not open the gate?'

"When they heard that, they said, 'This is one of our people calling.' A woman went then to the gate and opened. All at once a very cold wind blew through the gate—*ch'ua!* it blew; just like that, *ch'ua!* There was nothing to see; but, to hear, it was as if horses were crowding against one another, jostling through the gate, stirrup striking against stirrup. It scared a jump out of all the people in that courtyard; and the old woman at the gate, she was scared sick. She was just closing the gate when a voice called out, 'There is still some one behind us!' And, as she let the gate open again, there came in another, colder wind. That was I Ho entering the court of his home.

"The next day they were all in terror; for they did not know what was happening. The official notice had long come, of the death of those men. I Ho, they knew, had died in battle, and with him the men of Wulakai. They had prepared a coffin, as if for his body, and had already carried it out, empty, for burial. Now this that had happened was an omen, they feared, of something else, of something dreadful yet to happen. But then my uncle, the one from the ferry below Wulakai, came over to see them and told of the fifty who had crossed at his ferry. 'What do you fear?' he said. 'Were not they the men of the following of I Ho? There was not one lacking of the number. They all scattered, each to his own household. The announcement of their death came. You duly carried out the coffin of I Ho as if for burial, and now he has returned to his home. Honor him among your ancestors and let your hearts be at rest.' (For, if you think, the despatches had come by courier; and those couriers—at the slowest they rode several stages in a day, with relays of fresh horses prepared for them. But the returning dead, they rode as troops ride; where would they find relays of fresh horses prepared? March by march they rode the distance, and only in the time of marching troops could they reach at last their own homes.

"But indeed, that year, in every family holding throughout the countryside about Wulakai they were asking from family to family, 'Have yours come back?' They all came back. What do I say? The next month there came back another hundred, all in a body; and that time even their banners were seen.

"Five hundred men, six hundred men, were levied in the first levy from Wulakai and the steadings about it for a ride of thirty miles in the four quarters of the compass; and of the first levy, by the time that Turkistan was reduced to peace and leveled before us—which was a good many years—there came back only four men alive.

"I heard it all when I was yet a child, from the old people; and I heard the men who had come back tell of it. I Ho died in that first campaign, with Te Tsui-jen. They were each a captain of fifty in the troop of a man named Kuo, a Kirin man. In that year, after they had fought their way into the Red Temple (one of the names of Urumchi, now the capital of Chinese Turkistan) the Marshal despatched Kuo on the Ili road against the thieves, the rebels. Beyond Manass there is Ching Ho, the Crystal River; and there they had to ford the river, with thickets beyond it."

While the Old Man spoke thus accurately of the ford of Crystal River and the thickets beyond it, the tale became uncannily real to me. Two and a half years before, in the stillness just before dawn, my wife and I had ridden through that ford and out into those thickets, after an all-night ride on the road from Urumchi to Ili. It was getting light before we were through the thickets. Along that road you can still see ruined towns and villages, never inhabited again since the Mohammedan Rebellion. It made me almost uneasy to hear again, two thousand miles or so removed, the simple description of the place, given by a man to whom it meant only a distant savage place, whose name he had remembered from his boyhood, from the words of men who had fought there and seen their comrades die, sixty odd years ago.

*   *   *   *   *   *   *

"Now, Kuo," the Old Man went on, "was a fellow with a soft heart, and he was uneasy at the ford. I Ho and Te Tsui-jen urged him forward. They sent out scouts and the scouts returned, saying that only fifty or sixty men were beyond the river. But they did not know; the most part of the Mohammedans were hidden in the thickets. These two said: 'We cannot turn back, and there are only a few tens of them. If we withdraw, what report can we make? It is not here that we can turn back.' But Kuo would not go ahead; and, if you think, if the officers are always behind, how will the others fight? The officers must be in front.

"Then these two said: 'We will divide. You keep half the men here, and we will force the ford. If they fight by the river, we can fall back and you can support us. If they fight beyond, you can come up to reenforce us.'

"Then they forded the river. Those fifty or sixty Moslems gave ground. Then Te Tsui-jen and I Ho said, 'Straight ahead! After them!' They did not even pause to unfurl their banners. But those Mohammedans, their hearts were full of holes—they were very wily. As they gave ground and our men followed up, others came out from ambush behind and cut off our men from the river. Five or six hundred of them there were! Our men were always the better fighters; but you must think—they were but just one hundred and eighty men, and encircled, and still could they overcome five hundred, six hundred?

"I Ho said to Te Tsui-jen: 'This has finished our business. We two brothers, you and I, today we have met the real thing. But we can't let them have it all their own way.' Then they rallied their brothers and they said, 'If it be fighting, let it be fighting; if it be dying, let it be dying.' Kuo, from afar, saw that they had fallen into a trap; but, as for supporting them, he was not that man. He cast away his troops there in the road and fled by the way they had come.

"One hundred and eighty of our men, with those two, I Ho and Te Tsui-jen, all fell there in battle; all but twenty-five who got out of it. Even the bodies of the dead were abandoned there and could not be recovered.

"As for Kuo, if that fellow had not been related to the Marshal, it would have been all up with him. But, even so, you must not think too much of his being a relative; the Marshal cursed him a mouthful. He stood up in anger and slapped him in the face, this side one and that side one, and spun him around and kicked him in the behind. He said, 'Who are you to leave my men to die like that, good men like those two and a hundred and eighty men all but twenty-five?'

"But, to tell the truth of it, in that year those who died were many, and those who returned were few. There was another Marshal stationed at Chuguchak, Warden of the Marches of Tarbagatai. The Mohammedans butchered him like a sheep. The son of that Marshal swore a revenge; and he had all his dinner service made of Moslem skulls. In the course of time, when the victory was ours, he in his turn was Marshal at Chuguchak and Warden of the Marches of Tarbagatai; and then the Mohammedans ate bitterness. Of beating and cursing there is no need to speak; he killed them out of hand."

The Old Man was tired. He sat with his chin fallen on the ragged collar of his gown and his fingers tucked in his ragged sleeves. Then he sighed and stood up. "It is not early," he said; "will you not rest? I return to my own place."

●

CASTING THE RUNES

In the preface to *More Ghost Stories of an Antiquary* (1912), the book from which this one was taken, Dr James says that a good ghost story should "put the reader into the position of saying to himself, 'If I'm not very careful, something of this kind may happen to me!'" Certainly it is a telling rule in the case of this tale, in which a man going about his ordinary business becomes involved in a series of events not at all to his liking—events that might just as well have happened to you or me.—EDITOR.

M. R. James

CASTING THE RUNES

April 15th, 190—.

Dear Sir,—I am requested by the Council of the
. . . . Association to return to you the draft of a paper on *The Truth
of Alchemy*, which you have been good enough to offer to read at our
forthcoming meeting, and to inform you that the Council do not see
their way to including it in the programme.

　　　　　　　　I am,
　　　　　　　　　　　Yours faithfully,
　　　　　　　　　　　　. . . . . *Secretary.*

April 18th.

DEAR SIR,—I am sorry to say that my engagements do not permit of
my affording you an interview on the subject of your proposed paper.
Nor do our laws allow of your discussing the matter with a Committee

of our Council, as you suggest. Please allow me to assure you that the fullest consideration was given to the draft which you submitted, and that it was not declined without having been referred to the judgment of a most competent authority. No personal question (it can hardly be necessary for me to add) can have had the slightest influence on the decision of the Council.

Believe me (*ut supra*).

April 20th.

The Secretary of the .... Association begs respectfully to inform Mr. Karswell that it is impossible for him to communicate the name of any person or persons to whom the draft of Mr. Karswell's paper may have been submitted; and further desires to intimate that he cannot undertake to reply to any further letters on this subject.

"And who *is* Mr. Karswell?" inquired the Secretary's wife. She had called at his office, and (perhaps unwarrantably) had picked up the last of these three letters, which the typist had just brought in.

"Why, my dear, just at present Mr. Karswell is a very angry man. But I don't know much about him otherwise, except that he is a person of wealth, his address is Lufford Abbey, Warwickshire, and he's an alchemist, apparently, and wants to tell us all about it; and that's about all—except that I don't want to meet him for the next week or two. Now, if you're ready to leave this place, I am."

"What have you been doing to make him angry?" asked Mrs. Secretary.

"The usual thing, my dear, the usual thing: he sent in a draft of a paper he wanted to read at the next meeting, and we referred it to Edward Dunning—almost the only man in England who knows about these things—and he said it was perfectly hopeless, so we declined it. So Karswell has been pelting me with letters ever since. The last thing he wanted was the name of the man we referred his nonsense to; you saw my answer to that. But don't you say anything about it, for goodness' sake."

"I should think not, indeed. Did I ever do such a thing? I do hope, though, he won't get to know that it was poor Mr. Dunning."

"Poor Mr. Dunning? I don't know why you call him that;

he's a very happy man, is Dunning. Lots of hobbies and a comfortable home, and all his time to himself."

"I only meant I should be sorry for him if this man got hold of his name, and came and bothered him."

"Oh, ah! yes. I dare say he would be poor Mr. Dunning then."

The Secretary and his wife were lunching out, and the friends to whose house they were bound were Warwickshire people. So Mrs. Secretary had already settled it in her own mind that she would question them judiciously about Mr. Karswell. But she was saved the trouble of leading up to the subject, for the hostess said to the host, before many minutes had passed, "I saw the Abbot of Lufford this morning." The host whistled. "*Did* you? What in the world brings him up to town?" "Goodness knows; he was coming out of the British Museum gate as I drove past." It was not unnatural that Mrs. Secretary should inquire whether this was a real Abbot who was being spoken of. "Oh no, my dear: only a neighbour of ours in the country who bought Lufford Abbey a few years ago. His real name is Karswell." "Is he a friend of yours?" asked Mr. Secretary, with a private wink to his wife. The question let loose a torrent of declamation. There was really nothing to be said for Mr. Karswell. Nobody knew what he did with himself: his servants were a horrible set of people; he had invented a new religion for himself, and practised no one could tell what appalling rites; he was very easily offended, and never forgave anybody: he had a dreadful face (so the lady insisted, her husband somewhat demurring); he never did a kind action, and whatever influence he did exert was mischievous. "Do the poor man justice, dear," the husband interrupted. "You forget the treat he gave the school children." "Forget it, indeed! But I'm glad you mentioned it, because it gives an idea of the man. Now, Florence, listen to this. The first winter he was at Lufford this delightful neighbour of ours wrote to the clergyman of his parish (he's not ours, but we know him very well) and offered to show the school children some magic-lantern slides. He said he had some new kinds, which he thought would interest them. Well, the clergyman was rather surprised, because Mr. Karswell had shown himself inclined to be unpleasant to the children—complaining of their trespassing, or something of the sort; but of course he accepted, and the evening was fixed, and our friend went himself to see that everything went right. He said he never had been so thankful for anything as that his own children were all prevented from being there: they were at a children's party at our house, as a matter of fact. Because this Mr. Karswell had evidently set out with the intention of frightening these poor village children out of their wits, and I do believe, if he had been allowed to go on, he would actually have done so. He began with some comparatively mild things. Red Riding Hood was one, and even then, Mr. Farrer said, the wolf was so dreadful that several of the smaller children had to be taken out: and he said Mr. Karswell began the story by producing a noise like a wolf howling in the distance, which was the most gruesome thing he had ever heard. All the slides he showed, Mr. Farrer said, were most clever; they were absolutely realistic, and where he had got them or how he worked them he could not imagine. Well, the show went on, and the stories kept on becoming a little more terrifying each time, and the children were mesmerized into complete silence. At last he produced a series which represented a little boy passing through his own park—Lufford, I mean—in the evening. Every child in the room could recognize the place from the pictures. And this poor boy was followed, and at last pursued and overtaken, and either torn in pieces or somehow made away with, by a horrible hopping creature in white, which you saw first dodging about among the trees, and gradually it appeared more and more plainly. Mr. Farrer said it gave him one of the worst nightmares he ever remembered, and what it must have meant to the children doesn't bear thinking of. Of course this was too much, and he spoke very sharply indeed to Mr. Karswell, and said it couldn't go on. All *he* said was: 'Oh, you think it's time to bring our little show to an end and send them home to their beds? *Very* well!' And then, if you please, he switched on another slide, which showed a great mass of snakes, centipedes, and disgusting creatures with wings, and somehow or other he made it seem as if they were climbing out of the picture and getting in amongst the audience; and this was accompanied by a sort of dry rustling noise which sent the children nearly mad, and of course they stampeded. A good many of them were rather hurt in getting out of the room, and I don't suppose one of them closed an eye that night. There was the most dreadful trouble in the village afterwards. Of course the mothers threw a good part of the blame on poor Mr. Farrer, and, if they could have got past the gates, I believe the fathers would have broken every window in the Abbey. Well, now, that's Mr. Karswell: that's the Abbot of Lufford, my dear, and you can imagine how we covet *his* society."

"Yes, I think he has all the possibilities of a distinguished criminal, has Karswell," said the host. "I should be sorry for anyone who got into his bad books."

"Is he the man, or am I mixing him up with someone else?" asked the Secretary (who for some minutes had been wearing the frown of the man who is trying to recollect something). "Is he the man who brought out a *History of Witchcraft* some time back —ten years or more?"

"That's the man; do you remember the reviews of it?"

"Certainly I do; and what's equally to the point, I knew the author of the most incisive of the lot. So did you: you must remember John Harrington; he was at John's in our time."

"Oh, very well indeed, though I don't think I saw or heard anything of him between the time I went down and the day I read the account of the inquest on him."

"Inquest?" said one of the ladies. "What has happened to him?"

"Why, what happened was that he fell out of a tree and broke his neck. But the puzzle was, what could have induced him to get up there. It was a mysterious business, I must say. Here was this man—not an athletic fellow, was he? and with no eccentric twist about him that was ever noticed—walking home along a country road late in the evening—no tramps about—well known and liked in the place—and he suddenly begins to run like mad, loses his hat and stick, and finally shins up a tree—quite a difficult tree—growing in the hedgerow: a dead branch gives way, and he comes down with it and breaks his neck, and there he's found next morning with the most dreadful face of fear on him that could be imagined. It was pretty evident, of course, that he had been chased by something, and people talked of savage dogs, and beasts escaped out of menageries; but there was nothing to be made of that. That was in '89, and I believe his brother Henry (whom I remember as well at Cambridge, but *you* probably don't) has been trying to get on the track of an explanation ever since. He, of course, insists there was malice in it, but I don't know. It's difficult to see how it could have come in."

After a time the talk reverted to the *History of Witchcraft*. "Did you ever look into it?" asked the host.

"Yes, I did," said the Secretary. "I went so far as to read it."

"Was it as bad as it was made out to be?"

"Oh, in point of style and form, quite hopeless. It deserved all the pulverizing it got. But, besides that, it was an evil book. The man believed very word of what he was saying, and I'm very much mistaken if he hadn't tried the greater part of his receipts."

"Well, I only remember Harrington's review of it, and I must say if I'd been the author it would have quenched my literary ambition for good. I should never have held up my head again."

"It hasn't had that effect in the present case. But come, it's half-past three; I must be off."

On the way home the Secretary's wife said, "I do hope that horrible man won't find out that Mr. Dunning had anything to do with the rejection of his paper." "I don't think there's much chance of that," said the Secretary. "Dunning won't mention it himself, for these matters are confidential, and none of us will for the same reason. Karswell won't know his name, for Dunning hasn't published anything on the same subject yet. The only danger is that Karswell might find out, if he was to ask the British Museum people who was in the habit of consulting alchemical manuscripts: I can't very well tell them not to mention Dunning, can I? It would set them to talking at once. Let's hope it won't occur to him."

However, Mr. Karswell was an astute man.

This much is in the way of prologue. On an evening rather later in the same week, Mr. Edward Dunning was returning from the British Museum, where he had been engaged in Research, to the comfortable house in a suburb where he lived alone, tended by two excellent women who had been long with him. There is nothing to be added by way of description of him to what we have heard already. Let us follow him as he takes his sober course homewards.

A train took him to within a mile or two of his house, and an electric tram a stage farther. The line ended at a point some three hundred yards from his front door. He had had enough of reading when he got into the car, and indeed the light was not such as to allow him to do more than study the advertisements on the panes of glass that faced him as he sat. As was not unnatural, the advertisements in this particular line of cars were objects of his frequent contemplation, and, with the possible exception of the brilliant and convincing dialogue between Mr. Lamplough and an eminent K.C. on the subject of Puretic Saline, none of them afforded much scope to his imagination. I am wrong: there was one at the corner of the car farthest from him which did not seem familiar. It was in blue letters on a yellow ground, and all that he could read of it was a name—John Harrington—and something like a date. It could be of no interest to him to know more; but for all that, as the car emptied, he was just curious enough to move along the seat until he could read it well. He felt to a slight extent repaid for his trouble; the advertisement was *not* of the usual type. It ran thus: "In memory of John Harrington, F.S.A., of The Laurels, Ashbrooke. Died Sept. 18th, 1889. Three months were allowed."

The car stopped. Mr. Dunning, still contemplating the blue letters on the yellow ground, had to be stimulated to rise by a word from the conductor. "I beg your pardon," he said, "I was looking at that advertisement; it's a very odd one, isn't it?" The conductor read it slowly. "Well, my word," he said, "I never see that one before. Well, that is a cure, ain't it? Someone bin up to their jokes 'ere, I should think." He got out a duster and applied it, not without saliva, to the pane and then to the outside. "No," he said, returning, "that ain't no transfer; seems to me as if it was reg'lar *in* the glass, what I mean in the substance, as you may say. Don't you think so, sir?" Mr. Dunning examined it and rubbed it with his glove, and agreed. "Who looks after these advertisements, and gives leave for them to be put up? I wish you would inquire. I will just take a note of the words." At this moment there came a call from the driver: "Look alive, George, time's up." "All right, all right; there's somethink else what's up at this end. You come and look at this 'ere glass." "What's gorn with the glass?" said the driver, approaching. "Well, and oo's 'Arrington?

What's it all about?" "I was just asking who was responsible for putting the advertisements up in your cars, and saying it would be as well to make some inquiry about this one." "Well, sir, that's all done at the Company's orfice, that work is: it's our Mr. Timms, I believe, looks into that. When we put up to-night I'll leave word, and per'aps I'll be able to tell you to-morrer if you 'appen to be coming this way."

This was all that passed that evening. Mr. Dunning did just go to the trouble of looking up Ashbrooke, and found that it was in Warwickshire.

Next day he went to town again. The car (it was the same car) was too full in the morning to allow of his getting a word with the conductor: he could only be sure that the curious advertisement had been made away with. The close of the day brought a further element of mystery into the transaction. He had missed the tram, or else preferred walking home, but at a rather late hour, while he was at work in his study, one of the maids came to say that two men from the tramways were very anxious to speak to him. This was a reminder of the advertisement, which he had, he says, nearly forgotten. He had the men in—they were the conductor and driver of the car—and when the matter of refreshment had been attended to, asked what Mr. Timms had had to say about the advertisement. "Well, sir, that's what we took the liberty to step round about," said the conductor. "Mr. Timms 'e give William 'ere the rough side of his tongue about that: 'cordin' to 'im there warn't no advertisement of that description sent in, nor ordered, nor paid for, nor put up, nor nothink, let alone not bein' there, and we was playing the fool takin' up his time. 'Well,' I says, 'if that's the case, all I ask of you, Mr. Timms,' I says, 'is to take and look at it for yourself,' I says. 'Of course if it ain't there,' I says, 'you may take and call me what you like.' 'Right,' he says, 'I will': and we went straight off. Now, I leave it to you, sir, if that ad., as we term 'em, with 'Arrington on it warn't as plain as ever you see anythink—blue letters on yeller glass, and as I says at the time, and you borne me out, reg'lar *in* the glass, because, if you remember, you recollect of me swabbing it with my duster." "To be sure I do, quite clearly—well?" "You may say well, I don't think. Mr. Timms he gets in that car with a light—no, he told William to 'old the light outside. 'Now,' he says, 'where's your precious ad. what we've 'eard so much about?' ' 'Ere it is,' I says, 'Mr. Timms,' and I laid my hand on it." The conductor paused.

"Well," said Mr. Dunning, "it was gone, I suppose. Broken?"

"Broke!—not it. There warn't, if you'll believe me, no more trace of them letters—blue letters they was—on that piece o' glass, than—well, it's no good *me* talkin'. I never see such a thing. I leave it to William here if—but there, as I says, where's the benefit in me going on about it?"

"And what did Mr. Timms say?"

"Why 'e did what I give 'im leave to—called us pretty much anythink he liked, and I don't know as I blame him so much neither. But what we thought, William and me did, was as we seen you take down a bit of a note about that—well, that let- terin'——"

"I certainly did that, and I have it now. Did you wish me to speak to Mr. Timms myself, and show it to him? Was that what you came in about?"

"There, didn't I say as much?" said William. "Deal with a gent if you can get on the track of one, that's my word. Now perhaps, George, you'll allow as I ain't took you very far wrong to-night."

"Very well, William, very well; no need for you to go on as if you'd 'ad to frog's-march me 'ere. I come quiet, didn't I? All the same for that, we 'adn't ought to take up your time this way, sir; but if it so 'appened you could find time to step round to the Company's orfice in the morning and tell Mr. Timms what you seen for yourself, we should lay under a very 'igh obligation to you for the trouble. You see it ain't bein' called—well, one thing and another, as we mind, but if they got it into their 'ead at the orfice as we seen things as warn't there, why, one thing leads to another, and where we should be a twelvemunce 'ence—well, you can understand what I mean."

Amid further elucidations of the proposition, George, con- ducted by William, left the room.

The incredulity of Mr. Timms (who had a nodding acquaint- ance with Mr. Dunning) was greatly modified on the following day by what the latter could tell and show him; and any bad mark that might have been attached to the names of William and George was not suffered to remain on the Company's books; but explanation there was none.

Mr. Dunning's interest in the matter was kept alive by an incident of the following afternoon. He was walking from his club to the train, and he noticed some way ahead a man with a handful of leaflets such as are distributed to passers-by by agents of enterprising firms. This agent had not chosen a very crowded street for his operations: in fact, Mr. Dunning did not see him get rid of a single leaflet before he himself reached the spot. One was thrust into his hand as he passed: the hand that gave it touched his, and he experienced a sort of little shock as it did so. It seemed unnaturally rough and hot. He looked in passing at the giver, but the impression he got was so unclear that, however much he tried to reckon it up subsequently, nothing would come. He was walking quickly, and as he went on glanced at the paper. It was a blue one. The name of Harrington in large capitals caught his eye. He stopped, startled, and felt for his glasses. The next instant the leaflet was twitched out of his hand by a man who hurried past, and was irrecoverably gone. He ran back a few paces, but where was the passer-by? and where the distributor?

It was in a somewhat pensive frame of mind that Mr. Dunning passed on the following day into the Select Manuscript Room of the British Museum, and filled up tickets for Harley 3586, and some other volumes. After a few minutes they were brought to him, and he was settling the one he wanted first upon the desk, when he thought he heard his own name whispered behind him. He turned round hastily, and in doing so, brushed his little portfolio of loose papers on to the floor. He saw no one he recognized except one of the staff in charge of the room, who nodded to him, and he proceeded to pick up his papers. He thought he had them all, and was turning to begin work, when a stout gentleman at the table behind him, who was just rising to leave, and had collected his own belongings, touched him on the shoulder, saying, "May I give you this? I think it should be yours," and handed him a missing quire. "It is mine, thank you," said Mr. Dunning. In another moment the man had left the room. Upon finishing his work for the afternoon, Mr. Dunning had some conversation with the assistant in charge, and took occasion to ask who the stout gentleman was. "Oh, he's a man named Karswell," said the assistant;

"he was asking me a week ago who were the great authorities on alchemy, and of course I told him you were the only one in the country. I'll see if I can't catch him: he'd like to meet you, I'm sure."

"For heaven's sake don't dream of it!" said Mr. Dunning. "I'm particularly anxious to avoid him."

"Oh! very well," said the assistant, "he doesn't come here often: I dare say you won't meet him."

More than once on the way home that day Mr. Dunning confessed to himself that he did not look forward with his usual cheerfulness to a solitary evening. It seemed to him that something ill-defined and impalpable had stepped in between him and his fellow-men—had taken him in charge, as it were. He wanted to sit close up to his neighbours in the train and in the tram, but as luck would have it both train and car were markedly empty. The conductor George was thoughtful, and appeared to be absorbed in calculations as to the number of passengers. On arriving at his house he found Dr. Watson, his medical man, on his doorstep. "I've had to upset your household arrangements, I'm sorry to say, Dunning. Both your servants *hors de combat*. In fact, I've had to send them to the Nursing Home."

"Good heavens! what's the matter?"

"It's something like ptomaine poisoning, I should think: you've not suffered yourself, I can see, or you wouldn't be walking about. I think they'll pull through all right."

"Dear, dear! Have you any idea what brought it on?"

"Well, they tell me they bought some shell-fish from a hawker at their dinner-time. It's odd. I've made inquiries, but I can't find that any hawker has been to other houses in the street. I couldn't send word to you; they won't be back for a bit yet. You come and dine with me to-night, anyhow, and we can make arrangements for going on. Eight o'clock. Don't be too anxious."

The solitary evening was thus obviated; at the expense of some distress and inconvenience, it is true. Mr. Dunning spent the time pleasantly enough with the doctor (a rather recent settler), and returned to his lonely home at about 11.30. The night he passed is not one on which he looks back with any satisfaction. He was in bed and the light was out. He was wondering if the charwoman would come early enough to get him hot water next morning, when he heard the unmistakable sound of his study door opening. No step followed it on the passage floor, but the sound must mean mischief, for he knew that he had shut the door that evening after putting his papers away in his desk. It was rather shame than courage that induced him to slip out into the passage and lean over the banister in his nightgown, listening. No light was visible; no further sound came: only a gust of warm, or even hot air played for an instant round his shins. He went back and decided to lock himself into his room. There was more unpleasantness, however. Either an economical suburban company had decided that their light would not be required in the small hours, and had stopped working, or else something was wrong with the meter; the effect was in any case that the electric light was off. The obvious course was to find a match, and also to consult his watch: he might as well know how many hours of discomfort awaited him. So he put his hand into the well-known nook under the pillow: only, it did not get so far. What he touched was, according to his account, a mouth, with teeth, and with hair about it, and, he declares, not the mouth of a human being. I do not think it is any use to guess what he said or did; but he was in a spare room with the door locked and his ear to it before he was clearly conscious again. And there he spent the rest of a most miserable night, looking every moment for some fumbling at the door: but nothing came.

The venturing back to his own room in the morning was attended with many listenings and quiverings. The door stood open, fortunately, and the blinds were up (the servants had been out of the house before the hour of drawing them down); there was, to be short, no trace of an inhabitant. The watch, too, was in its usual place; nothing was disturbed, only the wardrobe door had swung open, in accordance with its confirmed habit. A ring at the back door now announced the charwoman, who had been ordered the night before, and nerved Mr. Dunning, after letting her in, to continue his search in other parts of the house. It was equally fruitless.

The day thus begun went on dismally enough. He dared not go to the Museum: in spite of what the assistant had said, Karswell might turn up there, and Dunning felt he could not cope with a probably hostile stranger. His own house was odious; he hated sponging on the doctor. He spent some little time in a call at the

Nursing Home, where he was slightly cheered by a good report of his housekeeper and maid. Towards lunch-time he betook himself to his club, again experiencing a gleam of satisfaction at seeing the Secretary of the Association. At luncheon Dunning told his friend the more material of his woes, but could not bring himself to speak of those that weighed most heavily on his spirits. "My poor dear man," said the Secretary, "what an upset! Look here: we're alone at home, absolutely. You must put up with us. Yes! no excuse: send your things in this afternoon." Dunning was unable to stand out: he was, in truth, becoming acutely anxious, as the hours went on, as to what that night might have waiting for him. He was almost happy as he hurried home to pack up.

His friends, when they had time to take stock of him, were rather shocked at his lorn appearance, and did their best to keep him up to the mark. Not altogether without success: but, when the two men were smoking alone later, Dunning became dull again. Suddenly he said, "Gayton, I believe that alchemist man knows it was I who got his paper rejected." Gayton whistled. "What makes you think that?" he said. Dunning told of his conversation with the Museum assistant, and Gayton could only agree that the guess seemed likely to be correct. "Not that I care much," Dunning went on, "only it might be a nuisance if we were to meet. He's a bad-tempered party, I imagine." Conversation dropped again; Gayton became more and more strongly impressed with the desolateness that came over Dunning's face and bearing, and finally—though with a considerable effort—he asked him point-blank whether something serious was not bothering him. Dunning gave an exclamation of relief. "I was perishing to get it off my mind," he said. "Do you know anything about a man named John Harrington?" Gayton was thoroughly startled, and at the moment could only ask why. Then the complete story of Dunning's experiences came out—what had happened in the tramcar, in his own house, and in the street, the troubling of spirit that had crept over him, and still held him; and he ended with the question he had begun with. Gayton was at a loss how to answer him. To tell the story of Harrington's end would perhaps be right; only, Dunning was in a nervous state, the story was a grim one, and he could not help asking himself whether there were not a connecting link between these two cases, in the person of Karswell. It was a difficult concession for a scientific man, but it could be eased by the phrase "hypnotic suggestion." In the end he decided that his answer to-night should be guarded; he would talk the situation over with his wife. So he said that he had known Harrington at Cambridge, and believed he had died suddenly in 1889, adding a few details about the man and his published work. He did talk over the matter with Mrs. Gayton, and, as he had anticipated, she leapt at once to the conclusion which had been hovering before him. It was she who reminded him of the surviving brother, Henry Harrington, and she also suggested that he might be got hold of by means of their hosts of the day before. "He might be a hopeless crank," objected Gayton. "That could be ascertained from the Bennetts, who knew him," Mrs. Gayton retorted; and she undertook to see the Bennetts the very next day.

It is not necessary to tell in further detail the steps by which Henry Harrington and Dunning were brought together.

The next scene that does require to be narrated is a conversation that took place between the two. Dunning had told Harrington of the strange ways in which the dead man's name had been brought before him, and had said something, besides, of his own subsequent experiences. Then he had asked if Harrington was disposed, in return, to recall any of the circumstances connected with his brother's death. Harrington's surprise at what he heard can be imagined: but his reply was readily given.

"John," he said, "was in a very odd state, undeniably, from time to time, during some weeks before, though not immediately before, the catastrophe. There were several things; the principal notion he had was that he thought he was being followed. No doubt he was an impressionable man, but he never had had such fancies as this before. I cannot get it out of my mind that there was ill-will at work, and what you tell me about yourself reminds me very much of my brother. Can you think of any possible connecting link?"

"There is just one that has been taking shape vaguely in my mind. I've been told that your brother reviewed a book very severely not long before he died, and just lately I have happened to cross the path of the man who wrote that book in a way he could resent."

"Don't tell me the man was called Karswell."

"Why not? that is exactly his name."

Henry Harrington leant back. "That is final to my mind. Now I must explain further. From something he said, I feel sure that my brother John was beginning to believe—very much against his will—that Karswell was at the bottom of his trouble. I want to tell you what seems to me to have a bearing on the situation. My brother was a great musician, and used to run up to concerts in town. He came back, three months before he died, from one of these, and gave me his programme to look at—an analytical programme: he always kept them. 'I nearly missed this one,' he said. 'I suppose I must have dropped it: anyhow, I was looking for it under my seat and in my pockets and so on, and my neighbour offered me his: said 'might he give it to me, he had no further use for it,' and he went away just afterwards. I don't know who he was—a stout, clean-shaven man. I should have been sorry to miss it; of course I could have bought another, but this cost me nothing.' At another time he told me that he had been very uncomfortable both on the way to his hotel and during the night. I piece things together now in thinking it over. Then, not very long after, he was going over these programmes, putting them in order to have them bound up, and in this particular one (which by the way I had hardly glanced at), he found quite near the beginning a strip of paper with some very odd writing on it in red and black —most carefully done—it looked to me more like Runic letters than anything else. 'Why!', he said, 'this must belong to my fat neighbour. It looks as if it might be worth returning to him; it may be a copy of something; evidently someone has taken trouble over it. How can I find his address?' We talked it over for a little and agreed that it wasn't worth advertising about, and that my brother had better look out for the man at the next concert, to which he was going very soon. The paper was lying on the book and we were both by the fire; it was a cold, windy summer evening. I suppose the door blew open, though I didn't notice it: at any rate a gust—a warm gust it was—came quite suddenly between us, took the paper and blew it straight into the fire: it was light, thin paper, and flared and went up the chimney in a single ash. 'Well,'

I said, 'you can't give it back now.' He said nothing for a minute: then rather crossly, 'No, I can't; but why you should keep on saying so I don't know.' I remarked that I didn't say it more than once. 'Not more than four times, you mean,' was all he said. I remember all that very clearly, without any good reason; and now to come to the point. I don't know if you looked at that book of Karswell's which my unfortunate brother reviewed. It's not likely that you should: but I did, both before his death and after it. The first time we made game of it together. It was written in no style at all—split infinitives, and every sort of thing that makes an Oxford gorge rise. Then there was nothing that the man didn't swallow: mixing up classical myths, and stories out of the *Golden Legend* with reports of savage customs of to-day—all very proper, no doubt, if you know how to use them, but he didn't: he seemed to put the *Golden Legend* and the *Golden Bough* exactly on a par, and to believe both: a pitiable exhibition, in short. Well, after the misfortune, I looked over the book again. It was no better than before, but the impression which it left this time on my mind was different. I suspected—as I told you—that Karswell had borne ill-will to my brother, even that he was in some way responsible for what had happened; and now his book seemed to me to be a very sinister performance indeed. One chapter in particular struck me, in which he spoke of 'casting the Runes' on people, either for the purpose of gaining their affection or of getting them out of the way—perhaps more especially the latter: he spoke of all this in a way that really seemed to me to imply actual knowledge. I've not time to go into details, but the upshot is that I am pretty sure from information received that the civil man at the concert was Karswell: I suspect—I more than suspect—that the paper was of importance: and I do believe that if my brother had been able to give it back, he might have been alive now. Therefore, it occurs to me to ask you whether you have anything to put beside what I have told you."

By way of answer, Dunning had the episode in the Manuscript Room at the British Museum to relate. "Then he did actually hand you some papers; have you examined them? No? because we must, if you'll allow it, look at them at once, and very carefully."

They went to the still empty house—empty, for the two servants were not yet able to return to work. Dunning's portfolio of papers was gathering dust on the writing-table. In it were the quires of small-sized scribbling paper which he used for his transcripts: and from one of these, as he took it up, there slipped and fluttered out into the room with uncanny quickness, a strip of thin light paper. The window was open, but Harrington slammed it to, just in time to intercept the paper, which he caught. "I thought so," he said; "it might be the identical thing that was given to my brother. You'll have to look out, Dunning; this may mean something quite serious for you."

A long consultation took place. The paper was narrowly examined. As Harrington had said, the characters on it were more like Runes than anything else, but not decipherable by either man, and both hesitated to copy them, for fear, as they confessed, of perpetuating whatever evil purpose they might conceal. So it has remained impossible (if I may anticipate a little) to ascertain what was conveyed in this curious message or commission. Both Dunning and Harrington are firmly convinced that it had the effect of bringing its possessors into very undesirable company. That it must be returned to the source whence it came they were agreed, and further, that the only safe and certain way was that of personal service; and here contrivance would be necessary, for Dunning was known by sight to Karswell. He must, for one thing, alter his appearance by shaving his beard. But then might not the blow fall first? Harrington thought they could time it. He knew the date of the concert at which the "black spot" had been put on his brother: it was June 18th. The death had followed on Sept 18th. Dunning reminded him that three months had been mentioned in the inscription on the car-window. "Perhaps," he added, with a cheerless laugh, "mine may be a bill at three months too. I believe I can fix it by my diary. Yes, April 23rd was the day at the Museum; that brings us to July 23rd. Now, you know, it becomes extremely important to me to know anything you will tell me about the progress of your brother's trouble, if it is possible for you to speak of it." "Of course. Well, the sense of being watched whenever he was alone was the most distressing thing to him. After a time I took to sleeping in his room, and he was the better for that: still, he talked a great deal in his sleep. What about? Is it wise to dwell on that, at least before things are straightened out? I think not, but I can tell you this: two things came for him by post during those weeks, both with a London postmark, and addressed in a commercial hand. One was a woodcut of Bewick's, roughly torn out of the page: one which shows a moonlit road and a man walking along it, followed by an awful demon creature. Under it were written the lines out of the 'Ancient Mariner' (which I suppose the cut illustrates) about one who, having once looked round——

> 'walks on,
> And turns no more his head,
> Because he knows a frightful fiend
> Doth close behind him tread.'

The other was a calendar, such as tradesmen often send. My brother paid no attention to this, but I looked at it after his death, and found that everything after Sept. 18 had been torn out. You may be surprised at his having gone out alone the evening he was killed, but the fact is that during the last ten days or so of his life he had been quite free from the sense of being followed or watched."

The end of the consultation was this. Harrington, who knew a neighbour of Karswell's, thought he saw a way of keeping a watch on his movements. It would be Dunning's part to be in readiness to try to cross Karswell's path at any moment, to keep the paper safe and in a place of ready access.

They parted. The next weeks were no doubt a severe strain upon Dunning's nerves: the intangible barrier which had seemed to rise about him on the day when he received the paper, gradually developed into a brooding blackness that cut him off from the means of escape to which one might have thought he might resort. No one was at hand who was likely to suggest them to him, and he seemed robbed of all initiative. He waited with inexpressible anxiety as May, June, and early July passed on, for a mandate from Harrington. But all this time Karswell remained immovable at Lufford.

At last, in less than a week before the date he had come to look upon as the end of his earthly activities, came a telegram: "Leaves Victoria by boat train Thursday night. Do not miss. I come to you to-night. Harrington."

He arrived accordingly, and they concocted plans. The train

left Victoria at nine and its last stop before Dover was Croydon
West. Harrington would mark down Karswell at Victoria, and
look out for Dunning at Croydon, calling to him if need were by a
name agreed upon. Dunning, disguised as far as might be, was to
have no label or initials on any hand luggage, and must at all costs
have the paper with him.

Dunning's suspense as he waited on the Croydon platform I
need not attempt to describe. His sense of danger during the last
days had only been sharpened by the fact that the cloud about him
had perceptibly been lighter; but relief was an ominous symptom,
and, if Karswell eluded him now, hope was gone; and there were
so many chances of that. The humour of the journey might be
itself a device. The twenty minutes in which he paced the platform and persecuted every porter with inquiries as to the boat train
were as bitter as any he had spent. Still, the train came, and Harrington was at the window. It was important, of course, that there
should be no recognition: so Dunning got in at the farther end of
the corridor carriage, and only gradually made his way to the compartment where Harrington and Karswell were. He was pleased,
on the whole, to see that the train was far from full.

Karswell was on the alert, but gave no sign of recognition.
Dunning took the seat not immediately facing him, and attempted,
vainly at first, then with increasing command of his faculties, to
reckon the possibilities of making the desired transfer. Opposite to
Karswell, and next to Dunning, was a heap of Karswell's coats on
the seat. It would be of no use to slip the paper into these—he
would not be safe, or would not feel so, unless in some way it
could be proffered by him and accepted by the other. There was a
handbag, open, and with papers in it. Could he manage to conceal
this (so that perhaps Karswell might leave the carriage without it),
and then find and give it to him? This was the plan that suggested
itself. If he could only have counselled with Harrington! But that
could not be. The minutes went on. More than once Karswell rose
and went out into the corridor. The second time Dunning was on
the point of attempting to make the bag fall off the seat, but he
caught Harrington's eye, and read in it a warning. Karswell, from
the corridor, was watching: probably to see if the two men recognized each other. He returned, but was evidently restless: and,
when he rose the third time, hope dawned, for something did slip

off his seat and fall with hardly a sound to the floor. Karswell went out once more, and passed out of range of the corridor window. Dunning picked up what had fallen, and saw that the key was in his hands in the form of one of Cook's ticket-cases, with tickets in it. These cases have a pocket in the cover, and within a very few seconds the paper of which we have heard was in the pocket of this one. To make the operation more secure, Harrington stood in the doorway of the compartment and fiddled with the blind. It was done, and done at the right time, for the train was now slowing down towards Dover.

In a moment more Karswell re-entered the compartment. As he did so, Dunning, managing, he knew not how, to suppress the tremble in his voice, handed him the ticket-case, saying, "May I give you this, sir? I believe it is yours." After a brief glance at the ticket inside, Karswell uttered the hoped-for response, "Yes, it is; much obliged to you, sir," and he placed it in his breast pocket.

Even in the few moments that remained—moments of tense anxiety, for they knew not to what a premature finding of the paper might lead—both men noticed that the carriage seemed to darken about them and to grow warmer; that Karswell was fidgety and oppressed; that he drew the heap of loose coats near to him and cast it back as if it repelled him; and that he then sat upright and glanced anxiously at both. They, with sickening anxiety, busied themselves in collecting their belongings; but they both thought that Karswell was on the point of speaking when the train stopped at Dover Town. It was natural that in the short space between town and pier they should both go into the corridor.

At the pier they got out, but so empty was the train that they were forced to linger on the platform until Karswell should have passed ahead of them with his porter on the way to the boat, and only then was it safe for them to exchange a pressure of the hand and a word of concentrated congratulation. The effect upon Dunning was to make him almost faint. Harrington made him lean up against the wall, while he himself went forward a few yards within sight of the gangway to the boat, at which Karswell had now arrived. The man at the head of it examined his ticket, and, laden with coats, he passed down into the boat. Suddenly the official called after him, "You, sir, beg pardon, did the other gentleman show his ticket?" "What the devil do you mean by the other gentleman?" Karswell's snarling voice called back from the deck. "The devil? Well, I don't know, I'm sure," Harrington heard him say to himself, and then aloud, "My mistake, sir; must have been your rugs! ask your pardon." And then, to a subordinate near him, " 'Ad he got a dog with him, or what? Funny thing: I could 'a' swore 'e wasn't alone. Well, whatever it was, they'll 'ave to see to it aboard. She's off now. Another week and we shall be gettin' the 'oliday customers." In five minutes more there was nothing but the lessening lights of the boat, the long line of the Dover lamps, the night breeze, and the moon.

Long and long the two sat in their room at the "Lord Warden." In spite of the removal of their greatest anxiety, they were oppressed with a doubt, not of the lightest. Had they been justified in sending a man to his death, as they believed they had? Ought they not to warn him, at least? "No," said Harrington; "if he is the murderer I think him, we have done no more than is just. Still, if you think it better—but how and where can you warn him?" "He was booked to Abbeville only," said Dunning. "I saw that. If I wired to the hotels there in Joanne's Guide, 'Examine your ticket-case, Dunning,' I should feel happier. This is the 21st: he will have a day. But I am afraid he has gone into the dark." So telegrams were left at the hotel office.

It is not clear whether these reached their destination, or whether, if they did, they were understood. All that is known is that, on the afternoon of the 23rd, an English traveller, examining the front of St. Wulfram's Church at Abbeville, then under extensive repair, was struck on the head and instantly killed by a stone falling from the scaffold erected round the north-western tower, there being, as was clearly proved, no workman on the scaffold at that moment: and the traveller's papers identified him as Mr. Karswell.

Only one detail shall be added. At Karswell's sale a set of Bewick, sold with all faults, was acquired by Harrington. The page with the woodcut of the traveller and the demon was, as he had expected, mutilated. Also, after a judicious interval, Harrington repeated to Dunning something of what he had heard his brother say in his sleep: but it was not long before Dunning stopped him.

●

LET's talk of graves, of worms, and epitaphs;
Make dust our paper, and with rainy eyes
Write sorrows on the bosom of the earth;
Let's choose executors and talk of wills:
And yet not so—for what can we bequeath
Save our deposed bodies to the ground?
Our lands, our lives, and all are Bolingbroke's,
And nothing can we call our own but death,
And that small model of the barren earth
Which serves as paste and cover to our bones.
For God's sake let us sit upon the ground
And tell sad stories of the death of kings:
How some have been depos'd, some slain in war,
Some haunted by the ghosts they have depos'd. . . .

—KING RICHARD THE SECOND

A MAN WITH TWO LIVES

Can Such Things Be?, the book from which this story is taken, contains a number of famous stories approved by sincere students of ghostly letters. *The Middle Toe of the Right Foot* and *The Damned Thing* are examples. I have rejected them in favor of this one, not because they are well-known and have been often reprinted, but because I want the stories in this book to be equally interesting to believers and outright skeptics. Bierce's obvious effort to persuade skeptics by a laboriously matter-of-fact style of reporting does not always suit his subject matter. In this little story the effort is not obtrusive; and the effect, to my way of thinking, is much better because of that.— EDITOR.

Ambrose Bierce

A
MAN WITH
TWO LIVES

Here is the queer story of David William Duck, related by himself. Duck is an old man living in Aurora, Illinois, where he is universally respected. He is commonly known, however, as "Dead Duck."

"In the autumn of 1866 I was a private soldier of the Eighteenth Infantry. My company was one of those stationed at Fort Phil Kearney, commanded by Colonel Carrington. The country is more or less familiar with the history of that garrison, particularly with the slaughter by the Sioux of a detachment of eighty-one men and officers—not one escaping—through disobedience of orders by its commander, the brave but reckless Captain Fetterman. When that occurred, I was trying to make my way with important dispatches to Fort C. F. Smith, on the Big Horn. As the country swarmed with hostile Indians, I traveled by night and concealed myself as best I could before daybreak. The better to do so, I went afoot, armed with a Henry rifle and carrying three days' rations in my haversack.

"For my second place of concealment I chose what seemed in the darkness a narrow cañon leading through a range of rocky hills. It contained many large bowlders, detached from the slopes of the hills. Behind one of these, in a clump of sage-brush, I made my bed for the day, and soon fell asleep. It seemed as if I had hardly closed my eyes, though in fact it was near midday, when I was awakened by the report of a rifle, the bullet striking the bowlder just above my body. A band of Indians had trailed me and had me nearly surrounded; the shot had been fired with an execrable aim by a fellow who had caught sight of me from the hillside above. The smoke of his rifle betrayed him, and I was no sooner on my feet than he was off his and rolling down the declivity. Then I ran in a stooping posture, dodging among the clumps of sage-brush in a storm of bullets from invisible enemies. The rascals did not rise and pursue, which I thought rather queer, for they must have known by my trail that they had to deal with only one man. The reason for their inaction was soon made clear. I had not gone a hundred yards before I reached the limit of my run—the head of the gulch which I had mistaken for a cañon. It terminated in a concave breast of rock, nearly vertical and destitute of vegetation. In that cul-de-sac I was caught like a bear in a pen. Pursuit was needless; they had only to wait.

"They waited. For two days and night, crouching behind a rock topped with a growth of mesquite, and with the cliff at my back, suffering agonies of thirst and absolutely hopeless of deliverance, I fought the fellows at long range, firing occasionally at the smoke of their rifles, as they did at that of mine. Of course, I did not dare to close my eyes at night, and lack of sleep was a keen torture.

"I remember the morning of the third day, which I knew was to be my last. I remember, rather indistinctly, that in my desperation and delirium I sprang out into the open and began firing my repeating rifle without seeing anybody to fire at. And I remember no more of that fight.

"The next thing that I recollect was my pulling myself out of a river just at nightfall. I had not a rag of clothing and knew nothing of my whereabouts, but all that night I traveled, cold and footsore, toward the north. At daybreak I found myself at Fort C. F. Smith, my destination, but without my dispatches. The first man that I met was a sergeant named William Briscoe, whom I knew very well. You can fancy his astonishment at seeing me in that condition, and my own at his asking who the devil I was.

" 'Dave Duck,' I answered; 'who should I be?'

"He stared like an owl.

" 'You do look it,' he said, and I observed that he drew a little away from me. 'What's up?' he added.

"I told him what had happened to me the day before. He heard me through, still staring; then he said:

" 'My dear fellow, if you are Dave Duck I ought to inform you that I buried you two months ago. I was out with a small scouting party and found your body, full of bullet-holes and newly scalped—somewhat mutilated otherwise, too, I am sorry to say—right where you say you made your fight. Come to my tent and I'll show you your clothing and some letters that I took from your person; the commandant has your dispatches.'

"He performed that promise. He showed me the clothing, which I resolutely put on; the letters, which I put into my pocket. He made no objection, then took me to the commandant, who heard my story and coldly ordered Briscoe to take me to the guardhouse. On the way I said:

" 'Bill Briscoe, did you really and truly bury the dead body that you found in these togs?'

" 'Sure,' he answered—'just as I told you. It was Dave Duck, all right; most of us knew him. And now, you damned impostor, you'd better tell me who you are.'

" 'I'd give something to know,' I said.

"A week later, I escaped from the guardhouse and got out of the country as fast as I could. Twice I have been back, seeking for that fateful spot in the hills, but unable to find it."

THE OPEN WINDOW

A pleasant kind of maliciousness distinguishes many of Saki's more notable characters, but we sometimes are not able to identify this quality in them until the story's last line; for Saki developed a new twist to the short story, quite as effective as, but usually much more subtle than, the surprise-ending of his contemporary, O. Henry.—EDITOR.

Saki (H.H.Munro)

THE OPEN WINDOW

"My aunt will be down presently, Mr. Nuttel," said a very self-possessed young lady of fifteen; "in the meantime you must try and put up with me."

Framton Nuttel endeavoured to say the correct something which should duly flatter the niece of the moment without unduly discounting the aunt that was to come. Privately he doubted more than ever whether these formal visits on a succession of total strangers would do much towards helping the nerve cure which he was supposed to be undergoing.

"I know how it will be," his sister had said when he was

preparing to migrate to this rural retreat; "you will bury yourself down there and not speak to a living soul, and your nerves will be worse than ever from moping. I shall just give you letters of introduction to all the people I know there. Some of them, as far as I can remember, were quite nice."

Framton wondered whether Mrs. Sappleton, the lady to whom he was presenting one of the letters of introduction, came into the nice division.

"Do you know many of the people round here?" asked the niece, when she judged that they had had sufficient silent communion.

"Hardly a soul," said Framton. "My sister was staying here, at the rectory, you know, some four years ago, and she gave me letters of introduction to some of the people here."

He made the last statement in a tone of distinct regret.

"Then you know practically nothing about my aunt?" pursued the self-possessed young lady.

"Only her name and address," admitted the caller. He was wondering whether Mrs. Sappleton was in the married or widowed state. An undefinable something about the room seemed to suggest masculine habitation.

"Her great tragedy happened just three years ago," said the child; "that would be since your sister's time."

"Her tragedy?" asked Framton; somehow in this restful country spot tragedies seemed out of place.

"You may wonder why we keep that window wide open on an October afternoon," said the niece, indicating a large French window that opened on to a lawn.

"It is quite warm for the time of the year," said Framton; "but has that window got anything to do with the tragedy?"

"Out through that window, three years ago to a day, her husband and her two young brothers went off for their day's shooting. They never came back. In crossing the moor to their favourite snipe-shooting ground they were all three engulfed in a treacherous piece of bog. It had been that dreadful wet summer, you know, and places that were safe in other years gave way suddenly without warning. Their bodies were never recovered. That was the dreadful part of it." Here the child's voice lost its self-possessed note and became flatteringly human. "Poor aunt always thinks that they will come back some day, they and the little brown spaniel that was lost with them, and walk in at that window just as they used to do. That is why the window is kept open every evening till it is quite dusk. Poor dear aunt, she has often told me how they went out, her husband with his white waterproof coat over his arm, and Ronnie, her youngest brother, singing, 'Bertie, why do you bound?' as he always did to tease her, because she said it got on her nerves. Do you know, sometimes on still, quiet evenings like this, I almost get a creepy feeling that they will all walk in through that window——"

She broke off with a little shudder. It was a relief to Framton when the aunt bustled into the room with a whirl of apologies for being late in making her appearance.

"I hope Vera has been amusing you?" she said.

"She has been very interesting," said Framton.

"I hope you don't mind the open window," said Mrs. Sappleton briskly; "my husband and brothers will be home directly from shooting, and they always come in this way. They've been out for snipe in the marshes today, so they'll make a fine mess over my poor carpets. So like you men-folk, isn't it?"

She rattled on cheerfully about the shooting and the scarcity of birds, and the prospects for duck in the winter. To Framton it was all purely horrible. He made a desperate but only partially successful effort to turn the talk on to a less ghastly topic; he was conscious that his hostess was giving him only a fragment of her attention, and her eyes were constantly straying past him to the open window and the lawn beyond. It was certainly an unfortunate coincidence that he should have paid his visit on this tragic anniversary.

"The doctors agree in ordering me complete rest, an absence of mental excitement, and avoidance of anything in the nature of violent physical exercise," announced Framton, who laboured under the tolerably wide-spread delusion that total strangers and chance acquaintances are hungry for the least detail of one's ailments and infirmities, their cause and cure. "On the matter of diet they are not so much in agreement," he continued.

"No?" said Mrs. Sappleton, in a voice which only replaced a yawn at the last moment. Then she suddenly brightened into alert attention—but not to what Framton was saying.

"Here they are at last!" she cried. "Just in time for tea, and don't they look as if they were muddy up to the eyes!"

Framton shivered slightly and turned towards the niece with a look intended to convey sympathetic comprehension. The child was staring out through the open window with dazed horror in her eyes. In a chill shock of nameless fear Framton swung round in his seat and looked in the same direction.

In the deepening twilight three figures were walking across the lawn towards the window; they all carried guns under their arms, and one of them was additionally burdened with a white coat hung over his shoulders. A tired brown spaniel kept close at their heels. Noiselessly they neared the house, and then a hoarse young voice chanted out of the dusk: "I said, Bertie, why do you bound?"

Framton grabbed wildly at his stick and hat; the hall-door, the gravel-drive, and the front gate were dimly noted stages in his headlong retreat. A cyclist coming along the road had to run into the hedge to avoid imminent collision.

"Here we are, my dear," said the bearer of the white mackintosh, coming in through the window; "fairly muddy, but most of it's dry. Who was that who bolted as we came up?"

"A most extraordinary man, a Mr. Nuttel," said Mrs. Sappleton; "could only talk about his illnesses, and dashed off without a word of good-bye or apology when you arrived. One would think he had seen a ghost."

"I expect it was the spaniel," said the niece calmly; "he told me he had a horror of dogs. He was once hunted into a cemetery somewhere on the banks of the Ganges by a pack of pariah dogs, and had to spend the night in a newly dug grave with the creatures snarling and grinning and foaming just above him. Enough to make anyone lose their nerve."

Romance at short notice was her speciality.

●

●

THE DEPARTED spirits know things past and to come,
yet are ignorant of things present. Agamemnon foretells
what should happen unto Ulysses, yet ignorantly inquires
what is become of his own son. The ghosts are afraid of
swords in Homer, yet Sibylla tells Æneas in Virgil, the thin
habit of spirits was beyond the force of weapons. The
spirits put off their malice with their bodies, and Caesar
and Pompey accord in Latin hell; yet Ajax, in Homer,
endures not a conference with Ulysses; and Deiphobus appears all mangled in Virgil's ghosts; yet we meet with
perfect shadows among the wounded ghosts of Homer.

—URN-BURIAL

THE WOMAN'S GHOST STORY

This tale has been a favorite with anthologists. I must confess, however, that I do not like it as well as a number of the other possible choices from Blackwood. It is included, as I have announced in the foreword, because in a book crowded full of ghost stories it seems legitimate to present a few for the deliberate reason that they call attention to technical problems of the type. Is the author justified in deliberately dispensing with the usual preliminaries to prepare us for the entry of the ghost? The reader must decide that question for himself.—EDITOR.

A l g e r n o n
B l a c k w o o d

THE
WOMAN'S
GHOST
STORY

"Yes," she said, from her seat in the dark corner, "I'll tell you an experience if you care to listen. And, what's more, I'll tell it briefly, without trimmings—I mean without unessentials. That's a thing story-tellers never do, you know," she laughed. "They drag in all the unessentials and leave their listeners to disentangle; but I'll give you just the essentials, and you can make of it what you please. But on one condition: that at the end you ask no questions, because I can't explain it and have no wish to."

We agreed. We were all serious. After listening to a dozen prolix stories from people who merely wished to "talk" but had nothing to tell, we wanted "essentials."

"In those days," she began, feeling from the quality of our silence that we were with her, "in those days I was interested in psychic things, and had arranged to sit up alone in a haunted house in the middle of London. It was a cheap and dingy lodging-house in a mean street, unfurnished. I had already made a preliminary examination in daylight that afternoon, and the keys from the care-taker, who lived next door, were in my pocket. The story was a good one—satisfied me, at any rate, that it was worth investigating; and I won't weary you with details as to the woman's murder and all the tiresome elaborations as to *why* the place was *alive*. Enough that it was.

"I was a good deal bored, therefore, to see a man, whom I took to be the talkative old caretaker, waiting for me on the steps when I went in at 11 P.M., for I had sufficiently explained that I wished to be there alone for the night.

" 'I wished to show you *the* room,' he mumbled, and of course I couldn't exactly refuse, having tipped him for the temporary loan of a chair and table.

" 'Come in, then, and let's be quick,' I said.

"We went in, he shuffling after me through the unlighted hall up to the first floor where the murder had taken place, and I pre-pared myself to hear his inevitable account before turning him out with the half-crown his persistence had earned. After lighting the gas I sat down in the arm-chair he had provided—a faded, brown, plush arm-chair—and turned for the first time to face him and get through with the performance as quickly as possible. And it was in that instant I got my first shock. The man was *not* the caretaker. It was not the old fool, Carey, I had interviewed earlier in the day and made my plans with. My heart gave a horrid jump.

" 'Now who are *you*, pray?' I said. 'You're not Carey, the man I arranged with this afternoon. Who are you?'

"I felt uncomfortable, as you may imagine. I was a 'psychical researcher,' and a young woman of new tendencies, and proud of my liberty, but I did not care to find myself in an empty house with a stranger. Something of my confidence left me. Confidence with women, you know, is all humbug after a certain point. Or perhaps you don't know, for most of you are men. But anyhow my pluck ebbed in a quick rush, and I felt afraid.

" 'Who are you?' I repeated quickly and nervously. The

follow was well dressed, youngish and good-looking, but with a face of great sadness. I myself was barely thirty. I am giving you essentials, or I would not mention it. Out of quite ordinary things comes this story. I think that's why it has value.

" 'No,' he said; 'I'm the man who was frightened to death.'

"His voice and his words ran through me like a knife, and I felt ready to drop. In my pocket was the book I had bought to make notes in. I felt the pencil sticking in the socket. I felt, too, the extra warm things I had put on to sit up in, as no bed or sofa was available—a hundred things dashed through my mind, foolishly and without sequence or meaning, as the way is when one is really frightened. Unessentials leaped up and puzzled me, and I thought of what the papers might say if it came out, and what my 'smart' brother-in-law would think, and whether it would be told that I had cigarettes in my pocket, and was a free-thinker.

" 'The man who was frightened to death!' " I repeated aghast.

" 'That's me,' he said stupidly.

"I stared at him just as you would have done—any one of you men now listening to me—and felt my life ebbing and flowing like a sort of hot fluid. You needn't laugh! That's how I felt. Small things, you know, touch the mind with great earnestness when terror is there—*real terror*. But I might have been at a middle-class tea-party, for all the ideas I had: they were so ordinary!

" 'But I thought you were the caretaker I tipped this afternoon to let me sleep here!' I gasped. 'Did—did Carey send you to meet me?'

" 'No,' he replied in a voice that touched my boots somehow. 'I am the man who was frightened to death. And what is more, I am frightened *now!*'

" 'So am I!' I managed to utter, speaking instinctively. 'I'm simply terrified.'

" 'Yes,' he replied in that same odd voice that seemed to sound within me. 'But you are still in the flesh, and I—*am not!*'

"I felt the need for vigorous self-assertion. I stood up in that empty, unfurnished room, digging the nails into my palms and clenching my teeth. I was determined to assert my individuality and my courage as a new woman and a free soul.

" 'You mean to say you are not in the flesh!' I gasped. 'What in the world are you talking about?'

"The silence of the night swallowed up my voice. For the first time I realised that darkness was over the city; that dust lay upon the stairs; that the floor above was untenanted and the floor below empty. I was alone in an unoccupied and haunted house, unprotected, and a woman. I chilled. I heard the wind round the house, and knew the stars were hidden. My thoughts rushed to policemen and omnibuses, and everything that was useful and comforting. I suddenly realised what a fool I was to come to such a house alone. I was icily afraid. I thought the end of my life had come. I was an utter fool to go in for psychical research when I had not the necessary nerve.

" 'Good God!' I gasped. 'If you're not Carey, the man I arranged with, who are you?'

"I was really stiff with terror. The man moved slowly towards me across the empty room. I held out my arm to stop him, getting up out of my chair at the same moment, and he came to a halt just opposite to me, a smile on his worn, sad face.

" 'I told you who I am,' he repeated quietly with a sigh, looking at me with the saddest eyes I have ever seen, 'and I am frightened *still.*'

"By this time I was convinced that I was entertaining either a rogue or a madman, and I cursed my stupidity in bringing the man in without having seen his face. My mind was quickly made up, and I knew what to do. Ghosts and psychic phenomena flew to the winds. If I angered the creature my life might pay the price. I must humour him till I got to the door, and then race for the street. I stood bolt upright and faced him. We were about of a height, and I was a strong, athletic woman who played hockey in winter and climbed Alps in summer. My hand itched for a stick, but I had none.

" 'Now, of course, I remember,' I said with a sort of stiff smile that was very hard to force. 'Now I remember your case and the wonderful way you behaved. . . .'

"The man stared at me stupidly, turning his head to watch me as I backed more and more quickly to the door. But when his face broke into a smile I could control myself no longer. I reached for the door in a run, and shot out on to the landing. Like a fool, I turned the wrong way, and stumbled over the stairs leading to the next storey. But it was too late to change. The man was after me, I was sure, though no sound of footsteps came; and I dashed up the next flight, tearing my skirt and banging my ribs in the darkness, and rushed headlong into the first room I came to. Luckily the door stood ajar, and, still more fortunate, there was a key in the lock. In a second I had slammed the door, flung my whole weight against it, and turned the key.

"I was safe, but my heart was beating like a drum. A second later it seemed to stop altogether, for I saw that there was some one else in the room besides myself. A man's figure stood between me and the window, where the street lamps gave just enough light to outline his shape against the glass. I'm a plucky woman, you know, for even then I didn't give up hope, but I may tell you that I have never felt so vilely frightened in all my born days. I had locked myself in with him!

"The man leaned against the window, watching me where I lay in a collapsed heap upon the floor. So there were two men in the house with me, I reflected. Perhaps other rooms were occupied too! What could it all mean? But, as I stared something changed in the room, or in me—hard to say which—and I realised my mistake, so that my fear, which had so far been physical, at once altered its character and became *psychical*. I became afraid in my soul instead of in my heart, and I knew immediately who this man was.

"'How in the world did you get up here?' I stammered to him across the empty room, amazement momentarily stemming my fear.

"'Now, let me tell you,' he began, in that odd far-away voice of his that went down my spine like a knife. 'I'm in different space, for one thing, and you'd find me in any room you went into; for according to your way of measuring, I'm *all over the house*. Space is a bodily condition, but I am out of the body, and am not affected by space. It's my condition that keeps me here. I want something to change my condition for me, for then I could get away. What I want is sympathy. Or, really, more than sympathy; I want affection—I want *love!*'

"While he was speaking I gathered myself slowly upon my feet. I wanted to scream and cry and laugh all at once, but I only succeeded in sighing, for my emotion was exhausted and a numbness was coming over me. I felt for the matches in my pocket and made a movement towards the gas jet.

" 'I should be much happier if you didn't light the gas,' he said at once, 'for the vibrations of your light hurt me a good deal. You need not be afraid that I shall injure you. I can't touch your body to begin with, for there's a great gulf fixed, you know; and really this half-light suits me best. Now, let me continue what I was trying to say before. You know, so many people have come to this house to see me, and most of them have seen me, and one and all have been terrified. If only, oh! if only some one would be *not* terrified, but kind and loving to me! Then, you see, I might be able to change my condition and get away!'

"His voice was so sad that I felt tears start somewhere at the back of my eyes; but fear kept all else in check, and I stood shaking and cold as I listened to him.

" 'Who are you then? Of course Carey didn't send you, I know now,' I managed to utter. My thoughts scattered dreadfully and I could think of nothing to say. I was afraid of a stroke.

" 'I know nothing about Carey, or who he is,' continued the man quietly, 'and the name my body had I have forgotten, thank God; but I am the man who was frightened to death in this house ten years ago, and I have been frightened ever since, and am frightened still; for the succession of cruel and curious people who come to this house to see the ghost, and thus keep alive its atmosphere of terror, only helps to render my condition worse. If only some one would be kind to me—*laugh*, speak gently and rationally with me, cry if they like, pity, comfort, soothe me—anything but come here in curiosity and tremble as you are now doing in that corner. Now, madam, won't you take pity on me?' His voice rose to a dreadful cry. 'Won't you step out into the middle of the room and try to love me a little?'

"A horrible laughter came gurgling up in my throat as I heard him, but the sense of pity was stronger than the laughter, and I found myself actually leaving the support of the wall and approaching the centre of the floor.

" 'By God!' he cried, at once straightening up against the window, 'you have done a kind act. That's the first attempt at sympathy that has been shown me since I died, and I feel better already. In life, you know, I was a misanthrope. Everything went wrong with me, and I came to hate my fellow men so much that I couldn't bear to see them even. Of course, like begets like, and this hate was returned. Finally I suffered from horrible delusions, and my room became haunted with demons that laughed and grimaced, and one night I ran into a whole cluster of them near the bed—and the fright stopped my heart and killed me. It's hate and remorse, as much as terror, that clogs me so thickly and keeps me here. If only some one could feel pity, and sympathy, and perhaps a little love for me, I could get away and be happy. When you came this afternoon to see over the house I watched you, and a little hope came to me for the first time. I saw you had courage, originality, resource—*love*. If only I could touch your heart, without frightening you, I knew I could perhaps tap that love you have stored up in your being there, and thus borrow the wings for my escape!'

"Now I must confess my heart began to ache a little, as fear left me and the man's words sank their sad meaning into me. Still, the whole affair was so incredible, and so touched with unholy quality, and the story of a woman's murder I had come to investigate had so obviously nothing to do with this thing, that I felt myself in a kind of wild dream that seemed likely to stop at any moment and leave me somewhere in bed after a nightmare.

"Moreover, his words possessed me to such an extent that I found it impossible to reflect upon anything else at all, or to consider adequately any ways and means of action or escape.

"I moved a little nearer to him in the gloom, horribly frightened, of course, but with the beginnings of a strange determination in my heart.

" 'You women,' he continued, his voice plainly thrilling at my approach, 'you wonderful women, to whom life often brings no opportunity of spending your great love, oh, if you only could know how many of *us* simply yearn for it! It would save our souls, if you but knew. Few might find the chance that you now have, but if you only spent your love freely, without definite object, just letting it flow openly for all who need, you would reach hundreds and thousands of souls like me, and *release us!* Oh, madam, I ask you again to feel with me, to be kind and gentle—and if you can to love me a little!'

"My heart did leap within me and this time the tears did

come, for I could not restrain them. I laughed too, for the way he called me 'madam' sounded so odd, here in this empty room at midnight in a London street, but my laughter stopped dead and merged in a flood of weeping when I saw how my change of feeling affected him. He had left his place by the window and was kneeling on the floor at my feet, his hands stretched out towards me, and the first signs of a kind of glory about his head.

" 'Put your arms round me and kiss me, for the love of God!' he cried. 'Kiss me, oh, kiss me, and I shall be freed! You have done so much already—now do this!'

"I stuck there, hesitating, shaking, my determination on the verge of action, yet not quite able to compass it. But the terror had almost gone.

" 'Forget that I'm a man and you're a woman,' he continued in the most beseeching voice I ever heard. 'Forget that I'm a ghost, and come out boldly and press me to you with a great kiss, and let your love flow into me. Forget yourself just for one minute and do a brave thing! Oh, love me, *love me*, LOVE ME! and I shall be free!'

"The words, or the deep force they somehow released in the centre of my being, stirred me profoundly, and an emotion infinitely greater than fear surged up over me and carried me with it across the edge of action. Without hesitation I took two steps forward towards him where he knelt, and held out my arms. Pity and love were in my heart at that moment, genuine pity, I swear, and genuine love. I forgot myself and my little tremblings in a great desire to help another soul.

" 'I love you! poor, aching, unhappy thing! I love you,' I cried through hot tears; 'and I am not the least bit afraid in the world.'

"The man uttered a curious sound, like laughter, yet not laughter, and turned his face up to me. The light from the street below fell on it, but there was another light too, shining all round it that seemed to come from the eyes and skin. He rose to his feet and met me, and in that second I folded him to my breast and kissed him full on the lips again and again."

All our pipes had gone out, and not even a skirt rustled in that dark studio as the story-teller paused a moment to steady her voice, and put a hand softly up to her eyes before going on again.

"Now, what can I say, and how can I describe to you, all you sceptical men sitting there with pipes in your mouths, the amazing sensation I experienced of holding an intangible, impalpable thing so closely to my heart that it touched my body with equal pressure all the way down, and then melted away somewhere into my very being? For it was like seizing a rush of cool wind and feeling a touch of burning fire the moment it had struck its swift blow and passed on. A series of shocks ran all over and all through me; a momentary ecstasy of flaming sweetness and wonder thrilled down into me; my heart gave another great leap—and then I was alone.

"The room was empty. I turned on the gas and struck a match to prove it. All fear had left me, and something was singing round me in the air and in my heart like the joy of a spring morning in youth. Not all the devils or shadows or hauntings in the world could then have caused me a single tremor.

"I unlocked the door and went all over the dark house, even into kitchen and cellar and up among the ghostly attics. But the house was empty. Something had left it. I lingered a short hour, analysing, thinking, wondering—you can guess what and how, perhaps, but I won't detail, for I promised only essentials, remember—and then went out to sleep the remainder of the night in my own flat, locking the door behind me upon a house no longer haunted.

"But my uncle, Sir Henry, the owner of the house, required an account of my adventure, and of course I was in duty bound to give him some kind of a true story. Before I could begin, however, he held up his hand to stop me.

" 'First,' he said, 'I wish to tell you a little deception I ventured to practise on you. So many people have been to that house and seen the ghost that I came to think the story acted on their imaginations, and I wished to make a better test. So I invented for their benefit another story, with the idea that if you did see anything I could be sure it was not due merely to an excited imagination.'

" 'Then what you told me about a woman having been murdered, and all that, was not the true story of the haunting?'

" 'It was not. The true story is that a cousin of mine went mad in that house, and killed himself in a fit of morbid terror following upon years of miserable hypochondriasis. It is his figure that investigators see.'

" 'That explains, then,' I gasped——

" 'Explains what?'

"I thought of that poor struggling soul, longing all these years for escape, and determined to keep my story for the present to myself.

" 'Explains, I mean, why I did not see the ghost of the murdered woman,' I concluded.

" 'Precisely,' said Sir Henry, 'and why, if you had seen anything, it would have had value, inasmuch as it could not have been caused by the imagination working upon a story you already knew.' "

●

BOLINGBROKE. Patience, good lady; wizards know their times:
Deep night, dark night, the silent of the night,
The time of night when Troy was set on fire;
The time when screech-owls cry, and ban-dogs howl,
And spirits walk, and ghosts break up their graves,
That time best fits the work we have in hand.

—SECOND PART OF KING HENRY THE SIXTH

●

. . . WHETHER THE complaint of Periander's wife be tolerable, that wanting her funeral burning she suffered intolerable cold in hell, according to the constitution of the infernal house of Pluto, wherein cold makes a great part of their tortures; it cannot pass without some question.

Why the female ghosts appear unto Ulysses, before the heroes and masculine spirits,—why the Psyche or soul of Tiresias is of the masculine gender, who being blind on earth sees more than all the rest in hell; why the funeral suppers consisted of eggs, beans, smallage, and lettuce, since the dead are made to eat asphodels about the Elysian meadows,—why, since there is no sacrifice acceptable, nor any propitiation for the covenant of the grave, men set up the deity of Morta, and fruitlessly adored divinities without ears, it cannot escape some doubt.

—URN-BURIAL

THE HAUNTED HOTEL

Everyone has heard of *The Moonstone*, by Wilkie Collins, a book that broke sharply away from the mystery tradition of the early 19th Century and set the style for the more modern type. Most of Collins' novels are too long for such a collection as this one. But *The Haunted Hotel* is of a satisfying length between novelette and full novel. It deals frankly with the supernatural, but the general style is one of realism. The reader of today should make fair allowances, however, for certain conventions of the mid-Victorian period which, although Collins reported them realistically, have come to seem artificial in the meanwhile.—EDITOR.

Wilkie Collins

THE
HAUNTED
HOTEL

THE FIRST PART

Chapter I

In the year 1860, the reputation of Doctor Wybrow as a London physician reached its highest point. It was reported on good authority that he was in receipt of one of the largest incomes derived from the practice of medicine in modern times.

One afternoon, towards the close of the London season, the Doctor had just taken his luncheon after a specially hard morning's work in his consulting-room, and with a formidable list of visits to patients at their own houses to fill up the rest of his day—when the servant announced that a lady wished to speak to him.

"Who is she?" the Doctor asked. "A stranger?"

"Yes, sir."

"I see no strangers out of consulting hours. Tell her what the hours are, and send her away."

"I have told her, sir."

"Well?"

"And she won't go."

"Won't go?" The Doctor smiled as he repeated the words. He was a humourist in his way; and there was an absurd side to the situation which rather amused him. "Has this obstinate lady given you her name?" he inquired.

"No, sir. She refused to give any name—she said she wouldn't keep you five minutes, and the matter was too important to wait till to-morrow. There she is in the consulting-room; and how to get her out again is more than I know."

Doctor Wybrow considered for a moment. His knowledge of women (professionally speaking) rested on the ripe experience of more than thirty years; he had met with them in all their varieties —especially the variety which knows nothing of the value of time, and never hesitates at sheltering itself behind the privileges of its sex. A glance at his watch informed him that he must soon begin his rounds among the patients who were waiting for him at their own houses. He decided forthwith on taking the only wise course that was open under the circumstance. In other words, he decided on taking to flight.

"Is the carriage at the door?" he asked.

"Yes, sir."

"Very well. Open the house-door for me without making any noise, and leave the lady in undisturbed possession of the consulting-room. When she gets tired of waiting, you know what to tell her. If she asks when I am expected to return, say that I dine at my club, and spend the evening at the theatre. Now then, softly, Thomas! If your shoes creak, I am a lost man."

He noiselessly led the way into the hall, followed by the servant on tip-toe.

Did the lady in the consulting-room suspect him? or did Thomas's shoes creak, and was her sense of hearing unusually keen? Whatever the explanation may be, the event that actually happened was beyond all doubt. Exactly as Doctor Wybrow passed his consulting-room, the door opened—the lady appeared on the threshold—and laid her hand on his arm.

"I entreat you, sir, not to go away without letting me speak to you first."

The accent was foreign; the tone was low and firm. Her fingers closed gently, and yet resolutely, on the Doctor's arm.

Neither her language nor her action had the slightest effect in inclining him to grant her request. The influence that instantly stopped him, on the way to his carriage, was the silent influence of her face. The startling contrast between the corpse-like pallor of her complexion and the over-powering life and light, the glittering metallic brightness in her large black eyes, held him literally spell-bound. She was dressed in dark colours, with perfect taste; she was of middle height, and (apparently) of middle age—say a year or two over thirty. Her lower features—the nose, mouth, and chin—possessed the fineness and delicacy of form which is oftener seen among women of foreign races than among women of English birth. She was unquestionably a handsome person, with the one serious drawback of her ghastly complexion, and with the less noticeable defect of a total want of tenderness in the expression of her eyes. Apart from his first emotion of surprise, the feeling she produced in the Doctor may be described as an overpowering feeling of professional curiosity. The case might prove to be something entirely new in his professional experience. "It looks like it," he thought; "and it's worth waiting for."

She perceived that she had produced a strong impression of some kind upon him, and dropped her hold on his arm.

"You have comforted many miserable women in your time," she said. "Comfort one more, to-day."

Without waiting to be answered, she led the way back into the room.

The Doctor followed her, and closed the door. He placed her in the patient's chair opposite the windows. Even in London the sun, on that summer afternoon, was dazzlingly bright. The radiant light flowed in on her. Her eyes met it unflinchingly, with the steely steadiness of the eyes of an eagle. The smooth pallor of her unwrinkled skin looked more fearfully white than ever. For the first time, for many a long year past, the Doctor felt his pulse quicken its beat in the presence of a patient.

Having possessed herself of his attention, she appeared, strangely enough, to have nothing to say to him. A curious apathy seemed to have taken possession of this resolute woman. Forced to speak first, the Doctor merely inquired, in the conventional phrase, what he could do for her.

The sound of his voice seemed to rouse her. Still looking straight at the light, she said abruptly: "I have a painful question to ask."

"What is it?"

Her eyes travelled slowly from the window to the Doctor's face. Without the slightest outward appearance of agitation, she put the "painful question" in these extraordinary words:

"I want to know, if you please, whether I am in danger of going mad?"

Some men might have been amused, and some might have been alarmed. Doctor Wybrow was only conscious of a sense of disappointment. Was this the rare case he had anticipated, judging rashly by appearances? Was the new patient only a hypochondriacal woman whose malady was a disordered stomach, and whose misfortune was a weak brain? "Why do you come to *me*," he asked sharply. "Why don't you consult a doctor whose special employment is the treatment of the insane?"

She had her answer ready on the instant.

"I don't go to a doctor of that sort," she said, "for the very reason that he *is* a specialist: he has the fatal habit of judging everybody by lines and rules of his own laying down. I come to *you*, because my case is outside of all lines and rules, and because you are famous in your profession for the discovery of mysteries in disease. Are you satisfied?"

He was more than satisfied—his first idea had been the right idea after all. Besides, she was correctly informed as to his professional position. The capacity which had raised him to fame and fortune, was his capacity (unrivalled among his brethren) for the discovery of remote disease.

"I am at your disposal," he answered. "Let me try if I can find out what is the matter with you."

He put his medical questions. They were promptly and plainly answered; and they led to no other conclusion than that the strange lady was, mentally and physically, in excellent health.

Not satisfied with questions, he carefully examined the great organs of life. Neither his hand nor his stethoscope could discover anything that was amiss. With the admirable patience and devotion to his art which had distinguished him from the time when he was a student, he still subjected her to one test after another. The result was always the same. Not only was there no tendency to brain disease—there was not even a perceptible derangement of the nervous system. "I can find nothing the matter with you," he said. "I can't even account for the extraordinary pallor of your complexion. You completely puzzle me."

"The pallor of my complexion is nothing," she answered a little impatiently. "In my early life, I had a narrow escape from death by poisoning. I have never had a complexion since—and my skin is so delicate, I cannot paint without producing a hideous rash. But that is of no importance, I wanted your opinion given positively. I believed in you, and you have disappointed me." Her head dropped on her breast. "And so it ends," she said to herself bitterly.

The Doctor's sympathies were touched. Perhaps it might be more correct to say that his professional pride was a little hurt. "It may end in the right way yet," he remarked, "if you choose to help me."

She looked up again with flashing eyes. "Speak plainly," she said. "How can I help you?"

"Plainly, madam, you come to me as an enigma, and you leave me to make the right guess by the unaided efforts of my art. My art will do much, but not all. For example something must have occurred—something quite unconnected with the state of your bodily health—to frighten you about yourself, or you would never have come here to consult me. Is that not true?"

She clasped her hands in her lap. "That is true!" she said eagerly. "I begin to believe in you again."

"Very well. You can't expect me to find out the moral cause which has alarmed you. I can positively discover that there is no physical cause for alarm; and (unless you admit me to your confidence) I can do no more."

She rose, and took a turn in the room. "Suppose I tell you?" she said. "But, mind, I shall mention no names!"

"There is no need to mention names. The facts are all I want."

"The facts are nothing," she rejoined. "I have only my own impressions to confess—and you will very likely think me a fanciful fool when you hear what they are. No matter. I will do my best to content you—I will begin with the facts that you want. Take my word for it, *they* won't do much to help you."

She sat down again. In the plainest possible words, she began the strangest and wildest confession that had ever reached the Doctor's ears.

Chapter II

"It is one fact, sir, that I am a widow," she said. "It is another fact that I am going to be married again in a week's time."

There she paused, and smiled at some thought that occurred to her. Doctor Wybrow was not favourably impressed by her smile —there was something at once sad and cruel in it. It came slowly, and it went away suddenly. He began to doubt whether he had been wise in acting on his first impression. His mind reverted to the commonplace patients and the discoverable maladies that were waiting for him, with a certain tender regret.

The lady went on.

"My approaching marriage," she said, "has one embarrassing circumstance connected with it. The gentleman whose wife I am to be, was engaged to another lady when he happened to meet with me, abroad; that lady, mind, being of his own blood and family, related to him as his cousin. I have innocently robbed her of her lover, and destroyed her prospects in life. Innocently, I say, —because he told me nothing of his engagement, until after I had accepted him. When we next met in England—and when there was danger, no doubt, of the affair coming to my knowledge— he told me the truth. I was naturally indignant. He had his excuse ready; he showed me a letter from the lady herself, releasing him from his engagement. A more noble, a more high-minded letter, I never read in my life. I cried over it—I who have no tears in me for sorrows of my own! If the letter had left him any hope of being forgiven, I would have positively refused to marry him. But the firmness of it—without anger, without a word of reproach, with heartfelt wishes even for his happiness—the firmness of it, I say, left him no hope. He appealed to my compassion; he appealed to his love for me. You know what women are. I too was soft-hearted—I said, Very well; yes! So it ended. In a week more (I tremble as I repeat it), we are to be married."

She did really tremble—she was obliged to pause and compose herself, before she could go on. The Doctor, waiting for more facts, began to fear that he stood committed to a long story.

"Forgive me for reminding you that I have suffering persons waiting to see me," he said. "The sooner you can come to the point, the better for my patients and for me."

The strange smile—at once so sad and so cruel—showed itself again on the lady's lips. "Every word I have said is to the point," she answered. "You will see it yourself in a moment more."

She resumed her narrative.

"Yesterday—you need fear no long story, sir; only yester-day—I was among the visitors at one of your English luncheon parties. A lady, a perfect stranger to me, came in late—after we had left the table, and had retired to the drawing-room, she happened to take a chair near me; and we were presented to each other. I knew her by name, as she knew me. It was the woman whom I had robbed of her lover, the woman who had written the noble letter. Now, listen! You were impatient with me for not interesting you in what I had said just now. I said it to satisfy your mind that I had no enmity of feeling towards the lady, on my side. I admired her, I felt for her—I had no cause to reproach myself. This is very important, as you will presently see. On her side, I have reason to be assured that the circumstances had been truly explained to her, and that she understood I was in no way to blame. Now, knowing all these necessary things, as you do, explain to me, if you can, why when I rose and met that woman's eyes looking at me, I turned cold from head to foot, and shuddered and shivered, and knew what a deadly panic of fear was, for the first time in my life."

The Doctor began to feel interested at last.

"Was there anything remarkable in the lady's personal appearance?" he asked.

"Nothing whatever!" was the vehement reply. "Here is the true description of her:—The ordinary English lady; the clear cold blue eyes, the fine rosy complexion, the inanimately polite manner, the large good-humoured mouth, the too plump cheeks and chin; these, and nothing more."

"Was there anything in her expression, when you first looked at her, that took you by surprise?"

"There was natural curiosity to see the woman who had been preferred to her; and perhaps some astonishment also, not to see a more engaging and more beautiful person; both those feelings restrained within the limits of good breeding, and both not lasting for more than a few moments—so far as I could see. I say 'so far', because the horrible agitation that she communicated to me disturbed my judgment. If I could have got to the door, I would have run out of the room, she frightened me so! I was not even able to stand up—I sank back in my chair; I stared horror-struck at the calm blue eyes that were only looking at me with a gentle surprise. To say they affected me like the eyes of a serpent is to say nothing. I felt her soul in them, looking into mine—looking, if such a thing can be, unconsciously to her own mortal self. I tell you my impression, in all its horror and in all its folly! That woman is destined (without knowing it herself), to be the evil genius of my life. Her innocent eyes saw hidden capabilities of wickedness in me that I was not aware of myself, until I felt them stirring under her look. If I commit faults in my life to come—if I am even guilty of crimes—she will bring the retribution, without (as I firmly believe) any conscious exercise of her own will. In one indescribable moment I felt all this—and I suppose my face showed it. The good artless creature was inspired by a sort of gentle alarm for me. 'I am afraid the heat of the room is too much for you; will you try my smelling-bottle?' I heard her say those kind words, and I remember nothing else—I fainted. When I recovered my senses the company had all gone; only the lady of the house was with me. For the moment I could say nothing to her; the dreadful impression that I have tried to describe to you came back to me with the coming back of my life. As soon as I could speak, I implored her to tell me the whole truth about the woman whom I had supplanted. You see, I had a faint hope that her good character might not really be deserved, that her noble letter was a skilful piece of hypocrisy—in short, that she secretly hated me, and was cunning enough to hide it. No! the lady had been her friend from her girlhood, was as familiar with her as if they had been sisters—knew her positively to be as good, as innocent, as incapable of hating anybody as the greatest saint that ever lived. My one last hope that I had only felt an ordinary forewarning of danger in the presence of an ordinary enemy, was a hope destroyed for ever. There was one more effort I could make, and I made it. I went next to the man whom I am to marry. I implored him to release me from my promise. He refused. I declared I would break my engagement. He showed me letters from his sisters, letters from his brothers and his dear friends—all entreating him to think again before he made me his wife; all repeating reports of me in Paris, Vienna, and London, which are so many vile lies. 'If you refuse to marry me,' he said, 'you admit that these reports are true —you admit that you are afraid to face society in the character of my wife.' What could I answer? There was no contradicting him —he was plainly right; if I persisted in my refusal, the utter destruction of my reputation would be the result. I consented to let the wedding take place as we had arranged it—and left him. The night has passed. I am here, with my fixed conviction—that innocent woman is ordained to have a fatal influence over my life. I am here with my one question to put, to the one man who can answer it. For the last time, sir, what am I—a demon who has seen the avenging angel? or only a poor mad woman, misled by the delusion of a deranged mind?"

Doctor Wybrow rose from his chair, determined to close the interview.

He was strongly and painfully impressed by what he had heard. The longer he had listened to her, the more irresistibly the conviction of the woman's wickedness had forced itself on him. He tried vainly to think of her as a person to be pitied—a person with a morbidly sensitive imagination, conscious of the capacities for evil which lie dormant in us all, and striving earnestly to open her heart to the counter-influence of her own better nature; the effort was beyond him. A perverse instinct in him said, as if in words, "Beware how you believe in her!"

"I have already given you my opinion," he said. "There is no sign of your intellect being deranged, or being likely to be deranged, that medical science can discover—as *I* understand it. As for the impressions you have confided to me, I can only say that yours is a case (as I venture to think) for spiritual rather than for medical advice. Of one thing be assured: what you have said to me in this room shall not pass out of it. Your confession is safe in my keeping."

She heard him, with a certain dogged resignation, to the end.

"Is that all?" she asked.

"That is all," he answered.

She put a little paper packet of money on the table. "Thank you, sir. There is your fee."

With those words she rose. Her wild black eyes looked upward with an expression of despair so defiant and so horrible in its silent agony, that the Doctor turned away his head, unable to endure the sight of it. The bare idea of taking anything from her —not money only, but anything even that she had touched—suddenly revolted him. Still without looking at her, he said, "Take it back; I don't want my fee."

She neither heeded nor heard him. Still looking upward, she said slowly to herself, "Let the end come. I have done with the struggle; I submit."

She drew her veil over her face, bowed to the Doctor, and left the room.

He rang the bell, and followed her into the hall. As the servant closed the door on her, a sudden impulse of curiosity—utterly unworthy of him, and at the same time utterly irresistible—sprang up in the Doctor's mind. Blushing like a boy, he said to the servant, "Follow her home, and find out her name." For one moment the man looked at his master, doubting if his own ears had not deceived him. Doctor Wybrow looked back at him in silence. The submissive servant knew what that silence meant—he took his hat and hurried into the street.

The Doctor went back to the consulting-room. A sudden revulsion of feeling swept over his mind. Had the woman left an infection of wickedness in the house, and had he caught it? What devil had possessed him to degrade himself in the eyes of his own servant? He had behaved infamously—he had asked an honest man, a man who had served him faithfully for years, to turn spy! Stung by the bare thought of it, he ran out into the hall again, and opened the door. The servant had disappeared; it was too late to call him back. But one refuge against his contempt for himself was now open to him—the refuge of work. He got into his carriage and went his rounds among his patients.

If the famous physician could have shaken his own reputation he would have done it that afternoon. Never before had he made himself so little welcome at the bedside. Never before had he put off until to-morrow the prescription which ought to have been written, the opinion which ought to have been given, to-day. He went home earlier than usual—unutterably dissatisfied with himself.

The servant had returned. Doctor Wybrow was ashamed to question him. The man reported the result of his errand, without waiting to be asked.

"The lady's name is the Countess Narona. She lives at——"

Without waiting to hear where she lived, the Doctor acknowledged the all-important discovery of her name, by a silent bend of the head, and entered his consulting-room. The fee that he had vainly refused still lay in its little white paper covering on the table. He sealed it up in an envelope; addressed it to the "Poor-box" of the nearest police-court; and, calling the servant in, directed him to take it to the magistrate the next morning. Faithful to his duties, the servant waited to ask the customary question, "Do you dine at home to-day, sir?"

After a moment's hesitation he said, "No: I shall dine at the club."

The most easily deteriorated of all the moral qualities, is the quality called "conscience." In one state of a man's mind, his conscience is the severest judge that can pass sentence on him. In another state, he and his conscience are on the best possible terms with each other in the comfortable capacity of accomplices. When Doctor Wybrow left his house for the second time, he did not even attempt to conceal from himself that his sole object, in dining at the club, was to hear what the world said of the Countess Narona.

Chapter III

There was a time when a man in search of the pleasures of gossip sought the society of ladies. The man knows better now. He goes to the smoking-room of his club.

Doctor Wybrow lit his cigar and looked round him, at his

brethren in social conclave assembled. The room was well filled; but the flow of talk was still languid. The Doctor innocently applied the stimulant that was wanted. When he inquired if anybody knew the Countess Narona, he was answered by something like a shout of astonishment. Never (the conclave agreed) had such an absurd question been asked before! Every human creature, with the slightest claim to a place in society, knew the Countess Narona. An adventuress with a European reputation of the blackest possible colour—such was the general description of the woman with the death-like complexion and the glittering eyes.

Descending to particulars, each member of the club contributed his own little stock of scandal to the memoirs of the Countess. It was doubtful whether she was really what she called herself—a Dalmatian lady. It was doubtful whether she had ever been married to the Count whose widow she assumed to be. It was doubtful whether the man who accompanied her in her travels (under the name of Baron Rivar, and in the character of her brother) was her brother at all. Report pointed to the Baron as a gambler at every "table" on the Continent. Report whispered that his so-called sister had narrowly escaped being implicated in a famous trial for poisoning at Vienna—that she had been known at Milan as a spy in the interest of Austria—that her "apartment" in Paris had been denounced to the police as nothing less than a private gambling-house—and that her present appearance in England was the natural result of that discovery. Only one member of the assembly in the smoking-room took the part of this much-abused woman, and declared that her character had been most cruelly and most unjustly assailed. But as the man was a lawyer, his interference went for nothing: it was naturally attributed to the spirit of contradiction inherent in his profession. He was asked derisively what he thought of the circumstances under which the Countess had become engaged to be married, and he made the characteristic answer, that he thought the circumstances highly creditable to both parties, and that he looked on the lady's future husband as a most enviable man.

Hearing this, the Doctor raised another shout of astonishment by inquiring the name of the gentleman whom the Countess was about to marry.

His friends in the smoking-room decided unanimously that

the celebrated physician must be a second "Rip-Van-Winkle," and that he had just awakened from a supernatural sleep of twenty years. It was all very well to say that he was devoted to his profession, and that he had neither time nor inclination to pick up fragments of gossip at dinner-parties and balls. A man who did not know that the Countess Narona had borrowed money at Homberg of no less a person than Lord Montbarry, and had then deluded him into making her a proposal of marriage, was a man who had probably never heard of Lord Montbarry himself. The younger members of the club, humouring the joke, sent a waiter for the "Peerage;" and read aloud the memoir of the nobleman in question, for the Doctor's benefit—with illustrative morsels of information interpolated by themselves.

"Herbert John Westwick. First Baron Montbarry, of Montbarry, King's County, Ireland. Created a Peer for distinguished military services in India. Born, 1812. Forty-eight years old, Doctor, at the present time. Not married. Will be married next week, Doctor, to the delightful creature we have been talking about. Heir presumptive, his lordship's next brother, Stephen Robert, married to Ella, youngest daughter of the Reverend Silas Marden, Rector of Runnigate, and has issue, three daughters. Younger brothers of his lordship, Francis and Henry, unmarried. Sisters of his lordship, Lady Barville, married to Sir Theodore Barville, Bart.; and Anne, widow of the late Peter Norbury, Esq., of Norbury Cross. Bear his lordship's relations well in mind, Doctor. Three brothers, Westwick, Stephen Francis, and Henry; and two sisters, Lady Barville and Mrs. Norbury. Not one of the five will be present at the marriage; and not one of the five will leave a stone unturned to stop it if the Countess will only give them a chance. Add to these hostile members of the family another offended relative not mentioned in the 'Peerage', a young lady."

A sudden outburst of protest in more than one part of the room stopped the coming disclosure, and released the Doctor from further persecution.

"Don't mention the poor girl's name; it's too bad to make a joke of that part of the business; she has behaved nobly under shameful provocation; there is but one excuse for Montbarry—he is either a madman or a fool." In these terms the protest expressed itself on all sides. Speaking confidentially to his next neighbour, the

Doctor discovered that the lady referred to was already known to him (through the Countess's confession) as the lady deserted by Lord Montbarry. Her name was Agnes Lockwood. She was described as being the superior of the Countess in personal attraction, and as being also by some years the younger woman of the two. Making all allowance for the follies that men committed every day in their relations with women, Montbarry's delusion was still the most monstrous delusion on record. In this expression of opinion every man present agreed—the lawyer even included. Not one of them could call to mind the innumerable instances in which the sexual influence has proved irresistible in the persons of women without even the pretension to beauty. The very members of the club whom the Countess (in spite of her personal disadvantages) could have most easily fascinated, if she had thought it worth her while, were the members who wondered most loudly at Montbarry's choice of a wife.

While the topic of the Countess's marriage was still the one topic of conversation, a member of the club entered the smoking-room whose appearance instantly produced a dead silence. Doctor Wybrow's next neighbour whispered to him, "Montbarry's brother—Henry Westwick!"

The new-comer looked round him slowly, with a bitter smile.

"You were all talking of my brother," he said. "Don't mind me. Not one of you can despise him more heartily than I do. Go on, gentlemen—go on!"

But one man present took the speaker at his word. That man was the lawyer who had already undertaken the defence of the Countess.

"I stand alone in my opinion," he said, "and I am not ashamed of repeating it in anybody's hearing. I consider the Countess Narona to be a cruelly-treated woman. Why shouldn't she be Lord Montbarry's wife? Who can say she has a mercenary motive in marrying him?"

Montbarry's brother turned sharply on the speaker. "*I* say it," he answered.

The reply might have shaken some men. The lawyer stood on his ground as firmly as ever.

"I believe I am right," he rejoined, "in stating that his lordship's income is not more than sufficient to support his station in life; also it is an income derived almost entirely from landed property in Ireland, every acre of which is entailed."

Montbarry's brother made a sign, admitting that he had no objection to offer so far.

"If his lordship dies first," the lawyer proceeded, "I have been informed that the only provision he can make for his widow consists in a rent charge on the property of no more than four hundred a year. His retiring pension and allowances, it is well-known, die with him. Four hundred a year is therefore all that he can leave to the Countess, if he leaves her a widow."

"Four hundred a year is *not* all," was the reply to this. "My brother has insured his life for ten thousand pounds; and he has settled the whole of it on the Countess, in the event of his death."

This announcement produced a strong sensation. Men looked at each other, and repeated the three startling words, "Ten thousand pounds!" Driven fairly to the wall, the lawyer made a last effort to defend his position.

"May I ask who made that settlement a condition of the marriage?" he said. "Surely it was not the Countess herself?"

Henry Westwick answered, "It was the Countess's brother;" and added, "which comes to the same thing."

After that, there was no more to be said—so long, at least, as Montbarry's brother was present. The talk flowed into other channels; and the Doctor went home.

But his morbid curiosity about the Countess was not set at rest yet. In his leisure moments he found himself wondering whether Lord Montbarry's family would succeed in stopping the marriage after all. And more than this he was conscious of a growing desire to see the infatuated man himself. Every day during the brief interval before the wedding, he looked in at the club, on the chance of hearing some news. Nothing had happened, so far as the club knew. The Countess's position was secure; Montbarry's resolution to be her husband was unshaken. They were both Roman Catholics, and they were to be married at the chapel in Spanish Place. So much the Doctor discovered about them—and no more.

On the day of the wedding, after a feeble struggle with himself, he actually sacrificed his patients and their guineas, and slipped away secretly to see the marriage. To the end of his life, he was angry with anybody who reminded him of what he had done on that day!

The wedding was strictly private. A closed carriage stood at the church door; a few people, mostly of the lower class, and mostly old women, were scattered about the interior of the building. Here and there Doctor Wybrow detected the faces of some of his brethren of the club, attracted by curiosity, like himself. Four persons only stood before the altar—the bride and bridegroom and their two witnesses. One of these last was a faded-looking woman, who might have been the Countess's companion or maid; the other was undoubtedly her brother, Baron Rivar. The bridal party (the bride herself included) wore their ordinary morning costume. Lord Montbarry, personally viewed, was a middle-aged military man of the ordinary type: nothing in the least remarkable distinguished him either in face or figure. Baron Rivar, again in his way, was another conventional representative of another well-known type. One sees his finely pointed moustache, his bold eyes, his crisply-curling hair, and his dashing carriage of the head, repeated hundreds of times over on the Boulevards of Paris. The only note-worthy point about him was of the negative sort—he was not in the least like his sister. Even the officiating priest was only a harmless, humble-looking old man, who went through his duties resignedly, and felt visible rheumatic difficulties every time he bent his knees. The one remarkable person, the Countess herself, only raised her veil at the beginning of the ceremony, and presented nothing in her plain dress that was worth a second look. Never, on the face of it, was there a less interesting and less romantic marriage than this. From time to time the Doctor glanced round at the door or up at the galleries, vaguely anticipating the appearance of some protesting stranger, in possession of some terrible secret, commissioned to forbid the progress of the service. Nothing in the shape of an event occurred—nothing extraordinary, nothing dramatic. Bound fast together as man and wife, the two disappeared, followed by their witnesses, to sign the registers; and still Doctor Wybrow waited, and still he cherished the obstinate hope that something worth seeing must certainly happen yet.

The interval passed, and the married couple, returning to the church, walked together down the nave to the door. Doctor Wybrow drew back as they approached. To his confusion and surprise, the Countess discovered him. He heard her say to her husband, "One moment; I see a friend." Lord Montbarry bowed and waited. She stepped up to the Doctor, took his hand, and wrung it hard. He felt her overpowering black eyes looking at him through her veil. "One step more, you see, on the way to the end!" She whispered those strange words, and returned to her husband. Before the Doctor could recover himself and follow her, Lord and Lady Montbarry had stepped into their carriage and had driven away.

Outside the church door stood the three or four members of the club who, like Doctor Wybrow, had watched the ceremony out of curiosity. Near them was the bride's brother, waiting alone. He was evidently bent on seeing the man whom his sister had spoken to, in broad daylight. His bold eyes rested on the Doctor's face, with a momentary flash of suspicion in them. The cloud suddenly cleared away; the Baron smiled with charming courtesy, lifted his hat to his sister's friend, and walked off.

The members constituted themselves into a club conclave on the church steps. They began with the Baron. "Damned ill-looking rascal!" They went on with Montbarry. "Is he going to take that horrid woman with him to Ireland?" "Not he! he can't face the tenantry; they know about Agnes Lockwood." "Well, but where *is* he going?" "To Scotland." "Does *she* like that?" "It's only for a fortnight; they come back to London, and go abroad." "And they will never return to England, eh?" "Who can tell? Did you see how she looked at Montbarry, when she had to lift her veil at the beginning of the service? In his place, I should have bolted. Did *you* see her, Doctor?" By this time Doctor Wybrow had remembered his patients, and had heard enough of the club gossip. He followed the example of Baron Rivar, and walked off.

"One step more, you see, on the way to the end," he repeated to himself, on his way home. "What end?"

Chapter IV

On the day of the marriage, Agnes Lockwood sat alone in the little drawing room of her London lodgings, burning the letters which had been written to her by Montbarry in the bygone time.

The Countess's maliciously smart description of her, addressed to Doctor Wybrow, had not even hinted at the charm that most distinguished Agnes—the artless expressions of goodness and purity which instantly attracted everyone who approached her. She looked by many years younger than she really was. With her fair complexion and shy manner, it seemed only natural to speak of her as "a girl", although she was now really advancing towards thirty years of age. She lived alone with an old nurse devoted to her, on a modest little income, which was just enough to support the two. There were none of the ordinary signs of grief in her face, as she slowly tore the letters of her false lover in two, and threw the pieces into the small fire which had been lit to consume them. Unhappily for herself she was one of those women who feel too deeply to find relief in tears. Pale and quiet, with cold, trembling fingers, she destroyed the letters one by one, without daring to read them again. She had torn the last of the series, and was still shrinking from throwing it after the rest into the swiftly destroying flame, when the old nurse came in, and asked if she would see "Master Henry",—meaning that youngest member of the Westwick family, who had publicly declared his contempt for his brother in the smoking-room of the club.

Agnes hesitated. A faint tinge of colour stole over her face.

There had been a long past time when Henry Westwick had owned that he loved her. She had made her confession to him, acknowledging that her heart was given to his eldest brother. He had submitted to his disappointment, and they had met thereafter as cousins and friends. Never before had she associated the idea of him with embarrassing recollections. But now, on the very day when his brother's marriage to another woman had consummated his brother's treason towards her, there was something vaguely repellent in the prospect of seeing him. The old nurse (who remembered them both in their cradles) observed her hesitation; and sympathising of course with the man, put in a timely word for Henry. "He says he's going away, my dear; and he only wants to shake hands and say good-bye." This plain statement of the case had its effect. Agnes decided on receiving her cousin.

He entered the room so rapidly that he surprised her in the act of throwing the fragments of Montbarry's last letter into the fire. She hurriedly spoke first.

"You are leaving London very suddenly, Henry. Is it business or pleasure?"

Instead of answering her, he pointed to the flaming letter, and to some black ashes of burnt paper lying lightly in the lower part of the fireplace.

"Are you burning letters?"

"Yes."

"*His* letters?"

"Yes."

He took her hand gently. "I had no idea I was intruding on you at a time when you must wish to be alone. Forgive me, Agnes —I shall see you when I return."

She signed to him, with a faint smile, to take a chair.

"We have known one another since we were children," she said. "Why should I feel a foolish pride about myself in your presence? why should I have any secrets from you? I sent back all your brother's gifts to me some time ago. I have been advised to do more, to keep nothing that can remind me of him—in short, to burn his letters. I have taken the advice; but I own I shrank a little from destroying the last of the letters. No—not because it was the last, but because it had this in it." She opened her hand and showed him a lock of Montbarry's hair, tied with a morsel of golden cord. "Well! well! let it go with the rest."

She dropped it into the flame. For awhile she stood with her back to Henry, leaning on the mantle-piece, and looking into the fire. He took the chair to which she had pointed, with a strange contradiction of expression in his face: the tears were in his eyes, while the brows above were knit close in an angry frown. He muttered to himself, "Damn him!"

She rallied her courage, and showed her face again when she spoke. "Well, Henry, and why are you going away?"

"I am out of spirits, Agnes, and I want a change."

She paused before she spoke again. His face told her plainly that he was thinking of *her* when he made that reply. She was grateful to him, but her mind was not with him: her mind was still with the man who had deserted her. She turned round again to the fire.

"Is it true," she asked, after a long silence, "that they have been married to-day?"

He answered ungraciously in the one necessary word:—"Yes."

"Did you go to the church?"

He resented the question with an expression of indignant surprise. "Go to the church?" he repeated. "I would as soon go to——." He checked himself there. "How can you ask?" he added in lower tones. "I have never spoken to Montbarry, I have not even seen him, since he treated you like the scoundrel and the fool that he is."

She looked at him suddenly, without saying a word. He understood her and begged her pardon. But he was still angry. "The reckoning comes to some men," he said, "even in this world. He will live to rue the day when he married that woman!"

Agnes took the chair by his side, and looked at him with a gentle surprise.

"Is it quite reasonable to be so angry with her because your brother preferred her to me?" she asked.

Henry turned on her sharply. "Do *you* defend the Countess, of all the people in the world?"

"Why not?" Agnes answered. "I know nothing against her. On the only occasion when we met, she appeared to be a singularly timid, nervous person, looking dreadfully ill; and *being* indeed so ill that she fainted under the heat of the room. Why should we not do her justice? We know that she was innocent of any intention to wrong me; we know that she was not aware of my engagement——"

Henry lifted his hand impatiently, and stopped her. "There is such a thing as being *too* just and *too* forgiving!" he interposed. "I can't bear to hear you talk in that patient way, after the scandalously cruel manner in which you have been treated. Try to forget them both, Agnes. I wish to God I could help you do it."

Agnes laid her hand on his arm. "You are very good to me, Henry; but you don't quite understand me. I was thinking of myself and my trouble in quite a different way, when you came in. I was wondering whether anything which has so entirely filled my heart, and so absorbed all that is best and truest in me, as my feeling for your brother, can really pass away as if it had never existed. I have destroyed the last visible things that remind me of him. In this world, I shall see him no more. But is the tie that once bound us, completely broken? Am I as entirely parted from the good and evil fortune of his life, as if we had never met and never loved? What do *you* think, Henry? I can hardly believe it."

"If you could bring the retribution on him that he has deserved," Henry Westwick answered sternly, "I might be inclined to agree with you."

As that reply passed his lips the old nurse appeared again at the door, announcing another visitor.

"I am sorry to disturb you, my dear. But here is little Mrs. Ferrari wanting to know when she may say a few words to you."

Agnes turned to Henry, before she replied. "You remember Emily Bidwell, my favourite pupil years ago at the village school, and afterwards my maid? She left me, to marry an Italian courier named Ferrari—and I am afraid it has not turned out very well. Do you mind my having her in here, for a minute or two?"

Henry rose to take his leave. "I should be glad to see Emily again at any other time," he said. "But it is best that I should go now. My mind is disturbed, Agnes; I might say things to you, if I stayed here any longer, which—which are better not said now. I shall cross the Channel by the mail to-night, and see how a few weeks' change will help me." He took her hand. "Is there anything in the world I can do for you?" he asked very earnestly. She thanked him, and tried to release her hand. He held it with a tremulous lingering grasp. "God bless you, Agnes!" he said in faltering tones, with his eyes on the ground. Her face flushed again, and the next instant turned paler than ever; she knew his heart as well as he knew it himself—she was too distressed to speak. He lifted her hand to his lips, kissed it fervently, and, without looking at her again, left the room. The nurse hobbled after him to the head of the stairs: she had not forgotten the time when the younger brother had been the unsuccessful rival of the elder for the hand of Agnes. "Don't be down-hearted, Master Hennery," whispered the old woman, with the unscrupulous common sense of persons in the lower rank of life. "Try her again, when you come back!"

Left alone for a few moments, Agnes took a turn in the room, trying to compose herself. She paused before a little water-coloured drawing on the wall, which had belonged to her mother: it was her own portrait when she was a child. "How much happier we should be," she thought to herself sadly, "if we never grew up!"

The courier's wife was shown in—a little meek melancholy woman, with white eyelashes, and watery eyes, who curtseyed deferentially and was troubled with a small chronic cough. Agnes shook hands with her kindly. "Well, Emily, what can I do for you?"

The courier's wife made rather a strange answer: "I'm afraid to tell you, Miss."

"Is it such a very difficult favour to grant? Sit down, and let me hear how you are going on. Perhaps the petition will slip out while we are talking. How does your husband behave to you?"

Emily's light grey eyes looked more watery than ever. She shook her head and sighed resignedly. "I have no positive complaint to make against him, Miss. But I'm afraid he doesn't care about me; and he seems to take no interest in his home—I may almost say he's tired of his home. It might be better for both of us, Miss, if he went travelling for a while—not to mention the money, which is beginning to be wanted sadly." She put her handkerchief to her eyes, and sighed again more resignedly than ever.

"I don't quite understand," said Agnes. "I thought your husband had an engagement to take some ladies to Switzerland and Italy?"

"That was his ill-luck, Miss. One of the ladies fell ill—and the others wouldn't go without her. They paid him a month's salary as compensation. But they had engaged him for the autumn and winter—and the loss is serious."

"I am sorry to hear it, Emily. Let us hope he will soon have another chance."

"It's not his turn, Miss, to be recommended when the next applications come to the courier's office. You see, there are so many of them out of employment just now. If he could be privately recommended——" She stopped, and left the unfinished sentence to speak for itself.

Agnes understood her directly. "You want my recommendation," she rejoined. "Why couldn't you say so at once?"

Emily blushed. "It would be such a chance for my husband," she answered confusedly. "A letter, inquiring for a good courier (a six months' engagement, Miss!) came to the office this morning.

It's another man's turn to be chosen—and the secretary will recommend him. If my husband could only send his testimonials by the same post—with just a word in your name, Miss—it might turn the scale, as they say. A private recommendation between two gentlefolks goes so far." She stopped again, and sighed again, and looked down at the carpet, as if she had some private reason for feeling a little ashamed of herself.

Agnes began to be rather weary of the persistent tone of mystery in which her visitor spoke. "If you want my interest with a friend of mine," she said, "why can't you tell me the name?"

The courier's wife began to cry. "I'm ashamed to tell you, Miss."

For the first time, Agnes spoke sharply. "Nonsense, Emily! Tell me the name directly—or drop the subject—whichever you like best."

Emily made a last desperate effort. She wrung her handkerchief hard in her lap, and let off the name as if she had been letting off a loaded gun:—"Lord Montbarry!"

Agnes rose and looked at her.

"You have disappointed me," she said very quietly, but with a look which the courier's wife had never seen in her face before. "Knowing what you know, you ought to be aware that it is impossible for me to communicate with Lord Montbarry. I always supposed you had some delicacy of feeling. I am sorry to find that I have been mistaken."

Weak as she was, Emily had spirit enough to feel the reproof. She walked in her meek noiseless way to the door. "I beg your pardon, Miss, I am not quite so bad as you think me. But I beg your pardon all the same."

She opened the door. Agnes called her back. There was something in the woman's apology that appealed irresistibly to her just and generous nature. "Come," she said; "we must not part in this way. Let me not misunderstand you, what *is* it that you expected me to do?"

Emily was wise enough to answer this time without any reserve. "My husband will send his testimonials, Miss, to Lord Montbarry, in Scotland. I only wanted you to let him say in his letter that his wife has been known to you since she was a child, and that you feel some little interest in his welfare on that account. I don't ask it now, Miss. You have made me understand that I was wrong."

Had she really been wrong? Past remembrances, as well as present troubles, pleaded powerfully with Agnes for the courier's wife. "It seems only a small favour to ask," she said, speaking under the impulse of kindness which was the strongest impulse in her nature. "But I am not sure that I ought to allow my name to be mentioned in your husband's letter. Let me hear again exactly what he wishes to say." Emily repeated the words—and then offered one of those suggestions, which have a special value of their own to persons unaccustomed to the use of their pens. "Suppose you try, Miss, how it looks in writing?" Childish as the idea was, Agnes tried the experiment. "If I let you mention me," she said, "we must at least decide what you are to say." She wrote the words in the briefest and plainest form:—"I venture to state that my wife has been known from her childhood to Miss Agnes Lockwood, who feels some little interest in my welfare on that account." Reduced to this one sentence, there was surely nothing in the reference to her name which implied that Agnes had permitted it, or that she was even aware of it. After a last struggle with herself, she handed the written paper to Emily, "Your husband must copy it exactly; without altering anything," she stipulated. "On that condition I grant your request." Emily was not only thankful—she was really touched. Agnes hurried the little woman out of the room. "Don't give me time to repent and take it back again," she said. Emily vanished.

"Is the tie that once bound us completely broken? Am I as entirely parted from the good and evil fortune of his life as if we had never met and never loved?" Agnes looked at the clock on the mantel-piece. Not ten minutes since, those serious questions had been on her lips. It almost shocked her to think of the commonplace manner in which they had already met with their reply. The mail of that night would appeal once more to Montbarry's remembrance of her—in the choice of a servant.

Two days later, the post brought a few lines from Emily. Her husband had got the place. Ferrari was engaged for six months certain, as Lord Montbarry's courier.

THE SECOND PART

Chapter V

After only one week of travelling in Scotland, my lord and my lady returned unexpectedly to London. Introduced to the mountains and lakes of the Highlands, her ladyship positively declined to improve her acquaintance with them. When she was asked for her reason, she answered with a Roman brevity, "I have seen Switzerland."

For a week more, the newly-married couple remained in London, in the strictest retirement. On one day in that week the nurse returned in a state of most uncustomary excitement from an errand on which Agnes had sent her. Passing the door of a fashionable dentist, she had met Lord Montbarry himself just leaving the house. The good woman's report described him, with malicious pleasure, as looking wretchedly ill. "His cheeks are getting hollow, my dear, and his beard is turning grey. I hope the dentist hurt him!"

Knowing how heartily her faithful old servant hated the man who had deserted her, Agnes made due allowance for a large infusion of exaggeration in the picture presented to her. The main impression produced on her mind was an impression of nervous uneasiness. If she trusted herself in the streets by daylight while Lord Montbarry remained in London, how could she be sure that his next chance-meeting might not be a meeting with herself? She waited at home, privately ashamed of her own superstitious fears for the next two days. On the third day the fashionable intelligence of the newspapers announced the departure of Lord and Lady Montbarry for Paris, on their way to Italy.

Mrs. Ferrari, calling the same evening, informed Agnes that her husband had left her with all reasonable expression of conjugal kindness; his temper being improved by the prospect of going abroad. But one other servant accompanied the travellers—Lady Montbarry's maid, rather a silent, unsociable woman, so far as Emily had heard. Her ladyship's brother, Baron Rivar, was already on the Continent. It had been arranged that he was to meet his sister and her husband at Rome.

One by one the dull weeks succeeded each other in the life of Agnes. She faced her position with admirable courage, seeing her friends, keeping herself occupied in her leisure hours with reading and drawing, leaving no means untried of diverting her mind from the melancholy remembrance of the past. But she had loved too faithfully, she had been wounded too deeply, to feel in any adequate degree the influence of the moral remedies which she employed. Persons who met with her in the ordinary relations of life, deceived by her outward serenity of manner, agreed that "Miss Lockwood seemed to be getting over her disappointment." But an old friend and school-companion who happened to see her during a brief visit to London, was inexpressibly distressed by the change that she detected in Agnes. This lady was Mrs. Westwick, the wife of that brother of Lord Montbarry who came next to him in age, and who was described in the "Peerage" as presumptive heir to the title. He was then away, looking after his interest in some mining property which he possessed in America. Mrs. Westwick insisted on taking Agnes back with her to her home in Ireland. "Come and keep me company while my husband is away. My three little girls will make you their playfellow, and the only stranger you will meet is the governess, whom I answer for your liking beforehand. Pack up your things, and I will call for you to-morrow on my way to the train." In those hearty terms the invitation was given. Agnes thankfully accepted it. For three happy months she lived under the roof of her friend. The girls hung round her neck in tears at her departure; the youngest of them wanted to go back with Agnes to London. Half in jest, half in earnest, she said to her old friend at parting, "If your governess leaves you, keep the place open for me." Mrs. Westwick laughed. The wiser children took it, seriously, and promised to let Agnes know.

On the very day when Miss Lockwood returned to London, she was recalled to those associations with the past which she was most anxious to forget. After the first kissings and greetings were over, the old nurse (who had been left in charge at the lodgings), had some startling information to communicate, derived from the courier's wife.

"Here has been little Mrs. Ferrari, my dear, in a dreadful state of mind, inquiring when you would be back. Her husband has left Lord Montbarry, without a word of warning—and nobody knows what has become of him."

Agnes looked at her in astonishment. "Are you sure of what you are saying?" she asked.

The nurse was quite sure. "Why, Lord bless you, the news comes from the courier's office in Golden Square—from the secretary, Miss Agnes, the secretary himself!" Hearing this, Agnes began to feel alarmed, as well as surprised. It was still early in the evening. She at once sent a message to Mrs. Ferrari, to say that she had returned.

In an hour more the courier's wife appeared, in a state of agitation which it was not easy to control. Her narrative, when she was at last able to speak connectedly, entirely confirmed the nurse's report of it.

After hearing from her husband with tolerable regularity from Paris, Rome, and Venice, Emily had twice written to him afterwards—and had received no reply. Feeling uneasy, she had gone to the office in Golden Square, to inquire if he had been heard of there. The post of the morning had brought a letter to the secretary from a courier then at Venice. It contained startling news of Ferrari. His wife had been allowed to take a copy of it, which she now handed to Agnes to read.

The writer stated that he had recently arrived in Venice. He had previously heard that Ferrari was with Lord and Lady Montbarry, at one of the old Venetian palaces which they had hired for a term. Being a friend of Ferrari, he had gone to pay him a visit. Ringing at the door that opened on the Grand Canal, and failing to make anyone hear him, he had gone round to a side entrance opening on one of the narrow lanes of Venice. Here, standing at the door, as if she was waiting for somebody—perhaps for the courier himself—he found a pale woman, with magnificent dark eyes, who proved to be no other than Lady Montbarry herself.

She asked, in Italian, what he wanted. He answered that he wanted to see the courier Ferrari, if it was quite convenient. She at once informed him that Ferrari had left the palace without assigning any reason, and without even leaving an address at which his monthly salary (then due to him), could be paid. Amazed at this reply, the courier inquired if any person had offended Ferrari, or quarrelled with him. The lady answered, "To my knowledge, certainly not. I am Lady Montbarry; and I can positively assure you that Ferrari was treated with the greatest kindness in this house. We are as much astonished as you are at his extraordinary disappearance. If you should hear of him, pray let us know, so that we may at least pay him the money which is due."

After one or two more questions (quite readily answered) relating to the date and the time of day at which Ferrari had left the palace, the courier took his leave.

He at once entered on the necessary investigations—without the slightest result so far as Ferrari was concerned. Nobody had seen him, nobody appeared to have been taken into his confidence. Nobody knew anything (that is to say, anything of the slightest importance), even about persons so distinguished as Lord and Lady Montbarry. It was reported that her ladyship's English maid had left her, before the disappearance of Ferrari, to return to her relatives in her own country, and that Lady Montbarry had taken no steps to supply her place. His lordship was described as being in delicate health. He lived in the strictest retirement—nobody was admitted to him, not even his own countrymen. A stupid old woman was discovered, who did the housework at the palace, arriving in the morning and going away again at night. She had never seen the lost courier—she had never seen even Lord Montbarry, who was then confined to his room. Her ladyship, "a most gracious and adorable mistress," was in constant attendance on her noble husband. There was no other servant then in the house (so far as the old woman knew), but herself. The meals were sent in from a restaurant. My lord, it was said, disliked strangers. My lord's brother-in-law, the Baron, was generally shut up in a remote part of the palace, occupied (the gracious mistress said) with experiments in chemistry. The experiments sometimes made a nasty smell. A doctor had latterly been called in to his lordship—an Italian doctor, long resident in Venice. Inquiries being addressed to this gentleman (a physician of undoubted capacity and respectability), it turned out that he also had never seen Ferrari, having been summoned to the palace (as his memorandum-book showed), at a date subsequent to the courier's disappearance. The doctor described Lord Montbarry's malady as bronchitis. So far, there was no reason to feel any anxiety, though the attack was a sharp one. If alarming symptoms should appear, he had arranged with her ladyship to call in another physician. For the rest, it was impossible to speak too highly of my lady; night and day she was at her lord's bedside.

With these particulars began and ended the discoveries made by Ferrari's courier-friend. The police were on the look-out for the lost man—and that was the only hope which could be held forth, for the present, to Ferrari's wife.

"What do you think of it, Miss?" the poor woman asked eagerly. "What would you advise me to do?"

Agnes was at a loss how to answer her; it was an effort even to listen to what Emily was saying. The references in the courier's letter to Montbarry—the report of his illness, the melancholy picture of his secluded life—had re-opened the old wound. She was not even thinking of the lost Ferrari; her mind was at Venice, by the sick man's bedside.

"I hardly know what to say," she answered. "I have had no experience in serious matters of this kind."

"Do you think it would help you, Miss, if you read my husband's letters to me? There are only three of them—they won't take long to read."

Agnes compassionately read the letters.

They were not written in a very tender tone. "Dear Emily," and "Yours affectionately"—these conventional phrases were the only phrases of endearment which they contained. In the first letter, Lord Montbarry was not very favourably spoken of:—"We leave Paris to-morrow. I don't much like my lord. He is proud and cold, and, between ourselves, stingy in money matters. I have had to dispute such trifles as a few centimes in the hotel bill; and twice already, some sharp remarks have passed between the newly-married couple, in consequence of her ladyship's freedom in purchasing pretty tempting things at the shops in Paris. 'I can't afford it, you must keep to your allowance.' She has had to hear those words already. For my part, I like her. She has the nice, easy foreign manners—*she* talks to me as if I was a human being like herself."

The second letter was dated from Rome.

"My lord's caprices" (Ferrari wrote) "have kept us perpetually on the move. He is becoming incurably restless. I suspect he is uneasy in his mind. Painful recollections I should say—I find him

constantly reading old letters, when her ladyship is not present.
We were to have stopped at Genoa; but he hurried us on. The
same thing at Florence. Here, at Rome, my lady insists on resting.
Her brother has met us at this place. There has been a quarrel
already (the lady's maid tells me) between my lord and the Baron.
The latter wanted to borrow money of the former. His lordship
refused in language which offended Baron Rivar. My lady pacified
them, and made them shake hands."

The third, and last letter, was from Venice.

"More of my lord's economy! Instead of going to an hotel, we
have hired a damp, mouldy, rambling old palace. My lady insists
on having the best suites of rooms wherever we go—and the palace
comes cheaper, for a two months' term. My lord tried to get it
for longer; he says the quiet of Venice is good for his nerves. But
a foreign speculator has secured the palace, and is going to turn it
into an hotel. The Baron is still with us, and there have been more
disagreements about money matters. I don't like the Baron—and
I don't find the attractions of my lady grow on me. She was much
nicer before the Baron joined us. My lord is a punctual pay-master;
it's a matter of honour with him; he hates parting with his money,
but he does it because he has given his word. I receive my salary
regularly at the end of each month—not a franc extra, though I
have done many things which are not part of a courier's proper
work. Fancy the Baron trying to borrow money of *me!* He is an
inveterate gambler. I didn't believe it when my Lady's maid first
told me so—but I have seen enough since to satisfy me that she
was right. I have seen other things besides, which—well! which
don't increase my respect for my lady and the Baron. The maid
says she means to give warning to leave. She is a respectable British
female, and doesn't take things quite as easily as I do. It is a dull
life here. No going into company—no company at home, not a
creature sees my lord—not even the consul, or the banker. When
he goes out, he goes alone, and generally towards nightfall. In-
doors, he shuts himself up in his own room with his books, and
sees as little of his wife and the Baron as possible. I fancy things
are coming to a crisis here. If my lord's suspicions are once awakened, the consequences will be terrible. Under certain provocations,
the noble Montbarry is a man who would stick at nothing. How-

ever, the pay is good—and I can't afford to talk of leaving the place, like my Lady's maid."

Agnes handed back the letters—so suggestive of the penalty paid already for his own infatuation by the man who had deserted her!—with feelings of shame and distress, which made her no fit counsellor for the helpless woman who depended on her advice.

"The one thing I can suggest," she said, after first speaking some kind words of comfort and hope, "is that we should consult a person of greater experience than ours. Suppose I write and ask my lawyer (who is also my friend and trustee) to come and advise us to-morrow after his business hours?"

Emily eagerly and gratefully accepted the suggestion. An hour was arranged for the meeting on the next day; the correspondence was left under the care of Agnes; and the courier's wife took her leave.

Weary and heartsick, Agnes lay down on the sofa, to rest and compose herself. The careful nurse brought in a reviving cup of tea. Her quaint gossip about herself and her occupations while Agnes had been away, acted as a relief to her mistress's overburdened mind. They were still talking quietly, when they were startled by a loud knock at the house door. Hurried footsteps ascended the stairs. The door of the sitting-room was thrown open violently; the courier's wife rushed in like a mad woman. "He's dead! they've murdered him!" Those wild words were all she could say. She dropped on her knees at the foot of the sofa—held out her hand, with something clasped in it—and fell back in a swoon.

The nurse, signing to Agnes to open the windows, took the necessary measures to restore the fainting woman. "What's this?" she exclaimed. "Here's a letter in her hand. See what it is, Miss."

The open envelope was addressed (evidently in a feigned handwriting) to "Mrs. Ferrari." The post-mark was "Venice." The contents of the envelope were a sheet of foreign note-paper, and a folded enclosure.

On the note-paper, one line only was written. It was again in a feigned handwriting, and it contained these words:——

"*To console you for the loss of your husband.*"

Agnes opened the enclosure next.

It was a Bank of England note for a thousand pounds.

Chapter VI

The next day, the friend and legal adviser of Agnes Lockwood, Mr. Troy, called on her by appointment in the evening.

Mrs. Ferrari—still persisting in the conviction of her husband's death—had sufficiently recovered to be present at the consultation. Assisted by Agnes, she told the lawyer the little that was known relating to Ferrari's disappearance, and then produced the correspondence connected with that event. Mr. Troy read (first) the three letters addressed by Ferrari to his wife; (secondly) the letter written by Ferrari's courier-friend, describing his visit to the palace and his interview with Lady Montbarry; and (thirdly) the one line of anonymous writing which had accompanied the extraordinary gift of a thousand pounds to Ferrari's wife.

Well known, at a later period, as the lawyer who acted for Lady Lydiard, in the case of theft, generally described as the case of "My Lady's Money," Mr. Troy was not only a man of learning and experience in his profession—he was also a man who had seen something of society at home and abroad. He possessed a keen eye for character, a quaint humour, and a kindly nature which had not been deteriorated even by a lawyer's professional experience of mankind. With all these personal advantages, it is a question nevertheless whether he was the fittest adviser whom Agnes could have chosen under the circumstances. Little Mrs. Ferrari, with many domestic merits, was an essentially commonplace woman. Mr. Troy was the last person living who was likely to attract her sympathies—he was the exact opposite of a commonplace man.

"She looks very ill, poor thing." In these words the lawyer opened the business of the evening, referring to Mrs. Ferrari as unceremoniously as if she had been out of the room.

"She has suffered a terrible shock," Agnes answered.

Mr. Troy turned to Mrs. Ferrari, and looked at her again, with the interest due to the victim of a shock. He drummed absently with his fingers on the table. At last he spoke to her.

"My good lady, you don't really believe that your husband is dead?"

Mrs. Ferrari put her handkerchief to her eyes. The word "dead" was ineffectual to express her feelings. "Murdered!" she said sternly, behind her handkerchief.

"Why? And by whom?" Mr. Troy asked.

Mrs. Ferrari seemed to find some difficulty in answering. "You have read my husband's letters, sir," she began. "I believe he discovered——" She got as far as that, and there she stopped.

"What did he discover?"

There are limits to human patience—even the patience of a bereaved wife. This cool question irritated Mrs. Ferrari into expressing herself plainly at last.

"He discovered Lady Montbarry and the Baron!" she answered, with a burst of hysterical vehemence. "The Baron is no more that vile woman's brother than I am. The wickedness of those two wretches came to my poor dear husband's knowledge. The lady's maid left her place on account of it. If Ferrari had gone away too, he would have been alive at this moment. They have killed him. I say they have killed him, to prevent it from getting to Lord Montbarry's ears." So in short, sharp sentences, and in louder and louder accents, Mrs. Ferrari stated *her* opinion of the case.

Still keeping his own view in reserve, Mr. Troy listened with an expression of satirical approval.

"Very strongly stated, Mrs. Ferrari," he said. "You build up your sentences well; you clench your conclusions in a workmanlike manner. If you had been a man, you would have made a good lawyer—you would have taken juries by the scruff of their necks. Complete the case, my good lady—complete the case. Tell us next who sent you this letter, enclosing the banknote. The 'two wretches' who murdered Mr. Ferrari would hardly put their hands in their pockets and send you a thousand pounds. Who is it—eh? I see the post-mark on the letter is 'Venice.' Have you any friend in that interesting city, with a large heart, and a purse to correspond, who has been let into the secret and who wishes to console you anonymously?"

It was not easy to reply to this. Mrs. Ferrari began to feel the first inward approaches of something like hatred towards Mr. Troy. "I don't understand you, sir," she answered. "I don't think this is a joking matter."

Agnes interfered, for the first time. She drew her chair a little nearer to her legal counsellor and friend.

"What is the most probable explanation, in your opinion?" she asked.

"I shall offend Mrs. Ferrari, if I tell you," Mr. Troy answered.

"No, sir, you won't!" cried Mrs. Ferrari, hating Mr. Troy undisguisedly by this time.

The lawyer leaned back in his chair. "Very well," he said, in his most good-humoured manner. "Let's have it out. Observe, madam, I don't dispute your view of the position of affairs at the palace in Venice. You have your husband's letters to justify you; and you have also the significant fact that Lady Montbarry's maid did really leave the house. We will say, then, that Lord Montbarry has presumably been made the victim of a foul wrong—that Mr. Ferrari was the first to find it out—and that the guilty persons had reasons to fear, not only that he would acquaint Lord Montbarry with his discovery, but that he would be a principal witness against them if the scandal was made public in a court of law. Now mark! Admitting all this, I draw a totally different conclusion from the conclusion at which you have arrived. Here is your husband left in this miserable household of three, under very awkward circumstances for *him*. What does he do? But for the bank-note and the written message sent to you with it, I should say that he had wisely withdrawn himself from association with a disgraceful discovery and exposure, by taking secretly to flight. The money modifies this view—unfavourably so far as Mr. Ferrari is concerned. I still believe he is keeping out of the way. But I now say he is paid for keeping out of the way—and that bank-note there on the table is the price of his absence, paid by the guilty persons to his wife."

Mrs. Ferrari's watery grey eyes brightened suddenly; Mrs. Ferrari's dull drab-coloured complexion became enlivened by a glow of brilliant red.

"It's false!" she cried. "It's a burning shame to speak of my husband in that way!"

"I told you I should offend you!" said Mr. Troy.

Agnes interposed once more—in the interests of peace. She took the offended wife's hand; she appealed to the lawyer to reconsider that side of his theory which reflected harshly on Ferrari. While she was still speaking, the servant interrupted her by entering the room with a visiting-card. It was the card of Henry Westwick; and there was an ominous request written on it in pencil.

"I bring bad news. Let me see you for a minute down stairs."
Agnes immediately left the room.

Alone with Mrs. Ferrari, Mr. Troy permitted his natural kindness of heart to show itself on the surface at last. He tried to make
his peace with the courier's wife.

"You have every claim, my good soul, to resent a reflection
cast upon your husband," he began. "I may even say that I respect
you for speaking so warmly in his defence. At the same time,
remember that I am bound, in such a serious matter as this, to tell
you what is really in my mind. I can have no intention of offending
you, seeing that I am a total stranger to you and to Mr. Ferrari.
A thousand pounds is a large sum of money; and a poor man may
excusably be tempted by it to do nothing worse than keep out of
the way for a while. My only interest, acting on your behalf, is
to get at the truth. If you will give me time, I see no reason to
despair of finding your husband yet."

Ferrari's wife listened, without being convinced: her narrow
little mind, filled to its extreme capacity by her unfavourable opinion of Mr. Troy, had no room left for the process of correcting
its first impression. "I am much obliged to you, sir," was all she
said. Her eyes were more communicative—her eyes added, in *their*
language, "You may say what you please; I will never forgive you
to my dying day."

Mr. Troy gave it up. He composedly wheeled his chair round,
put his hands in his pockets and looked out of the window.

After an interval of silence, the drawing-room door was
opened.

Mr. Troy wheeled round again briskly to the table, expecting
to see Agnes. To his surprise there appeared, in her place, a perfect
stranger to him—a gentleman, in the prime of life, with a marked
expression of pain and embarrassment on his handsome face. He
looked at Mr. Troy, and bowed gravely.

"I am so unfortunate as to have brought news to Miss Agnes
Lockwood which has greatly distressed her," he said. "She has
retired to her room. I am requested to make her excuse, and to
speak to you in her place."

Having introduced himself in those terms, he noticed Mrs.
Ferrari, and held out his hand to her kindly. "It is some years
since we last met, Emily," he said. "I am afraid you have almost

forgotten the 'Master Henry' of old times." Emily, in some little confusion, made her acknowledgments, and begged to know if she could be of any use to Miss Lockwood. "The old nurse is with her," Henry answered; "they will be better left together." He turned once more to Mr. Troy. "I ought to tell you," he said, "that my name is Henry Westwick. I am the younger brother of the late Lord Montbarry."

"The *late* Lord Montbarry!" Mr. Troy exclaimed.

"My brother died at Venice, yesterday evening. There is the telegram." With that startling answer, he handed the paper to Mr. Troy.

The message was in these words:

"Lady Montbarry, Venice. To Stephen Robert Westwick, Newbury's Hotel, London. It is useless to take the journey. Lord Montbarry died of bronchitis, at 8:40 this evening. All needful details by post."

"Was this expected, sir?" the lawyer asked.

"I cannot say that it has taken us entirely by surprise," Henry answered. "My brother Stephen (who is now the head of the family) received a telegram three days since, informing him that alarming symptoms had declared themselves, and that a second physician had been called in. He telegraphed back to say that he had left Ireland for London, on his way to Venice, and to direct that any further message might be sent to his hotel. The reply came in a second telegram. It announced that Lord Montbarry was in a state of insensibility, and that, in his brief intervals of consciousness, he recognised nobody. My brother was advised to wait in London for later information. The third telegram is now in your hands. That is all I know, up to the present time."

Happening to look at the courier's wife, Mr. Troy was struck by the expression of blank fear which showed itself in the woman's face.

"Mrs. Ferrari," he said, "have you heard what Mr. Westwick has just told me?"

"Every word of it, sir."

"Have you any questions to ask?"

"No, sir."

"You seem to be alarmed," the lawyer persisted. "Is it still about your husband?"

"I shall never see my husband again, sir. I have thought so all along, as you know. I feel sure of it now."

"Sure of it, after what you have just heard?"

"Yes, sir."

"Can you tell me why?"

"No, sir. It's a feeling I have. I can't tell why."

"Oh, a feeling?" Mr. Troy repeated, in a tone of compassionate contempt. "When it comes to feelings, my good soul——!" He left the sentence unfinished, and rose to take his leave of Mr. Westwick. The truth is, he began to feel puzzled himself, and he did not choose to let Mrs. Ferrari see it.

"Accept the expression of my sympathy, sir," he said to Mr. Westwick politely. "I wish you good evening."

Henry turned to Mrs. Ferrari as the lawyer closed the door. "I have heard of your trouble, Emily, from Miss Lockwood. Is there anything I can do to help you?"

"Nothing, sir, thank you. Perhaps I had better go home after what has happened? I will call to-morrow, and see if I can be of any use to Miss Agnes. I am very sorry for her." She stole away, with her formal courtesy, her noiseless step, and her obstinate resolution to take the gloomiest view of her husband's case.

Henry Westwick looked round him in the solitude of the little drawing-room. There was nothing to keep him in the house, and yet he lingered in it. It was something to be even near Agnes—to see the things belonging to her that were scattered about the room. There, in one corner was her chair, with her embroidery on the work-table by its side. On the little easel near the window was her last drawing, not quite finished yet. The book she had been reading lay on the sofa, with her tiny pencil-case in it to mark the place at which she had left off. One after another, he looked at the objects that reminded him of the woman whom he loved—took them up tenderly—and laid them down again with a sigh. Ah, how far, how unattainably far from him, she was still! "She will never forget Montbarry," he thought to himself as he took up his hat to go. "Not one of us feels his death as she feels it. Miserable, miserable wretch—how she loved him!"

In the street, as Henry closed the house-door, he was stopped by a passing acquaintance—a wearisome inquisitive man—doubly unwelcome to him, at that moment. "Sad news, Westwick, this about your brother. Rather an unexpected death, wasn't it? We never heard at the club that Montbarry's lungs were weak. What will the insurance offices do?"

Henry started; he had never thought of his brother's life insurance. What could the offices do but pay? A death by bronchitis, certified by two physicians, was surely the least disputable of all deaths. "I wish you hadn't put that question into my head!" he broke out irritably. "Ah!" said his friend, "you think the widow will get the money? So do I! so do I!"

CHAPTER VII

Some days later, the insurance offices (two in number) received the formal announcement of Lord Montbarry's death, from her ladyship's London solicitors. The sum insured in each office was five thousand pounds—on which one year's premium only had been paid. In the face of such a pecuniary emergency as this, the Directors thought it desirable to consider their position. The medical advisers of the two offices, who had recommended the insurance of Lord Montbarry's life, were called into council over their own reports. The result excited some interest among persons connected with the business of life insurance. Without absolutely declining to pay the money, the two offices (acting in concert) decided on sending a commission of inquiry to Venice, "for the purpose of obtaining further information."

Mr. Troy received the earliest intelligence of what was going on. He wrote at once to communicate his news to Agnes; adding, what he considered to be a valuable hint, in these words:

"You are intimately acquainted, I know, with Lady Barville, the late Lord Montbarry's eldest sister. The solicitors employed by her husband, are also the solicitors to one of the two insurance offices. There may possibly be something in the Report of the commission of inquiry touching on Ferrari's disappearance. Ordinary persons would not be permitted, of course, to see such a document. But a sister of the late lord is so near a relative as to be an exception to general rules. If Sir Theodore Barville puts it on that footing, the lawyers, even if they do not allow his wife to look at the Report, will at least answer any discreet questions she may ask referring to it."

The reply was received by return of post. Agnes declined to avail herself of Mr. Troy's proposal.

"My interference, innocent as it was," she wrote, "has already been productive of such deplorable results, that I cannot and dare not stir any further in the case of Ferrari. If I had not consented to let that unfortunate man refer to me by name, the late Lord Montbarry would never have engaged him, and his wife would have been spared the misery and suspense from which she is suffering now. I would not even look at the Report to which you allude if it was placed in my hands—I have heard more than enough of that hideous life in the palace at Venice. If Mrs. Ferrari chooses to address herself to Lady Barville (with your assistance), that is of course quite another thing. But, even in this case, I must make it a positive condition that my name shall not be mentioned. Forgive me, dear Mr. Troy! I am very unhappy, and very unreasonable—but I am only a woman, and you must not expect too much from me."

Foiled in this direction, the lawyer next advised making the attempt to discover the present address of Lady Montbarry's English maid. This excellent suggestion had one drawback: it could only be carried out by spending money—and there was no money to spend. Mrs. Ferrari shrunk from the bare idea of making any use of the thousand pound note. It had been deposited in the safe keeping of a bank. If it was even mentioned in her hearing, she shuddered and referred to it, with melodramatic fervour, as "my husband's blood-money!"

So, under stress of circumstances, the attempt to solve the mystery of Ferrari's disappearance was suspended for awhile.

It was the last month of the year 1860. The commission of inquiry was already at work; having begun its investigations on December 6. On the 10th, the term for which the late Lord Montbarry had hired the Venetian Palace expired. News by telegram reached the insurance offices that Lady Montbarry had been advised by her lawyers to leave for London with as little delay as possible. Baron Rivar, it was believed, would accompany her to England, but would not remain in that country, unless his services were absolutely required by her ladyship. The Baron, "well known as an enthusiastic student of chemistry," had heard of certain recent discoveries in connection with that science, in the United States, and was anxious to investigate them personally.

These items of news, collected by Mr. Troy, were duly communicated to Mrs. Ferrari, whose anxiety about her husband made her a frequent, a too frequent, visitor at the lawyer's office. She attempted to relate what she had heard to her good friend and protectress. Agnes steadily refused to listen, and positively forbade any further conversation relating to Lord Montbarry's wife, now that Lord Montbarry was no more. "You have Mr. Troy to advise you," she said, "and you are welcome to what little money I can spare, if money is wanted. All I ask in return is that you will not distress me. I am trying to separate myself from remembrances——" her voice faltered; she paused to control herself——"from remembrances," she resumed, "which are sadder than ever since I have heard of Lord Montbarry's death. Help me by your silence to recover my spirits, if I can. Let me hear nothing more, until I can rejoice with you that your husband is found."

Time advanced to the 13th of the month; and more information of the interesting sort reached Mr. Troy. The labours of the insurance commission had come to an end—the Report had been received from Venice on that day.

Chapter VIII

On the 14th the Directors and their legal advisers met for the reading of the Report, with closed doors. These were the terms in which the Commissioners related the results of their inquiry:

"*Private and Confidential.*

"We have the honour to inform our Directors that we arrived in Venice on December 6, 1860. On the same day we proceeded to the palace inhabited by Lord Montbarry at the time of his last illness and death.

"We were received with all possible courtesy by Lady Montbarry's brother, Baron Rivar. 'My sister was her husband's only attendant throughout his illness,' the Baron informed us. 'She is overwhelmed by grief and fatigue—or she would have been here to receive you personally. What are your wishes, gentlemen? and what can I do for you in her ladyship's place?'

"In accordance with our instructions, we answered that the

death and burial of Lord Montbarry abroad made it desirable to obtain more complete information relating to his illness, and to the circumstances which had attended it, than could be conveyed in writing. We explained that the law provided for the lapse of a certain interval of time before the payment of the sum assured, and we expressed our wish to conduct the inquiry with the most respectful consideration for her ladyship's feelings, and for the convenience of any other members of the family inhabiting the house.

"To this the Baron replied, 'I am the only member of the family living here, and I and the palace are entirely at your disposal.' From first to last we found this gentleman perfectly straightforward, and most amiably willing to assist us.

"With the one exception of her ladyship's room, we went over the whole of the palace the same day. It is an immense place, only partially furnished. The first floor and part of the second floor were the portions of it that had been inhabited by Lord Montbarry and the members of the household. We saw the bedchamber, at one extremity of the palace, in which his lordship died, and the small room communicating with it, which he used as a study. Next to this was a large apartment or hall, the doors of which he habitually kept locked, his object being (as we were informed) to pursue his studies uninterruptedly in perfect solitude. On the other side of the large hall were the bedchamber occupied by her ladyship, and the dressing-room in which the maid slept previous to her departure for England. Beyond these were the dining and reception rooms, opening into an antechamber, which gave access to the grand staircase of the palace.

"The only inhabited rooms on the second floor were the sitting-room and bed-room occupied by Baron Rivar, and another room at some distance from it, which had been the bed-room of the courier Ferrari.

"The rooms on the third floor and on the basement were completely unfurnished, and in a condition of great neglect. We inquired if there was anything to be seen below the basement— and we were at once informed that there were vaults beneath, which we were at perfect liberty to visit.

"We went down, so as to leave no part of the palace unexplored. The vaults were, it was believed, used as dungeons in the

old times—say some centuries since. Air and light were only partially admitted to these dismal places by two long shafts of winding construction, which communicated with the back yard of the
palace, and the openings of which, high above the ground, were
protected by iron gratings. The stone stairs leading down into the
vaults could be closed at will by a heavy trap-door in the back
hall, which we found open. The Baron himself led the way down
the stairs. We remarked that it might be awkward if that trap-door
fell down and closed the opening behind us. The Baron smiled at
the idea. 'Don't be alarmed, gentlemen,' he said; 'the door is safe.
I had an interest in seeing to it myself, when we first inhabited the
palace. My favourite study is the study of experimental chemistry
—and my workshop, since we have been in Venice, is down here.'

"These words explained a curious smell in the vaults, which
we noticed the moment we entered them. We can only describe
the smell by saying that it was of a two-fold sort—faintly aromatic
as it were, in its first effect, but with some after odour very sickening in our nostrils. The Baron's furnaces and retorts, and other
things, were all there to speak for themselves, together with some
packages of chemicals, having the name and address of the person
who had supplied them, plainly visible on their labels. 'Not a
pleasant place for a study,' Baron Rivar observed, 'but my sister
is timid. She has a horror of chemical smells and explosions—and
she has banished me to these lower regions, so that my experiments
may neither be smelt nor heard.' He held out his hands, on which
we had noticed that he wore gloves in the house. 'Accidents will
happen sometimes,' he said, 'no matter how careful a man may be.
I burnt my hands severely in trying a new combination the other
day, and they are only recovering now.'

"We mention these otherwise unimportant incidents, in order
to show that our exploration of the palace was not impeded by any
attempt at concealment. We were even admitted to her ladyship's
own room—on a subsequent occasion when she went out to take
the air. Our instructions recommended us to examine his lordship's
residence, because the extreme privacy of his life at Venice, and
the remarkable departure of the only two servants in the house,
might have some suspicious connection with the nature of his
death. We found nothing to justify suspicion from first to last.

"As to his lordship's retired way of life, we have conversed on the subject with the consul and the banker—the only two strangers who held any communication with him. He called once at the bank to obtain money on his letter of credit, and excused himself from accepting an invitation to visit the banker at his private residence, on the ground of his delicate health. His lordship wrote to the same effect on sending his card to the consul, to excuse himself from personally returning that gentleman's visit to the palace. We have seen the letter, and we beg to offer the following copy of it. 'Many years passed in India have injured my constitution. I have ceased to go into society; the one occupation of my life now is the study of Oriental literature. The air of Italy is better for me than the air of England, or I should never have left home. Pray accept the apologies of a student and an invalid. The active part of my life is at an end.' The self-seclusion of his lordship seems to us to be explained in these brief lines. We have not, however, on that account spared our inquiries in other directions. Nothing to excite a suspicion of anything wrong has come to our knowledge.

"As to the departure of the lady's maid, we have seen the woman's receipt for her wages, in which it is expressly stated that she left Lady Montbarry's service because she disliked the Continent, and wished to get back to her own country. This is not an uncommon result of taking English servants to foreign parts. Lady Montbarry has informed us that she abstained from engaging another maid, in consequence of the extreme dislike which his lordship expressed to having strangers in the house, in the state of his health at that time.

"The disappearance of the courier Ferrari is, in itself, unquestionably a suspicious circumstance. Neither her ladyship nor the Baron can explain it; and no investigation that we could make has thrown the smallest light on this event, or has justified us in associating it, directly or indirectly, with the object of our inquiry. We have even gone the length of examining the portmanteau which Ferrari left behind him. It contains nothing but clothes and linen—no money, and not even a scrap of paper in the pockets of the clothes. The portmanteau remains in charge of the police.

"We have also found opportunities of speaking privately to the old woman who attends to the rooms occupied by her ladyship and the Baron. She was recommended to fill this situation by the keeper of the restaurant who has supplied the meals to the family throughout the period of their residence at the palace. Her character is most favourably spoken of. Unfortunately, her limited intelligence makes her of no value as a witness. We were patient and careful in questioning her, and we found her perfectly willing to answer us; but we could elicit nothing which is worth including in the present Report.

"On the second day of our inquiries, we had the honour of an interview with Lady Montbarry. Her ladyship looked miserably worn and ill, and seemed to be quite at a loss to understand what we wanted with her. Baron Rivar, who introduced us, explained the nature of our errand in Venice, and took pains to assure her that it was a purely formal duty on which we were engaged. Having satisfied her ladyship on this point, he discreetly left the room.

"The questions which we addressed to Lady Montbarry related mainly, of course, to his lordship's illness. The answers, given with great nervousness of manner, but without the slightest appearance of reserve, informed us of the facts that follow:

"Lord Montbarry had been out of order for some time past—nervous and irritable. He first complained of having taken cold on November 13 last; he passed a wakeful and feverish night, and remained in bed the next day. Her ladyship proposed sending for medical advice. He refused to allow her to do this, saying that he could quite easily be his own doctor in such a trifling matter as a cold. Some hot lemonade was made at his request, with a view to producing perspiration. Lady Montbarry's maid having left her at that time, the courier Ferrari (then the only servant in the house) went out to buy the lemons. Her ladyship made the drink with her own hands. It was successful in producing perspiration—and Lord Montbarry had some hours of sleep afterwards. Later in the day, having need of Ferrari's services, Lady Montbarry rang for him. The bell was not answered. Baron Rivar searched for the man, in the palace and out of it, in vain. From that time forth not a trace of Ferrari could be discovered. This happened on November 14.

"On the night of the 14th, the feverish symptoms accompanying his lordship's cold returned. They were in part perhaps attributable to the annoyance and alarm caused by Ferrari's mysterious disappearance. It had been impossible to conceal the circumstance, as his lordship rang repeatedly for the courier; insisting that the man should relieve Lady Montbarry and the Baron by taking their place during the night at his bedside.

"On the 15th (the day on which the old woman first came to do the housework), his lordship complained of sore throat, and of a feeling of oppression on the chest. On this day, and again on the 16th, her ladyship and the Baron entreated him to see a doctor. He still refused. 'I don't want strange faces about me; my cold will run its course, in spite of the doctor,' that was his answer. On the 17th he was so much worse, that it was decided to send for medical help whether he liked it or not. Baron Rivar, after inquiry at the consul's, secured the services of Doctor Bruno, well known as an eminent physician in Venice; with the additional recommendation of having resided in England, and having made himself acquainted with English forms of medical practice.

"Thus far, our account of his lordship's illness has been derived from statements made by Lady Montbarry. The narrative will now be most fitly continued in the language of the doctor's own report, herewith subjoined.

" 'My medical diary informs me that I first saw the English Lord Montbarry, on November 17. He was suffering from a sharp attack of bronchitis. Some precious time had been lost, through his obstinate objection to the presence of a medical man at his bedside. Generally speaking, he appeared to be in a delicate state of health. His nervous system was out of order—he was at once timid and contradictory. When I spoke to him in English, he answered in Italian; and when I tried him in Italian, he went back to English. It mattered little—the malady had already made such progress that he could only speak a few words at a time, and those in a whisper.

" 'I at once applied the necessary remedies. Copies of my prescriptions (with translation into English) accompany the present statements, and are left to speak for themselves.

" 'For the next three days I was in constant attendance on my patient. He answered to the remedies employed, improving slowly, but decidedly. I could conscientiously assure Lady Montbarry that no danger was to be apprehended thus far. She was indeed a most devoted wife. I vainly endeavoured to induce her to accept the services of a competent nurse: she would allow nobody to attend on her husband but herself. Night and day this estimable woman was at his bedside. In her brief intervals of repose, her brother watched the sick man in her place. This brother was, I must say, very good company, in the intervals when we had time for a little talk. He dabbled in chemistry, down in the horrid underwater vaults of the palace; and he wanted to show me some of his experiments. I have enough of chemistry in writing prescriptions—and I declined. He took it quite good-humouredly.

" 'I am straying away from my subject. Let me return to the sick lord.

" 'Up to the 20th, then, things went well enough. I was quite unprepared for the disastrous change that showed itself, when I paid Lord Montbarry my morning visit on the 21st. He had relapsed and seriously relapsed. Examining him to discover the cause, I found symptoms of pneumonia—that is to say, in unmedical language, inflammation of the substance of the lungs. He breathed with difficulty, and was only partially able to relieve himself by coughing. I made the strictest inquiries, and was assured that his medicine had been administered as carefully as usual, and that he had not been exposed to any changes of temperature. It was with great reluctance that I added to Lady Montbarry's distress; but I felt bound, when she suggested a consultation with another physician, to own that I too thought there was really need for it.

" 'Her ladyship instructed me to spare no expense, and to get the best medical opinion in Italy. The best opinion was happily within our reach. The first and foremost of Italian physicians, is Torello of Padua. I sent a special messenger for the great man. He arrived on the evening of the 21st, and confirmed my opinion that pneumonia had set in, and that our patient's life was in danger. I told him what my treatment of the case had been, and he approved of it in every particular. He made some valuable suggestions, and (at Lady Montbarry's express request) he consented to defer his return to Padua until the following morning.

" 'We both saw the patient at intervals in the course of the night. The disease, steadily advancing, set our utmost resistance at defiance. In the morning Doctor Torello took his leave. "I can be of no further use," he said to me. "The man is past all help—and he ought to know it."

" 'Later in the day I warned my lord, as gently as I could, that his time had come. I am informed that there are serious reasons for my stating what passed between us on this occasion in detail, and without any reserve. I comply with the request.

" 'Lord Montbarry received the intelligence of his approaching death with becoming composure, but with a certain doubt. He signed to me to put my ear to his mouth. He whispered faintly, "Are you sure?" It was no time to deceive him; I said, "Positively sure." He waited a little, gasping for breath, and then he whispered again, "Feel under my pillow." I found under his pillow a letter, sealed and stamped, ready for the post. His next words were just audible, and no more—"Post it yourself." I answered of course, that I would do so—and I did post the letter with my own hand. I looked at the address. It was directed to a lady in London. The street I cannot remember. The name I can perfectly recall: it was an Italian name—"Mrs. Ferrari."

" 'That night my lord nearly died of asphyxia. I got him through it for the time; and his eyes showed me that he understood me when I told him, the next morning, that I had posted the letter. This was his last effort of consciousness. When I saw him again he was sunk in apathy. He lingered in a state of insensibility, supported by stimulants, until the 25th, and died (unconscious to the last) on the evening of that day.

" 'As to the cause of his death, it seems (if I may be excused for saying so) simply absurd to ask the question. Bronchitis, terminating in pneumonia—there is no more doubt that this, and this only, was the malady of which he expired, than that two and two make four. Doctor Torello's own note of the case is added here to a duplicate of my certificate, in order (as I am informed) to satisfy some English offices in which his lordship's life was insured. The English offices must have been founded by that celebrated saint and doubter, mentioned in the New Testament, whose name was Thomas!'

"Doctor Bruno's narrative ends here.

"Reverting for a moment to our inquiries addressed to Lady Montbarry, we have to report that she can give us no information on the subject of the letter which the doctor posted at Lord Montbarry's request. When his lordship wrote it? what it contained? why he kept it a secret from Lady Montbarry (and from the Baron also)? and why he should write at all to the wife of his courier? these are questions to which we find it simply impossible to obtain any replies. It seems even useless to say that the matter is open to suspicion. Suspicion implies conjecture of some kind—and the letter under my lord's pillow baffles all conjecture. Application to Mrs. Ferrari may perhaps clear up the mystery. Her residence in London will be easily discovered at the Italian Couriers' Office, Golden Square.

"Having arrived at the close of the present Report, we have now to draw your attention to the conclusion which is justified by the results of our investigation.

"The plain question before our Directors and ourselves appears to be this: Has the inquiry revealed any extraordinary circumstances which render the death of Lord Montbarry open to suspicion? The inquiry has revealed extraordinary circumstances beyond all doubt—such as the disappearance of Ferrari, the remarkable absence of the customary establishment of servants in the house, and the mysterious letter which his lordship asked the doctor to post. But where is the proof that any one of these circumstances is associated—suspiciously and directly associated—with the only event which concerns us, the event of Lord Montbarry's death? In the absence of any such proof, and in the face of the evidence of two eminent physicians, it is impossible to dispute the statement on the certificate that his lordship died a natural death. We are bound, therefore, to report, that there are no valid grounds for refusing the payment of the sum for which the late Lord Montbarry's life was assured.

"We shall send these lines to you by the post of to-morrow, December 10; leaving time to receive your further instructions (if any), in reply to our telegram of this evening announcing the conclusion of the inquiry."

CHAPTER IX

"Now, my good creature, whatever you have to say to me, out with it at once! I don't want to hurry you needlessly; but these are business hours, and I have other people's affairs to attend to besides yours."

Addressing Ferrari's wife, with his usual blunt good-humour, in these terms, Mr. Troy registered the lapse of time by a glance at the watch on his desk, and then waited to hear what his client had to say to him.

"It's something more, sir, about the letter with the thousand pound note," Mrs. Ferrari began. "I have found out who sent it to me."

Mr. Troy started. "This is news indeed!" he said. "Who sent you the letter?"

"Lord Montbarry sent it, sir."

It was not easy to take Mr. Troy by surprise. But Mrs. Ferrari threw him completely off his balance. For awhile he could only look at her in silent surprise. "Nonsense!" he said, as soon as he had recovered himself. "There is some mistake—it can't be!"

"There is no mistake," Mrs. Ferrari rejoined, in her most positive manner. "Two gentlemen from the insurance offices called on me this morning, to see the letter. They were completely puzzled—especially when they heard of the bank-note inside. But they know who sent the letter. His lordship's doctor in Venice posted it at his lordship's request. Go to the gentlemen yourself, sir, if you don't believe me. They were polite enough to ask if I could account for Lord Montbarry writing to me and sending me the money. I gave them my opinion directly—I said it was like his lordship's kindness."

"Like his lordship's kindness?" Mr. Troy repeated, in blank amazement.

"Yes, sir! Lord Montbarry knew me, like all the other members of the family, when I was at school on the estate in Ireland. If he could have done it, he would have protected my poor dear husband. But he was helpless himself in the hands of my lady and the Baron—and the only kind thing he could do was to provide for me in my widowhood, like the true nobleman he was!"

"A very pretty explanation!" said Mr. Troy. "What did your visitors from the insurance offices think of it?"

"They asked me if I had any proof of my husband's death?"

"And what did you say?"

"I said, 'I give you better than proof, gentlemen; I give you my positive opinion.'"

"That satisfied them, of course?"

"They didn't say so in words, sir. They looked at each other —and wished me good morning."

"Well, Mrs. Ferrari, unless you have some more extraordinary news for me, I think I shall wish you good morning, too. I can take a note of your information (very startling information, I own); and, in the absence of proof, I can do no more."

"I can provide you with proof, sir,—if that is all you want," said Mrs. Ferrari, with great dignity. "I only wish to know, first, whether the law justifies me in doing it. You may have seen in the fashionable intelligence of the newspapers that Lady Montbarry has arrived in London, at Newbury's Hotel. I propose to go and see her."

"The deuce you do! May I ask for what purpose?"

Mrs. Ferrari answered in a mysterious whisper. "For the purpose of catching her in a trap! I shan't send in my name—I shall announce myself as a person on business, and the first words I say to her will be these: 'I come, my lady, to acknowledge the receipt of the money sent to Ferrari's widow.' Ah! you may well start, Mr. Troy! It almost takes *you* off your guard, doesn't it? Make your mind easy, sir; I shall find the proof that everybody asks me for in her guilty face. Let her only change colour by the shadow of a shade—let her eyes only drop for half an instant—I shall discover her! The one thing I want to know is does the law permit it?"

"The law permits it," Mr. Troy answered gravely; "but whether her ladyship will permit it, is quite another question. Have you really courage enough, Mrs. Ferrari, to carry out this notable scheme of yours? You have been described to me, by Miss Lockwood, as rather a nervous, timid sort of person—and, if I may trust my own observation, I should say you justify the description."

"If you had lived in the country, sir, instead of living in London," Mrs. Ferrari replied, "you would sometimes have seen a sheep turn on a dog. I am far from saying that I am a bold woman —quite the reverse. But when I stand in that wretch's presence, and think of my murdered husband, the one of us two who is likely to be frightened is not *me*. I am going there now, sir. You shall hear how it ends. I wish you good morning."

With those brave words the courier's wife gathered her mantle about her and walked out of the room.

Mr. Troy smiled—not satirically, but compassionately. "The little simpleton!" he thought to himself. "If half of what they say of Lady Montbarry is true, Mrs. Ferrari and her trap have but a poor prospect before them. I wonder how it will end?"

All Mr. Troy's experience failed to forewarn him of how it *did* end.

CHAPTER X

In the meantime, Mrs. Ferrari held to her resolution. She went straight from Mr. Troy's office to Newbury's Hotel.

Lady Montbarry was at home, and alone. But the authorities of the hotel hesitated to disturb her when they found that the visitor declined to mention her name. Her ladyship's new maid happened to cross the hall while the matter was still in debate. She was a Frenchwoman, and, on being appealed to, she settled the question in the swift, easy, rational French way. "Madame's appearance was perfectly respectable. Madame might have reasons for not mentioning her name which Miladi might approve. In any case, there being no orders forbidding the introduction of a strange lady, the matter clearly rested between Madame and Miladi. Would Madame, therefore, be good enough to follow Miladi's maid up the stairs?"

In spite of her resolution, Mrs. Ferrari's heart beat as if it would burst out of her bosom, when her conductress led her into an ante-room, and knocked at a door opening into a room beyond. But it is remarkable that persons of sensitively-nervous organization are the very persons who are capable of forcing themselves (apparently by the exercise of a spasmodic effort of will) into the performance of acts of the most audacious courage. A low, grave voice from the inner room said, "Come in." The maid, opening the door, announced, "A person to see you, Miladi, on business," and immediately retired. In the one instant while these events passed, timid little Mrs. Ferrari mastered her own throbbing heart; stepped over the threshold, conscious of her clammy hands, dry lips, and burning head; and stood in the presence of Lord Montbarry's widow, to all outward appearances as supremely self-possessed as her ladyship herself.

It was still early in the afternoon, but the light in the room was dim. The blinds were drawn down. Lady Montbarry sat with her back to the windows, as if even the subdued daylight was disagreeable to her. She had altered sadly for the worse in her per-

sonal appearance since the memorable day when Doctor Wybrow
had seen her in his consulting-room. Her beauty was gone—her
face had fallen away to mere skin and bone; the contrast between
her ghastly complexion and her steely glittering black eyes was
more startling than ever. Robed in dismal black, relieved only by
the brilliant whiteness of her widow's cap—reclining in a panther-
like suppleness of attitude on a little green sofa—she looked at the
stranger who had intruded on her, with a moment's languid
curiosity, than dropped her eyes again to the hand-screen which
she held between her face and the fire. "I don't know you," she
said. "What do you want with me?"

Mrs. Ferrari tried to answer. Her first burst of courage had
already worn itself out. The bold words that she had determined
to speak were living words still in her mind, but they died on
her lips.

There was a moment of silence. Lady Montbarry looked
round again at the speechless stranger. "Are you deaf?" she asked.
There was another pause. Lady Montbarry quietly looked back
again at the screen, and put another question. "Do you want
money?"

"Money!" That one word roused the sinking spirit of the
courier's wife. She recovered her courage; she found her voice.
"Look at me, my lady, if you please," she said, with a sudden
outbreak of audacity.

Lady Montbarry looked round for the third time. The fatal
words passed Mrs. Ferrari's lips.

"I come, my lady, to acknowledge the receipt of the money
sent to Ferrari's widow."

Lady Montbarry's glittering black eyes rested with steady
attention on the woman who had addressed her in those terms.
Not the faintest expression of confusion or alarm, not even a mo-
mentary flutter of interest stirred the deadly stillness of her face.
She reposed as quietly, she held the screen as composedly, as ever.
The test had been tried, and had irretrievably, utterly failed.

There was another silence. Lady Montbarry considered with
herself. The smile that came slowly and went away suddenly—
the smile at once so sad and so cruel—showed itself on her thin
lips. She lifted her screen, and pointed with it to a seat at the

farther end of the room. "Be so good as to take that chair," she said.

Helpless under her first bewildering sense of failure—not knowing what to say or what to do next—Mrs. Ferrari mechanically obeyed. Lady Montbarry, rising on the sofa for the first time, watched her with undisguised scrutiny as she crossed the room—then sank back in a reclining position once more. "No," she said to herself quietly, "the woman walks steadily; she is not intoxicated—the only other possibility is that she may be mad."

She had spoken loud enough to be heard. Stung by the insult Mrs. Ferrari instantly answered her. "I am no more drunk or mad than you are!"

"No?" said Lady Montbarry. "Then you are only insolent? The ignorant English mind (I have observed) is apt to be insolent in the exercise of unrestrained English liberty. This is very noticeable to us foreigners among you people in the streets. Of course I can't be insolent to you, in return. I hardly know what to say to you. My maid was imprudent in admitting you so easily to my room. I suppose your respectable appearance misled her. I wonder who you are? You mentioned the name of a courier who left us very strangely. Was he married by any chance? Are you his wife? And do you know where he is?"

Mrs. Ferrari's indignation burst its way through all restraints. She advanced to the sofa; she feared nothing, in the fervour and rage of her reply.

"I am his widow—and you know it, you wicked woman! Ah! it was in an evil hour, when Miss Lockwood recommended my husband to be his lordship's courier——"

Before she could add another word, Lady Montbarry sprang from the sofa with the stealthy suddenness of a cat—seized her by both shoulders—and shook her with the strength and frenzy of a madwoman. "You lie! you lie! you lie!" She dropped her hold at the third repetition of the accusation, and threw up her hands wildly with a gesture of despair. "Oh, Jesu Maria! is it possible?" she cried. "*Can* the courier have come to me through that woman?" She turned like lightning on Mrs. Ferrari, and stopped her as she was escaping from the room. "Stay here, you fool—stay here, and answer me! If you cry out, as sure as the heavens are above you, I'll strangle you with my own hands. Sit down again—and fear nothing. Wretch! It is I who am frightened—frightened out of my senses. Confess that you lied, when you used Miss Lockwood's name just now! No! I don't believe you on your oath; I will believe nobody but Miss Lockwood herself. Where does she live? Tell me that, you noxious stinging little insect—and you may go." Terrified as she was, Mrs. Ferrari hesitated. Lady Montbarry lifted her hands threateningly, with the long, lean, yellow-white fingers outspread and crooked at the tips. Mrs. Ferrari shrank at the sight of them, and gave the address. Lady Montbarry pointed contemptuously to the door—then changed her mind. "No! not yet! you will tell Miss Lockwood what has happened, and she may refuse to see me. I will go there at once, and you shall go with me. As far as the house—not inside of it. Sit down again. I am going to ring for my maid. Turn your back to the door—you cowardly face is not fit to be seen!"

She rang the bell. The maid appeared.

"My cloak and bonnet—instantly!"

The maid produced the cloak and bonnet from the bed-room.

"A cab at the door—before I can count ten!"

The maid vanished. Lady Montbarry surveyed herself in the glass, and wheeled round again, with her cat-like suddenness, to Mrs. Ferrari.

"I look more than half dead already, don't I?" she said, with a grim outburst of irony. "Give me your arm."

She took Mrs. Ferrari's arm and left the room. "You have nothing to fear, so long as you obey," she whispered, on the way downstairs. "You leave me at Miss Lockwood's door, and never see me again."

In the hall, they were met by the landlady of the hotel. Lady Montbarry graciously presented her companion. "My good friend Mrs. Ferrari; I am so glad to have seen her." The landlady accompanied them to the door. The cab was waiting. "Get in first, good Mrs. Ferrari," said her ladyship; "and tell the man where to go."

They were driven away. Lady Montbarry's variable humour changed again. With a low groan of misery, she threw herself back in the cab. Lost in her own dark thoughts, as careless of the woman whom she had bent to her iron will, as if no such person sat by her side, she preserved a sinister silence, until they reached the house where Miss Lockwood lodged. In an instant, she roused herself to action. She opened the door of the cab, and closed it again on Mrs. Ferrari, before the driver could get off his box.

"Take that lady a mile farther on her way home!" she said, as she paid the man his fare. The next moment she had knocked at the house-door. "Is Miss Lockwood at home?" "Yes, ma'am." She stepped over the threshold—the door closed on her.

"Which way, ma'am?" asked the driver of the cab.

Mrs. Ferrari put her hand to her head, and tried to collect her thoughts. Could she leave her friend and benefactress helpless at Lady Montbarry's mercy? She was still vainly endeavouring to decide on the course that she ought to follow—when a gentleman, stopping at Miss Lockwood's door, happened to look towards the cab-window, and saw her.

"Are you going to call on Miss Agnes, too?" he asked.

It was Henry Westwick. Mrs. Ferrari clasped her hands in gratitude as she recognised him.

"Go in, sir!" she cried. "Go in, directly. That dreadful woman is with Miss Agnes. Go and protect her!"

"What woman?" Henry asked.

The answer literally struck him speechless. With amazement and indignation in his face, he looked at Mrs. Ferrari as she pronounced the hated name of "Lady Montbarry." "I'll see to it," was all he said. He knocked at the house-door; and he too, in his turn, was let in.

CHAPTER XI

"Lady Montbarry, Miss."

Agnes was writing a letter, when the servant astonished her by announcing the visitor's name. Her first impulse was to refuse to see the woman who had intruded on her. But Lady Montbarry had taken care to follow close on the servant's heels. Before Agnes could speak she had entered the room.

"I beg to apologise for my intrusion, Miss Lockwood. I have a question to ask you, in which I am very much interested. No one can answer me but yourself." In low hesitating tones, with her glittering black eyes bent modestly on the ground, Lady Montbarry opened the interview in those words.

Without answering, Agnes pointed to a chair. She could do this, and, for the time, she could do no more. All that she had read of the hidden and sinister life in the palace at Venice; all that she heard of Montbarry's melancholy death and burial in a foreign land; all that she knew of the mystery of Ferrari's disappearance, rushed into her mind, when the black-robed figure confronted her, standing just inside the door. The strange conduct of Lady Montbarry added a new perplexity to the doubts and misgivings that troubled her. There stood the adventuress whose character had left its mark on society all over Europe—the Fury who had terrified Mrs. Ferrari at the hotel—inconceivably transformed into a timid shrinking woman! Lady Montbarry had not once ventured to look at Agnes, since she had made her way into the room. Advancing to take the chair that had been pointed out to her, she hesitated, put her hand on the rail to support herself, and still remained standing. "Please give me a moment to compose myself," she said faintly. Her head sank on her bosom: she stood before Agnes like a conscious culprit before a merciless judge.

The silence that followed was literally the silence of fear on both sides. In the midst of it the door was opened once more—and Henry Westwick appeared.

He looked at Lady Montbarry with a moment's steady attention—bowed to her with formal politeness—and passed on in silence. At the sight of her husband's brother, the sinking spirit of the woman sprang to life again. Her drooping figure became erect. Her eyes met Westwick's look, brightly defiant. She returned his bow with an icy smile of contempt.

Henry crossed the room to Agnes.

"Is Lady Montbarry here by your invitation?" he asked quietly.

"No."

"Do you wish to see her?"

"It is very painful to me to see her."

He turned and looked at his sister-in-law. "Do you hear that?" he asked coldly.

"I hear it," she answered more coldly still.

"Your visit is, to say the least of it, ill-timed."

"Your interference is, to say the least of it, out of place."

With that retort, Lady Montbarry approached Agnes. The presence of Henry Westwick seemed at once to relieve and embolden her. "Permit me to ask my question, Miss Lockwood," she said, with graceful courtesy. "It is nothing to embarrass you. When the courier Ferrari applied to my late husband for employment, did you——." Her resolution failed her, before she could say more. She sank trembling into the nearest chair, and, after a moment's struggle, composed herself again. "Did you permit Ferrari," she resumed, "to make sure of being chosen for our courier, by using your name?"

Agnes did not reply with her customary directness. Trifling as it was, the reference to Montbarry, proceeding from *that* woman of all others, confused and agitated her.

"I have known Ferrari's wife, for many years," she began. "And I take an interest——"

Lady Montbarry abruptly lifted her hands with a gesture of entreaty. "Ah, Miss Lockwood, don't waste time by talking of his wife! Answer my plain question, plainly!"

"Let me answer her," Henry whispered. "I will undertake to speak plainly enough."

Agnes refused by a gesture. Lady Montbarry's interruption had roused her sense of what was due to herself. She resumed her reply in plainer terms.

"When Ferrari wrote to the late Lord Montbarry," she said, "he did certainly mention my name."

Even now, she had innocently failed to see the object which her visitor had in view. Lady Montbarry's impatience became ungovernable. She started to her feet, and advanced to Agnes.

"Was it with your knowledge and permission that Ferrari used your name?" she asked. "The whole soul of my question is in *that*. For God's sake, answer me—Yes, or No!"

"Yes."

That one word struck Lady Montbarry as a blow might have struck her. The fierce life that had animated her face the instant before, faded out of it, suddenly, and left her like a woman turned to stone. She stood, mechanically confronting Agnes, with a stillness so rapt and perfect that not even the breath she drew was perceptible to the two persons who were looking at her.

Henry spoke to her roughly. "Rouse yourself," he said. "You have received your answer."

She looked round at him. "I have received my sentence," she rejoined—and turned slowly to leave the room.

To Henry's astonishment, Agnes stopped her. "Wait a moment, Lady Montbarry. I have something to ask on my side."

Lady Montbarry paused on the instant—silently submissive as if she had heard a word of command. Henry drew Agnes away to the other end of the room, and remonstrated with her. "You do wrong to call that person back," he said.——"No," Agnes whispered, "I have had time to remember."——"To remember what?"——"To remember Ferrari's wife: Lady Montbarry may have heard something of the lost man."——"Lady Montbarry may have heard, but she won't tell."——"It may be so, Henry, but, for Emily's sake, I must try."——Henry yielded. "Your kindness is inexhaustible," he said with his admiration of her kindling in his eyes. "Always thinking of others; never of yourself!"

Meanwhile, Lady Montbarry waited with a resignation that could endure any delay. Agnes returned to her, leaving Henry by himself. "Pardon me for keeping you waiting," she said in her gentle, courteous way. "You have spoken of Ferrari. I wish to speak of him too."

Lady Montbarry bent her head in silence. Her hand trembled as she took out her handkerchief and passed it over her forehead. Agnes detected the trembling, and shrank back a step. "Is the subject painful to you?" she asked timidly.

Still silent, Lady Montbarry invited her by a wave of the hand to go on. Henry approached, attentively watching his sister-in-law. Agnes went on.

"No trace of Ferrari has been discovered in England," she said. "Have you any news of him? And will you tell me (if you have heard anything), in mercy to his wife?"

Lady Montbarry's thin lips suddenly relaxed into their sad and cruel smile.

"Why do you ask *me* about the lost courier?" she said. "You will know what has become of him, Miss Lockwood, when the time is ripe for it."

Agnes started. "I don't understand you," she said. "How shall I know? Will some one tell me?"

"Some one will tell you."

Henry could keep silence no longer. "Perhaps your ladyship may be the person," he interrupted with ironical politeness.

She answered him with contemptuous ease. "You may be

right, Mr. Westwick. One day or another, I may be the person who tells Miss Lockwood what has become of Ferrari, if——" She stopped; with her eyes fixed on Agnes.

"If what?" Henry asked.

"If Miss Lockwood forces me to it."

Agnes listened in astonishment. "Force you to it?" she repeated. "How can I do that? Do you mean to say my will is stronger than yours?"

"Do *you* mean to say that the candle doesn't burn the moth, when the moth flies into it?" Lady Montbarry rejoined. "Have you ever heard of such a thing as the fascination of terror. I am drawn to you by the fascination of terror. I have no right to visit you. I have no wish to visit you: you are my enemy. For the first time in my life, against my own will, I submit to my enemy. See! I am waiting, because you told me to wait—and the fear of you (I swear it!) creeps through me while I stand here. Oh, don't let me excite your curiosity or your pity! Follow the example of Mr. Westwick. Be hard and brutal, and unforgiving, like him. Grant me my release. Tell me to go."

The frank and simple nature of Agnes could discover but one intelligible meaning in this strange outbreak.

"You are mistaken in thinking me your enemy," she said. "The wrong you did me when you gave your hand to Lord Montbarry was not one intentionally done. I forgave you my sufferings in his lifetime. I forgive you even more freely now that he has gone."

Henry heard her with mingled emotions of admiration and distress! "Say no more!" he exclaimed. "You are too good to her; she is not worthy of it."

The interruption passed unheeded by Lady Montbarry. The simple words in which Agnes had replied seemed to have absorbed the whole attention of this strangely-changeable woman. As she listened, her face settled slowly into an expression of hard and tearless sorrow. There was a marked change in her voice when she spoke next. It expressed that last worst resignation which has done with hope.

"You good innocent creature," she said, "what does your amiable forgiveness matter? What are your poor little wrongs, in the reckoning for greater wrongs which is demanded of me?

I am not trying to frighten you: I am only miserable about myself. Do you know what it is to have a firm presentiment of calamity that is coming to you—and yet to hope that your own positive conviction will not prove true? When I first met you, before my marriage, and first felt your influence over me, I had that hope. It was a starveling sort of hope that lived a lingering life in me until to-day. *You* struck it dead, when you answered my question about Ferrari."

"How have I destroyed your hopes?" Agnes asked. "What connection is there between my permitting Ferrari to use my name to Lord Montbarry, and the strange and dreadful things you are saying to me now?"

"The time is near, Miss Lockwood, when you will discover that for yourself. In the meanwhile, you shall know what my fear of you is, in the plainest words I can find. On the day when I took your hero from you and blighted your life—I am firmly persuaded of it!—you were made the instrument of the retribution that my sins of many years had deserved. Oh, such things have happened before to-day. One person has, before now, been the means of innocently ripening the growth of evil in another. You have done that already—and you have more to do yet. You have still to bring me to the day of discovery, and to the punishment that is my doom. We shall meet again—here in England, or there in Venice where my husband died—and meet for the last time."

In spite of her better sense, in spite of her natural superiority to superstitions of all kinds, Agnes was impressed by the terrible earnestness with which those words were spoken. She turned pale as she looked at Henry. "Do *you* understand her?" she asked.

"Nothing is easier than to understand her," he replied contemptuously. "She knows what has become of Ferrari; and she is confusing you in a cloud of nonsense, because she daren't own the truth. Let her go!"

If a dog had been under one of the chairs, and had barked, Lady Montbarry could not have proceeded more impenetrably with the last words she had to say to Agnes.

"Advise your interesting Mrs. Ferrari to wait a little longer," she said. "*You* will know what has become of her husband, and you will tell her. There will be nothing to alarm you. Some trifling event will bring us together the next time—as trifling, I dare say, as the engagement of Ferrari. Sad nonsense, Mr. Westwick, is it not? But you make allowances for women; we all talk nonsense. Good morning, Miss Lockwood."

She opened the door—suddenly, as if she was afraid of being called back for the second time—and left them.

CHAPTER XII

"Do you think she is mad?" Agnes asked.

"I think she is simply wicked. False, superstitious, inveterately cruel—but not mad. I believe her main motive in coming here was to enjoy the luxury of frightening you."

"She *has* frightened me. I am ashamed to own it—but so it is."

Henry looked at her, hesitated for a moment, and seated himself on the sofa by her side.

"I am very anxious about you, Agnes," he said. "But for the fortunate chance which led me to call here to-day—who knows what that vile woman might not have said or done, if she had found you alone? My dear, you are leading a sadly unprotected solitary life. I don't like to think of it; I want to see it changed— especially after what has happened to-day. No! no! it is useless to tell me that you have your old nurse. She is too old; she is not in your rank of life—there is no sufficient protection in the companionship of such a person for a lady in your position. Don't mistake me, Agnes! what I say, I say in the sincerity of my devotion to you." He paused, and took her hand. She made a feeble effort to withdraw it—and yielded. "Will the day never come," he pleaded, "when the privilege of protecting you may be mine? when you will be the pride and joy of my life, as long as my life lasts?" He pressed her hand gently. She made no reply. The colour came and went on her face: her eyes were turned away from him. "Have I been so unhappy as to offend you?" he asked.

She answered that—she said, almost in a whisper, "No."

"Have I distressed you?"

"You have made me think of the sad days that are gone." She said no more; she only tried to withdraw her hand from his for the second time. He still held it; he lifted it to his lips.

"Can I never make you think of other days than those—of the happier days to come? Or, if you must think of the time that is passed, can you not look back to the time when I first loved you?"

She sighed as he put the question. "Spare me, Henry," she answered sadly. "Say no more!"

The colour rose again in her cheeks; her hand trembled in his. She looked lovely, with her eyes cast down and her bosom heaving gently. At that moment he would have given everything he had in the world to take her in his arms and kiss her. Some mysterious sympathy, passing from his hand to hers, seemed to tell her what was in his mind. She snatched her hand away, and suddenly looked up at him. The tears were in her eyes. She said nothing; she let her eyes speak for her. They warned him—without anger, without unkindness—but still they warned him to press her no further that day.

"Only tell me that I am forgiven," he said, as he rose from the sofa.

"Yes," she answered quietly, "you are forgiven."

"I have not lowered myself in your estimation, Agnes?"

"Oh, no!"

"Do you wish me to leave you?"

She rose, in her turn, from the sofa, and walked to her writing table before she replied. The unfinished letter which she had been writing when Lady Montbarry interrupted her, lay open on the blotting-book. As she looked at the letter, and then looked at Henry, the smile that charmed everybody showed itself in her face.

"You must not go just yet," she said: "I have something to tell you. I hardly know how to express it. The shortest way perhaps will be to let you find it out for yourself. You have been speaking of my lonely unprotected life here. It is not a very happy life, Henry—I own that." She paused, observing the growing anxiety of his expression as he looked at her, with a shy satisfaction that perplexed her. "Do you know that I have anticipated your idea?" she went on. "I am going to make a great change in my life—if your brother Stephen and his wife will only consent to it." She opened the desk of the writing-table while she spoke, took a letter out, and handed it to Henry.

He received it from her mechanically. Vague doubts, which he hardly understood himself, kept him silent. It was impossible that the "Change in her life" of which she had spoken could mean that she was about to be married—and yet he was conscious of a perfectly unreasonable reluctance to open the letter.

Their eyes met; she smiled again. "Look at the address," she said. "You ought to know the handwriting—but I dare say you don't."

He looked at the address. It was in the large, irregular, uncertain writing of a child. He opened the letter instantly.

"Dear Aunt Agnes,——Our governess is going away. She has had money left to her, and a house of her own. We have had cake and wine to drink her health. You promised to be our governess if we wanted another. We want you. Mamma knows nothing about this. Please come before Mamma can get another governess. Your loving Lucy, who writes this. Clara and Blanche have tried to write too. But they are too young to do it. They blot the paper."

"Your eldest niece," Agnes exclaimed, as Henry looked at her in amazement. "The children used to call me aunt when I was staying with their mother in Ireland, in the autumn. The three girls were my inseparable companions—they are the most charming children I know. It is quite true that I offered to be their governess, if they ever wanted one, on the day when I left them to return to London. I was writing to propose it to their mother, just before you came."

"Not seriously!" Henry exclaimed.

Agnes placed her unfinished letter in his hand. Enough of it had been written to show that she did seriously propose to enter the household of Mr. and Mrs. Stephen Westwick as governess to their children! Henry's bewilderment was not to be expressed in words.

"They won't believe you are in earnest," he said.

"Why not?" Agnes asked quietly.

"You are my brother Stephen's cousin; you are his wife's old friend!"

"All the more reason, Henry, for trusting me with the charge of their children."

"But you are their equal; you are not obliged to gain your living by teaching. There is something absurd in your entering their service as a governess!"

"What is there absurd in it? The children love me; the mother loves me; the father has shown me innumerable instances of his true friendship and regard. I am the very woman for the place—and, as to my education, I must have completely forgotten it indeed, if I am not fit to teach three children, the eldest of whom is only eleven years old. You say I am their equal. Are there no other women who serve as governesses, and who are the equals of the persons whom they serve? Besides, I don't know that I *am* their equal. Have I not heard that your brother Stephen was the next heir to the title? Will he not be the new lord? Never mind answering me! We won't dispute whether I am right or wrong in turning governess—we will wait the event. I am weary of my lonely useless existence here, and eager to make my life more happy and more useful in the household of all others in which I should most like to have a place. If you will look again, you will see that I have these personal considerations still to urge before I finish my letter. You don't know your brother and his wife as well as I do, if you doubt their answer. I believe they have courage enough and heart enough to say Yes."

Henry submitted without being convinced.

He was a man who disliked all eccentric departures from custom and routine; and he felt especially suspicious of the change proposed in the life of Agnes. With new interests to occupy her mind, she might be less favourably disposed to listen to him, on the next occasion when he urged his suit. The influence of the "lonely useless existence" of which she complained, was distinctly an influence in his favour. While her heart was empty, her heart was accessible. But with his nieces in full possession of it, the clouds of doubt overshadowed his prospects. He knew the sex well enough to keep these purely selfish perplexities to himself. The waiting policy was especially the policy to pursue with a woman as sensitive as Agnes. If he once offended her delicacy he was lost. For the moment he wisely controlled himself and changed the subject.

"My little niece's letter has had an effect," he said, "which the child never contemplated in writing it. She has just reminded me of one of the objects that I had in calling on you to-day."

Agnes looked at the child's letter. "How does Lucy do that?" she asked.

"Lucy's governess is not the only lucky person who has had

money left her," Henry answered. "Is your old nurse in the house?"

"You don't mean to say that nurse has got a legacy?"

"She has got a hundred pounds. Send for her, Agnes, while I show you the letter."

He took a handful of letters from his pocket, and looked through them, while Agnes rang the bell. Returning to him, she noticed a printed letter among the rest, which lay open on the table. It was a "prospectus," and the title of it was "Palace Hotel Company of Venice (Limited)." The two words, "Palace" and "Venice," instantly recalled her mind to the unwelcome visit of Lady Montbarry. "What is that?" she asked, pointing to the title.

Henry suspended his search, and glanced at the prospectus. "A really promising speculation," he said. "Large hotels always pay well, if they are well managed. I know the man who is appointed to be manager of this hotel, when it is opened to the public; and I have such entire confidence in him that I have become one of the share-holders of the Company."

The reply did not appear to satisfy Agnes. "Why is the hotel called the 'Palace Hotel'?" she inquired.

Henry looked at her, and at once penetrated her motive for asking the question. "Yes," he said, "it *is* the palace that Montbarry hired at Venice; and it has been purchased by the Company to be changed into an hotel."

Agnes turned away in silence, and took a chair at the farther end of the room. Henry had disappointed her. His income as a younger son stood in need, as she well knew, of all the additions that he could make to it by successful speculation. But she was unreasonable enough, nevertheless, to disapprove of his attempting to make money already out of the house in which his brother had died. Incapable of understanding this purely sentimental view of a plain matter of business, Henry returned to his papers, in some perplexity at the sudden change in the manner of Agnes towards him. Just as he found the letter of which he was in search, the nurse made her appearance. He glanced at Agnes, expecting that she would speak first. She never even looked up, when the nurse came in. It was left to Henry to tell the old woman why the bell had summoned her to the drawing-room.

"Well, nurse," he said, "you have had a windfall of luck. You have had a legacy left you of a hundred pounds."

The nurse showed no outward signs of exultation. She waited a little to get the announcement of the legacy well settled in her mind—and then she said quietly, "Master Henry, who gives me that money, if you please?"

"My late brother, Lord Montbarry, gives it to you." (Agnes instantly looked up, interested in the matter for the first time.) Henry went on: "His will leaves legacies to the surviving old servants of the family. There is a letter from his lawyers, authorising you to apply to them for the money."

In every class of society, gratitude is the rarest of all human virtues. In the nurse's class it is especially rare. Her opinion of the man who had deceived and deserted her mistress remained the same opinion still, perfectly undisturbed by the passing circumstance of the legacy.

"I wonder who reminded my lord of the old servants?" she said. "He would never have heart enough to remember them himself!"

Agnes suddenly interposed. Nature, always abhorring monotony, institutes reserves of temper as elements in the composition of the gentlest women living. Even Agnes could, on rare occasions, be angry. The nurse's view of Montbarry's character seemed to have provoked her beyond endurance.

"If you have any sense of shame in you," she broke out, "you ought to be ashamed of what you have just said! Your ingratitude disgusts me. I leave you to speak with her, Henry—*you* won't mind it!" With this significant intimation that he too had dropped out of his customary place in her good opinion, she left the room.

The nurse received the smart reproof administered to her with every appearance of feeling rather amused by it than not. When the door had closed, this female philosopher winked at Henry.

"There's a power of obstinacy in young women," she remarked. "Miss Agnes wouldn't give my lord up as a bad one, even when he jilted her. And now she's sweet on him after he's dead. Say a word against him, and she fires up as you see. All obstinacy! It will wear out with time. Stick to her, Master Henry—stick to her!"

"She doesn't seem to have offended you," said Henry.

"*She?*" the nurse repeated in amazement—"she offend me? I like her in her tantrums; it reminds me of her when she was a baby. Lord bless you! when I go to bid her good night, she'll give me a big kiss, poor dear—and say, Nurse, I didn't mean it! About this money, Master Henry? If I was younger I should spend it in dress and jewellery. But I'm too old for that. What shall I do with my legacy when I have got it?"

"Put it out at interest," Henry suggested. "Get so much a year for it, you know."

"How much shall I get?" the nurse asked.

"If you put your hundred pounds into the Funds, you will get between three and four pounds a year."

The nurse shook her head. "Three or four pounds a year? That won't do! I want more than that. Look here, Master Henry. I don't care about this bit of money—I never did like the man who has left it to me, though he *was* your brother. If I lost it all to-morrow, I shouldn't break my heart; I'm well enough off, as it is, for the rest of my days. They say you're a speculator. Put me in for a good thing, there's a dear! Neck-or-nothing—and *that* for the Funds!" She snapped her fingers to express her contempt for security of investment at three per cent.

Henry produced the prospectus of the Venetian Hotel Company. "You're a funny old woman," he said. "There, you dashing speculator—there is neck-or-nothing for you! You must keep it a secret from Miss Agnes, mind. I'm not at all sure that she would approve of my helping you to this investment."

The nurse took out her spectacles. "Six per cent, guaranteed," she read; "and the Directors have every reason to believe that ten per cent, or more, will be ultimately realized to the shareholders by the hotel. Put me into that, Master Henry! And, wherever you go, for Heaven's sake, recommend the hotel to your friends!"

So the nurse, following Henry's mercenary example, had *her* pecuniary interest, too, in the house in which Lord Montbarry had died.

Three days passed before Henry was able to visit Agnes again. In that time, the little cloud between them had entirely passed away. Agnes received him with even more than her customary kindness. She was in better spirits than usual. Her letter to Mrs. Stephen Westwick had been answered by return of post; and her proposal had been joyfully accepted, with one modification. She was to visit the Westwicks for a month—and, if she really liked teaching the children, she was then to be governess, aunt, and cousin, all in one—and was only to go away in an event which her friends in Ireland persisted in contemplating, the event of her marriage.

"You see I was right," she said to Henry.

He was still incredulous. "Are you really going?" he asked.

"I am going next week."

"When shall I see you again?"

"You know you are always welcome at your brother's house. You can see me when you like." She held out her hand. "Pardon me for leaving you—I am beginning to pack up already."

Henry tried to kiss her at parting. She drew back directly.

"Why not? I am your cousin," he said.

"I don't like it," she answered.

Henry looked at her, and submitted. Her refusal to grant him his privilege as a cousin was a good sign,—it was indirectly an act of encouragement to him in the character of her lover.

On the first day in the new week, Agnes left London on her way to Ireland. As the event proved, this was not destined to be the end of her journey. The way to Ireland was only the first stage on her way to the palace at Venice.

THE THIRD PART

CHAPTER XIII

In the spring of the year 1861, Agnes was established at the country-seat of her good friends—now promoted (on the death of the first lord, without offspring) to be the new Lord and Lady Montbarry. The old nurse was not separated from her mistress. A place, suited to her time of life, had been found for her in the pleasant Irish household. She was perfectly happy in her new sphere; and she spent her first half-year's dividend from the Venice Hotel Company, with characteristic prodigality, in presents for the children.

Early in the year, also, the directors of the life insurance offices, submitted to circumstances, and paid the ten thousand pounds. Immediately afterwards, the widow of the first Lord Montbarry (otherwise, the dowager Lady Montbarry) left England, with Baron Rivar, for the United States. The Baron's object was announced in the scientific columns of the newspapers to be investigation into the present state of experimental chemistry in the great American republic. His sister informed inquiring friends that she accompanied him, in the hope of finding consolation in change of scene after the bereavement that had fallen on her. Hearing this news from Henry Westwick (then paying a visit at his brother's house), Agnes was conscious of a certain sense of relief. "With the Atlantic between us," she said, "surely I have done with that terrible woman now!"

Barely a week passed after those words had been spoken, before an event happened which reminded Agnes of "the terrible woman" once more.

On that day, Henry's engagements had obliged him to return to London. He had ventured, on the morning of his departure, to press his suit once more on Agnes; and the children, as he had anticipated, proved to be innocent obstacles in the way of his success. On the other hand, he had privately secured a firm ally in his sister-in-law. "Have a little patience," the new Lady Montbarry had said; "and leave me to turn the influence of the children in the right direction; they can persuade her to listen to you—and they shall!"

The two ladies had accompanied Henry, and some other guests who went away at the same time, to the railway station, and had just driven back to the house, when the servant announced that "a person, of the name of Rolland, was waiting to see her ladyship."

"Is it a woman?"

"Yes, my lady."

Young Lady Montbarry turned to Agnes.

"This is the very person," she said, "whom your lawyer thought likely to help him, when he was trying to trace the lost courier."

"You don't mean the English maid who was with Lady Montbarry at Venice?"

"My dear! don't speak of Montbarry's horrid widow, by the name which is *my* name now. Stephen and I have arranged to call her by her foreign title, before she was married. I am 'Lady Montbarry,' and she is 'the Countess.' In that way there will be no confusion.—Yes, Mrs. Rolland was in my service before she became the Countess's maid. She was a perfectly trustworthy person, with one defect that obliged me to send her away—a sullen temper which led to perpetual complaints of her in the servants' hall. Would you like to see her?"

Agnes accepted the proposal, in the faint hope of getting some information for the courier's wife. The complete defeat of every attempt to trace the lost man had been accepted as final by Mrs. Ferrari. She had deliberately arrayed herself in widow's mourning; and was earning her livelihood in an employment which the unwearied kindness of Agnes had procured for her in London. The last chance of penetrating the mystery of Ferrari's disappearance seemed to rest now on what Ferrari's former fellow-servant might be able to tell. With highly-wrought expectations, Agnes followed her friend into the room in which Mrs. Rolland was waiting.

A tall, bony woman, in the autumn of life, with sunken eyes and iron-grey hair, rose stiffly from her chair, and saluted the ladies with stern submission as they opened the door. A person of unblemished character, evidently—but not without visible drawbacks. Big bushy eyebrows, an awfully deep and solemn voice, a harsh unbending manner, a complete absence in her figure of the undulating lines characteristic of the sex, presented Virtue in this excellent person under its least alluring aspect. Strangers, on a first introduction to her, were accustomed to wonder why she was not a man.

"Are you pretty well, Mrs. Rolland?"

"I am as well as I can expect to be, my lady, at my time of life."

"Is there anything I can do for you?"

"Your ladyship can do me a great favour, if you will please speak to my character while I was in your service. I am offered a place, to wait on an invalid lady who has lately come to live in this neighbourhood."

"Ah, yes—I have heard of her. A Mrs. Carbury, with a very

pretty niece I am told. But, Mrs. Rolland, you left my service some time ago. Mrs. Carbury will surely expect you to refer to the last mistress by 'whom you were employed."

A flash of virtuous indignation irradiated Mrs. Rolland's sunken eyes. She coughed before she answered, as if her "last mistress" stuck in her throat.

"I have explained to Mrs. Carbury, my lady, that the person I last served—I really cannot give her her title in your ladyship's presence!—has left England for America. Mrs. Carbury knows that I quitted the person of my own free will, and knows why, and approves of my conduct so far. A word from your ladyship will be amply sufficient to get me the situation."

"Very well, Mrs. Rolland, I have no objection to be your reference, under the circumstances. Mrs. Carbury will find me at home to-morrow until two o'clock."

"Mrs. Carbury is not well enough to leave the house, my lady. Her niece, Miss Haldane, will call and make the inquiries, if your ladyship has no objection."

"I have not the least objection. The pretty niece carries her own welcome with her. Wait a minute, Mrs. Rolland. This lady is Miss Lockwood—my husband's cousin, and my friend. She is anxious to speak to you about the courier who was in the late Lord Montbarry's service at Venice."

Mrs. Rolland's bushy eyebrows frowned in stern disapproval of the new topic of conversation. "I regret to hear it, my lady," was all she said.

"Perhaps, you have not been informed of what happened, after you left Venice?" Agnes ventured to add. "Ferrari left the palace secretly; and he has never been heard of since."

Mrs. Rolland mysteriously closed her eyes—as if to exclude some vision of the lost courier which was of a nature to disturb a respectable woman. "Nothing that Mr. Ferrari could do would surprise me," she replied in her deepest bass tones.

"You speak rather harshly of him," said Agnes.

Mrs. Rolland suddenly opened her eyes again. "I speak harshly of nobody without reason," she said. "Mr. Ferrari behaved to me, Miss Lockwood, as no man living has ever behaved—before or since."

"What did he do?"

Mrs. Rolland answered with a stony stare of horror:—"He took liberties with me."

Young Lady Montbarry suddenly turned aside, and put her handkerchief over her mouth in convulsions of suppressed laughter.

Mrs. Rolland went on, with a grim enjoyment of the bewilderment which her reply had produced in Agnes. "And when I insisted on an apology, Miss, he had the audacity to say that the life at the palace was dull, and he didn't know how else to amuse himself!"

"I am afraid I have hardly made myself understood," said Agnes. "I am not speaking to you out of any interest in Ferrari. Are you aware that he is married?"

"I pity his wife," said Mrs. Rolland.

"She is naturally in great grief about him," Agnes proceeded.

"She ought to thank God she is rid of him," Mrs. Rolland interposed.

Agnes still persisted. "I have known Mrs. Ferrari from her childhood, and I am sincerely anxious to help her in this matter. Did you notice anything, while you were at Venice, that would account for her husband's extraordinary disappearance? On what sort of terms, for instance, did he live with his master and mistress?"

"On terms of familiarity with his mistress," said Mrs. Rolland, "which was simply sickening to a respectable English servant. She used to encourage him to talk to her about all his affairs—how he got on with his wife, and how pressed he was for money, and such like—just as if they were equals. Contemptible—that's what I call it."

"And his master?" Agnes continued. "How did Ferrari get on with Lord Montbarry?"

"My lord used to live shut up with his studies and his sorrows," Mrs. Rolland answered, with a hard solemnity expressive of respect for his lordship's memory. "Mr. Ferrari got his money when it was due; and he cared for nothing else. 'If I could afford it, I would leave the place too; but I can't afford it.' Those were the last words he said to me, on the morning when I left the palace. I made no reply. After what had happened (on that other occasion) I was naturally not on speaking terms with Mr. Ferrari."

"Can you really tell me nothing which will throw any light on this matter?"

"Nothing," said Mrs. Rolland, with an undisguised relish of the disappointment that she was inflicting.

"There was another member of the family at Venice," Agnes resumed, determined to sift the question to the bottom while she had the chance. "There was Baron Rivar."

Mrs. Rolland lifted her large hands, covered with rusty black gloves, in mute protest against the introduction of Baron Rivar as a subject of inquiry. "Are you aware, Miss," she began, "that I left my place in consequence of what I observed——?"

Agnes stopped her there. "I only wanted to ask," she explained, "if anything was said or done by Baron Rivar which might account for Ferrari's strange conduct?"

"Nothing that I know of," said Mrs. Rolland. "The Baron and Mr. Ferrari (if I may use such an expression) were 'birds of a feather,' so far as I could see—I mean, one was as unprincipled as the other. I am a just woman; and I will give you an example. Only the day before I left, I heard the Baron say (through the open door of his room while I was passing along the corridor), 'Ferrari, I want a thousand pounds. What would you do for a thousand pounds?' And I heard Mr. Ferrari answer, 'Anything, sir, as long as I was not found out.' And then they both burst out laughing. I heard no more than that. Judge for yourself, Miss."

Agnes reflected for a moment. A thousand pounds was the sum that had been sent to Mrs. Ferrari in the anonymous letter. Was that enclosure in any way connected, as a result, with the conversation between the Baron and Ferrari? It was useless to press any more inquiries on Mrs. Rolland. She could give no further information which was of the slightest importance to the object in view. There was no alternative but to grant her her dismissal. One more effort had been made to find a trace of the lost man—and once again the effort had failed.

They were a family party at the dinner-table that day. The only guest left in the house was a nephew of the new Lord Montbarry—the eldest son of his sister, Lady Barville. Lady Montbarry could not resist telling the story of the first (and last) attack made on the virtue of Mrs. Rolland, with a comically-exact imitation of Mrs. Rolland's deep and dismal voice. Being asked by her husband what had brought that formidable person to the house, she naturally mentioned the expected visit of Miss Haldane. Arthur Barville, unusually silent and preoccupied so far, suddenly struck into the conversation with a burst of enthusiasm. "Miss Haldane is the most charming girl in all Ireland!" he said. "I caught sight of her yesterday, over the wall of her garden, as I was riding by. What time is she coming to-morrow? Before two? I'll look into the drawing-room by accident—I am dying to be introduced to her!"

Agnes was amused by his enthusiasm. "Are you in love with Miss Haldane already?" she asked.

Arthur answered gravely, "It's no joking matter. I have been all day at the garden wall, waiting to see her again! It depends on Miss Haldane to make me the happiest or the wretchedest man living."

"You foolish boy! How can you talk such nonsense?"

He was talking nonsense undoubtedly. But, if Agnes had only known it, he was doing something more than that. He was innocently leading her another stage nearer on the way to Venice.

Chapter XIV

As the summer-months advanced, the transformation of the Venetian palace into the modern hotel proceeded rapidly towards completion.

The outside of the building, with its fine Palladian front looking on the canal, was wisely left unaltered. Inside, as a matter of necessity, the rooms were almost rebuilt—so far at least as the size and the arrangement of them were concerned. The vast saloons were partitioned off into "apartments" containing three or four rooms each. The broad corridors in the upper regions, afforded spare space enough for rows of little bed chambers, devoted to servants and to travellers with limited means. Nothing was spared but the solid floors and the finely-carved ceilings. These last, in excellent preservation as to workmanship, merely required cleaning, and regilding here and there, to add greatly to the beauty and importance of the best rooms in the hotel. The only exception to the complete re-organisation of the interior was at one extremity of the edifice, on the first and second floors. Here there happened, in each case, to be rooms of such comparatively moderate size, and so attractively decorated, that the architect suggested leaving them as they were. It was afterwards discovered that these were no other than the apartments respectively occupied by Lord Mont-barry (on the first floor), and by Baron Rivar (on the second). The room in which Montbarry had died was still fitted up as a bedroom, and was now distinguished as Number Fourteen. The room above it, in which the Baron had slept, took its place on the hotel-register as Number Thirty-eight. With the ornaments on the walls and ceilings cleaned and brightened up, and with the heavy old-fashioned beds, chairs, and tables replaced by bright, pretty and luxurious modern furniture, these two promised to be at once the most attractive and most comfortable bedchambers in the hotel. As for the once-desolate and disused ground floor of the building, it was now transformed, by means of splendid dining-rooms, reception-rooms, billiard-rooms, and smoking-rooms, into a palace by itself. Even the dungeon-like vaults beneath, now lighted and ventilated on the most approved modern plan, had been turned as if by magic into kitchens, servants' offices, ice-rooms, and wine cellars, worthy of the splendour of the grandest hotel in Italy, in the now bygone period of seventeen years since.

Passing from the lapse of the summer months at Venice, to the lapse of the summer months in Ireland, it is next to be re-corded that Mrs. Rolland obtained the situation of attendant on the invalid Mrs. Carbury and that the fair Miss Haldane, like a female Cæsar, came, saw, and conquered, on her first day's visit to the new Lord Montbarry's house.

The ladies were as loud in her praises as Arthur Barville him-self. Lord Montbarry declared that she was the only perfectly pretty woman he had ever seen, who was really unconscious of her own attractions The old nurse said she looked as if she had just stepped out of a picture, and wanted nothing but a gilt frame round her to make her complete. Miss Haldane, on her side, re-turned from her first visit to the Montbarrys charmed with her new acquaintances. Later on the same day, Arthur called with an offer-ing of fruit and flowers for Mrs. Carbury, and with instructions to ask if she was well enough to receive Lord and Lady Montbarry and Miss Lockwood on the morrow. In a week's time, the two households were on the friendliest terms. Mrs. Carbury, confined to the sofa by a spinal malady, had been hitherto dependent on her niece for one of the few pleasures she could enjoy, the pleasure of having the best new novels read to her as they came out. Discovering this, Arthur volunteered to relieve Miss Haldane, at intervals, in the office of reader. He was clever at mechanical contrivances of all sorts, and he introduced improvements in Mrs. Carbury's couch, and in the means of conveying her from the bed-chamber to the drawing-room, which alleviated the poor lady's sufferings and brightened her gloomy life. With these claims on the gratitude of the aunt, aided by the personal advantages which he unquestionably possessed, Arthur advanced rapidly in the favour of the charming niece. She was, it is needless to say, perfectly well aware that he was in love with her, while he was himself modestly reticent on the subject—so far as words went. But she was not equally quick in penetrating the nature of her own feeling towards Arthur. Watching the two young people with keen powers of observation, necessarily concentrated on them by the complete seclusion of her life, the invalid lady discovered signs of roused sensibility in Miss Haldane, when Arthur was present, which had never yet shown themselves in her social relations with other admirers eager to pay their addresses to her. Having drawn her own conclusions in private, Mrs. Carbury took the first favourable opportunity (in Arthur's interests) of putting them to the test.

"I don't know what I shall do," she said one day, "when Arthur goes away."

Miss Haldane looked up quickly from her work. "Surely he is not going to leave us!" she exclaimed.

"My dear! he has already stayed at his uncle's house a month longer than he intended. His father and mother naturally expect to see him at home again."

Miss Haldane met this difficulty with a suggestion, which could only have proceeded from a judgment already disturbed by the ravages of the tender passion. "Why can't his father and mother go and see him at Lord Montbarry's?" she asked. "Sir Theodore's place is only thirty miles away, and Lady Barville is Lord Montbarry's sister. They needn't stand on ceremony."

"They may have other engagements," Mrs. Carbury remarked.

"My dear aunt, we don't know that! Suppose you ask Arthur?"

"Suppose *you* ask him?"

Miss Haldane bent her head again over her work. Suddenly as it was done, her aunt had seen her face—and her face betrayed her.

When Arthur came the next day, Mrs. Carbury said a word to him in private, while her niece was in the garden. The last new novel lay neglected on the table. Arthur followed Miss Haldane into the garden. The next day, he wrote home, enclosing in his letter a photograph of Miss Haldane. Before the end of the week, Sir Theodore and Lady Barville arrived at Lord Montbarry's, and formed their own judgment of the fidelity of the portrait. They had themselves married early in life—and, strange to say, they did not object on principle to the early marriages of other people. The question of age being thus disposed of, the course of true love had no other obstacles to encounter. Miss Haldane was an only child, and was possessed of an ample fortune. Arthur's career at the university had been creditable, but certainly not brilliant enough to present his withdrawal in the light of a disaster. As Sir Theodore's eldest son, his position was already made for him. He was two-and-twenty years of age; and the young lady was eighteen. There was really no producible reason for keeping the lovers waiting, and no excuse for deferring the wedding-day beyond the first week in September. In the interval while the bride and bridegroom would be necessarily absent on the inevitable tour abroad, a sister of Mrs. Carbury volunteered to stay with her during the temporary separation from her niece. On the conclusion of the honeymoon, the young couple were to return to Ireland, and were to establish themselves in Mrs. Carbury's spacious and comfortable house.

These arrangements were decided upon early in the month of August. About the same date, the last alterations in the old palace at Venice were completed. The rooms were dried by steam; the cellars were stocked; the manager collected round him his army of skilled servants; and the new hotel was advertised all over Europe to open in October.

Chapter XV

(Miss Agnes Lockwood to Mrs. Ferrari.)

"I promised to give you some account, dear Emily, of the marriage of Mr. Arthur Barville and Miss Haldane. It took place ten days since. But I have had so many things to look after in the absence of the master and mistress of this house, that I am only able to write to you to-day.

"The invitations to the wedding were limited to members of the families, on either side, in consideration of the ill-health of Miss Haldane's aunt. On the side of the Montbarry family, there were present, besides Lord and Lady Montbarry, Sir Theodore and Lady Barville; Mrs. Norbury (whom you may remember as his lordship's second sister); and Mr. Francis Westwick, and Mr. Henry Westwick. The three children and I attended the ceremony as bridesmaids. We were joined by two young ladies, cousins of the bride and very agreeable girls. Our dresses were white, trimmed with green in honour of Ireland; and we each had a handsome gold bracelet given to us as a present from the bridegroom. If you add to the persons whom I have already mentioned, the elder members of Mrs. Carbury's family, and the old servants in both houses— privileged to drink the healths of the married pair at the lower end of the room—you will have the list of the company at the wedding-breakfast complete.

"The weather was perfect, and the ceremony (with music) was beautifully performed. As for the bride, no words can describe how lovely she looked, or how well she went through it all. We were very merry at the breakfast, and the speeches went off on the whole quite well enough. The last speech, before the party broke up, was made by Mr. Henry Westwick, and was the best of all. He made a happy suggestion, at the end, which has produced a very unexpected change in my life here.

"As well as I remember he concluded in these words:—'On one point, we are all agreed—we are sorry that the parting hour is near, and we should be glad to meet again. Why should we not meet again? This is the autumn time of the year; we are most of us leaving home for the holidays. What do you say (if you have no engagements that will prevent it) to joining our young married friends before the close of their tour, and renewing the social success of this delightful breakfast by another festival in honour of the honeymoon? The bride and bridegroom are going to Germany and the Tyrol, on their way to Italy. I propose that we allow them a month to themselves, and that we arrange to meet them afterwards in the north of Italy—say at Venice.'

"This proposal was received with great applause, which was changed into shouts of laughter by no less a person than my dear old nurse. The moment Mr. Westwick pronounced the word 'Venice,' she started up among the servants at the lower end of the room, and called out at the top of her voice, 'Go to our hotel, ladies and gentlemen! We get six per cent on our money already; and if you will only crowd the place and call for the best of everything, it will be ten per cent in our pockets in no time. Ask Master Henry!'

"Appealed to in this irresistible manner, Mr. Westwick had no choice but to explain that he was concerned as a shareholder in a new Hotel Company at Venice, and that he had invested a small sum of money for the nurse (not very considerately as I think) in the speculation. Hearing this, the company, by way of humouring the joke, drank a new toast:—Success to the nurse's hotel, and a speedy rise in the dividend!

"When the conversation returned in due time to the more serious question of the proposed meeting at Venice, difficulties began to present themselves, caused of course by invitations for the autumn which many of the guests had already accepted. Only two members of Mrs. Carbury's family were at liberty to keep the proposed appointment. On our side we were more at leisure to do as we pleased. Mr. Henry Westwick decided to go to Venice in advance of the rest, to test the accommodation of the new hotel on the opening day. Mrs. Norbury and Mr. Francis Westwick volunteered to follow him; and, after some persuasion, Lord and Lady Montbarry consented to a species of compromise. His lordship could not conveniently spare time enough for the journey to Venice, but he and Lady Montbarry arranged to accompany Mrs. Norbury and Mr. Francis Westwick as far on their way to Italy as Paris. Five days since they took their departure to meet their travelling companions in London; leaving me here in charge of the three dear children. They begged hard of course to be taken with papa and mamma. But it was thought better not to interrupt the progress of their education and not to expose them (especially the two younger girls) to the fatigues of travelling.

"I have had a charming letter from the bride, this morning, dated Cologne. You cannot think how artlessly and prettily she assures me of her happiness. Some people, as they say in Ireland, are born to good luck—and I think Arthur Barville is one of them.

"When you next write, I hope to hear that you are in better health and spirits, and that you continue to like your employment. Believe me, sincerely your friend.——A. L."

Agnes had just closed and directed her letter, when the eldest of her three pupils entered the room with the startling announcement that Lord Montbarry's travelling-servant had arrived from Paris! Alarmed by the idea that some misfortune had happened, she ran out to meet the man in the hall. Her face told him how seriously he had frightened her, before she could speak. "There's nothing wrong, Miss," he hastened to say. "My lord and my lady are enjoying themselves in Paris. They only want you and the young ladies to be with them." Saying these amazing words, he handed to Agnes a letter from Lady Montbarry.

"Dearest Agnes" (she read), "I am so charmed with the delightful change in my life—it is six years, remember, since I last travelled on the Continent—that I have exerted all my fascinations to persuade Lord Montbarry to go on to Venice. And, what is more to the purpose, I have actually succeeded! He has just gone to his room to write the necessary letters of excuse in time for the post to England. May you have as good a husband, my dear, when your time comes! In the meanwhile, the one thing wanting now to make my happiness complete, is to have you and the darling children with us. Montbarry is just as miserable without them as I am—though he doesn't confess it so freely. You will have no difficulties to trouble you. Louis will deliver these hurried lines, and will take care of you on the journey to Paris. Kiss the children for me a thousand times—and never mind their education for the present! Pack up instantly, my dear, and I will be fonder of you than ever. Your affectionate friend, Adela Montbarry."

Agnes folded up the letter; and, feeling the need of composing herself, took refuge for a few minutes in her own room.

Her first natural sensations of surprise and excitement at the prospect of going to Venice were succeeded by impressions of a less agreeable kind. With the recovery of her customary composure came the unwelcome remembrance of the parting words spoken to her by Montbarry's widow:—"We shall meet again—here in England, or there in Venice where my husband died—and meet for the last time."

It was an odd coincidence, to say the least of it, that the march of events should be unexpectedly taking Agnes to Venice, after those words had been spoken! Was the woman of the mysterious warnings and the wild black eyes, still thousands of miles away in America? Or was the march of events taking her unexpectedly, too, on the journey to Venice? Agnes started out of her chair, ashamed of even the momentary concession to superstition which was implied by the mere presence of such questions as these in her mind.

She rang the bell, and sent for her little pupils, and announced their approaching departure to the household. The noisy delight of the children, the inspiriting effort of packing up in a hurry, roused all her energies. She dismissed her own absurd misgivings from consideration with the contempt that they deserved. She worked as only women *can* work, when their hearts are in what they do. The travellers reached Dublin that day, in time for the boat to England. Two days later, they were with Lord and Lady Montbarry at Paris.

THE FOURTH PART

Chapter XVI

It was only the twentieth of September, when Agnes and the children reached Paris. Mrs. Norbury and her brother Francis had then already started on their journey to Italy—at least three weeks before the date at which the new hotel was to open for the reception of travellers.

The person answerable for this premature departure was Francis Westwick.

Like his younger brother Henry, he had increased his pecuniary resources by his own enterprise and ingenuity; with this differ-

ence, that his speculations were connected with the Arts. He had
made money in the first instance, by a weekly newspaper; and he
had then invested his profits in a London Theatre. This latter
enterprise, admirably conducted, had been rewarded by the public
with steady and liberal encouragement. Pondering over a new form
of theatrical attraction for the coming winter season, Francis had
determined to revive the languid public taste for the "ballet" by
means of an entertainment of his own invention, combining dramatic interest with dancing. He was now, accordingly, in search
of the best dancer (possessed of the indispensable personal attractions) who was to be found in the theatres of the Continent. Hearing from his foreign correspondents of two women who had made
successful first appearances, one at Milan and one at Florence,
he had arranged to visit those cities, and to judge of the merits of
the dancers for himself, before he joined the bride and bridegroom. His widowed sister, having friends at Florence whom she
was anxious to see, readily accompanied him. The Montbarrys
remained at Paris, until it was time to present themselves at the
family meeting in Venice. Henry found them still in the French
capital, when he arrived from London on his way to the opening of
the new hotel.

Against Lady Montbarry's advice, he took the opportunity of
renewing his addresses to Agnes. He could hardly have chosen a
more unpropitious time for pleading his cause with her. The gaie-
ties of Paris (quite incomprehensibly to herself as well as to everyone about her) had a depressing effect on her spirits. She had no
illness to complain of; she shared willingly in the ever varying succession of amusements offered to strangers by the ingenuity of the
liveliest people in the world—but nothing roused her: she remained
persistently dull and weary through it all. In this frame of mind
and body, she was in no humour to receive Henry's ill-timed addresses with favour, or even with patience: she plainly and positively refused to listen to him. "Why do you remind me of what
I have suffered?" she asked petulantly. "Don't you see that it has
left its mark on me for life?"

"I thought I knew something of women by this time," Henry
said, appealing privately to Lady Montbarry for consolation. "But
Agnes completely puzzles me. It is a year since Montbarry's
death; and she remains as devoted to his memory as if he had died

faithful to her—she still feels the loss of him, as none of *us* feel it!"

"She is the truest woman that ever breathed the breath of life," Lady Montbarry answered. "Remember that, and you will understand her. Can such a woman as Agnes give her love or refuse it, according to circumstances? Because the man was unworthy of her, was he less the man of her choice? The truest and best friend to him (little as he deserved it) in his lifetime, she naturally remains the truest and best friend to his memory now. If you really love her, wait; and trust to your two best friends— to time and to me. There is my advice; let your own experience decide whether it is not the best advice that I can offer. Resume your journey to Venice to-morrow; and when you take leave of Agnes, speak to her as cordially as if nothing had happened."

Henry wisely followed this advice. Thoroughly understanding him, Agnes made the leave-taking friendly and pleasant on her side. When he stopped at the door for a last look at her, she hurriedly turned her head so that her face was hidden from him. Was that a good sign? Lady Montbarry, accompanying Henry down the stairs, said, "Yes, decidedly! Write when you get to Venice. We shall wait here to receive letters from Arthur and his wife, and we shall time our departure for Italy accordingly."

A week passed, and no letter came from Henry. Some days later, a telegram was received from him. It was despatched from Milan, instead of from Venice; and it brought this strange message:—"I have left the hotel. Will return on the arrival of Arthur and his wife. Address, meanwhile, Albergo Reale, Milan."

Preferring Venice before all other cities of Europe, and having arranged to remain there until the family meeting took place, what unexpected event had led Henry to alter his plans? and why did he state the bare fact, without adding a word of explanation? Let the narrative follow him—and find the answer to those questions at Venice.

Chapter XVII

The Palace Hotel, appealing for encouragement mainly to English and American travellers, celebrated the opening of its doors, as a matter of course, by the giving of a grand banquet, and the delivery of a long succession of speeches.

Delayed on his journey, Henry Westwick only reached Venice in time to join the guests over their coffee and cigars. Observing the splendour of the reception-rooms, and taking note especially of the artful mixture of comfort and luxury in the bed-chambers, he began to share the old nurse's views of the future, and to contemplate seriously the coming dividend of ten per cent. The hotel was beginning well, at all events. So much interest in the enterprise had been aroused, at home and abroad, by profuse advertising, that the whole accommodation of the building had been secured by travellers of all nations for the opening night. Henry only obtained one of the small rooms on the upper floor, by a lucky accident—the absence of the gentleman who had written to engage it. He was quite satisfied, and was on his way to bed, when another accident altered his prospects for the night, and moved him into another and a better room.

Ascending on his way to the higher regions as far as the first floor of the hotel, Henry's attention was attracted by an angry voice protesting, in a strong New England accent, against one of the greatest hardships that can be inflicted on a citizen of the United States—the hardship of sending him to bed without gas in his room.

The Americans are not only the most hospitable people to be found on the face of the earth—they are (under certain conditions) the most patient and good-tempered people as well. But they are human; and the limit of American endurance is found in the obsolete institution of a bedroom candle. The American traveller, in the present case, declined to believe that his bedroom was in a completely finished state without a gas-burner. The manager pointed to the fine antique decorations (renewed and regilt) on the walls and ceiling, and explained that the emanations of burning gas-light would certainly spoil them in the course of a few months. To this the traveller replied that it was possible, but that he did not understand decorations. A bedroom with gas in it was what he was used to, was what he wanted, and was what he was determined to have. The compliant manager volunteered to ask some other gentleman, housed on the inferior upper story (which was lit throughout with gas), to change rooms. Hearing this, and being quite willing to exchange a small bed-chamber for a large one, Henry volunteered to be the other gentleman. The excellent

American shook hands with him on the spot. "You are a cultured person, sir," he said; "and *you* will no doubt understand the decorations."

Henry looked at the number of the room on the door as he opened it. The number was Fourteen.

Tired and sleepy, he naturally anticipated a good night's rest. In the thoroughly healthy state of his nervous system, he slept as well in a bed abroad as in a bed at home. Without the slightest assignable reason, however, his just expectations were disappointed. The luxurious bed, the well-ventilated room, the delicious tranquillity of Venice by night, all were in favour of his sleeping well. He never slept at all. An indescribable sense of depression and discomfort kept him waking through darkness and daylight alike. He went down to the coffee-room as soon as the hotel was astir, and ordered some breakfast. Another unaccountable change in himself appeared with the appearance of the meal. He was absolutely without appetite. An excellent omelette and cutlets cooked to perfection, he sent away untasted—he, whose appetite never failed him, whose digestion was still equal to any demands on it!

The day was bright and fine. He sent for a gondola, and was rowed to the Lido.

Out on the airy Lagoon, he felt like a new man. He had not left the hotel ten minutes before he was fast asleep in the gondola. Waking, on reaching the landing-place, he crossed the Lido, and enjoyed a morning's swim in the Adriatic. There was only a poor restaurant on the island, in those days; but his appetite was now ready for anything; he eat whatever was offered to him, like a famished man. He could hardly believe, when he reflected on it, that he had sent away untasted his excellent breakfast at the hotel.

Returning to Venice, he spent the rest of the day in the picture-galleries and the churches. Towards six o'clock his gondola took him back, with another fine appetite, to meet some travelling-acquaintances with whom he had engaged to dine at the table d'hote.

The dinner was deservedly rewarded with the highest approval by every guest in the hotel but one. To Henry's astonishment, the appetite with which he had entered the house mysteriously and completely left him when he sat down to table. He could drink some wine, but he could literally eat nothing. "What in the world is the matter with you?" his travelling-acquaintances asked. He could honestly answer, "I know no more than you do."

When night came, he gave his comfortable and beautiful bedroom another trial. The result of the second experiment was a repetition of the result of the first. Again he felt the all-pervading sense of depression and discomfort. Again he passed a sleepless night. And once more, when he tried to eat his breakfast, his appetite completely failed him!

This personal experience of the new hotel was too extraordinary to be passed over in silence. Henry mentioned it to his friends in the public room, in the hearing of the manager. The manager, naturally zealous in defence of the hotel, was a little hurt at the implied reflection cast on Number Fourteen. He invited the travellers present to judge for themselves whether Mr. Westwick's bedroom was to blame for Mr. Westwick's sleepless nights; and he especially appealed to a grey-headed gentleman, a guest at the breakfast-table of an English traveller, to take the lead in the investigation. "This is Doctor Bruno, our first physician in Venice," he explained, "I appeal to him to say if there are any unhealthy influences in Mr. Westwick's room."

Introduced to Number Fourteen, the doctor looked round him with a certain appearance of interest which was noticed by everyone present. "The last time I was in this room," he said, "was on a melancholy occasion. It was before the palace was changed into an hotel. I was in professional attendance on an English nobleman who died here." One of the persons present inquired the name of the nobleman. Doctor Bruno answered (without the slightest suspicion that he was speaking before a brother of the dead man), "Lord Montbarry."

Henry quietly left the room, without saying a word to anybody.

He was not, in any sense of the term, a superstitious man. But he felt, nevertheless, an insurmountable reluctance to remaining in the hotel. He decided on leaving Venice. To ask for another room would be, as he could plainly see, an offence in the eyes of the manager. To remove to another hotel, would be to openly abandon an establishment in the success of which he had a pecuniary interest. Leaving a note for Arthur Barville, on his arrival in Venice, in which he merely mentioned that he had gone to look at the Italian lakes, and that a line addressed to his hotel at Milan would bring him back again, he took the afternoon train to Padua—and dined with his usual appetite, and slept as well as ever that night.

The next day, a gentleman and his wife, returning to England by way of Venice, arrived at the hotel and occupied Number Fourteen.

Still mindful of the slur that had been cast on one of his best bed-chambers, the manager took occasion to ask the travellers the next morning how they liked their room. They left him to judge for himself how well they were satisfied, by remaining a day longer in Venice than they had originally planned to do, for the sole purpose of enjoying the excellent accommodation offered to them by the new hotel. "We have met with nothing like it in Italy," they said; "you may rely on our recommending you to all our friends."

On the day when Number Fourteen was again vacant, an English lady travelling alone with her maid arrived at the hotel, saw the room, and at once engaged it.

The lady was Mrs. Norbury. She had left Francis Westwick at Milan, occupied in negotiating for the appearance at his theatre of the new dancer at the Scala. Not having heard to the contrary, Mrs. Norbury supposed that Arthur Barville and his wife had already arrived at Venice. She was more interested in meeting the young married couple than in waiting the result of the hard bargaining which delayed the engagement of the new dancer; and she volunteered to make her brother's apologies, if his theatrical business caused him to be late in keeping his appointment at the honeymoon festival.

Mrs. Norbury's experience of Number Fourteen differed entirely from her brother Henry's experience of the room.

Falling asleep as readily as usual, her repose was disturbed by a succession of frightful dreams; the central figure in every one of them being the figure of her dead brother, the first Lord Montbarry. She saw him starving in a loathsome prison; she saw him pursued by assassins, and dying under their knives; she saw him drowning in immeasurable depths of dark water; she saw him in a bed of fire, burning to death in the flames; she saw him tempted by a shadowy creature to drink, and dying of the poisonous draught. The reiterated horror of these dreams had such an effect on her that she rose with the dawn of day, afraid to trust herself again in bed. In the old times, she had been noted in the family as the one member of it who lived on affectionate terms with Montbarry. His other sister and his brothers were constantly quarrelling with him. Even his mother owned that her eldest son was of all her children the child whom she least liked. Sensible and resolute woman as she was, Mrs. Norbury shuddered with terror as she sat at the window of her room, watching the sunrise, and thinking of her dreams.

She made the first excuse that occurred to her, when her maid came in at the usual hour, and noticed how ill she looked. The woman was of so superstitious a temperament that it would have been in the last degree indiscreet to trust her with the truth. Mrs. Norbury merely remarked that she had not found the bed quite to her liking, on account of the large size of it. She was accustomed at home, as her maid knew, to sleep in a small bed. Informed of this objection later in the day, the manager regretted that he could only offer to the lady the choice of one other bed-chamber, numbered Thirty-eight, and situated immediately over the bed-chamber which she desired to leave. Mrs. Norbury accepted the proposed change of quarters. She was now about to pass her second night in the room occupied in the old days of the palace by Baron Rivar.

Once more, she fell asleep as usual. And, once more, the frightful dreams of the first night terrified her; following each other in the same succession. This time her nerves, already shaken, were not equal to the renewed torture of terror inflicted on them. She threw on her dressing-gown, and rushed out of her room in the middle of the night. The porter, alarmed by the banging of the door, met her hurrying headlong down the stairs, in search of the first human being she could find to keep her company. Considerably surprised at this last new manifestation of the famous "English eccentricity," the man looked at the hotel register, and led the lady upstairs again to the room occupied by her maid. The maid was not asleep, and more wonderful still, was not even undressed. She received her mistress quietly. When they were alone, and when Mrs. Norbury had, as a matter of necessity, taken her attendant into her confidence, the woman made a very strange reply.

"I have been asking about the hotel, at the servants' supper to-night," she said. "The valet of one of the gentlemen staying here has heard that the late Lord Montbarry was the last person who lived in the palace, before it was made into an hotel. The room he died in, ma'am, was the room you slept in last night. Your room to-night is the room just above it. I said nothing for fear of frightening you. For my own part, I have passed the night as you see, keeping my light in, and reading my Bible. In my opinion, no member of your family can hope to be happy or comfortable in this house."

"What do you mean?"

"Please to let me explain myself, ma'am. When Mr. Henry Westwick was here (I have this from the valet, too) he occupied the room his brother died in (without knowing it) like you. For two nights he never closed his eyes. Without any reason for it (the valet heard him tell the gentlemen in the coffee-room) he could *not* sleep; he felt so low and so wretched in himself. And what is more, when daytime came, he couldn't even eat while he was under this roof. You may laugh at me, ma'am—but even a servant may draw her own conclusions. It's my conclusion that something happened to my lord, which we none of us know about, when he died in this house. His ghost walks in torment until he can tell it! The living persons related to him are the persons who feel he is near them—the persons who may yet see him in the time to come. Don't, pray don't stay any longer in this dreadful place! I wouldn't stay another night here myself—no, not for anything that could be offered me!"

Mrs. Norbury at once set her servant's mind at ease on this last point.

"I don't think about it as you do," she said gravely. "But I should like to speak to my brother of what has happened. We will go back to Milan."

Some hours necessarily elapsed before they could leave the hotel, by the first train in the forenoon.

In that interval, Mrs. Norbury's maid found an opportunity of confidentially informing the valet of what had passed between her mistress and herself. The valet had other friends to whom he related the circumstances in his turn. In due course of time, the narrative, passing from mouth to mouth, reached the ears of the manager. He instantly saw that the credit of the hotel was in danger, unless something was done to retrieve the character of the room numbered Fourteen. English travellers, well acquainted with the peerage of their native country, informed him that Henry Westwick and Mrs. Norbury were by no means the only members of the Montbarry family. Curiosity might bring more of them to the hotel, after hearing what had happened. The manager's ingenuity easily hit on the obvious means of misleading them, in this case. The numbers of all the rooms were enamelled in blue, on white china plates, screwed to the doors. He ordered a new plate to be prepared, bearing the number "13 A"; and he kept the room empty, after its tenant for the time being had gone away, until the plate was ready. He then re-numbered the room, placing the removed Number Fourteen on the door of his own room (on the second floor), which, not being to let, had not previously been numbered at all. By this device, Number Fourteen, disappeared at once and forever, from the books of the hotel, as the number of a bedroom to let.

Having warned the servants to beware of gossipping with travellers on the subject of the changed numbers, under penalty of being dismissed, the manager composed his mind with the reflection that he had done his duty to his employers. "Now," he thought to himself, with an excusable sense of triumph, "let the whole family come here if they like! The hotel is a match for them!"

Chapter XVIII

Before the end of the week, the manager found himself in relations with "the family" once more. A telegram from Milan announced that Mr. Francis Westwick would arrive in Venice on the next day, and would be obliged if Number Fourteen, on the first floor, could be reserved for him, in the event of its being vacant at the time.

The manager paused to consider, before he issued his directions.

The re-numbered room had been last let to a French gentleman. It would be occupied on the day of Mr. Francis Westwick's arrival, but it would be empty again on the day after. Would it be well to reserve the room for the special occupation of Mr. Francis? and when he had passed the night unsuspiciously and comfortably in "No. 13 A," to ask him in the presence of witnesses how he liked his bed-chamber? In this case, if the reputation of the room happened to be called in question again, the answer would vindicate it, on the evidence of a member of the very family which had first given Number Fourteen a bad name. After a little reflection, the manager decided on trying the experiment, and directed that "13 A" should be reserved accordingly.

On the next day Francis Westwick arrived, in excellent spirits.

He had signed agreements with the most popular dancer in Italy; he had transferred the charge of Mrs. Norbury to his brother Henry, who had joined him in Milan; and he was now at full liberty to amuse himself by testing in every possible way the extraordinary influence exercised over his relatives by the new hotel. When his brother and sister first told him what their experience had been, he instantly declared that he would go to Venice in the interest of his theatre. The circumstances related to him contained invaluable hints for a ghost-drama. The title occurred to him in the railway: "The Haunted Hotel." Post that in red letters six feet high, on a black ground, all over London—and trust the excitable public to crowd into the theatre!

Received with the politest attention by the manager, Francis met with a disappointment on entering the hotel. "Some mistake, sir. No such room on the first floor as Number Fourteen. The room bearing that number is on the second floor, and has been occupied by me from the day when the hotel opened. Perhaps you meant number 13 A on the first floor? It will be at your service to-morrow—a charming room. In the meantime, we will do the best we can for you, to-night."

A man who is the successful manager of a theatre is probably the last man in the civilized universe who is capable of being impressed with favourable opinions of his fellow-creatures. Francis privately set the manager down as a humbug, and the story about the numbering of the rooms as a lie.

On the day of his arrival he dined by himself in the restaurant, before the hour of the table d'hote, for the express purpose of questioning the waiter, without being overheard by anybody. The answer led him to the conclusion that "13 A" occupied the situation in the hotel which had been described by his brother and sister as the situation of "14." He asked next for the Visitors' List, and found that the French gentleman who then occupied "13 A" was the proprietor of a theatre in Paris, personally well known to him. Was the gentleman then in the hotel? He had gone out, but would certainly return for the table d'hote. When the public dinner was over, Francis entered the room, and was welcomed by his Parisian colleague, literally, with open arms. "Come and have a cigar in my room," said the friendly Frenchman. "I want to hear whether you have really engaged that woman at Milan or not." In this easy way Francis found his opportunity of comparing the interior of the room with the description which he had heard of it at Milan.

Arriving at the door, the Frenchman bethought himself of his travelling companion. "My scene-painter is here with me," he said, "on the lookout for materials. An excellent fellow, who will take it as a kindness if we ask him to join us. I'll tell the porter to send him up when he comes in." He handed the key of his room to Francis. "I will be back in a minute. It's at the end of the corridor—13 A."

Francis entered the room alone. There were the decorations on the walls and the ceiling, exactly as they had been described to him! He had just time to perceive this at a glance, before his attention was diverted to himself and his own sensations, by a grotesquely-disagreeable occurrence which took him completely by surprise.

He became conscious of a mysteriously-offensive odour in the room, entirely new in his experience of revolting smells. It was composed (if such a thing could be) of two mingling exhalations, which were separately-discoverable exhalations nevertheless. This strange blending of odours consisted of something faintly and unpleasantly aromatic, mixed with another underlying smell, so unutterably sickening that he threw open the window, and put his head out into the fresh air, unable to endure the horribly-infected atmosphere for a moment longer.

The French proprietor joined his English friend, with his cigar already lit. He started back in dismay at a sight terrible to his countrymen in general—the sight of an open window. "You English people are perfectly mad on the subject of fresh air!" he exclaimed. "We shall catch our deaths of cold."

Francis turned, and looked at him in astonishment. "Are you really not aware of the smell there is in the room?" he asked.

"Smell!" repeated his brother manager. "I smell my own good cigar. Try one yourself. And for Heaven's sake shut the window!"

Francis declined the cigar by a sign. "Forgive me," he said. "I will leave you to close the window. I feel faint and giddy—I had better go out." He put his handkerchief over his nose and mouth, and crossed the room to the door.

The Frenchman followed the movements of Francis, in such a state of bewilderment that he actually forgot to seize the opportunity of shutting out the fresh air. "Is it so nasty as that?" he asked, with a broad stare of amazement.

"Horrible!" Francis muttered behind his handkerchief. "I never smelt anything like it in my life!"

There was a knock at the door. The scene-painter appeared. His employer instantly asked him if he smelt anything.

"I smell your cigar. Delicious! Give me one directly!"

"Wait a minute. Besides my cigar, do you smell anything else —vile, abominable, overpowering, indescribable, never-never-never smelt before!"

The scene-painter appeared to be puzzled by the vehement energy of the language addressed to him. "The room is as fresh and sweet as a room can be," he answered. As he spoke, he looked back with astonishment at Francis Westwick, standing outside in the corridor, and eyeing the interior of the bed-chamber with an expression of undisguised disgust.

The Parisian director approached his English colleague, and looked at him with grave and anxious scrutiny.

"You see, my friend, here are two of us, with as good noses as yours, who smell nothing. If you want evidence from more noses, look there!" He pointed to two little English girls, at play in the corridor. "The door of my room is wide open—and you know how fast a smell can travel. Now listen, while I appeal to these innocent noses, in the language of their own dismal island. My little loves, do you sniff a nasty smell here—ha?" The children burst out laughing, and answered emphatically, "No." "My good Westwick," the

Frenchman resumed, in his own language, "the conclusion is surely plain? There is something wrong, very wrong, with your own nose. I recommend you to see a medical man."

Having given that advice, he returned to his room, and shut out the horrid fresh air with a loud exclamation of relief. Francis left the hotel, by the lanes that led to the Square of St. Mark. The night-breeze soon revived him. He was able to light a cigar, and to think quietly over what had happened.

Chapter XIX

Avoiding the crowd under the colonnades, Francis walked slowly up and down the noble open space of the square, bathed in the light of the rising moon.

Without being aware of it himself, he was a thorough materialist. The strange effect produced on him by the room—following on the other strange effects produced on the other relatives of his dead brother—exercised no perplexing influence over the mind of this sensible man. "Perhaps," he reflected, "my temperament is more imaginative than I supposed it to be—and this is a trick played on me by my own fancy? Or, perhaps, my friend is right; something is physically amiss with me? I don't feel ill, certainly. But that is no safe criterion sometimes. I am not going to sleep in that abominable room to-night—I can well wait till to-morrow to decide whether I shall speak to a doctor or not. In the meantime, the hotel doesn't seem likely to supply me with the subject of a piece. A terrible smell from an invisible ghost is a perfectly new idea. But it has one drawback. If I realise it on the stage, I shall drive the audience out of the theatre."

As his strong common sense arrived at this facetious conclusion, he became aware of a lady, dressed entirely in black, who was observing him with marked attention. "Am I right in supposing you to be Mr. Francis Westwick?" the lady asked, at the moment when he looked at her.

"That is my name, madam. May I inquire to whom I have the honour of speaking?"

"We have only met once," she answered, a little evasively, "when your late brother introduced me to the members of his family. I wonder if you have quite forgotten my big black eyes and my hideous complexion?" She lifted her veil as she spoke, and turned so that the moonlight rested on her face.

Francis recognised at a glance the woman of all others whom he most cordially disliked—the widow of his dead brother, the first Lord Montbarry. He frowned as he looked at her. His experience on the stage, gathered at innumerable rehearsals with actresses who had sorely tried his temper, had accustomed him to speak roughly to women who were distasteful to him. "I remember you," he said, "I thought you were in America!"

She took no notice of his ungracious tone and manner; she simply stopped him when he lifted his hat, and turned to leave her.

"Let me walk with you for a few minutes," she quietly replied. "I have something to say to you."

He showed her his cigar. "I am smoking," he said.

"I don't mind smoking."

After that, there was nothing to be done (short of downright brutality) but to yield. He did it with the worst possible grace. "Well?" he resumed. "What do you want of me?"

"You shall hear directly, Mr. Westwick. Let me first tell you what my position is. I am alone in the world. To the loss of my husband has now been added another bereavement, the loss of my companion in America, my brother—Baron Rivar."

The reputation of the Baron, and the doubt which scandal had thrown on his assumed relationship to the Countess, were well known to Francis. "Shot in a gambling-saloon?" he asked brutally.

"The question is a perfectly natural one on your part," she said with the impenetrably-ironical manner which she could assume on certain occasions. "As a native of horse-racing England, you belong to a nation of gamblers. My brother died no extraordinary death, Mr. Westwick. He sank, with many other unfortunate people, under a fever prevalent in a Western city which we happened to visit. The calamity of his loss made the United States unendurable to me. I left by the first steamer that sailed from New York—a French vessel which brought me to Havre. I continued my lonely journey to the South of France. And then I went on to Venice."

"What does all this matter to me?" Francis thought to himself.

She paused, evidently expecting him to say something. "So you have come to Venice?" he said carelessly. "Why?"

"Because I couldn't help it," she answered.

Francis looked at her with cynical curiosity. "That sounds odd," he remarked. "Why couldn't you help it?"

"Women are accustomed to act on impulse," she explained. "Suppose we say that an impulse has directed my journey? And yet, this is the last place in the world that I wish to find myself in. Associations that I detest are connected with it in my mind. If I had a will of my own, I would never see it again. I hate Venice. As you see, however, I am here. When did you meet with such an unreasonable woman before? Never, I am sure!" She stopped, eyed him for a moment, and suddenly altered her tone. "When is Miss Agnes Lockwood expected to be in Venice?" she asked.

It was not easy to throw Francis off his balance, but that extraordinary question did it. "How the devil did you know that Miss Lockwood was coming to Venice?" he exclaimed.

She laughed—a bitter, mocking laugh. "Say, I guessed it."

Something in her tone, or perhaps something in the audacious defiance of her eyes as they rested on him, roused the quick temper that was in Francis Westwick. "Lady Montbarry——!" he began.

"Stop there!" she interposed. "Your brother Stephen's wife calls herself Lady Montbarry now. I share my title with no woman. Call me by my name, before I committed the fatal mistake of marrying your brother. Address me, if you please, as Countess Narona."

"Countess Narona," Francis resumed, "if your object in claiming my acquaintance is to mystify me, you have come to the wrong man. Speak plainly, or permit me to wish you good evening."

"If your object is to keep Miss Lockwood's arrival in Venice a secret," she retorted, "speak plainly, Mr. Westwick, on *your* side, and say so."

Her intention was evidently to irritate him; and she succeeded. "Nonsense!" he broke out petulantly. "My brother's travelling arrangements are secrets to nobody. He brings Miss Lockwood here, with Lady Montbarry and the children. As you seem so well informed, perhaps you know why she is coming to Venice?"

The Countess had suddenly become grave and thoughtful. She had made no reply. The two strangely-associated companions, having reached one extremity of the square were now standing before the church of St. Mark. The moonlight was bright enough to show the architecture of the grand cathedral in its wonderful variety of detail. Even the pigeons of St. Mark were visible, in dark, closely packed rows, roosting in the archways of the great entrance doors.

"I never saw the old church look so beautiful by moonlight," the Countess said quietly; speaking, not to Francis, but to herself. "Goodbye, St. Mark's by moonlight! I shall not see you again."

She turned away from the church, and saw Francis listening to her with wondering looks. "No," she resumed, placidly picking up the lost thread of the conversation, "I don't know why Miss Lockwood is coming here, I only know that we are to meet in Venice!"

"By previous appointment?"

"By Destiny," she answered, with her head on her breast, and her eyes on the ground. Francis burst out laughing. "Or if you like it better," she instantly resumed, "by what fools call Chance."

Francis answered easily, out of the depths of his strong common sense. "Chance seems to be taking a queer way of bringing the meeting about," he said. "We have all arranged to meet at the Palace Hotel. How is it that your name is not on the Visitors' List? Destiny ought to have brought you to the Palace Hotel, too."

She abruptly pulled down her veil. "Destiny may do that yet!" she said. "The Palace Hotel?" she repeated, speaking once more to herself. "The old hell, transformed into the new purgatory. The place itself. Jesu Maria! the place itself!" She paused and laid her hand on her companion's arm. "Perhaps Miss Lockwood is not going there with the rest of you?" she burst out with sudden eagerness. "Are you positively sure she will be at the hotel?"

"Positively! Haven't I told you that Miss Lockwood travels with Lord and Lady Montbarry? and don't you know that she is a member of the family? You will have to move, Countess, to our hotel."

She was perfectly impenetrable to the bantering tone in which he spoke. "Yes," she said faintly, "I shall have to move to your hotel." Her hand was still on his arm—he could feel her shivering from head to foot while she spoke. Heartily as he disliked and distrusted her, the common instinct of humanity obliged him to ask if she felt cold.

"Yes," she said. "Cold and faint."

"Cold and faint, Countess, on such a night as this?"

"The night has nothing to do with it, Mr. Westwick. How do you suppose the criminal feels on the scaffold, while the hangman is putting the rope round his neck? Cold and faint, too, I should think. Excuse my grim fancy. You see destiny has got the rope round *my* neck—and *I* feel it."

She looked about her. They were at that moment close to the famous cafe known as "Florian's." "Take me in there," she said; "I must have something to revive me. You had better not hesitate. You are interested in reviving me. I have not said what I wanted to say to you yet. It's business, and it's connected with your theatre."

Wondering inwardly what she could possibly want with his theatre, Francis reluctantly yielded to the necessities of the situation, and took her into the cafe. He found a quiet corner in which they could take their places without attracting notice. "What will you have?" he inquired resignedly. She gave her own orders to the waiter, without troubling him to speak for her.

"Maraschino. And a pot of tea."

The waiter stared; Francis stared. The tea was a novelty (in connection with maraschino) to both of them. Careless whether she surprised them or not, she instructed the waiter, when her directions had been complied with, to pour a large wine-glass full of the liqueur into a tumbler, and to fill it up from the teapot. "I can't do it for myself," she remarked, "my hand trembles so." She drank the strange mixture eagerly, hot as it was. "Maraschino punch—will you taste some of it?" she said. "I inherit the discovery of this drink. When your English Queen Caroline was on the Continent, my mother was attached to her court. That much injured Royal Person invented, in her happier hours, maraschino punch. Fondly attached to her gracious mistress, my mother shared her tastes. And I, in my turn, learnt from my mother. Now, Mr. Westwick, suppose I tell you what my business is. You are manager of a theatre. Do you want a new play?"

"I always want a new play—provided it's a good one."

"And you pay, if it's a good one?"

"I pay liberally—in my own interests."

"If *I* write the play, will you read it?"

Francis hesitated. "What has put writing a play into your head?" he asked.

"Mere accident," she answered. "I had once occasion to tell my late brother of a visit I paid to Miss Lockwood, when I was last in England. He took no interest in what happened at the interview, but something struck him in my way of relating it. He said, 'You describe what passed between you and the lady with the point and contrast of good stage dialogue. You have the dramatic instinct—try if you can write a play. You might make money.' *That* put it into my head."

These last words seemed to startle Francis. "Surely you don't want money!" he exclaimed.

"I always want money. My tastes are expensive. I have nothing but my poor little four hundred a year—and the wreck that is left of the other money. About two hundred pounds in circular notes, no more."

Francis knew that she was referring to the ten thousand pounds paid by the insurance offices. "All those thousands gone already!" he exclaimed.

She blew a little puff of air over her fingers. "Gone like that!" she answered coolly.

"Baron Rivar?"

She looked at him with a flash of anger in her hard black eyes.

"My affairs are my own secret, Mr. Westwick. I have made you a proposal—and you have not answered me yet. Don't say No, without thinking first. Remember what a life mine has been. I have seen more of the world than most people, playwrights included. I have had strange adventures; I have heard remarkable stories; I have observed; I have remembered. Are there no materials, here in my head, for writing a play—if the opportunity is granted to me?" She waited a moment, and suddenly repeated her strange question about Agnes. "When is Miss Lockwood expected to be in Venice?"

"What has that to do with your new play, Countess?"

The Countess appeared to feel some difficulty in giving that question its fit reply. She mixed another tumbler full of the maraschino punch, and drank one good half of it before she spoke again.

"It has everything to do with my new play," was all she said. "Answer me." Francis answered her.

"Miss Lockwood may be here in a week. Or for all I know to the contrary, sooner than that."

"Very well. If I am a living woman and a free woman, in a week's time—or if I am in possession of my senses in a week's time (don't interrupt me; I know what I am talking about)—I shall go to England, and I shall write a sketch or outline of my play, as a specimen of what I can do. Once again, will you read it?"

"I will certainly read it. But, Countess, I don't understand——"

She held up her hand for silence, and finished the second tumbler of maraschino punch.

"I am a living enigma—and you want to know the right reading of me," she said. "Here is the reading, as your English phrase goes, in a nutshell. There is a foolish idea in the minds of many persons that the natives of the warm climates are imaginative people. There never was a greater mistake. You will find no such unimaginative people anywhere as you find in Italy, Spain, Greece, and the other Southern countries. To anything fanciful, to anything spiritual, their minds are deaf and blind by nature. Now and then, in the course of centuries, a great genius springs up amongst them; and he is the exception which proves the rule. Now see! I, though I am no—genius—I am, in my little way (as I suppose) an exception too. To my sorrow, I have some of that imagination, which is so common among the English and the Germans—so rare among the Italians, the Spaniards, and the rest of them! And what is the result? I think it has become a disease in me. I am filled with presentiments which make this wicked life of mine one long terror to me. It doesn't matter, just now, what they are. Enough that they absolutely govern me—they drive me over land and sea at their own horrible will; they are in me, and torturing me, at this moment! Why don't I resist them? Ha! but I do resist them. I am trying (with the help of the good punch) to resist them now. At intervals I cultivate the difficult virtue of sound sense. Sometimes sound sense makes a hopeful woman of me. At one time, I had the hope that what seemed reality to me was only mad delusion, after all—I even asked the question of an English doctor! At other times, other sensible doubts of myself beset me. Never mind dwelling on them now—it always ends in the old terrors and superstitions taking possession of me again. In a week's time, I shall know whether Destiny does indeed decide my future for me, or whether I decide it for myself. In the last case, my resolution is to absorb this self-tormenting fancy of mine in the occupation that I have told you of already. Do you understand me a little better now? And, our business being settled, dear Mr. Westwick, shall we get out of this hot room into the nice cool air again?"

They rose to leave the cafe. Francis privately concluded that the maraschino punch offered the only discoverable explanation of what the Countess had said to him.

CHAPTER XX

"Shall I see you again?" she asked, as she held out her hand to take leave. "It is quite understood between us, I suppose, about the play?"

Francis recalled his extraordinary experience of that evening in the re-numbered room. "My stay in Venice is uncertain," he replied. "If you have anything more to say about this dramatic venture of yours, it may be as well to say it now. Have you decided on a subject already? I know the public taste in England better than you do—I might save you some waste of time and trouble, if you have not chosen your subject wisely."

"I don't care what subject I write about, so long as I write," she answered carelessly. "If *you* have got a subject in your head, give it to me. I answer for the characters and the dialogue."

"You answer for the characters and the dialogue," Francis repeated. "That's a bold way of speaking for a beginner! I wonder if I should shake your sublime confidence in yourself, if I suggested the most ticklish subject to handle which is known to the stage? What do you say, Countess, to entering the lists with Shakespeare, and trying a drama with a ghost in it? A true story, mind! founded on events in this very city in which you and I are interested."

She caught him by the arm, and drew him away from the crowded colonnade into the solitary middle space of the square. "Now tell me!" she said eagerly. "Here, where nobody is near us. How am I interested in it? How? how?"

Still holding his arm, she shook him in her impatience to hear the coming disclosure. For a moment he hesitated. Thus far, amused by her ignorant belief in herself, he had merely spoken in jest. Now, for the first time, impressed by her irresistible earnestness, he began to consider what he was about from a more serious point of view. With her knowledge of all that had passed in the old palace, before its transformation into an hotel, it was surely possible that she might suggest some explanation of what had happened to his brother and sister, and himself. Or, failing to do this, she might accidentally reveal some event in her own experience which, acting as a hint to a competent dramatist, might prove to be the making of a play. The prosperity of his theatre was his one serious object in life. "I may be on the trace of another 'Corsican Brothers,'" he thought. "A new piece of that sort would be ten thousand pounds in my pocket at least."

With these motives (worthy of the single-hearted devotion to dramatic business which made Francis a successful manager) he related, without further hesitation, what his own experience had been, and what the experience of his relatives had been, in the haunted hotel. He even described the outbreak of superstitious terror which had escaped Mrs. Norbury's ignorant maid. "Sad stuff, if you look at it reasonably," he remarked. "But there is something dramatic in the notion of the ghostly influence making itself felt by the relations in succession, as they one after another enter the fatal room—until the once chosen relative comes who will see the Unearthly Creature and know the terrible truth. Material for a play, Countess—first-rate material for a play!"

There he paused. She neither moved nor spoke. He stooped and looked closer at her.

What impression had he produced? It was an impression which his utmost ingenuity had failed to anticipate. She stood by his side—just as she had stood before Agnes when her question about Ferrari was plainly answered—like a woman turned to stone. Her eyes were vacant and rigid; all the life in her face had faded out of it. Francis took her by the hand. Her hand was cold as the pavement they were standing on. He asked her if she was ill.

Not a muscle in her moved. He might as well have spoken to the dead.

"Surely," he said, "you are not foolish enough to take what I have been telling you seriously?"

Her lips moved slowly. As it seemed, she was making an effort to speak to him.

"Louder," he said. "I can't hear you."

She struggled to recover possession of herself. A faint light began to soften the dull cold stare of her eyes. In a moment more she spoke so that he could hear her.

"I never thought of the other world," she murmured, in low dull tones like a woman talking in her sleep.

Her mind had gone back to the day of her last memorable interview with Agnes; she was slowly recalling the confession that had escaped her, the warning words which she had spoken at that past time. Necessarily incapable of understanding this, Francis looked at her in perplexity. She went on in the same dull vacant tone, steadily following out her own train of thought, with her heedless eyes on his face, and her wandering mind far away from him.

"I said some trifling event would bring us together the next time. I was wrong. No trifling event will bring us together. I said I might be the person who told her what had become of Ferrari, if she forced me to it. Shall I feel some other influence than hers? Will *he* force me to it? When *she* sees him, shall *I* see him too?"

Her head sank a little; her heavy eyelids dropped slowly; she heaved a long, low, weary sigh. Francis put her arm in his, and made an attempt to rouse her.

"Come, Countess, you are weary and over-wrought. We have had enough talking to-night. Let me see you safe back to your hotel. Is it far from here?"

She started when he moved, and obliged her to move with him, as if he had suddenly awakened her out of a deep sleep.

"Not far," she said faintly. "The old hotel on the quay. My mind's in a strange state; I have forgotten the name."

"Danieli's?"

"Yes!"

He led her on slowly. She accompanied him in silence as far as the end of the Piazzetta. There, when the full view of the moon-lit Lagoon revealed itself, she stopped him as he turned toward the Riva degli Schiavoni. "I have something to ask you. I want to wait and think."

She recovered her lost idea, after a long pause.

"Are you going to sleep in the room to-night?" she asked.

He told her that another traveller was in possession of the room that night. "But the manager has reserved it for me to-morrow," he added, "if I wish to have it."

"No," she said. "You must give it up."

"To whom?"

"To me."

He started. "After what I have told you, do you really wish to sleep in that room to-morrow night?"

"I *must* sleep in it."

"Are you not afraid?"

"I am horribly afraid."

"So I should have thought, after what I have observed in you to-night. Why should you take the room? You are not obliged to occupy it, unless you like."

"I was not obliged to go to Venice, when I left America," she answered. "And yet I came here. I must take the room and keep the room, until——" She broke off at those words. "Never mind the rest," she said. "It doesn't interest you."

It was useless to dispute with her. Francis changed the subject. "We can do nothing to-night," he said. "I will call on you to-morrow morning, and hear what you think of it then."

They moved on again to the hotel. As they approached the door, Francis asked if she was staying in Venice under her own name.

She shook her head. "As your brother's widow, I am known here. As Countess Narona, I am known here. I want to be un-known, this time, to strangers in Venice; I am travelling under a common English name." She hesitated, and stood still. "What has come to me?" she muttered to herself. "Some things I remember; and some I forget. I forgot Danieli's—and now I forget my Eng-lish name." She drew him hurriedly into the hall of the hotel, on the wall of which hung a list of visitors' names. Running her finger slowly down the list, she pointed to the English name that she had assumed:—"Mrs. James."

"Remember that when you call to-morrow," she said. "My head is heavy. Good night."

Francis went back to his own hotel, wondering what the events of the next day would bring forth. A new turn in his affairs had taken place in his absence. As he crossed the hall, he was requested by one of the servants to walk into the private office. The manager was waiting there with a gravely pre-occupied manner, as if he had something serious to say. He regretted to hear that Mr. Francis Westwick had, like other members of the family, discovered mysterious sources of discomfort in the new hotel. He had been informed in strict confidence of Mr. Westwick's extraordinary objection to the atmosphere of the bedroom upstairs. Without presuming to discuss the matter, he must beg to be excused from reserving the room for Mr. Westwick after what had happened.

Francis answered sharply, a little ruffled by the tone in which the manager had spoken to him. "I might, very possibly, have declined to sleep in the room, if you had reserved it," he said. "Do you wish me to leave the hotel?"

The manager saw the error that he had committed, and hastened to repair it. "Certainly not, sir! We will do our best to make you comfortable, while you stay with us. I beg your pardon if I have said anything to offend you. The reputation of an establishment like this is a matter of very serious importance. May I hope that you will do us the great favour to say nothing about what has happened upstairs? The two French gentlemen have kindly promised to keep it a secret."

This apology left Francis no polite alternative but to grant the manager's request. "There is an end to the Countess's wild scheme," he thought to himself, as he retired for the night. "So much better for the Countess!"

He rose late the next morning. Inquiring for his Parisian friends, he was informed that both the French gentlemen had left for Milan. As he crossed the hall, on his way to the restaurant, he noticed the head porter chalking the numbers of the rooms on some articles of luggage which were waiting to go upstairs. One trunk attracted his attention by the extraordinary number of old travelling labels left on it. The porter was marking it at the moment—and the number was, "13 A." Francis instantly looked at the card fastened on the lid. It bore the common English name, "Mrs. James!" He at once inquired about the lady. She had arrived early that morning, and she was then in the Reading Room. Looking into the room, he discovered a lady in it alone. Advancing a little nearer, he found himself face to face with the Countess.

She was seated in a dark corner, with her head down and her arms crossing over her bosom. "Yes," she said in a tone of weary impatience, before Francis could speak to her. "I thought it best not to wait for you—I determined to get here before anybody else could take the room."

"Have you taken it for long?" Francis asked.

"You told me Miss Lockwood would be here in a week's time. I have taken it for a week."

"What has Miss Lockwood to do with it?"

"She has everything to do with it—she must sleep in the room. I shall give the room up to her when she comes here."

Francis began to understand the superstitious purpose that she had in view. "Are you (an educated woman) really of the same opinion as my sister's maid!" he exclaimed. "Assuming your absurd superstition to be a serious thing, you are taking the wrong means to prove it true. If I and my brother and sister have seen nothing, how should Agnes Lockwood discover what was not revealed to Us? She is only distantly related to the Montbarrys—she is only our cousin."

"She was nearer to the heart of the Montbarry who is dead than any of you," the Countess answered sternly. "To the last day of his life, my miserable husband repented his desertion of her. She will see what none of you have seen—she shall have the room."

Francis listened, utterly at a loss to account for the motives that animated her. "I don't see what interest *you* have in trying this extraordinary experiment," he said.

"It is my interest not to try it! It is my interest to fly from Venice, and never set eyes on Agnes Lockwood or any of your family again!"

"What prevents you from doing that?"

She started to her feet and looked at him wildly. "I know no more what prevents me than you do!" she burst out. "Some will that is stronger than mine drives me on to my destruction, in spite of my own self!" She suddenly sat down again, and waved her hand for him to go. "Leave me," she said. "Leave me to my thoughts."

Francis left her, firmly persuaded by this time that she was out of her senses. For the rest of the day, he saw nothing of her. The night, so far as he knew, passed quietly. The next morning he breakfasted early, determining to wait in the restaurant for the appearance of the Countess. She came in and ordered her breakfast quietly, looking dull and worn and self-absorbed, as she had looked when he last saw her. He hastened to her table, and asked if anything had happened in the night.

"Nothing," she answered.

"You have rested as well as usual?"

"Quite as well as usual. Have you had any letters this morning? Have you heard when she is coming?"

"I have had no letters. Are you really going to stay here? Has your experience of last night not altered the opinion which you expressed to me yesterday?"

"Not in the least."

The momentary gleam of animation which had crossed her face when she questioned him about Agnes, died out of it again when he answered her. She looked, she spoke, she eat her breakfast, with a vacant resignation, like a woman who had done with hopes, done with interests, done with everything but the mechanical movements and instincts of life.

Francis went out, on the customary travellers' pilgrimage to the shrines of Titian and Tintoret. After some hours of absence, he found a letter waiting for him when he got back to the hotel. It was written by his brother Henry, and it recommended him to return to Milan immediately. The proprietor of a French theatre, recently arrived from Venice, was trying to induce the famous dancer whom Francis had engaged, to break faith with him and accept a higher salary.

Having made this startling announcement, Henry proceeded to inform his brother that Lord and Lady Montbarry, with Agnes and the children, would arrive in Venice in three days more. "They know nothing of our adventures at the hotel," Henry wrote; "and they have telegraphed to the manager for the accommodation that they want. There would be something absurdly superstitious in our giving them a warning which would frighten the ladies and children out of the best hotel in Venice. We shall be a strong party this time—too strong a party for ghosts! I shall meet the travellers on their arrival of course, and try my luck again at what you call the Haunted Hotel. Arthur Barville and his wife have already got as far on their way as Trent; and two of the lady's relations have arranged to accompany them on the journey to Venice."

Naturally indignant at the conduct of his Parisian colleague, Francis made his preparations for returning to Milan by the train of that day.

On his way out, he asked the manager if his brother's telegram had been received. The telegram had arrived, and, to the surprise of Francis, the rooms were already reserved. "I thought you would refuse to let any more of the family into the house," he said satirically. The manager answered (with the due dash of respect) in the same tone. "Number 13 A is safe, sir, in the occupation of a stranger. I am the servant of the Company; and I dare not turn money out of the hotel."

Hearing this Francis said good-bye—and said nothing more. He was ashamed to acknowledge it to himself, but he felt an irresistible curiosity to know what would happen when Agnes arrived at the hotel. Besides "Mrs. James" had reposed confidence in him. He got into his gondola, respecting the confidence of "Mrs. James."

Toward evening on the third day, Lord Montbarry and his travelling companions arrived, punctual to their appointment.

"Mrs. James," sitting at the window of her room watching for them, saw the new lord land from his gondola first. He handed his wife from the steps. The three children were next committed to his care. Last of all, Agnes appeared in the little black doorway of the gondola-cabin; and, taking Lord Montbarry's hand, passed in her turn to the steps. She wore no veil. As she ascended to the door of the hotel, the Countess (eyeing her through an opera-glass) noticed that she paused to look at the outside of the building, and that her face was very pale.

CHAPTER XXI

Lord and Lady Montbarry were received by the housekeeper; the manager being absent for a day or two on business connected with the affairs of the hotel.

The rooms reserved for the travellers on the first floor were three in number; consisting of two bedrooms opening into each other, and communicating on the left, with a drawing-room. Complete so far, the arrangements proved to be less satisfactory in reference to the third bedroom required for Agnes and for the eldest daughter of Lord Montbarry, who usually slept with her on their travels. The bed-chamber on the right of the drawing-room was already occupied by an English widow lady. Other bed-chambers at the other end of the corridor were also let in every case. There was accordingly no alternative but to place at the disposal of Agnes a comfortable room on the second floor. Lady Montbarry vainly complained of this separation of one of the members of her travelling party from the rest. The housekeeper hinted that it was impossible for her to ask other travellers to give up their rooms. She could only express her regret, and assure Miss Lockwood that her bed-chamber on the second floor was one of the best rooms in that part of the hotel.

On the retirement of the housekeeper, Lady Montbarry noticed that Agnes had seated herself apart, feeling apparently no interest in the question of the bedrooms. Was she ill? No; she felt a little unnerved by the railway journey, and that was all. Hearing this, Lord Montbarry proposed that she should go out with him, and try the experiment of half an hour's walk in the cool evening air. Agnes gladly accepted the suggestion. They directed their steps towards the square of St. Mark, so as to enjoy the breeze blowing over the lagoon. It was the first visit of Agnes to Venice. The fascination of the wonderful city of the waters exerted its full influence over her sensitive nature. The proposed half hour of the walk had passed away, and was fast expanding to half an hour more, before Lord Montbarry could persuade his companion to remember that dinner was waiting for them. As they returned, passing under the colonnade, neither of them noticed a lady in deep mourning, loitering in the open space of the square. She started as she recognised Agnes walking with the new Lord Montbarry—hesitated for a moment—and then followed them, at a discreet distance, back to the hotel.

Lady Montbarry received Agnes in high spirits—with news of an event which had happened in her absence.

She had not left the hotel more than ten minutes, before a little note in pencil was brought to Lady Montbarry by the house-keeper. The writer proved to be no less a person than the widow lady who occupied the room on the other side of the drawing-room, which her ladyship had vainly hoped to secure for Agnes. Writing under the name of Mrs. James, the polite widow ex-plained that she had heard from the housekeeper of the disappoint-ment experienced by Lady Montbarry in the matter of the rooms. Mrs. James was quite alone; and as long as her bed-chamber was airy and comfortable, it mattered nothing to her whether she slept on the first or second floor of the house. She had accordingly much pleasure in proposing to change rooms with Miss Lockwood. Her luggage had already been removed, and Miss Lockwood had only to take possession of the room (Number 13 A), which was now entirely at her disposal.

"I immediately proposed to see Mrs. James," Lady Montbarry continued, "and to thank her personally for her extreme kindness. But I was informed that she had gone out, without leaving word at what hour she might be expected to return. I have written a little note of thanks, saying that we hope to have the pleasure of personally expressing our sense of Mrs. James's courtesy to-mor-row. In the meantime, Agnes, I have ordered your boxes to be removed downstairs. Go!—and judge for yourself, my dear, if that good lady has not given up to you the prettiest room in the house!"

With these words, Lady Montbarry left Miss Lockwood to make a hasty toilet for dinner.

The new room at once produced a favourable impression on Agnes. The large window, opening into a balcony, commanded an admirable view of the canal. The decorations on the walls and ceiling, were carefully copied from the exquisitely graceful designs of Raphael in the Vatican. The massive wardrobe possessed com-partments of unusual size, in which double the number of dresses that Agnes possessed might have been conveniently hung at full length. In the inner corner of the room, near the head of the bed-stead, there was a recess which had been turned into a little dressing-room, and which opened by a second door on the inferior staircase of the hotel, commonly used by the servants. Noticing these aspects of the room at a glance, Agnes made the necessary change in her dress, as quickly as possible. On her way back to the drawing-room she was addressed by a chambermaid in the corridor who asked for her key. "I will put your room tidy for the night, Miss," the woman said, "and I will then bring the key back to you in the drawing-room."

While the chambermaid was at her work, a solitary lady, loitering about the corridor of the second story, was watching her over the bannisters. After awhile, the maid appeared, with her pail in her hand, leaving the room by way of the dressing-room and the back stairs. As she passed out of sight, the lady on the second floor (no other, it is needless to add, than the Countess herself) ran swiftly down the stairs, entered the bed-chamber by the principal door, and hid herself in the empty side compartment of the wardrobe. The chambermaid returned, completed her work, locked the door of the dressing-room on the inner side, locked the principal entrance door on leaving the room, and returned the key to Agnes in the drawing-room.

The travellers were just sitting down to their late dinner, when one of the children noticed that Agnes was not wearing her watch. Had she left it in her bed-chamber in the hurry of chang-ing her dress? She rose from the table at once, in search of her watch; Lady Montbarry advising her, as she went out, to see to the security of her bed-chamber in the event of there being thieves in the house. Agnes found her watch, forgotten on the toilet table, as she had anticipated. Before leaving the room again, she acted on Lady Montbarry's advice, and tried the key in the lock of the dressing-room door. It was properly secured. She left the bed-chamber, locking the main door behind her.

Immediately on her departure, the Countess, oppressed by the confined air in the wardrobe, ventured on stepping out of her hiding-place into the empty room.

Entering the dressing-room on tip-toe, she listened at the door, until the silence outside informed her that the corridor was empty. Upon this, she unlocked the door, and passing out, closed it again softly; leaving it to all appearances (when viewed on the inner side) as carefully secured as Agnes had seen it when she tried the key in the lock with her own hand.

While the Montbarrys were still at dinner, Henry Westwick joined them, arriving from Milan.

When he entered the room, and again when he advanced to shake hands with her, Agnes was conscious of a latent feeling which secretly reciprocated Henry's unconcealed pleasure on meeting her again. For a moment only, she returned his look; and in that moment her own observation told her that she had silently encouraged him to hope. She saw it in the sudden glow of happiness which over-spread his face; and she confusedly took refuge in the usual conventional inquiries relating to the relatives whom he had left at Milan.

Taking his place at the table, Henry gave a most amusing account of the position of his brother Francis between the mercenary opera-dancer on one side, and the unscrupulous manager of the French theatre on the other. Matters had proceeded to such extremities, that the law had been called on to interfere, and had decided the dispute in favour of Francis. On winning the victory the English manager had at once left Milan, recalled to London by the affairs of his theatre. He was accompanied on the journey back, as he had been accompanied on the journey out, by his sister. Resolved, after passing two nights of terror in the Venetian hotel, never to enter it again, Mrs. Norbury asked to be excused from appearing at the family festival, on the ground of ill-health. At her age, travelling fatigued her, and she was glad to take advantage of her brother's escort to return to England.

While the talk at the dinner-table flowed easily onward, the evening-time advanced to night—and it became necessary to think of sending the children to bed.

As Agnes rose to leave the room, accompanied by the eldest girl, she observed with surprise that Henry's manner suddenly changed. He looked serious and pre-occupied; and when his niece wished him good night, be abruptly said to her, "Marian, I want to know what part of the hotel you sleep in?" Marian, puzzled by the question, answered that she was going to sleep as usual with "Aunt Agnes." Not satisfied with that reply, Henry next inquired whether the bedroom was near the room occupied by the other members of the travelling party. Answering for the child, and wondering what Henry's object could possibly be, Agnes mentioned the polite sacrifice made to her convenience by Mrs. James. "Thanks to that lady's kindness," she said, "Marian and I are only on the other side of the drawing-room." Henry made no remark; he looked incomprehensibly discontented as he opened the door for Agnes and her companion to pass out. After wishing them good night, he waited in the corridor until he saw them enter the fatal corner-room—and then he called abruptly to his brother, "Come out, Stephen, and let us smoke."

As soon as the two brothers were at liberty to speak together privately, Henry explained the motive which had led to his strange inquiries about the bedrooms. Francis had informed him of the meeting with the Countess at Venice, and of all that had followed it; and Henry now carefully repeated the narrative to his brother in all its details. "I am not satisfied," he added, "about that woman's purpose in giving up her room. Without alarming the ladies by telling them what I have just told you, can you not warn Agnes to be careful in securing her door?"

Lord Montbarry replied, that the warning had been already given by his wife, and that Agnes might be trusted to take good care of herself and her little bedfellow. For the rest, he looked upon the story of the Countess and her superstitions as a piece of theatrical exaggeration, amusing enough in itself, but quite unworthy of a moment's serious attention.

While the gentlemen were absent from the hotel, the room which had been already associated with so many startling circumstances, became the scene of another strange event in which Lady Montbarry's eldest child was concerned.

Little Marian had been got ready for bed as usual, and had (so far) taken hardly any notice of the new room. As she knelt down to say her prayers, she happened to look up at that part of the ceiling above her which was just over the head of the bed. The next instant she alarmed Agnes, by starting to her feet with a cry of terror, and pointing to a small brown spot on one of the white panelled spaces of the carved ceiling. "It's a spot of blood!" the child exclaimed. "Take me away! I won't sleep here!"

Seeing plainly that it would be useless to reason with her while she was in the room, Agnes hurriedly wrapped Marian in a dressing-gown, and carried her back to her mother in the drawing-room. Here, the ladies did their best to soothe and reassure the trembling girl. The effort proved to be useless; the impression that had been produced on the young and sensitive mind was not to be removed by persuasion. Marian could give no explanation of the panic of terror that had seized her. She was quite unable to say why the spot on the ceiling looked like the colour of a spot of blood. She only knew that she should die of terror if she saw it again. Under these circumstances, but one alternative was left. It was arranged that the child should pass the night in the room occupied by her two younger sisters and the nurse.

In half an hour more, Marian was peacefully asleep with her arm round her sister's neck. Lady Montbarry went back with Agnes to her room to see the spot on the ceiling which had so strangely frightened the child. It was so small as to be only just perceptible, and had in all probability been caused by the careless-ness of a workman, or by a dripping from water accidentally spilt on the floor of the room above.

"I really cannot understand why Marian should place such a terrible interpretation on such a trifling thing," Lady Montbarry remarked.

"I suspect the nurse is in some way answerable for what has happened," Agnes suggested. "She may quite possibly have been telling Marian some tragic nursery story which has left its mis-chievous impression behind it. Persons in her position are sadly ignorant of the danger of exciting a child's imagination. You had better caution the nurse to-morrow."

Lady Montbarry looked round the room with admiration. "Is it not prettily decorated?" she said. "I suppose, Agnes, you don't mind sleeping here by yourself?"

Agnes laughed. "I feel so tired," she replied, "that I was think-ing of bidding you good-night, instead of going back to the draw-ing-room."

Lady Montbarry turned towards the door. "I see your jewel-case on the table," she resumed. "Don't forget to lock the other door there, in the dressing-room."

"I have already seen to it, and tried the key myself," said Agnes. "Can I be of any use to you before I go to bed?"

"No, my dear, thank you; I feel sleepy enough to follow your example. Good-night, Agnes—and pleasant dreams on your first night in Venice."

Chapter XXII

Having closed and secured the door on Lady Montbarry's departure, Agnes put on her dressing-gown, and, turning to her open boxes, began the business of unpacking. In the hurry of making her toilet for dinner, she had taken the first dress that lay uppermost in the trunk, and had thrown her travelling costume on the bed. She now opened the doors of the wardrobe for the first time, and began to hang her dresses on the hooks in the large compartment on one side.

After a few minutes only of this occupation, she grew weary of it, and decided on leaving the trunks as they were, until the next morning. The oppressive south wind which had blown throughout the day, still prevailed at night. The atmosphere of the room felt close; Agnes threw a shawl over her head and shoulders, and, opening the window, stepped into the balcony to look at the view.

The night was heavy and overcast; nothing could be distinctly seen. The canal beneath the window looked like a black gulf, opposite houses were barely visible as a row of shadows, dimly relieved against the starless and moonless sky. At long intervals, the warning cry of a belated gondolier was just audible, as he turned the corner of a distant canal, and called to invisible boats which might be approaching him in the darkness. Now and then, the nearer dip of an oar in the water told of the viewless passage of other gondolas bringing guests back to the hotel. Excepting these rare sounds, the mysterious night-silence of Venice was literally the silence of the grave.

Leaning on the parapet of the balcony, Agnes looked vacantly into the black void beneath. Her thoughts reverted to the miserable man who had broken his pledged faith to her, and who had died in that house. Some change seemed to have come over her, since her arrival in Venice; some new influence appeared to be at work. For the first time in her experience of herself, compassion and regret were not the only emotions aroused in her by the remembrance of the dead Montbarry. A keen sense of the wrong that she had suffered, never yet felt by that gentle and forgiving nature, was felt by it now. She found herself thinking of the bygone days of her humiliation almost as harshly as Henry Westwick had thought of them—she who had rebuked him the last time he had spoken slightingly of his brother in her presence! A sudden fear and doubt of herself startled her physically as well as morally. She turned from the shadowy abyss of the dark water as if the mystery and the gloom of it had been answerable for the emotions which had taken her by surprise. Abruptly closing the window, she threw aside her shawl, and lit the candles on the mantel-piece, impelled by a sudden craving for light in the solitude of her room.

The cheering brightness round her, contrasting with the black gloom outside, restored her spirits. She felt herself enjoying the light like a child!

Would it be well (she asked herself) to get ready for bed? No! The sense of drowsy fatigue that she had felt half an hour since was gone. She returned to the dull employment of unpacking her boxes. After a few minutes only, the occupation became tiresome to her once more. She sat down by the table, and took up a guide-book. "Suppose I inform myself," she thought, "on the subject of Venice?"

Her attention wandered from the book, before she had turned the first page of it.

The image of Henry Westwick was the present image in her memory now. Recalling the minutest incidents and details of the evening, she could think of nothing which presented him under other than a favourable and interesting aspect. She smiled to herself softly, her colour rose by fine gradations, as she felt the full luxury of dwelling on the perfect truth and modesty of his devotion to her. Was the depression of spirits from which she had suffered so persistently on her travels attributable, by any chance, to their long separation from each other—embittered perhaps by her own vain regret when she remembered her harsh reception of him in Paris? Suddenly conscious of this bold question, and of the self-abandonment which it implied, she returned mechanically to her book, startled by the unrestrained liberty of her own thoughts. What lurking temptations to forbidden tenderness find their hiding places in a woman's dressing-gown, when she is alone in her room at night! With her heart in the tomb of the dead Montbarry, could Agnes even think of another man, and think of love? How shameful! how unworthy of her! For the second time, she tried to interest herself in the guide-book—and once more she tried in vain. Throwing the book aside, she turned desperately to the one resource that was left, to her luggage—resolved to fatigue herself without mercy, until she was weary enough and sleepy enough to find a safe refuge in bed.

For some little time, she persisted in the monotonous occupation of transferring her clothes from her trunk to the wardrobe. The large clock in the hall, striking midnight, reminded her that it was getting late. She sat down for a moment in an arm-chair by the bedside, to rest.

The silence in the house now caught her attention, and held it—held it disagreeably. Was everybody in bed and asleep but herself? Surely it was time for her to follow the general example? With a certain irritable nervous haste, she rose again and undressed herself. "I have lost two hours of rest," she thought, frowning at the reflection of herself in the glass, as she arranged her hair for the night. "I shall be good for nothing to-morrow!"

She lit the night-light, and extinguished the candles—with one exception, which she removed to a little table, placed on the side of the bed opposite the side occupied by the arm-chair. Having put her travelling-box of matches and guide-book near the candle, in case she might be sleepless and might want to read, she blew out the light, and laid her head on the pillow.

The curtains of the bed were looped back to let the air pass freely over her. Lying on her left side, with her face turned away from the table, she could see the arm-chair by the dim night-light. It had a chintz covering—representing large bunches of roses scattered over a pale green ground. She tried to weary herself into drowsiness by counting over and over again the bunches of roses that were visible from her point of view. Twice her attention was distracted from the counting, by sounds outside—by the clock chiming the half-hour past twelve; and then again, by the fall of a pair of boots on the upper floor, thrown out to be cleaned, and with that barbarous disregard of the comforts of others, which is observable in humanity when it inhabits an hotel. In the silence that followed these passing disturbances, Agnes went on counting the roses on the arm-chair more and more slowly. Before long she confused herself in the figures—tried to begin counting again—

thought she would wait a little first—felt her eyelids drooping, and her head sinking lower and lower on the pillow—sighed faintly—and sank into sleep.

How long that first sleep lasted she never knew. She could only remember, in the after-time, that she awoke instantly.

Every faculty and perception in her passed the boundary line between insensibility and consciousness, so to speak, at a leap. Without knowing why, she sat up suddenly in the bed, listening for she knew not what. Her head was in a whirl; her heart beat furiously, without any assignable cause. But one trivial event had happened during the interval while she had been asleep. The night-light had gone out; and the room, as a matter of course, was in total darkness.

She felt for the match-box, and paused after finding it. A vague sense of confusion was still in her mind. She was in no hurry to light the match. The pause in the darkness was, strangely enough, agreeable to her.

In the quieter flow of her thoughts during this interval, she could ask herself the natural question—What cause had awakened her so suddenly, and had so strangely shaken her nerves? Had it been the influence of a dream? She had not dreamed at all—or, to speak more correctly, she had no waking remembrance of having dreamed. The mystery was beyond her fathoming: the darkness began to oppress her. She struck the match on the box, and lit her candle.

As the welcome light diffused itself over the room, she turned from the table and looked towards the other side of the bed.

In the moment when she turned, the chill of a sudden terror gripped her round the heart, as with the clasp of an icy hand.

She was not alone in the room!

There—in the chair at the bedside—there, suddenly revealed under the flow of light from the candle, was the figure of a woman reclining. Her head lay back over the chair. Her face, turned up to the ceiling, had the eyes closed, as if she was wrapped in a deep sleep.

The shock of the discovery held Agnes speechless and help-less. Her first conscious action, when she was in some degree mistress of herself again, was to lean over the bed, and to look closer at the woman who had so incomprehensibly stolen into her room in the dead of night. One glance was enough: she started back with a cry of amazement. The person in the chair was no other than the widow of the dead Montbarry—the woman who had warned her that they were to meet again, and that the place might be Venice!

Her courage returned to her, stung into action by the natural sense of indignation which the presence of the Countess provoked.

"Wake up!" she called out. "How dare you come here? How did you get in? Leave the room—or I will call for help!"

She raised her voice at the last words. It produced no effect. Leaning farther over the bed, she boldly took the Countess by the shoulder and shook her. Not even this effort succeeded in rousing the sleeping woman. She still lay back in the chair, possessed by a torpor like the torpor of death—insensible to sound, insensible to touch. Was she really sleeping? Or had she fainted?

Agnes looked closer at her. She had not fainted. Her breathing was audible, rising and falling in deep heavy gasps. At intervals she ground her teeth savagely. Beads of perspiration stood thickly on her forehead. Her clenched hands rose and fell slowly from time to time on her lap. Was she in the agony of a dream or was she spiritually conscious of something hidden in the room?

The doubt involved in that last question was unendurable. Agnes determined to rouse the servants who kept watch in the hotel at night.

The bell-handle was fixed to the wall, on the side of the bed by which the table stood.

She raised herself from the crouching position which she had assumed in looking close at the Countess; and, turning towards the other side of the bed, stretched out her hand to the bell. At the same instant, she stopped and looked upward. Her hand fell helplessly at her side. She shuddered, and sank back on the pillow.

What had she seen?

She had seen another intruder in her room.

Midway between her face and the ceiling, there hovered a human head—severed at the neck, like a head struck from the body by the guillotine.

Nothing visible, nothing audible, had given her warning of its appearance. Silently and suddenly, the head had taken its place above her. No supernatural change had passed over the room, or was perceptible in it now. The dumbly-tortured figure in the chair; the broad window opposite the foot of the bed, with the black night beyond it; the candle burning on the table—these, and all other objects in the room, remain unaltered. One object more, unutterably horrid, had been added to the rest. That was the only change—no more, no less.

By the yellow candle-light she saw the head distinctly, hovering in mid-air above her. She looked at it steadfastly, spell-bound by the terror that held her.

The flesh of the face was gone. The shrivelled skin was darkened in hue, like the skin of an Egyptian mummy—except at the neck. There it was of a lighter colour; there it showed spots and splashes of the hue of that brown spot on the ceiling, which the child's fanciful terror had distorted into the likeness of a spot of blood. The remains of a discoloured moustache and whiskers, hanging over the upper lip, and over the hollows where the cheeks had once been, made the head just recognisable as the head of a man. Over all the features death and time had done their obliterating work. The eyelids were closed. The hair on the skull, discoloured like the hair on the face, had been burnt away in places. The bluish lips, parted in a fixed grin, showed the double row of teeth. By slow degrees the hovering head (perfectly still when she first saw it) began to descend towards Agnes as she lay beneath. By slow degrees that strange double-blended odour, which the Commissioners had discovered in the vaults of the old palace— which had sickened Francis Westwick in the bed-chamber of the new hotel—spread its fetid exhalations over the room. Downward and downward the hideous apparition made its slow progress, until it stopped close over Agnes—stopped, and turned slowly, so that the face of it confronted the upturned face of the woman in the chair.

After that there came a pause. Then a momentary movement disturbed the rigid repose of the dead face.

The closed eyelids opened slowly. The eyes revealed themselves, bright with the glassy film of death—and fixed their dreadful look on the woman in the chair.

Agnes saw that look; saw the reclining woman rise, as if in obedience to some silent command—and saw no more.

Her next conscious impression was of the sunlight pouring in at the window; of the friendly presence of Lady Montbarry at the bedside; and of the children's wondering faces peeping in at the door.

Chapter XXIII

"You have some influence over Agnes. Try what you can do, Henry, to make her take a sensible view of the matter. There is really nothing to make a fuss about. My wife's maid knocked at her door early in the morning, with the customary cup of tea. Getting no answer she went round to the dressing-room—found the door on that side unlocked—and discovered Agnes on the bed in a fainting fit. With my wife's help they brought her to herself again; and she told the extraordinary story which I have just repeated to you. You must have seen for yourself that she has been over-fatigued, poor thing, by our long railway journeys; her nerves are out of order—and she is just the person to be easily terrified by a dream. She obstinately refuses, however, to accept this rational view. Don't suppose that I have been severe with her! All that a man can do to humour her I have done. I have writen to the Countess (in her assumed name) offering to restore the room to her. She writes back, positively declining to return to it. I have accordingly arranged (so as not to have the thing known in the hotel) to occupy the room for one or two nights, and to leave Agnes to recover her spirits under my wife's care. Is there anything more that I can do? Whatever questions Agnes has asked of me I have answered to the best of my ability; she knows all that you told me about Francis and the Countess last night. But try as I may I can't quiet her mind. I have given up the attempt in despair, and left her in the drawing-room. Go, like a good fellow, and try what you can do to compose her."

In those words, Lord Montbarry stated the case to his brother from the rational point of view. Henry made no remark, he went straight to the drawing-room.

He found Agnes walking rapidly backwards and forwards, flushed and excited. "If you come here to say what your brother has been saying to me," she broke out before he could speak, "spare yourself the trouble. I don't want common sense—I want a true friend who will believe in me."

"I am that friend, Agnes," Henry answered quietly, "and you know it."

"You really believe that I am not deluded by a dream?"

"I know that you are not deluded—in one particular, at least."

"In what particular?"

"In what you have said of the Countess. It is perfectly true——"

Agnes stopped him there. "Why do I only hear this morning that the Countess and Mrs. James are one and the same person?" she asked distrustfully. "Why was I not told of it last night?"

"You forget that you had accepted the exchange of rooms before I reached Venice," Henry replied. "I felt strongly tempted to tell you, even then—but your sleeping arrangements for the night were all made; I should only have inconvenienced and alarmed you. I waited till the morning, after hearing from my brother that you had yourself seen to your security from any intrusion. How that intrusion was accomplished it is impossible to say. I can only declare that the Countess's presence by your bedside last night was no dream of yours. On her own authority I can testify that it was a reality."

"On her own authority?" Agnes repeated eagerly. "Have you seen her this morning?"

"I have seen her not ten minutes since."

"What was she doing?"

"She was busily engaged in writing. I could not even get her to look at me until I thought of mentioning your name."

"She remembered me, of course?"

"She remembered you with some difficulty. Finding that she wouldn't answer me on any other terms, I questioned her as if I had come direct from you. Then she spoke. She not only admitted that she had the same superstitious motive for placing you in that room which she had acknowledged to Francis—she even owned that she had been by your bedside, watching through the night, 'to see what you saw,' as she expressed it. Hearing this, I tried to persuade her to tell me how she got into the room. Unluckily, her manuscript on the table caught her eyes; she returned to her writing. 'The Baron wants money,' she said, 'I must get on with my play.' What she saw, or dreamed, while she was in your room last night, it is at present impossible to discover. But judging by my brother's account of her, as well as by what I remember of her myself, some recent influence has been at work which has produced a marked change in this wretched woman for the worse. Her mind is, in certain respects, unquestionably deranged. One proof of it is that she spoke to me of the Baron as if he were still a living man. When Francis saw her, she declared that the Baron was dead, which is the truth. The United States Consul at Milan showed us the announcement of the death in an American newspaper. So far as I can see, such sense as she still possesses seems to be entirely absorbed in one absurd idea—the idea of writing a play for Francis to bring out at his theatre. He admits that he encouraged her to hope that she might get money in this way. I think he did wrong. Don't you agree with me?"

Without heeding the question, Agnes rose abruptly from her chair.

"Do me one more kindness, Henry," she said. "Take me to the Countess at once."

Henry hesitated. "Are you composed enough to see her, after the shock that you have suffered?" he asked.

She trembled, the flush on her face died away, and left it deadly pale. But she held to her resolution. "You have heard of what I saw last night?" she said faintly.

"Don't speak of it!" Henry interposed. "Don't uselessly agitate yourself."

"I must speak! My mind is full of horrid questions about it. I know I can't identify it—and yet I ask myself over and over again, in whose likeness did it appear? Was it in the likeness of Ferrari or was it——?" she stopped, shuddering. "The Countess knows, I must see the Countess!" she resumed vehemently. "Whether my courage fails me or not, I must make the attempt. Take me to her before I have time to feel afraid of it!"

Henry looked at her anxiously. "If you are really sure of your own resolution," he said, "I agree with you—the sooner you see her the better. You remember how strangely she talked of your influence over her, when she forced her way into your room in London?"

"I remember it perfectly. Why do you ask?"

"For this reason. In the present state of her mind, I doubt if she will be much longer capable of realising her wild idea of you as the avenging angel who is to bring her to a reckoning for her evil deeds. It may be well to try what your influence can do while she is still capable of feeling it."

He waited to hear what Agnes would say. She took his arm and led him in silence to the door.

They ascended to the second floor, and, after knocking, entered the Countess's room.

She was still busily engaged in writing. When she looked up from the paper, and saw Agnes, a vacant expression of doubt was the only expression in her wild black eyes. After a few moments, the lost remembrances and associations appeared to return slowly to her mind. The pen dropped from her hand. Haggard and trembling, she looked closer at Agnes, and recognised her at last. "Has the time come already?" she said in low awe-stricken tones. "Give me a little longer respite, I haven't done my writing yet!"

She dropped on her knees, and held out her clasped hands entreatingly. Agnes was far from having recovered, after the shock that she had suffered in the night: her nerves were far from being equal to the strain that was now laid on them. She was so startled by the change in the Countess that she was at a loss what to say or to do next. Henry was obliged to speak to her, "Put your questions while you have the chance," he said, lowering his voice. "See! the vacant look is coming over her face again."

Agnes tried to rally her courage. "You were in my room last night——" she began. Before she could add a word more, the Countess lifted her hands, and wrung them above her head with a low moan of horror. Agnes shrank back, and turned as if to leave the room. Henry stopped her, and whispered to her to try again. She obeyed him after an effort. "I slept last night in the room that you gave up to me," she resumed. "I saw——"

The Countess suddenly rose to her feet. "No more of that," she cried. "Oh, Jesu Maria! do you think I want to be told what you saw? Do you think I don't know what it means for you and for me? Decide for yourself, Miss. Examine your own mind. Are you well assured that the day of reckoning has come at last? Are you ready to follow me back, through the crimes of the past, to the secrets of the dead?"

She turned again to the writing-table, without waiting to be answered. Her eyes flashed: she looked like her old self once more as she spoke. It was only for a moment. The old ardour and impetuosity were nearly worn out. Her head sank; she sighed heavily as she unlocked a desk which stood on the table. Opening a drawer in the desk, she took out a leaf of vellum, covered with faded writing. Some ragged ends of silken thread were still attached to the leaf, as if it had been torn out of a book.

"Can you read Italian?" she asked, handing the leaf to Agnes. Agnes answered silently by an inclination of her head.

"The leaf," the Countess proceeded, "once belonged to a book in the old library of the palace, while this building was still a palace. By whom it was torn out you have no need to know. For what purpose it was torn out you may discover for yourself, if you will. Read it first—at the fifth line from the top of the page."

Agnes felt the serious necessity of composing herself. "Give me a chair," she said to Henry. "And I will do my best." He placed himself behind her chair so that he could look over her shoulder and help her to understand the writing on the leaf. Rendered into English, it ran as follows:——

"I have now completed my literary survey of the first floor of the palace. At the desire of my noble and gracious patron, the lord of this glorious edifice, I next ascend to the second floor, and continue my catalogue or description of the pictures, decorations, and other treasures of art therein contained. Let me begin with the corner room at the western extremity of the palace, called the Room of the Caryatides, from the statues which support the mantel-piece. This work is of comparatively recent execution: it dates from the eighteenth century only, and reveals the corrupt taste of the period in every part of it. Still, there is a certain interest which attaches to the mantel-piece: it conceals a cleverly constructed hiding-place between the floor of the room and the ceiling of the room beneath, which was made during the last evil days of the Inquisition in Venice, and which is reported to have saved an ancestor of my gracious lord pursued by that terrible tribunal. The machinery of this curious place of concealment has been kept in good order by the present lord, as a species of curiosity. He condescended to show me the method of working it. Approaching the two Caryatides, rest your hand on the forehead (midway between the eyebrows) of the figure which is on your left as you stand opposite to the fireplace, then press the head inwards as if you were pushing it against the wall behind. By doing this, you set in motion the hidden machinery in the wall which turns the hearthstone on a pivot, and discloses the hollow place below. There is room enough in it for a man to lie easily at full length. The method of closing the cavity again is equally simple. Place both your hands on the temples of the figure; pull as if you were pulling it towards you—and the hearthstone will revolve into its proper position again."

"You need read no further," said the Countess. "Be careful to remember what you have read."

She put the page of vellum in her writing-desk, locked it, and led the way to the door.

"Come!" she said; "and see what the mocking Frenchman called, 'The beginning of the end.'"

Agnes was barely able to rise from her chair; she trembled from head to foot. Henry gave her his arm to support her. "Fear nothing," he whispered; "I shall be with you."

The Countess proceeded along the westward corridor, and stopped at the door numbered Thirty-eight. This was the room which had been inhabited by Baron Rivar in the old days of the palace; the room situated immediately over the bed-chamber in which Agnes had passed the night. For the last two days it had been empty. The absence of luggage in it when they opened the door, showed that it had not yet been let.

"You see!" said the Countess, pointing to the carved figure at the fireplace; "and you know what to do. Have I deserved that you should temper justice with mercy?" she went on in lower tones. "Give me a few hours more to myself. The Baron wants money—I must get on with my play."

She smiled vacantly, and imitated the action of writing with her right hand as she pronounced the last words. The effort of concentrating her weakened mind on other and less familiar topics than the constant want of money in the Baron's lifetime, and the vague prospect of gain from the still unfinished play, had evidently exhausted her poor reserves of strength. When her request had been granted, she addressed no expressions of gratitude to

Agnes; she only said, "Feel no fear, Miss, of my attempting to escape you. Where you are, there I must be till the end comes."

Her eyes wandered round the room with a last weary and stupefied look. She returned to her writing with slow and feeble steps, like the steps of an old woman.

Chapter XXIV

Henry and Agnes were left alone in the Room of the Caryatides.

The person who had written the description of the palace—probably a poor author or artist—had correctly pointed out the defects of the mantel-piece. Bad taste, exhibiting itself on the most costly and splendid scale, was visible in every part of the work. It was, nevertheless, greatly admired by ignorant travellers of all classes; partly on account of its imposing size, and partly on account of the number of variously-coloured marbles which the sculptor had contrived to introduce into his design. Photographs of the mantel-piece were exhibited in the public rooms, and found a ready sale among English and American visitors to the hotel.

Henry led Agnes to the figure on the left, as they stood facing the empty fire-place. "Shall I try the experiment," he asked, "or will you?" She abruptly drew her arm away from him, and turned back to the door. "I can't even look at it," she said. "That merciless marble face frightens me!"

Henry put his hand on the forehead of the figure. "What is there to alarm you, my dear, in this conventionally classical face?" he asked, jestingly. Before he could press the head inwards, Agnes hurriedly opened the door. "Wait till I am out of the room!" she cried. "The bare idea of what you may find there horrifies me!" She looked back into the room as she crossed the threshold. "I won't leave you altogether," she said, "I will wait outside."

She closed the door. Left by himself, Henry lifted his hand once more to the marble forehead of the figure.

For the second time, he was checked on the point of setting the machinery of the hiding-place in motion. On this occasion, the interruption came from an outbreak of friendly voices in the corridor. A woman's voice exclaimed, "Dearest Agnes, how glad I am to see you again!" A man's voice followed, offering to introduce some friend to "Miss Lockwood." A third voice (which Henry recognised as the voice of the manager of the hotel) became audible next, directing the housekeeper to show the ladies and gentlemen the vacant apartments at the other end of the corridor. "If more accommodation is wanted," the manager went on, "I have a charming room to let here." He opened the door as he spoke, and found himself face to face with Henry Westwick.

"This is indeed an agreeable surprise, sir!" said the manager cheerfully. "You are admiring our famous chimney-piece, I see. May I ask, Mr. Westwick, how you find yourself in the hotel, this time? Have the supernatural influences affected your appetite again?"

"The supernatural influences have spared me, this time," Henry answered. "Perhaps you may yet find that they have affected some other member of the family." He spoke gravely, resenting the familiar tone in which the manager had referred to his previous visit to the hotel. "Have you just returned?" he asked, by way of changing the topic.

"Just this minute, sir. I had the honour of travelling in the same train with friends of yours who have arrived at the hotel—Mr. and Mrs. Arthur Barville, and their travelling companions. Miss Lockwood is with them, looking at the rooms. They will be here before long, if they find it convenient to have an extra room at their disposal."

This announcement decided Henry on exploring the hiding-place before the interruption occurred. It had crossed his mind, when Agnes left him, that he ought perhaps to have a witness, in the not very probable event of some alarming discovery taking place. The too-familiar manager, suspecting nothing, was there at his disposal. He turned again to the Caryan figure, maliciously resolving to make the manager his witness.

"I am delighted to hear that our friends have arrived, at last," he said. "Before I shake hands with them, let me ask you a question about this queer work of art here. I see photographs of it downstairs. Are they for sale?"

"Certainly, Mr. Westwick."

"Do you think the chimney-place is as solid as it looks?" Henry proceeded. "When you came in, I was just wondering whether this figure here had not accidentally got loosened from the wall behind it." He laid his hand on the marble forehead, for the third time. "To my eye, it looks a little out of the perpendicular. I almost fancy I could jog the head just now, when I touched it." He pressed the head inwards as he said those words.

A sound of jarring iron was instantly audible behind the wall. The solid hearthstone in front of the fire-place turned slowly at the feet of the two men, and disclosed a dark cavity below. At the same moment, the strange and sickening combination of odours, hitherto associated with the vaults of the old palace and with the bed-chamber beneath, now floated up from the open recess, and filled the room.

The manager started back. "Good God, Mr. Westwick!" he exclaimed, "what does this mean?"

Remembering, not only what his brother Francis had felt in the room beneath, but what the experience of Agnes had been on the previous night, Henry was determined to be on his guard. "I am as much surprised as you are," was his only reply.

"Wait for me one moment, sir," said the manager. "I must stop the ladies and gentlemen outside from coming in."

He hurried away—not forgetting to close the door after him. Henry opened the window, and waited there breathing the purer air. Vague apprehensions of the next discovery to come, filled his mind for the first time. He was doubly resolved, now, not to stir a step in the investigation without a witness.

The manager returned with a wax taper in his hand, which he lighted as soon as he entered the room.

"We need fear no interruption now," he said. "Be so kind, Mr. Westwick, as to hold the light. It is *my* business to find out what this extraordinary discovery means."

Henry held the taper. Looking into the cavity, by the dim and flickering light, they both detected a dark object at the bottom of it. "I think I can reach the thing," the manager remarked, "if I lie down, and put my hand into the hole."

He knelt on the floor—and hesitated. "Might I ask you, sir, to give me my gloves?" he said. "They are in my hat, on the chair behind you."

Henry gave him the gloves. "I don't know what I may be going to take hold of," the manager explained, smiling rather uneasily as he put on his right glove.

He stretched himself at full length on the floor, and passed his right arm into the cavity. "I can't say exactly what I have got hold of," he said. "But I have got it."

Half raising himself, he drew his hand out.

The next instant he started to his feet with a shriek of terror. A human head dropped from his nerveless grasp on the floor, and rolled to Henry's feet. It was the hideous head that Agnes had seen hovering above her, in the vision of the night!

The two men looked at each other, both struck speechless by the same emotion of horror. The manager was the first to control himself. "See to the door, for God's sake!" he said. "Some of the people outside may have heard me."

Henry moved mechanically to the door.

Even when he had his hand on the key, ready to turn it in the lock in case of necessity, he still looked back at the appalling object on the floor. There was no possibility of identifying those decayed and distorted features with any living creature whom he had seen —and yet, he was conscious of feeling a vague and awful doubt which shook him to the soul. The questions which tortured the mind of Agnes, were now *his* questions too. *He* asked himself, "In whose likeness might I have recognised it before the decay set in? The likeness of Ferrari? or the likeness of——?" He paused trembling, as Agnes had paused trembling before him. Agnes! The name, of all women's names the dearest to him, was a terror to him now! What was he to say to her? What might be the consequence if he trusted her with the terrible truth?

No footsteps approached the door; no voices were audible outside. The travellers were still occupied in the rooms at the eastern end of the corridor.

In the brief interval that had passed, the manager had sufficiently recovered himself to be able to think once more of the first and foremost interest of his life—the interest of the hotel.

"If this frightful discovery becomes known," he said, "the closing of the hotel, and the ruin of the Company will be the inevitable results. I feel sure that I can trust your discretion, sir, so far?"

"You can certainly trust me," Henry answered. "But surely discretion has its limits," he added, "after such a discovery as we have made?"

The manager understood that the duty which they owed to the community as honest and law-abiding men, was the duty to which Henry now referred. "I will at once find the means," he said, "of conveying the remains privately out of the house, and I will myself place them in the care of the police-authorities. Will you leave the room with me? or do you not object to keep watch here, and help me when I return?"

While he was speaking, the voices of the travellers made themselves heard again at the end of the corridor. Henry instantly consented to wait in the room. He shrank from facing the inevitable meeting with Agnes if he showed himself in the corridor at that moment.

The manager hastened his departure, in the hope of escaping notice. He was discovered by his guests before he could reach the head of the stairs. Henry heard the voices plainly as he turned the key. While the terrible drama of discovery was in progress on one side of the door, trivial questions about the amusements of Venice and facetious discussions on the relative merits of French and Italian cookery were proceeding on the other. Little by little the sound of the talking grew fainter. The visitors, having arranged their plans of amusement for the day, were on their way out of the hotel. In a minute or two there was silence once more.

Henry turned to the window, thinking to relieve his mind by looking at the bright view over the canal. He soon grew wearied of the familiar scene. The morbid fascination which seems to be exercised by all horrible sights, drew him back again to the ghastly object on the floor.

Dream or reality, how had Agnes survived the sight of it? As the question passed through his mind, he noticed for the first time something lying on the floor near the head. Looking closer, he perceived a thin little plate of gold, with three false teeth attached to it, which had apparently dropped out (loosened by the shock) when the manager let the head fall on the floor.

The importance of this discovery, and the necessity of not too readily communicating it to others, instantly struck Henry. Here surely was a chance—if any chance remained—of identifying the shocking relic of humanity which lay before him, the dumb witness of a crime! Acting on this idea, he took possession of the teeth, purposing to use them as a last means of inquiry when other attempts at investigation had been tried and had failed.

He went back again to the window: the solitude of the room began to weigh on his spirits. As he looked out again at the view, there was a soft knock at the door. He hastened to open it—and checked himself in the act. A doubt occurred to him. Was it the manager who had knocked? He called out, "Who is there?"

The voice of Agnes answered him. "Have you anything to tell me, Henry?"

He was hardly able to reply. "Not just now," he said, confusedly. "Forgive me if I don't open the door. I will speak to you a little later."

The sweet voice made itself heard again, pleading with him piteously. "Don't leave me alone, Henry! I can't go back to the happy people downstairs."

How could he resist that appeal? He heard her sigh—he heard the rustling of her dress as she moved away in despair. The very thing that he had shrunk from doing but a few minutes since was the thing that he did now! He joined Agnes in the corridor. She turned as she heard him, and pointed trembling in the direction of the closed room. "Is it so terrible as that?" she asked faintly.

He put his arm round her to support her. A thought came to him as he looked at her, waiting in doubt and fear for his reply. "You shall decide the question for yourself," he said, "if you will first put on your hat and cloak, and come out with me."

She was naturally surprised. "Can you tell me your object in going out?" she asked.

He owned what his object was unreservedly. "I want, before all things," he said, "to satisfy your mind and mine on the subject of Montbarry's death. I am going to take you to the doctor who attended him in his illness, and to the consul who followed him to the grave."

Her eyes rested on Henry gratefully. "Oh, how well you understand me!" she said. The manager joined them at the same moment, on his way up the stairs. Henry gave him the key of the room, and then called to the servants in the hall to have a gondola ready at the steps. "Are you leaving the hotel?" the manager asked. "In search of evidence," Henry whispered, pointing to the key. "If the authorities want me, I shall be back in an hour."

Chapter XXV

The day had advanced to evening. Lord Montbarry and the bridal party had gone to the opera. Agnes alone, pleading the excuse of fatigue, remained at the hotel. Having kept up appearances by accompanying his friends to the theatre, Henry Westwick slipped away after the first act and joined Agnes in the drawing-room.

"Have you thought of what I said to you earlier in the day?" he asked, taking a chair at her side. "Do you agree with me that the one dreadful doubt which oppressed us both is at least set at rest?"

Agnes shook her head sadly. "I wish I could agree with you, Henry—I wish I could honestly say that my mind is at ease."

The answer would have discouraged most men. Henry's patience (where Agnes was concerned) was equal to any demands on it.

"If you will only look back at the events of the day," he said, "you must surely admit that we have not been completely baffled. Remember how Doctor Bruno disposed of our doubts—'After thirty years of medical practice, do you think I am likely to mistake the symptoms of death by bronchitis?' If ever there was an unanswerable question, there it is! Was the consul's testimony doubtful in any part of it? He called at the palace to offer his services, after hearing of Lord Montbarry's death; he arrived at the time when the coffin was in the house; he himself saw the corpse placed in it, and the lid screwed down. The evidence of the priest was equally beyond dispute. He remained in the room with the coffin, reciting the prayers for the dead, until the funeral left the palace. Bear all these statements in mind, Agnes; and how can you deny that the question of Montbarry's death and burial is a question set at rest? We have really but one doubt left: we have still to ask ourselves whether the remains which I discovered are the remains of the lost courier or not. There is the case as I understand it. Have I stated it fairly?"

Agnes could not deny that he had stated it fairly.

"Then what prevents you from experiencing the same sense of relief that I feel?" Henry asked.

"What I saw last night prevents me," Agnes answered. "When we spoke of this subject, after our inquiries were over, you reproached me with taking, what you called, the superstitious view. I don't quite admit that—but I do acknowledge that I should find the superstitious view intelligible if I heard it expressed by some other person. Remembering what your brother and I once were to each other in the bygone time, I can understand the apparition making itself visible to Me, to claim the mercy of Christian burial, and the vengeance due to a crime. I can even perceive some faint possibility of truth in the explanation which you described as the mesmeric theory—that what I saw might be the result of magnetic influence communicated to me, as I lay between the remains of the murdered husband above me and the guilty wife suffering the tortures of remorse at my bedside. But what I do *not* understand is, that I should have passed through that dreadful ordeal; having no previous knowledge of the murdered man in his lifetime, or only knowing him (if you suppose that I saw the apparition of Ferrari) through the interest which I took in his wife. I can't dispute your reasoning, Henry. But I feel in my heart of hearts that you are deceived. Nothing will shake my belief that we are still as far from having discovered the dreadful truth as ever."

Henry made no further attempt to dispute with her. She had impressed him with a certain reluctant respect for her own opinion in spite of himself.

"Have you thought of any better way of arriving at the truth?" he asked. "Who is to help us? No doubt there is the Countess, who has the clue of the mystery in her own hands. But, in the present state of her mind, is her testimony to be trusted—even if she were willing to speak? Judging by my own experience, I should say decidedly not."

"You don't mean that you have seen her again?" Agnes eagerly interposed.

"Yes, I had half an hour to spare before dinner; and I disturbed her once more over her endless writing."

"And you told her what you found when you opened the hiding-place?"

"Of course I did!" Henry replied. "I said, in so many words, that I held her responsible for the discovery, and that I expected her to reveal the whole truth. She went on with her writing—as if

I had spoken in an unknown tongue! I was equally obstinate, on my side. I told her plainly that the head had been placed under the care of the police, and that the manager and I had signed our declarations and given our evidence. She paid not the slightest heed to me. By way of tempting her to speak, I added that the whole investigation was to be kept a secret, and that she might depend on my discretion. For the moment I thought I had succeeded. She looked up from her writing with a passing flash of curiosity, and said, 'What are they going to do with it?'—meaning, I suppose, the head. I answered that it was to be privately buried, after photographs of it had first been taken. I even went the length of communicating the opinion of the surgeon.consulted, that some chemical means of arresting decomposition had been used, and had only partially succeeded—and I asked her point-blank if the surgeon was right? The trap was not a bad one—but it completely failed. She said in the coolest manner, 'Now you are here, I should like to consult you about my play; I am at a loss for some new incidents.' Mind! there was nothing satirical in this. She was really eager to read her wonderful work to me—evidently supposing that I took a special interest in such things, because my brother is the manager of a theatre! I left her, making the first excuse that occurred to me. So far as I am concerned, I can do nothing with her. But it is possible that *your* influence may succeed with her again, as it has succeeded already. Will you make the attempt, to satisfy your own mind? She is still upstairs; and I am quite ready to accompany you."

Agnes shuddered at the bare suggestion of another interview with the Countess.

"I can't! I daren't!" she exclaimed. "After what has happened in that horrible room, she is more repellent to me than ever. Don't ask me to do it, Henry! Feel my hand—you have turned me as cold as death only with talking of it!"

She was not exaggerating the terror that possessed her. Henry hastened to change the subject.

"Let us talk of something more interesting," he said. "I have a question to ask you about yourself. Am I right in believing that the sooner you get away from Venice the happier you will be?"

"Right?" she repeated, excitedly. "You are more than right! No words can say how I long to be away from this horrible place.

But you know how I am situated—you heard what Lord Montbarry said at dinner-time?"

"Suppose he has altered his plans since dinner-time?" Henry suggested.

Agnes looked surprised. "I thought he had received letters from England which obliged him to leave Venice to-morrow," she said.

"Quite true," Henry admitted. "He had arranged to start for England to-morrow, and to leave you and Lady Montbarry and the children to enjoy your holiday in Venice under my care. Circumstances have occurred, however, which have forced him to alter his plans. He must take you all back with him to-morrow, because I am not able to assume the charge of you. I am obliged to give up my holiday in Italy, and return to England, too."

Agnes looked at him in some little perplexity: she was not quite sure whether she understood him or not. "Are you really obliged to go back?" she asked.

Henry smiled as he answered her. "Keep the secret," he said, "or Montbarry will never forgive me!"

She read the rest in his face. "Oh!" she exclaimed, blushing brightly, "you have not given up your pleasant holiday in Italy on my account?"

"I shall go back with you to England, Agnes. That will be holiday enough for *me*."

She took his hand in an irrepressible outburst of gratitude. "How good you are to me!" she murmured tenderly. "What should I have done in the troubles that have come to me, without your sympathy? I can't tell you, Henry, how I feel your kindness."

She tried impulsively to lift his hand to her lips. He gently stopped her. "Agnes," he said, "are you beginning to understand how truly I love you?"

That simple question found its own way to her heart. She owned the whole truth, without saying a word. She looked at him—and then looked away again.

He drew her to his bosom. "My own darling!" he whispered —and kissed her. Softly and tremulously, the sweet lips lingered, and touched his lips in return. Then her head drooped. She put

her arms round his neck, and hid her face in his bosom. They
spoke no more.

The charmed silence had lasted but a little while, when it
was mercilessly broken by a knock at the door.

Agnes started to her feet. She placed herself at the piano:
the instrument being opposite to the door, it was impossible, when
she seated herself on the music-stool, for any person entering the
room to see her face. Henry called out irritably, "Come in."

The door was not opened. The person on the other side
asked a strange question.

"Is Mr. Henry Westwick alone?"

Agnes instantly recognised the voice of the Countess. She
hurried to a second door, which communicated with one of the
bedrooms. "Don't let her come near me!" she whispered nervously. "Good night, Henry! good night!"

If Henry could, by an effort of will, have transported the
Countess to the uttermost ends of the earth, he would have made
the effort without remorse. As it was, he only repeated, more
irritably than ever, "Come in!"

She entered the room slowly with her everlasting manuscript
in her hand. Her step was unsteady; a dark flush appeared on her
face, in place of its customary pallor; her eyes were bloodshot and
widely dilated. In approaching Henry, she showed a strange in-
capability of calculating her distances—she struck against the table
near which he happened to be sitting. When she spoke, her articu-
lation was confused, and her pronunciation of some of the longer
words was hardly intelligible. Most men would have suspected
her of being under the influence of some intoxicating liquor.
Henry took a truer view—he said, as he placed a chair for her,
"Countess, I am afraid you have been working too hard: you
look as if you wanted rest."

She put her hand to her head. "My invention has gone," she
said. "I can't write my fourth act. It's all a blank—all a blank!"

Henry advised her to wait till the next day. "Go to bed,"
he suggested; "and try to sleep."

She waved her hand impatiently. "I must finish the play,"
she answered. "I only want a hint from you. You must know
something about plays. Your brother has got a theatre. You must
often have heard him talk about fourth and fifth acts—you must

have seen rehearsals, and all the rest of it." She abruptly thrust the manuscript into Henry's hand. "I can't read it to you," she said, "I feel giddy when I look at my own writing. Just run your eye over it, there's a good fellow—and give me a hint."

Henry glanced at the manuscript. He happened to look at the list of the persons of the drama. As he read the list he started and turned abruptly to the Countess, intending to ask her for some explanation. The words were suspended on his lips. It was but too plainly useless to speak to her. Her head lay back on the upper rail of the chair. She seemed to be half asleep already. The flush on her face had deepened: she looked like a woman who was in danger of having a fit.

He rang the bell, and directed the man who answered it to send one of the chambermaids upstairs. His voice seemed to partially rouse the Countess; she opened her eyes in a slow drowsy way. "Have you read it?" she asked.

It was necessary as a mere act of humanity to humour her. "I will read it willingly," said Henry, "if you will go upstairs to bed. You shall hear what I think of it to-morrow morning. Our heads will be clearer, we shall be better able to make the fourth act in the morning."

The chambermaid came in while he was speaking. "I am afraid the lady is ill," Henry whispered. "Take her up to her room." The woman looked at the Countess and whispered back, "Shall we send for a doctor, sir?"

Henry advised taking her upstairs first, and then asking the manager's advice. There was great difficulty in persuading her to rise, and accept the support of the chambermaid's arm. It was only by reiterated promises to read the play that night, and to make the fourth act in the morning, that Henry prevailed on the Countess to return to her room.

Left to himself, he began to feel a certain languid curiosity in relation to the manuscript. He looked over the pages, reading a line here and a line there. Suddenly he changed colour as he read —and looked up from the manuscript like a man bewildered. "Good God! what does this mean?" he said to himself.

His eyes turned nervously to the door by which Agnes had left him. She might return to the drawing-room; she might want to see what the Countess had written. He looked back again at the passage which startled him—considered with himself for a moment—and suddenly and softly left the room.

Chapter XXVI

Entering his own room on the upper floor, Henry placed the manuscript on his table, open at the first leaf. His nerves were unquestionably shaken; his hand trembled as he turned the pages; he started at chance noises on the staircase of the hotel.

The scenario, or outline, of the Countess's play began with no formal prefatory phrases. She presented herself and her work with the easy familiarity of an old friend.

"Allow me, dear Mr. Francis Westwick, to introduce to you the persons in my proposed Play. Behold them, arranged symmetrically in a line.

"My Lord. The Baron. The Courier. The Doctor. The Countess.

"I don't trouble myself, you see, to invent fictitious family names. My characters are sufficiently distinguished by their social titles, and by the striking contrast which they present one with another.

"The First Act opens——

"No! Before I open the First Act, I must announce, in justice to myself, that this Play is entirely the work of my own invention. I scorn to borrow from actual events; and, what is more extraordinary still, I have not stolen one of my ideas from the Modern French drama. As the manager of an English theatre, you will naturally refuse to believe this. It doesn't matter. Nothing matters—except the opening of my first act.

"We are at Homburg, in the famous Salon d'Or, at the height of the season. The Countess (exquisitely dressed) is seated at the green table. Strangers of all nations are standing behind the players, venturing their money or only looking on. My Lord is among the strangers. He is struck by the Countess's personal appearance in which beauties and defects are fantastically mingled in the most attractive manner. He watches the Countess's game, and places his money where he sees her deposit her own little stake. She looks round at him, and says, 'Don't trust to my colour; I have been unlucky the whole evening. Place your stake on the other colour, and you may have a chance of winning.' My Lord (a true Englishman) blushes, bows, and obeys. The Countess proves a true prophet. She loses again. My Lord wins twice the sum that he has risked.

"The Countess rises from the table. She has no more money, and she offers my Lord her chair.

"Instead of taking it, he politely places his winnings in her hand, and begs her to accept the loan as a favour to himself. The Countess stakes again, and loses again. My Lord smiles superbly, and presses a second loan on her. From that moment her luck turns. She wins, and wins largely. Her brother, the Baron, trying his fortune in another room, hears of what is going on, and joins my Lord and the Countess.

"Pay attention, if you please, to the Baron. He is delineated as a remarkable and interesting character.

"This noble person has begun life with a single-minded devotion to the science of experimental chemistry, very surprising in a young and handsome man with a brilliant future before him. A profound knowledge of the occult sciences has persuaded the Baron that it is possible to solve the famous problem called the 'Philosopher's Stone.' His own pecuniary resources have long since been exhausted by his costly experiment. His sister has next supplied him with the small fortune at her disposal; reserving only the family jewels, placed in the charge of her banker and friend at Frankfort. The Countess's fortune also being swallowed up, the Baron has in a fatal moment sought for new supplies at the gaming table. He proves, at starting on his perilous career, to be a favourite of fortune; wins largely, and alas! profanes his noble enthusiasm for science by yielding his soul to the all-debasing passion of the gamester.

"At the period of the Play the Baron's good fortune has deserted him. He sees his way to a crowning experiment in the fatal search after the secret of transmuting the baser metals into gold. But how is he to pay the preliminary expenses? Destiny like a mocking echo, answers, How?

"Will his sister's winnings (with my Lord's money) prove large enough to help him? Eager for this result, he gives the Countess his advice how to play. From that disastrous moment the infection of his own adverse fortune spreads to his sister. She loses again, and again—loses to the last farthing.

"The amiable and wealthy Lord offers a third loan; but the scrupulous Countess positively refuses to take it. On leaving the table, she presents her brother to my Lord. The gentlemen fall into pleasant talk. My Lord asks leave to pay his respects to the Countess, the next morning, at her hotel. The Baron hospitably invites him to breakfast. My Lord accepts, with a last admiring glance at the Countess which does not escape her brother's observation, and takes his leave for the night.

"Alone with his sister, the Baron speaks out plainly. 'Our affairs,' he says, 'are in a desperate condition, and must find a desperate remedy. Wait for me here while I make inquiries about my Lord. You have evidently produced a strong impression on him. If we can turn that impression into money, no matter at what sacrifice, the thing must be done.'

"The Countess now occupies the stage alone, and indulges in a soliloquy which develops her character.

"It is at once a dangerous and attractive character. Immense capacities for good are implanted in her nature, side by side with equally remarkable capacities for evil. It rests with circumstances to develop either the one or the other. Being a person who produces a sensation wherever she goes, this noble lady is naturally made the subject of all sorts of scandalous reports. To one of these reports (which falsely and abominably points to the Baron as her lover instead of her brother) she now refers with just indignation. She has just expressed her desire to leave Homburg, as the place in which the vile calumny first took its rise, when the Baron returns, overhears her last words, and says to her, 'Yes, leave Homburg by all means; provided you leave it in the character of my Lord's betrothed wife!'

"The Countess is startled and shocked. She protests that she does not reciprocate my Lord's admiration for her. She even goes the length of refusing to see him again. The Baron answers, 'I must positively have command of money. Take your choice, between marrying my Lord's income, in the interest of my grand discovery—or leave me to sell myself and my title to the first rich woman of low degree who is ready to buy me.'

"The Countess listens in surprise and dismay. Is it possible that the Baron is in earnest? He is horribly in earnest. 'The woman who will buy me,' he says, 'is in the next room to us at this moment. She is the wealthy widow of a Jewish usurer. She has the money I want to reach the solution of the great problem. I have only to be that woman's husband, and to make myself master of untold millions of gold. Take five minutes to consider what I have said to you, and tell me on my return which of us is to marry for the money I want, you or I.'

"As he turns away, the Countess stops him.

"All the noblest sentiments in her nature are exalted to the highest pitch. 'Where is the true woman,' she exclaims, 'who wants time to consummate the sacrifice of herself, when the man to whom she is devoted demands it?' She does not want five minutes —she does not want five seconds—she holds out her hand to him, and she says, 'Sacrifice me on the altar of your glory! Take as stepping-stones on the way to your triumph, my love, my liberty, and my life!'

"On this grand situation the curtain falls. Judging by my first act, Mr. Westwick, tell me truly, and don't be afraid of turning my head:—Am I not capable of writing a good play?"

Henry paused between the First and Second Acts; reflecting, not on the merits of the Play, but on the strange resemblance which the incidents so far presented to the incidents that had attended the disastrous marriage of the first Lord Montbarry.

Was it possible that the Countess, in the present condition of her mind, supposed herself to be exercising her invention when she was only exercising her memory?

The question involved consideration too serious to be made the subject of a hasty decision. Reserving his opinion, Henry turned the page, and devoted himself to the reading of the next act. The manuscript proceeded as follows:——

"The Second Act opens at Venice. An interval of four months has elapsed since the date of the scene at the gambling table. The action now takes place in the reception-room of one of the Venetian palaces.

"The Baron is discovered, alone, on the stage. He reverts to the events which have happened since the close of the First Act.

The Countess has sacrificed herself; the mercenary marriage has taken place—but not without obstacles, caused by difference of opinion on the question of marriage settlements.

"Private inquiries, instituted in England, have informed the Baron that my Lord's income is derived chiefly from what is called entailed property. In case of accidents, he is surely bound to do something for his bride? Let him, for example, insure his life for a sum proposed by the Baron, and let him so settle the money that his widow shall have it, if he dies first.

"My Lord hesitates. The Baron wastes no time in useless discussion. 'Let us by all means' (he says) 'consider the marriage as broken off.' My Lord shifts his ground, and pleads for a smaller sum than the one proposed. The Baron briefly replies, 'I never bargain.' My Lord is in love; the natural result follows—he gives way.

"So far, the Baron has no cause to complain. But my Lord's turn comes, when the marriage has been celebrated, and when the honeymoon is over. The Baron has joined the married pair at a palace which they have hired in Venice. He is still bent on solving the problem of the 'Philosopher's Stone.' His laboratory is set up in the vaults beneath the palace—so that smells from chemical experiments may not incommode the Countess, in the higher regions of the house. The one obstacle in the way of his grand discovery is, as usual, the want of money. His position at the present time has become truly critical. He owes debts of honour to gentlemen in his own rank of life, which must positively be paid; and he proposes, in his own friendly manner, to borrow the money of my Lord. My Lord positively refuses, in the rudest terms. The Baron applies to his sister to exercise her conjugal influence. She can only answer that her noble husband (being no longer distractedly in love with her) now appears in his true character, as one of the meanest men living. The sacrifice of the marriage has been made, and has already proved useless.

"Such is the state of affairs at the opening of the second act.

"The entrance of the Countess suddenly disturbs the Baron's reflections. She is in a state bordering on frenzy. Incoherent expressions of rage burst from her lips: it is some time before she can sufficiently control herself to speak plainly. She has been doubly insulted—first, by a menial person in her employment;

secondly, by her husband. Her maid, an English woman, has declared that she will serve the Countess no longer. She will give up her wages, and return at once to England. Being asked her reason for this strange proceeding, she insolently hints that the Countess's service is no service for an honest woman, since the Baron has entered the house. The Countess does, what any lady in her position would do; she indignantly dismisses the wretch on the spot.

"My Lord, hearing his wife's voice raised in anger, leaves the study in which he is accustomed to shut himself up over his books, and asks what this disturbance means. The Countess informs him of the outrageous language and conduct of her maid. My Lord not only declares his entire approval of the woman's conduct; but expresses his own abominable doubts of his wife's fidelity, in language of such horrible brutality that no lady could pollute her lips by repeating it. 'If I had been a man,' the Countess says: 'and if I had had a weapon in my hand, I would have struck him dead at my feet!'

"The Baron, listening silently so far, now speaks. 'Permit me to finish the sentence for you,' he says. 'You would have struck your husband dead at your feet; and by that rash act, you would have deprived yourself of the insurance money settled on the widow—the very money which is wanted to relieve your brother from the unendurable pecuniary position which he now occupies!'

"The Countess gravely reminds the Baron that this is no joking matter. After what my Lord has said to her, she has little doubt that he will communicate his infamous suspicions to his lawyers in England. If nothing is done to prevent it, she may be divorced and disgraced, and thrown on the world, with no resource but the sale of her jewels to keep her from starving.

"At this moment, the Courier who has been engaged to travel with my Lord from England, crosses the stage with a letter to take to the post. The Countess stops him, and asks to look at the address on the letter. She takes it from him for a moment, and shows it to her brother. The handwriting is my Lord's; and the letter is directed to his lawyers in London.

"The Courier proceeds to the post-office. The Baron and the Countess look at each other in silence. No words are needed. They thoroughly understand the position in which they are placed; they clearly see the terrible remedy for it. What is the plain alternative before them? Disgrace and ruin—or my Lord's death!

"The Baron walks backwards and forwards in great agitation, talking to himself. The Countess hears fragments of what he is saying. He speaks of my Lord's constitution probably weakened in India—of a cold which my Lord has caught two or three days since—of the remarkable manner in which such slight things as colds sometimes end in serious illness and death.

"He observes that the Countess is listening to him, and asks if she has anything to propose. She is a woman who, with many defects, has the great merit of speaking out. 'Is there no such thing as a serious illness,' she asks, 'corked up in one of those bottles of yours in the vaults downstairs?'

"The Baron answers by gravely shaking his head. What is he afraid of?—a possible examination of the body after death? No; he can set any post-mortem examination at defiance. It is the process of administering the poison that he dreads. A man so distinguished as my Lord cannot be taken seriously ill without medical attendance. Where there is a Doctor there is always danger of discovery. Then, again, there is the Courier, faithful to my Lord as long as my Lord pays him. Even if the Doctor sees nothing suspicious, the Courier may discover something. The poison, to do its work with the necessary secrecy, must be repeatedly administered in graduated doses. One trifling miscalculation or mistake may rouse suspicion. The insurance office may hear of it, and may refuse to pay the money. As things are, the Baron will not risk it, and will not allow his sister to risk it in his place.

"My Lord himself is the next character who appears. He has repeatedly rung for the Courier, and the bell has not been answered. 'What does this insolence mean?'

"The Countess (speaking with quiet dignity—for why should her infamous husband have the satisfaction of knowing how deeply he has wounded her?) reminds my Lord that the Courier has gone to the post. My Lord asks suspiciously if she has looked at the letter. The Countess informs him coldly that she has no curiosity about his letters. Referring to the cold from which he is suffering, she inquires if he thinks of consulting a medical man. My Lord answers roughly that he is quite old enough to be capable of doctoring himself.

"As he makes this reply, the Courier appears, returning from the post. My Lord gives him orders to go out again and buy some lemons. He proposes to try hot lemonade as a means of inducing perspiration in bed. In that way he has formerly cured colds, and in that way he will cure the cold from which he is suffering now.

"The Courier obeys in silence. Judging by appearances he goes very reluctantly on this second errand.

"My Lord turns to the Baron (who thus far has taken no part in the conversation) and asks him, in a sneering tone, how much longer he proposes to prolong his stay in Venice. The Baron answers quietly, 'Let us speak plainly to one another, my Lord. If you wish me to leave your house, you have only to say the word, and I go.' My Lord turns to his wife, and asks if she can support the calamity of her brother's absence—laying a grossly insulting emphasis on the word 'brother.' The Countess preserves her impenetrable composure; nothing in her betrays the deadly hatred with which she regards the titled ruffian who has insulted her. 'You are master in this house, my Lord,' is all she says. 'Do as you please.'

"My Lord looks at his wife; looks at the Baron—and suddenly alters his tone. Does he perceive in the composure of the Countess and her brother something lurking under the surface that threatens him? This is at least certain, he makes a clumsy apology for the language that he has used. (Abject wretch!)

"My Lord's excuses are interrupted by the return of the Courier with the lemons and hot water.

"The Countess observes for the first time that the man looks ill. His hands tremble as he places the tray on the table. My Lord orders his Courier to follow him and make the lemonade in the bedroom. The Countess remarks, that the Courier seems hardly capable of obeying his orders. Hearing this, the man admits that he is ill. He, too, is suffering from a cold; he has been kept waiting in a draught at the shop where he bought the lemons; he feels alternately hot and cold, and he begs permission to lie down for a little while on his bed.

"Feeling her humanity appealed to, the Countess volunteers to make the lemonade herself. My Lord takes the Courier by the arm, leads him aside, and whispers these words to him, 'Watch her, and see that she puts nothing into the lemonade; then bring it to me with your own hands; and, then, go to bed, if you like.'

"Without a word more to his wife, or to the Baron, my Lord leaves the room.

"The Countess makes the lemonade, and the Courier takes it to his master.

"Returning, on the way to his own room, he is so weak, and feels, he says, so giddy, that he is obliged to support himself by the backs of the chairs as he passes them. The Baron, always considerate to persons of low degree, offers his arm. 'I am afraid, my poor fellow,' he says, 'that you are really ill.' The Courier makes this extraordinary answer: 'It's all over with me, Sir; I have caught my death.'

"The Countess is naturally startled. 'You are not an old man,' she says, trying to rouse the Courier's spirits. 'At your age, catching cold doesn't surely mean catching your death?' The Courier fixes his eyes despairingly on the Countess.

" 'My lungs are weak, my Lady,' he says, 'I have already had two attacks of bronchitis. The second time, a great physician joined my own Doctor in attendance on me. He considered my recovery almost in the light of a miracle. "Take care of yourself," he said. "If you have a third attack of bronchitis, as certainly as two and two make four, you will be a dead man." I feel the same inward shivering, my Lady, that I felt on those two former occasions—and I tell you again, I have caught my death in Venice.'

"Speaking some comforting words, the Baron leads him to his room. The Countess is left alone on the stage.

"She seats herself, and looks towards the door by which the Courier has been led out. 'Ah! my poor fellow,' she says, 'if you could only change constitutions with my Lord, what a happy result would follow for the Baron and for me! If *you* could only get cured of a trumpery cold with a little hot lemonade, and if *he* could only catch his death in your place——!'

"She suddenly pauses—considers for awhile—and springs to her feet, with a cry of triumphant surprise; the wonderful, the unparalleled idea has crossed her mind like a flash of lightning. Make the two men change names and places; and the deed is done! Where are the obstacles? Remove my Lord (by fair means or foul) from his room; and keep him secretly prisoner in the palace, to live or die as future necessity may determine. Place the Courier in the vacant bed, and call in the doctor to see him—ill, in my Lord's character, and (if he dies) dying under my Lord's name."

The manuscript dropped from Henry's hands. A sickening sense of horror overpowered him. The question which had occurred to his mind at the close of the First Act of the Play assumed a new and terrible interest now. As far as the scene of the Countess's soliloquy, the incidents of the Second Act had reflected the events of his late brother's life as faithfully as the incidents of the First Act. Was the monstrous plot, revealed in the lines which he had just read, the offspring of the Countess's morbid imagination? or had she, in this case also, deluded herself with the idea that she was inventing when she was really writing under the influence of her own guilty remembrance of the past? If the latter interpretation were the true one, he had just read the narrative of the contemplated murder of his brother, planned in cold blood by a woman who was at that moment inhabiting the same house with him. While, to make the fatality complete, Agnes herself had innocently provided the conspirators with the one man who was fitted to be the passive agent of their crime.

Even the bare doubt that it might be so, was more than he could endure. He left his room; resolved to force the truth out of the Countess, or to denounce her before the authorities as a murderess at large.

Arrived at her door, he was met by a person just leaving the room. The person was the manager. He was hardly recognisable; he looked and spoke like a man in a state of desperation.

"Oh, go in if you like!" he said to Henry. "Mark this, sir! I am not a superstitious man; but I do begin to believe that crimes carry their own curse with them. This hotel is under a curse. What happens in the morning? We discover a crime committed in the old days of the palace. The night comes, and brings another dreadful event with it—a death; a sudden and shocking death, in the house. Go in, and see for yourself! I shall resign my situation, Mr. Westwick; I can't contend with fatalities that pursue me here!"

Henry entered the room.

The Countess was stretched on her bed. The doctor on one side and the chambermaid on the other, were standing looking at her. From time to time, she drew a heavy stertorous breath, like a person oppressed in sleeping. "Is she likely to die?" Henry asked.

"She is dead," the doctor answered. "Dead of the rupture of a blood-vessel on the brain. Those sounds that you hear are purely mechanical—they may go on for hours."

Henry looked at the chambermaid. She had little to tell. The Countess had refused to go to bed, and had placed herself at her desk to proceed with her writing. Finding it useless to remonstrate with her, the maid had left the room to speak to the manager. In the shortest time, the doctor was summoned to the hotel, and found the Countess dead on the floor. There was this to tell—and no more.

Looking at the writing-table as he went out, Henry saw the sheet of paper on which the Countess had traced her last lines of writing. The characters were almost illegible. Henry could just distinguish the words, "First Act," and "Persons of the Drama." The lost wretch had been thinking of her Play to the last, and had begun it all over again!

Chapter XXVII

Henry returned to his room.

His first impulse was to throw aside the manuscript, and never to look at it again. The one chance of relieving his mind from the dreadful uncertainty that oppressed it, by obtaining positive evidence of the truth, was a chance annihilated by the Countess's death. What good purpose could be served, what relief could he anticipate, if he read more?

He walked up and down the room. After an interval, his thoughts took a new direction; the question of the manuscript presented itself under another point of view. Thus far, his reading had only informed him that the conspiracy had been planned. How did he know that the plan had been put in execution?

The manuscript lay just before him on the floor. He hesitated —then picked it up; and, returning to the table, read on as follows, from the point at which he had left off:

"While the Countess is still absorbed in the bold yet simple combination of circumstances which she has discovered, the Baron returns. He takes a serious view of the case of the Courier; it may be necessary, he thinks, to send for medical advice. No servant is left in the palace, now the English maid has taken her departure. The Baron himself must fetch the doctor, if the doctor is really needed.

" 'Let us have medical help, by all means,' his sister replies. 'But wait and hear something that I have to say to you first.' She then electrifies the Baron by communicating her idea to him. What danger of discovery have they to dread? My Lord's life in Venice has been a life of absolute seclusion: nobody but his banker knows him, even by personal appearance. He has presented his letter of credit as a perfect stranger; and he and his banker have never seen each other since that first visit. He has given no parties, and gone to no parties. On the few occasions when he has hired a gondola or taken a walk, he has always been alone. Thanks to the atrocious suspicion which makes him ashamed of being seen with his wife, he has led the very life which makes the proposed enterprise easy of accomplishment.

"The cautious Baron listens—but gives no positive opinion as yet. 'See what you can do with the Courier,' he says; 'and I will decide when I hear the result. One valuable hint I may give you before you go. Your man is easily tempted by money—if you only offer him enough. The other day I asked him, in jest, what he would do for a thousand pounds. He answered, "Anything." Bear that in mind; and offer your highest bid without bargaining.'

"The scene changes to the Courier's room, and shows the poor wretch with a photographic portrait of his wife in his hand, crying. The Countess enters.

"She wisely begins by sympathising with her contemplated accomplice. He is duly grateful; he confides his sorrows to his gracious mistress. Now that he believes himself to be on his death-bed, he feels remorse for his neglectful treatment of his wife. He could resign himself to die; but despair overpowers him when he remembers that he has saved no money, and that he will leave his widow, without resources, to the mercy of the world.

"On this hint the Countess speaks. 'Suppose you were asked to do a perfectly easy thing,' she says; 'and suppose you were rewarded for doing it by a present of a thousand pounds, as a legacy for your widow?'

"The Courier raises himself on his pillow, and looks at the Countess with an expression of incredulous surprise. She can hardly be cruel enough (he thinks) to joke with a man in his miserable plight. Will she say plainly what this perfectly easy thing is, the doing of which will meet with such a magnificent reward?

"The Countess answers that question by confiding her project to the Courier, without the slightest reserve.

"Some minutes of silence follow when she has done. The Courier is not weak enough yet to speak without stopping to think first. Still keeping his eyes on the Countess, he makes a quaintly insolent remark on what he has just heard. 'I have not hitherto been a religious man; but I feel myself on the way to it. Since your ladyship has spoken to me, I believe in the Devil.' It is the Countess's interest to see the humorous side of this confession of faith. She takes no offence. She only says, 'I will give you half an hour by yourself, to think over my proposal. You are in danger of death. Decide, in your wife's interests, whether you will die worth nothing, or die worth a thousand pounds.'

"Left alone, the Courier seriously considers his position—and decides. He rises with difficulty; writes a few lines on a leaf taken from his pocket-book; and with slow and faltering steps leaves the room.

"The Countess, returning at the expiration of the half-hour's interval, finds the room empty. While she is wondering, the Courier opens the door. What has he been doing out of bed? He answers, 'I have been protecting my own life, my Lady, on the bare chance that I may recover from the bronchitis for the third time. If you or the Baron attempt to hurry me out of this world, or to deprive me of my thousand pounds reward, I shall tell the doctor where he will find a few lines of writing, which describe your ladyship's plot. I may not have strength enough, in the case supposed, to betray you by making a complete confession with my own lips; but I can employ my last breath to speak the half-dozen words which will tell the doctor where he is to look. Those words it is needless to add, will be addressed to your ladyship, if I find your engagements towards me faithfully kept.'

"With this audacious preface, he proceeds to state the conditions on which he will play his part in the conspiracy, and die (if he does die) worth a thousand pounds.

"Either the Countess or the Baron are to taste the food and drink brought to his bedside, in his presence, and even the medicines which the doctor may prescribe for him. As for the money, it is to be produced in one bank note, folded in a sheet of paper, on which a line is to be written, dictated by the Courier. The two enclosures are then to be sealed up in an envelope, addressed to his wife, and stamped ready for the post. This done, the letter is to be placed under his pillow; the Baron or the Countess being at liberty to satisfy themselves, day by day at their own time, that the letter remains in its place, with the seal unbroken, as long as the doctor has any hope of his patient's recovery. The last stipulation follows. The Courier has a conscience; and with a view to keeping it easy, insists that he shall be left in ignorance of that part of the plot which relates to the sequestration of my Lord. Not that he cares particularly what becomes of his miserly master—but he does dislike taking other people's responsibilities on his own shoulders.

"These conditions being agreed to, the Countess calls in the Baron, who has been waiting events in the next room.

"He is informed that the Courier has yielded to temptation; but he is still too cautious to make any compromising remarks. Keeping his back turned on the bed, he shows a bottle to the Countess. It is labelled 'Chloroform.' She understands that my Lord is to be removed from his room in a convenient state of insensibility. In what part of the palace is he to be hidden? As they open the door to go out, the Countess whispers that question to the Baron. The Baron whispers back, 'In the vaults!' On those words, the curtain falls."

Chapter XXVIII

So the Second Act ended.

Turning to the Third Act, Henry looked wearily at the pages as he let them slip through his fingers. Both in mind and body, he began to feel the need of repose.

In one important respect, the latter portion of the manuscript differed from the pages which he had just been reading. Signs of an overwrought brain showed themselves, here and there, as the outlines of the Play approached its end. The handwriting grew worse and worse. Some of the longer sentences were left unfinished. In the exchange of dialogue, questions and answers were not always attributed respectively to the right speaker. At certain intervals the writer's failing intelligence seemed to recover itself for awhile; only to relapse again, and to lose the thread of the narrative more hopelessly than ever.

After reading one or two of the more coherent passages, Henry recoiled from the ever-darkening horror of the story. He closed the manuscript, heartsick and exhausted, and threw himself on his bed to rest. The door opened almost at the same moment. Lord Montbarry entered the room.

"We have just returned from the Opera," he said; "and we have heard the news of that miserable woman's death. They say you spoke to her in her last moments; and I want to hear how it happened."

"You shall hear how it happened," Henry answered; "and more than that. You are now the head of the family, Stephen; and I feel bound, in the position which oppresses me, to leave you decide what ought to be done."

With those introductory words, he told his brother how the Countess's Play had come into his hands. "Read the first few pages," he said, "I am anxious to know whether the same impression is produced on both of us."

Before Lord Montbarry had got half way through the First Act, he stopped, and looked at his brother. "What does she mean by boasting of this as her own invention," he asked. "Was she too crazy to remember that these things really happened?"

This was enough for Henry: the same impression had been produced on both of them. "You will do as you please," he said. "But if you will be guided by me, spare yourself the reading of those pages to come, which describe our brother's terrible expiation of his heartless marriage."

"Have *you* read it all, Henry?"

"Not all. I shrank from reading some of the latter part of it. Neither you nor I saw much of our elder brother after we left school; and, for my part, I felt, and never scrupled to express my feeling, that he behaved infamously to Agnes. But when I read that unconscious confession of the murderous conspiracy to which he fell a victim, I remembered, with something like remorse, that the same mother bore us. I have felt for him to-night, what I am ashamed to think I never felt for him before."

Lord Montbarry took his brother's hand.

"You are a good fellow, Henry," he said; "but are you quite sure that you have not been needlessly distressing yourself? Because some of this crazy creature's writing accidentally tells what we know to be the truth, does it follow that all the rest is to be relied on to the end?"

"There is no possible doubt of it," Henry replied.

"No possible doubt?" his brother repeated. "I shall go on with my reading, Henry—and see what justification there may be for that confident conclusion of yours."

He read on steadily, until he had reached the conclusion of the Second Act. Then he looked up.

"Do you really believe that the mutilated remains which you discovered this morning are the remains of our brother?" he asked. "And do you believe it on such evidence as this?"

Henry answered silently, by a sign in the affirmative.

Lord Montbarry checked himself—evidently on the point of entering an indignant protest.

"You acknowledge that you have not read the later scenes of the piece," he said. "Don't be childish, Henry! If you persist in pinning your faith on such stuff as this, the least you can do is to make yourself thoroughly acquainted with it. Will you read the Third Act? No? Then I shall read it to you."

He turned to the Third Act, and ran over those fragmentary passages which were clearly enough expressed to be intelligible to the mind of a stranger.

"Here is a scene in the vaults of the palace," he began. "The victim of the conspiracy is sleeping on his miserable bed; and the Baron and the Countess are considering the position in which they stand. The Countess (as well as I can make it out) has raised the money that is wanted, by borrowing on the security of her jewels at Frankfort; and the Courier upstairs is still declared by the doctor to have a chance of recovery. What are the conspirators to do, if the man does recover? The cautious Baron suggests setting the prisoner free. If he ventures to appeal to the law, it is easy to declare that he is subject to insane delusion, and to call his own wife as a witness. On the other hand, if the Courier dies, how is the sequestrated and unknown nobleman to be put out of the way? Passively, by letting him starve in his prison? No: the Baron is a man of refined tastes; he dislikes needless cruelty. The active policy remains. Say, assassination by the knife of a hired bravo? The Baron objects to trusting an accomplice: also to spending money on any one but himself. Shall they drop their prisoner into the canal? The Baron declines to trust water—water will show him on the surface. Shall they set his bed on fire? An excellent idea; but the smoke might be seen. No: poisoning is no doubt an easier death than he deserves, but there is really no other safe way out of it than to poison him. Is it possible, Henry, that you believe this consultation really took place?"

Henry made no reply. The succession of questions that had just been read to him exactly followed the succession of the dreams that had terrified Mrs. Norbury, on the two nights which she had passed at the hotel. It was useless to point out this coincidence to his brother. He only said, "Go on."

Lord Montbarry turned the pages until he came to the next intelligible passage.

"Here," he proceeded, "is a double scene on the stage—so far as I can understand the sketch of it. The doctor is upstairs, innocently writing the certificate of my Lord's decease, by the dead Courier's bedside. Down in the vault the Baron stands by the corpse of the murdered lord, preparing the strong chemical acids which are to reduce it to a heap of ashes.—Surely, it is not worth while to trouble ourselves with deciphering such melodramatic horrors as these? Let us get on! let us get on!"

He turned the leaves again; attempting vainly to discover the meaning of the confused scenes that followed. On the last page but one he found the last intelligible sentences.

"The Third Act," he said, "seems to be divided into two Parts or Tableaux. I think I can read the writing at the beginning of the Second Part. The Baron and the Countess open the scene. The Baron's hands are mysteriously concealed by gloves. He has reduced the body to ashes, by his own system of cremation, with the exception of the head——"

Henry interrupted his brother there. "Don't read any more!" he exclaimed.

"Let us do the Countess justice," Lord Montbarry persisted. "There are not half a dozen lines more that I can make out. The accidental breaking of his jar of acid has burnt the Baron's hands severely. He is still unable to proceed to the destruction of the head—and the Countess is woman enough (with all her wickedness) to shrink from attempting to take his place—when the first news is received of the coming arrival of the commission of inquiry despatched by the Insurance Offices. The Baron feels no alarm. Inquire as the commission may, it is the natural death of the Courier (in my Lord's character) that they are blindly investigating. The head not being destroyed, the obvious alternative is to hide it—and the Baron is equal to the occasion. His studies in the old library have informed him of a safe place of concealment in the palace. The Countess may recoil from handling the acids, and watching the process of cremation. But she can surely sprinkle a little disinfecting powder——"

"No more!" Henry reiterated. "No more."

"There is no more that can be read, my dear fellow. The last page looks like sheer delirium. She may well have told you that her invention had failed her!"

"Face the truth honestly, Stephen—and save her memory."

Lord Montbarry rose from the table at which he had been sitting, and looked at his brother with pitying eyes.

"Your nerves are out of order, Henry," he said. "And no wonder, after that frightful discovery under the hearthstone. We won't dispute about it; we will wait a day or two until you are quite yourself again. In the meantime, let us understand each other on one point at least. You leave the question of what is to be done with these pages of writing to me, as the head of the family?"

"I do."

Lord Montbarry quietly took up the manuscript, and threw it into the fire. "Let this rubbish be of some use," he said, holding the pages down with the poker. "The room is getting chilly—let the Countess's Play set some of these charred logs flaming again." He waited a little at the fire-place, and returned to his brother. "Now, Henry, I have a last word to say, and then I have done. I am ready to admit that you have stumbled, by an unlucky chance, on the proof of a crime committed in the old days of the palace, nobody knows how long ago. With that one concession, I dispute everything else. Rather than agree in the opinion you have formed, I won't believe anything that has happened. The super-natural influence that some of us felt when we first slept in this hotel—your loss of appetite, our sister's dreadful dreams, the smell that overpowered Francis, and the head that appeared to Agnes —I declare them all to be sheer delusions! I believe in nothing, noth-ing, nothing!" He opened the door to go out, and looked back into the room. "Yes," he resumed, "there is one thing I believe in. My wife has committed a breach of confidence—I believe Agnes will marry you. Good night, Henry. We leave Venice the first thing to-morrow morning."

So Lord Montbarry disposed of the mystery of The Haunted Hotel.

POSTSCRIPT

A last means of deciding the difference of opinion between the two brothers was still in Henry's possession. He had his own idea of the use to which he might put the false teeth, as a means of inquiry, when his fellow-travellers returned to England.

The only surviving depository of the domestic history of the family in past years was Agnes Lockwood's old nurse. Henry took his first opportunity of trying to revive her personal recollections of the deceased Lord Montbarry. But the nurse had never forgiven the great man of the family for his desertion of Agnes: she flatly refused to consult her memory. "Even the bare sight, of my lord, when I last saw him in London," said the old woman, "made my finger-nails itch to set their marks on his face. I was sent on an errand by Miss Agnes, and I met him coming out of the dentist's door—and, thank God, that's the last I saw of him."

Thanks to the nurse's quick temper and quaint way of ex-pressing herself, the object of Henry's inquiries was gained already! He ventured on asking if she had noticed the situation of the house. She had noticed, and still remembered the situation— "did Master Henry suppose she had lost the use of her senses, because she had happened to be nigh on eighty years old?" The same day, he took the false teeth to the dentist, and set all further doubt (if doubt had still been possible) at rest for ever. The teeth had been made for the first Lord Montbarry.

Henry never revealed the existence of this last link in the chain of discovery to any living creature, his brother Stephen included. He carried his terrible secret with him to the grave.

There was one other event in the memorable past on which he preserved the same compassionate silence. Little Mrs. Ferrari never knew that her husband had been—not as she supposed, the Countess's victim—but the Countess's accomplice. She still believed that the late Lord Montbarry had sent her the thousand pound note, and still recoiled from making use of a present, which she persisted in declaring had "the stain of her husband's blood on it." Agnes, with the widow's entire approval, took the money to the Children's Hospital; and spent it in adding to the number of the beds.

In the spring of the new year the marriage took place. At the special request of Agnes, the members of the family were the only persons present at the ceremony: the three children acted as bridesmaids. There was no wedding breakfast—and the honeymoon was spent in the retirement of a cottage on the banks of the Thames.

During the last few days of the residence of the newly-married couple by the riverside, Lady Montbarry's children were invited to enjoy a day's play in the garden. The eldest girl overheard (and reported to her mother) a little conjugal dialogue which touched on the subject of The Haunted Hotel.

"Henry, I want you to give me a kiss."

"There it is, my dear."

"Now, I am your wife, may I speak to you about something?"

"What is it?"

"Something that happened the day before we left Venice. You saw the Countess during the last six hours of her life. Won't you tell me whether she made any confession to you?"

"No conscious confession, Agnes—and therefore no confession that I need distress you by repeating."

"Did she say nothing about what she saw or heard, on that dreadful night in my room?"

"Nothing. We only know by the event, that her mind never recovered from the terror of it."

Agnes was not quite satisfied. The subject troubled her. Even her own brief intercourse with her miserable rival of other days suggested questions that perplexed her. She remembered the Countess's prediction. "You have to bring me to the day of discovery, and to the punishment that is my doom." Had the prediction simply failed like other mortal prophecies? Or had it been fulfilled, on the memorable night when she had seen the apparition, and when she had innocently tempted the Countess to watch her in her room?

Let it, however, be recorded, among the other virtues of Mrs. Henry Westwick, that she never again attempted to persuade her husband into betraying his secrets. Other men's wives, hearing of this extraordinary conduct (and being trained in the modern school of morals and manners) naturally regarded her with compassionate contempt. They always spoke of Agnes, from that time forth, as "rather an old-fashioned person."

Is that all?

That is all.

Is there no explanation of the mystery of The Haunted Hotel?

Ask yourself if there is any explanation of the mystery of your own life and death.—Farewell.

●

The learned Henry Jacob, fellow of Merton College in Oxford, died at Dr. Jacob's, M.D. house in Canterbury. About a week after his death, the doctor being in bed and awake, and the moon shining bright, saw his cousin Henry standing by his bed, in his shirt, with a white cap on his head and his beard-mustachoes turning up, as when he was alive. The doctor pinched himself, and was sure he was awoked: he turned to the other side from him; and, after some time, took courage to turn the other way again towards him, and Henry Jacob stood there still; he should have spoken to him but he did not; for which he has been ever since sorry. About half an hour after, he vanished. Not long after this, the cook-maid, going to the wood-pile to fetch wood to dress supper, saw him standing in his shirt upon the wood-pile. This account I had in a letter from Doctor Jacob, 1673, relating to his life, for Mr. Anthony Wood; which is now in his hands.

—John Aubrey

CLORINDA WALKS IN HEAVEN

It was my desire to include in this volume an example of the sort of story in which a personality walks out of its earthly body and into an afterlife, as a logical progression. The choice came down to that between certain passages from Cabell's *Jurgen* and this story of Coppard's. *Clorinda* won out because it is a self-sufficient short story. But I hope this hint will send some readers back for comparison to the pleasant allegory of Jurgen's visits to Hell and Heaven.— EDITOR.

A. E. Coppard

CLORINDA
WALKS IN
HEAVEN

Miss Smith, Clorinda Smith, desired not to die
on a wet day. Her speculations upon the possibilities of one's
demise were quite ingenuous and had their mirth, but she shrunk
from that figure of her dim little soul—and it was only dimly that
she could figure it at all—approaching the pathways of the Boundless in a damp, bedraggled condition.

"But the rain couldn't harm your spirit," declared her comforting friends.

"Why not?" asked Clorinda, "if there is a ghost of me, why
not a ghost of the rain?"

There were other aspects, delectable and illusive, of this
imagined apotheosis, but Clorinda always hoped—against hope be

it said—that it wouldn't be wet. On three evenings there had been a bow in the sky, and on the day she died rain poured in fury. With a golden key she unlocked the life out of her bosom and moved away without fear, as if a great light had sprung suddenly under her feet in a little dark place, into a region where things became starkly real and one seemed to live like the beams rolling on the tasselled corn in windy acres. There was calmness in those translucent leagues and the undulation amid a vast implacable light until she drifted, like a feather fallen from an unguessed star, into a place which was extraordinarily like the noon-day world, so green and warm was its valley.

A little combe lay between some low hills of turf, and on a green bank beside a few large rocks was a man mending a ladder of white new-shaven willow studded with large brass nails, mending it with hard knocks that sounded clearly. The horizon was terraced only just beyond and above him, for the hills rolled steeply up. Thin pads of wool hung in the arch of the ultimate heavens, but towards the end of the valley the horizon was crowded with clouds torn and disbattled. Two cows, a cow of white and a cow of tan, squatted where one low hill held up, as it were, the sunken limits of the sky. There were larks—in such places the larks sing for ever—and thrushes—the wind vaguely active—seven white ducks—a farm. Each nook was a flounce of blooms and a bower for birds. Passing close to the man—he was sad and preoccupied, dressed in a little blue tunic—she touched his arm as if to enquire a direction, saying "Jacob!"

She did not know what she would have asked of him, but he gave her no heed and she again called to him "Jacob!" He did not seem even to see her, so she went to the large white gates at the end of the valley and approached a railway crossing. She had to wait a long time for trains of a vastness and grandeur were passing, passing without sound. Strange advertisements on the hoardings and curious direction posts gathered some of her attention. She observed that in every possible situation, on any available post or stone, people had carved initials, sometimes a whole name, often with a date, and Clorinda experienced a doubt of the genuineness of some of these, so remote was the antiquity implied. At last, the trains were all gone by, and as the barriers swung back she crossed the permanent way.

There was neither ambiguity in her movements nor surprise in her apprehensions. She just crossed over to a group of twenty or thirty men who moved to welcome her. They were barelegged, sandal-footed, lightly clad in beautiful loose tunics of peacock and cinnamon, which bore not so much the significance of colour as the quality of light; one of them rushed eagerly forward, crying "Clorinda!" offering to her a long coloured scarf. Strangely, as he came closer, he grew less perceivable; Clorinda was aware in a flash that she was viewing him by some other mechanism than that of her two eyes. In a moment he utterly disappeared and she felt herself wrapt into his being, caressed with faint caresses, and troubled with dim faded ecstasies and recognitions not wholly agreeable. The other men stood grouped around them, glancing with half-closed cynical eyes. Those who stood farthest away were more clearly seen: in contiguity a presence could only be divined, resting only—but how admirably!—in the nurture of one's mind.

"What is it?" Clorinda asked: and all the voices replied, "Yes, we know you!"

She felt herself released, and the figure of the man rejoined the waiting group. "I was your husband Reuben," said the first man slowly, and Clorinda, who had been a virgin throughout her short life, exclaimed "Yes, yes, dear Reuben!" with momentary tremors and a queer fugitive drift of doubt. She stood there, a spook of comprehending being, and all the uncharted reefs in the map of her mind were anxiously engaging her. For a time she was absorbed by this new knowledge.

Then another voice spoke:

"I was your husband Raphael!"

"I know, I know," said Clorinda, turning to the speaker, "we lived in Judea."

"And we dwelt in the valley of the Nile," said another, "in the years that are gone."

"And I too . . . and I too . . . and I too," they all clamoured, turning angrily upon themselves.

Clorinda pulled the strange scarf from her shoulders where Reuben had left it, and, handling it so, she became aware of her many fugitive sojournings upon the earth. It seemed that all of her past had become knit in the scarf into a compact pattern of beauty and ugliness of which she was entirely aware, all its mul-

tiplexity being immediately resolved . . . the habitations with
cave men, and the lesser human unit of the lesser later day. Pata-
gonian, Indian, Cossack, Polynesian, Jew . . . of such stuff the
pattern was intimately woven, and there were little plangent
perfect moments of the past that fell into order in the web.
Clorinda watching the great seabird with pink feet louting above
the billows that roared upon Iceland, or Clorinda hanging her
girdle upon the ebony hooks of the image of Tanteelee. She had
taken voyaging drafts upon the whole world, cataract jungle and
desert, ingle and pool and strand, ringing the changes upon a whole
gamut of masculine endeavour . . . from a prophet to a haber-
dasher. She could feel each little life lying now as in a sarsenet
of cameos upon her visible breasts: thereby for these . . . these
men . . . she was draped in an eternal wonder. But she could
not recall any image of her past life in *these* realms, save only
that her scarf was given back to her on every return by a man
of these men.

She could remember with humility her transient passions
for them all. None, not one, had ever given her the measure of
her own desire, a strong harsh flame that fashioned and tempered
its own body; nothing but a nebulous glow that was riven into
embers before its beam had sweetened into pride. She had gone
from them childless always and much as a little child.

From the crowd of quarrelling ghosts a new figure detached
itself, and in its approach it subdued that vague vanishing which
had been so perplexing to Clorinda. Out of the crowd it slipped,
and loomed lovingly beside her, took up her thought and the interrogation that came into her mind.

"No," it said gravely, "there is none greater than these. The
ultimate reaches of man's mind produce nothing but images of
men."

"But," said Clorinda, "do you mean that our ideals, previsions
of a vita-nuova . . ."

"Just so," it continued, "a mere intoxication. Even here you
cannot escape the singular dower of dreams . . . you can be
drunk with dreams more easily and more permanently than with
drugs."

The group of husbands had ceased their quarrelling to listen;

Clorinda swept them with her glances thoughtfully and doubt-fully.

"Could mankind be so poor," the angel resumed, "as poor as these, if it housed something greater than itself?"

With a groan the group of outworn husbands drew away. Clorinda turned to her companion with disappointment and some dismay . . . "I hardly understand yet . . . is this all then just . . ."

"Yes," it replied, "just the ghost of the world."

She turned unhappily and looked back across the gateway into the fair combe with its cattle, its fine grass, and the man working diligently therein. A sense of bleak loneliness began to possess her; here, then, was no difference save that there were no correlations, no consequences; nothing had any effect except to produce the ghost of a ghost. There was already in the hinterland of her apprehensions a ghost, a ghost of her new ghostship; she was to be followed by herself, pursued by figures of her own ceaseless being!

She looked at the one by her side: "Who are you?" she asked, and at the question the group of men drew again very close to them.

"I am your unrealized desire," it said: "Did you think that the dignity of virginhood, rarely and deliberately chosen, could be so brief and barren? Why, that pure idea was my own immaculate birth, and I was born, the living mate of you."

The hungry-eyed men shouted with laughter.

"Go away!" screamed Clorinda to them; "I do not want you."

Although they went she could hear the echoes of their sneer-ing as she took the arm of her new lover. "Let us go," she said, pointing to the man in the combe, "and speak to him." As they approached the man he lifted his ladder hugely in the air and dashed it to the ground so passionately that it broke.

"Angry man! angry man!" mocked Clorinda. He turned towards her fiercely. Clorinda began to fear him; the muscles and knots of his limbs were uncouth like the gnarl of old trees; she made a little pretence of no more observing him.

"Now what is it like," said she jocularly to the angel at her side, and speaking of her old home, "what is it like now at Weston-super-Mare?"

At that foolish question the man with the ladder reached forth an ugly hand and twitched the scarf from her shoulders.

It cannot now be told to what remoteness she had come, or on what roads her undirected feet had travelled there, but certain it is that in that moment she was gone. . . . Why, where, or how cannot be established: whether she was swung in a blast of annihilation into the uttermost gulfs, or withdrawn for her beauty into that mysterious Nox, into some passionate communion with the eternal husbands, or into some eternal combat with their passionate other wives . . . from our scrutiny at least she passed for ever.

It is true there was a beautiful woman of this name who lay for a month in a deep trance in the West of England. On her recovery she was balladed about in the newspapers and upon the halls for quite a time, and indeed her notoriety brought requests for her autograph from all parts of the world, and an offer of marriage from a Quaker potato merchant. But she tenderly refused him and became one of those faded grey old maids who wear their virginity like antiquated armour.

●

PUCK. My fairy lord, this must be done with haste,
For night's swift dragons cut the clouds full fast,
And yonder shines Aurora's harbinger;
At whose approach, ghosts, wandering here and there,
Troop home to churchyards: damned spirits all,
That in cross-ways and floods have burial,
Already to their wormy beds are gone;
For fear lest day should look their shames upon,
They wilfully themselves exile from light,
And must for aye consort with black-brow'd night.

—MIDSUMMER NIGHT'S DREAM

●

THEREFORE, for spirits, I am so far from denying their existence, that I could easily believe, that not only whole countries, but particular persons have their tutelary and guardian angels . . . for there is in this universe a stair, or manifest scale of creatures, rising not disorderly, or in confusion, but with a comely method and proportion. Between creatures of mere existence and things of life, there is a large disproportion of nature; between plants and animals and creatures of sense, a wider difference; between them and man, a far greater: and if the proportion hold on, between man and angels there should be yet a greater.

—RELIGIO MEDICI

BEOWULF: THE GRENDEL EPISODE

With the possible exception of a few lyrics, *Beowulf* is the earliest work of literature written in the language that became English. Part of it is a ghost story, and I have tried to separate that part from the rest. In doing so, it has been necessary not only to omit the earlier and later matter, but to cut a number of passages within the episode itself that are pertinent to the story as a whole but not to the particular case of Grendel. Such surgery I regard with a proper horror, but there would have been no justification for including all of *Beowulf* in this book, as the omitted matter is twice as long as the part here presented. *Beowulf* is of course in verse. The modern verse versions, which try to reflect the original meter and alliteration, are rather hard to read. I have consequently chosen the most readable prose version I know of, and am particularly fortunate in having this sample to present in advance of the publication of the translation as a whole. I am much indebted to the translator for permitting this unusual procedure, and take this occasion for public assurance that the copyright automatically obtained herewith will be assigned to him at once. On my own responsibility I have deleted the Christian references that appear in the existing manuscripts of a story of pre-Christian origin. A number of scholars hold that these were not late interpolations, but were inserted in the first formally composed version of an old story that had come down by word of mouth. I have no scholarship to judge of that, but I know that artistically they do not belong against the background of "weird" that sets off the rest of the story.— EDITOR.

Beowulf
(Anglo-Saxon)

THE
GRENDEL
EPISODE

How King Hrothgar Built Him a Great Mead-Hall

Then Hrothgar was granted good speed in war, glory in battle, so that his comrades and kinsmen followed him eagerly and the youth waxed and became a great company of fighting men. It came to his mind that he would bid men build him a great hall and mead-house, mightier than the sons of men had ever heard of; and there he would deal out to young and old what God might give him, saving public lands and the lives of men. Then, I have heard, the work of building the house was ordered forth among many tribes about this earth. It befell him that early and in good time it was all ready, this hugest of hall-buildings; he gave it the name of Heorot (Hart), for his word was powerful far and wide. Nor did he neglect his boast, but dealt out riches and jewels at the feast. The hall towered, high, horn-gabled; it was free of ruinous flame and loathly fire; nor was it for a long time yet that sword-hate together with slaughter must rise against the king.

Of Grendel, and His Raids of Heorot

Then a certain strong ghost who dwelt in darkness endured with pain (for a long time) to hear each day the joy that was loud in the hall, wherein was the sound of the harp and the sweet singing of the scop; who spoke, knowing how to recount from afar back, of the beginning of men, and told how the Almighty wrought the earth, lovely land engirled with water, and in triumph set up the sun and moon as luminaries to light the land-dwellers, and made fair the corners of the world with leafy boughs and likewise created life for everything that moves and lives. So the men-at-arms lived in happiness until this fiend of hell began to do deeds of wickedness. This grim ghost was named Grendel—a huge wanderer of the marches—and he kept the moors and the fens and the fastnesses.

He went then when night fell to look about the high house and to see how the Ring-Danes had settled it after their beer-bout. He found therein a company of aethelings sleeping after the feast; they knew not sorrow, the misery of men. The unholy wight, grim and greedy, was soon ready, fierce and fell, and took thirty thegns that were at their rest; then glorying in his spoil he went back to his home with his fill of houses to raid. Then at dawn of day the war-craft of Grendel was made clear to man; and when it was known a weeping went up, a great mourning-song. The lord of the people, the peerless aetheling, sat there unhappy and felt and endured great sorrow for his thegns, after they had seen the bitter traces of the ghastly demon. The trial was all too strong, dismal and longsome! Nor was this the first time by much; for after about one night he did more murder, and did not shrink therefor from wrack and woe; he was too fast in it; then was it easy to find him who sought his rest farther away, a bed in a house; for there was shown and clearly set forth the hatred of this hall-thegn; then he who would flee from the fiend kept himself more distant and safer. So he held sway and fought against the right, alone against them all, until this best of houses stood empty. And so for a long time; for twelve winter-tides the friend of the Scyldings bore the affliction, every kind of woe, of wide sorrow; for it became known to men and the sons of men, in sad story, how Grendel fought awhile with Hrothgar, and held him in hostility, and wrought wrack and ruin for many a season, in a long struggle; he would make peace with no man of the Danish nation, to pay the blood-price or settle the fee, nor did any one of the counsellors think they could look for better shift at the hands of the slayer. But the monster ever ravaged them, the dark death-shadow; about the youth and the fighting men he hovered and plotted. He kept to the night eternal of the misty moors; and no man knows whither the hellions will turn and wander.

So the son of Healfdene was fretted with cares that lasted a long time, nor might the wily warrior put away his woe. That struggle was all too strong, bitter and longsome that fell upon the land; grim grief it was, the worst of night-horrors.

OF BEOWULF, AND HOW HE SAILED TO THE LAND OF THE DANES

The thegn of Higelac, goodly among the Geats, heard of these things at home, of the deeds of Grendel. He was the strongest man of might among mankind at this time of life, well-born and big. He bade them get him ready a good wave-splitter, and said that over the swan's road he would seek the war-king, the goodly lord, since he needed men. His shrewd carles blamed him not at all for this venture, though he was dear to them; they sharpened his valour and looked to the omens. The hero had chosen out of the Geatish men the boldest champions he could find; with fourteen others he took to the sea-wood, and a warrior, skilled in seacraft, showed them the land-marks. The time came, the ship was on the waves, the boat beneath the cliffs; the young men stepped eagerly into the stem, while the currents eddied and the water by the shore; the fighters loaded their shining gear, their stately armour, into the ship's bosom; the men pushed off the well-built ship on their welcome voyage. Sped by the wind the foamy-throated ship, most like to a bird, went over the tossing sea until about the same time of the second day after the curved ship had set out; then the seafarers sighted land, the ocean cliffs a-glitter, the steep crags and the wide sea-nesses. Then the sea was crossed, their voyage at an end. Thence swiftly the Weder men set their wooden ship upon the shore and left it; their mail-shirts, the weeds of battle, clanked; they thanked God that the sea-ways had been made easy for them.

How the Watchman on the Danish Coast Met with Beowulf

Then from the wall the watchman of the Scyldings, whose duty it was to hold the sea-cliffs, espied the bright bucklers borne over the gangway, and the ready armour; and curiosity stirred his thought as to what men they were. The thegn of Hrothgar went then riding a-horseback to the shore, and flourished his great spear in his strong hands, and questioned them in formal words:

"Who are you among armoured men, fended by mail-sarks, that are come thus over the ocean bringing your tall ship across the sea-roads? Look you, I was guarding the coast for this while and holding the sea-watch, so that no foe with a viking-army might do scathe in the land of the Danes. Men with shields have never approached here more as if they knew the place, nor did you know that the leave of the warriors would be granted you, the consent of the rulers. Never on earth have I seen a bigger warrior than is one of you, a fighter in armour; armed as he is with his weapons, he is no hall-thegn, or else his looks, his gallant appearance, gives him the lie. Now I look to learn your stock ere you go much farther hence as spies upon the land of the Danes. Now, far-dwellers, sea-farers, you have heard my plain thought; it is best that I know speedily whence you are come."

Him the lord, the leader of the company, answered, unlocking his word-hoard: "We are of the race of Geats, and hearth-companions to Higelac. My father was known to men as a noble chief, Ecgtheow was his name; he endured many a winter ere he went his way, aged, from the dwelling place; all counsellors about the wide earth were ready to hearken to him. We are come in friendly spirit to seek your lord the son of Healfdene, the shield of the people; may you be of good counsel to us. With that great man, the lord of the Danes, we have a mighty errand; nor shall any of it be secret, of that I am sure. You know, if it is in truth as we hear tell, that among the Scyldings some foe, I know not what, a secret destroyer by the dark of night, shows terribly an unheard-of evilness, and does scathe and slaughter. Touching this, out of my large wisdom I may advise Hrothgar as to how, ancient and goodly, he may overpower the fiend—if a change and relief from his cares may ever come and the seething sorrow turn cooler; else he must always have sorrow and bitterness as long as this tallest of houses keeps its high place."

The warder, the fearless guardian, answered sitting there on his horse: "A sharp warrior should be a judge alike of words and deeds, if he thinks aright. I take it this is a company friendly to the lord of the Scyldings. Go, bring forth your arms and armour, I shall guide you; thus I will tell my young thegns to hold your boat, your fresh-tarred vessel, on the sand against any foe, until your curving ship bears you back, longed-for men, over the sea-streams to the Weder-march, every one to whom, doing bravely, it is granted to be given up hale by the battle-storm."

How Beowulf Went to Heorot

Then they set forth; the boat abode fast, the broad-beamed vessel lay at mooring, fast at anchor. The figure of the boar shone over their helmets, wrought of gold, gleaming and fire-tempered; and forward went the warlike men. They hasted, marching together, until they might reach the timbered hall, grand and gold-decked. That was the foremost hall among men under heaven, in which the high one dwelt; its light shone far over many a land. Then the battle-brave warrior pointed out to them the bright hall, that they might get them forward to it; the warrior wih his men turned his horse about, then said:

"It is time for me to go. I will to the sea, to hold my ward safe against any attacking host."

The street was paved, the way directed the men and kept them together. The mail-shirts close-linked by hand glittered, the sheer iron meshes of their armour clashed, when first they came in their grim gear to the hall. Sea-weary, they set their broad shields aside, laid their sturdy bucklers against the wall of the building. Then they stooped down to the benches; their byrnies rang, the armour of warriors; their spears, the weapons of seamen, ashwood gray-seeming from above, stood together. This iron-clad company was well fitted with weapons.

How Wulfgar the Chamberlain Told Hrothgar of Beowulf's Coming

Then a haughty hero asked of the noble fighters: "Whence are you come bearing plated shields, gray hauberks, helmet-masks and store of battle-spears? I am Hrothgar's servant herald. Never have I seen so many foreign men of braver aspect. I think that in high spirits—not at all in exile but out of high-heartedness—you have come to seek Hrothgar."

Then the powerful proud lord of the Weders answered him and spoke a stout word from under his helm: "We are board-companions of Higelac; Beowulf is my name. I wish to tell my errand to the mighty prince, the son of Healfdene, your lord, if he will grant us that we greet him, goodly as he is."

Wulfgar—he was a man of the Wendels, and his spirit, worth and wisdom were known to many—answered: "I will question the liege of the Danes, the lord of the Scyldings, the giver of bounty, as you have asked me to do; I will question the noble lord about your voyage, and his answer, which I think will be a good one, shall be known to you forthwith."

He turned then quickly to where Hrothgar sat, old and very hoary, among his throng of earls. The strong man advanced until he stood by the shoulder of the king of the Danes; he knew the way of the warrior. Said Wulfgar to his lord:

"Here are Geatish men come from afar over the sweep of the ocean; his fighters call the leader Beowulf. They have prayed, my lord, that they may traffic in words with you; do not refuse them an answer, gladman Hrothgar! In their war-weeds they seem worthy of the esteem of earls; moreover their chief, who has led them hither, is a stout man."

Then Hrothgar, the helm of the Scyldings, made answer:

"I knew of him when he was a boy. His aged father was called Ecgtheow, to whom Hrethel of the Geats gave his only daughter in marriage; and now his hardy son is come hither and has sought a friendly lord. At that time when the seafarers brought the gifts here in thanksgiving they said that the man-at-arms had the strength of thirty men in his handclasp. Out of his kindness, as I think, the Holy Lord has sent him to us West-Danes, against the grimness of Grendel. For his spirit I shall bestow gifts upon this goodly man. Go you with all speed and tell all this company of kinsmen to come in together and see me. Tell them also in words that they are welcome to the Danish people."

Then Wulfgar went to the door of the hall and from within spoke them a word: "My victorious lord, the prince of the East-Danes, has bidden me tell you that he knows your noble stock, and you stout-hearted men are welcome hither over the sea-surges. Now you may go in, in your war-sarks, and visit Hrothgar in your battle-masks; leave your war-shields here, your wooden battle-shafts likewise, to await the upshot of your talk."

How Beowulf Came Before Hrothgar

Then the prince rose up, and about him many a young fighter, a warlike group of thegns. Some bided there to watch their war-gear, as the hardy chief commanded them. They hastened together, a hero leading them, under the roof of Heorot; the warrior went forward, hardy beneath his helm, until he stood upon the hearth. Beowulf spoke, and his byrnie glittered upon him, wrought by the skill of the smith:

"Hrothgar, wassail! I am kinsman and thegn of Higelac and have dared many a great deed in my youth. The matter of Grendel has been made clearly known to me in my own land; the sea-farers say that this hall, this most mighty building, stands idle and useless after the evenlight is hidden in the hold of heaven. Then my people, the best of them, wily carles, lord Hrothgar, urged me to seek you; for they know my might. Themselves were by when I came out of battle, gory from my foe, what time I bound five of them and slew the race of giants, and killed the water-monsters by night beneath the waves, and underwent hard distress and avenged the ills of the Weders—for these had worked them woe—

and ground them in their wrath; and now I purpose to have to do, alone, with the fiend Grendel. Now therefore, lord of the Bright-Danes, bulwark of the Scyldings, I shall ask of you one boon; that you do not deny me, protector of warriors, liege of the folk— now that I am come so far—that I alone with my company of earls, this hardy troop, may cleanse out Heorot. I have learned that the monster in his recklessness takes no heed of weapons; then, so may my lord Higelac be kindly to me, I despise to bear sword or broad shield of yellow into the fight, but with my grip I shall lay hold on the fiend and struggle for my life, hate for hate; and whom death shall take shall be left to the Lord's will. I know that if he can compass it he will eat the Geatish people unafraid in the war-hall, as often he has done, the best of men. You need not bury my head, but he will have me all blood-spattered, if death takes me; he bears away a bloody corpse with intent to feed on it; he eats it, the lone-farer, ruthlessly, and stains his moor-dwelling. You will need sorrow no longer over the cheer of my body. Send to Hige-lac, if the battle takes me, this best of byrnies that guards my breast, this finest of hauberks; it was left by Hraedla, it is the work of Weland. Fate goes ever whither it must."

Of Hrothgar's Welcome

Hrothgar spoke, the helm of the Scyldings: "Friend Beowulf, you have sought us for deed-doing, out of kindliness. It is sorrow in my heart to say to any among men what ruin, what slaughter Grendel has brought to pass in Heorot by his hatred. My war-company, my battle-troop, has waned away, their wyrd has swept them away into the wrath of Grendel. Full often the fighters, drunk with beer, boasted over the ale-can that in the beer-hall they would abide Grendel's onset with the wrath of the sword-blade. Then in the morning-tide, when day lightened, this high mead-hall was a-reek with blood, and all the benches were splashed with blood, and the hall gory from the fight; and I had the fewer good men, beloved warriors, when death had taken them away. Sit now to the feast, victorious among men, and speak forth meetly as your mood whets you."

Then for all the Geat-folk together the benches were cleared in the beer-hall; they went mightily to sit, proud in their strength.

A thegn looked to the service, bearing in his hands the wrought tankard, and poured the shining drink. A clear-voiced scop sang the while in Heorot. There was joy to the warriors, for there were many young men of the Danes and Weders.

Wealtheow came forth, Hrothgar's queen, mindful of her kinsmen, and greeted the gold-crowned man in the hall; and the stately woman first gave a cup to the overlord of the East-Danes, bade him be blithe at the beer-drinking, lief to his people; gladly he took the draught and the hall-cup, that king hardy in battle. Then the lady of the Helmings went about to each of the young men and the fighters, giving them a share of precious vessel, until the time came when the crowned queen bore a mead-cup to Beowulf. She greeted the lord of the Geats and wise of words thanked God that her wish had come to pass, that she might trust in any earl for relief from slaughter. The stark-slaying fighter took the cup at the hands for Wealtheow; then, set for combat, he spoke:

"I vowed when I went upon the sea and sat in the seaboat with my troop of warriors that I would surely work the wish of your people, or else fall a corpse fast in the grip of my foe. I shall do a deed of earl-like might, or else abide the end of my day's in this mead-hall."

These words, the boasting speech of the Geat, liked the woman well; she went gold-crowned, a stately queen of the folk, to sit beside her lord.

How Beowulf and His Thegns Were Left to Guard the Hall

Then again, as erewhiles, there were mighty words spoken in the hall, and a troop within the place, and the noise of a gallant people, until presently the son of Healfdene would seek his evening rest. He knew that the ogre had been bent on war against the high hall from the time when they could see the sunlight until the lowering night, the shaper of shadow-helms, came striding dark beneath the welkin over all. Every man arose. Hrothgar greeted Beowulf man to man, bade him good speed and the keeping of the wine-hall, and added this word:

"Never to any men, since I might lay hand to shield, have I trusted the keeping of this great hall of the Danes, save to you now. Have then and hold this best of houses, think of your valour, make known your huge strength, ward against the wrath of your foe. You shall lack no wished-for thing if you come out of this strong battle with your life."

Then the stalwart Beowulf of the Geats spoke a few words of boasting before he took to the couch:

"I count myself no worse in vigour at works of war than Grendel deems himself; for this I will not slay him with the sword and so bereave him of life, though well I might. He knows nothing of these good things nor can he strike against me and hew at my buckler, rough though he be at bitter deeds; but in the night we shall forgo the sword, if he dare seek a fight without weapons."

Then the daring in battle leaned down, and the pillow took the cheek of the earl, and about him many a brisk sea-rover lay down to his hall-bed. Not one of them thought that he would ever again seek his lovely home, his folk or free-city where he was bred.

How Grendel Lost His Arm

In the dark of night the Shadow-goer came stalking. The spearmen who were to hold that horned hall were sleeping, all but one. Beowulf watching in anger abode fiercely the onset of battle.

Then Grendel came on his way from the moors, under the misty hills, and he bore God's anger. The man-scather was minded to ensnare some men in that high hall. He walked beneath the welkin until he knew that the wine-hall, the gold-room of men, was right at hand. Nor was that the first journey he had made against Hrothgar's home; never in the days of his life, before or since, did he find harder cheer, harder hall-thegns. So the mirthless warrior came to visit the hall. Soon the door, made fast with forged bonds, sprang apart, after he had laid hands on it; then wrathful-minded, being in anger, he burst through the mouth of the hall. Swiftly thereafter the fiend trod upon the wrought floor, and strode in ire, and an evil light like flame shot from his eyes. He saw many a warrior in the hall, a kindred troop sleeping all together, a group of strong fighters. Then his heart laughed out; the evil ogre thought that ere day should come he would sunder life and body for each one of them, when his hope of feasting would be granted. Yet it was not fated that he should feed upon mankind beyond that night. The strong kinsman of Higelac watched to see how the man-scather would fare in a sudden grip. The monster did not look for that from a man, but on his first attack he seized swiftly on a sleeping man, slit him without wavering, bit through his bones, drank the blood from his veins, swallowed him in great gobbets; soon he had eaten the dead man, hands, feet and all. He stepped forth nearer, laid hands upon the strong-hearted one in his bed, reached toward his opponent with his hand; Beowulf gripped him suddenly and fiercely, and sat up, leaning on his arm. Soon that shepherd of vile deeds found that never in the reaches of the mid-lying earth might he meet another man with a greater hand-grip. He turned frightened in heart and soul; but not the sooner could he get away. His heart longed to be hence, he wanted to seek cover, and look for his company of devils; nor was his luck there such as he had ever found it in the days of his life.

Then the hero kinsman of Higelac remembered his evening-speech, stood upright, and grappled fast with him. The fingers burst. The ogre made for outdoors, the earl stepped ahead of him. The monster was minded whensoever he might to get farther off and flee to the fen-fastnesses; for he knew that his fingers were in the power of the grim man's grip. That was a bitter visit that the scather made to Heorot. The folk-hall dinned; all the Danish earls, the camp-dwellers, were sadly frightened. Both of these eager hallwards were enraged. The hall was in an uproar. Terror fell on all the brave Danish earls who dwelt about. Both grim keepers of the hall were in anger. Then was it a great wonder that the wine-hall held up against the daring in battle, that it did not fall to the ground, this fair land-hall; but it was made fast inside and outside with bonds of iron shrewdly smithied. Then from the floor, as I have heard, there sprang up many a mead-bench inlaid with gold, where the grim men struggled. The wise men of the Scyldings had never thought that any man might in any wise break it apart, gorgeous and horn-trimmed, and smash it at will, unless the circle of fire were to swallow it in its jaws. A scream went up, startling enough; deathly terror stood among the North-Danes, each of those who from the wall heard the weeping, the adversary of God singing a grisly lay, a song void of triumph, the knave of hell howling in his pain. He that held him fast was the strongest of might among mankind at that day of life.

The guarder of earls by no means wished that the killer should get away alive, nor did he count his life-days useful to any people. Then many an earl of Beowulf drew his ancient blade, wishing to fend the life of their lord, their mighty leader, wheresoever they might. They did not know where the hardy warriors were struggling together, and thought to hew about on either hand and seek out the life of the foe; but no war-brand of choice iron on earth could reach the destroyer, for he had laid a spell on every sword-edge. Yet the end of his days must come, pitifully, on that day of his life on earth, and the strong ghost wander far into the power of the fiends. Then he who of old had in mirth of mind done many a scathe to mankind found that his body would not hold out for him, but the high-hearted kinsman of Higelac had him by the hands. Either while alive was hateful to the other. The dark demon abode, body-sore; a wound opened to view on his shoulder, the sinews sprang apart, the bone-locks snapped asunder. War-strength was granted to Beowulf, and Grendel must flee thence, sick to death, under the fen-steeps to find his cheerless home. He knew too well this his days were sped and the number of his days. After the storm of battle the wish of the Danes was brought to pass. Then he who had come from afar, shrewd and stalwart, had rinsed the hall of Hrothgar and beaten off the foe. He had joy of his night's work, his deeds of strength. The lord of the Geats had proved his boast to the East-Danes, had given them aid in their great distress, the sorrow that they had suffered and must perforce endure, no small grief. That was a clear token when the lief of battle laid down the hand, arm and shoulder—and therein was all the grip of Grendel—under the gabled roof.

How the Danes and the Geats Made Merry

Then in the morning, I have heard, there was many a fighter about the gift-hall; the folk-leaders came from afar and near about the wide ways to see the wonder, the prints of the loathely one. His death did not seem a grievous thing to any of those who looked upon his shameful tracks and saw how, weary of heart and beaten in battle, he had taken his way, doomed and fugitive, to the mere

of monsters. There the water was a-welter with blood, and the black swing of the waves was all bestreaked with hot blood, boiling with battle-gore. Doomed he dived; and afterward, joyless in the fen-deep he laid down his life and hell took him.

Then the warrior, the son of Ecglaf, was more quiet in his boasting over works of war, when the aethelings saw the hand and fingers of the fiend hung by the earl's craft from the high roof. All gathered before the stark nails, most like to steel, awful and ghastly. Everyone said that no hard sword might hit him so as to cut away the bloody battle-hand of the monster.

And Gave Him Gifts at the Feasting

Then speedily they bade clear Heorot within by hand, and many a man and woman was there to make ready that guest-hall. Gold-gleaming the webs shone upon the walls, there was many a wondrous sight for any man to stare upon. That bright room was badly battered, though all fastened within with bonds of iron, and the hinges were split apart. The roof alone had come through unscathed when the ogre, reeking from his deeds of wrath, turned in flight without hope of life.

Then it was time for the son of Healfdene to go to the hall; the king himself would partake of the feast. I have not heard of a greater group of men better behaved about their lord. The noble men sat down to the benches and ate their fill, merrily draining many a mead-cup; the men were high-spirited in that lofty hall, Hrothgar and Hrothulf. Heorot was filled within with friends; at that time the Theod-Scyldings designed no runes of treachery. Then the son of Healfdene gave to Beowulf a golden standard in guerdon for his triumph, with a plated staff, and a helm and byrnie. Many saw a man bear a great treasure-sword before him. Beowulf was given a cup in the hall. He need not be ashamed before the spearmen of the precious gift. I have not heard of many men giving four gold-decked gifts to another in friendlier fashion at the ale-bench. About the top of the helm a ridge wound with wire guarded the head, so that no hard-showering blade might harm him much when the shield-fighter should go against grim men. Then the fender of earls bade lead eight rich-bridled horses upon the floor, in under the enclosure. On one of these lay a saddle glitteringly wrought, loaded with gems; that was the war-seat of the battle-king, when the son of Healfdene would chance the sword-play—never did the fury of the famous man flag in the forefront, when the men were falling dead. And the lord of the Ingwines gave to Beowulf both alike, horses and harness, and bade him use them well. In such manly wise did the strong lord, the treasure-holder, repay the battle-stormer with horses and wealth, so that never a man may blame him who will speak soothly and righteously.

The hall was noisy. Wealtheow spoke out before the assembly: "Have joy of this ring, dear Beowulf, and wassail; and use this byrnie, from the folk-treasure, and luck be with you; make yourself known through your strength, and be of good counsel to these young lads. I will remember this service. You have so done that forever and ever men shall praise you far and near, as far as the sea, the home of the winds, bends about the walls. Henceforth, aetheling, live and be happy. I wish you many a treasure. Be seemly of deeds to my sons, and give them joy. Here every earl is true to the other, mild of mood, faithful to his lord; the thegns are loyal, the people ready, the men-at-arms drink well. Do as I bid you."

OF GRENDEL'S MOTHER. HOW SHE WOULD AVENGE HER SON

Then she went to her seat. There was the best of banquets, and the men drank wine. They did not think of wyrd, grim ordained fate, as it should befall many an earl after evening came and Hrothgar took his way to his own house, the mighty one to his rest. Countless earls kept the hall, as they had often done before. They cleared the bench-boards; the beds and pillows were spread. Many a beer-drinker, close to fate, lay down on the floor to sleep. They set at their heads their battle-bucklers, their bright board-shields. There on a bench over each aetheling might easily be seen his battle-steep helm, his ringed byrnie, and his brisk spear. Their custom was often to be ready for fighting, whether at home or on a viking, or at either of these times whenever their leader felt the need. It was a good way.

Then they sank to sleep. One of them paid sorely for his evening rest, as had full often befallen when Grendel haunted the gold-hall, and did unrighteousness, until that end overtook him, death after his sins. That was seen and made widely known to men, that an avenger lived after the strife, for a long while after the troublesome struggle. Grendel's mother, the queen of monster-wives, held a grudge, she who must dwell in the deadly water, the cold streams, would make a baleful onslaught, and avenge her son's death.

And How She Carried Off Aeschere from Heorot

She came then to Heorot where the Ring-Danes were sleeping about that hall. Then soon came a changed state for the earls, when Grendel's mother reached in for them. The grim one was less strong by as much as the craft of women, of a war-grim wife, is less than that of a weaponed man, when the bound sword, hammer-wrought, doughty of edge, shears the swine on the helm that faces it. Then in the hall was many a hard-edged sword drawn by the settles, and many a one had his wide shield fast in his hands; no one thought of his helm or broad byrnie when the grim one saw him. She was in haste, and wished to get hence and save her life after she was seen; and swiftly she had gripped fast one of the aethelings and gone to the fen. He whom she slew at his rest was the dearest of heroes in comradeship to Hrothgar by the two seas, a noble shield-fighter, a renowned man. Beowulf was not there, but already another place had been assigned after the treasure-giving to the mighty Geat. A shouting went up in Heorot; she had taken the bloody hand of Grendel they knew well; care was renewed in the wick. Nor was that good chaffering, when they must pay on either side with the lives of their friends.

How Beowulf Undertook a Second Venture

Then the old king, the hoary war-lord, was in troubled mood, after he had heard that his aldor-thegn was no more, that the dearest of all was dead. With speed Beowulf was fetched to the bower, the fighter ready for triumph. He came at dawn together with his earls, an aetheling fighter, himself and his friends, where the wise man asked him, to see if after the spell of woes the All-Wielder might ever grant him respite. The stalwart man went up the floor with his body-guard, and the hall-wood rang; then spoke words to the wise liege of the Ingwines, asked him if the night had sped as his heart would wish.

Hrothgar spoke, the helm of the Scyldings: "Ask not about my happiness! Sorrow is renewed for the people of the Danes. Dead is Aeschere, the elder brother of Yrmenlaf, my counsellor and rede-giver, my henchman, when we fended our heads in battle, when the squadrons clashed and the boars' heads struck together. So should an earl be, a peerless aetheling, such as Aeschere was! The wandering death-ghost was his bane in Heorot. I do not know whither the monster, glorying in carrion, gorged with her meal, has drawn away. She has wreaked revenge for that yesternight you killed Grendel roughly with your hard hands, since all too long he had wasted and haunted my people. He fell in fight, forfeit of life, and now is come another mighty man-scather who would avenge her kin, and has from afar caused atonement of the feud, as is known of many a thegn who weeps from his heart over the boon-giver. It is a hard heart-bale; and now the hand lies low that was kind to you in all that you wished.

"I have heard dwellers of my land, my folk and counsellors, say that they have seen two such march-steppers holding the moors, two ghosts from afar. Of these one, as clearly as they might see, was in the likeness of a woman; the other trod his roving way in the shape of a man, save that he was mightier than any other. Him the earth-dwellers named Grendel in days of yore; they do not know about his father, whether he had any among the strange goblins. They dwell in the dim land of the wolf-hills, the windy nesses and forbidding fen-ways, where the water-fall tumbles beneath the gloom of the nesses, an underground flood. It is not many miles hence that the mere stands. Over it hang frosted groves, and a root-fast wood overshadows the water. There any night one may see a deathly wonder, fire on the lake. No one of the sons of men lives who is so wise as to know that ground; yet when, harried by hounds, a strong-horned heath-faring stag seeks the holtwood, far-driven, he sooner yields up his life upon the bank than go in and save his head. That is no happy place! Thence arises a churning of water, dark beneath the welkin, when the wind stirs up the bitter weather, until the sky is darkened and the heavens weep. Now is help at hand from you alone. You do not yet know the home, the evil place where you may find the sinful spirit. Seek it if you dare. I will pay you richly for the struggle, with ancient treasures and twisted gold as I did before, if you come on your way thence."

Beowulf spoke, the son of Ecgtheow: "Do not sorrow, wise man! It is better for anyone to avenge his friend, when he mourns overmuch. Each of us must await the end of his earthly life; let him work what he can of daring before his death. So it will be best for a man-at-arms when he is no more. Arise, keeper of the kingdom, go forth quickly and look at the track of Grendel's kinswoman. I promise you this; she shall not get to cover, neither in the arms of the earth nor the woods of the mountains nor the floor of the ocean, go where she will. Have patience this day through every woe, as I think you will."

The Mere of Grendel's Mother

Then the old man sprang up and thanked God, the mighty Lord, for what the man had said. A horse was bridled for Hrothgar, a curly-maned charger. The wise king rode in state, and a band of shield-men stepped after him on foot. The prints were seen far over the wold-paths, the tracks along the ground, where she had fared forward over the murky moor bearing, all lifeless, the best of the kin-thegns who dwelt at home with Hrothgar. Then the child of aethelings went over steep stone-slopes, narrow paths, strait single-tracks, an unknown way over sheer nesses and many a monster's den; he went ahead with a few skilled men to find the way, until of a sudden he saw mountain trees leaning over the hoar-gray stone, a joyless wood; and under it stood water, bloody and turgid. Then it was hard for the hearts of all the Danes, lords of the Scyldings, to suffer, and grief to many a thegn and all the earls, when they found Aeschere's head on the sea-cliff. The water welled with blood as they looked at it, with hot battle-gore. Time and again the horn sang out an eager war-song. The foot-soldiers all sat down. Then they saw about the water many of the worm-kind, strange sea-drakes, exploring the sound, and lying on the ness-slopes such water-monsters as often in the morning take their sorrowful way to the sea-roads, worms and wild beasts. They slipped on their way, bitter and swollen with wrath; they had heard the clear noise, the winding of the war-horn. A man of the Geats tore one from life as he swam, with a shaft from his bow, the hard war-arrow hitting him to the death; he was the slower at swimming in the sea when death took him. Swiftly he was caught with the barbed boar-spear, assailed in anger, and drawn up on the ness, a wondrous wave-cleaver; the men stared at the grisly guest.

How Beowulf Went Down into the Mere

Beowulf donned his earl's weeds, and troubled not at all about his life; his war-byrnie, hard woven by hand, wide and well-wrought, must have a try at swimming, for it knew how to guard his body so that the war-grip and the bitter clasp of anger might not scathe his heart or his life; but his head was fended by the stout helm which was to scrape against the floor of the mere and seek the swirl of waters—richly wrought it was, and ringed about with lovely chains, as in the days of old the weapon-smith fashioned it and furnished it with wondrous ornament, and set it about with the likenesses of boars, so that thereafter neither brand nor battlemace might bite the wearer. Nor was that thing the smallest of help that the spokesman of Hrothgar gave him at his need. A hafted sword it was, named Hrunting. It was peerless among ancient treasures. The blade was of iron, brilliant with poison-bands, hardened with battle-blood. Never in battle had it failed anyone who swung it with his hands, who durst make deadly raids and do battle with his foes. That was not the first time that it was to do rough work. Indeed the son of Ecglaf, crafty of might, did not remember what he had said when drunk with wine, when he lent this weapon to a better swordsman. He himself durst not risk his life under the struggling waves and prove his valour; for which he forwent glory and praise of goodly deeds. Not so was it with the other, when he had geared himself for battle.

Beowulf spoke, the son of Ecgtheow: "Remember now, great kinsman of Healfdene, king of wise men, gold-lord of people—now that I am ready for the venture—what we two agreed before, if I should lose my life in your behalf, that you would ever take the place of father to me even in death. Be a bulwark to my companions and kin-thegns, if the fight takes me; and such treasure as you have given me send, dear Hrothgar, to Higelac. Then the liege of the Geats, the son of Hraedla, may see when he gazes on that store that I found a giver of rings good in all manliness, and enjoyed it while I might. And let Unferth, the far-famed man, have my old blade, my wondrous hard-edged war-sword; I shall win glory for myself with Hrunting until death shall take me."

After these words the lord of the Geats hastened in might, and would not wait for any answer; the helm of the water swallowed the fighter. It was some time of the day before he might see the bottom.

How They Fought Beneath the Water

Then she who in sword-ghastliness had held the circle of the lake for a hundred half-years, grim and greedy, saw that some one of stranger men was coming into her garth from above. She grappled with him, and gripped the warrior in her cruel claws, but none the sooner for this did she scathe his hale body; his chain-armour ringed him about, so that she could not clutch through the coat-of-mail, the locked sark, with her fell fingers. Then the water-wolf bore the ring-prince down toward her home till she came to the bottom, so that—and he was angry for it—he could not wield his weapons; but many strange creatures beset him as he swam, and many a sea-beast bruised his battle-sark with his deadly tusks, and monsters pursued him. Then the earl saw that he was in some kind of death-hall where the water hindered him not at all, and the sudden grip of the lake might not reach him by reason of the roofed building. He saw a firelight, a bleak glimmer shining brightly.

Then the goodly man was aware of the demon of the lake-floor, the mighty mere-wife. He gave a huge heave to his war-brand, swung his hand without holding back, so that the greedy, war-lief, ring-hilted blade sang against her head. Then the stranger found that the battle-light would not cut her nor scathe her life, but the edge failed its lord at his need. It had gone through many a hand-fight, and often had shorn through helmets and the armour of a doomed man; this was the first time for the dear treasure that its worth flagged.

Then the kinsman of Higelac, mindful of glory, was hearty, and in no wise let go of his valour. The warrior in anger threw away the wondrously-bound, curve-hilted sword so that it lay on the ground, stout and steel-edged. He trusted in his strength, in the hand-grip of his might. So should a man do, when he thinks to win long-lasting praise in battle; nor does he care about his life. The lord of the War-Geats, troubling not at all for her rage, gripped Grendel's mother by the shoulder; in anger the battle-hard bent back his deadly foe, so that he threw her to the floor. She swiftly paid him back with her grim claws, and grappled with him; then weary-hearted the strongest of warriors, the foot-sol-dier, stumbled so that he had a fall. Then she sat on the hall-guest and drew her dirk, broad and bright-edge; she would avenge her child, her only son. On his shoulder lay his woven breast-net, and that guarded his life and withstood the entry of point or edge. Then would the son of Ecgtheow have gone under the wide ground, the champion of the Geats, if his war-byrnie, the hard battle-net, had not helped him.

How Beowulf Slew Grendel's Mother with a Giant Sword

Then among the armour he saw a victorious brand, an old sword of the Giants, mighty of edge, the glory of fighters; it was the best of weapons, but it was so vast that no other man could have borne it to battle, goodly and glorious as it was, and the work of giants. The bold Scylding, raging and war-grim, seized the linked haft, and despairing of life swung the ring-hilted sword, and slashed in wrath, so that the hard blade took her at the neck and broke the circle of bones. The brand split clean through her doomed body, and she shuddered to the floor, and the blade was bloody, and the man rejoiced in his work.

And Cut Off Grendel's Head

The flame flickered, the light within shone clearly as shines from heaven the candle of the sky. He looked along the hall; then he turned by the wall, and held the weapon hard by the hilt, the determined and wrathful thegn of Higelac; for the blade was not useless to the warrior, but he wished with all speed to pay out Grendel for all those deeds of slaughter he had wrought upon the Danes, on more than one raid, when he slew Hrothgar's hearth-mates in sleep, and ate fifteen sleeping men of the Danish folk, and also carried off another, loathsome spoil. The stark champion paid him off that score when he saw Grendel, war-weary, lying at rest, lifeless from the hurt he had got in the fight at Heorot. The corpse sprang wide apart when it suffered a stroke after death, a hard deadly swing that carved off the head.

But the Men-at-arms, Seeing Blood in the Water, Were Afraid

Soon the shrewd carles who with Hrothgar were watching the lake saw that the swirl of the waves was all streaked and the water reeking with blood. The graybeards, the old men about the good king, said together that they did not think that the aetheling would ever come back in triumph to seek the great lord; and so thought many a one, that the water-wolf had killed him. Then came the ninth hour of the day. The sturdy Scyldings did not give up, but the gold-lord of men went away home. The strangers sat sick at heart and stared upon the mere; they wished, but did not hope, to see their free-lord himself.

Until They Saw Their Champion Swimming Ashore

Then that war-brand began to melt with the gore into bloody icicles; it was a wonderful thing how it all melted much like ice. The lord of the Weder-Geats did not take any more of the treasures that were in that place, though he saw many; only that head, and the hilt with it, richly inlaid; the damascened sword had already melted, burned away, so hot was the blood, and the strong ghost that died there. Soon he who abode through the struggle the fall of his foes was a-swimming, and dived up through the water; the waters were made clean, and the large lands, when the strong ghost let go of her life-days and the world of this life.

How Beowulf Took Leave of Hrothgar

Then the warder of shieldmen came swimming mightily ashore; he rejoiced in his sea-booty, in the great burden of things he had with him. And they went to meet him, and thanked God, this lusty crowd of thegns, and had great joy of their lord, that they might see him safe and sound. Then from the strong man helm and byrnie were loosened with all speed. The lake stagnated, the water beneath the sky, all splotched with gore. They fared forth thence afoot, joyous of heart, and measured the earthway, the known road; and the king-bold men bore from the seacliff the head that had been horrible to all their valiant men. Four men with some ado bore Grendel's head on a pikestaff to the goldhall; and anon fourteen bold battle-brisk Geats came marching to the hall, and with them their leader, gallant among the throng, stepped over the meadows. Then the ealdorman of thegns, the man covered with glory, the hale battle-hero, went in to greet Hrothgar. On the floor Grendel's head was set before the old man, where the men were drinking, ghastly for the earls and the queen that was with them, a wondrous sight to see; and the men looked upon it.

The Geat was merry of mood, he went straightway to the settle. Then, as before, there was fair speech among the sturdy floor-sitters. The helm of night gloomed darkly over the men. The young warriors stood up, for the ancient, grizzled Scylding was about to retire. The Geat, the stout shield-fighter, was wondrously well pleased to rest; soon a hall-thegn guided the far-comer forth, weary as he was from his venture, and in courtesy he looked to every need of the thegn, as the sea-farers were wont to be courteous in those days.

How They Took Farewell of Each Other on the Morrow

Then the great-hearted man rested; the hall towered, gabled and gold-gleaming; the guest slept within until the black raven, blithe-hearted, foretold the brightening of the sky. Then came the sun scattering light over the shadows; the warriors made haste, the aethelings were eager to fare back to their people; the bold stranger would go to his ship far away.

GREEN THOUGHTS

I have referred to *The Beast With Five Fingers* as a ghost story in the modern manner. Here is another variant, and here again the rules are laid down. The typical behavior of the principal non-human character is not at all what one would expect—but it plays no favorites, even as between two human beings and a cat and mouse. Once we know the nature of Mr Collier's tale, it is true to its own internal fantastic logic. It takes none of the liberties with time and space that gave Gothic ghosts such an unfair advantage over those whom they haunted.—EDITOR.

John Collier

G R E E N
THOUGHTS

Annihilating all that's made
To a green thought in a green shade.
—MARVELL.

The orchid had been sent among the effects of his friend, who had come by a lonely and mysterious death on the expedition. Or he had bought it among a miscellaneous lot, "unclassified," at the close of the auction. I forget which, but one or the other it certainly was: moreover, even in its dry, brown, dormant root state, this orchid had a certain sinister quality. It

749

looked, with its bunched and ragged projections, like a huge dead insect, or a rigid yet a gripping hand, hideously gnarled, or a grotesquely whiskered, threatening face. Would you not have known what sort of an orchid it was?

Mr. Mannering did not know. He read nothing but catalogues and books on fertilisers. He unpacked the new acquisition with a solicitude absurd enough in any case, towards any orchid, or primrose either, in the twentieth century, but idiotic, foolhardy, doom-eager, when extended to an orchid thus come by, in appearance thus. And in his traditional obtuseness he at once planted it in what he called "the Observation Ward," facetious fellow! a hot-house built against the south wall of his dumpy red dwelling. Here he set always the most interesting additions to his collection, and especially weak and sickly plants, for there was a glass door in his study wall, through which he could see into this hot-house, so that the weak and sickly plants could encounter no crisis without his immediate knowledge and his tender care.

This plant, however, proved hardy enough. At the ends of thick and stringy stalks, it opened out bunches of darkly shining leaves, and soon it spread in every direction, usurping so much space that first one, then another, then all its neighbours had to be removed to a hot-house at the end of the garden. It was, Cousin Jane said, a regular hop-vine. The comparison was little to the point. At the ends of the stalks, just before the leaves began, were set groups of tendrils, which hung idly, serving no apparent purpose. Mr. Mannering thought that very probably these were vestigial organs, a heritage from some period when the plant had been a climber. But when were the vestigial tendrils of an ex-climber half or quarter so thick and strong?

After a long time, sets of tiny buds appeared here and there among the extravagant foliage. Soon they opened into small flowers, miserable little things: they looked like flies' heads. How disappointed I should have been, and you would too, I hope, or Doyle and Wells have lived and writ in vain. One naturally expects a large, garish, sinister bloom, like a sea anemone, or a Chinese lantern, or a hippopotamus yawning, on any important orchid; and should it be an unclassified one as well, I think one has every right to insist on a sickly and overpowering scent into the bargain.

Mr. Mannering did not mind at all. Indeed, apart from his

joy and happiness in being the discoverer and god-father of a new sort of orchid, he felt only a mild and scientific interest in the fact that the paltry blossoms were so very much like flies' heads. Could it be to attract other flies for food, or as fertilisers? But then, why like their heads?

It was a few days later that Cousin Jane's cat disappeared. This was a great blow to Cousin Jane, but Mr. Mannering was not, in his heart of hearts, greatly sorry. He was not fond of the cat, for he could not open the smallest chink in a glass roof, for ventilation, but that creature would squeeze through somehow, to enjoy the warmth, and in this way it had broken many a tender shoot. But before poor Cousin Jane had lamented two days, something happened that so engrossed Mr. Mannering that he had no mind left at all with which to sympathise with her affliction, nor to make at breakfast kind and hypocritical enquiries after the lost cat. A strange new bud appeared on the orchid. It was clearly evident that there would be two quite different sorts of bloom on this one plant, as sometimes happens in such fantastic corners of the vegetable world, and that the new flower would be very different in size and structure from the earlier ones. It grew bigger and bigger, till it was as big as one's fist.

And just then, it could never have been more inopportune, an affair of the most unpleasant, the most distressing nature summoned Mr. Mannering to town. It was his wretched nephew, in trouble again: and this time so deeply and so very disgracefully that it took all Mr. Mannering's generosity, and all his influence too, to extricate the worthless young man. Indeed as soon as he saw the state of affairs, he told the prodigal that this was the very last time he might expect assistance, that his vices and his ingratitude had long cancelled all affection between them, and that for this last helping hand he was indebted only to his mother's memory, and to no faith on the part of his uncle either in his repentance or his reformation. He wrote, moreover, to Cousin Jane, to relieve his feelings, telling her of the whole business, and adding that the only thing to do was to cut the young man off entirely. He begged her, also, to send immediate news of any development on the part of his orchid.

When he got back to Torquay, Cousin Jane had disappeared. The situation was extremely annoying. Their only servant was a cook, who was very old, and very stupid, and very deaf. She suffered, besides, from an obsession, due to the fact that for many years Mr. Mannering had had no conversation with her in which he had not included an impressive reminder that she must always, no matter what might happen, keep the big kitchen stove up to a certain pitch of activity. For this stove, besides supplying the house with hot water, heated the pipes in the "Observation Ward," to which the daily gardener who had charge of the other hot-houses had no access. By this time she had come to regard her duties as stoker as her chief *raison d'être*, and it was difficult to penetrate her deafness with any question which her stupidity and her obsession did not somehow transmute into an enquiry after the stove, and this, of course, was especially the case when Mr. Mannering spoke to her. All he could disentangle was what she had volunteered on first seeing him, that his cousin had not been seen for three days, that she had left without saying a word. Mr. Mannering was perplexed and annoyed, but, being a man of method, secretary, indeed, of his County's Lodge of the Royal Antedeluvian Order of Orchid Growers, he thought it best to postpone further enquiries until he had refreshed himself a little after his long and tiring journey. A full supply of energy was necessary to extract any information from the old cook: besides, there was probably a note somewhere. It was only natural that before he went to his room, Mr. Mannering should peep into the hot-house, just to make sure that the wonderful orchid had come to no harm during the inconsiderate absence of Cousin Jane. As soon as he opened the door, his eyes fell upon the bud: it had changed in shape very considerably, and had increased in size to the bigness of a human head. It is no exaggeration to state that Mr. Mannering remained rooted to the spot, with his eyes fixed upon this wonderful bud, for fully five minutes.

But, you will ask, why did he not see her clothes on the floor? Well, as a matter of fact, to be perfectly plain and straightforward (it is a delicate point), there were no clothes on the floor. To avoid all shilly-shallying, I must tell you that Cousin Jane, though of course, she was thoroughly, entirely estimable in every respect, though she was well over forty, too, was given to the study, and in fact to the practice, of certain of the very latest ideas on the dual culture of the soul and body. Swedish, and German, neo-

Greek and all that. You will understand, no doubt. And the orchid-house was the warmest place available. I must proceed with the order of events.

Mr. Mannering at length withdrew his eyes from this stupendous bud, and (disciplined in his pleasures as all great souls are) decided that he must temporarily abandon this . . . this positive Peak in Darien, and devote his attention to the grey exigencies of everyday life. But although his body dutifully ascended the stairs, heart, mind and soul all remained, like the three kings of old, in adoration of the plant. Here we see another side to Mr. Mannering's character. Although he was philosophical to the point of insensibility over the miserable smallness of the earlier flowers, yet he was now as much gratified by the magnitude of the great new bud as you or I might be. Is not the orchid-grower a man with a heart—like you? Hence, it was not unnatural that Mr. Mannering, while in his bath, should be full of the most exalted visions of the blossoming of his heart's darling, his vegetable god-child. It would be the largest known, by far: complex as a dream, or dazzlingly simple. It would open like a dancer, or like the sun rising. Why, it might be opening at this very moment! At this thought Mr. Mannering could restrain himself no longer; he rose from the steamy water, and, wrapping his bath-towel robe about him, hurried down to the hot-house, scarcely staying to dry himself, though he was subject to colds.

The bud had not yet opened: it still reared its unbroken head among the glossy, fleshy foliage, and he now saw, what he had had no eyes for previously, how very exuberant that foliage had grown. Suddenly he realised with astonishment that this huge bud was not that which had appeared before he went away. That one had been lower down on the plant. Where was it now, then? Why, this new thrust and spread of foliage concealed it from him. He walked across, and discovered it. It had opened into a bloom. And as he looked at this bloom, his astonishment grew to stupefaction, one might say to petrification, for it is a fact that Mr. Mannering remained rooted to the spot, with his eyes fixed on the flower, for fully fifteen minutes. The flower was an exact replica of the head of Cousin Jane's lost cat. The similitude was so exact, so life-like that Mr. Mannering's first movement, after the fifteen minutes, was to seize his bath-towel robe, to draw it about him, for he was a modest man, and the cat, though bought for a Tom, had proved to be quite the reverse. I relate this to show how much character, spirit, *presence*, call it what you will, there was upon this floral cat's face. But although he made to seize his bath-towel robe, it was too late: he could not move; the new lusty foliage had closed in unperceived, the too lightly dismissed tendrils were everywhere upon him: he gave a few weak cries and sank to the ground, and there, as the Mr. Mannering of ordinary life, he passes out of this story. Just fancy!

Mr. Mannering sank into a coma, into an insensibility so deep that a black eternity passed before the first faint elements of his consciousness reassembled themselves in his brain. For of his brain was the centre of a new bud being made. Indeed, it was two or three days before this at first almost shapeless and quite primitive lump of organic matter had become sufficiently mature to be called Mr. Mannering at all. These days, which passed quickly enough, in a certain mild, not unpleasant excitement, in the outer world, seemed to the dimly working mind within the bud to resume the whole history of the development of our species, in a great many epochal parts.

A process analogous to the mutations of the embryo was being enacted here. At last the entity which was thus being rushed down an absurdly foreshortened vista of the ages arrived, slowing up, into the foreground. It became recognisable. The Seven Ages of Mr. Mannering were presented, as it were, in a series of close-ups, as in an educational film; his consciousness settled and cleared; the bud was mature, ready to open. At this point, I believe, Mr. Mannering's state of mind was exactly that of a patient, who, struggling up from vague dreams, wakening from under an anæsthetic, asks plaintively, "Where am I?" Then the bud opened, and he knew.

There was the hot-house, but seen from an unfamiliar angle; there, through the glass door, was his study, and there below him was the cat's head (Oh! *now* he knew) and there, and there beside him was Cousin Jane. He could not say a word, but then, neither could she. Perhaps it was as well. At the very least, he would have been forced to own that she had been in the right in an argument of long standing; she had always maintained that in the end no good would come of his pre-occupation with "those unnatural flowers."

Yet it must be admitted that Mr. Mannering was not at first greatly put about by this extraordinary upheaval in his daily life. This, I think, was because he was interested, not only in private and personal matters, but in the wider and more general, one might say the biological, aspects of his metamorphosis: to the rest, simply because he was now a vegetable, he responded with a vegetable reaction. The impossibility of locomotion, for example, did not trouble him in the least, nor even the absence of body and limbs, any more than the cessation of that stream of rashers and tea, biscuits and glasses of milk, luncheon cutlets and so forth that had flowed in at his mouth for over fifty years, but which had now been reversed to a gentle, continuous, scarcely noticeable feeding from below. All the powerful influence of the physical upon the mental, therefore, inclined him towards tranquillity. But the physical is not all. Although no longer a man, he was still Mr. Mannering. Dear me! And from this anomaly, as soon as his scientific interest had subsided, issued a host of woes, mainly subjective in origin.

He was fretted, for instance, by the thought that he would now have no opportunity to name his orchid, nor to write a paper upon it, and, still worse, there grew up in his mind the abominable conviction that, as soon as his plight was discovered, it was he who would be named and classified, and that he himself would be the subject of a paper; possibly, even, of comment and criticism in the lay press. Like all orchid collectors, he was excessively shy and sensitive, and in his present situation these qualities brought him to the verge of wilting. Worse yet was the fear of being transplanted, thrust into some unfamiliar, draughty, probably public place. Being dug up! Ugh! A violent shudder pulsated through all the heavy foliage that sprang from Mr. Mannering's division of the plant. He awoke to consciousness of ghostly and remote sensations in the stem below, and in certain tufts of leaves that sprouted from it; they were somehow reminiscent of spine and heart and limbs. He felt quite a dryad.

In spite of all, however, the sunshine was very pleasant. The rich odour of hot spicy earth filled the hot-house. From a special fixture on the hot-water pipes a little warm steam oozed into the air. Mr. Mannering began to abandon himself to a feeling of *laissez-aller*. Just then, up in the corner of the glass roof, at the

ventilator, he heard a persistent buzzing. Soon the note changed
from one of irritation to a more complacent sound; a bee had
managed to find his way, after some difficulty, through one of the
tiny chinks in the metal work. The visitor came drifting down and
down through the still, green air, as if into some sub-aqueous
world, and he came to rest on one of those petals which were Mr.
Mannering's eye-brows. Thence he commenced to explore one
feature after another, and at last he settled heavily on the lower
lip, which drooped under his weight and allowed him to crawl
right into Mr. Mannering's mouth. This was quite a considerable
shock, of course, but on the whole the sensation was neither as
alarming nor as unpleasant as might have been expected; indeed,
strange as it may sound, the appropriate word seemed to be something like . . . refreshing. Perhaps the little tongue had been
coated.

But Mr. Mannering soon ceased his drowsy toying with the
mot juste, when he saw the departed bee, after one or two lazy
circlings, settle directly upon the maiden lip of Cousin Jane. Ominous as lightning, a simple botanical principle flashed across the
mind of her wretched relative. Which principle? It is only too well
known. Even the very babes and sucklings are familiar with it. Is
it not drummed into their jaded ears by parents and governesses,
curates and the family doctor: is it not Exercise One in the principal subject on the kindergarten curriculum? Cousin Jane was
aware of it also, although, being the product of an earlier age, she
might have remained still blessedly ignorant had not her cousin,
vain, garrulous, proselytising fool, attempted for years past to
interest her in the rudiments of botany. How the miserable man
upbraided himself now!

He saw two bunches of leaves just below the flower tremble
and flutter, and rear themselves painfully upward into the very
likeness of two shocked and protesting hands. He saw the soft and
orderly petals of his cousin's face ruffle and incarnadine with rage
and embarrassment, then turn sickly as a gardenia with horror and
dismay. He thought, absurdly enough, of York and Lancaster.
But what was he to do? All the rectitude implanted by his careful
training, all the chivalry proper to an orchid-collector, boiled and
surged beneath a paralytically calm exterior. He positively trav-
ailed in the effort to activate the muscles of his face, to assume

an expression of grief, manly contrition, helplessness in the face of fate, willingness to make all honourable amends, all suffused with the light of a vague but solacing optimism; but it was all in vain. When he had strained till his nerves seemed likely to tear under the tension, the only movement he could achieve was a trivial flutter of the left eyelid—worse than nothing.

This incident completely aroused Mr. Mannering from his vegetable lethargy. He rebelled against the limitations of the form into which he had thus been cast while subjectively he remained all too human. Was he not still at heart a man, with a man's hopes, ideals, aspirations? And capacity for suffering.

When dusk came, and the opulent and sinister shapes of the great plant dimmed to a suggestiveness more powerfully impressive than had been its bright noonday luxuriance, and the atmosphere of a tropical forest filled the orchid-house like an exile's dream, or the nostalgia of the saxophone; when the cat's whiskers drooped and even Cousin Jane's eyes slowly closed, the unhappy man remained awake, staring into the gathering darkness. Suddenly the light in the study was switched on. Two men entered the room. One of them was his lawyer, the other was his nephew.

"This is his study, as you know, of course," said the wicked nephew. "There's nothing here. I looked round when I came over on Wednesday."

"Ah! well," said the lawyer. "It's a very queer business, an absolute mystery." He had evidently said so more than once before; they must have been discussing matters in another room. "Well, we must hope for the best. In the meantime, in all the circumstances, it's perhaps as well that you, as next-of-kin, should take charge of things here. We must hope for the best."

Saying this, the lawyer turned, about to go, and Mr. Mannering saw a malicious smile overspread the young man's face. The uneasiness which had overcome him at first sight of his nephew was intensified to fear and trembling at the sight of this smile.

When he had shown the lawyer out, the nephew returned to the study and looked around with a lively and sinister satisfaction. Then he cut a caper on the hearthrug. Mr. Mannering thought he had never seen anything so diabolical as this solitary expression of the glee of a venomous nature, at the prospect of unchecked sway here whence he had been outcast, license where he had been condemned. How vulgar petty triumph appeared, beheld thus; how disgusting petty spite, how appalling revengefulness and hardness of heart! He remembered suddenly that his nephew had been notable, in his repulsive childhood, for his cruelty to flies, tearing their wings off, and for his barbarity towards cats. A sort of dew might have been noticed upon the good man's forehead. It seemed to him that his nephew had only to glance that way and all would be discovered, although he might have remembered that it was impossible to see from the lighted room into the darkness in the hot-house. His own vision of events inside the room was, of course, only too clear.

On the mantelpiece stood a large unframed photograph of Mr. Mannering. His nephew soon caught sight of this, and strode across to confront it with a triumphant and insolent sneer. "What? You old Pharisee," said he, "taken her off for a trip to Brighton, have you? My God! How I hope you'll never come back! How I hope you've fallen over the cliffs, or got swept off by the tide or something! Anyway . . . I'll make hay while the sun shines. Ugh! you old skinflint, you!" And he reached forward his hand, on which the thumb held the middle finger bent and in check, and that finger, then released, rapped viciously upon the nose in the photograph. Then the usurping rascal left the room, and left all the lights on, presumably preferring the dining room with its tantalus and cellarette to the scholarly austerities of the study.

All night long the glare of electric light from the study fell full upon Mr. Mannering and his Cousin Jane, like the glare of a cheap and artificial sun. You, who have seen at midnight, in the park, a few insomniac asters standing stiff and startled under an arc-light, all their weak colour bleached out of them by the drenching chemical radiance, neither asleep nor awake, but held fast in a tense, a neurasthenic trance, you can form an idea of how the night passed with this unhappy pair.

And towards morning an incident occurred, trivial in itself, no doubt, but sufficient then and there to add the last drop to poor Cousin Jane's discomfiture, and to her relative's embarrassment and remorse. Along the edge of the great earth-box in which the orchid was planted, ran a small black mouse. It had wicked red eyes, a naked, evil snout and huge repellent ears, queer as a bat's. This creature ran straight over the lower leaves of Cousin Jane's part of the plant. It was simply appalling: the stringy main-stem writhed like a hair on a coal-fire, the leaves contracted in an agonised spasm, like seared mimosa; the terrified lady nearly uprooted herself in her convulsive horror. I think she would actually have done so, had not the mouse hurried on past her.

But it had not gone more than a foot or so when it looked up and saw, bending over it, and seeming positively to bristle with life, that flower which had once been called Tib. There was a breathless pause. The mouse was obviously paralysed with terror, the cat could only look and long. Suddenly the more human watchers saw a sly frond of foliage curve softly outward and close in behind the hypnotised creature. Cousin Jane, who had been thinking exultantly, "Well, now it'll go away and never, never, never come back," suddenly became aware of hideous possibilities. Summoning all her energy, and you must remember that she had been "out" some days longer than her cousin, and so had much more control of her leaves, she achieved a spasmodic flutter, enough to break the trance that held the mouse, so that, like a clockwork toy, it swung round and fled. But already the fell arm of the orchid had cut off its retreat, the mouse leapt straight at it, like a flash five tendrils at the end caught the fugitive and held it fast, and soon its body dwindled and was gone. Now the heart of Cousin Jane was troubled with horrid fears, and slowly and painfully she turned her weary face first to one side, then to the other, in a fever of anxiety as to where the new bud would appear. A sort of sucker, green and sappy, which twisted lightly about her main stem, and reared a blunt head, much like a tip of asparagus, close to her own, suddenly began to swell in the most suspicious manner. She squinted at it, fascinated and appalled. Could it be her imagination? It was not. . . . But, after all, what are these trifles?

Next evening the door opened again, and again the nephew entered the study. This time he was alone, and it was evident that he had come straight from table. He carried in his hand a decanter of whiskey capped by an inverted glass. Under his arm was a syphon. His face was distinctly flushed, and such a smile as is often seen in saloon bars played about his lips. These lips he occasionally pursed, while simultaneously his cheeks became a little distended: then they would suddenly collapse. He put down his burdens, and, turning to Mr. Mannering's cigar cabinet, produced a bunch of keys which he proceeded to try upon the lock, muttering vindictively at each abortive attempt, until it opened, when he helped himself from the best of its contents. Annoying as it was to witness this insolent appropriation of his property, and mortifying to see the contempt with which the cigar was smoked, the good gentleman found deeper cause for uneasiness in the thought that, with the possession of the keys, his abominable nephew had access to every private corner that was his.

At present, however, the usurper seemed indisposed to carry on investigations; he splashed a great deal of whiskey into the tumbler, and, relaxing into an attitude of extravagant comfort, proceeded to revolt his unseen audience by an exhibition of those animal grossnesses in which a certain type of man is wont to indulge when he fancies himself alone with his Maker. I mean wide, shameless yawning, sucking the teeth, or picking them with a finger-nail, eructations, hawking, spitting even. But after a while, the young man began to tire of his own company; he had not yet had time to gather any of his pot-house companions into his uncle's home, and repeated resource to the whiskey bottle only increased his longing for something to relieve the monotony. His eye fell upon the door of the orchid house. Sooner or later it was bound to have come to pass. Does this thought greatly console the condemned man when the fatal knock sounds upon the door of his cell? No. Nor were the hearts of the trembling pair in the hothouse at all succoured by the reflection.

As the nephew fumbled with the handle of the glass door, Cousin Jane slowly raised two fronds of leaves that grew on each side, high up on her stem, and sank her troubled head behind them. Mr. Mannering observed, in a sudden rapture of hope, that by this device she was fairly well concealed from any casual glance. Hastily he strove to follow her example. Unfortunately, he had not yet gained sufficient control of his—his limbs?—and all his tortured efforts could not raise them beyond an agonised horizontal. The door had opened, the nephew was feeling for the electric light switch just inside. It was a moment for one of the superlative achievements of panic. Mr. Mannering was well equipped for the occasion. Suddenly, at the cost of indescribable effort, he succeeded in raising the right frond, not straight upwards, it is true, but in a series of painful jerks along a curve outward and backward, and ascending by slow degrees till it attained the position of an arm held over the possessor's head from behind. Then, as the light flashed on, a spray of leaves at the very end of this frond spread out into a fan, rather like a very fleshy horse-chestnut leaf in structure, and covered the anxious face below. What a relief! And now the nephew advanced into the orchid-house, and now the hidden pair simultaneously remembered the fatal presence of the cat. Simultaneously also, their very sap stood still in their veins. The nephew was walking along by the plant. The cat, a sagacious beast, "knew" with the infallible intuition of its kind that this was an idler, a parasite, a sensualist, gross and brutal, disrespectful to age, insolent to weakness, barbarous to cats. Therefore it remained very still, trusting to its low and somewhat retired position on the plant, and to protective mimicry and such things, and to the half-drunken condition of the nephew, to avoid his notice. But all in vain.

"What?" said the nephew. "What, a cat?" And he raised his hand to offer a blow at the harmless creature. Something in the dignified and unflinching demeanour of his victim must have penetrated into even his besotted mind, for the blow never fell, and the bully, a coward at heart as bullies invariably are, shifted his gaze from side to side to escape the steady, contemptuous stare of the courageous cat. Alas! his eye fell on something glimmering whitely behind the dark foliage. He brushed aside the intervening leaves that he might see what it was. It was Cousin Jane.

"Oh! Ah!" said the young man, in great confusion. "*You're* back. But what are you hiding there for?"

His sheepish stare became fixed, his mouth opened in bewilderment: then the true condition of things dawned upon his mind. Most of us would have at once instituted some attempts at communication, or at assistance of some kind, or at least have knelt down to thank our Creator that we had, by His grace, been spared such a fate, or perhaps have made haste from the orchid-house to ensure against accidents. But alcohol had so inflamed the young man's hardened nature that he felt neither fear nor awe nor gratitude, and as for any spirit of helpfulness, that was as far as ever from his hard revengeful heart. As he grasped the situation a devilish smile overspread his face.

"Ha! Ha! Ha!" said he, "but where's the old man?"

He peered about the plant, looking eagerly for his uncle. In a moment he had located him, and raising the inadequate vizor of leaves, discovered beneath it the face of our hero, troubled with a hundred bitter emotions.

"Hullo, Narcissus!" said the nephew.

A long silence ensued. The nephew was so pleased that he could not say a word. He rubbed his hands together, and licked his lips, and stared and stared as a child might at a new toy.

"You're properly up a tree now," he said. "Yes, the tables are turned now all right, aren't they? Ha! Ha! Do you remember last time we met?"

A flicker of emotion passed over the face of the suffering blossom, betraying consciousness.

"Yes, you can hear what I say," added the tormentor. "Feel too, I expect. What about that?"

As he spoke, he stretched out his hand, and, seizing a delicate frill of fine, silvery filaments that grew as whiskers grow round the lower half of the flower, he administered a sharp tug. The result would have interested that ingenious experimenter, Sir J. C. Bose. Without pausing to note, however, even in the interests of science, the subtler shades of his uncle's reaction, content with the general effect of that devastating wince, the wretch chuckled with satisfaction, and, taking a long pull from the reeking butt of the stolen cigar, puffed the vile fumes straight into his victim's centre. The brute!

"How do you like that, John the Baptist?" he asked with a leer. "Good for the blight, you know. Just what you want!"

Something rustled upon his coat sleeve. Looking down, he saw a long stalk, well adorned with the fatal tendrils, groping its way over the arid and unsatisfactory surface. In a moment it had reached his wrist, he felt it fasten, but knocked it off as one would a leech, before it had time to establish its hold.

"Ugh!" said he, "so that's how it happens, is it? I think I'll keep outside till I get the hang of things a bit. *I* don't want to be made an Aunt Sally of. Though I shouldn't think they could get you with your clothes on." Struck by a sudden thought, he looked from his uncle to Cousin Jane, and from Cousin Jane back to his uncle again. He scanned the floor, and saw a single crumpled bath-towel robe lying in the shadow.

"Why?" he said, "*well!* . . . Haw! Haw! Haw!" And with an odious backward leer, he made his way out of the orchid-house.

Mr. Mannering felt that his suffering was capable of no increase. Yet he dreaded the morrow. His fevered imagination patterned the long night with waking nightmares, utterly fantastic visions of humiliation and torture. Torture! It was absurd, of course, for him to fear cold-blooded atrocities on the part of his nephew, but how he dreaded some outrageous whim that might tickle the youth's sense of humour, and lead him to *any* wanton freak, especially if he were drunk at the time. He thought of slugs and snails, espaliers and topiary. Oh! Oh! Oh! If only the monster would rest content with insults and mockery, with wasting his substance, ravaging his cherished possessions before his eyes, with occasional pulling at the whiskers, even! Then it might be possible to turn gradually from all that still remained in him of man, to subdue the passions, no longer to admire or desire to go native, as it were, relapsing into the Nirvana of a vegetable dream. But in the morning he found this was not so easy.

In came the nephew, and, pausing only to utter the most perfunctory of jeers at his relatives in the glass-house, he sat at the desk and unlocked the top drawer. He was evidently in search of money, his eagerness betrayed that; no doubt he had run through all he had filched from his uncle's pockets, and had not yet worked out a scheme for getting direct control of his bank account. However, the drawer held enough to cause the scoundrel to rub his hands with satisfaction, and, summoning the housekeeper, to bellow into her ear a reckless order upon the wine and spirit merchant.

"Get along with you," he shouted, when he had at last made her understand. "I shall have to get someone a bit more on the spot to wait on me! I can tell you that. Yes," he added to himself as the poor old woman hobbled away, deeply hurt by his bullying manner, "yes, a nice little parlour-maid . . . a nice little parlour-maid."

He hunted in the Buff Book for the number of the local registry office. That afternoon he interviewed a succession of maidservants in his uncle's study. Those that happened to be plain, or too obviously respectable, he treated curtly and coldly; they soon made way for others. It was only when a girl was attractive (according to the young man's depraved tastes, that is), and also

bore herself in a fast or brazen manner, that the interviews were
at all prolonged. In these cases the nephew would conclude in a
fashion that left no doubt at all in the minds of any of his auditors
as to his real intentions. Once, for example, leaning forward, he
took the girl by the chin, saying with an odious smirk, "There's
no one else but me, and so you'd be treated just like one of the
family; d'you see, my dear?" To another he would say, slipping
his arm round her waist, "Do you think we shall get on well together? Will you make me nice and cosy and comfortable, eh?"
He addressed one as "Baby," another as "Chicken." I can't imagine
what poor Cousin Jane must have thought.

After this conduct had sent two or three in confusion from
the room, there entered a young person of the most regrettable
description, one whose character, betrayed as it was in her mere-
tricious finery, her crude cosmetics and her tinted hair, showed yet
more clearly in florid gesture and too facile smile. The nephew lost
no time in coming to an arrangement with this creature. Indeed,
her true nature was so obvious that the depraved young man only
went through the farce of an ordinary interview as a sauce to his
anticipations, enjoying the contrast between conventional dialogue
and unbridled glances. She was to come next day. Mr. Mannering
feared more for his unhappy cousin than for himself. "What
scenes may she not have to witness," he thought, "that yellow
cheek of hers to incarnadine?" If he only could have said a few
words!

But that evening, when the nephew came to take his ease in
the study, it was obvious that he was far more under the influence
of liquor than had been the case before. His face, flushed patchily
by the action of the spirits, wore a sullen sneer, an ominous light
burned in that bleared eye, he muttered savagely under his breath.
Clearly this fiend in human shape was what is known as "fighting
drunk," clearly some trifle had set his vile temper in a blaze.

It is interesting to note, even at this stage, a sudden change in
Mr. Mannering's reactions. They now seemed entirely egotistical,
and were to be elicited only by stimuli directly associated with
physical matters. The nephew kicked a hole in a screen in his
drunken fury, he flung a burning cigar-end down on the carpet, he
scratched matches on the polished table. His uncle witnessed this
with the calm of one whose sense of property and of dignity has

become numbed and paralysed; he felt neither fury nor mortifica-tion. Had he, by one of those sudden strides by which all such development takes place, approached much nearer to his goal, complete vegetation? His concern for the threatened modesty of Cousin Jane, which had moved him so strongly only a few hours earlier, must have been the last dying flicker of exhausted altru-ism; that most human characteristic had faded from him. He felt that relief which certain sick people feel when they first notice the influence of a drug as an irregular blur on their consciousness of pain, or which unhappy lovers enjoy when they first rub their hands and skip about the room in a morning ecstasy of (probably illusory) indifference. But instead of running to the glass and rapturously greeting himself as a long-lost friend, as this latter class generally do, Mr. Mannering soberly prepared to bid his personality farewell. The change, however, in its present stage, was not an unmixed blessing. Narrowing in from the wider and more expressly human regions of his being, his consciousness now left outside its focus not only pride and altruism, which had been responsible for much of his woe, but fortitude and detachment also, which, with quotation from the Greeks, had been his support before the whole battery of his distresses. Moreover, within its constricted circle, his ego was not reduced but concentrated; his serene, flower-like indifference towards the ill-usage of his furni-ture was balanced by the absorbed, flower-like single-mindedness of his terror at the thought of similar ill-usage directed towards himself. It is important now to appreciate this white, intense light of Mr. Mannering's apprehensions.

What a strange shock it would be, if, shall we say, in the third act of 'Hamlet,' the mind, dispread in contemplation of diverse forces converging harmoniously on some still-distant con-summation, was suddenly *jabbed* (as a sea anemone by a stick) by the spectacle of the King treading by chance upon Hamlet's toe, and causing him such annoyance, that, in a flash . . .

Inside the study the nephew still fumed and swore. On the mantelpiece stood an envelope, addressed in Mr. Mannering's hand-writing to Cousin Jane. In it was the letter he had written from Town, describing his nephew's disgraceful conduct. The young man's eye fell upon this, and, unscrupulous, impelled by idle curiosity, he took it up and drew out the letter. As he read, his face grew a hundred times blacker than before.

"What?" he muttered, " '. . . a mere racecourse cad . . . a worthless vulgarian . . . a scoundrel of the sneaking sort' . . . and what's this? . . . '. . . cut him off absolutely' . . . What?" said he, with a horrifying oath, "*Would* you cut me off absolutely? Two can play at that game, you old devil!"

And he snatched up a large pair of scissors that lay on the desk, and burst into the hot-house.

Among fish, the dory, they say, screams when it is seized upon by man; among insects, the caterpillar of the death's-head moth is capable of a still, small shriek of terror; in the vegetable world, only the mandrake could voice its agony—till now.

●

What gentle ghost, besprent with April dew,
Hails me so solemnly to yonder yew?

—BEN JONSON

●

The dress of the fairies. They wear a red conical cap; a mantle of green cloth, inlaid with wild flowers; green pantaloons, buttoned with bobs of silk; and silver shoon. They carry quivers of adder-slough, and bows made of the ribs of a man buried where "three lairds' lands meet;" their arrows are made of bog-reed, tipped with white flints, and dipped in the dew of hemlock; they ride on steeds whose hoofs would not "dash the dew from the cup of a harebell."

—CROMEK

THE TELL-TALE HEART

Those who consider themselves sane, and who find it uncomfortable to believe in ghosts, are likely to ascribe all ghostly phenomena to madness. *The Horla*, and one or two other stories herein, gain much of their effect by setting up a conflict in the reader's own mind over the question of the spokesman's sanity. In this story, with all its terrible brevity, we are spared such doubts. The effect is that of a man obviously mad from the first sentence, betraying his own madness by his effort to appear reasonable and sane.—EDITOR.

Edgar Allan Poe

THE TELL-
TALE HEART

True! nervous, very, very dreadfully nervous I had been and am; but why *will* you say that I am mad? The disease had sharpened my senses, not destroyed, not dulled them. Above all was the sense of hearing acute. I heard all things in the heaven and in the earth. I heard many thing in hell. How, then, am I mad? Hearken! and observe how healthily—how calmly I can tell you the whole story.

It is impossible to say how first the idea entered my brain; but once conceived, it haunted me day and night. Object there was none. Passion there was none. I loved the old man. He had never wronged me. He had never given me insult. For his gold I had no desire. I think it was his eye! yes, it was this! One of his eyes resembled that of a vulture—a pale blue eye, with a film over it. Whenever it fell upon me, my blood ran cold; and so by degrees, very gradually, I made up my mind to take the life of the old man, and thus rid myself of the eye for ever.

Now this is the point. You fancy me mad. Madmen know nothing. But you should have seen *me*. You should have seen how wisely I proceeded—with what caution—with what foresight, with what dissimulation, I went to work. I was never kinder to the old man than during the whole week before I killed him. And every night, about midnight, I turned the latch of his door and opened it—oh, so gently! And then, when I had made an opening sufficient for my head, I put in a dark lantern, all closed, closed, so that no light shone out, and then I thrust in my head. Oh, you would have laughed to see how cunningly I thrust it in! I moved it slowly, very, very slowly, so that I might not disturb the old man's sleep. It took me an hour to place my whole head within the opening so far that I could see him as he lay upon his bed. Ha! would a mad-man have been so wise as this? And then, when my head was well in the room, I undid the lantern cautiously—oh, so cautiously— cautiously (for the hinges creaked), I undid it just so much that a single thin ray fell upon the vulture eye. And this I did for seven long nights, every night just at midnight, but I found the eye always closed, and so it was impossible to do the work; for it was not the old man who vexed me, but his Evil Eye. And every morn- ing, when the day broke, I went boldly into the chamber, and spoke courageously to him, calling him by name in a hearty tone, and inquiring how he had passed the night. So you see he would have been a very profound old man, indeed, to suspect that every night, just at twelve, I looked in upon him while he slept.

Upon the eighth night I was more than usually cautious in opening the door. A watch's minute hand moves more quickly than did mine. Never before that night had I *felt* the extent of my own powers, of my own sagacity. I could scarcely contain my feelings of triumph. To think that there I was, opening the door, little by little, and he not even to dream of my secret deeds or thoughts. I fairly chuckled at the idea; and perhaps he heard me; for he moved on the bed suddenly, as if startled. Now you may think that I drew back—but no. His room was as black as pitch with the thick darkness (for the shutters were close fastened through fear of robbers), and so I knew that he could not see the opening of the door, and I kept pushing it on steadily, steadily.

I had my head in, and was about to open the lantern, when my thumb slipped upon the tin fastening, and the old man sprang up in the bed, crying out, "Who's there?"

I kept quite still and said nothing. For a whole hour I did not move a muscle, and in the meantime I did not hear him lie down. He was still sitting up in the bed listening; just as I have done, night after night, hearkening to the death watches in the wall.

Presently I heard a slight groan, and I knew it was the groan of mortal terror. It was not a groan of pain or grief—oh no! it was the low stifled sound that arises from the bottom of the soul when overcharged with awe. I knew the sound well. Many a night, just at midnight, when all the world slept, it has welled up from my own bosom, deepening, with its dreadful echo, the terrors that distracted me. I say I knew it well. I knew what the old man felt, and pitied him, although I chuckled at heart. I knew that he had been lying awake ever since the first slight noise, when he had turned in the bed. His fears had been ever since growing upon him. He had been trying to fancy them causeless, but could not. He had been saying to himself, "It is nothing but the wind in the chimney, it is only a mouse crossing the floor," or "It is merely a cricket which has made a single chirp." Yes, he has been trying to comfort himself with these suppositions; but he had found all in vain. *All in vain;* because Death, in approaching him, had stalked with his black shadow before him, and enveloped the victim. And it was the mournful influence of the unperceived shadow that caused him to feel, although he neither saw nor heard, to *feel* the presence of my head within the room.

When I had waited a long time, very patiently, without hearing him lie down, I resolved to open a little—a very, very little crevice in the lantern. So I opened it—you cannot imagine how stealthily, stealthily—until, at length, a single dim ray, like the thread of the spider, shot out from the crevice and fell upon the vulture eye.

It was open—wide, wide open—and I grew furious as I gazed upon it. I saw it with perfect distinctness—all a dull blue, with a hideous veil over it that chilled the very marrow in my bones;

but I could see nothing else of the old man's face or person: for I had directed the ray as if by instinct, precisely upon the damned spot.

And now have I not told you that what you mistake for madness is but over-acuteness of the senses? Now, I say, there came to my ears a low, dull, quick sound, such as a watch makes when enveloped in cotton. I knew *that* sound well too. It was the beating of the old man's heart. It increased my fury, as the beating of a drum stimulates the soldier into courage.

But even yet I refrained and kept still. I scarcely breathed. I held the lantern motionless. I tried how steadily I could maintain the ray upon the eye. Meantime the hellish tattoo of the heart increased. It grew quicker and quicker, and louder and louder every instant. The old man's terror *must* have been extreme! It grew louder, I say, louder every moment!—do you mark me well? I have told you that I am nervous: so I am. And now at the dead hour of the night, amid the dreadful silence of that old house, so strange a noise as this excited me to uncontrollable terror. Yet, for some minutes longer I refrained and stood still. But the beating grew louder, louder! I thought the heart must burst. And now a new anxiety seized me—the sound would be heard by a neighbor! The old man's hour had come! With a loud yell, I threw open the lantern and leaped into the room. He shrieked once—once only. In an instant I dragged him to the floor, and pulled the heavy bed over him. I then smiled gaily, to find the deed so far done. But, for many minutes, the heart beat on with a muffled sound. This, however, did not vex me; it would not be heard through the wall. At length it ceased. The old man was dead. I removed the bed and examined the corpse. Yes, he was stone, stone dead. I placed my hand upon the heart and held it there many minutes. There was no pulsation. He was stone dead. His eye would trouble me no more.

If still you think me mad, you will think so no longer when I describe the wise precautions I took for the concealment of the body. The night waned, and I worked hastily, but in silence. First of all I dismembered the corpse. I cut off the head and the arms and the legs.

I then took up three planks from the flooring of the chamber, and deposited all between the scantlings. I then replaced the boards so cleverly, so cunningly, that no human eye—not even *his*—could have detected anything wrong. There was nothing to wash out—no stain of any kind—no blood-spot whatever. I had been too wary for that. A tub had caught all—ha! ha!

When I had made an end of these labors, it was four o'clock—still dark as midnight. As the bell sounded the hour, there came a knocking at the street door. I went down to open it with a light heart, for what had I *now* to fear? There entered three men, who introduced themselves, with perfect suavity, as officers of the police. A shriek had been heard by a neighbor during the night: suspicion of foul play had been aroused; information had been lodged at the police office, and they (the officers) had been deputed to search the premises.

I smiled,—for *what* had I to fear? I bade the gentlemen welcome. The shriek, I said, was my own in a dream. The old man, I mentioned, was absent in the country. I took my visitors all over the house. I bade them search—search *well*. I led them, at length, to *his* chamber. I showed them his treasures, secure, undisturbed. In the enthusiasm of my confidence, I brought chairs into the room, and desired them *here* to rest from their fatigues, while I myself, in the wild audacity of my perfect triumph, placed my own seat up on the very spot beneath which reposed the corpse of the victim.

The officers were satisfied. My *manner* had convinced them. I was singularly at ease. They sat, and while I answered cheerily, they chatted of familiar things. But, ere long, I felt myself getting pale and wished them gone. My head ached, and I fancied a ringing in my ears: but still they sat and still they chatted. The ringing became more distinct;—it continued and became more distinct: I talked more freely to get rid of the feeling: but it continued and gained definitiveness—until, at length, I found that the noise was *not* within my ears.

No doubt I now grew *very* pale;—but I talked more fluently, and with a heightened voice. Yet the sound increased—and what could I do? It *was a low, dull, quick sound—much such a sound as a watch makes when enveloped in cotton.* I gasped for breath—and yet the officers heard it not. I talked more quickly—more vehemently; but the noise steadily increased. I arose and argued about trifles, in a high key and with violent gesticulations, but the noise steadily increased. Why *would* they not be gone? I paced the floor to and fro with heavy strides, as if excited to fury by the observation of the men—but the noise steadily increased. Oh God! what *could* I do? I foamed—I raved—I swore! I swung the chair upon which I had been sitting, and grated it upon the boards, but the noise arose over all and continually increased. It grew louder —louder—*louder!* And still the men chatted pleasantly, and smiled. Was it possible they heard not? Almighty God!—no, no! They heard!—they suspected!—they *knew!*—they were making a *mockery* of my horror!—this I thought, and this I think. But anything was better than this agony! Anything was more tolerable than this derision! I could bear those hypocritical smiles no longer! I felt that I must scream or die!—and now—again!—hark! louder! louder! louder! *louder!*——

"Villains!" I shrieked, "dissemble no more! I admit the deed! —tear up the planks!—here, here!—it is the beating of his hideous heart!"

●

In the most high and palmy state of Rome,
A little ere the mightiest Julius fell,
The graves stood tenantless and the sheeted dead
Did squeak and gibber in the Roman streets.

—Hamlet

●

DR. —— TWISS, minister of the new church at West-minister, told me that his father, (Dr. Twiss, prolocutor of the assembly of divines, and author of *Vindiciae Gratiæ*) when he was a school-boy at Winchester, saw the phantom of a school-fellow of his, deceased, (a rakehell) who said to him "I am damned." This was the occasion of Dr. Twiss's (the father's) conversion, who had been before that time, as he told his son, a very wicked boy; he was hypochondriacal. There is a story like this, of the conversion of St. Bruno, by an apparition: upon which he became mighty devout, and founded the order of the Carthusians.

—JOHN AUBREY

A VISITOR FROM DOWN UNDER

"Down Under," in England, means the antipodes. Specifically it means Australia. Perhaps the author intends a double meaning, in this story. *A Visitor from Down Under* had acquired fame even before it first appeared in book form, in *The Killing Bottle:* 1932. It has been reprinted in several anthologies. I present it again here chiefly as an excellent example of the out-and-out ghost story in the modern manner, gaining power in contrast with the Gothic romance by the very fact that it leaves out the fantastic appurtenances of such stories of a century ago, and uses thoroughly commonplace surroundings.—EDITOR.

L. P. Hartley

A VISITOR
FROM DOWN
UNDER

"And who will you send to fetch him away?"

After a promising start, the March day had
ended in a wet evening. It was hard to tell whether rain or fog
predominated. The loquacious 'bus-conductor said "A foggy evening" to those who rode inside, and "A wet evening" to such as
were obliged to ride outside. But in or on the 'buses, cheerfulness
held the field, for their patrons, inured to discomfort, made light
of climatic inclemency. All the same, the weather was worth
remarking on: the most scrupulous conversationalist could refer to
it without feeling self-convicted of banality. How much more the
conductor, who, in common with most of his kind, had a considerable conversational gift.

The 'bus was making its last journey through the heart of London before turning in for the night. Inside it was only half full. Outside, as the conducter was aware by virtue of his sixth sense, there still remained a passenger too hardy or too lazy to seek shelter. And now, as the 'bus rattled rapidly down the Strand, the footsteps of this person could be heard shuffling and creaking upon the metal-shod stairs.

"Anyone on top?" asked the conductor, addressing an errant umbrella-point and the hem of a mackintosh.

"I didn't notice anyone," the man replied.

"It's not that I don't trust you," remarked the conductor, pleasantly giving a hand to his alighting fare; "but I think I'll go up and make sure."

Moments like these, moments of mistrust in the infallibility of his observation, occasionally visited the conductor. They came at the end of a tiring day, and if he could he withstood them. They were signs of weakness, he thought; and to give way to them matter for self-reproach. "Going barmy, that's what you are," he told himself, and he casually took a fare inside to prevent his mind dwelling on the unvisited outside. But his unreasoning disquietude survived this distraction, and murmuring against himself he started to climb the stairs.

To his surprise, almost stupefaction, he found that his misgivings were justified. Breasting the ascent, he saw a passenger sitting on the right-hand front seat; and the passenger, in spite of his hat turned down, his collar turned up and the creased white muffler that showed between the two, must have heard him coming; for though the man was looking straight ahead, in his outstretched left hand, wedged between the first and second fingers, he held a coin.

"Jolly evening, don't you think," asked the conductor, who wanted to say something. The passenger made no reply, but the penny, for such it was, slipped the fraction of an inch lower in the groove between the pale freckled fingers.

"I said it was a damn wet night," the conductor persisted irritably, annoyed by the man's reserve. Still no reply.

"Where you for?" asked the conductor, in a tone suggesting that, wherever it was, it must be a discreditable destination.

"Carrick Street."

"Where?" the conductor demanded. He had heard all right, but a slight peculiarity in the passenger's pronunciation made it appear reasonable to him, and possibly humiliating to the passenger, that he should not have heard.

"Carrick Street."

"Then why don't you say Carrick Street?" the conductor grumbled as he punched the ticket.

There was a moment's pause, then "Carrick Street," the passenger repeated.

"Yes, I know, I know; you needn't go on telling me," fumed the conductor, fumbling with the passenger's penny. He couldn't get hold of it from above, it had slipped too far, so he passed his hand underneath the other's and drew the coin from between his fingers.

It was cold, even where it had been held.

"Know?" said the stranger suddenly, "what do you know?"

The conductor was trying to draw his fare's attention to the ticket, but could not make him look round. "I suppose I know you are a clever chap," he remarked. "Look here now. Where do you want this ticket? In your buttonhole?"

"Put it here," said the passenger.

"Where?" asked the conductor. "You aren't a blooming letter-rack."

"Where the penny was," replied the passenger. "Between my fingers."

The conductor felt reluctant, he did not know why, to oblige the passenger in this. The rigidity of the hand disconcerted him: it was stiff, he supposed, or perhaps paralysed. And since he had been standing on the top his own hands were none too warm. The ticket doubled up and grew limp under his repeated efforts to push it in. He bent lower, for he was a good-hearted fellow, and using both hands, one above and one below, he slid the ticket into its bony slot.

"Right you are, Kaiser Bill."

Perhaps the passenger resented this jocular allusion to his physical infirmity; perhaps he merely wanted to be quiet. All he said was:

"Don't speak to me again."

"Speak to you!" shouted the conductor, losing all self-control. "Catch me speaking to a stuffed dummy!"

Muttering to himself, he withdrew into the bowels of the 'bus.

At the corner of Carrick Street quite a number of people got on board. All wanted to be first, but pride of place was shared by three women, who all tried to enter simultaneously.

The conductor's voice made itself audible above the din: "Now then, now then, look where you're shoving! This isn't a bargain-sale. Gently, *please*, lady, he's only a pore old man." In a moment or two the confusion abated, and the conductor, his hand on the cord of the bell, bethought himself of the passenger on top whose destination Carrick Street was. He had forgotten to get down. Yielding to his good nature, for the conductor was averse to further conversation with his uncommunicative fare, he mounted the stairs, put his head over the top and shouted, "Carrick Street! Carrick Street!" That was the utmost he could bring himself to do. But his admonition was without effect; his summons remained unanswered; nobody came. "Well, if he wants to stay up there he can," muttered the conductor, still aggrieved. "I won't fetch him down, cripple or no cripple." The 'bus moved on. He slipped by me, thought the conductor, while all that Cup-tie crowd was getting in.

The same evening, some five hours earlier, a taxi turned into Carrick Street and pulled up at the door of a small hotel. The street was empty. It looked like a cul-de-sac, but in reality it was pierced at the far end by an alley, like a thin sleeve, which wound its way into Soho.

"That the last, sir?" enquired the driver, after several transits between the cab and the hotel.

"How many does that make?"

"Nine packages in all, sir."

"Could you get all your worldly goods into nine packages, driver?"

"That I could; into two."

"Well, have a look inside and see if I have left anything."

The cabman felt about among the cushions. "Can't find nothing, sir."

"What do you do with anything you find?" asked the stranger.

"Take it to New Scotland Yard, sir," the driver promptly replied.

"Scotland Yard?" said the stranger. "Strike a match, will you, and let me have a look."

But he, too, found nothing, and, reassured, followed his luggage into the hotel.

A chorus of welcome and congratulation greeted him. The manager, the manager's wife, the ministers without portfolio of which all hotels are full, the porters, the lift-man, all clustered around him.

"Well, Mr. Rumbold, after all these years! We thought you'd forgotten us! And wasn't it odd, the very night your telegram came from Australia, we'd been talking about you! And my husband said, 'Don't you worry about Mr. Rumbold! He'll fall on his feet all right. Some fine day he'll walk in here a rich man.' Not that you weren't always well-off, but my husband meant a millionaire."

"He was quite right," said Mr. Rumbold slowly, savouring his words; "I am."

"There, what did I tell you?" the manager exclaimed, as though one recital of his prophecy was not enough. "But I wonder you're not too grand to come to Rossall's Hotel."

"I've nowhere else to go," said the millionaire shortly. "And if I had, I wouldn't. This place is like home to me."

His eyes softened as they scanned the familiar surroundings. They were light-grey eyes, very pale, and seeming paler from their setting in his tanned face. His cheeks were slightly sunken and very deeply lined; his blunt-ended nose was straight. He had a thin straggling moustache, straw-coloured, which made his age difficult to guess. Perhaps he was nearly fifty, so wasted was the skin on his neck, but his movements, unexpectedly agile and decided, were those of a younger man.

"I won't go up to my room now," he said, in response to the manageress's question. "Ask Clutsam—he's still with you?—good— to unpack my things. He'll find all I want for the night in the green suit-case. I'll take my despatch-box with me. And tell them to bring me a sherry-and-bitters in the lounge."

As the crow flies, it was not far to the lounge. But by way of the tortuous, ill-lit passages, doubling on themselves, yawning with dark entries, plunging into kitchen stairs—the catacombs so dear to the habitués of Rossall's Hotel—it was a considerable distance. Anyone posted in the shadow of these alcoves, or arriving at the head of the basement staircase, could not have failed to notice the air of utter content which marked Mr. Rumbold's leisurely progress: the droop of his shoulders, acquiescing in weariness; the hands turned inwards and swaying slightly, but quite forgotten by their owner; the chin, always prominent, now pushed forward so far that it looked relaxed and helpless, not at all defiant. The unseen witness would have envied Mr. Rumbold, perhaps even grudged him his holiday airs, his untroubled acceptance of the present and the future.

A waiter whose face he did not remember brought him the *apéritif* which he drank slowly, his feet propped unconventionally upon a ledge of the chimney-piece; a pardonable relaxation, for the room was empty. Judge therefore his surprise when, out of a fire-engendered drowsiness, he heard a voice which seemed to come from the wall above his head. A cultivated voice, perhaps too cultivated, slightly husky, yet careful and precise in its enunciation. Even while his eyes searched the room to make sure that no one had come in, he could not help hearing everything the voice said. It seemed to be talking to him, and yet the rather oracular utterance implied a less restricted audience. The utterance of a man who was aware that, though it was a duty for him to speak, for Mr. Rumbold to listen would be both a pleasure and a profit.

"——A Children's Party," the voice announced in an even, neutral tone, nicely balanced between approval and distaste, between enthusiasm and boredom: "six little girls and six little" (a faint lift in the voice, expressive of tolerant surprise) "boys. The Broadcasting Company has invited them to tea, and they are anxious that you should share some of their fun." (At the last word the voice became almost positively colourless.) "I must tell you that they have had tea, and enjoyed it, didn't you, children?" (A cry of "Yes," muffled and timid, greeted this leading question.) "We should have liked you to hear our table-talk, but there wasn't much of it, we were so busy eating." For a moment the voice identified itself with the children. "But we can tell you what we ate. Now, Percy, tell us what you had."

A piping little voice recited a long list of comestibles: like the children in the treacle-well, thought Rumbold, Percy must have been, or soon would be, very ill. A few others volunteered the items of their repast. "So you see," said the voice, "we have not done so badly. And now we are going to have crackers, and afterwards" (the voice hesitated and seemed to dissociate itself from the words) "children's games." There was an impressive pause, broken by the muttered exhortation of a little girl: "Don't cry, Philip, it won't hurt you." Fugitive sparks and snaps of sound followed; more like a fire being mended, thought Rumbold, than crackers. A murmur of voices pierced the fusillade. "What have you got, Alec, what have you *got?*" "I've got a cannon." "Give it to me." "No." "Well, lend it to me." "What do you want it for?" "I want to shoot · Jimmy."

Mr. Rumbold started. Something had disturbed him. Was it imagination, or did he hear, above the confused medley of sound, a tiny click? The voice was speaking again. "And now we're going to begin the games." As though to make amends for past luke-warmness a faint flush of anticipation gave colour to the decorous voice. "We will commence with that old favourite, Ring-a-ring-of-Roses."

The children were clearly shy, and left each other to do the singing. Their courage lasted for a line or two, and then gave out. But fortified by the Speaker's baritone, powerful though subdued, they took heart, and soon were singing without assistance or direc-tion. Their light wavering voices had a charming effect. Tears stood in Mr. Rumbold's eyes. "Oranges and Lemons" came next. A more difficult game, it yielded several unrehearsed effects before it finally got under way. One could almost see the children being marshalled into their places as though for a figure in the Lancers. Some of them no doubt had wanted to play another game; children are contrary, and the dramatic side of "Oranges and Lemons," though it appeals to many, always affrights a few. The disinclina-tion of these last would account for the pauses and hesitations which irritated Mr. Rumbold, who, as a child, had always had a strong fancy for this particular game. When, to the tramping and stamping of many small feet, the droning chant began, he leaned back and closed his eyes in ecstasy. He listened intently for the final accelerando which leads up to the catastrophe. Still the prologue maundered on, as though the children were anxious to extend the period of security, the joyous care-free promenade which the great Bell of Bow by his inconsiderate profession of ignorance, was so rudely to curtail. The Bells of Old Bailey pressed their usurers' question; the Bells of Shoreditch answered with becoming flippancy; the Bells of Stepney posed their ironical query, when suddenly before the great Bell of Bow had time to get his word in, Mr. Rumbold's feelings underwent a strange revolution. Why couldn't the game continue, all sweetness and sunshine? Why drag in the fatal issue? Let payment be deferred; let the bells go on chiming and never strike the hour. But heedless of Mr. Rumbold's squeamishness, the game went its way. After the eating comes the reckoning.

> "Here is a candle to light you to bed,
> And here comes a chopper to chop off your head!
> Chop, chop, chop . . ."

A child screamed, and there was silence.

Mr. Rumbold felt quite upset, and great was his relief when, after a few more half-hearted rounds of "Oranges and Lemons," the voice announced, "Here we come gathering Nuts and May." At least there was nothing sinister in that. Delicious sylvan scene, comprising in one splendid botanical inexactitude all the charms of winter, spring, and autumn.

What superiority to circumstance was implied in the conjunction of nuts and may! What defiance of cause and effect! What a testimony to coincidence! For cause and effect are against us, as witness the fate of Old Bailey's Debtor; but coincidence is always on our side, always teaching us how to eat our cake and have it! The long arm of coincidence; Mr. Rumbold would have liked to clasp it by the hand.

Meanwhile his own hand conducted the music of the revels and his foot kept time. Their pulses quickened by enjoyment, the children put more heart into the singing; the game went with a swing; the ardour and rhythm of it invaded the little room where Mr. Rumbold sat. Like heavy fumes the waves of sound poured

in, so penetrating, they ravished the sense, so sweet they intoxicated it, so light they fanned it to a flame. Mr. Rumbold was transported. His hearing, sharpened by the subjugation and quiescence
of his other faculties, began to take in new sounds; the names, for
instance, of the players who were "wanted" to make up each side
and of the champions who were to pull them over. For the lis-
teners-in, the issues of the struggles remained in doubt. Did Nancy
Price succeed in detracting Percy Kinkham from his allegiance?
Probably. Did Alec Wharton prevail against Maisie Drew? It was
certainly an easy win for someone: the contest lasted only a
second, and a ripple of laughter greeted it. Did Violet Kingham
make good against Horace Gold? This was a dire encounter,
punctuated by deep irregular panting. Mr. Rumbold could see, in
his mind's eye, the two champions straining backwards and forwards across the white motionless handkerchief, their faces red
and puckered with exertion. Violet or Horace, one of them had
to go: Violet might be bigger than Horace, but then Horace was
a boy: they were evenly matched: they had their pride to maintain.
The moment when the will was broken and the body went limp
in surrender would be like a moment of dissolution. Yes, even this
game had its stark, uncomfortable side. Violet or Horace, one of
them was smarting now; crying perhaps under the humiliation of
being fetched away.

The game began afresh. This time there was an eager ring in
the children's voices: two tried antagonists were going to meet: it
would be a battle of giants. The chant throbbed into a war-cry.

> "Who will you have for your Nuts and May,
>   Nuts and May, Nuts and May?
> Who will you have for your Nuts and May
>   On a cold and frosty morning?"

They would have Victor Rumbold for Nuts and May, Victor
Rumbold, Victor Rumbold; and from the vindictiveness in their
voices they might have meant to have his blood too.

> "And who will you send to fetch him away,
>   Fetch him away, fetch him away?
> Who will you send to fetch him away
>   On a cold and frosty morning?"

Like a clarion call, a shout of defiance, came the reply:

> "We'll send Jimmy Hagberd to fetch him away,
>   Fetch him away, fetch him away;
> We'll send Jimmy Hagberd to fetch him away,
>   On a wet and foggy evening."

This variation, it might be supposed, was intended to promote the contest from the realms of pretence into the world of reality. But Mr. Rumbold probably did not hear that his abduction had been antedated. He had turned quite green and his head was lolling against the back of the chair.

"Any wine, sir?"

"Yes, Clutsam, a bottle of champagne."

"Very good, sir."

Mr. Rumbold drained the first glass at one go.

"Anyone coming in to dinner besides me, Clutsam?" he presently enquired.

"Not now, sir, it's nine o'clock," replied the waiter, his voice edged with reproach.

"Sorry, Clutsam, I didn't feel up to the mark before dinner, so I went and lay down."

The waiter was mollified.

"Thought you weren't looking quite yourself, sir. No bad news, I hope?"

"No, nothing. Just a bit tired after the journey."

"And how did you leave Australia, sir?" enquired the waiter, to accommodate Mr. Rumbold, who seemed anxious to talk.

"In better weather than you have here," Mr. Rumbold replied, finishing his second glass, and measuring with his eye the depleted contents of the bottle.

The rain kept up a steady patter on the glass roof of the coffee room.

"Still, a good climate isn't everything: it isn't like home, for instance," the waiter remarked.

"No, indeed."

"There's many parts of the world as would be glad of a good day's rain," affirmed the waiter.

"There certainly are," said Mr. Rumbold, who found the conversation sedative.

"Did you do much fishing when you were abroad, sir?" the waiter pursued.

"A little."

"Well, you want rain for that," declared the waiter, as one who scores a point. "The fishing isn't preserved in Australia, like what it is here?"

"No."

"Then there ain't no poaching," concluded the waiter philosophically. "It's every man for himself."

"Yes, that's the rule in Australia."

"Not much of a rule, is it?" the waiter took him up. "Not much like law, I mean."

"It depends what you mean by law."

"Oh, Mr. Rumbold, sir, you know very well what I mean. I mean the police. Now, if you was to have done a man in out in Australia—murdered him, I mean—they'd hang you for it if they caught you, wouldn't they?"

Mr. Rumbold teased the champagne with the butt-end of his fork and drank again.

"Probably they would, unless there were special circumstances."

"In which case you might get off?"

"I might."

"That's what I mean by law," pronounced the waiter. "You know what the law is: you go against it, and you're punished. Of course I don't mean you, sir; I only say 'you' as—as an illustration to make my meaning clear."

"Quite, quite."

"Whereas if there was only what you call a rule," the waiter pursued, deftly removing the remains of Mr. Rumbold's chicken, "it might fall to the lot of any man to round you up. Might be anybody; might be me."

"Why should you or they," asked Mr. Rumbold, "want to round me up? I haven't done you any harm, or them."

"Oh, but we should have to, sir."

"Why?"

"We couldn't rest in our beds, sir, knowing you was at large. You might do it again. Somebody'd have to see to it."

"But supposing there was nobody?"

"Sir?"

"Supposing the murdered man hadn't any relatives or friends; supposing he just disappeared, and no one ever knew that he was dead?"

"Well, sir," said the waiter, winking portentously, "in that case he'd have to get on your track himself. He wouldn't rest in his grave, sir, no, not he, and knowing what he did."

"Clutsam," said Mr. Rumbold suddenly, "bring me another bottle of wine and don't trouble to ice it."

The waiter took the bottle from the table and held it up to the light. "Yes, it's dead, sir."

"Dead?"

"Yes, sir, finished—empty—dead."

"You're right," Mr. Rumbold agreed. "It's quite dead."

It was nearly eleven o'clock. Mr. Rumbold again had the lounge to himself. Clutsam would be bringing his coffee presently. Too bad of Fate to have him haunted by these casual reminders; too bad, his first day at home. "Too bad, too bad," he muttered, while the fire warmed the soles of his slippers. But it was excellent champagne, he would take no harm from it: the brandy Clutsam was bringing him would do the rest. Clutsam was a good sort, nice, old-fashioned servant . . . nice, old-fashioned house. . . . Warmed by the wine, his thoughts began to pass out of his control.

"Your coffee, sir," said a voice at his elbow.

"Thank you, Clutsam, I'm very much obliged to you," said Mr. Rumbold, with the exaggerated civility of slight intoxication. "You're an excellent fellow. I wish there were more like you."

"I hope so, too, I'm sure," said Clutsam, trying in his muddle-hearted way to deal with both observations at once.

"Don't seem many people about," Mr. Rumbold remarked. "Hotel pretty full?"

"Oh yes, sir, all the suites are let, and the other rooms too. We're turning people away every day. Why, only to-night a gentleman rang up. Said he would come round late, on the off-chance. But, bless me, he'll find the birds have flown."

"Birds?" echoed Mr. Rumbold.

"I mean, there aren't any more rooms, not for love nor money."

"Well, I'm sorry for him," said Mr. Rumbold, with ponderous sincerity. "I'm sorry for any man, friend or foe, who has to go tramping about London on a night like this. If I had an extra bed in my room, I'd put it at his disposal."

"You have, sir," the waiter said.

"Why, of course I have. How stupid! Well, well. I'm sorry for the poor chap. I'm sorry for all homeless ones, Clutsam, wandering on the face of the earth."

"Amen to that," said the waiter devoutly.

"And doctors and such, pulled out of their beds at midnight. It's a hard life. Ever thought about a doctor's life, Clutsam?"

"Can't say I have, sir."

"Well, well, but it's hard; you can take that from me."

"What time shall I call you in the morning, sir?" the waiter asked, seeing no reason why the conversation should ever stop.

"You needn't call me Clutsam," replied Mr. Rumbold in a sing-song voice, and running the words together as though he were excusing the waiter from addressing him by the waiter's own name. "I'll get up when I'm ready. And that may be pretty late, pretty late." He smacked his lips over the words. "Nothing like a good lie, eh, Clutsam?"

"That's right, sir. You have your sleep out," the waiter encouraged him. "You won't be disturbed."

"Good night, Clutsam, you're an excellent fellow, and I don't care who hears me say so."

"Good night, sir."

Mr. Rumbold returned to his chair. It lapped him round, it ministered to his comfort; he felt at one with it. At one with the fire, the clock, the tables, all the furniture. Their usefulness, their goodness, went out to meet his usefulness, his goodness, met and were friends. Who could bind their sweet influences or restrain them in the exercise of their kind offices? No one. No one; certainly not a shadow from the past. The room was perfectly quiet. Street sounds reached it only as a low continuous hum, infinitely reassuring. Mr. Rumbold fell asleep.

He dreamed that he was a boy again, living in his old home

in the country. He was possessed, in the dream, by a master-passion; he must collect fire-wood whenever and wherever he saw it. He found himself one autumn afternoon in the woodhouse; that was how the dream began. The door was partly open, admitting a little light, but he could not recall how he got in. The floor of the shed was littered with bits of bark and thin twigs; but, with the exception of the chopping block which he knew could not be used, there was nowhere a log of sufficient size to make a fire. Though he did not like being in the woodhouse alone he stayed long enough to make a thorough search. But he could find nothing. The compulsion he knew so well descended on him, and he left the woodhouse and went into the garden. His steps took him to the foot of a high tree, standing by itself in a tangle of long grass at some distance from the house. The tree had been lopped; for half its height it had no branches, only leafy tufts, sticking out at irregular intervals. He knew what he would see when he looked up into the dark foliage. And there, sure enough it was; a long dead bough, bare in patches where the bark had peeled off, and crooked in the middle like an elbow.

He began to climb the tree. The ascent proved easier than he expected, his body seemed no weight at all. But he was visited by a terrible oppression, which increased as he mounted. The bough did not want him; it was projecting its hostility down the trunk of the tree. And every second brought him nearer to an object which he had always dreaded: a growth, people called it. It stuck out from the trunk of the tree, a huge circular swelling thickly matted with twigs. Victor would have rather died than hit his head against it.

By the time he reached the bough twilight had deepened into night. He knew what he had to do: sit astride the bough, since there was none near by from which he could reach it, and press with his hands until it broke. Using his legs to get what purchase he could, he set his back against the tree, and pushed with all his might downwards. To do this he was obliged to look beneath him, and he saw, far below him on the ground, a white sheet spread out as though to catch him; and he knew at once that it was a shroud.

Frantically he pulled and pushed at the stiff brittle bough; a lust to break it took hold of him; leaning forward his whole length, he seized the bough at the elbow joint and strained it away from him. As it cracked he toppled over and the shroud came rushing upwards. . . .

Mr. Rumbold waked in a cold sweat to find himself clutching the curved arm of the chair on which the waiter had set his brandy. The glass had fallen over, and the spirit lay in a little pool on the leather seat. "I can't let it go like that," he thought, "I must get some more." A man he did not know answered the bell. "Waiter," he said, "bring me a brandy and soda in my room in a quarter of an hour's time. Rumbold, the name is." He followed the waiter out of the room. The passage was completely dark except for a small blue gas-jet, beneath which was huddled a cluster of candlesticks. The hotel, he remembered, maintained an old-time habit of deference towards darkness. As he held the wick to the gas-jet, he heard himself mutter, "Here is a candle to light you to bed." But he recollected the ominous conclusion of the distich, and, fuddled as he was, he left it unspoken.

Shortly after Mr. Rumbold's retirement the door-bell of the hotel rang. Three sharp peals, and no pause between them. "Someone in a hurry to get in," the night porter grumbled to Clutsam, who was on duty till midnight. "Expect he's forgotten his key." He made no haste to answer the summons, it would do the forgetful fellow good to wait: teach him a lesson. So dilatory was he that by the time he reached the hall-door the bell was tinkling again. Irritated by such importunity, he deliberately went back to set straight a pile of newspapers before letting this impatient devil in. To mark his indifference he even kept behind the door while he opened it; so that his first sight of the visitor only took in his back. But this limited inspection sufficed to show that the man was a stranger and not a guest at the hotel.

In the long black cape which fell almost sheer one side and on the other stuck out as though he had a basket under his arm, he looked like a crow with a broken wing. A bald-headed crow, thought the porter, for there's a patch of bare skin between that white linen thing and his hat.

"Good evening, sir," he said, "what can I do for you?"

The stranger made no answer, but glided to a side table and began turning over some letters with his right hand.

"Are you expecting a message?" asked the porter.

"No," the stranger replied. "I want a room for the night."

"Was you the gentleman who telephoned for a room this evening?"

"Yes."

"In that case I was to tell you we're afraid you can't have one, the hotel's booked right up."

"Are you quite sure?" asked the stranger. "Think again."

"Them's my orders, sir. It don't do me no good to think." At this moment the porter had a curious sensation as though some important part of him, his life maybe, had gone adrift inside him and was spinning round and round. The sensation ceased when he began to speak.

"I'll call the waiter, sir," he said.

But before he called the waiter appeared, intent on an errand of his own.

"I say, Bill," he began, "what's the number of Mr. Rumbold's room? He wants a drink taken up, and I forgot to ask him."

"It's thirty-three," said the porter unsteadily. "The double room."

"Why, Bill, what's up?" the waiter exclaimed. "You look as if you'd seen a ghost."

Both men stared round the hall, and then back at each other. The room was empty.

"God," said the porter. "I must have had the horrors. But he was here a moment ago. Look at this."

On the stone flags lay an icicle, an inch or two long, around which a little pool was fast collecting.

"Why, Bill," cried the waiter, "how did that get here? It's not freezing."

"*He* must have brought it," the porter said.

They looked at each other in consternation, which changed into terror as the sound of a bell made itself heard, coming from the depths of the hotel.

"Clutsam's there," whispered the porter. "He'll have to answer it, whoever it is."

Clutsam had taken off his tie, and was getting ready for bed. What on earth could anyone want in the lounge at this hour? He pulled on his coat and went upstairs.

Standing by the fire he saw the same figure whose appearance and disappearance had so disturbed the porter. "Yes, sir," he said.

"I want you to go to Mr. Rumbold," said the stranger, "and ask him if he is prepared to put the other bed in his room at the disposal of a friend."

In a few moments Clutsam returned.

"Mr. Rumbold's compliments, sir, and he wants to know who it is." The stranger went to the table in the centre of the room. An Australian newspaper was lying on it, which Clutsam had not noticed before. The aspirant to Mr. Rumbold's hospitality turned over the pages. Then with his finger, which appeared, even to Clutsam standing by the door, unusually pointed, he cut out a rectangular slip, about the size of a visiting card, and, moving away, motioned the waiter to take it.

By the light of the gas-jet in the passage Clutsam read the excerpt. It seemed to be a kind of obituary notice; but of what possible interest could it be to Mr. Rumbold, to know that the body of Mr. James Hagberd had been discovered in circumstances which suggested that he had met his death by violence?

After a longer interval Clutsam returned, looking puzzled and a little frightened.

"Mr. Rumbold's compliments, sir, but he knows no one of that name."

"Then take this message to Mr. Rumbold," said the stranger. "Say 'would he rather that I went up to him, or that he came down to me?'"

For the third time Clutsam went to do the stranger's bidding. He did not, however, upon his return open the door of the smoking-room, but shouted through it:

"Mr. Rumbold wishes you to Hell, sir, where you belong, and says 'Come up if you dare.'"

Then he bolted.

A minute later, from his retreat in an underground coal-cellar, he heard a shot fired. Some old instinct, danger-loving or danger-disregarding, stirred in him, and he ran up the stairs quicker than he had ever run up them in his life. In the passage he stumbled over Mr. Rumbold's boots. The bed-room door was ajar. Putting his head down he rushed in. The brightly lit room was empty. But almost all the movables in it were overturned, and the bed was in a frightful mess. The pillow with its fivefold perforation was the first object on which Clutsam noticed blood-stains. Thenceforward he seemed to see them everywhere. But what sickened him and kept him so long from going down to rouse the others was the sight of an icicle on the window-sill, a thin claw of ice curved like a Chinaman's nail, with a bit of flesh sticking to it.

That was the last he saw of Mr. Rumbold. But a policeman patrolling Carrick Street noticed a man in a long black cape who seemed, from the position of his arm, to be carrying something heavy. He called out to the man and ran after him; but though he did not seem to be moving very fast the policeman could not overtake him.

●

ONE LAMBERT, a gun-smith at Hereford, was at Caermarthen, to mend and put in order the ammunition of that county, before the expedition to Scotland, which was in 1639. He was then a young man, and walking on the sand by the sea side, a man came to him (he did verily believe it was a man) and asked him if he knew Hereford? yes, quoth he, I am a Hereford man. Do you know it well, quoth the other; perfectly well, quoth Lambert. "That city shall be begirt" (he told me he did not know what the word begirt meant then) "by a foreign nation, that will come and pitch their camp in the Haywood, and they shall batter such a gate," which they did, (I have forgot the name of it) "and shall go away and not take it."

The Scots came in 1645, and encamped before Hereford in the Hay-wood, and stormed the ——— gate, and raised the siege. Lambert did well remember this discourse, but did not heed it till they came to the Hay-wood. Many of the city had heard of this story, but when the ——— gate was stormed, Lambert went to all the guards of the town, and encouraged them with more than ordinary confidence: and contrary to all human expectation, when the besieged had no hope of relief, the Scots raised the siege, September 2, 1645, and went back into Scotland, *re infecta*. I knew this Lambert and took this account from his own mouth; he is a modest poor man, of a very innocent life, lives poor, and cares not to be rich.

—JOHN AUBREY

THE FOGHORN

An interesting comparison can be made between this story and *The Yellow Wall Paper*. The device is the same in both cases, but Mrs Gilman, writing in the '90s, used the epistolary method of self-revelation perfected early in the 18th Century, while Mrs Atherton's story, written in 1933, takes advantage of the more recently developed stream-of-consciousness technic. The following story, as the reader will realize at the conclusion, could not have been written at all in the epistolary style.—EDITOR.

Gertrude Atherton

THE FOGHORN

What an absurd vanity to sleep on a hard pillow and forgo that last luxurious burrowing into the very depths of a mass of baby pillows! . . . her back was already as straight as —a chimney? . . . who was the Frenchman that said one must reject the worn counters? . . . but this morning she would have liked that sensuous burrowing, and the pillow had never seemed so hard, so flat . . . yet how difficult it was to wake up! She had had the same experience once before when the doctor had given her veronal for insomnia . . . could Ellen, good creature, have put a tablet in the cup of broth she took last thing at night: 'as a wise precaution,' the doctor had said genially. What a curse insomnia was! But she had a congenital fear of drugs and had told no one of this renewal of sleeplessness, knowing it would pass.

And, after all, she didn't mind lying awake in the dark; she could think, oh, pleasant lovely thoughts, despite this inner perturbation—so cleverly concealed. How thankful she was to be tall enough to carry off this new fashion in sleeves! If trains would only come in again, she would dress her hair high some night (just for fun) and look—not like her beloved Mary Stewart, for Mary was almost ugly if one analyzed her too critically. Charm? How much more charm counted than mere beauty, and she herself had it 'full measure and running over,' as that rather fresh admirer had announced when drinking her health at her coming-out party . . . what was his name? . . . six years ago. He was only a college boy . . . how could one remember? There had been so many since.

Ninon de l'Enclos? She was passable in her portraits but famous mainly for keeping young . . . Diane de Poictiers? She must have needed charm double-distilled if she looked anything like an original portrait of her hung at a loan exhibition in Paris: flaxen hair, thin and straight, drawn severely from a bulging brow above insufferably sensual eyes—far too obvious and 'easy' for the fastidious male of today—a flaxen complexion, no highlights; not very intelligent. Interesting contrast in taste centuries apart—perhaps.

Madame Récamier? Better-looking than most of the historic beauties: hair piled high—but then she wore a slip of an Empire gown . . . well, never mind. . . .

She ranked as a beauty herself, although perhaps charm had something to do with it. Her mouth was rather wide, but her teeth were exquisite. Something rather obscure was the matter in that region of brilliant enamel this morning. A toothache? She had never had a toothache. Well, there was no pain . . . what matter . . . something wrong, though; she'd go to the dentist during the day. Her nose was a trifle tip-tilted, but very straight and thin, and anyhow the tilt suited the way she carried her head, 'flung in the air.' Her complexion and hair and eyes were beyond all cavil . . . she was nothing so commonplace as a downright blonde or brunette . . . how she should hate being catalogued! The warm, bright waving masses of her hair had never been cut since her second birthday. They, too, were made for burrowing.

Her mother's wedding dress had a long train. But the delicate ivory of the satin had waxed with time to a sickly yellow. Her mother hadn't pressed the matter when she was engaged to John St. Rogers, but she had always expressed a wish that each of her daughters should wear the dress to the altar. Well, she had refused outright, but had consented to have her own gown trimmed with the lace: yards and yards of *point d'Alençon*—and a veil that reached halfway down the train. What a way to spend money! Who cared for lace now? Not the young, anyhow. But Mother was rather a dear, and she could afford to be quite unselfish for once, as it certainly would be becoming. When the engagement was broken, they told the poor old darling that she cried because she would have another long wait before watching all that lace move up the aisle on a long slender figure that made her think pridefully of the graceful skeleton hidden within one hundred and seventy resented pounds.

Well, she would never wear that lace—nor any wedding gown. If she were lucky enough to marry at all, the less publicity the better . . . a mere announcement (San Francisco papers please copy) . . . a quiet return from Europe . . . a year or two in one of those impersonal New York apartment-houses where no one knew the name of his next-door neighbor . . . no effacement in a smaller city for her!

How strange that she of all girls should have fallen in love with a married man—or, at all events, accepted the dire consequences. With a father that had taken to drugs and then run off with another woman—luckily before Mother had come in for Granddad's fortune—and . . . what was it Uncle Ben had once said, Queer twists in this family since 'way back.' It had made her more conventional than her natural instincts would have prompted; but, no, let her do herself justice: she had cultivated a high standard of character and planted her mind with flowers both sturdy and fair—that must have been the reason she had fallen in love at last, after so many futile attempts. No need for her to conceal from him the awful truth that she read the Greek and Latin classics in the original text, attended morning classes over at the University . . . odd, how men didn't mind if you 'adored' music and pictures, but if they suspected you of being intellectual, they either despised or feared you, and faded away. . . .

Fog on the Bay. Since childhood she had loved to hear that long-drawn-out, almost-human moan of the foghorn as she lay warm and sheltered in bed. It was on a night of fog they had spoken for the first time, although they had nodded at three or four formal dinners given to the newcomers who had brought letters to the elect. Bostonians were always popular in San Francisco; they had good manners and their formality was only skin-deep. The men were very smart; some of the women, too; but as a rule they lacked the meticulous grooming and well-set-up appearance of their men. She had been impressed the first time she had met him: six feet (she herself was five feet six), somewhere in the thirties, very spare, said to be a first-rate tennis player, and had ranked as an all-round athlete at Harvard; had inherited a piece of property in San Francisco which was involving him in litigation, but he was in no haste to leave, even before they met.

That had been at the Jeppers', and as the house commanded a fine view of the Bay, and she was tired of being torn from some man every time they had circled the ballroom, she had managed to slip away and had hidden behind the curtains of the deep bow window at the end of the hall. In a moment she was aware that someone had followed her, and oddly enough she knew who it was, although she didn't turn her head; and they stood in silence and gazed together at the sharp dark outlines of the mountains on the far side of the Bay; the gliding spheroids of golden light that were the ferry boats, the islands with their firm, bold outlines, now almost visibly drooping in slumber . . . although there always seemed to her to be an atmosphere of unrest about Alcatraz, psychic emanation of imprisoned men under rigid military rule, and officials no doubt as resentful in that dull monotonous existence on a barren rock . . . A light flickered along a line of barred upper windows; doubtless a guard on his rounds. . . .

The band of pulsing light on the eastern side of the Bay: music made visible . . . stars as yellow and bright above, defying the thin silver of the hebetic moon . . . lights twinkling on Sausolito opposite, standing out boldly from the black mass of Tamalpais high-flung above. Her roving eyes moved to the Golden Gate, narrow entrance between two crouching forts, separating that harbor of arrogant beauty from the gray waste of the Pacific—ponderous, rather stupid old ocean. . . .

For the first time he spoke: 'The fog! Chief of San Francisco's many beauties.'

She nodded, making no other reply, watching that dense yet imponderable white mass push its way through the Golden Gate like a laboring ship . . . then riding the waters more lightly, rolling a little, writhing, whiffs breaking from the bulk of that ghostly ship to explore the hollows of the hills, resting there like puffs of white smoke. Then, over the cliffs and heights on the northern side of the Bay, a swifter, more formless, but still lovely white visitant that swirled over the inland waters, enshrouding the islands, Sausolito, where so many Englishmen lived, the fulgent zone in the east; but a low fog—the moon and stars still visible . . . the foghorns, one after the other, sending forth their long-drawn-out moans of utter desolation. . . .

With nothing more to look at, they had seated themselves on a small sofa, placed there for reticent couples, and talked for an hour—a desultory exploring conversation. She recalled none of it. A few mornings later they had met on the Berkeley ferryboat, accidentally no doubt, and he had gone on with her in the train and as far as the campus. . . . Once again. . . . After that, when the lecture was over, in the Greek Theatre . . . wonderful hours . . . how easy to imagine themselves in Greece of the fifth century B.C., alone in that vast gray amphitheatre, the slim, straight tenebrous trees above quivering with the melody of birds!

Never a word of love—not for months. This novel and exciting companionship was enough . . . depths of personality to explore—in glimpses! Sometimes they roamed over the hills, gay and carefree. They never met anyone they knew.

Winter. Weeks of pouring rain. They met in picture galleries, remote corners of the Public Library, obscure restaurants of Little Italy under the shadow of Telegraph Hill. Again they were unseen, undiscovered.

He never came to the house. Since her mother's death and the early marriages of the girls, Uncle Ben had come to live with her in the old house on Russian Hill; the boys were East at school; she was free of all family restrictions, but her old servants were intimate with all the other servants on the Hill. She barely knew his wife. He never spoke of her.

Spring. A house-party in the country, warm and dry after the last of the rains. After dinner they had sat about on the terraces, smoking, drinking, listening to a group singing within, admiring the 'ruins' of a Roman temple at the foot of the lawn lit by a blazing moon.

He and she had wandered off the terrace, and up an almost perpendicular flight of steps on the side of the mountain that rose behind the house . . . dim aisles of redwoods, born when the earth was young, whose long trunks never swayed, whose high branches rarely sang in the wind—unfriendly trees, but protective, sentinel-like, shutting out the modern world; reminiscent those closely planted aisles were of ancient races . . . forgotten races . . . godlike races, perhaps.

Well, they had felt like gods that night. How senseless to try to stave off a declaration of love . . . to fear . . . to wonder . . . to worry . . . How inevitable . . . natural . . . when it came! Hour of hours . . .

They had met the next day in a corner of their favorite little restaurant, over a dish of spaghetti, which she refused to eat as it had liver in it, and talked the matter out. No, she would not enter upon a secret intrigue; meeting him in some shady quarter of the town, where no questions were asked, in some horrible room which had sheltered thousands of furtive 'lovers' before them . . . she would far rather never see him again. . . . He had smiled at the flight taken by an untrained imagination, but nodded. . . . No, but she knew the alternative. He had no intention of giving her up. No hope of a divorce. He had sounded his wife; tentatively at first, then told her outright he loved another woman. She had replied that he could expect no legal release from her. It was her chance for revenge and she would take it. . . . A week or two and his business in San Francisco would be settled . . . he had an independent fortune . . . would she run away with him? Elope in good old style? Could she stand the gaff? All Europe for a perpetual honeymoon—unless his wife were persuaded by her family later on to divorce him. Then he would return and work at something. He was not a born idler.

She had consented, of course, having made up her mind before they met. She had had six years of 'the world.' She knew what she wanted. One might 'love' many times, but not more than once find completion, that solidarity which makes two as one against the malignant forces of life. She had no one to consider but herself. Her mother was dead. Her sisters, protected by husbands, wealth, position, would merely be 'thrilled.' The boys and Uncle Ben, of course, would be furious. Men were so hopelessly conservative.

For the rest of the world she cared exactly nothing.

That foghorn. What was it trying to tell her? A boat . . . fog . . . why was it so hard to remember? So hard to awaken? Ellen must have given her an overdose. Fragmentary pictures . . . slipping down the dark hill to the wharf . . . her low delighted laugh echoed back to her as he helped her into the boat . . . one more secret lark before they flung down the gage. . . . How magnificently he rowed . . . long, sweeping, easy strokes as he smiled possessively into her eyes and talked of the future. . . . No moon, but millions of stars that shed a misty golden light . . . rows of light on the steep hillsides of the city. The houses dark and silent . . . a burst of music from Fort Mason. . . .

Out through the Golden Gate, still daring . . . riding that oily swell . . . his chuckle as she had dared him to row straight across to China. . . . Her sharp anxious cry as she half-rose from her seat and pointed to a racing mountain of snow-white mist.

He had swept about at once and made for the beach below Sutro Heights. Too late. Almost as he turned, they were engulfed. Even an old fisherman would have lost his sense of direction. And then the foghorns began their warnings. The low, menacing roar from Point Benito. The wailing siren on Alcatraz. Sausolito's throaty bass. The deep-toned bell on Angel Island. She knew them all, but they seemed to come from new directions.

A second . . . a moment . . . an hour . . . later . . . a foreign but unmistakable note. Ships—two of them. . . . Blast and counter-blast. . . . She could barely see his white rigid face through the mist as he thrust his head this way and that trying to locate those sounds. . . . Another abrupt swerve . . . crash . . . shouts . . . her own voice shrieking as she saw his head almost severed—the very fog turn red. . . .

She could hear herself screaming yet. It seemed to her that she had been screaming since the beginning of time.

She sat up in bed, clasping her head between her hands, and rocked to and fro. This bare small room, just visible in the gray dawn. . . . She was in a hospital, of course. Was it last night or the night before they had brought her here? She wondered vaguely that she felt no inclination to scream any more, now that she had struggled to full consciousness. . . . Too tired, perhaps . . . the indifference of exhaustion. . . . Even her eyes felt singularly dry, as if they had been baked in a hot oven. She recalled a line, the only memorable line, in Edwin Arnold's 'Light of Asia,' 'Eyepits red with rust of ancient tears.' . . . Did her eyes look like that? But she did not remember crying . . . only screaming. . . .

Odd that she should be left alone like this. Uncle Ben and the girls must have been summoned. If they had gone home, tired out, they should have left a nurse in constant attendance . . . and surely they might have found her a better room. . . . Or had she been carried into some emergency hospital? . . . Well, she could go home today.

Her hands were still clasping her head when another leaf of awareness turned over, rattling like parchment. Hair. Her lovely abundant hair. . . . She held her breath as her hands moved exploringly over her head. Harsh short bristles almost scratched them.

She had had brain fever, then. Ill a long time . . . weeks . . . months, perhaps. . . . No wonder she felt weak and spent and indifferent! But she must be out of danger, or they would not leave her like this. . . . Would she suffer later, with renewed mocking strength? Or could love be burnt out, devoured by fever germs? A short time before, while not yet fully conscious, she had relived all the old hopes, fears, dreams, ecstasies; reached out triumphantly to a wondrous future, arrogantly sure of herself and the man, contemptuous of the world and its makeshift conventions. . . . And now she felt nothing. . . .

But when she was well again? Twenty-four! Forty, fifty, years more; they were a long-lived family. Her mother had been killed at a railroad crossing. . . . Well, she had always prided herself on her strength. She would worry through the years somehow.

Had the town rung with the scandal when the newspapers flared forth next morning? No girl goes rowing at night with a married man unless there is something between them. Had his wife babbled? Were the self-righteous getting off the orthodoxies of their kind? Punished for their sin. Retributive justice meted out to a girl who would break up a home and take a married man for her lover.

Retributive justice! As if there were any such thing in life as justice. All helpless victims of the law of cause and effect. Futile, aspiring, stupidly confident links in the inexorable chain of Circumstance. . . . Commonplace minds croaking, 'Like father like daughter' . . .

How she hated, hated, *hated*, self-righteousness, smug hypocrisy . . . illogical minds—one sheep bleating like another sheep— not one of them with the imagination to guess that she never would have stooped to a low secret intrigue. . . .

She had been pounding her knee with her fist in a sudden access of energy. As it sputtered out and she felt on the verge of collapse, her hand unfolded and lay palm down on the quilt. . . . She felt her eyes bulging. . . . She uttered her first sound: a low almost inarticulate cry.

Her hand? That large-veined, skinny thing? She had beautiful long white hands, with skin as smooth as the breast of a dove. Of no one of her beauty's many parts had she been prouder, not even when she stood now and then before the cheval glass and looked critically, and admiringly, at the smooth, white, rounded perfection of her body. She had given them a golden manicure set on one of her birthdays, a just tribute; and they were exquisitely kept, although she hated conspicuous nails. . . .

A delusion? A nightmare? She spread the other hand beside it . . . side by side the two on the dingy counterpane . . . old hands. . . . Shorn hair will grow again . . . but hands . . .

Mumbling. Why mumbling? She raised one of those withered yellow hands to her mouth. It was empty. Her shaking fingers unbuttoned the high night-gown, and she glanced within. Pendent dugs, brown and shrivelled.

Brain fever! The sun had risen. She looked up at the high barred window. She understood.

Voices at the door. She dropped back on the pillow and closed her eyes and lay still.

The door was unlocked, and a man and woman entered: doctor and nurse, as was immediately evident. The doctor's voice was brisk and business-like and deeply mature; the woman's, young and deferential.

'Do you think she'll wake again, doctor?'

'Probably not. I thought she would be gone by now, but she is still breathing.' He clasped the emaciated wrist with his strong fingers. 'Very feeble. It won't be long now.'

'Is it true, doctor, that sometimes, just before death, reason is restored and they remember and talk quite rationally?'

'Sometimes. But not for this case. Too many years. Look in every hour, and when it is over, ring me up. There are relatives to be notified. Quite important people, I believe.'

'What are they like?'

'Never seen them. The law firm in charge of her estate pays the bills. Why should they come here? Couldn't do her any good, and nothing is so depressing as these melancholia cases. It's a long time now since she was stark raving. That was before my time. Come along. Six wards after this one. . . . Don't forget to look in. Good little girl. I know you never forget.'

They went out and locked the door.

●

●

At——, in the Moorlands in Staffordshire, lived a poor old man, who had been a long time lame. One Sunday, in the afternoon, he being alone, one knocked at his door: he bade him open it, and come in. The Stranger desired a cup of beer; the lame man desired him to take a dish and draw some, for he was not able to do it himself. The stranger asked the poor old man how long he had been ill? the poor man told him. Said the Stranger, "I can cure you. Take two or three balm leaves steeped in your beer for a fortnight or three weeks, and you will be restored to your health; but constantly and zealously serve God." The poor man did so, and became perfectly well. This Stranger was in a purple-shag gown, such as was not seen or known in those parts. And no body in the street after even song did see any one in such a coloured habit. Doctor Gilbert Sheldon, since Archbishop of Canterbury, was then in the Moorlands, and justified the truth of this to Elias Ashmole, Esq., from whom I had this account, and he hath inserted it in some of his memoirs, which are in the Musæum at Oxford.

—John Aubrey

THE CHERRY TREE

I think that an editor who holds conscientiously to his main task can be permitted an occasional vagary—if he confesses on the spot. Frankly, then, I have included this story more out of a desire to give it a wider audience than because it belongs strictly in this volume. I cannot remember any piece of prose writing, long or short, to which my thoughts have returned oftener than to *The Cherry Tree*.—EDITOR.

A. E. Coppard

THE CHERRY
T R E E

There was uproar somewhere among the back-
yards of Australia Street. It was so alarming that people at
their midday meal sat still and stared at one another. A fortnight
before murder had been done in the street, in broad daylight with
a chopper; people were nervous. An upper window was thrown
open and a startled and startling head exposed.

"It's that young devil, Johnny Flynn, again! Killing rats!"
shouted Mrs. Knatchbole, shaking her fist towards the Flynns'
backyard. Mrs. Knatchbole was ugly; she had a goitred neck and a
sharp skinny nose with an orb shining at its end, constant as grief.

"You wait, my boy, till your mother comes home, you just wait!" invited this apparition, but Johnny was gazing sickly at the body of a big rat slaughtered by the dogs of his friend George. The uproar was caused by the quarrelling of the dogs, possibly for honours, but more probably, as is the custom of victors, for loot.

"Bob down!" warned George, but Johnny bobbed up to catch the full anger of those baleful Knatchbole eyes. The urchin put his fingers promptly to his nose.

"Look at that for eight years old!" screamed the lady. "Eight years old 'e is! As true as God's my maker I'll . . ."

The impending vow was stayed and blasted for ever, Mrs. Knatchbole being taken with a fit of sneezing, whereupon the boys uttered some derisive "Haw haws!"

So Mrs. Knatchbole met Mrs. Flynn that night as she came from work, Mrs. Flynn being a widow who toiled daily and dreadfully at a laundry and perforce left her children, except for their school hours, to their own devices. The encounter was an emphatic one and the tired widow promised to admonish her boy.

"But it's all right, Mrs. Knatchbole, he's going from me in a week, to his uncle in London he is going, a person of wealth, and he'll be no annoyance to ye then. I'm ashamed that he misbehaves but he's no bad boy really."

At home his mother's remonstrances reduced Johnny to repentance and silence; he felt base indeed; he wanted to do something great and worthy at once to offset it all; he wished he had got some money, he'd have gone and bought her a bottle of stout —he knew she liked stout.

"Why do ye vex people so, Johnny?" asked Mrs. Flynn wearily. "I work my fingers to the bone for ye, week in and week out. Why can't ye behave like Pomony?"

His sister was a year younger than he; her name was Mona which Johnny's elegant mind had disliked. One day he re-baptized her; Pomona she became and Pomona she remained. The Flynns sat down to supper. "Never. mind, mum," said the boy, kissing her as he passed, "talk to us about the cherry tree!" The cherry tree, luxuriantly blooming, was the crown of the mother's memories of her youth and her father's farm; around the myth of its wonderful blossoms and fruit she could weave garlands of romance, and to her own mind as well as to the minds of her children it became a heavenly symbol of her old lost home, grand with acres and delightful with orchard and full pantry. What wonder that in her humorous narration the joys were multiplied and magnified until even Johnny was obliged to intervene. "Look here, how many horses *did* your father have, mum . . . really, though?" Mrs. Flynn became vague, cast a furtive glance at this son of hers and then gulped with laughter until she recovered her ground with "Ah, but there *was* a cherry tree!" It was a grand supper—actually a polony and some potatoes. Johnny knew this was because he was going away. Ever since it was known that he was to go to London they had been having something special like this, or sheep's trotters or a pig's tail. Mother seemed to grow kinder and kinder to him. He wished he had some money, he would like to buy her a bottle of stout—he knew she liked stout.

Well, Johnny went away to live with his uncle, but alas he was only two months in London before he was returned to his mother and Pomony. Uncle was an engine-driver who disclosed to his astounded nephew a passion for gardening. This was incomprehensible to Johnny Flynn. A great roaring boiling locomotive was the grandest thing in the world. Johnny had rides on it, so he knew. And it was easy for him to imagine that every gardener cherished in the darkness of his disappointed soul an unavailing passion for a steam engine, but how an engine-driver could immerse himself in the mushiness of gardening was a baffling problem. However, before he returned home he discovered one important thing from his uncle's hobby, and he sent the information to his sister:

Dear Pomona—
Uncle Harry has got a alotment and grow veggutables. He says what makes the mold is worms. You know we puled all the worms out off our garden and chukked them over Miss Natchbols wall. Well you better get some more quick a lot ask George to help you and I bring som seeds home when I comes next week by the xcursion on Moms birthday
                    Your sincerely brother
                                        John Flynn

On mother's birthday Pomona met him at the station. She kissed him shyly and explained that mother was going to have a half holiday to celebrate the double occasion and would be home with them at dinner time.

"Pomony, did you get them worms?"

Pomona was inclined to evade the topic of worms for the garden, but fortunately her brother's enthusiasm for another gardening project tempered the wind of his indignation. When they reached home he unwrapped two parcels he had brought with him; he explained his scheme to his sister; he led her into the garden. The Flynns' backyard, mostly paved with bricks, was small and so the enclosing walls, truculently capped by chips of glass, although too low for privacy, were yet too high for the growth of any cherishable plant. Johnny had certainly once reared a magnificent exhibit of two cowslips, but these had been mysteriously destroyed by the Knatchbole cat. The dank little enclosure was charged with sterility; nothing flourished there except a lot of beetles and a dauntless evergreen bush, as tall as Johnny, displaying a profusion of thick shiny leaves that you could split on your tongue and make squealers with. Pomona showed him how to do this and they then busied themselves in the garden until the dinner siren warned them that Mother would be coming home. They hurried into the kitchen and Pomona quickly spread the cloth and the plates of food upon the table, while Johnny placed conspicuously in the centre, after laboriously extracting the stopper with a fork and a hair-pin, a bottle of stout brought from London. He had been much impressed by numberless advertisements upon the hoardings respecting this attractive beverage. The children then ran off to meet their mother and they all came home together with great hilarity. Mrs. Flynn's attention having been immediately drawn to the sinister decoration of her dining table, Pomona was requested to pour out a glass of the nectar. Johnny handed this gravely to his parent, saying:

"Many happy returns of the day, Mrs. Flynn!"

"O, dear, dear!" gasped his mother merrily, "you drink first!"

"Excuse me, no, Mrs. Flynn," rejoined her son, "many happy returns of the day!"

When the toast had been honoured Pomona and Johnny looked tremendously at each other.

"Shall we?" exclaimed Pomona.

"O yes," decided Johnny; "come on, mum, in the garden, something marvellous!"

She followed her children into that dull little den, and fortuitously the sun shone there for the occasion. Behold, the dauntless evergreen bush had been stripped of its leaves and upon its blossomless twigs the children had hung numerous couples of ripe cherries, white and red and black.

"What do you think of it, mum?" cried the children, snatching some of the fruit and pressing it into her hands, "what do you think of it?"

"Beautiful!" said the poor woman in a tremulous voice. They stared silently at their mother until she could bear it no longer. She turned and went sobbing into the kitchen.

●

WHAT IS more cheerful, now, in the fall of the year, than an open wood-fire? Do you hear those little chirps and twitters coming out of that piece of apple-wood? Those are the ghosts of the robins and bluebirds that sang upon the bough when it was in blossom last Spring. In Summer whole flocks of them come fluttering about the fruit-trees under the window: so I have singing birds all the year round.

—THOMAS BAILEY ALDRICH

AFTERWARD

It would ill-beseem me as an editor to pick and choose between the stories presented in this volume, but if I were put to the task of selecting the most effective *technic* for the ghost story, Edith Wharton's *Afterward* would inevitably come first to mind. The tale would be interesting and compelling without a ghost; but, as I have indicated in the foreword, the addition of a ghost makes a good story into a superb one.—EDITOR.

Edith Wharton

AFTERWARD

"Oh, there *is* one, of course, but you'll never know it."

The assertion, laughingly flung out six months earlier in a bright June garden, came back to Mary Boyne with a new perception of its significance as she stood, in the December dusk, waiting for the lamps to be brought into the library.

The words had been spoken by their friend Alida Stair, as they sat at tea on her lawn at Pangbourne, in reference to the very house of which the library in question was the central, the pivotal "feature." Mary Boyne and her husband, in quest of a country place in one of the southern or southwestern counties, had, on their arrival in England, carried their problem straight to Alida

Stair, who had successfully solved it in her own case; but it was not until they had rejected, almost capriciously, several practical and judicious suggestions that she threw out: "Well, there's Lyng, in Dorsetshire. It belongs to Hugo's cousins, and you can get it for a song."

The reason she gave for its being obtainable on these terms—its remoteness from a station, its lack of electric light, hot-water pipes, and other vulgar necessities—were exactly those pleading in its favour with two romantic Americans perversely in search of the economic drawbacks which were associated, in their tradition, with unusual architectural felicities.

"I should never believe I was living in an old house unless I was thoroughly uncomfortable," Ned Boyne, the more extravagant of the two, had jocosely insisted; "the least hint of 'convenience' would make me think it had been bought out of an exhibition, with the pieces numbered, and set up again." And they had proceeded to enumerate, with humorous precision, their various doubts and demands, refusing to believe that the house their cousin recommended was *really* Tudor till they learned it had no heating system, or that the village church was literally in the grounds till she assured them of the deplorable uncertainty of the water-supply.

"It's too uncomfortable to be true!" Edward Boyne had continued to exult as the avowal of each disadvantage was successively wrung from her; but he had cut short his rhapsody to ask, with a relapse to distrust: "And the ghost? You've been concealing from us the fact that there is no ghost!"

Mary, at the moment, had laughed with him, yet almost with her laugh, being possessed of several sets of independent perceptions, had been struck by a note of flatness in Alida's answering hilarity.

"Oh, Dorsetshire's full of ghosts, you know."

"Yes, yes; but that won't do. I don't want to have to drive ten miles to see somebody else's ghost. I want one of my own on the premises. *Is* there a ghost at Lyng?"

His rejoinder had made Alida laugh again, and it was then that she had flung back tantalisingly: "Oh, there *is* one, of course, but you'll never know it."

"Never know it?" Boyne pulled her up. "But what in the

world constitutes a ghost except for the fact of its being known for one?"

"I can't say. But that's the story."

"That there's a ghost, but that nobody knows it's a ghost?"

"Well—not till afterward, at any rate."

"Till afterwards?"

"Not till long afterward."

"But if it's once been identified as an unearthly visitant, why hasn't its *signalement* been handed down in the family? How has it managed to preserve its incognito?"

Alida could only shake her head. "Don't ask me. But it has."

"And then suddenly"—Mary spoke up as if from cavernous depths of divination—"suddenly, long afterward, one says to one's self *'That was it?'*"

She was startled at the sepulchral sound with which her question fell on the banter of the other two, and she saw the shadow of the same surprise flit across Alida's pupils. "I suppose so. One just has to wait."

"Oh, hang waiting!" Ned broke in. "Life's too short for a ghost who can only be enjoyed in retrospect. Can't we do better than that, Mary?"

But it turned out that in the event they were not destined to, for within three months of their conversation with Mrs. Stair they were settled at Lyng, and the life they had yearned for, to the point of planning it in advance in all its daily details, had actually begun for them.

It was to sit, in the thick December dusk, by just such a wide-hooded fireplace, under just such black oak rafters, with the sense that beyond the mullioned panes the downs were darkened to a deeper solitude: it was for the ultimate indulgence of such sensations that Mary Boyne, abruptly exiled from New York by her husband's business, had endured for nearly fourteen years the soul-deadening ugliness of a Middle Western town, and that Boyne had ground on doggedly at his engineering till, with a suddenness that still made her blink, the prodigious windfall of the Blue Star Mine had put them at a stroke in possession of life and the leisure to taste it. They had never for a moment meant their new state to be one of idleness; but they meant to give themselves only to harmonious activities. She had her vision of painting and gardening (against a background of grey walls), he dreamed of the production of his long-planned book on the "Economic Basis of Culture"; and with such absorbing work ahead no existence could be too sequestered: they could not get far enough from the world, or plunge deep enough into the past.

Dorsetshire had attracted them from the first by an air of remoteness out of all proportion to its geographical position. But to the Boynes it was one of the ever-recurring wonders of the whole incredibly \compressed island—a nest of counties, as they put it—that for the production of its effects so little of a given quality went so far: that so few miles made a distance, and so short a distance a difference.

"It's that," Ned had once enthusiastically explained, "that gives such depth to their effects, such relief to their contrasts. They've been able to lay the butter so thick on every delicious mouthful."

The butter had certainly been laid on thick at Lyng: the old house hidden under a shoulder of the downs had almost all the finer marks of commerce with a protracted past. The mere fact that it was neither large nor exceptional made it, to the Boynes, abound the more completely in its special charm—the charm of having been for centuries a deep dim reservoir of life. The life had probably not been of the most vivid order: for long periods, no doubt, it had fallen as noiselessly into the past as the quiet drizzle of autumn fell, hour after hour, into the fish-pond between the yews; but these back-waters of existence sometimes breed, in their sluggish depths, strange acuities of emotion, and Mary Boyne had felt from the first the mysterious stir of intenser memories.

The feeling had never been stronger than on this particular afternoon when, waiting in the library for the lamps to come, she rose from her seat, and stood among the shadows of the hearth. Her husband had gone off, after luncheon, for one of his long tramps on the downs. She had noticed of late that he preferred to go alone; and, in the tried security of their personal relations, had been driven to conclude that his book was bothering him, and that he needed the afternoons to turn over in solitude the problems left from the morning's work. Certainly the book was not going as smoothly as she had thought it would, and there were lines of perplexity between his eyes such as had never been there in his engineering days. He had often, then, looked fagged to the verge of illness, but the native demon of "worry" had never branded his brow. Yet the few pages he had so far read to her—the introduction, and a summary of the opening chapter—showed a firm hold on his subject, and an increasing confidence in his powers.

The fact threw her into deeper perplexity, since, now that he had done with "business" and its disturbing contingencies, the one other possible source of anxiety was eliminated. Unless it were his health, then? But physically he had gained since they had come to Dorsetshire, grown robuster, ruddier and fresher-eyed. It was only within the last week that she had felt in him the undefinable change which made her restless in his absence, and as tongue-tied in his presence as though it were *she* who had a secret to keep from him!

The thought that there *was* a secret somewhere between them struck her with a sudden rap of wonder, and she looked about her down the long room.

"Can it be the house?" she mused.

The room itself might have been full of secrets. They seemed to be piling themselves up, as evening fell, like the layers and layers of velvet shadow dropping from the low ceiling, the rows of books, the smoke-blurred sculpture of the hearth.

"Why—of course—the house is haunted!" she reflected.

The ghost—Alida's imperceptible ghost—after figuring largely in the banter of their first month or two at Lyng, had been gradually left aside as too ineffectual for imaginative use. Mary had, indeed, as became the tenant of a haunted house, made the customary inquiries among her rural neighbours, but, beyond a vague "The du say so, Ma'am," the villagers had nothing to impart. The elusive spectre had apparently never had sufficient identity for a legend to crystallise about it, and after a time the Boynes had set the matter down to their profit-and-loss account, agreeing that Lyng was one of the few houses good enough in itself to dispense with supernatural enhancements.

"And I suppose, poor ineffectual demon, that's why it beats its beautiful wings in vain in the void," Mary had laughingly concluded.

"Or, rather," Ned answered in the same strain, "why, amid so much that's ghostly, it can never affirm its separate existence as *the* ghost!" And thereupon their invisible housemate had finally dropped out of their references, which were numerous enough to make them soon unaware of the loss.

Now, as she stood on the hearth, the subject of their earlier curiosity revived in her with a new sense of its meaning—a sense gradually acquired through daily contact with the scene of the lurking mystery. It was the house itself, of course, that possessed the ghost-seeing faculty, that communed visually but secretly with its own past; if one could only get into close enough communion with the house, one might surprise its secret, and acquire the ghost-sight on one's own account. Perhaps, in his long hours in this very room, where she never trespassed till the afternoon, her husband *had* acquired it already, and was silently carrying about the weight of whatever it had revealed to him. Mary was too well versed in the code of the spectral world not to know that one could not talk about the ghosts one saw: to do so was almost as great a breach of taste as to name a lady in a club. But this explanation did not really satisfy her. "What, after all, except for the fun of the shudder," she reflected, "would he really care for any of their old ghosts?" And thence she was thrown back once more on the fundamental dilemma: the fact that one's greater or less susceptibility to spectral influences had no particular bearing on the case, since, when one *did* see a ghost at Lyng, one did not know it.

"Not till long afterward," Alida Stair had said. Well, supposing Ned *had* seen one when they first came, and had known only within the last week what had happened to him? More and more under the spell of the hour, she threw back her thoughts to the early days of their tenancy, but at first only to recall a lively confusion of unpacking, settling, arranging of books, and calling to each other from remote corners of the house as, treasure after treasure, it revealed itself to them. It was in this particular connection that she presently recalled a certain soft afternoon of the previous October, when, passing from the first rapturous flurry of exploration to a detailed inspection of the old house, she had pressed (like a novel heroine) a panel that opened on a flight of corkscrew stairs leading to a flat ledge of the roof—the roof which, from below, seemed to slope away on all sides too abruptly for any but practised feet to scale.

The view from this hidden coign was enchanting, and she had flown down to snatch Ned from his papers and give him the freedom of her discovery. She remembered still how, standing at her side, he had passed his arm about her while their gaze flew to the long tossed horizon-line of the downs, and then dropped contentedly back to trace the arabesque of yew hedges about the fishpond, and the shadow of the cedar of the lawn.

"And now the other way," he had said, turning her about within his arm; and closely pressed to him, she had absorbed, like some long satisfying draught, the picture of the grey-walled court, the squat lions on the gates, and the lime-avenue reaching up to the highroad under the downs.

It was just then, while they gazed and held each other, that she had felt his arm relax, and heard a sharp "Hullo!" that made her turn to glance at him.

Distinctly, yes, she now recalled that she had seen, as she glanced, a shadow of anxiety, of perplexity, rather, fall across his face; and, following his eyes, had beheld the figure of a man—a man in loose greyish clothes, as it appeared to her—who was sauntering down the lime-avenue to the court with the doubtful gait of a stranger who seeks his way. Her short-sighted eyes had given her but a blurred impression of slightness and greyishness, with something foreign, or at least unlocal, in the cut of the figure or its dress; but her husband had apparently seen more—seen enough to make him push past her with a hasty "Wait!" and dash down the stairs without pausing to give her a hand.

A slight tendency to dizziness obliged her, after a provisional clutch at the chimney against which they had been leaning, to follow him first more cautiously; and when she had reached the landing she paused again, for a less definite reason, leaning over the banister to strain her eyes through the silence of the brown sun-flecked depths. She lingered there till, somewhere in those depths, she heard the closing of a door; then, mechanically impelled, she went down the shallow flights of steps till she reached the lower hall.

The front door stood open on the sunlight of the court, and hall and court were empty. The library door was open, too, and after listening in vain for any sound of voices within, she crossed the threshold, and found her husband alone, vaguely fingering the papers on his desk.

He looked up, as if surprised at her entrance, but the shadow of anxiety had passed from his face, leaving it even, as she fancied, a little brighter and clearer than usual.

"What was it? Who was it?" she asked.

"Who?" he repeated, with the surprise still all on his side.

"The man we saw coming toward the house."

He seemed to reflect. "The man? Why, I thought I saw Peters; I dashed after him to say a word about the stable drains, but he had disappeared before I could get down."

"Disappeared? But he seemed to be walking so slowly when we saw him."

Boyne shrugged his shoulders. "So I thought; but he must have got up steam in the interval. What do you say to our trying a scramble up Meldon Steep before sunset?"

That was all. At the time the occurrence had been less than nothing, had, indeed, been immediately obliterated by the magic of their first vision from Meldon Steep, a height which they had dreamed of climbing ever since they had first seen its bare spine rising above the roof of Lyng. Doubtless it was the mere fact of the other incident's having occurred on the very day of their ascent to Meldon that had kept it stored away in the fold of memory from which it now emerged; for in itself it had no mark of the portentous. At the moment there could have been nothing more natural than that Ned should dash himself from the roof in the pursuit of dilatory tradesmen. It was the period when they were always on the watch for one or the other of the specialists employed about the place; always lying in wait for them, and rushing out at them with questions, reproaches or reminders. And certainly in the distance the grey figure had looked like Peters.

Yet now, as she reviewed the scene, she felt her husband's explanation of it to have been invalidated by the look of anxiety on his face. Why had the familiar appearance of Peters made him anxious? Why, above all, if it was of such prime necessity to confer with him on the subject of the stable drains, had the failure to find him produced such a look of relief? Mary could not say that any one of these questions had occurred to her at the time, yet, from the promptness with which they now marshalled themselves at her summons, she had a sense that they must all along have been there, waiting their hour.

II

Weary with her thoughts, she moved to the window. The library was now quite dark, and she was surprised to see how much faint light the outer world still held.

As she peered out into it across the court, a figure shaped itself far down the perspective of bare limes: it looked a mere blot of deeper grey in the greyness, and for an instant, as it moved toward her, her heart thumped to the thought "It's the ghost!"

She had time, in that long instant, to feel suddenly that the man of whom, two months earlier, she had had a distant vision from the roof, was now, at his predestined hour, about to reveal himself as *not* having been Peters; and her spirit sank under the impending fear of the disclosure. But almost with the next tick of the clock the figure, gaining substance and character, showed itself even to her weak sight as her husband's; and she turned to meet him, as he entered, with the confession of her folly.

"It's really too absurd," she laughed out, "but I never *can* remember!"

"Remember what?" Boyne questioned as they drew together.

"That when one sees the Lyng ghost one never knows it."

Her hand was on his sleeve, and he kept it there, but with no response in his gesture or in the lines of his preoccupied face.

"Did you think you'd seen it?" he asked, after an appreciable interval.

"Why, I actually took *you* for it, my dear, in my mad determination to spot it!"

"Me—just now?" His arm dropped away, and he turned from her with a faint echo of her laugh. "Really, dearest, you'd better give it up, if that's the best you can do."

"Oh, yes, I give it up. Have *you?*" she asked, turning round on him abruptly.

The parlour-maid had entered with letters and a lamp, and the light struck up into Boyne's face as he bent above the tray she presented.

"Have *you?*" Mary perversely insisted, when the servant had disappeared on her errand of illumination.

"Have I what?" he rejoined absently, the light bringing out the sharp stamp of worry between his brows as he turned over the letters.

"Given up trying to see the ghost." Her heart beat a little at the experiment she was making.

Her husband, laying his letters aside, moved away into the shadow of the hearth.

"I never tried," he said, tearing open the wrapper of a newspaper.

"Well, of course," Mary persisted, "the exasperating thing is that there's no use trying, since one can't be sure till so long afterward."

He was unfolding the paper as if he had hardly heard her; but after a pause, during which the sheets rustled spasmodically between his hands, he looked up to ask, "Have you any idea *how long?*"

Mary had sunk into a low chair beside the fireplace. From her seat she glanced over, startled, at her husband's profile, which was projected against the circle of lamplight.

"No; none. Have *you?*" she retorted, repeating her former phrase with an added stress of intention.

Boyne crumpled the paper into a bunch, and then, inconsequently, turned back with it toward the lamp.

"Lord, no! I only meant," he explained, with a faint tinge of impatience, "is there any legend, any tradition, as to that?"

"Not that I know of," she answered; but the impulse to add "What makes you ask?" was checked by the reappearance of the parlour-maid, with tea and a second lamp.

With the dispersal of shadows, and the repetition of the daily domestic office, Mary Boyne felt herself less oppressed by that sense of something mutely imminent which had darkened her afternoon. For a few moments she gave herself to the details of her task, and when she looked up from it she was struck to the point of bewilderment by the change in her husband's face. He had seated himself near the farther lamp, and was absorbed in the perusal of his letters; but was it something he had found in them, or merely the shifting of her own point of view, that had restored his features to their normal aspect? The longer she looked the more definitely the change affirmed itself. The lines of tension had vanished, and such traces of fatigue as lingered were of the kind easily attributable to steady mental effort. He glanced up, as if drawn by her gaze, and met her eyes with a smile.

"I'm dying for my tea, you know; and here's a letter for you," he said.

She took the letter he held out in exchange for the cup she proffered him, and, returning to her seat, broke the seal with the languid gesture of the reader whose interests are all enclosed in the circle of one cherished presence.

Her next conscious motion was that of starting to her feet, the letter falling to them as she rose, while she held out to her husband a newspaper clipping.

"Ned! What's this? What does it mean?"

He had risen at the same instant, almost as if hearing her cry before she uttered it; and for a perceptible space of time he and she studied each other, like adversaries watching for an advantage, across the space between her chair and his desk.

"What's what? You fairly made me jump!" Boyne said at length, moving toward her with a sudden half-exasperated laugh. The shadow of apprehension was on his face again, not now a look of fixed foreboding, but a shifting vigilance of lips and eyes that gave her the sense of his feeling himself invisibly surrounded.

Her hand shook so that she could hardly give him the clipping.

"This article—from the *Waukesha Sentinel*—that a man named Elwell has brought suit against you—that there was something wrong about the Blue Star Mine. I can't understand more than half."

They continued to face each other as she spoke, and to her astonishment she saw that her words had the almost immediate effect of dissipating the strained watchfulness of his look.

"Oh, *that!*" He glanced down the printed slip, and then folded it with the gesture of one who handles something harmless and familiar. "What's the matter with you this afternoon, Mary? I thought you'd got bad news."

She stood before him with her undefinable terror subsiding slowly under the reassurance of his tone.

"You knew about this, then—it's all right?"

"Certainly I knew about it; and it's all right."

"But what *is* it? I don't understand. What does this man accuse you of?"

"Pretty nearly every crime in the calendar." Boyne had tossed the clipping down, and thrown himself into an arm-chair near the fire. "Do you want to hear the story? It's not particularly interesting—just a squabble over interests in the Blue Star."

"But who is this Elwell? I don't know the name."

"Oh, he's a fellow I put into it—gave him a hand up. I told you all about him at the time."

"I daresay. I must have forgotten." Vainly she strained back among her memories. "But if you helped him, why does he make this return?"

"Probably some shyster lawyer got hold of him and talked him over. It's all rather technical and complicated. I thought that kind of thing bored you."

His wife felt a sting of compunction. Theoretically, she deprecated the American wife's detachment from her husband's professional interests, but in practice she had always found it difficult to fix her attention on Boyne's report of the transactions in which his varied interests involved him. Besides, she had felt during their years of exile, that, in a community where the amenities of living could be obtained only at the cost of efforts as arduous as her husband's professional labours, such brief leisure as he and she could command should be used as an escape from immediate preoccupations, a flight to the life they always dreamed of living. Once or twice, now that this new life had actually drawn its magic circle about them, she had asked herself if she had done right; but hitherto such conjectures had been no more than the retrospective excursions of an active fancy. Now, for the first time, it startled her a little to find how little she knew of the material foundation on which her happiness was built.

She glanced at her husband, and was again reassured by the composure of his face; yet she felt the need of more definite grounds for her reassurance.

"But doesn't this suit worry you? Why have you never spoken to me about it?"

He answered both questions at once. "I didn't speak of it at first because it *did* worry me—annoyed me, rather. But it's all ancient history now. Your correspondent must have got hold of a back number of the *Sentinel*."

She felt a quick thrill of relief. "You mean it's over? He's lost his case?"

There was a just perceptible delay in Boyne's reply. "The suit's been withdrawn—that's all."

But she persisted, as if to exonerate herself from the inward charge of being too easily put off. "Withdrawn it because he saw he had no chance?"

"Oh, he had no chance," Boyne answered.

She was still struggling with a dimly felt perplexity at the back of her thoughts.

"How long ago was it withdrawn?"

He paused, as if with a slight return of his former uncertainty. "I've just had the news now; but I've been expecting it."

"Just now—in one of your letters?"

"Yes; in one of my letters."

She made no answer, and was aware only, after a short interval of waiting, that he had risen, and, strolling across the room, had placed himself on the sofa at her side. She felt him, as he did so, pass an arm about her, she felt his hand seek hers and clasp it, and turning slowly, drawn by the warmth of his cheek, she met his smiling eyes.

"It's all right—it's all right?" she questioned, through the flood of her dissolving doubts; and "I give you my word it was never righter!" he laughed back at her, holding her close.

III

One of the strangest things she was afterward to recall out of all the next day's strangeness was the sudden and complete recovery of her sense of security.

It was in the air when she woke in her low-ceiled, dusky room; it went with her down-stairs to the breakfast-table, flashed out at her from the fire, and re-duplicated itself from the flanks of the urn and the sturdy flutings of the Georgian teapot. It was as if, in some roundabout way, all her diffused fears of the previous day, with their moment of sharp concentration about the newspaper article—as if this dim questioning of the future, and startled return upon the past, had between them liquidated the arrears of some haunting moral obligation. If she had indeed been careless of her husband's affairs, it was, her new state seemed to prove, because her faith in him instinctively justified such carelessness; and his right to her faith had now affirmed itself in the very face of menace and suspicion. She had never seen him more untroubled, more naturally and unconsciously himself, than after the cross-examination to which she had subjected him: it was almost as if he had been aware of her doubts, and had wanted the air cleared as much as she did.

It was as clear, thank Heaven! as the bright outer light that surprised her almost with a touch of summer when she issued from the house for her daily round of the gardens. She had left Boyne at his desk, indulging herself, as she passed the library door, by a last peep at his quiet face, where he bent, pipe in mouth, above his papers; and now she had her own morning's task to perform. The task involved, on such charmed winter days, almost as much happy loitering about the different quarters of her demesne as if spring were already at work there. There were such endless possibilities still before her, such opportunities to bring out the latent graces of the old place, without a single irreverent touch of alteration, that the winter was all too short to plan what spring and autumn executed. And her recovered sense of safety gave, on this particular morning, a peculiar zest to her progress through the sweet still place. She went first to the kitchen-garden, where the espaliered pear-trees drew complicated patterns on the walls, and pigeons were fluttering and preening about the silvery-slated roof of their cot. There was something wrong about the piping of the hot-house, and she was expecting an authority from Dorchester, who was to drive out between trains and make a diagnosis of the boiler. But when she dipped into the damp heat of the green-houses, among the spiced scents and waxy pinks and reds of old-fashioned exotics—even the flora of Lyng was in the note!—she learned that the great man had not arrived, and, the day being too rare to waste in an artificial atmosphere, she came out again and paced along the springy turf of the bowling-green to the gardens behind the house. At their farther end rose a grass terrace, looking across the fish-pond and yew hedges to the long house-front with its twisted chimney-stacks and blue roof angles all drenched in the pale gold moisture of the air.

Seen thus, across the level tracery of the gardens, it sent her, from open windows and hospitably smoking chimneys, the look of some warm human presence, of a mind slowly ripened on a sunny wall of experience. She had never before had such a sense of her intimacy with it, such a conviction that its secrets were all beneficent, kept, as they said to children, "for one's good," such a trust in its power to gather up her life and Ned's into the harmonious pattern of the long, long story it sat there weaving in the sun.

She heard steps behind her, and turned, expecting to see the gardener accompanied by the engineer from Dorchester. But only one figure was in sight, that of a youngish slightly built man, who, for reasons she could not on the spot have given, did not remotely resemble her notion of an authority on hothouse boilers. The new-comer, on seeing her, lifted his hat, and paused with the air of a gentleman—perhaps a traveller—who wishes to make it known that his intrusion is involuntary. Lyng occasionally attracted the more cultivated traveller, and Mary half-expected to see the stranger dissemble a camera, or justify his presence by producing it. But he made no gesture of any sort, and after a moment she asked, in a tone responding to the courteous hesitation of his attitude: "Is there any one you wish to see?"

"I came to see Mr. Boyne," he answered. His intonation, rather than his accent, was faintly American, and Mary, at the note, looked at him more closely. The brim of his soft felt hat cast a shade on his face, which, thus obscured, wore to her short-sighted gaze a look of seriousness, as of a person arriving "on business," and civilly but firmly aware of his rights.

Past experience had made her equally sensible to such claims; but she was jealous of her husband's morning hours, and doubtful of his having given any one the right to intrude on them.

"Have you an appointment with my husband?" she asked.

The visitor hesitated, as if unprepared for the question.

"I think he expects me," he replied.

It was Mary's turn to hesitate. "You see this is his time for work: he never sees any one in the morning."

He looked at her a moment without answering; then, as if

accepting her decision, he began to move away. As he turned, Mary saw him pause and glance up at the peaceful house-front. Something in his air suggested weariness and disappointment, the dejection of the traveller who has come from far off and whose hours are limited by the time-table. It occurred to her that if this were the case her refusal might have made his errand vain, and a sense of compunction caused her to hasten after him.

"May I ask if you have come a long way?"

He gave her the same grave look. "Yes—I have come a long way."

"Then, if you'll go to the house, no doubt my husband will see you now. You'll find him in the library."

She did not know why she had added the last phrase, except from a vague impulse to atone for her previous inhospitality. The visitor seemed about to express his thanks, but her attention was distracted by the approach of the gardener with a companion who bore all the marks of being the expert from Dorchester.

"This way," she said, waving the stranger to the house; and an instant later she had forgotten him in the absorption of her meeting with the boiler-maker.

The encounter led to such far-reaching results that the engineer ended by finding it expedient to ignore his train, and Mary was beguiled into spending the remainder of the morning in absorbed confabulation among the flower-pots. When the colloquy ended, she was surprised to find that it was nearly luncheon-time, and she half expected, as she hurried back to the house, to see her husband coming out to meet her. But she found no one in the court but an under-gardener raking the gravel, and the hall, when she entered it, was so silent that she guessed Boyne to be still at work.

Not wishing to disturb him, she turned into the drawing-room, and there, at her writing-table, lost herself in renewed calculations of the outlay to which the morning's conference had pledged her. The fact that she could permit herself such follies had not yet lost its novelty; and somehow, in contrast to the vague fears of the previous days, it now seemed an element of her recovered security, of the sense that, as Ned had said, things in general had never been "righter."

She was still luxuriating in a lavish play of figures when the parlour-maid, from the threshold, roused her with an enquiry as to the expediency of serving luncheon. It was one of their jokes that Trimmle announced luncheon as if she were divulging a state secret, and Mary, intent upon her papers, merely murmured an absent-minded assent.

She felt Trimmle wavering doubtfully on the threshold, as if in rebuke of such unconsidered assent; then her retreating steps sounded down the passage, and Mary, pushing away her papers, crossed the hall—and went to the library door. It was still closed, and she wavered in her turn, disliking to disturb her husband, yet anxious that he should not exceed his usual measure of work. As she stood there, balancing her impulses, Trimmle returned with the announcement of luncheon, and Mary, thus impelled, opened the library door.

Boyne was not at his desk, and she peered about her, expecting to discover him before the book-shelves, somewhere down the length of the room; but her call brought no response, and gradually it became clear to her that he was not there.

She turned back to the parlour-maid.

"Mr. Boyne must be up-stairs. Please tell him that luncheon is ready."

Trimmle appeared to hesitate between the obvious duty of obedience and an equally obvious conviction of the foolishness of the injunction laid on her. The struggle resulted in her saying: "If you please, Madam, Mr. Boyne's not up-stairs."

"Not in his room? Are you sure?"

"I'm sure, Madam."

Mary consulted the clock. "Where is he, then?"

"He's gone out," Trimmle announced, with the superior air of one who has respectfully waited for the question that a well-ordered mind would have put first.

Mary's conjecture had been right, then. Boyne must have gone to the gardens to meet her, and since she had missed him, it was clear that he had taken the shorter way by the south door, instead of going round to the court. She crossed the hall to the French window opening directly on the yew garden, but the parlour-maid, after another moment of inner conflict, decided to bring out: "Please, Madam, Mr. Boyne didn't go that way."

Mary turned back. "Where *did* he go? And when?"

"He went out of the front door, up the drive, Madam." It was a matter of principle with Trimmle never to answer more than one question at a time.

"Up the drive? At this hour?" Mary went to the door herself, and glanced across the court through the tunnel of bare limes. But its perspective was as empty as when she had scanned it on entering.

"Did Mr. Boyne leave no message?"

Trimmle seemed to surrender herself to a last struggle with the forces of chaos.

"No, Madam. He just went out with the gentleman."

"The gentleman? What gentleman?" Mary wheeled about, as if to front this new factor.

"The gentleman who called, Madam," said Trimmle resignedly.

"When did a gentleman call? Do explain yourself, Trimmle!"

Only the fact that Mary was very hungry, and that she wanted to consult her husband about the greenhouses, would have caused her to lay so unusual an injunction on her attendant; and even now she was detached enough to note in Trimmle's eye the dawning defiance of the respectful subordinate who has been pressed too hard.

"I couldn't exactly say the hour, Madam, because I didn't let the gentleman in," she replied, with an air of discreetly ignoring the irregularity of her mistress's course.

"You didn't let him in?"

"No, Madam. When the bell rang I was dressing, and Agnes——"

"Go and ask Agnes, then," said Mary.

Trimmle still wore her look of patient magnanimity. "Agnes would not know, Madam, for she had unfortunately burnt her hand in trimming the wick of the new lamp from town"—Trimmle, as Mary was aware, had always been opposed to the new lamp—"and so Mrs. Dockett sent the kitchen-maid instead."

Mary looked again at the clock. "It's after two! Go and ask the kitchen-maid if Mr. Boyne left any word."

She went into luncheon without waiting, and Trimmle presently brought her there the kitchen-maid's statement that the gentleman had called about eleven o'clock, and that Mr. Boyne had gone out with him without leaving any message. The kitchen-maid did not even know the caller's name, for he had written it on a slip of paper, which he had folded and handed to her, with the injunction to deliver it at once to Mr. Boyne.

Mary finished her luncheon, still wondering, and when it was over, and Trimmle had brought the coffee to the drawing-room, her wonder had deepened to a first faint tinge of disquietude. It was unlike Boyne to absent himself without explanation at so unwonted an hour, and the difficulty of identifying the visitor whose summons he had apparently obeyed made his disappearance the more unaccountable. Mary Boyne's experience as the wife of a busy engineer, subject to sudden calls and compelled to keep irregular hours, had trained her to the philosophic acceptance of surprises; but since Boyne's withdrawal from business he had adopted a Benedictine regularity of life. As if to make up for the dispersed and agitated years, with their "stand-up" lunches, and dinners rattled down to the joltings of the dining-cars, he culti-vated the last refinements of punctuality and monotony, discour-aging his wife's fancy for the unexpected, and declaring that to a delicate taste there were infinite gradations of pleasure in the re-currences of habit.

Still, since no life can completely defend itself from the un-foreseen, it was evident that all Boyne's precautious would sooner or later prove unavailable, and Mary concluded that he had cut short a tiresome visit by walking with his caller to the station, or at least accompanying him for part of the way.

This conclusion relieved her from farther preoccupation, and she went out herself to take up her conference with the gardener. Thence she walked to the village post-office, a mile or so away; and when she turned toward home the early twilight was setting in.

She had taken a foot-path across the downs, and as Boyne, meanwhile, had probably returned from the station by the high-road, there was little likelihood of their meeting. She felt sure, however, of his having reached the house before her; so sure that, when she entered it herself, without even pausing to inquire of Trimmle, she made directly for the library. But the library was still empty, and with an unwonted exactness of visual memory she observed that the papers on her husband's desk lay precisely as they had lain when she had gone in to call him to luncheon.

Then of a sudden she was seized by a vague dread of the unknown. She had closed the door behind her on entering, and as she stood alone in the long silent room, her dread seemed to take shape and sound, to be there breathing and lurking among the shadows. Her short-sighted eyes strained through them, half-discerning an actual presence, something aloof, that watched and knew; and in the recoil from that intangible presence she threw herself on the bell-rope and gave it a sharp pull.

The sharp summons brought Trimmle in precipitately with a lamp, and Mary breathed again at this sobering reappearance of the usual.

"You may bring tea if Mr. Boyne is in," she said, to justify her ring.

"Very well, Madam. But Mr. Boyne is not in," said Trimmle, putting down the lamp.

"Not in? You mean he's come back and gone out again?"

"No, Madam. He's never been back."

The dread stirred again, and Mary knew that now it had her fast.

"Not since he went out with—the gentleman?"

"Not since he went out with the gentleman."

"But who *was* the gentleman?" Mary insisted, with the shrill note of some one trying to be heard through a confusion of noises.

"That I couldn't say, Madam." Trimmle, standing there by the lamp, seemed suddenly to grow less round and rosy, as though eclipsed by the same creeping shade of apprehension.

"But the kitchen-maid knows—wasn't it the kitchen-maid who let him in?"

"She doesn't know either, Madam, for he wrote his name on a folded paper."

Mary, through her agitation, was aware that they were both designating the unknown visitor by a vague pronoun, instead of the conventional formula which, till then, had kept their allusions within the bounds of conformity. And at the same moment her mind caught at the suggestion of the folded paper.

"But he must have a name! Where's the paper?"

She moved to the desk, and began to turn over the documents that littered it. The first that caught her eye was an unfinished letter in her husband's hand, with his pen lying across it, as though dropped there at a sudden summons.

"My dear Parvis"—who was Parvis?—"I have just received your letter announcing Elwell's death, and while I suppose there is now no farther risk of trouble, it might be safer——"

She tossed the sheet aside, and continued her search; but no folded paper was discoverable among the letters and pages of manuscript which had been swept together in a heap, as if by a hurried or a startled gesture.

"But the kitchen-maid *saw* him. Send her here," she commanded, wondering at her dulness in not thinking sooner of so simple a solution.

Trimmle vanished in a flash, as if thankful to be out of the room, and when she reappeared, conducting the agitated underling, Mary had regained her self-possession, and had her questions ready.

The gentleman was a stranger, yes—that she understood. But what had he said? And above all, what had he looked like? The first question was easily enough answered, for the disconcerting reason that he had said so little—had merely asked for Mr. Boyne, and, scribbling something on a bit of paper, had requested that it should at once be carried in to him.

"Then you don't know what he wrote? You're not sure it *was* his name?"

The kitchen-maid was not sure, but supposed it was, since he had written it in answer to her inquiry as to whom she should announce.

"And when you carried the paper in to Mr. Boyne, what did he say?"

The kitchen-maid did not think that Mr. Boyne had said anything, but she could not be sure, for just as she had handed him the paper and he was opening it, she had become aware that the visitor had followed her into the library, and she had slipped out, leaving the gentlemen together.

"But then, if you left them in the library, how do you know that they went out of the house?"

This question plunged the witness into a momentary inarticulateness, from which she was rescued by Trimmle, who, by means of ingenious circumlocutions, elicited the statement that before she could cross the hall to the back passage she had heard the two gentlemen behind her, and had seen them go out of the front door together.

"Then, if you saw the strange gentleman twice, you must be able to tell me what he looked like."

But with this final challenge to her powers of expression it became clear that the limit of the kitchen-maid's endurance had been reached. The obligation of going to the front door to "show in" a visitor was in itself so subversive of the fundamental order of things that it had thrown her faculties into hopeless disarray, and she could only stammer out, after various panting efforts: "His hat, mum, was different-like, as you might say——"

"Different? How different?" Mary flashed out, her own mind, in the same instant, leaping back to an image left on it that morning, and then lost under layers of subsequent impressions.

"His hat had a wide brim, you mean? and his face was pale —a youngish face?" Mary pressed her, with a white-lipped intensity of interrogation. But if the kitchen-maid found any adequate answer to this challenge, it was swept away for her listener down the rushing current of her own convictions. The stranger— the stranger in the garden! Why had Mary not thought of him before? She needed no one now to tell her that it was he who had called for her husband and gone away with him. But who was he, and why had Boyne obeyed him?

IV

It leaped out at her suddenly, like a grin out of the dark, that they had often called England so little—"such a confoundedly hard place to get lost in."

A confoundedly hard place to get lost in! That had been her husband's phrase. And now, with the whole machinery of official investigation sweeping its flashlights from shore to shore, and across the dividing straits; now, with Boyne's name blazing from the walls of every town and village, his portrait (how that wrung her!) hawked up and down the country like the image of a hunted criminal; now the little compact populous island, so policed, surveyed and administered, revealed itself as a Sphinx-like guardian of abysmal mysteries, staring back into his wife's anguished eyes as if with the wicked joy of knowing something they would never know!

In the fortnight since Boyne's disappearance there had been no word of him, no trace of his movements. Even the usual misleading reports that raise expectancy in tortured bosoms had been few and fleeting. No one but the kitchen-maid had seen Boyne leave the house, and no one else had seen "the gentleman" who accompanied him. All enquiries in the neighbourhood failed to elicit the memory of a stranger's presence that day in the neighbourhood of Lyng. And no one had met Edward Boyne, either alone or in company, in any of the neighbouring villages, or on the road across the downs, or at either of the local railway-stations. The sunny English noon had swallowed him as completely as if he had gone out into the Cimmerian night.

Mary, while every official means of investigation was working at its highest pressure, had ransacked her husband's papers for any trace of antecedent complications, of entanglements or obligations unknown to her, that might throw a ray into the darkness. But if any such had existed in the background of Boyne's life, they had vanished like the slip of paper on which the visitor had written his name. There remained no possible thread of guidance except—if it were indeed an exception—the letter which Boyne had apparently been in the act of writing when he received his mysterious summons. That letter, read and reread by his wife, and submitted by her to the police, yielded little enough to feed conjecture.

"I have just heard of Elwell's death, and while I suppose there is now no farther risk of trouble, it might be safer——" That was all. The "risk of trouble" was easily explained by the newspaper clipping which had apprised Mary of the suit brought against her husband by one of his associates in the Blue Star enterprise. The only new information conveyed by the letter was the fact of its showing Boyne, when he wrote it, to be still apprehensive of the results of the suit, though he had told his wife that it had been withdrawn, and though the letter itself proved that the plaintiff was dead. It took several days of cabling to fix the identity of the "Parvis" to whom the fragment was addressed, but even after these enquiries had shown him to be a Waukesha lawyer, no new facts concerning the Elwell suit were elicited. He appeared to have had no direct concern in it, but to have been conversant with the facts merely as an acquaintance, and possible intermediary; and he declared himself unable to guess with what object Boyne intended to seek his assistance.

This negative information, sole fruit of the first fortnight's search, was not increased by a jot during the slow weeks that followed. Mary knew that the investigations were still being carried on, but she had a vague sense of their gradually slackening, as the actual march of time seemed to slacken. It was as though the days, flying horror-struck from the shrouded image of the one inscrutable day, gained assurance as the distance lengthened, till at last they fell back into their normal gait. And so with the human imaginations at work on the dark event. No doubt it occupied them still, but week by week and hour by hour it grew less absorbing, took up less space, was slowly but inevitably crowded out of the foreground of consciousness by the new problems perpetually bubbling up from the cloudy caldron of human experience.

Even Mary Boyne's consciousness gradually felt the same lowering of velocity. It still swayed with the incessant oscillations of conjecture; but they were slower, more rhythmical in their beat. There were even moments of weariness when, like the victim of some poison which leaves the brain clear, but holds the body motionless, she saw herself domesticated with the Horror, accepting its perpetual presence as one of the fixed conditions of life.

These moments lengthened into hours and days, till she passed into a phase of stolid acquiescence. She watched the routine of daily life with the incurious eye of a savage on whom the meaningless processes of civilisation make but the faintest impression. She had come to regard herself as part of the routine, a spoke of the wheel, revolving with its motion; she felt almost like the furniture of the room in which she sat, an insensate object to be dusted and pushed about with the chairs and tables. And this deepening apathy held her fast at Lyng, in spite of the entreaties of friends and the usual medical recommendation of "change." Her friends supposed that her refusal to move was inspired by the belief that her husband would one day return to the spot from which he had vanished, and a beautiful legend grew up about this imaginary state of waiting. But in reality she had no such belief: the depths

of anguish enclosing her were no longer lighted by flashes of hope.
She was sure that Boyne would never come back, that he had gone
out of her sight as completely as if Death itself had waited that
day on the threshold. She had even renounced, one by one, the
various theories as to his disappearance which had been advanced
by the press, the police, and her own agonised imagination. In
sheer lassitude her mind turned from these alternatives of horror,
and sank back into the blank fact that he was gone.

No, she would never know what had become of him—no one
would ever know. But the house *knew;* the library in which she
spent her long lonely evenings knew. For it was here that the last
scene had been enacted, here that the stranger had come, and
spoken the word which had caused Boyne to rise and follow him.
The floor she trod had felt his tread; the books on the shelves had
seen his face; and there were moments when the intense consciousness of the old dusky walls seemed about to break out into some
audible revelation of their secret. But the revelation never came,
and she knew it would never come. Lyng was not one of the
garrulous old houses that betray the secrets entrusted to them. Its
very legend proved that it had always been the mute accomplice,
the incorruptible custodian, of the mysteries it had surprised. And
Mary Boyne, sitting face to face with its silence, felt the futility
of seeking to break it by any human means.

V

"I don't say it *wasn't* straight, and yet I don't say it *was*
straight. It was business."

Mary, at the words, lifted her head with a start, and looked
intently at the speaker.

When, half an hour before, a card with "Mr. Parvis" on it had
been brought up to her, she had been immediately aware that the
name had been a part of her consciousness ever since she had read
it at the head of Boyne's unfinished letter. In the library she had
found awaiting her a small sallow man with a bald head and gold
eye-glasses, and it sent a tremor through her to know that this was
the person to whom her husband's last known thought had been
directed.

Parvis, civilly, but without vain preamble—in the manner of

a man who has his watch in his hand—had set forth the object of his visit. He had "run over" to England on business, and finding himself in the neighbourhood of Dorchester, had not wished to leave it without paying his respects to Mrs. Boyne; and without asking her, if the occasion offered, what she meant to do about Bob Elwell's family.

The words touched the spring of some obscure dread in Mary's bosom. Did her visitor, after all, know what Boyne had meant by his unfinished phrase? She asked for an elucidation of his question, and noticed at once that he seemed surprised at her continued ignorance of the subject. Was it possible that she really knew as little as she said?

"I know nothing—you must tell me," she faltered out; and her visitor thereupon proceeded to unfold his story. It threw, even to her confused perceptions, and imperfectly initiated vision, a lurid glare on the whole hazy episode of the Blue Star Mine. Her husband had made his money in that brilliant speculation at the cost of "getting ahead" of some one less alert to seize the chance; and the victim of his ingenuity was young Robert Elwell, who had "put him on" to the Blue Star scheme.

Parvis, at Mary's first cry, had thrown her a sobering glance through his impartial glasses.

"Bob Elwell wasn't smart enough, that's all; if he had been, he might have turned round and served Boyne the same way. It's the kind of thing that happens every day in business. I guess it's what the scientists call the survival of the fittest—see?" said Mr. Parvis, evidently pleased with the aptness of his analogy.

Mary felt a physical shrinking from the next question she tried to frame: it was as though the words on her lips had a taste that nauseated her.

"But then—you accuse my husband of doing something dishonourable?"

Mr. Parvis surveyed the question dispassionately. "Oh, no, I don't. I don't even say it wasn't straight." He glanced up and down the long lines of books, as if one of them might have supplied him with the definition he sought. "I don't say it *wasn't* straight, and yet I don't say it *was* straight. It was business." After all, no definition in his category could be more comprehensive than that.

Mary sat staring at him with a look of terror. He seemed to her like the indifferent emissary of some evil power.

"But Mr. Elwell's lawyers apparently did not take your view, since I suppose the suit was withdrawn by their advice."

"Oh, yes; they knew he hadn't a leg to stand on, technically. It was when they advised him to withdraw the suit that he got desperate. You see, he'd borrowed most of the money he lost in the Blue Star, and he was up a tree. That's why he shot himself when they told him he had no show."

The horror was sweeping over Mary in great deafening waves.

"He shot himself? He killed himself because of *that?*"

"Well, he didn't kill himself, exactly. He dragged on two months before he died." Parvis emitted the statement as unemotionally as a gramophone grinding out its "record."

"You mean that he tried to kill himself, and failed? And tried again?"

"Oh, he didn't have to *try* again," said Parvis grimly.

They sat opposite each other in silence, he swinging his eyeglasses thoughtfully about his finger, she, motionless, her arms stretched along her knees in an attitude of rigid tension.

"But if you knew all this," she began at length, hardly able to force her voice above a whisper, "how is it that when I wrote you at the time of my husband's disappearance you said you didn't understand his letter?"

Parvis received this without perceptible embarrassment: "Why, I didn't understand it—strictly speaking. And it wasn't the time to talk about it, if I had. The Elwell business was settled when the suit was withdrawn. Nothing I could have told you would have helped you to find your husband."

Mary continued to scrutinise him. "Then why are you telling me now?"

Still Parvis did not hesitate. "Well, to begin with, I supposed you knew more than you appear to—I mean about the circumstances of Elwell's death. And then people are talking of it now; the whole matter's been raked up again. And I thought if you didn't know you ought to."

She remained silent, and he continued: "You see, it's only come out lately what a bad state Elwell's affairs were in. His wife's a proud woman, and she fought on as long as she could, going to work, and taking sewing at home when she got too sick—something with the heart, I believe. But she had his mother to look after, and the children, and she broke down under it, and finally had to ask for help. That called attention to the case, and the papers took it up, and a subscription was started. Everybody out there liked Bob Elwell, and most of the prominent names in the place are down on the list, and people began to wonder why——"

Parvis broke off to fumble in an inner pocket. "Here," he continued, "here's an account of the whole thing from the *Sentinel* —a little sensational, of course. But I guess you'd better look it over."

He held out a newspaper to Mary, who unfolded it slowly, remembering, as she did so, the evening when, in that same room, the perusal of a clipping from the *Sentinel* had first shaken the depths of her security.

As she opened the paper, her eyes, shrinking from the glaring headlines, "Widow of Boyne's Victim Forced to Appeal for Aid," ran down the column of text to two portraits inserted in it. The first was her husband's, taken from a photograph made the year they had come to England. It was the picture of him that she liked best, the one that stood on the writing-table up-stairs in her bedroom. As the eyes in the photograph met hers, she felt it would be impossible to read what was said of him, and closed her lids with the sharpness of the pain.

"I thought if you felt disposed to put your name down——" she heard Parvis continue.

She opened her eyes with an effort, and they fell on the other portrait. It was that of a youngish man, slightly built, with features somewhat blurred by the shadow of a projecting hat-brim. Where had she seen that outline before? She stared at it confusedly, her heart hammering in her ears. Then she gave a cry.

"This is the man—the man who came for my husband!"

She heard Parvis start to his feet, and was dimly aware that she had slipped backward into the corner of the sofa, and that he was bending above her in alarm. She straightened herself, and reached out for the paper, which she had dropped.

"It's the man! I should know him anywhere!" she persisted in a voice that sounded to her own ears like a scream.

Parvis's answer seemed to come to her from far off, down endless fog-muffled windings.

"Mrs. Boyne, you're not very well. Shall I call somebody? Shall I get a glass of water?"

"No, no, no!" She threw herself toward him, her hand frantically clutching the newspaper. "I tell you, it's the man! I *know* him! He spoke to me in the garden!"

Parvis took the journal from her, directing his glasses to the portrait. "It can't be, Mrs. Boyne. It's Robert Elwell."

"Robert Elwell?" Her white stare seemed to travel into space. "Then it was Robert Elwell who came for him."

"Came for Boyne? The day he went away from here?" Parvis's voice dropped as hers rose. He bent over, laying a fraternal hand on her, as if to coax her gently back into her seat. "Why, Elwell was dead! Don't you remember?"

Mary sat with her eyes fixed on the picture, unconscious of what he was saying.

"Don't you remember Boyne's unfinished letter to me—the one you found on his desk that day? It was written just after he'd heard of Elwell's death." She noticed an odd shake in Parvis's unemotional voice. "Surely you remember!" he urged her.

Yes, she remembered: that was the profoundest horror of it. Elwell had died the day before her husband's disappearance; and this was Elwell's portrait; and it was the portrait of the man who had spoken to her in the garden. She lifted her head and looked slowly about the library. The library could have borne witness that it was also the portrait of the man who had come in that day to call Boyne from his unfinished letter. Through the misty surgings of her brain she heard the faint boom of half-forgotten words—words spoken by Alida Stair on the lawn at Pangbourne before Boyne and his wife had ever seen the house at Lyng, or had imagined that they might one day live there.

"This was the man who spoke to me," she repeated.

She looked again at Parvis. He was trying to conceal his disturbance under what he probably imagined to be an expression of indulgent commiseration; but the edges of his lips were blue. "He thinks me mad; but I'm not mad," she reflected; and suddenly there flashed upon her a way of justifying her strange affirmation.

She sat quiet, controlling the quiver of her lips, and waiting till she could trust her voice; then she said, looking straight at Parvis: "Will you answer me one question, please? When was it that Robert Elwell tried to kill himself?"

"When—when?" Parvis stammered.

"Yes; the date. Please try to remember."

She saw that he was growing still more afraid of her. "I have a reason," she insisted.

"Yes, yes. Only I can't remember. About two months before, I should say."

"I want the date," she repeated.

Parvis picked up the newspaper. "We might see here," he said, still humouring her. He ran his eyes down the page. "Here it is. Last October—the——"

She caught the words from him. "The 20th, wasn't it?" With a sharp look at her, he verified. "Yes, the 20th. Then you *did* know?"

"I know now." Her gaze continued to travel past him. "Sunday, the 20th—that was the day he came here first."

Parvis's voice was almost inaudible. "Came *here* first?"

"Yes."

"You saw him twice, then?"

"Yes, twice." She just breathed it at him. "He came first on the 20th of October. I remember the date because it was the day we went up Meldon Steep for the first time." She felt a faint gasp of inward laughter at the thought that but for that she might have forgotten.

Parvis continued to scrutinise her, as if trying to intercept her gaze.

"We saw him from the roof," she went on. "He came down the lime-avenue toward the house. He was dressed just as he is in that picture. My husband saw him first. He was frightened, and ran down ahead of me; but there was no one there. He had vanished."

"Elwell had vanished?" Parvis faltered.

"Yes." Their two whispers seemed to grope for each other. "I couldn't think what had happened. I see now. He *tried* to come then; but he wasn't dead enough—he couldn't reach us. He had to wait for two months to die; and then he came back again—and Ned went with him."

She nodded at Parvis with the look of triumph of a child who has worked out a difficult puzzle. But suddenly she lifted her hands with a desperate gesture, pressing them to her temples.

"Oh, my God! I sent him to Ned—I told him where to go! I sent him to this room!" she screamed.

She felt the walls of books rush toward her, like inward falling ruins; and she heard Parvis, a long way off, through the ruins, crying to her, and struggling to get at her. But she was numb to his touch, she did not know what he was saying. Through the tumult she heard but one clear note, the voice of Alida Stair, speaking on the lawn at Pangbourne.

"You won't know till afterward," it said. "You won't know till long, long afterward."

●

THE COUNTESS of Thanet (Earl John's Lady) saw as she was in bed with her Lord in London, her daughter my Lady Hatton, who was then in Northamptonshire, at Horton Kirby; the candle was burning in her chamber. Since, viz. *anno* 1675, this Lady Hatton was blown up with gunpowder set on fire by lightning, in the castle at Guernsey, where her Lord was Governor.*

* See Mr. Baxter's Treatise of Spirits.

—JOHN AUBREY

ACKNOWLEDGMENTS

All copyright material in this collection has been reprinted with the permission of the authors and the following publishers and holders of copyright to whom especial thanks are due:

Edward Arnold & Company, London: *Casting the Runes* and *The Treasure of Abbot Thomas* from *The Collected Ghost Stories of M. R. James*.

Gertrude Atherton and Houghton Mifflin Company, Boston: *The Foghorn* from *The Foghorn* by Gertrude Atherton, copyright, 1935.

Ernest Benn Limited, London: *The Ghost-Ship* from *The Ghost-Ship* by Richard Middleton.

Brandt & Brandt, New York: *Adam and Eve and Pinch Me, Clorinda Walks in Heaven, The Cherry Tree* and *The King of the World* from *Adam and Eve and Pinch Me* by A. E. Coppard, copyright, 1922, published by Alfred A. Knopf, Inc.; *Perez* by W. L. George, from *Georgian Stories*, copyright, 1922, published by Chapman & Hall, Ltd., London.

Katharine Beecher Stetson Chamberlin: *The Yellow Wall Paper* by Charlotte Perkins Gilman.

Norman Collins: *The New Statesman and Nation*, London: *Justice* from *The Gibsons* and *Climax for a Ghost Story* by I. A. Ireland.

J. M. Dent & Sons Ltd., London: *August Heat* from *Midnight House* by W. F. Harvey.

Doubleday, Doran & Company, Inc., Garden City, New York: *The Furnished Room* from *The Four Million* by O. Henry, copyright, 1905, 1933, by Doubleday, Doran & Company, Inc.

E. P. Dutton & Company, Inc., New York: *The Wendigo* from *The Lost Valley* by Algernon Blackwood; *The Woman's Ghost Story* from *The Listener* by Algernon Blackwood; *The Story of Glam* from *The Saga of Gretter The Strong*, translated from the Islandic by George Ainslie Hight. (Published in the Everyman's Library); and *The Beast with Five Fingers* from *The Beast with Five Fingers* by W. F. Harvey.

847

Farrar & Rinehart, Inc., New York: *The Feather Cloak of Hawaii* from *Myths and Legends of the Polynesians* by Johannes C. Andersen; *The Half Pint Flask* by DuBose Heyward, copyright, 1927, 1929.

Hill & Peters, New York: *Green Thoughts* by John Collier, originally published in the *London Mercury*, May 1931.

Alfred A. Knopf, Inc., New York: *The Horla* from *The Horla* by Guy de Maupassant and *The White People* from *The House of Souls* by Arthur Machen.

Owen Lattimore: *The Ghosts of Wulakai* by Owen Lattimore, originally published in *Asia Magazine*, March 1934.

Little, Brown & Company, Boston: *The Story of Ming-Y* from *Some Chinese Ghosts* by Lafcadio Hearn.

The Macmillan Company, New York: *Where Their Fire Is Not Quenched* from *Uncanny Stories* by May Sinclair.

Peaslee and Brigham, New York: *The Screaming Skull* from *Wandering Ghosts* by F. Marion Crawford. Published by The Macmillan Company.

James B. Pinker & Son, London: *The Monkey's Paw* from *The Lady of the Barge* by W. W. Jacobs, published by Harper & Bros., copyright, 1902.

G. P. Putnam's Sons, New York: *An Occurrence at Owl Creek Bridge* from *In the Midst of Life* by Ambrose Bierce, and *A Man With Two Lives* by Ambrose Bierce.

Charles Scribner's Sons, New York: *Markheim* from *The Merry Men* by Robert Louis Stevenson, and *Afterward* from *Tales of Men and Ghosts* by Edith Wharton.

The University of Chicago Press, Chicago: *The Brahman, the Thief, and the Ghost* from *The Panchatantra*, translated by Arthur W. Ryder (1925).

The Viking Press, New York: *Laura* and *The Open Window* from *The Short Stories of Saki* (H. H. Munro), copyright, 1930, by The Viking Press, Inc. (originally published in *Beasts and Super Beasts*, 1914); and *Full Fathom Five* from *While Rome Burns* by Alexander Woollcott, copyright, 1934.

Ann Watkins, Inc., New York: *The Gentleman from America* from *Mayfair*, by Michael Arlen; and *A Visitor From Down Under* from *The Killing Bottle* by L. P. Hartley.